SUMMER BREEZE

M

SUMMER BREEZE

WITHDRAWN

CATHERINE PALMER
& GARY CHAPMAN

WALKER LARGE PRINT

An imprint of Thomson Gale, a part of The Thomson Corporation

THOMSON

✴

GALE

Detroit • New York ... ille, Maine • London

THOMSON

GALE

LIBRARY OF CONGRESS CATALOGING-IN-PUBLICATION DATA

Palmer, Catherine, 1956–
　　Summer breeze / by Catherine Palmer & Gary Chapman.
　　　p. cm. — (Four seasons ; #2)
　　ISBN-13: 978-0-7862-9615-6 (alk. paper)
　　ISBN-10: 0-7862-9615-1 (alk. paper)
　　ISBN-13: 978-1-59415-191-0 (pbk. : alk. paper)
　　ISBN-10: 1-59415-191-1 (pbk. : alk. paper)
　　1. Marriage — Fiction. 2. Ozarks, Lake of the (Mo.) — Fiction. 3. Large type books. I. Chapman, Gary D., 1938– II. Title.
PS3566.A495S857 2007b
813'.54—dc22
　　　　　　　　　　　　　　　　　　　　　　　　　　2007024419

Published in 2007 by arrangement with Tyndale House Publishers, Inc.

Printed in the United States of America on permanent paper
10 9 8 7 6 5 4 3 2 1

For Shannon & Frances Bledsoe.
My deepest gratitude for your
assistance,
your encouragement,
and most of all your faithful prayers.

C.P.

When two people are under the influence of the most violent, most insane, most delusive, and most transient of passions, they are required to swear that they will remain in that excited, abnormal, and exhausting condition continuously until death do them part.

George Bernard Shaw
Getting Married

NOTE TO READERS

There's nothing like a good story! I'm excited to be working with Catherine Palmer on a fiction series based on the concepts in my book *The Four Seasons of Marriage.* You hold in your hands the second book in this series.

My experience, both in my own marriage and in counseling couples for more than thirty years, suggests that marriages are always moving from one season to another. Sometimes we find ourselves in winter — discouraged, detached, and dissatisfied; other times we experience springtime, with its openness, hope, and anticipation. On still other occasions we bask in the warmth of summer — comfortable, relaxed, enjoying life. And then comes fall with its uncertainty, negligence, and apprehension. The cycle repeats itself many times throughout the life of a marriage, just as the seasons repeat themselves in nature. These concepts are described in *The Four Seasons of Marriage,* along with seven proven strategies to help couples move away from the unsettledness of fall or the alienation and coldness of winter toward the hopefulness of spring or the warmth and closeness of summer.

Combining what I've learned in my counseling practice with Catherine's excellent writing skills has led to this series of four novels. In the lives of the characters you'll meet in these pages, you will see the choices I have observed people making over and over again through the years, the value of caring friends and neighbors, and the hope of marriages moving to a new and more pleasant season.

In *Summer Breeze* and the other stories in the Four Seasons fiction series, you will meet newlyweds, blended families, couples who are deep in the throes of empty-nest adjustment, and senior couples. Our hope is that you will see yourself or someone you know in these characters. If you are hurting, this book can give you hope — and some ideas for making things better. Be sure to check out the discussion questions at the end of the book for further ideas.

And whatever season you're in, I know

you'll enjoy the people and the stories in Deepwater Cove.

Gary D. Chapman, PhD

ACKNOWLEDGMENTS

So many people affect the writing and publication of a novel. For his valuable information about the Missouri Water Patrol, Officer Shannon Bledsoe has earned my admiration and gratitude. Any errors in the manuscript are my own. For inspiration as well as prayer support, the young wives and mothers in Michael Vitelli's Bible study class have my deepest thanks. Frances, Carolynn, Tammara, Liz, and many others, may God bless and reward you for your faithful service. For sharing both laughter and tears, my longtime friends are treasures I cherish. Janice, Mary, Roxie, Kristie, BB, Lucia — I love you. My prayer support team holds me up before God, and I can't thank you enough — Mary, Andrew, Nina, and Marilyn.

I also thank my Tyndale family for all you have meant to me during these past ten years. Ron Beers and Karen Watson, bless you for making this series not only a reality but a pleasure. Kathy Olson, I can't imagine having the courage to write a single word without you. Your careful editing and precious friendship are truly gifts from the Lord. Travis and Keri, Andrea, Babette, Mavis, Victor, the amazing sales team, the wonderful design department — thank you all from the bottom of my heart.

Though I often leave them for last, first on my list of supporters, encouragers, and loved ones are my family. Tim, Geoffrey, and Andrei, I love you so much.

CHAPTER ONE

The crackle of the two-way radio mounted in his boat alerted Officer Derek Finley to a call from Water Patrol headquarters in Jefferson City.

"Boater in distress," the dispatcher said. "Boater in distress at the twenty-mile mark in front of Green Oaks Condominiums. Dan Becker is reporting the incident. Repeat, Dan Becker. He says he's in the path of other boats, and he believes he is creating a possible hazard in navigation."

"Ten-four, Jeff City." Derek began to turn the twenty-nine-foot Donzi the Patrol had assigned him. With its twin outboard motors — each at 250 horsepower — the boat could go sixty-five miles an hour. But he wouldn't push it to that speed on a routine call like this one.

"Okay, Jeff," he told the dispatcher. "I will be en route from the twenty-five-mile mark."

As he increased speed, Derek scanned for other boats in his path. On such a warm, beautiful day, the first day of the long Memorial Day weekend, the water would be busy. Without doubt, several folks would be boating while intoxicated. Though Missouri had many lakes, rivers, and streams, Lake of the Ozarks had the highest number of BWI arrests in the state. Working the night shift, which began at three in the afternoon and wouldn't end until three the next morning, he had already stopped a boat after spotting a woman who had decided to sunbathe on a bow gunwale lacking adequate rails. Later, he had taken a call about a personal watercraft operating in a no-wake zone near someone's dock. Many PWC operators had no idea they were supposed to obey the same rules as a full-size craft.

The Donzi cut through the sparkling water, and as he often did, Derek reflected on how much he enjoyed his job. Though he had graduated from college with a degree in business and had worked behind a desk for almost a year, he'd quit the minute he heard the state was recruiting. Not long after, he'd passed the background check and the physical fitness test. His work with the Water Patrol provided the perfect blend of

16

excitement, enjoyment of nature, public service, and — during the rare criminal investigation — intellectual challenge.

Now approaching the twenty-mile mark, Derek spotted the stranded boat — a twenty-five-foot Challenger bobbing mid-channel as other vessels zipped around it. Two middle-aged couples, sunburned and hatless, began waving the moment they saw him.

"Jeff, I am 10-23 with the boater in distress," Derek told the dispatcher. He slowed the Donzi as he approached the stranded vessel. "How're you folks doing today? Is there a Dan Becker on board?"

"That's me," one of the men answered. "It's my boat. I'm the one who called."

"I understand you broke down."

"Yeah, looks that way. We were out all morning fishing. Then we headed home and got this close to our dock, and suddenly the motor died."

"We've tried everything," the other man said. "The boat won't start."

"You got gas?"

"We had a full tank when we left the dock." Dan Becker scratched the rosy bald spot on his head. "We can't have used all that up. Lemme check." In a moment, he groaned. "Empty. Oh, brother. I never even

17

thought of that."

Derek smiled. Though the common boating mishaps that took most of his time could feel a little routine, he enjoyed helping people — whether it was seeing an intoxicated person out of danger to himself or others, guiding someone who'd gotten lost on the lake, or assisting a couple of stalled fishermen. Derek felt a sense of purpose and accomplishment at the end of each day. "Happens all the time," he told Dan. "How about a tow? I can take you to your slip. Or there's a gas dock about a half mile down. Mermaid Marina. You can fill up there."

Fanning themselves, the women begged to be taken to their personal slip near the condominium. But Dan and his buddy prevailed. "Let's get some gas. Might as well take care of it, since we've got you here, Officer."

Expecting that answer, Derek was already gathering the tow rope. "I'm going to throw this across. Hook it to the bow eye."

As the two men worked to clip the rope to their boat, Derek checked the black tow post mounted on his Donzi. When they signaled him, Derek stepped into the shade of the canopy to the operator's position and took the wheel. As his Donzi moved forward, the tow rope tightened, and the Challenger began floating safely behind.

Out of gas, he thought with a chuckle and a shake of his head. How many times had he heard that one? His Donzi and the nineteen other Water Patrol boats that constantly roamed Lake of the Ozarks carried officers to answer complaint calls and emergencies. Success depended on control, wits, courage, and skill. Most of the time, the calls were run-of-the-mill, but he had to stay always alert in case of a real problem.

He mentally recounted the list of reasons people gave for their boats stalling in the water. "Officer, our motor broke." "My boat won't start." "Our outdrive is busted." "We were pullin' a skier and our motor fell off!" But by far the most common was "We ran out of gas."

Towing the Challenger alongside the Mermaid Marina dock, Derek noted the college-aged young women who worked the gas pumps and encouraged people to visit the lake-view restaurant just uphill from the dock. He tipped his cap as a pleasant reminder that he'd be patrolling the area for boaters who might have had too much to drink.

Then he turned to Dan Becker and his companions. "Well, you're here safe and sound," he said as they unhooked the tow

19

rope and tossed it back to him. "You folks have a great day now."

"Say, Officer," Dan called, "what do we owe you for the tow?"

"Part of the job." Derek waved as he pulled away and reported to the dispatcher. "Jeff, I'm 10-24 and 10-8."

With the assignment completed, he was back in service. As Derek steered into open water again, a fellow officer radioed him, and they agreed to meet at the fifteen-mile mark to touch base. With overlapping shifts, the men often met on the water to discuss ongoing investigations and recent incidents. In the past ten years, Derek figured he had seen just about everything. But the recent unusual drowning had him and the other officers puzzled. Five days earlier, Derek had found a body floating in a tangle of fishing line near Deepwater Cove. So far there were no clues as to the victim's identity. And no one had reported a missing person.

Surveying the many boats on the lake as he passed them, Derek knew the unresolved incident was nagging at him. But without more information, there was nothing he could do.

Dark hair flying, the ten-year-old pressed back hard on the pedals of her bicycle. Girl and bike skidded to a stop in the driveway of the gray, wood-framed house with its window boxes full of draping, hot pink petunias. As the bike's front wheel rammed into the post that supported the mailbox, the child's mother gasped aloud.

"Lydia, where is your helmet?" Kim called from the front porch of the lakefront house. "I told you never to ride your bike without a helmet. Go to your room and put it on this instant!"

"I'm done riding for the day," Lydia announced, dropping her bicycle in the driveway and flouncing toward the house. She wore a midriff-revealing, spaghetti-strapped T-shirt; a pair of tight aqua shorts; and sparkly flip-flops. "I called Dad while you and Luke were at the doctor. He wants to talk to you."

A chill of dread swirled through Kim's stomach. "Lydia, you're not supposed to talk to your father unless I'm in the room. That's a court order."

"Court order, court order! I'm sick to death of court orders. Who cares, anyhow?"

Lydia tried to step past her mother, but Kim blocked her way with an outstretched arm.

"What?" the girl snapped. "Let me by! I need to call Tiffany."

21

"Sit down here on the porch with me a minute," Kim ordered. Seeing the stubborn tilt to her daughter's chin, she added more softly, "Please."

"Mom, I need to find out what Tiffany's wearing to church tomorrow." Lydia, all skinny brown legs and lanky arms, dropped onto a wicker chair. "Her mom's going to let her wear shorts to church, because it's already a week past Memorial Day, and everybody knows Memorial Day is the start of summer."

"You're not wearing shorts to church," Kim declared. Two years older and a grade ahead of Lydia in school, Tiffany had little parental supervision. Lydia's best friend, she often accompanied the Finley family to church and on other outings, but her mother never joined them. In fact, Kim had never met the woman, who seemed to allow her daughter to do whatever she wanted any time of the day or night.

Kim shook her head. "I don't think shorts are appropriate for church, and —"

"They're appropriate if everyone else is wearing them!" Lydia glared at her mother with narrowed eyes. "You don't know anything."

Taking a deep breath, Kim settled onto a wicker love seat beside her daughter. As she

22

studied Lydia, she attempted to pray away her ire while focusing on the lovely young woman emerging from childhood before her eyes.

"Lydia," she began, stifling the urge to scold, "you know all the rules are for your own safety. The helmet is to protect your head, and the court order is to regulate your father's contact with you. He hasn't been abiding by our agreements, and I'm this close to calling my attorney about it. The last thing I need is for *you* to be calling *him*."

"How long is this lecture going to take?" Lydia cut in. "Tiffany wants me to call her right after she gets home from the mall."

"Interrupting me is rude and unacceptable," Kim retorted. "I'd better not see you riding that bike without your helmet again, or I'll ground you from it. And you can forget about wearing shorts to church. The ones you have on are too short. Don't you realize what you look like these days? You're almost a teenager, Lydia. You have to start behaving more maturely, and that includes being aware of the way you dress. And if I hear that you've called your father again, young lady, you're going to have serious consequences. Now go move that bicycle out of the driveway before Derek comes home and runs over it."

"Would you relax?" Lydia asked, her voice just at the edge of a sneer. She pushed up from the chair and started across the porch, headed for her bicycle. "You're so grouchy. You yell at everyone and preach at us all the time. We used to have fun when you were home, but now I can't wait until you go back to work. You're making Luke and me miserable. I'm surprised Derek even bothers to come home. All you do is bite his head off."

"You're exaggerating, Lydia. I don't yell at you and Luke, and I never . . ." Kim's voice faltered as her daughter defiantly swung a leg over the bike, settled onto the saddle, and pedaled off up the road. As Lydia's glossy brown hair vanished around a curve, Kim knotted her fists and battled down a cry of rage. This was not supposed to happen!

The focus of the family ought to be on Luke, not Lydia. Luke was the twin with diabetes. In order to stay alive, Luke needed the right diet, enough exercise, and regular monitoring of his blood glucose level. In the past few weeks, Kim had reexamined everything she knew about nutrition and basic general health. And then she'd had to absorb an enormous amount of new information. Things like syringes, glucose monitors, and lancet needles were part of every-day life now. She easily used new terms such as *beta cells, HLA markers, hypoglycemia, ketones,* and *triglycerides.* Day and night for the month since Luke's first symptoms and then the diagnosis, she had watched over her son. She spent hours praying for his health, worrying over any sign of a possible problem, and phoning to discuss each development with his endocrinologist.

Unwilling to send Luke to the sports and recreational camps the twins usually attended in the summer, Kim had asked permission to take a leave of absence from her work as a hygienist for a dentist in Camdenton. Dr. Groene was sympathetic and kind, and he'd hired temporary help for the short term. But Kim's paychecks had stopped, and the family was finding it hard to make ends meet.

A voice broke into her thoughts. "Where's Lydia?" Luke pushed open the screen door and stepped onto the porch. "I thought I heard her out here. Tiffany just called."

"She's riding her bike," Kim told her son. She signaled for Luke to join her by patting the wicker love seat. "How are you doing, honey? Are you shaky or nauseous like this morning?"

"I'm fine, Mom." He plopped down in the

chair where his sister had sat moments before. "I wish I felt like riding my bike."

"Well, why don't you? Do you feel dizzy or anything like that? Do you have a headache?" She reached toward him. "Let me see if you're sweaty."

"Mom, stop. I'm okay." Luke pulled his knees to his chin and wrapped his arms around them. "You're treating me like a baby! I checked my blood. Nothing's wrong with me. Leave me alone."

"Then get your helmet and go catch up to your sister. I'm sure she'd enjoy the company."

"No." Glaring over his knees, he frowned out at the world. "I don't feel like doing anything. And I'm not wearing that stupid helmet anymore."

Kim sighed. Growing up in a home in which her parents' constant fighting had led to divorce, she had learned to cope with the unexpected. Her alcoholic mother had moved the children from town to town as drinking cost her one job after another. Kim had been determined never to repeat her parents' mistakes. The summer after graduating from high school, she'd gone to work for Dr. Groene as a receptionist and moved into a small apartment. Soon her next-door neighbor had charmed his way into her heart, and she happily married the handsome marine-engine repairman.

It wasn't long before Kim realized she had done exactly what she'd hoped to avoid. Every now and then — seemingly out of the blue — Joe became loud and mean. She was just past her first trimester with the twins the first time he slapped her. After that, her life became a nightmare.

Terrified to leave her husband and terrified to stay with him, she walked on eggshells and prayed that she could safely deliver her babies. Soon after they were born, Kim had started attending the Lake Area Ministry Bible Chapel. At LAMB Chapel, as it was called, she found strength and courage she had never known in her life. With the help and support of several women in the church, especially Patsy Pringle, she had managed to escape her husband and take refuge at an abuse crisis center. After divorcing Joe and winning custody of the twins, she settled into what she hoped could be a normal life.

And then she'd met Derek Finley. Even as she thought of the wonderful man who had stepped into her life and swept her off her feet three years before, Kim saw his truck rolling along the lake road toward their home in Deepwater Cove.

"Hey, here comes Derek!" Luke shouted. "I wonder if he brought me any cherry strings."

"You can't have —" Kim bit off the rest of the words. If Luke wanted to eat a snack now and then, he would simply have to monitor his blood sugar and keep everything in balance. He had learned to do that already. She needed to start trusting him. But a ten-year-old boy? It was so hard not to worry.

"Look, he's got Lydia's bike in the back!" Luke jumped off his chair and raced across the porch and down the steps. "I bet she fell off! I bet she wasn't wearing her helmet!"

"Oh no!" Kim ran toward the approaching truck. "Derek? Is Lydia all right?"

"Of course I am." Lydia opened the door on the passenger side and slid out onto the driveway. "Derek saw me riding near the highway to Tranquility, and he picked me up. Hey, Luke, want some trail mix? It's cheese flavored."

Before Kim could react, Luke had stuck his hand into the bag. She was trying to say something about it being almost supper-time and not good for his glucose level when Derek swept her up in his arms and planted a warm kiss on her lips. She resisted for a moment — fears, worries, and frustration still at the forefront of her mind — and then she smelled his sun-heated skin. Melting into her husband, she wrapped her arms around his neck and slid her hand down the soft hair at the back of his head.

"Surprise," he said, kissing her cheek and then the side of her neck. "I hope you made enough supper for one extra. The captain saw I was getting bleary-eyed and sent me home for a couple of hours to eat and put my feet up."

"Bleary-eyed?" Kim murmured. "Not you. And surely not in Party Cove."

He laughed and swatted her playfully as he followed her to the porch. They both knew that in his ten years on patrol, Derek had become jaded by the skimpily clad twentysomethings who cavorted from boat to boat in the notorious cove.

With more than a little pride, Kim opened the front door to a home filled with the aroma of homemade spaghetti sauce and toasted garlic bread. As it was a Saturday, she had been able to start the morning by tackling the laundry that piled up through the week and scrubbing the master bath-room.

In the midst of tensions converging like a line of thunderstorms capable of producing tornadoes, Kim always tried to keep the house peaceful and clean. She knew she was sometimes discouraged or grumpy, but she hoped her husband and children understood how much she cared by the things she did for them.

"The doctor says Luke is doing very well at monitoring his glucose levels," she told Derek as they stepped into the kitchen. That morning, Kim had fed the twins an early lunch before driving her son to his pediatrician's office. Afterward, she'd had time to finish the laundry and vacuum the living room.

"I knew the boy could conquer this thing," Derek said. "He's tough as nails, that kid. How's Lydia been today?"

"The same." Kim lifted the lid on the spaghetti sauce and gave it a stir. "She wants to wear shorts to church tomorrow."

"Why not? She's a pretty little gal, just like her mom. Both of you look cute in shorts. Besides, it's summer."

"Don't you dare side with her, Derek," Kim warned. "She's already pushing every limit we've set. She called Joe this afternoon when we weren't home. She won't wear her bike helmet. And now she's determined to wear shorts to church just because Tiffany's mother is letting Tiffany wear them."

"Does God have something against shorts?"

Kim pursed her lips to keep from saying something she might regret. The only thing that had caused her to doubt the wisdom of marrying Derek Finley was his disinterest in church. She had read about the importance of sharing a religious faith with your spouse, but she hadn't realized how much it would mean to her until they were already married. Then she saw that Derek slept in on his work-free Sunday mornings, and he never made anything but indifferent comments when Kim tried to talk to him about her beliefs. He certainly didn't try to lead the family in prayer or direct their thoughts toward heaven. Still, in every other way, he had proven himself just about perfect.

"Oh, baby, that is the best-smelling sauce in the world." Derek sighed as he leaned over to savor the scent. "You are the queen of cooks, and I mean that. My mom could make some pretty decent spaghetti, but you have her beat hands down."

Kim smiled as she set an extra place at the table. Derek's mother was exactly opposite to hers. Kim's mom had barely been able to afford the clothes she needed to wear to apply for work, while Derek had been brought up in a lovely home in Clayton, near St. Louis. Before he was killed in an automobile accident, Derek's father had worked as an award-winning freelance photographer for various wildlife and exploration magazines. His mother always dressed in linen and pearls. She belonged to a country club and several volunteer organizations. And she never failed to point out the small flaws in her son's chosen life partner.

"I got my spaghetti recipe from that chef I told you about," Kim said as Derek washed his hands in the kitchen sink. She had asked him a hundred times to wash up in the bathroom. He never noticed the coat of grime he left on her white porcelain sink.

"The guy your mother worked for when you lived in Joplin?" he asked, shedding droplets across the countertop as he reached for the towel. "He taught you a lot. I owe that fellow. If we ever get down south, we'll stop by the restaurant so I can shake his hand and thank him for turning my wife into the best cook ever."

"You would have liked him. His name was Marcel, and he was from France. But he could make just about anything, including spaghetti."

"He let you hang around in his kitchen?"

"Well, not at the restaurant. My mom got fired only a couple of weeks after we moved

32

to Joplin. But she and Marcel had already struck up a thing for each other, so we moved in with him for a while. I can't remember how long that one lasted. Anyway, he used to cook for us after work, and I would watch him."

Derek came up behind Kim and slipped his strong arms around her waist as she checked the pasta. "I don't know how a woman like you could have emerged from that kind of past," he murmured. "But I sure am glad I found you."

Kim turned her head and kissed his cheek. "God brought us together," she told him. "And I have no idea how He feels about shorts in church."

"Go easy on Lydia, Kim. I bet if Luke starts acting more like himself, Lydia will follow."

Kim stepped out of her husband's embrace and took down bowls for the sauce and pasta. She generally respected the way Derek handled the kids, but when they disagreed, it was all she could do to keep from reminding him that they were *her* children, and he ought to just back off. This time, as usual, he was right.

"I'm probably being too hard on both of them," Kim admitted. "I talked it over with Patsy last week, and she thought maybe

Lydia's rebellion is her way of responding to all the changes we've had to make because of Luke. It made sense. I know I'm overprotecting him and making both of the kids as afraid as I am."

"Really, Lydia's doing pretty well, considering." Derek sat down at the table as Kim called the twins to dinner. "The shorts, the helmet, even calling Joe . . . none of those things is all that bad. Not like the stuff I see going on with girls just a few years older than Lydia. She's a great kid."

"What do you mean calling Joe is not that bad? You know what kind of a man he is. I can't believe you think Lydia's behavior today is okay."

"Calm down, honey. Joe only contacts the kids because it makes you crazy. There's no way he's getting anywhere near them. Don't get so upset."

"You'd be upset too if you really understood what that man put us through. You may be used to dealing with out-of-control drunks, but I'm not! The kids and I were his victims long enough, and the thought of him being in contact with them still scares me."

"You're a strong woman, Kim."

"Maybe so, but Joe is stronger." She shook her head in frustration. "You know what he's like, Derek, but you're never willing to discuss it with me. You won't do anything about it, either. You just keep telling me it's going to be okay. Sometimes I wonder if you even hear what I'm saying. Where's your concern for me? Where's the protection you ought to be offering the children? Joe is out there, and he scares me to death."

"But he can't hurt any of you, Kim. The law protects you, I'll protect you, and you can stand up for yourself. At some point you need to trust yourself — and the kids."

"They're only children, Derek. They're ten years old." Kim glared at him as she took the chair across the table. "Things have changed. I realize the twins are almost eleven, and I've left them alone in the past. Summers have been filled with camps and clubs and some free time at home. But with Joe making trouble and with Luke's problems, I can't imagine doing that now."

"Listen, I had an idea —"

"Hey, Derek, did you find out who drowned the other day?" Luke skipped into the kitchen, followed closely by his sister. "Did some drunk fall out of a boat again? Or was it a murder? That would be cool!"

"He's not going to say anything about it," Lydia admonished her brother. "I already asked him."

"Your sister's right — I can't talk about an ongoing investigation," Derek told Luke, reaching over to rumple his hair. "You know that, buddy. Besides, who wants to hear that kind of thing at the table? Look at this awesome dinner your mom made."

"I hate spaghetti," Lydia announced. "I'm not eating it. She leaves chunks of tomatoes floating around so you can see them. It's disgusting."

"Lydia," Kim began.

"Are we going to pray?" Luke cut in. "I'm so hungry I feel like I'm going to throw up."

"Hunger and nausea. That's a blood sugar imbalance!" Kim started to leap up from the table, but Derek caught her arm.

Luke scowled. "Mom, just feed me, okay? I'll be fine in a minute."

"Just feed him," Lydia insisted, her face going pale. "Feed him, Mom!" Suddenly bursting into tears, she grabbed her brother's plate and ladled spaghetti sauce onto it. "Eat, Lukey," she said, pressing a spoonful toward his mouth. "Eat! Eat this right now."

"Stop it, you idiot!" Luke knocked the spoon out of his sister's hand, splattering the kitchen floor and wall with red sauce. "I'm not gonna die! Everybody quit freaking out! I hate the way you guys treat me all the time. You make me feel like I'm dying, and I'm not!"

"Whoa there." Derek laid his hand firmly on Luke's shoulder. "Nobody thinks you're dying. You're *not* dying, kiddo; you're living. You're doing great with everything, and your mom and I are so proud of you we could just about bust. So, let's all settle down and have some dinner. Kim, how about if I pray?"

It was the first time in their marriage that Derek had even mentioned prayer, let alone offered to ask a blessing. Kim was so astonished she couldn't speak.

Keeping one hand on Luke's shoulder and the other on his wife's arm, Derek bowed his head. "We're all a little off-balance here," he began, "and we need to settle down and realize that someone bigger than us is in control. Please help Luke get to feeling comfortable managing his diabetes, and help Lydia to accept the change in her brother without getting too upset. And be with Kim, who trusts in You to look out for her family. Amen."

Everyone lifted their heads at the same time. Kim swallowed in grateful amazement that for the first time, her husband had acknowledged the existence of a heavenly power. Maybe Derek hadn't used God's name or mentioned Christ, but at least he

37

had offered up a prayer. It was a beginning — a huge beginning.

A smile softening her heart, Kim lifted the bowl of pasta and passed it to her husband. "Thank you, honey," she said. "That was exactly what we needed."

Derek grinned as he dished out a plateful of noodles. "And here's something else that'll help us all feel better — an answer to my prayer right off the bat. I was about to mention this earlier, but I got interrupted. Kim, you're going to be able to go back to work on Monday, and the twins will be safe and sound right here at home." He looked around the table. "My mother called this afternoon. Kids, your grandma Finley's on her way down here from St. Louis for a nice long visit!"

CHAPTER TWO

"Well, howdy-doody," Pete said, waggling his eyebrows as Patsy settled onto the weather-beaten gray bench beside him on the dock. "I've never seen you without all your gear."

"What gear?" She stretched out her legs and drank down a breath of cool air off the lake. "Pete, if you start talking about how I change my hair color all the time or the fact that I enjoy wearing makeup or how many pairs of high heels I own, I'll go home and take a nap."

"All right; I won't say a word." He leaned over and gave her a little peck on the cheek. "But I sure do like the look of those bare toes."

It was the first time Pete had come close to even touching Patsy, let alone kissing her, and she just about fell off the bench into the lake. Instead, she grabbed the iron post that supported the dock's roof. Taking a deep breath, she tried to calm herself.

Under normal circumstances, Sunday afternoon called for a nap. But lately the order of Patsy's Sundays had altered, and she liked the change. Nowadays, she met Pete Roberts in the sanctuary. They sat together on her favorite pew near the front of the chapel, where the music and preaching could keep her awake. After that, she and the owner of Rods-N-Ends dined at Aunt Mamie's Good Food in Camdenton. You couldn't find a better place for fried chicken, roast beef, hot homemade dinner rolls, and mashed potatoes with creamy brown gravy.

Today Pete had persuaded Patsy to accompany him to Deepwater Cove's community dock for a little postlunch fishing. It was the worst time of day for the crappie to bite, but Patsy figured the dock might be a good place to accidentally on purpose run into the Finleys. The twins loved to swim, and Patsy often spotted the family at the lakeshore in the afternoon.

Unwilling to admit that Pete's kiss had startled her, Patsy dipped her toes into the water. "Any sign of the Finleys?" she asked, looking around. "I'd like to ask Kim how things are going with Luke."

Aware of Pete's shoulder next to hers,

Patsy kept her focus trained on the lake. For umpteen years, she had shampooed, trimmed, dyed, curled, and styled people's hair. She knew the feel of long hair, short hair, fine hair, coarse hair, limp hair, and overpermed, overbleached, over-blow-dried hair. But Patsy couldn't remember the last time she had felt the brush of a man's mustache and beard against her cheek.

Not that she particularly *liked* it, she told herself as Pete went back to his minnow. Facial hair held no appeal to Patsy. It hid a man's best features — his mouth and jaw-line — not to mention the crumbs and other junk that could get caught in it.

But that kiss . . .

It had caught her off guard and sent a shiver down her spine. Patsy absently stuck her hand in Pete's minnow bucket and came up with one of the small, wriggling silver bait fish. Did her reaction to a kiss on the cheek mean Patsy's well-barricaded heart was softening to the man?

She poked her hook through the minnow and cast the fishing line out across the open water that surrounded the dock. The afternoon sun glinted off the blue-gray surface, casting spangles of light on the dock's corrugated tin roof. On this weekend, one of the busiest of the year, Lake of the Ozarks

41

bustled with traffic. Runabouts pulled inner tubes, skiers, and wakeboarders. Pontoon boats drifted along, loaded down with families who were barbecuing or fishing. Jet Skis zoomed by, ripping up the water and making conversation difficult.

Despite the hectic activity on the lake, its surroundings remained peaceful. Thick forests of maple, oak, dogwood, redbud, and hickory trees draped with ivy and carpeted with layers of fallen leaves and mushrooms reached down to the water's edge. Red and yellow limestone bluffs formed caves for bats and sanctuaries for all kinds of wildlife. Overhead, in a blue sky dotted with puffs of white clouds, ravens circled, gulls searched for fish, and flocks of geese winged toward secret nests.

Patsy would have enjoyed the scenery if not for that kiss Pete had given her. Boy, oh boy. She could not afford to let her comfortable, well-ordered life get thrown off-kilter by a man. Especially not Pete Roberts. Everything he had told her about his past made her uncomfortable — two divorces, enough DWIs to send him to jail, a stint in a rehabilitation center, and a job that barely let him make ends meet. He had been known to chew tobacco and spit wherever it was convenient, including the flower box outside Patsy's salon. He was pudgy, hairy, and annoying. Other than that, she didn't mind him too much.

"Nice day for fishing," Pete drawled as he turned the crank on his reel. "What did you think of the sermon this morning?"

"I liked it." Truth be told, Patsy had already forgotten the topic of the message, but she admired Pastor Andrew and knew he had probably preached on something she agreed with.

"Fishing for men," Pete said. "Craziest thing I ever heard. Anyone who knows fishing knows that when you pull a fish out of water, it's gonna die. No ifs, ands, or buts. That fish is doomed. So why on earth would Jesus tell the disciples to go fishing for men? Pastor Andrew talked on and on about it, saying we were supposed to be like that and go fishing for men too. I wanted to stand up and ask him if he was missin' a few shingles from his roof."

"It was a *story*, Pete. Jesus didn't mean it to be taken exactly the way it sounds." Patsy reeled in the last of her line, noticed that her minnow was gone, and reached for another. "It was a whatchamacallit . . . a metaphor or an allegory or something like that."

"A parable?"

"Well, I don't know what it's called, but Jesus was saying that He wants us to go find other people and tell them about Him."

"Yeah, but He shouldn't have told us to be fishers of men. It makes me think of a stringer of dead folks, and what good is that?"

"Oh, Pete." Patsy shook her head. How strange the Bible's teachings must sound to someone who had rarely heard them.

"What I'm saying is that if you fish for men," Pete muttered, "then you're gonna have a problem on your hands. You'd think Jesus would have been smart enough to know that, Him living out by Lake Galilee."

"He was smart, all right," Patsy countered. "The thing is . . . people *do* have to die once they get caught by Jesus. You know how Pastor Andrew always reminds us that we have to die to ourselves?"

"How — like that business about taking up our cross?"

"Yes, and giving up our life in order to save it. All those famous verses from the Bible. If the true Fisher of Men reels you in, Pete, you are going to die to your old self and be born again."

"Born again." With a snort of disgust, Pete laid his rod on the bench and took a round can of snuff from the back pocket of his

jeans. "I've heard that one before. I never wanted to be one of those born-again kind of Christians. Holy Rollers is what my dad called them. Crazy-sounding folks, if you ask me."

As Pete reached for a pinch of tobacco, Patsy snatched the can away and flung it out across the lake. It made a couple of skips over the water, then disappeared beneath a wave.

The moment she realized what she'd done, Patsy dropped her pole onto the dock and covered her mouth with her hand. "Oh, Pete, I am *so* sorry," she said. "Sometimes I act without thinking, and it never turns out right. I'll get you another can of snuff. In fact, I'll drive over to the convenience store right this minute —"

"Calm down," he said, patting her bare knee with his minnow-baiting hand. "Don't you worry about it, pudd'n. I need to quit chewing anyhow. Dr. Groene says it's bad for my teeth and gums."

Patsy glanced over at him. "You're not mad?"

"Naw. Hey, look who's coming up the dock. It's Steve and Brenda Hansen. And they've got Cody, too."

He waved at the handsome couple strolling hand in hand. Behind them sauntered the thin, curly-haired young man who had found both residence and employment among the homeowners in Deepwater Cove. Cody was a little slow to figure things out, but he was the hardest worker Patsy had ever employed at her salon. He kept the place spic-and-span, and he was polite to the patrons too.

"Caught anything?" Steve Hansen asked.

"Nothing but this pretty gal here," Pete answered, sticking a thumb in Patsy's direction. "We're just warming up our rods. You going out in your boat?"

"Yeah, we thought we'd look for a quieter cove. Brenda wants to try to teach Cody how to swim."

"I don't want to swim," Cody said. "My daddy always told me that swimming is for fish, and I am not a fish."

"You'll be fine," Brenda assured him. "I taught my three kids, and they love it. Once you learn how, you'll enjoy swimming. It's fun."

"Okay." Cody gave the word a backwoods Missouri twang — *oh-kye.* "Patsy and Pete have minnows in their bucket. You can eat them if you're real hungry, Patsy, but I wouldn't if I was you. They don't taste too good."

"Thanks for the warning, Cody." Patsy

smiled at him. "You sure are looking dandy today. I believe we've finally got your hair just the right length."

The young man blushed and clapped his hand on his head. "You always cut my hair good, Patsy Pringle. Especially the first time."

"We'll never forget that big event; will we, Brenda?" Patsy murmured, grinning at Steve's lovely wife. After a difficult adjustment to the empty nest, Brenda and Steve Hansen seemed to be back on track. In fact, today they looked as chipper as a pair of lovebirds perched side by side in the summer sunlight.

"Cody came out from under all that hair and surprised every one of us ladies," Brenda said.

"And you came out from that rocking chair you were always sitting in too." Cody nodded at Brenda. "You did, huh? You were sad all the time, and you didn't want to talk to me. But now you're happy."

"That's right, Cody. I'm feeling lots better." Brenda smiled at Pete and Patsy. "I wanted to tell you we found a roofer whose bid was reasonable. He'll be starting work in a couple of weeks."

"That reminds me," Pete said. "Thanks for patching the leak over my cash register,

Steve. I'll be glad when they put a new roof on the whole shebang. I mailed my rent check on Friday, by the way. You ought to have it by Tuesday."

"Mine, too," Patsy echoed.

Steve and Brenda had recently purchased the strip of attached shops in the nearby town of Tranquility. Now they were busy tending to the many repairs neglected by the former owner.

"And did you hear our good news?" Brenda asked, leaning one shoulder against the dock's iron post. "We found a renter for the empty store."

"Who?" Pete and Patsy asked at the same time.

"Her name is Bitty Sondheim," Steve said. "She's new to the area, and she'll be opening a little restaurant called the Pop-In. Just breakfast and lunch."

"There goes my hot dog business," Pete lamented.

"Uh-oh." Cody shook his head.

Everyone knew that Pete's hot dogs were among Cody's favorite foods. Patsy could see that the young man was crestfallen, and to tell the truth, she didn't feel so good about the information herself.

"I doubt you're going to lose much traffic to the new place," Brenda told Pete. "It'll have a different kind of food than yours. The owner wants to serve mostly omelets and sandwiches."

"Sounds too much like my tearoom," Patsy said. "I'm happy you didn't rent the space to that man who wanted to open an adult video store, but I don't know what I'll do if people stop coming by for tea. It's helped so much financially, and I've got those local ladies baking for me. They count on that extra income. I really can't afford the competition."

"Don't worry," Steve said. "This new place is missing the one thing you've got, Patsy: chairs. Tables, too, in fact. There's just a kitchen, a front counter for ordering, and a little bit of standing room. People won't be able to sit around and chew the fat."

"Patsy doesn't serve fat," Cody spoke up. "She serves chocolate cake. It comes in squares, just the way I like it."

"You mean no one can sit down to eat?" Patsy asked. "So this little restaurant is going to serve fast food?"

Brenda nodded. "Basically you're right — only it won't taste like fast food. That's what the owner assured us. Bitty got the idea from a little beachfront restaurant in California. It'll be omelets-to-go and sandwiches-to-go. She wraps everything in parchment paper, warm and easy to hold. Real cute, too, and reasonable prices. She's got a simple menu that one or two cooks can handle — with no need for waitresses or busboys."

Steve slipped his arm around his wife. "Brenda is going to do the interior design for the place. She has some great ideas for a color scheme and decorations."

"Now there's a good idea," Patsy said. "I don't think any house at the lake is as pretty as yours."

"Hey, you haven't seen mine," Pete protested.

"You're my friend, Pete, but I shudder to think what your place looks like."

"Shudder all you want. I'll have you know I'm as neat as a pin, handy with tools, and a fanatic about my yard. I built all those planter boxes for the shops, didn't I? You've never seen flowers as happy as the ones in my garden at home. And how about that soundproof wall I put up between your salon and my store? I can do carpentry with the best of 'em. Not to mention my cooking, which I must say is pretty up-and-walkin' good. I make the tastiest chili anybody ever ate. When I fry up a mess of fish and hush puppies, there's not a soul around that can stay away."

"You're mighty skilled at bragging, too," Patsy added. "Well, one of these days maybe Cody and I will come over and inspect this house and yard you're so proud of, Pete. Meanwhile, I'm glad Brenda is going to put her artistic skills to work on the new shop. If you have any ideas about improving the looks of my salon, honey, I'd be happy to hear them."

"I'll give it some thought," Brenda said. "Well, we'd better head out in the boat if I'm going to begin teaching Cody to swim before sunset."

"I don't want to swim," Cody said. "My daddy always told me that swimming is for fish."

As Brenda and Steve started toward their boat, Cody dawdled behind. When the couple was safely out of earshot, he leaned over and spoke in Patsy's ear.

"I . . . am . . . not . . . a . . . *fish*," he emphatically enunciated.

"I know you're not a fish," she whispered back. "People swim too. Now go get on the boat."

"Okay," Cody said forlornly.

Pete was chuckling as he cast his line out across the water again. "That Cody's got more brains than folks think. He knows he's not a fish, and that's just exactly what I've been trying to tell you. Jesus missed the mark when He told His friends to be fishers of men. That idea is plumb loco, and don't try to explain to me about being born again, Patsy Pringle. I got born once, and that was plenty."

Patsy pinched her lips shut and reeled in her line. Pete sure thought he knew a lot about everything. But he had no idea that the woman on the bench next to him was fishing for more than crappie and bass. She was fishing for *him,* and if she had her way, Pete Roberts would be born again before the summer was out.

As Kim Finley and her twins approached the lakeshore, she waved at the couple on the end of the dock. It was nice to see Pete Roberts and Patsy Pringle sitting so comfortably together, she thought. They made a perfect couple. Though Patsy was reluctant to admit it, everyone else knew Pete had fixed his eye on her the moment he opened his bait shop next to her salon. She enjoyed his company too, even though she complained about him. Kim wondered how long it would take for Patsy to come to her senses. It hadn't taken Derek long to win Kim's heart, she recalled as she watched

Luke and Lydia race ahead of her toward the water.

A short distance from the swimming area stood Deepwater Cove's dock — a double row of boat slips with decking in between and a roof overhead. Today, nearly all the boats were out on the water as full-timers and weekenders made the most of the beautiful weather. The place where the neighborhood's families could picnic and swim featured a large parklike patch of green grass, several shady trees, a bench, and a few tables and chairs. A square wooden swim dock floated in the center of a roped-off area of water.

It was a little late in the day for a swim, but Kim had finally given in to her twins' desire to join the neighborhood's other children on the beach. She packed a basket of thick towels, snorkels, masks, flippers, and healthy snacks. Then she added the zippered bag she had put together for Luke to keep with him at all times. Syringes, a monitor, needles, insulin, and glucose pills filled the bag they had come to call his "insulin kit." As the kids raced to the water, Kim spread out a blanket and settled in the shade to watch them paddle around and splash each other.

"Well, that was a major flop." The cheerful voice behind Kim belonged to Brenda Hansen. Hair damp, the slightly older woman sat down cross-legged on the blanket. "I hope you don't mind if I join you, Kim. I could definitely use some female companionship after what I just went through."

"Sure, I'd love your company. Derek's working, and I'm keeping an eye on the twins." Kim could see the outline of Brenda's wet bathing suit beneath her T-shirt. "What happened?"

"I tried to teach Cody how to swim."

"Uh-oh." Kim was sympathetic, but aware of Cody's quirks, she couldn't hold back a smile. "Trouble?"

"First he started yelling, 'I am not a fish! I am not a fish!' over and over."

"Oh, dear."

"When I finally got him off the boat and into the water, he thrashed around so much that he nearly drowned both of us."

"Did he have on a life jacket?"

"Of course, but that made no difference to Cody. He was petrified. The next thing I knew, he had lost his swimsuit."

Kim threw back her head and laughed. "You're kidding! How did that happen?"

"He hadn't tied the string around his waist, and the elastic was too loose. There

54

we were — flailing around, Cody and I hollering at each other, Steve yelling at both of us as we all searched for Cody's trunks. And then here came a Water Patrol boat."

"Was it Derek?"

"I wish. The officer thought we were trying to drown a poor naked man. He jumped into the water and so did Steve. There we all were, churning up waves and struggling to hear each other over Cody's hysterics. It was ridiculous! Cody kept grabbing the ladder on the boat and trying to haul himself out of the lake before we had found his swimsuit."

"Oh, I can't wait to tell Derek!" Kim giggled. "This will rival some of his stories, for sure."

"I finally found the trunks snagged on the propeller, and Steve and the officer got them free while Cody sobbed his heart out. You would have thought we really had been trying to do him in. Poor guy. Then the officer happened to mention the drowning near Deepwater Cove, and that made Cody cry even harder. Finally Steve helped him get dressed, the officer went on his way, and we all got back in the boat and came home."

"Wow, you must be exhausted. Where's Cody now?"

"He and Steve went up to the house.

Cody was eager to frost a cake we baked before we left."

"Let me guess — chocolate?" Kim asked, and the two women shared a smile. "I can't picture Steve baking a cake. Does he cook often?"

"He never used to lift a finger in the kitchen, but lately he's been doing a lot of grilling for us. He discovered he likes to bake, too."

"That's fantastic. Derek helps when he can, but his hours are so unreliable that most of the cooking has fallen to me."

"That's how we used to be. But in the last couple of months, things have been a lot better."

"I'm so glad, Brenda. I didn't want to pry, but I've been concerned. You seemed very depressed. It reminded me of how I felt during my divorce. You look so much happier now."

Brenda reached over and gave her a hug. "Thanks for caring, Kim. Now that I think back on what happened, I can see that things hadn't been great between Steve and me for a long time. But we really started to fall apart about the time Jessica and Justin went off to college and Steve got so busy selling real estate. His new agency kept him away from home constantly. I've learned that I need my husband to spend quality time with me. Steve simply didn't have any time to give. That hurt me so much that I withdrew from him into myself, and nothing could make me feel better."

"But you were remodeling your basement — painting it all those wonderful colors and —"

"None of that helped," Brenda interrupted, holding up a hand to stop Kim. "Trust me; things were bad. I got to the point where I was down all the time. I didn't even feel like I could pray. Steve and I . . . well, we were in trouble. But things turned around, thank God. And I mean that literally. You and the other ladies came over to help me. Steve finally began to understand that I missed him and needed time with him. I saw that I had pulled my love and support away right when he needed it most. I hated his job, and I resented the long hours he put into selling houses, but I realized I had to change my attitude if I wanted to hold our marriage together."

"It looks like you sorted everything out."

"Well, we're working on it. We still have a long way to go. Sometimes Steve gets busy and ignores me. Sometimes I still withdraw from him. But we're making a real effort to forgive the past and support each other. I've been joining Steve for dinners with his clients, and he's become very enthusiastic about my interest in interior design. It surprised me that only just now is he beginning to appreciate what I've been doing all these years. Plus, we bought the shops in Tranquility, and we're working to revitalize the strip."

"I'll bet that's drawn you closer together."

"It has, and it's added some stress to our lives. But we're doing pretty well with the problems that crop up. I'm sure there will be more rough spots to come, but I pray we don't let our guard down. Neither of us wants to allow things to get that bad again — ever."

"That's a good way to look at it." Kim watched Lydia cannonball into the water next to her brother and come up laughing. "My first marriage was a nightmare. When Joe started hitting me, I knew I had to get out. He refused to acknowledge the problem, and nothing I tried helped at all. It took a long time — and the help of some good friends — before I accepted the truth, but there was no room to work on a relationship that threatened my life."

"I'm sure things are different with Derek."

"Like night and day," Kim said. "He's the most loving man I ever met. He treats me so well, and the twins adore him. It hasn't been easy on him, either. He'd never been married before or spent much time around kids. As an only child, he had to work pretty hard to get out from under his mother's wing. Miranda is a nice woman, but she kept Derek on a tight rein, so he focused his attention on getting through college and then working with the Water Patrol. Luke and Lydia can be a handful, but Derek is wonderful with them. Last night, he came home for supper, and we were all upset over Luke's health. Brenda, you won't believe this. . . . Derek had us sit down at the table, and he prayed for us."

Brenda's mouth parted in delighted surprise. "Oh, Kim! We've been asking God for this to happen. How wonderful!"

"I was shocked. But he did it as if it was almost natural. You know how Derek has always said he wasn't sure if there even was a God. But last night, he actually acknowledged that there was someone bigger than us, someone in control. It wasn't the all-out change we've been praying for, but I was thrilled."

"Kim, that's great. How are the twins doing? Has Luke's diabetes changed things at home?"

"Everything." Kim studied her children as

they paddled, around among the others in the swim area. "Sometimes I feel the way I did when they were toddlers — unwilling to take my eyes off them for a second."

"I can't imagine how hard it must be."

"Until the diagnosis, I was comfortable leaving the twins home alone for a few hours after school. I used to let them ride their bikes unaccompanied. And they were free to go down to the lake anytime they wanted."

"They're strong swimmers," Brenda said. "Unlike *some* people we know. Luke and Lydia remind me so much of my three. They stayed tan and healthy every summer from the sunshine and exercise they got living here at Deepwater Cove."

"Derek and I thought it was the perfect place to raise children. Until diabetes." As Kim spoke, she realized she had come to view the disease as a monster that hovered over her family, lurking and watching, waiting for the first slipup before pouncing on Luke.

"The doctor told me to treat it as a normal part of living," Kim told her friend, "but I just can't shrug it off like that. It threatens my son's life."

"I know," Brenda said in a hushed voice.

"And even though I have Derek, I still see

60

myself as Luke's main protector."

"That's understandable." Brenda nodded.

"I dread the thought of going back to work, but I have no choice. Dr. Groene needs me. And . . . well . . . I know I should be grateful but . . . Derek's mother is coming for a visit. Miranda is supposed to get here later this evening. She'll look after the kids while I'm out during the day."

"I can't remember meeting her. What's she like?"

"Perfect."

"You two should get along great then."

"Ha, ha," Kim said dryly.

"I mean it. You're so organized, and the twins always look great. You and Derek love each other. You're supportive of his work. He's happy. You have a nice, tidy home — all the good things. To my way of thinking, you're perfect."

"That's a stretch, Brenda. I'm keeping up with the house, but other than that, I'm just functioning. And since Luke's diagnosis . . . barely. Now I'm adding my job at Dr. Groene's office *and* a guest to my workload."

"How long will your mother-in-law be here?"

"Who knows? It could be a while. With her husband gone, she doesn't have much to hold her in St. Louis. She worries constantly about Derek. When she finds out about all the extra work the drowning has caused him, she'll be really uptight."

"And she's concerned about the twins, too, of course."

"Luke and Lydia are not really her grandchildren, you know. Stepgrandchildren. Miranda reminds me of that now and then, just in case I forget. I'm sure she cares about them, but in the past I've felt that . . . well, that they get on her nerves."

"What kid doesn't? That's part of their job description."

"I guess so." Kim leaned back on her elbows and pointed her toes out toward the water. If she could just stay calm and relaxed while Derek's mother was visiting, then things would be so much easier. She had to trust Miranda Finley with her children; there was no other option.

"Want some chocolate cake? We brought plates and forks, too."

Kim turned to find Cody and Steve holding out their newly frosted sheet cake. And behind them stood Miranda Finley — blonde, tan, fit — with a paper plate of chocolate cake in her hand.

"Hey, there!" she greeted Kim. "No, don't get up!"

"Miranda!" Kim got to her feet anyway and embraced her mother-in-law. "I'm sorry I didn't hear your car pull up. This is Brenda Hansen, and it looks like you've already met her husband, Steve, and our friend Cody Goss."

"Nice to meet you, Brenda," Miranda said. She was wearing a white sweater set with a pair of white linen shorts and matching sandals. "I stopped at the house, Kim, and when no one answered, I drove around and spotted you down here. I hope you don't mind if I join in."

"No, of course not," Kim told her.

As Steve and Cody put squares of cake on wobbly paper plates, Miranda slipped off her sandals and stepped onto the blanket. She reminded Kim of a vintage Barbie doll. Tall, thin, her hair highlighted and her makeup expertly applied. So ladylike and genteel. The fragrance of expensive perfume drifted from her neck, where two gold chains hung in perfect symmetry.

Steve and Cody joined the women, hunkering down in the grass to eat their cake. The sun hung low in the sky and cast a shimmer of bronze, orange, and red across the lake. A blue heron flapped its huge wings as it swept over the water to find a roost for the night.

The cake was good, and Kim had never minded if the kids snacked occasionally before supper. Now, of course, she had to help Luke watch everything he put into his mouth. He would come home ravenous, as he always did after swimming. She had a large pot of pasta, alfredo sauce, and baked chicken nuggets waiting.

"This is delicious," Miranda told Steve and Cody. "I love chocolate cake."

"Me too," Cody said. "In squares."

"Squares are definitely best," she agreed. Then she glanced expectantly at her daughter-in-law. "The twins will each want a piece. Oh, Kim, I just thought of something. You did remember to put sunscreen on the children, didn't you?"

Kim's stomach knotted. "Not today. It was so late when we came out."

"I just read an article that said ultraviolet rays can reflect off the water no matter how late in the day. Can you imagine? Thank goodness, I always kept Derek coated when we were at the pool. With children, you never can be too careful."

Kim glanced down at the basket she had packed. She was sure she had taken care of everything the twins could possibly need or want. But as always, Miranda Finley had found her Achilles' heel.

"What a sweet picture this is." Miranda sighed. "Parents and children. A sunset and a lake. Good friends and —"

"And chocolate cake," Cody added. "But no more swimming. Not for me, huh, Brenda? That's because what my daddy always said was true. Swimming is for fish. And now we all know the truth about that: I am not a fish."

CHAPTER THREE

"Hello?" Derek said into the empty house. "Anyone there? Kim?" He'd just arrived home after working the late shift and had been surprised to spot a light in the living room. Had Kim waited up for him? Or was it his mother? The memory of coming home after a date to find Miranda waiting for him gave Derek a jolt of apprehension. Surely not. He was thirty-four and had been out of the nest for well over a decade.

He'd steeled himself for trouble ever since moving his mother to Deepwater Cove. Not only did his family increase by one, but Miranda Finley had about as hard a head as anyone he'd ever known.

No one answered his greeting, so he stepped into the foyer and loosened the straps on the heavy bulletproof vest he had begun wearing recently.

To be honest, he was glad no one had waited up for him. He was hoping to have a few minutes of privacy to call one of the other officers he'd chatted with on the lake that day. Though Derek thought Jerry had a good head on his shoulders, he was afraid the guy wasn't taking his work seriously enough.

"Derek?" Kim's low voice drifted from the shadows. "Hi, honey. I guess I drifted off to sleep on the couch. Welcome home."

The sound of her voice startled him. "What are you doing up so late, babe?" he asked as Kim approached. "I thought you'd be in bed by now."

"I was waiting for you," she said.

"Is that right? Well, I'm glad." Though he was happy to see his wife, Derek was annoyed at having to wait another day to call Jerry. If the officer was in over his head, Derek wanted to do what he could to help, and the sooner the better.

Instead, Kim was taking his hand and leading him toward the kitchen. "Lydia and I baked you some brownies. Have a seat, and I'll get you one."

"Brownies?" Preoccupied with his friend's situation, Derek tried to readjust his focus on his wife.

"Baking brownies was the only thing I could think of to calm Lydia down," Kim said. "You won't believe what she did. She got on the computer again — without permission. This time she looked up diabetes."

"Uh-oh," he said. With this news, Derek realized he not only couldn't call Jerry, but he had better start paying closer attention to Kim. Though it bothered him to neglect something that was such a concern, he took a closer look at Kim's face and saw that those deep brown eyes he loved so much were puffy from crying. As he settled into a chair, Derek tried to tear his thoughts away from his friend and focus on dessert and a distraught wife.

Kim slid a plate with a brownie on it in front of him, and then she poured him a large glass of milk.

He sighed and took a bite. "Good," he said. "Pecans . . . my favorite. Lydia helped with these? I didn't think she was interested in cooking."

"She's not, but I had to find something for her to do after your mother called me today in a panic."

"Uh-oh," Derek said again. The bite of brownie began to sink like a stone into his gut. "Mom called you at work?"

"Yes, and I was right in the middle of helping Dr. Groene with an extraction. Lydia knows she's not allowed to be on the computer unless one of us is around. But the minute you walked out the door for work, she talked your mother into letting her use it. Then she found . . ." Kim's face crumpled as she tried to force out the words. "She found a Web site. It was about diabetes. And it said . . . it said the life expectancy for a child with type 1 is shortened by fifteen years."

"Aw, Kim, come here, sweetheart," Derek whispered, pulling his wife into his lap and sliding his arms around her. "That's just some stupid statistic. It doesn't mean it will happen to Luke. He's young and healthy, and we're taking good care of him. More important, he's learning how to manage his own symptoms. The kid is bright — a bona fide genius. Both of them are, and they know how to look out for each other."

"That's partly what I'm worried about," she said. "If anything bad happens to Luke, you know Lydia will blame herself. They're twins, Derek! When things began to get so bad with their father — or maybe it was before that — I told them to keep an eye on each other. I shouldn't have done it. You can't expect a child to take on such a heavy responsibility."

"But that's why my mom came down from St. Louis. She's here to help."

Kim's lips shut tight, and she rose from his lap. "Your mother had *no* idea what to do today," she told him as she tucked aluminum foil around the brownie pan with a lot more force than Derek thought necessary. "When she called, she sounded practically hysterical. I was sure Luke had gone into a coma or the house was burning down or something."

"Hysterical?"

"Dr. Groene and I were working on a difficult wisdom tooth extraction when the receptionist opened the door to say I had an emergency call. You know how Dr. Groene feels about interruptions during surgery, but what could I do? When I answered the phone, your mother was so frantic that I couldn't make heads or tails of what had happened. Lydia was crying in the background, and Miranda was babbling, and it was pure bedlam. Guess who finally got on the line? Luke. He told me that Lydia and Grandma Finley were both freaking out. Your mother was trying to turn off the computer in the middle of Lydia's efforts to print the diabetes data. Luke was furious. Just like the other evening, he insisted that we all think he's going to die, and maybe we even want him to die so he won't bug us so much, and —"

"Now hold on, honey," Derek cut in. "I'll set Luke straight on that nonsense in the morning. He's got this crazy notion in his head, and everyone's reinforcing it by pushing the panic button every two minutes. I'll talk to Lydia, too. She violated the house rules by using the computer. Did you ground her?"

"I couldn't. Oh, Derek, I didn't have the heart. I know they fight like cats and dogs sometimes, but Lydia loves her brother so much. That's why she was researching diabetes on the Internet."

"Which is against the rules. What did you say to her about that?"

"What could I say? There wasn't anything I could do. I just left work as soon as I could, drove home, and made brownies with her."

"Kim, you can't do that to Dr. Groene. He relies on you."

"I know. Of course I know! He tells me all the time. He postponed a lot of appointments while I took all that time off. But, Derek, this was about family."

"You can't intervene every time there's a problem at home. Mom and the twins have to learn to manage things. If you come running whenever they have the least bit of trouble, you're going to lose your job."

"Is that what you care about? My job?"

"I care about it, but —"

"Don't you see what's happening, Derek? Everything is falling apart. I need to be here for the kids —"

"*No.* No, you don't." He stood, took her shoulders, and turned her around to face him. "Kim, you're as spooked as Lydia, and it's not doing Luke a bit of good."

"How can you say that? I'm the one who helped him learn to take care of himself. I keep my eye on him constantly in case something happens. I monitor him and check on him —"

"Yeah, you watch him like a hawk. The kid is scared he's going to get pounced on every time he moves. You're too protective, Kim. You've got to let him go a little bit — Lydia, too."

"You're the one who wanted to ground Lydia." She pulled away and set the brownies on top of the microwave. "Sometimes you can be so harsh, Derek. All your rules and regulations! It's like you don't understand how this has affected all of us. You were happy when everything was normal, but now that Luke is sick, you're coming down too hard on us."

Derek gritted his teeth, trying to keep from saying something he might regret. He had been married to Kim for three years, and he certainly did know how the family interacted. He also knew that these so-called rules and regulations were what kept things functioning. Exhausted from hours on the water and frustrated with the drowning case that was drawing so many blanks, he had little energy for an argument with his wife in the middle of the night.

They both needed sleep. They needed a break from the chaos.

"Let's just hit the hay," he said.

"Derek, I waited up for you because I wanted us to talk! We have to *do* something. I'm giving this all I can, and you have to do your part. We have to take some kind of action here. You make these rules, but I'm telling you things feel out of control."

"Whether you like it or not, Kim, rules are important. That's how the world functions — laws and regulations. Everything needs order so the people in charge can have some control."

"But you won't even talk to me about *what* rules and regulations. We need to sit down and make a plan."

"I'll make the rules right now: Computers are still off-limits without you or me around. Helmets and kneepads still have to be worn while biking. Grandma watches the twins if

73

they want to swim. And Luke's kit goes everywhere."

Kim tucked a tendril of her dark brown hair behind one ear. "Yes, Officer Finley." She gave him a mock salute. "Aye aye."

Derek gazed at her long, pretty neck and the soft sweep of her nightgown. He reached for her and took her in his arms. "Will that make it better, baby?" he murmured against her ear. "You know I love you. I'll do everything in my power to make you happy. You are the most beautiful, amazing lady," he said, tracing a finger down her neck. "All these years, and I finally found you. I don't know how I got so lucky."

"It wasn't luck, Derek. God brought us together," she said softly. "We have to trust Him to keep us strong."

Confident that he had solved Kim's latest crisis, Derek began unbuckling his gun belt. He was pulling it from his waist when he heard something slide off a shelf in the living room and land on the floor with a crash. In a split second, Derek had snapped his .40-caliber Glock from its holster and aimed it in the direction of the noise.

"Who's there?" he called out.

"Ow! Ouch!" His mother's voice echoed clearly into the kitchen. "Oh, nuts. Now what? Derek? Derek, honey? Is that you? I heard something . . . people talking . . . arguing. I can't find the light switch, and I've knocked something off the piano, and, well . . . I'm barefoot. Derek?"

Letting out a deep breath, he felt the adrenaline rush begin to subside. He pushed his weapon back into the holster and snapped it shut.

Kim's dark eyes flashed up at him. "We don't have a piano," she whispered.

"But we do have my mother," he muttered back.

Kim laid her head against his shoulder. Derek wrapped one arm around her, flipped on the foyer light, and stepped into the living room to assess the damage.

"The meeting of the Tea Lovers' Club will now come to order," Esther Moore announced as she tapped her china cup with the side of her spoon.

Patsy Pringle watched in amusement as the clusters of tea drinkers ignored poor Esther. The group had been gathering around tables in a sunny corner of Just As I Am every Wednesday afternoon since the club formed. And from day one, Esther Moore had been trying to impose *Robert's Rules of Order* on the others.

Several times Esther had referred to

herself as the club's president, only to be reminded that the TLC had no officers. She regularly took meeting minutes and kept them tucked away in her purse. But whenever she brought out her notebook to read, the whole room begged her not to keep any records in case someone had accidentally gossiped the week before. So far as Patsy knew, "no gossiping" was the only rule the group kept, and she had laid down that law herself.

"I have several updates from last week," Esther said, still tapping her teacup. "I think you should all hear the minutes."

Cody Goss, seated beside Patsy, began snickering. "Minutes," he whispered to her. "Minutes are on a clock, not in a notebook. The big hand points to them, because Brenda told me that. . . . Hey, Mrs. Moore," he called out, reaching clear across the table to bump her elbow for attention. Manners were not Cody's strong suit. "Hey, nobody can hear what you're saying, Mrs. Moore. If you want people to listen up, you might as well stop hitting your teacup with that spoon and just whistle."

Before Patsy could react, Cody lifted his fingers to his mouth and blew. The earsplitting screech brought conversation in the salon to an instant halt as everyone clapped their hands over their ears. Everyone, that is, except Opal Jones, who was ninety-four and deaf as a fence post. She owned a pair of hearing aids but hated to wear them. While the echoes of Cody's whistle died down, Opal took a sip of tea and then calmly rearranged her napkin on her lap.

"There," he announced, grinning from ear to ear. "My daddy taught me how to get people to pay attention. Whistling is pretty easy if you practice."

"Gracious sakes alive, Cody Goss!" Esther frowned at him. "You've nearly scared the dickens out of us."

"Okay," Cody said nervously, eyeing Brenda Hansen.

Patsy knew Brenda had been making a valiant attempt to teach Cody some social skills. The look on Esther's face would have withered most people's confidence. But Cody was cut from a different cloth.

He glanced at the ladies gathered around the room and said, "I'll help anyone learn how to whistle. I'm good at it."

"Thank you, Cody," Brenda spoke up. "Maybe after the meeting. *Outside.*"

"Okay." He nodded and poked a bite of chocolate cake into his mouth.

"As I was saying," Esther resumed while she fished around in her purse for her meeting notebook, "I believe we should begin. Kim, would you like to introduce your guest?"

Kim Finley stood and laid a gentle hand on the shoulder of the slender, deeply tanned woman beside her. "This is Derek's mother, Miranda Finley, from St. Louis. She's here to spend time with the twins while I'm at work."

"Well, isn't that nice," Esther commented. "We're pleased you could join us this afternoon. I guess Derek is watching Luke?"

Kim reddened slightly at the obvious reference to her son's medical problems. Patsy hadn't been able to talk to Kim last Sunday at the dock, though she had tried. There were just too many people — Cody, Steve and Brenda Hansen, and Miranda Finley had all clustered around her and the twins. Even with that many people clamoring for Kim's attention, Patsy knew how private her friend was. Kim wouldn't want to discuss her son's diabetes in such a large group.

Acknowledging Esther's question with a nod, Kim sat down beside her mother-in-law. Miranda had been chatting with everyone at their table. Patsy was pleased to note that Miranda's short, spiky hair tipped with pale blonde highlights was going to need regular care at a good beauty salon. Her roots were showing already.

"First I'd like to catch us up on last week's items of discussion," Esther continued. "One of our dear founding members, Ashley Hanes, was kind enough to ask her husband to build a bridge over the Hansens' drainage ditch. Brad completed the project last week, and he did a lovely job. But with the summer construction business heating up, he doesn't have time to paint it. Would some of us like to take on that job?" By now she had her notebook out and was running a pencil down her list.

Patsy decided to check the tea bag supply. These women tended to deplete it in a hurry. Cody could just about gulp a teacupful in one swallow.

Besides, she didn't need to hear the minutes. Patsy knew more about the goings-on in Deepwater Cove than anyone. While she styled hair or painted fingernails, her customers talked. Sometimes she had trouble concentrating on the topic, like when they were explaining how to crochet an afghan or deal with the latest hitches in Social Security or Medicare. But usually she listened.

As Patsy restocked the tea bags and sugar cubes, she noticed Brenda Hansen across the room. The lovely blonde woman reminded Patsy of a golden yellow crocus bud emerging from a deep blanket of snow — the first sign of spring after a long, bleak winter. Hope flourished in her bright green eyes, and joy radiated from her glowing pink cheeks. If Patsy guessed right, Brenda was beginning to fall in love. And the object of her blossoming affection was none other than her good-looking husband himself.

"All right, we've got a painting committee," Esther said, keeping a fragile hold on her authority as the women began to refill their teacups. They had started murmuring again, so Esther raised her voice a little. "Now, Brenda and several others — including me, if I may say so — pitched in and fixed up Patsy Pringle's front flower bed the other day. How do you like it, honey?"

Patsy sat down again and nodded. She wasn't much for speeches. "It was a real nice surprise when I drove up to my house," she said. "I like it just fine. Thank you all for helping me out."

"You're welcome," Cody replied, though Patsy was fairly sure he hadn't been a part of that particular project. In fact, Cody spent most of his time going from the salon to various houses in Deepwater Cove — dusting, mowing, gutter cleaning, window washing, and doing myriad other tasks the neighbors paid him to perform. A couple of weeks ago, Brenda had helped him open a bank account, and Patsy imagined the boy would be close to a zillionaire before — as he liked to put it — he crossed the Jordan and passed on to glory.

"Does anyone else have a project they want help with?" Esther asked. When no one volunteered right away, she continued. "Then let's turn our attention to new business and catch up on our members. Opal, how's your colon?"

Opal was adjusting her pearls as she gazed out the window toward the forest on the other side of the highway. She looked so peaceful sitting there, and Patsy thought how comforting it might be to go deaf.

But Esther was clearly anxious for a report from Opal. Ashley Hanes tapped her shoulder, and Opal looked around in surprise.

"Your colon!" Ashley shouted. "Mrs. Moore wants to know how it's getting along!"

"My colon? Well, mercy." Opal narrowed her eyes at Esther for a moment; then she turned to the others. "If you must know, yesterday I ate some chocolate pie that my sister Mabel brought over. I'm not supposed to, but I did. Boy, oh boy, did I pay for it.

You betcha. Besides that, I planted tomatoes again this year, and I'm going to eat 'em, too. I know I shouldn't, but why not?"

"Because you had cancer," Ashley reminded her loudly. "They took out most of your colon!"

"I know what they did. Good gravy." For a moment, Opal pursed her lips and rolled her eyes. Then she spoke up again. "I hear tell somebody drowned in the cove. Who was it?"

At that, everyone turned and looked at Kim Finley. With all the attention suddenly focused on her once again, Kim shrank back into her chair. Patsy's heart went out to her. Kim had been through a lot more than people knew.

Luke and Lydia had been the only bright spot in Kim's desolate life until three years ago, when Officer Derek Finley of the Missouri Water Patrol walked into Dr. Groene's office needing a root canal. Then he came in for a filling. And a good polishing. And some whitening. By the time his teeth were so shiny they could knock you over when he smiled, Derek had won Kim's heart.

The little family was about as happy as they come, but this past spring the warmth of their love had been hit full force by Luke's diabetes diagnosis. And now Kim's mother-in-law had moved into the Finley household. Patsy was no psychologist, but it didn't take much to figure out that could turn into a recipe for disaster.

"The drowning?" Kim asked, as if she wasn't quite sure what Opal had been referring to. "I haven't heard anything new. Derek is working on it, but he can't say anything about an ongoing investigation."

"An investigation!" Esther cried out, as though she had struck gold. "Does that mean there was some kind of crime?"

Kim shifted in her chair. "Most deaths call for an investigation. Accidental or not."

"I haven't read about the drowning in the local paper since the first mention of it," Brenda said. "Do they have any idea who it was, Kim?"

"Yeah, who was it?" Ashley echoed. The young redhead wore a skinny tank top and a necklace of homemade beads. "Brad doesn't like the idea of someone drowning so near us. He says Deepwater Cove is too quiet a part of the lake for people to go around drowning. It's not like Party Cove or the main channel, where they're always drinking and acting crazy. He thinks that because Derek is having to spend so much overtime looking into the death, the drowning might be a murder."

"Murder?" Esther exclaimed. "Now, that doesn't seem possible. Not around here. We're so peaceful. Parents and neighbors are always out watching the kids swim. Kim, could it have been a murder?"

As she sat amid the busy, nosy flock of women, Kim Finley reminded Patsy of a lone, straight oak tree rising above the forest floor. Strong, quiet, faithful, she looked like someone you could rely on, a friend who would never betray or hurt you. But a blast of chilly wind had torn at her leaves, turning them from green and gold into brown, fragile wisps. She wouldn't die, and she wouldn't collapse. But she might be facing a winter that would threaten her to the core.

"Derek and I don't discuss his work," Kim told the women. She squared her shoulders and spoke almost defiantly. "If there's a crime, the press will report it. There are confidentiality laws, of course, but that doesn't stop the television crews and newspaper reporters. I doubt the drowning is anything unusual. Lake of the Ozarks is known for its troubled waters. Last year we had the most BWI arrests in the state. The Water Patrol worked more than a hundred and fifty boating accidents with nearly a dozen fatalities. Derek does his job, and he does it well. But the last thing he wants to talk about when he comes home is drunk boaters and drownings."

"I suppose you're right," Esther said. She appeared slightly put out that Kim hadn't succumbed to the group's pleas for details. While canvassing the neighborhood in his golf cart, Esther's husband usually picked up every snippet of local gossip to be had. Charlie related the news to Esther before he told anyone else, and the Moores took pride in knowing everything about everyone — or as they put it, having a deep concern for the welfare of the Deepwater Cove community.

Charlie, a retired mail carrier, had once told Patsy his intuition was so finely tuned that he could tell what was in a letter just by lifting the envelope. The mere sight of stilted writing on an address or a stamp stuck on sideways had taught him trouble was headed for the recipient. Charlie had six senses, he liked to tell people: sight, smell, hearing, taste, touch . . . and mail. The last, he insisted, was the most dependable. He could read the mood of a family by the glint in their dog's eyes. He knew what was happening in a household by the way the curtains were drawn, the grass mowed, or the sprinklers set. A neighborhood kept no secrets when Charlie Moore was on his rounds. And even though he had retired, Deepwater Cove still benefited from the daily patrols he took in his golf cart.

But Patsy was proud of Kim for sticking to her guns. If Derek wasn't supposed to discuss his work, then so be it. Patsy had done her share of trying to pry information about the drowning out of Officer Finley, and she felt pretty bad about it.

As Kim was obviously not going to say another word, Esther wrote something in her notebook of meeting minutes. "Thank you for that report, Kim," she said. "And now I'd like to find out more about the new shop moving into Tranquility. Brenda, we hear it's a restaurant."

"Was it a man or a woman?" Cody asked in a loud voice before Brenda could respond. "The dead person in the water — was it a him or a her? Because if it was a him, then maybe nobody would come looking. My daddy told me that hims can disappear off the face of the earth and nobody might miss them. But people would look for a her. She might be a mother or daughter or sister, and that means someone loves her and wants her to come home. That's how it is with women, but a man could run off and even take his son with him. And if that man was not someone's favorite person in the world, and if the son didn't know but to do as he was told, then the two of them could leave forever. That's how it could be."

The hush in the tea area was broken only by the whine of a blow-dryer over in the salon. Was that what had happened to Cody? Patsy had heard that a letter found in the young man's pants pocket told how he came to be wandering around the lake homeless, filthy, and hungry. Cody's father wrote that his wife had died. Was that true? Or was it possible that the man had run off with Cody when he was just a little boy? Had no one ever gone looking for the two of them? Could there be a woman somewhere — an aunt, a sister, or even a mother — who might want to know what had happened to that child?

Patsy glanced at Brenda, who had gone pale as a sheet. Then Patsy looked at Esther, whose mouth hung so far open it looked like her teeth might drop into the teacup. Last, Patsy focused on Kim, who wasn't moving a muscle.

She had the most awful feeling that no one would say anything, and then Cody might blurt out something even more shocking.

But Kim, bless her heart, chose that moment to stand up and settle her purse strap on her shoulder. "I don't know if the person who drowned was a man or a woman, Cody," she said. "But I do know that we would all miss you very much if you suddenly disappeared."

Cody beamed. "That's because I'm in the club. And I work hard to keep everything span. And I take showers and wear clean clothes." His face sobered. "Swimming is not for me, though. I am not a fish."

"I won't go near the water either, Cody," Esther sang out as she put her notebook away. "No one cares about that, honey. We love you just the way you are. Say, did you eat all the chocolate cake, Cody? I noticed it was cut into squares, the way I like it."

"Me too! I'll get you a piece, Mrs. Moore. There's lots left."

Cody leaped up and headed for the dessert counter as the women broke into relieved chatter. Patsy leaned back in her chair and watched as Kim Finley crossed the salon and disappeared through the front door.

CHAPTER FOUR

Kim didn't know when she had ever looked forward to a weekend so much. Or dreaded one so intensely. As she gathered up her purse and car keys in the staff room at Dr. Groene's office, she heaved a deep sigh.

"Everything all right?" The dentist's gentle voice drifted in from the doorway. "I hope I haven't overloaded you this first week back in the office, Kim. We had a few cases I just couldn't put off any longer. Old Abe is about to lose his teeth. If we don't take some action, he's going to lose every last one of them."

Kim reflected on the shabbily dressed and slightly odorous man who had come into the office several times lately. Dr. Groene was doing his best to preserve the fellow's few remaining teeth, but one of his molars was just begging to be pulled.

"It's pretty obvious that Abe Fugal hasn't ever been to a doctor — or a dentist, for that matter," Kim agreed. At some point in life, the fellow had broken several fingers, and the bones had fused in such a way as to render his left hand almost useless. His eyesight was poor, and he blinked repeatedly as he asked about the sterilized tools spread out on the tray next to his chair. And as for his mouth . . . well, it was safe to say those teeth hadn't seen a toothbrush in many a long year. "You know," Kim continued, "even though we didn't need to use gas today, I was concerned about him driving. Doesn't he usually have a woman here with him?"

"Yes, June Bixby — long gray hair and brown eyes. She's been here a few times. I was hoping to get a look at her teeth one of these days too." Dr. Groene tugged off his white coat and dropped it into the laundry bin. "Well, anyway, I hope it hasn't been too much for you this week."

Though they worked closely together, Kim rarely spoke to the dentist at any length. She viewed her role as one of support and assistance. Occasionally he chose to consult with her about a perplexing situation, but usually he chatted with the patient and ignored Kim almost completely. She didn't mind. Ben Groene had an excellent reputation in the area, and his office

90

was filled with patients from the moment Kim arrived in the morning until she left each evening. He paid her well, provided excellent health and retirement benefits, and treated her with respect.

"The extra hours are fine," she assured him. "I appreciate your willingness to let me take so much time off for Luke."

"Not a problem," he said. "Seems like one of my six is always into some kind of trouble — a broken arm, a fever, a loose tooth, a skinned knee. The older ones run my poor wife around the bend with their hormone surges. If they aren't in love, they're sobbing their eyes out in the bathroom. The dramatics would do Shakespeare proud."

Kim laughed. "Lydia is almost eleven, and I'm starting to see some of that. She constantly challenges our rules."

"Eleven's about the right age for the rebellion to start. My wife taught me the secret to good discipline. If anyone knows how to manage kids, it's my Mary. When they're little, the occasional time-out or a single swat on the backside will do the trick. About the time the pimples start, be ready to ground them when they misbehave. No TV, movies, time with friends — that kind of thing. When they hit fifteen, you've *really* got the keys to good behavior."

With a sly grin, he pulled a key ring from his pocket and jangled it to emphasize his point. "Threaten to take away the car keys, and they'll do anything you want," he declared. "You see these? They're Jordan's. He's eighteen and thinks he rules the world. But Dad owns the car. And when Jordan misses his curfew by an hour, Dad takes the keys. You can bet that kid will come home on time from here on out."

Recalling the night Lydia had screamed and Luke had knocked the spoon from his frantic sister's hand, Kim wondered if Dr. Groene's parenting technique was really that simple. And it didn't take into account the fact that her own family now had another authority figure living with them.

What would make Grandma Finley a help rather than a hindrance?

"I guess Luke is getting along pretty well these days," Dr. Groene commented as he took a bottle of cold water from the refrigerator and twisted the cap until the seal broke. "Good thing Derek's mother was able to come down from St. Louis and help out for a while. It shouldn't be long before your boy gets his routine figured out."

"He's managing, but . . . it's hard to be away from him. Even when I'm deep in the middle of a procedure, I realize I'm worrying about Luke."

Dr. Groene nodded. "Yes, I can imagine." He eyed her as he took a sip from his water bottle. "I remember how my wife worried the first few months after I was diagnosed."

"You? Are you . . . are *you* a diabetic?" Kim stammered.

He smiled. "You make it sound like you just found out I'm an alien. Diabetics are not as rare as you think. I was nineteen when my doctor diagnosed me with type 1. Mary and I had been married less than a month."

"I never knew. All these years."

"I don't let the disease own me. I like to be the boss, you know." He winked as he stepped toward the door. "Here's my motto: If you've got to be a diabetic, be a good one. Be disciplined. Monitor yourself. Get a buddy to keep an eye on you for signs of trouble. Mary knows that if I start acting odd, she needs to take charge right away. When my blood sugar gets low, I dislike be-ing compliant, and sometimes I'm even a little combative. But years ago we made a pact, and I've learned to obey my wife. The kids have known about my diabetes all their lives, and we're used to it. In fact, I don't even bother to look for a private room to give myself insulin. We can be watching TV or fooling around in the backyard, and I'll whip out the ol' kit."

Kim stood staring at him, stunned. Never once had Dr. Groene mentioned having diabetes. He acted so normal about it. Even casual. As if it weren't really a factor in his life.

Heading out the back door toward his car, he spoke over his shoulder. "All I'm saying is, Luke will be fine. Don't worry."

The door closed behind him, and Kim walked to the front of the building to lock up. Was it really possible to be a diabetic and still have a full, happy life? Ben and Mary Groene had enjoyed a long marriage. They had six healthy children. They lived on the lakeshore in a large, beautiful home. Their oldest daughter attended Yale University.

As she settled into her car and drove toward Deepwater Cove, Kim reflected on the serenity with which Dr. Groene conducted his life. Everything went like clockwork at the office. She had always thought that was simply a reflection of his tranquil personality and the calm demeanor of the staff he had hired. But maybe he had taught himself to be orderly and careful so he could keep his blood sugar levels regulated. *"If you've got to be a diabetic, be a good one,"* he had told her. Ben Groene must be among the best.

As she pulled into the driveway of the Finley house, Kim realized that her employer had given her the advice she'd been looking for ever since the endocrinologist had uttered Luke's frightening diagnosis.

Order, she thought. *Serenity. Peace.* Pondering how she could implement this atmosphere at home, Kim was stepping out of the car when the front door flew open. Lydia hurtled through it, with Derek in hot pursuit.

"No way!" Lydia screamed at him as she tore across the porch and into the yard. "I won't! I will not take it off, and you can't make me!"

"Get back here, Lydia!" Derek caught up to the girl in a matter of seconds. With one arm, he snagged her around the waist. His knee gently knocked her feet out from under her, and she slumped backward onto the grass.

"You can't do this!" she shrieked as he stood above her, hands at his waist. "You're not my real father! You have no power over me. Let me go, you jerk!"

"Lydia!" Kim cried out, rushing toward them. "Derek, what's going on?"

"Get up, kid," Derek barked in a tone Kim

had never heard. His forehead furrowed, he glanced at his wife. Then he turned back to the skinny girl writhing on the lawn. "I said — *get up!* Now!"

"Ow! He hurt me!" Lydia hollered as she curled into a ball. "I'm calling the police! I'm calling the child-abuse hotline!"

"What on earth — ?" Kim dropped her purse and fell to her knees. Memories of her first husband flooded Kim's mind. She had been thrown across a room, knocked onto a couch, slapped on the cheek so hard her ears rang.

"Lydia, are you all right?" she asked, gathering her daughter in her arms. "Sweetie, what are you doing? What happened?"

"*He* did it!" Lydia spat. "He said I had to . . . to . . . ."

Fear filling her heart, Kim stared up at Derek. "What did you do to my daughter?"

Wearing his Water Patrol uniform, Derek stood over them. Kim was taken aback by the fury in his eyes. Her husband never got angry. Part of what had drawn her to the man was his composure, his detachment even in the midst of crisis. But now she feared he might whip out his baton or even his gun — as he had the other night when he'd thought there was an intruder in the living room.

"Take a look at *your* daughter," Derek said. "Then ask her what happened."

Kim's focus shifted to Lydia. Dark smudges of mascara streaked toward her temples. Deep blue eye shadow stained her lids. A thick layer of foundation ended at her jawline, as though she were wearing a mask. Two spots of bright pink on her cheeks matched the glossy sheen on her pouting lips.

Stepping out of the painful memory of her own past, Kim was suddenly able to see her daughter's face. Her fear turned to confusion. "Lydia, why are you wearing my makeup?"

"It's not yours. It's mine. I bought it with my allowance, and I have the right to wear it."

"But you're only ten years old, honey," Kim said in dismay. "You don't wear makeup."

"I'm almost eleven, and I can wear it if I want to. I'm going to spend the night at Tiffany's house. She gets to wear makeup. Her mom even helps her with it."

"Well, I don't care what Tiffany and her mother do together," Kim said firmly. "You don't have our permission."

"I don't need Derek's permission," Lydia

sneered. "He's not my dad."

Kim fell silent for a moment as she tried to remember what Dr. Groene's life had shown her: order, serenity, peace. She had been raised with so much discord and confusion that she had rarely known what was allowed or what wasn't. Her mother had been sober only part of the time, and rules seemed to ebb and flow with the alcohol.

At a loss, Kim studied the comical looking child in the grass and then turned her attention to her husband. "Derek, what happened?"

"I'll tell you what's happening." The voice came from Miranda Finley, who was crossing the lawn toward the others. She had on a pale pink knit top, matching linen shorts, and a pair of pink beaded sandals. "These children are a mess, Kim. All Luke wants to do the entire day is play games on his little machines. Lydia is either on the phone or the computer. When I try to get them up and outside, they argue with me. I tell them I'll go with them down to the lake to swim, but they refuse. I offered to take them shopping at the outlet mall. Only Lydia agreed, so we had to leave Luke at home."

"You left Luke by himself?" Kim cried.

"Derek was home," Miranda pointed out.

"But you came here for Luke, not Lydia. He's the one who needs to be watched."

"Which is exactly what I was doing the whole time this little imp was upstairs getting carried away with her makeover."

"*You* helped me buy the makeup, Grandma Finley," Lydia retorted. "You even picked out the lip gloss."

"You let her buy this junk?" Derek turned on his mother. "Lydia doesn't have permission to wear makeup! She's ten, for crying out loud."

"Every girl should learn to use a touch of cosmetics," Miranda shot back. "And who better to teach her than me? My mother took me for a professional consultation when I was ready to start doing my face. I don't think Lydia is too young to practice."

"She's too young to go to her friend's house looking like that," Derek said. "Lydia is sweet and innocent. She's pretty, like her mother, and I don't want that to change." His tone had softened as he spoke, but his face went grim again when he touched his gun belt. "I've gotta go. I'm about to be late to work."

"But what about taking me to Tiffany's house?" Lydia whined. "You promised, Derek! You told me you would drive me —"

"Grounded," Kim said, cutting her off.

Dr. Groene's wise words formed in her mind as she stood and pulled Lydia up from the grass. Taking her daughter by the shoulders, Kim spoke firmly. "You are not going to Tiffany's house this weekend, and you won't go next weekend either. If you can follow the household rules until then, I'll consider letting you invite her over here for the night. Now walk back inside and take that stuff off your face."

"I'm sick of this stupid, ridiculous family!" Lydia shrieked as she marched across the yard. Fists clenched, she shook her head. "I wish I lived with my real father."

"You do live with your real father!" Kim retorted loudly as she watched her daughter slam the door. Derek had already backed his truck out of the garage, and he drove off without even a glance at his wife. Turning to her mother-in-law, Kim eyed the blonde, spiky hair and the bright blue eyes rimmed in dark liner. Come to think of it, Miranda Finley wore far too much makeup for Kim's taste.

Unable to think what to say to the woman, Kim picked up her purse. "I'd better help Lydia find the cold cream," she murmured.

"I have an exfoliating cleanser that works so much better," Miranda called after her. "Cold cream can really clog young pores!"

■ ■ ■ ■

As Derek steered his boat toward the mile marker where he and another officer had agreed to meet that afternoon, the recent unusual drowning nagged him. But for some reason, Lydia's unexpected outburst bothered him even more. The child had sassed her stepfather with more venom than most of the belligerent drunk boaters he'd ticketed. Worst of all, her rage seemed to come out of nowhere.

He had been crossing the living room to greet Kim before heading to work when he spotted Lydia on the stairs. At the sight of her heavily made-up face, he had stopped dead in his tracks. All he said was "Whoa," and the kid lit into him. It was almost as if she knew he would forbid her to go out wearing makeup, so she had preplanned her temper tantrum.

But why had that one word triggered such a response? Why had Lydia kept mentioning her *real* father, when she and Luke always dreaded spending time with Joe? And how about the way Kim had rushed to Lydia's side before even stopping to talk to him? That bugged him more than he cared to admit. Then his mother had jumped into the fray.

"Women," he muttered as he pulled up beside Larry Marshall's patrol boat.

"What's that?" the other officer asked.

"Too many women at home," Derek groused. "Mother, wife, daughter. All on my case."

"Yow, that bites." Larry paused. "Speaking of women, did you hear the news? We just got the call from headquarters in Jefferson City. The unidentified Code 4 you found over by Deepwater Cove was a female."

A wash of disbelief ran through Derek. "No kidding? I would have sworn on a stack of Bibles it was a man. The jeans, the boots, the T-shirt."

"Me too. I had it pegged as a male all the way. But you've gotta admit, the decomposition was pretty bad."

Derek frowned at the memory of the body he had found tangled in fishing line not far from the small cove where he and Kim made their home. That afternoon, a light breeze had carried an odor in his direction, and he recognized it immediately. As a patrolman, he had worked deaths on the lake before, but he'd never been the one to locate the remains. It was an image he would just as soon forget.

Trained to treat every death as a homicide, they would have to wait until that scenario was ruled out. All the same, such circumstances were rare at Lake of the Ozarks.

"My guess is she was drinking on a dock or a boat," Larry said. "She sure wouldn't be the first drunk to fall into the lake, and she won't be the last. Probably passed out and drowned."

Derek shrugged. "If you'd seen the way the line was wrapped around her, you might think differently."

"You really believe it could have been a homicide?"

"It's possible. Then again, who would wrap a person in fishing line?"

"Someone who wanted to immobilize her?"

"I can snap that line with my bare hands," Derek said. "I checked."

"Yeah, but this was a woman."

"True, and there was an awful lot of line. I just can't believe that no one has called her in as a missing person."

Derek shook his head at the realization that not only was the woman still unidentified, but she hadn't had a funeral, nor had her body been buried. Whether her death was a homicide or an accident, she had once been a living, breathing human.

"I'd better get on over to Party Cove," he told his friend as he checked his watch. "It's prime drunk-hunting time."

"I reckon we've got five or six hundred boats out there," Larry told him. "People are starting to head home so they can get ready to go barhopping."

"Every weekend they cut the animals free."

Larry chuckled. "It's Sodom and Gomorrah all right."

As Derek parted from his friend, he thought about Larry's reference. Derek knew that Sodom and Gomorrah were bad places, but he had no idea why. He thought it might be from the Bible, but he had grown up in a home where God was rarely mentioned, and his limited knowledge of the Bible came from the few times his grandparents had taken him to church.

In that area, Kim couldn't be more different. On free evenings or weekends, she always had her nose in one of her religious books. She tried to read the Bible every day, and she kept markers in all kinds of how-to manuals, self-help books, and Christian novels.

Not that Kim was overly holy by any means. Derek reflected on his wife as he steered the Donzi toward the Glaize arm of

Lake of the Ozarks. The breeze cooled his skin, and the hum of the twin motors soothed his nerves. To Derek, Kim was more attractive than ever. The way she made him feel sent goose bumps down his arms. It was hard to imagine how her first husband could have been so stupid as to let her get away.

Kim was a great woman. She took good care of her children, she cooked delicious meals, she kept the house tidy, and she satisfied his every need. Even her religious bent appealed to Derek. Kim's Christian faith had given her a gentle and kind spirit that he treasured. She loved him more deeply than he would ever have believed possible. What more could a man want? How big a loser did you have to be to start knocking around a woman that wonderful? And she had been pregnant at the time. With twins!

"Lydia." He uttered the name in frustration. All this time, Derek had done his best to be a good father figure to Luke and Lydia. He had provided for them much better than the worthless alcoholic whose genes they carried. He loved those kids as if they were his own. There was nothing Derek wouldn't do for his family.

But he refused to allow his ten-year-old stepdaughter to be turned into one of those pint-size beauty queens by some friend whose mother was too permissive. As Derek steered into Anderson Hollow, he fumed over the memory of Lydia's mascara-blackened eyelashes and petulant pink lips. Young girls looking provocatively older than their true age could get into trouble so fast they might never know what hit them, he thought as he surveyed the mayhem in Party Cove.

This summer weekend was no different from all the rest. Lines of boats had been anchored to the lake bed and then tethered together. The tangled music from hundreds of sound systems rose in a cacophony of drumbeats, steel guitars, and wailing singers. Crumpled beer cans drifted in the water. An empty foam cooler bobbed past. The distinct smell of burning marijuana mingled with the tobacco smoke that hung in the evening air. Girls in bikinis danced while guys grabbed at them, laughing and teasing. The thought that pretty, dark-haired Lydia might ever become one of these young women turned Derek's stomach.

A couple of his fellow officers were already patrolling the area, but there were never enough to keep the place under complete control. Despite the obvious drunkenness, loud music, and near nudity, it was difficult to make arrests. Though driving a boat while intoxicated was illegal, Missouri had no law against drinking alcohol while boating. Someone sipping from a beer could steer right past a Water Patrol boat without getting a ticket. Catching pot smokers proved nearly impossible. At the first sign of the authorities, a user could easily dispose of his stash. Patrolmen mainly served to deter all-out anarchy and to put a stop to blatant violations.

"Welcome to the cove, Officer Finley," a voice said, communicating by private frequency over the radio in Derek's patrol boat. "You want to take a run by the Gauntlet and see what's going on?"

Derek signaled that he would swing over toward the most notorious section of the inlet. He double-checked his gun belt, a habit that had started years ago. One hand on the steering wheel, he felt his way around the heavy black strap at his waist — two magazines with fifteen rounds each, an extra-bright flashlight, his expandable baton, the radio, a can of pepper spray, a pair of handcuffs, his .40-caliber Glock, a state-issued cell phone, and a pocket recorder. All in place and ready to go.

As Derek headed in the direction of the Gauntlet, he could see a row of houseboats moored along the shoreline, as always. Across a narrow stretch of lake, a second chain of vessels faced the houseboats.

Shaking his head more in resignation than dismay, Derek watched a twenty-five-foot Challenger rumble toward the Gauntlet. As it entered the stretch of water between the houseboats and the chain of vessels, party-ers sprayed the Challenger with huge water guns. Mechanical launchers tossed water balloons. Several topless girls stood up on the Challenger's deck and began shimmy-ing around while they got drenched.

"Great," Derek murmured, focusing his attention on the path of open water ahead as he sped up to intercept the Challenger at the other end of the Gauntlet. Though charged with enforcing the state's sexual misconduct law, Derek doubted he'd have to take the situation that far.

He understood the appeal of alcohol, but other questions plagued him. What was the attraction of partying this way weekend after weekend? Why did people bring their chil-dren onto the lake and out to this cove? This was fun?

"We've got a 10-38 in Anderson Hollow near the entrance to the cove." The dis-patcher on Derek's radio voiced the call for immediate assistance just as he steered the last few feet toward the end of the Gauntlet. "There's a fight in progress with several people involved. . . ."

As the dispatcher at the Water Patrol's general headquarters in Jefferson City gave further information and directions, Derek swung the Donzi away from the Challenger. So much for stopping the boaters for a polite chat about public indecency. Officer Finley was needed elsewhere.

Sodom and Gomorrah, he thought as he navigated past a group of swimmers waving beer bottles to the beat of the music coming from their houseboat. A girl screamed from a nearby vessel, and several people yelled as she yanked up her bikini top and flashed the patrolman speeding by. Derek turned his head away, and kept driving. Were people in the Bible ever as crazy as this?

Chapter Five

Pete Roberts was cleaning a clump of grass from a Weedwhacker's motor when Cody Goss pushed open the front door of Rods-N-Ends. Pete smiled at the young man. The rack of rotisserie hot dogs drew Cody to the tackle shop at least once a week. Now that he had some money of his own, Cody indulged himself once in a while.

"Hey, Pete," he said as he stepped up to the heated case to watch the wieners rotate on the racks. "How are your hot dogs today?"

"Fresh and sizzling, as usual." Pete moved to the sink he had installed near his work area and began washing his hands. "How many you want this time, kiddo? Two or three?"

Cody's tongue slipped out and licked his lips. "Three, please. I'm not fat yet. Not as fat as you anyhow. I think I could have three."

"I reckon you could." Pete grinned at the young man's well-known frankness. Though Cody had offended some with his blunt honesty, Pete enjoyed the fact that the kid said exactly what was on his mind. "You think I'm fat, Cody?"

The blue eyes darted to Pete's face. "I sure do. Don't you?"

"I guess I am, now that you mention it."

"If you looked into a mirror, you would know that you're wider around the middle than anywhere else. Patsy Pringle thinks you're fat. She says you look like a big, shaggy ol' bear."

Pete chuckled as he unwound the wire tie on a bag of buns. "Are you sure she wasn't talking about my beard needing a trim?"

"I don't think so. I'm pretty sure she was talking about your stomach." Cody drummed his fingers on the counter while Pete squirted ketchup and mustard on the three hot dogs. "Hey," he piped up after a moment, "did you hear that the drowned person Officer Finley found in the lake was a lady?"

"I read that in the paper this morning. Where'd you hear it?"

"At Patsy's next door. All the ladies are talking about it, and I was washing windows on the inside, so that's how I heard. It's not polite to listen to other people's conversations. That's what Brenda told me. But if they talk loud, you can't help it. When the blow-dryers are going, those ladies talk loud."

"I'll bet they do." Pete slid the hot dogs into their paper sleeves one by one. "It's kind of unusual to have a female drown, I hear. I reckon she must have been drunk and fell off of a boat or something."

"She was wrapped in fishing line."

"I heard that. Nasty business. Hard to believe she washed up so close to us."

"Officer Finley found her. The women next door said nobody has called to ask about a missing lady. I don't understand why not. My daddy told me that a man could disappear, or even a man and a little boy that nobody wanted, and no one would bother to look for them. But if a woman went missing, people would search for her. Do you think that's true?"

Pete pushed the three hot dogs across the counter toward Cody, who had laid the exact amount of cash — including tax — right next to the register. He couldn't imagine why the boy was so caught up in this drowning incident. As far as Pete was concerned, the less folks talked about it the better. Drownings and such were bad for

112

business. Tourists liked to think of the lake as a place for sun, water, and lots of fun. Unpleasant news ought to be buried on the back page of the paper, Pete thought. Or left out altogether.

"I reckon people probably have called the police or the Water Patrol about the woman," he told Cody. "No one goes missing without somebody noticing."

"Not even a man? a man and a little boy that nobody wanted?"

Pete frowned as he strolled back to the area of his shop where he repaired small engines. The Weedwhacker would be easy enough to fix. Just getting the moldy old grass out was a good start.

"Cody, who's this man and boy you're talking about?" he asked. "The person who drowned was a woman. Did you know someone who turned up missing?"

The young man wandered across the room, uncharacteristically abandoning his hot dogs on the counter. "That man might be my daddy," he said in a low voice. "And I think that little boy might be me."

Pete looked up in surprise. "You? What makes you say that? Why would your father run off with you, Cody?"

"Hmmm." Cody pushed his hands into the front pockets of his jeans. Then he pushed them into the back pockets. "It might be because nobody wanted me. Not even my mother. Because . . . because I am dumb."

"Dumb, huh?" Pete pointed at Cody with the end of a screwdriver. "You're not dumb, kiddo. I can promise you that. Who ever said you were?"

"Lots of people. One time some men hit me and called me names. They said I was dumb, stupid, idiot, crazy, nuts."

"Good golly, Miss Molly. You mean to tell me you got beat up by a bunch of thugs?"

"They were men, and they hit me because I'm dumb."

"And I'm here to tell you that's a flat-out lie. Did you ever go to school, Cody Goss?"

"No. But I learned my Bible verses real good. Do you want to hear Psalm 139? It's my favorite."

"I don't want to hear no Bible verses. Not right now. I want to know why your daddy didn't put you in school."

"Because the other boys might make fun of me, because I'm dumb."

"Would you quit saying that, kid? You're not dumb! There's not a mother alive who wouldn't be proud to have you for a son and miss you to pieces if your daddy ran off with you."

"Really?"

Cody stared with such intensity that Pete began to wonder if he'd said too much. Flustered, he went back to work cleaning up the Weedwhacker. "Your hot dogs are getting cold," he told the boy. "You better eat them."

Hanging his head, Cody muttered, "Okay."

Pete worked a moment longer on the whacker; then he looked up at the young man, who was still standing there staring at him. "Well, are you going to eat your hot dogs, or not?"

"Do you think I might have a mother?" Cody asked.

"Well, you had a mother once; I know that much. At one time, everyone has a mother. That's how you get born. You grow in her — inside the mother's innards. Then one day, you pop out, and there you are."

"I popped out of a mother?"

"You've got a belly button, ain't you?"

Cody lifted his T-shirt and checked. "Yes, I do."

"Then you were born from some woman just like all the rest of us."

"Where is she?" Cody asked. "Where's my mother?"

Pete swallowed. "Listen, you'd better get

115

over there and eat your hot dogs. You need to go finish washing Patsy's windows. If she finds out we've been jabbering, she'll hang me up by my thumbnails."

"No, she won't," Cody said. "Patsy would never do that. She's nice."

Trying to ignore the kid, Pete studied the Weedwhacker long and hard. It definitely needed oil. And some new line. Probably just a good cleaning would do the trick. People could be pretty ignorant when it came to small engines. They would walk into Rods-N-Ends hauling a perfectly good hand vacuum or chain saw and tell him it was shot. All he had to do was add a belt or work out a kink and the owner was back in business. Good money for not much work. Exactly what Pete liked best.

"I want to see her," Cody said suddenly. "Where is she?"

"Next door. You know Patsy — she never leaves the salon until she's done for the day and ready to lock up."

"Not Patsy. My mother. I want to see my mother. Where is she?"

"Now how would I know that?" Pete asked, wondering how to get the lid back onto *this* can of worms. "Go eat them hot dogs, boy, and let me work."

"I want to see my mother!" Cody said

more loudly. As he continued to speak, his voice rose to a wail. "I want her! I want to know where she is! Why did she let me go? Why didn't she find me? Where is my mother?"

"Whoa, kiddo, pipe down!" Pete grabbed his cell phone from the pocket of his overalls and quickly dialed. When a voice answered, he said, "Hey, where's Patsy? This is Pete, next door. Send her over here pronto; you hear me? I got a pack of trouble on my hands, and his name is Cody Goss."

As tears started to roll down Cody's cheeks, Pete lunged for the hot dogs. He snatched them up and waved them in front of the boy's nose. "Looka here. Hot dogs! Yum! How about a bite, okay? Stop your blubbering now, kid. I mean it. Eat your lunch."

"Where is she? Why isn't she looking for me?" Cody's nose was running. "I don't understand. What if she drowned? What if she got wrapped in fishing line and fell off a boat? Maybe my mother is the lady that Officer Finley found! In the water! Dead!"

Pete felt so awful that he was considering ducking out the back of his store and locking the door behind him when he saw Patsy marching, shoulders back and jaw set, toward Rods-N-Ends. Thank the good

Lord! There must be a God, Pete thought, and at this moment, he didn't even mind about the fishing-for-men story Jesus had told. He had needed help, and here came Patsy.

"What's going on?" she demanded as she pushed open the door and stepped inside. "Pete Roberts, what have you done to Cody?"

"I didn't do anything!" he protested. "He's got this idea in his head —"

"Cody doesn't make things up out of thin air!" She grabbed a wad of napkins from the stainless steel holder near the hot dog grill. "Poor Cody. What happened, honeybunch? What did Pete say to you?"

"Everyone has a mother, even me," Cody sobbed. "Pete said so."

"Good gravy, Pete! Did you have to go and bring that up?"

"Now wait just a —"

"Blow your nose, Cody," Patsy ordered. "There you go. And again. Good. Now, what's this all about? Tell Patsy."

"I have got a belly button," Cody said, sniffling.

Patsy gave Pete a look that would wither grass. "Yes, so do I. What about belly buttons, Cody?"

"Everyone has a belly button, and everyone has a mother that they popped out of."

"Popped out?" Again she eyed Pete.

He shrugged helplessly. "Well? How else would you describe it?"

"I wouldn't!" Patsy snapped. "I'd let Brenda Hansen do it. You're the last person in the world to be telling this young man about the birds and the bees. What were you thinking?"

"Where is my mother?" Cody asked. "Did she get drunk and wrapped in fishing line and drowned?"

"That's not your mother. That's the woman who washed up in Deepwater Cove. She could be anyone."

"She could be my mother."

"Well, she's not."

"Then where is my mother?"

Patsy sighed. "Cody, do you remember the letter Brenda and Steve found in your pocket? Your father had written it, and he said your mother passed away. I'm very sorry to have to say it, but your mother died."

"I don't want her to be dead."

"Oh, for mercy's sake, let's go call Brenda. Grab your hot dogs, Cody. We'll get Brenda to drive over to the salon and sort everything out. And next time, don't bother asking Mr. Roberts here any questions."

Cody gathered the three hot dogs and held them against his chest as Patsy led him toward the front door of the tackle shop. His eyes focused on Pete. Patsy, too, cast a backward glance. Then she shook her head, grabbed Cody's elbow, and ushered him out onto the sidewalk.

"Hey, Patsy," Pete hollered after her. "Stop telling people I look like a bear!"

Patsy paused a moment, gazing at him through the plate glass window. Then she burst into giggles as she led Cody toward the haven of Just As I Am.

Saturday evening, the telephone rang while Kim was in the kitchen wrapping potatoes in aluminum foil. She reached for the receiver, but when she held it to her ear, she could already hear her mother-in-law's voice on the spare room's extension.

"You've reached the Finley family!" Miranda sang out. "Derek, Kim, Miranda, Luke, and Lydia — all at home and eager to chat. How may I help you?"

Kim winced at the inclusion of their guest's name in the family lineup, but she couldn't deny that Miranda was now definitely a part of the household structure. In the two weeks since her arrival, she had wedged herself firmly into place — like a queen who had arrived to rule an upstart realm from the comfort of her bedroom.

During that short time, the woman had managed to alter just about every routine Kim had established. Miranda's high blood pressure meant less salt in the meals. She hated nuts, so pecans had to be left out of the brownies and walnuts omitted from the Waldorf salad. Peanut-butter sandwiches went straight onto the no-no list. Miranda's clothing added an extra load or two on laundry day. Thank goodness the woman was willing to iron her own linen shorts and slacks and to hand wash her filmy silk blouses. She insisted on a mug of coffee every morning and a cup of chamomile tea at night, and she let it be known if they weren't made just the way she liked them.

Even worse in Kim's mind, Miranda wasn't the least bit interested in church or God, and she often started eating her meal before the blessing had been asked. Her favorite activity was shopping, so the twins had to accompany her on frequent and lengthy trips to the outlet mall. Lydia didn't mind, but Luke deplored being dragged from one store to another. Yet with both parents gone during the daytime in the second week, he was left with no choice. In fact, no matter what the Finleys planned,

Miranda had to be figured into the picture.

For the first few days of her mother-in-law's visit, Kim had accommodated the changes. She told herself that Miranda was essentially a kind woman. Nothing would have to be modified all that much.

Though able to ignore the dominating presence for a short while, Kim soon found her patience tested. When she wanted to scream in frustration, she made up her mind to be polite. Her waning goodwill lasted four or five days longer. By the end of the second week, she was downright angry.

Now poised to cut her mother-in-law out of the phone conversation, Kim heard the voice on the other end of the line speak up.

"Oh, is this Miranda Finley?" Kim recognized Brenda Hansen's sweet tone at once. "For a moment I thought you might be Lydia."

"Lydia? Gracious, that would be odd, wouldn't it? We're not even related."

Kim flinched. Derek loved the twins like a father, and Kim had prayed that his own mother would see them as her grandchildren. But Miranda kept the lines clearly drawn between herself and the twins.

"I was hoping to speak to Kim for a minute," Brenda told Miranda over the phone. "Something has come up, and I'd like her advice."

"Oh, dear, I'm all the way down the hall in my room, and Kim is in the kitchen," Miranda said. "She's baking potatoes for dinner, though why, I surely don't know. We've had enough carbohydrates today to sink a ship. She started us out this morning with French toast. Then she fed us sandwiches and chips for lunch. Now it's baked potatoes, and I think I even saw her getting out a box of rice. Can you imagine? I'm afraid I'll outgrow my clothes in no time if she keeps this up."

"I've always thought Kim was a great cook," Brenda said.

"I'm right here," Kim spoke up. "I heard the phone ring. It's okay, Miranda; I'll take the call now."

"Well, I did have something to ask Brenda, if you don't mind, Kim. She has such a way with decor, and I've been eyeing the lace curtains in the living room. I don't mean to be critical, of course, but with the twill sofa and the two leather chairs, I'm wondering if lace is the right texture for the windows. I was thinking maybe a simple sheer fabric would be better in there. You could pick one of the colors from the sofa. Say that soft yellow, for example. Or the muted green. What do you think, Brenda?"

There was a momentary pause. "I . . . uh, I can't really picture the curtains in my mind right at the moment, Miranda."

"They're sort of a thick lace with roses strewn everywhere. Very feminine. Now I don't want to sound the least bit disapproving of Kim's decisions about this lovely home, but I just have a feeling the curtains don't work well with the leather."

By this time, Kim had wandered into the living room and was studying the beautiful lace curtains she'd found several years ago in an antique shop. The tag said they'd been made in Brussels, and Kim was delighted to discover that they fit her windows perfectly. What was wrong with leather, twill, and lace? To her, they made a perfect combination.

"I'll come over and take a look sometime," Brenda told Miranda.

"Why not now?" Miranda suggested. "Kim's potatoes will take an hour at least, and we're not doing a thing. Come by and see what you think. Then you and Kim can discuss whatever was on your mind."

Kim could think of about fifty things she needed to be doing, but she decided to echo her mother-in-law's invitation. "Miranda's right," she told her friend. "I'd love to see you if you have a minute, Brenda."

"Well, I've got Cody here with me at the house. But I guess we could come over for a little while before Steve gets home. He and I are taking one of his clients to the country club for dinner at seven. Cody's spending the night with Esther and Charlie Moore."

Before Kim could utter another word, Miranda had said good-bye and hung up. Replacing the receiver, Kim watched as her mother-in-law came sashaying down the hall in her spotless white slacks, matching leather belt, and pink-striped tank top.

Miranda clapped her hands when she spotted Kim. "I hope you don't mind that I invited Brenda over, though I wish she didn't have to bring that young man. He strikes me as odd. But she's so sweet, and more my age than yours anyway. I really enjoy Brenda. In fact, I think one day we might be good friends. She knows how it feels to lose your loved ones and be left alone day after day."

"Brenda stays busy," Kim inserted. "There was a time when she felt a little adrift. But she teaches Cody, and she helps Steve manage their rentals in Tranquility. I think she's even been doing some decorating in the homes he has up for sale."

"Now isn't that wonderful?" Miranda had

lifted one of the lace curtains, and she began examining it. "What are these flowers anyway? Roses or peonies? Well, Brenda will know exactly what to do about the windows. Lace is such a feminine fabric, and you've got all this masculine twill and leather in here, Kim. Not to mention the wood floors and coffee table. Don't you think lace is a little jarring to the eye?"

No, Kim wanted to retort. *I love my lace curtains.* But the doorbell was ringing, and it would be Brenda. Kim asked her mother-in-law to let in their visitors, and then she returned to the kitchen to finish up the potatoes.

So what if the Finleys ate carbohydrates now and then? They had fresh fruits and vegetables, meats, and dairy products, too. Kim fumed as she pushed the tray of foil-wrapped potatoes into the hot oven beside the large, onion-coated slab of beef that had already been roasting for several hours. She always checked to make sure Luke carefully counted his carbohydrates. Often they worked together to save up carbs so he could join the rest of the family in treats like an ice cream sundae or a slice of cake. What right did Miranda Finley have to come into her home and criticize the way she cooked? And how dare she disapprove of her beautiful European curtains?

"Hey, Kim! Do you have any chocolate cake in your kitchen?" Cody stood in the doorway, hands pushed down into the front pockets of his blue jeans. "I like chocolate cake, and Esther doesn't make it because of Charlie's diabetes. I'm sleeping at Esther and Charlie's house tonight, and they won't have any chocolate cake. Do you?"

"No, I don't, Cody," Kim told him. The sight of the earnest young man took her frustration level down several notches. "I'm sorry. I've got chocolate-chip cookies, though."

"Those are not my favorite."

"How about if I invite you over the next time I make chocolate cake?"

Cody grinned. "Okay."

"You know, I had forgotten that Charlie has diabetes," Kim said as she checked the pot of green beans on the stove. "So does my Luke."

"I know your Luke. He's a twin to Lydia. That means they popped out of you at the same time."

"Actually, Luke came first and then Lydia arrived about five minutes later. And believe me, Cody, neither one of them popped out."

"Pete Roberts told me that babies pop out of their mothers, and everyone has a mother, even me, because I have a belly button."

Kim blinked for a moment, trying to process the information. "I suppose Pete is right. I'm the mother of Luke and Lydia, and they both have belly buttons."

Cody's eyes crinkled and his nose scrunched up as if he were about to cry. "I don't know what happened to my mother. My daddy wrote in a letter that she was dead, but I want to know why. What happened to her? What if she died from getting drunk and wrapped in fishing line like that woman in the lake?"

"Now, Cody," Brenda said in a warning tone as she stepped into the kitchen and put her arm around the young man. "We've been over this too many times for you to keep repeating it. Your mother died a long time ago. We don't know exactly what happened, but the woman who drowned in the lake was *not* your mother."

"But she might be," he said mournfully, "because nobody knows who the drowned lady was. And I don't know who my mother was. So maybe they're the same person."

"Oh, Cody." Brenda sighed and glanced at Kim as if seeking assistance. "He doesn't seem to understand the passage of time the way we do. Evidently Pete Roberts mentioned to Cody that everyone has a mother, so now we've got this huge issue to deal with."

Kim set the pot holders on the counter. "Cody, did your daddy tell you anything at all about your mother? Ever?"

He shook his head. "He just said when men disappear, no one comes looking."

"Well, I'm sure your father thought he was telling you the truth, but I'm afraid he was wrong. Derek looks for missing men quite often."

"Derek is Officer Finley," Cody stated. "He found the drowned lady."

"Sometimes people do get lost, Cody," Kim said gently. "And then the police, the Highway Patrol, the Water Patrol, and lots of others start looking for them. Men and women get lost. Children too. People search for the lost ones until they're found."

"But does anyone ever get lost and then nobody goes looking for them?"

"Once in a while. No one has mentioned missing a woman near the lake, for example. So that's why this particular drowning case has been in the newspaper a lot."

"I am missing a woman," he said firmly. "I am missing a mother."

"But you have Brenda. And what about Esther and Patsy? Those women look after you and love you just like a mother would. You have me, too, Cody. I care about you very much. So do Ashley Hanes and Opal and all the members of the TLC."

"But you're not my mother. None of those ladies is my mother. Everyone here has a real, true family. Everyone but me. What if I have a sister? Or maybe a brother? Or an aunt or uncle?"

"I don't know. Maybe someone at some point could help search to find out if you have any relatives."

"Which someone at which point?"

"I could do it," Miranda offered. She had been leaning against the kitchen doorway, one of the living room's lace curtains in her arms. "I traced my husband's genealogy all the way back to Ireland in the 1600s. And I've followed my own family to the Civil War. It gets rather complicated there, but I'm not giving up. I'm actually quite good at finding people's relatives."

Kim and Brenda both turned to Miranda and stared at her. Hardly knowing how to respond, Kim watched in astonishment as Cody threw his arms around Miranda.

"Thank you," he said. "I don't know who you are yet, but you must be a Christian, because only a Christian would help somebody find their relatives."

Miranda stiffened and carefully detached Cody from her neck. "I am not a Christian," she told him. "I believe that many paths lead to God — Buddhism, Hinduism, Islam, even paganism. I'm proud to say that I've looked into just about every world religion that is now practiced or ever existed in the past, and I'm convinced there can be any number of roads toward divinity."

Cody looked at Brenda, his eyes blinking in wonderment. "Did you hear that? She's not a Christian. What's her name?"

"My name is Miranda Finley," the woman herself answered. "I'm Officer Derek Finley's mother. We met the day I arrived — by the lake."

Gaping, Cody eyed her in silence for a moment. "Only a Christian would give you chocolate cake," he murmured.

"That's not true, young man. There are plenty of good, caring people in the world, and not all of them are Christians. I would give you chocolate cake."

"Right now?" he asked, brightening.

"No. But if I made some cake, I would share it with you. I'm a very nice person, and I'm not a Christian. I'm not even particularly fond of Christians, truth be told. They're pushy."

Miranda's eyes focused on Kim for an

instant; then she trained them on Cody again. "Now then, you need to be quiet while Brenda, Kim, and I chat."

"But what about my relatives?"

"I'll start looking for them on Monday morning. Meanwhile, stand aside, Cody." She stepped between him and the other two women and held up the Belgian lace curtain. "What do you think of this, Brenda? Isn't it a little too flowery to go well with leather and twill?"

Chapter Six

Derek couldn't believe his good fortune at finding Kim awake in bed when he got off work after a twelve-hour shift that Saturday. The twins had been asleep for a while, he knew, and evidently his mother had shut herself into the guest bedroom for the night. This was definitely a positive sign, and he planned to make the most of it. Derek had been out on the lake all day, spending some of it snacking on a bag of nacho cheese–flavored tortilla chips. He would need to take a quick shower and brush his teeth before giving his wife the kind of kiss her eyes were begging from him.

"You look like heaven itself," he told Kim, his voice low as he unbuttoned his shirt. She was wearing one of his favorite nightgowns, a blue scrap that was slinky and silken. "I must have seen a couple dozen half-naked girls in Anderson Hollow today, and not a one of them could hold a candle to you."

"Though I'm sure you didn't spend much time comparing, right?"

"Right," he said with a grin. "Of course not."

Like most of the other officers on the water, Derek was careful about what he looked at in Party Cove. If he spotted some young gal exposing herself, he turned his head quickly. Focusing on contacting the dispatcher and navigating through clusters of swimmers on his way to intercept the woman's boat, he kept his attention in the right place.

A Water Patrolman's hours were long, the sun hot, and the temptation great. Of Derek's entire graduating class, only three officers remained on duty. The job — like most in law enforcement — took a toll on marriages and other relationships. Before committing himself to a wife and children, Derek had made very sure he knew how to handle his assignment and not get into trouble. With a woman like Kim waiting for him at the end of each shift, he didn't have much to worry about.

"I was thankful for my canopy today," he told her. "The sun was blistering. I hope you and the twins stayed inside."

"Most of the time. The three of us drove

over to Just As I Am for a cup of tea at about four this afternoon. Luke wanted to go as badly as Lydia."

"Three of you? Didn't my mom tag along?"

"She elected to stay home and wax her legs. Evidently she can't find anyone down here who does it as well as her salon in St. Louis."

Derek made a face. "Wax her legs?"

"Whatever floats your boat."

He shook off the thought and focused on his wife again. "Oh, babe, I can't wait to hold you in my arms. Can you give me five minutes to shower and wash off the day?"

Kim shrugged as she gazed at him. Just the sight of her dark, liquid eyes and bare shoulders sent currents through Derek's stomach.

"Actually, I stayed up because I was hoping we could talk," she said. "There are some things going on that I want to tell you about. I need your opinion."

"Talk?" He froze, his belt halfway out of its loops. "Are you serious?"

"Yes." She swung her legs over the side of the bed. "Listen, Derek, I know what's on your mind, but I'm exhausted tonight. I've spent the whole day on the house, trying to put things back in order after working all week. I must have done fifteen loads of laundry. I made French toast for everyone for breakfast, and then I fixed ham-and-cheese sandwiches for lunch. And then I put in a pot roast and I thought I would bake . . . bake some . . . potatoes. . . ."

"Kim? Are you crying?" He couldn't believe this. He had walked into the bedroom to find his wife looking like a seductress. Setting all his hopes on kissing her sweet lips, he discovered she only wanted to talk about her day . . . it wasn't possible. Laundry and French toast?

"I'm not crying," she said, sniffling and wiping a finger beneath one eye. "I'm fine. It's just that you know I do everything I can to show you and the kids that I love you. I never ask anything of you except to watch the twins when you can. I do all the cleaning, the cooking, and the washing, plus I hold down a full-time job. I'm happy to do it. But then I find out I've hung the wrong curtains in the living room."

"Curtains? Wait a minute. . . . What?" Derek had a bad feeling his wife was upset that he didn't help around the house more. He had been steeling himself to apologize when her train of conversation took a sudden twist, like that last unexpected loop on a roller coaster ride.

Curtains. Derek tried to remember the living room drapes. How could curtains matter after a long, tiring day? What they both needed was to hold each other and ease their stress with some welcome loving.

"I don't know about curtains, baby," he said, stepping toward her and gathering her in his arms. "All I know is that you look delicious in that little blue thing. I could just eat you up."

Usually Kim slipped her hands around him and began drawing circles on his bare back. This time she laid her head on his shoulder and let out a deep sigh.

"The curtains are lace," she murmured. "From Belgium. I think they're wonderful, but even Brenda Hansen said they might look better in the dining room. Can you believe that?"

Derek made a valiant attempt to concentrate on his wife's words instead of on the warm, pliant figure pressed against him. He mumbled in her ear, "So, what was Brenda Hansen doing here?"

"*Your mother* asked her to come!" With that, Kim pushed on his chest until he plopped down on the edge of the bed. She began pacing. "Your mother said she thought our house needed Brenda's decorating expertise. Brenda Hansen is a good friend, but it's not like she knows everything there is about home decor. She doesn't have a degree in interior design. I don't think she even went to college. But everyone around here considers her the expert."

Reaching the wall, Kim made a U-turn. "Well, I happen to like those curtains," she went on. "I love them, in fact. And I think they go perfectly well with the leather chairs and the twill couch. I don't want them hanging in the dining room, because that's where we have the best lake view. Those windows ought to be left bare, just the way I have them."

Another U-turn at the opposite wall. "It's not like I hire Cody Goss to do anything for us. I do it. I do everything myself, because it's the best way I know to show you all how much I love you. I want you to eat a good, hot meal and hear that food whispering that your wife loves you. When you put on your uniform, it should let you know that I care about you, and that's why I take the time to wash it and iron it and fold it so neatly."

Derek began to feel like he was watching a tennis match.

"And I bought those Belgian lace curtains specifically because they were soft and pretty. I keep them washed and bleached and ironed and hung on their rods, because

I love my family. Your mother just doesn't get that. All she can think about is re-arranging our home and criticizing my baked potatoes."

Derek did his best to concentrate, but he had no idea what she was talking about. All he could see were her long, tanned legs; her graceful neck; that slender waist; and the outlined curves beneath her little blue gown.

But now she turned all of a sudden, hands on her hips and brown eyes boring into him. Like a turtle frozen in the middle of a highway, he held his breath and tried to think clearly. The last thing he recalled Kim saying was something about potatoes, but he couldn't remember what.

"I love your potatoes," he fumbled out.

She let out a muffled cry of exasperation. "Don't you get it? She's sabotaging me with the kids. Now they think we eat too many carbohydrates! Lydia said that very thing, mimicking her exact words right at me. Derek, you know I'm doing everything I can to feed our family a balanced menu. I make sure Luke counts his carbs."

"Of course you do," Derek affirmed. Was Kim upset about Luke's diabetes? Or had Brenda Hansen criticized her cooking? That didn't sound like something Brenda would do.

139

"And now she's volunteering to help Cody look for his relatives," Kim went on. "Can you believe that? She thinks that because she knows how to trace genealogy, she can find people who've been absent from his life for nearly twenty years. People who might not even exist. Ancestors and missing families are not the same! Besides, it's bound to upset Cody, no matter how it turns out. But she just can't keep her nose out of things."

Derek stood and rubbed his chest. He hadn't seen Kim this upset in a long time, and he couldn't imagine why she was. If Brenda Hansen wanted to look for Cody's relatives, let her. Chances were slim anyone would be found.

"Honey, why has this got you so worked up?" he asked. "You have your own life. Let this other stuff go. Come here and let me hold you."

Kim resumed pacing. "And you know what else? You never tell me anything."

"What? Yes, I do. I tell you I love you. I tell you I think you're beautiful, and I'm crazy about the kids. I love our house, and you're a great cook, and most of all . . . you're beautiful." He shrugged. "And I think you make the best baked potatoes I've ever eaten in my life."

140

She glared at him from across the room. "I *mean* you don't talk to me about your work! People are constantly asking me about that drowning, and you never even told me it was a woman. I had to find out from someone else. So what do you know about the case? How old was the woman? What color was her hair? How did she die, and why did the body wash up near Deepwater Cove?"

"You know I don't talk about ongoing investigations, Kim."

"Why can't you tell me? Don't you trust me? I'm your wife, and you ought to trust me."

"Why would you even want to know?"

"Because of Cody. He's all confused. He thinks the dead woman might be his mother, but this afternoon I couldn't say, 'No, she's not. I can assure you of that because of the information Derek gave me.' Everyone expected me to know about the body in the cove, but I didn't. You never say anything to me about your day except that I'm prettier than all the half-naked women in Party Cove."

"Well, you are."

"Derek, that's shallow. That's not even real conversation. When you talk to me, you don't say anything. You just toss out compliments like candy at a parade. And I'm supposed to think that's wonderful?"

Whatever flames of passion Derek had been feeling were growing colder by the minute. How could she dismiss his loving words so easily? Nothing communicated love and approval more than a compliment. Not only did Kim rarely return his sentiments; now she was acting like she didn't even appreciate all the kind things he made a point of saying to her.

In three years of marriage, he had never seen his wife this worked up. She was actually wringing her hands. Derek could confront a boater in violation of the law, chase down a jet-skier, or handcuff a belligerent drunk. But this was different. This was an agitated wife in a skimpy gown at the end of a long, hard day.

"Okay," he said, starting for the bathroom. "You made your point, whatever it was, so I'm going to take my shower and get some sleep. If you want to keep talking about all this, we'll try it again in the morning."

"Derek!"

He pushed open the bathroom door and turned to her. "Look, Kim, I'm tired."

"But what about the curtains? And your mom? And Cody? And why won't you tell me about your work?"

"I don't want to fight, babe. Arguing is not my style. You know that. Now get back in bed and try to rest. Things always look better in the morning."

He shut the door behind him and glanced in the mirror. Wow, he'd gotten a lot of sun during the day. His nose was beet red. He would put some lotion on it after his shower.

As he started running the water, he thought about Kim waiting up for him just so she could stalk back and forth across the bedroom floor. Whatever had upset her surely wasn't worth that much energy. Curtains? How trivial could you get? He didn't give a hoot about curtains; that's for sure.

And why all this sudden interest in the drowning case? Kim had never pried into his work, and he didn't ask about hers. They shared highlights once in a while, sure, but he couldn't fake an interest in dental hygiene any more than she could pretend to care how many boaters he had ticketed on a particular day.

Derek stepped into the shower and let the warm water run down his tired body. Why had she put on that blue teddy if all she intended was to rant about Cody Goss and Brenda Hansen? No, the longer he weighed the situation, the more certain he felt that

Kim had been preparing for some late-night passion. Maybe these other things had crept into her mind while she waited for him to get home. And maybe . . . just maybe . . . by the time he got out of the shower, she would have remembered her original goal for the evening. As he lifted his face into the spray of water, Derek smiled.

A particularly stubborn head of dark brown curls made Patsy late to the meeting of the Tea Lovers' Club that Wednesday afternoon. The client, a woman from Iowa who had recently bought a house near Camdenton, wanted highlights. Not merely a few gently glowing streaks, either. She insisted on bright gold stripes that Patsy had worried would make her look like she had on a tiger-skin cap.

Not only did the woman's curls have a mind of their own, but that brown color did not want to bleach out. Patsy's first effort wound up auburn, which she thought looked downright pretty. But the new client was newly divorced, and she was out to make a statement. She had on a V-neck top down to here and a miniskirt up to there, and she looked like she was about to spill out everywhere. No matter how much Patsy tried to talk her into a more sensible color combination, the woman was determined that her hair be brown and gold.

By the time Patsy made it to the table with her cup of tea and a buttermilk scone, she was about fried. Tiger Lady had left the salon, pleased at last, but then Patsy'd had to rush through Steve Hansen's trim and Opal Jones's toenails in order to get to the meeting before everyone left. Opal wasn't pleased to be kept waiting either, but she had an appointment that she intended to keep. At ninety-four, she was too stiff to reach her feet and needed Patsy to work on them every once in a while.

"What color did you paint my nails?" Opal asked loudly as she sat down beside Patsy.

"Red!" Patsy shouted into her left ear, which worked better than the right one. "Same as always!"

Opal smiled and took a sip of tea. Patsy knew that no matter how old the widow got, she took great pride in her appearance. She enjoyed wearing high heels to church, and she regularly drove herself to the outlet mall in Osage Beach to shop the sales. Today Opal had on a yellow knit top sprinkled with butterflies and a pair of matching slacks along with her pretty open-toed sandals.

Letting out a deep breath and trying to relax the muscles in her calves and back,

145

Patsy lifted her cup to her lips. Evidently Esther Moore was putting forth her usual effort to impose an agenda on the club. She was jotting down "new business" in her little notebook. This new business included a plan for a Fourth of July decorating spree in which every home in Deepwater Cove and every shop and restaurant in Tranquility would be transformed by members of the TLC.

"The dollar store has red, white, and blue bunting for sale," Esther was saying as Patsy nibbled on her scone. "I think we ought to drape some on the front of each golf cart in the neighborhood. Does anyone know where we can find affordable flags?"

"Our restaurant manager at the country club accidentally ordered too many flags for the tables," Ashley Hanes spoke up. "They're fairly small, but I bet he'd let us have the extras for free. We could put one in every yard."

Patsy noted that the redhead's neck was encircled five-deep in strands of handmade beads, which she fiddled with when she talked. Her skinny tank top and tight shorts bore evidence that the young woman wasn't the least bit pregnant, though Ashley had secretly confided in almost everyone that she and Brad were trying to have a baby.

Still starry-eyed about her handsome husband, Ashley took great joy in showing off her engagement ring with its large diamond. It was as though she couldn't quite believe she had actually married the high school's most popular athlete.

Ashley hadn't had her hair trimmed for a while, Patsy realized. The redhead had never been one to sit quietly in the salon chair, and Patsy knew she would always get a full update on how things were going between the newlyweds. Maybe after the club meeting Patsy could schedule Ashley an appointment for a trim. Her ends were getting a bit straggly.

"That is a wonderful idea, Ashley," Esther said, beaming. "If you'll get us those flags, we'll be just about set. Does anyone else have an idea for what we might do to celebrate the independence of our great country?"

"We could put on a fireworks show down at the commons area by the water," Ashley suggested. "Brad loves fireworks. He'd be happy to organize it if people would chip in a little money."

At this, Esther's lips pinched shut. Everyone knew that shooting off fireworks on the commons was against the Deepwater Cove bylaws, and everyone but Brad Hanes was glad. The young man turned into a kid nearly every holiday, blowing up who knew how much money on bottle rockets, Roman candles, and other pyrotechnics. Patsy herself didn't mind fireworks, but she felt sure Ashley's suggestion would be voted down.

"I appreciate the thought," Esther said, "but you know my dog is terrified by fireworks or thunder, or any loud noises. Poor Boofer tries to get behind the sofa, but these days he's too fat. He wedges in as far as he can go, and then he gets stuck. It's all Charlie and I can do to pull him out."

"I'll have to agree with Esther about fireworks," Brenda Hansen spoke up. "My cat feels the same way Boofer does about loud noises. I'll never forget the night lightning struck an electric pole near the house and Ozzie jumped into a pan of pink paint. I thought I'd never get him clean."

Ashley shrugged, her face suddenly forlorn. "Well, if that's how you feel. Most people enjoy watching fireworks on the Fourth. It's traditional, you know."

"How about barbecuing pork steaks on the commons instead?" Patsy put in brightly.

Pork steaks might as well be added to Missouri's official seal. As far as Patsy knew, there had never been a gathering of people in the Show-Me State without someone serving pork steaks.

"Folks could bring their portable grills," she went on, "and we could have a potluck supper with the steaks, casseroles, and different salads."

"Steve will be happy to churn homemade ice cream," Brenda offered. Her husband had kissed her cheek before departing the salon a few minutes ago when Patsy finished his trim.

"I have a great seven-layer dip if people want to contribute bags of chips." Kim Finley hadn't said much till now. As a rule, she was fairly quiet, but when she did have something on her mind, she expressed it well. "And I'll bring the fixings for sundaes, too. There's nothing like hot fudge, pecans, maraschino cherries, and whipped cream on a sundae."

"What's happening on Sunday?" Opal asked, elbowing Patsy.

"We're talking about the Fourth of July!" Patsy disliked yelling, but she didn't have much choice since Opal had left her hearing aids at home. "We plan to barbecue pork steaks on the commons!"

"I didn't realize the Fourth was on a Sunday this year," Opal declared. "I guess I'll bring a couple of my apple pies."

No one could deny that Opal Jones made the best apple pie in the county. As everyone clapped, Esther called the meeting to a close, and the women resumed their chatter. Several rose to refill their cups, while others prepared to leave.

Patsy took delight in the comfortable crowd gathered in her tea area. Since the founding of the TLC, she had come to think of it as a garden — a safe, quiet place set aside for nourishment, growth, and support. As the music of her favorite trio, Color of Mercy, drifted in the air, Patsy studied her patch of blossoms, birds, and butterflies.

Ashley Hanes, still in the springtime blush of marriage, seemed to be settling down a little now, just as flowers sank their roots into the soil in preparation for summer. Orange-red canna lilies blossomed in Patsy's mind when she looked at Ashley. With her flame of long hair and her stacks of beaded necklaces, Ashley came across as tropical and exotic.

Patsy loved canna lilies, and she planted a cluster of them near her mailbox every year. They were tall, showy, and bright all summer, but they didn't last long once the first frost hit. And that was the trouble with cannas — in winter, their raggedy blooms fell off, and their leaves faded from green to brown to black. In Missouri, cannas died out altogether unless you dug them from the ground and hid them in a warm place until the following spring.

Chatting with Esther Moore, Ashley projected a confidence and strength as hardy as a canna's with its thick stem and broad leaves. But Patsy wondered what would happen if winter ever struck the Hanes marriage the way it had Brenda and Steve Hansen's.

Thank goodness, these days Brenda was perking right up. She made Patsy think of another lily that was common all over Missouri. Unlike cannas, surprise lilies could survive the harshest freezes and ice storms. As soon as spring arrived, they sent up long green leaves as a sign that they were still alive. But it wasn't until summer, after the leaves had long since vanished, that these bulbs surprised everyone by bursting out of the ground to show off their prettiest pink ruffles. Leafless, the blossoms danced in the breeze on long stems, nodding as if to welcome everything else in the garden.

Not only was Brenda showing signs of a lovely summertime outlook, but Esther Moore continued to reflect that season too. Calm, comfortable, and satisfied in her long marriage to Charlie, she was a honeysuckle vine. Hardy green foliage and a sweet perfume announced that the honeysuckle, like Esther, was perfectly happy and showing no signs of fading.

"What do you think about bananas?" Brenda asked Kim Finley.

For a second, Patsy feared the others at the table had been reading her mind. Then Brenda finished her thought.

"Steve is crazy about banana splits. He'd rather eat a banana split than a steak dinner. In fact, that's why we bought the ice cream maker."

"I'll bring plenty of bananas," Kim assured her. "Derek likes them too. Lydia won't touch a banana, but Luke might as well be half monkey."

Both Kim and Brenda were seated at the table with Patsy and Opal. While Opal serenely sipped her tea and studied the scene outside the salon, Patsy continued to take account of her tea garden. For some reason Cody hadn't shown up for the TLC meeting, which wasn't like him at all. Some of the women were beginning to leave, and Patsy regretted missing most of the fellowship. She hoped Kim and Brenda would linger awhile, even though she knew they had such busy lives.

"He's doing better each day," Kim was

telling her friend when Patsy began listening to them again. "Luke is much more conscientious than I had expected. He's actually pretty good at keeping track of his blood sugar and figuring out his insulin doses."

"That's wonderful. My Justin wouldn't be that responsible. He's still in college, but he barely passes each semester. So unlike Jennifer and Jessica."

Patsy thought Kim looked a little weary today. In the garden of women Patsy nurtured, Kim had never been a summer girl. Life had taken a toll on her, and these days she seemed a bit faded — beautiful but worn, like a cluster of chrysanthemums at the end of the season. Maybe once they had been golden or purple, but now the flowers were losing their color and the leaves were starting to wilt.

"Kim, could we talk about your curtains?" Brenda spoke up all of a sudden.

The way she leaned forward and laid her hand on Kim's arm startled Patsy from her gardening reverie.

"Don't worry about it," Kim said, her lips forming a halfhearted smile. "You're probably right about the lace. I've been thinking about taking them —"

"No!" Brenda's grip tightened on Kim's

arm. "Please don't take down those curtains. I mean that seriously. I've done some thinking, and I've looked through my home-decor magazines since I was at our house, and now I realize that lace goes quite well with more masculine furnishings. It provides a balance. Harmony of texture and sensibility. The truth is, those curtains are gorgeous, Kim. Once I got a closer look, I could see they were delicate and unusual — maybe even handmade. I think they should stay exactly where you hung them."

"But you said —"

"I know what I said, and I wish I'd had more time to think it all through before I spoke a single word. The way your mother-in-law was going on about the leather chairs and the twill sofa, I felt overwhelmed. Somehow I thought maybe *you* wanted to replace the curtains. But then as I was leaving, I saw your face, and I realized how much you love them. I think they go perfectly in your living room, Kim. I mean that."

"But lace is a very different texture than leather and twill."

"Exactly. They complement each other. Listen, Kim, I enjoy decorating, and I'm learning more all the time. But I'm no expert. I do what feels natural to me, and that's not always right for everyone else. You've seen my house. Yours is very different, but that doesn't make it wrong. In fact, I've always loved your home and felt totally comfortable there."

"If you think I should leave the curtains, I will. But Miranda won't be happy."

"Well, whose house is it, anyway?" Brenda shot back.

At that, Kim fell silent. She folded her paper napkin into a tiny square. Then she set it on the table and pushed it up against her plate. "I'm not sure," she said finally, glancing at Brenda and then at Patsy with a look of apology in her eyes.

"That house belongs to you and Derek, of course," Patsy blurted out. She had no idea what the big deal was about lace curtains, but she had sat on the Deepwater Cove Association's board of directors long enough to know what belonged to whom. "You own a house, a slip in the community dock, two cars, and a boat."

"But I think . . ." Kim picked up her napkin and unfolded it again. "I think Miranda might be taking over."

Her voice was low when she said the words, and Patsy knew this would be a good time for her to grab Opal by the arm and make an exit. Clearly Kim was burdened, and she had chosen to share her heart with Brenda. But Patsy was sitting right there, and by golly, after being on her feet all day, she didn't feel like getting up. She would do her best to keep her mouth shut and concentrate on the song Color of Mercy was singing. It happened to be one of her favorites, and she might even hum along. Opal, of course, wouldn't hear anything.

"The family unit consists of you, Derek, and the twins," Brenda was saying as Patsy tried not to listen. "Miranda is not part of your immediate family. She can't take over."

"But Derek won't discuss it with me. I tried the other night. I was upset about the curtains —"

"Oh, Kim, I'm so sorry!"

"It's not your fault, Brenda. Miranda instigated the whole issue about the curtains, and then she even had the gall to take one of them down from the window. When Derek got home that night, I did my best to tell him the things that have been on my mind — like how I try to do things for him so that he'll know I love him and how much I want him to tell me about his work. He keeps it all inside and won't share anything with me. Derek actually got upset with me that night. I know he was angry, even though he didn't let on. You know what he did? He walked away and took a shower."

"Who's having a shower?" Opal asked, blinking at Patsy. "I'm not too old to celebrate with everyone else, and I don't want to be left out this time. You make sure my name is on the list, Patsy. I love to shop for babies."

CHAPTER SEVEN

As dearly as Kim loved Patsy Pringle, she was grateful when the salon owner gathered Opal Jones and led the widow away to pay for her pedicure. Kim didn't mind Patsy's knowing about the trouble over her lace curtains. If anyone could be trusted to keep her mouth shut, it was Patsy.

But right now, Kim felt as though Brenda Hansen would truly understand her problems. Like Kim, Brenda had struggled with depression, marital troubles, and the challenges of raising children. Maybe she even had a meddling mother-in-law.

"Men can be so confusing," Brenda commented as she returned to the table with two more cups of tea and a couple of plain butter cookies. "They think *we're* temperamental! At least we know we have feelings, and we're pretty sure what they are. It sounds like Derek is bottling things inside. That's typical, isn't it? Steve used to stare at me while I talked, and I finally realized he wasn't listening at all. If I got the least bit upset, he would walk away."

"Derek told me confrontation wasn't his style," Kim confessed.

"Yeah, right, and he works for the Water Patrol. Officer Derek Finley confronts people every day. He just doesn't want to argue with *you*."

"But I need to tell him some things he might not want to hear."

"First you have to get him to listen," Brenda said. "Steve is only now catching on to that concept. Somehow you need to get some time alone with Derek, away from his mom and the kids. Make sure he's not too tired or hungry. If Steve is hungry, forget about talking. He's like a grouchy old grizzly, and he won't hear a word. Once you've fed Derek, you can tell him everything."

Kim wished she felt like Brenda's idea would work. "Derek doesn't want to hear anything negative. He focuses on the positive. But for me, life isn't always sunny. Derek throws out compliments and encouragement all day long. That's what I first loved about him. But when things aren't perfect, he wants to run and hide. Brenda, I've been through a lot, and very little of it was good. My life is better right now than it's ever been, but I'm so . . . I'm just so scared. I'm afraid I'll lose him if I can't feel wonderful about everything."

"It's okay that you and Derek are different, isn't it? You don't have to both be Little Merry Sunshine. Let Derek have that role. Someone needs to deal with the fact that Luke has a serious health condition. And someone has to keep the house running and the family fed and the laundry done. If Derek walks around glowing with happiness and showering you with compliments, that's fine. Let him be who he is. You be you. Derek loves you, Kim. He's not going to leave you just because things get rough sometimes."

"I hope you're right."

"Listen, Steve still loves me after all I put him through. And I love him back. Let me tell you; that's a miracle. Based on what we've gone through, I can assure you that Derek will stick it out too. No one's marriage is a fairy tale with a guaranteed happily-ever-after ending. It's hard work."

Kim sighed. "Nobody knows that better than I do."

"You're doing great," Brenda said, squeezing Kim's hand. "I mean that."

"I wish he would tell me more about his job," Kim told her friend. "I'd really like to know —"

"Did we miss the meeting of the TLC?" Cody Goss blurted out as he stepped in front of the table where the two women were talking. "Because I wanted to come, but *she* said we had to go to the library, and that place is full to the brim of books."

"Cody, did you interrupt us?" Brenda asked gently. "Kim and I were talking."

"Yes, I did interrupt, but I don't want to miss the meeting."

"Well, I'm sorry, but it's over. And that's no excuse for bad manners."

Cody hung his head. "Okay. I'm sorry too."

"There you are!" Miranda materialized at Cody's side, while Luke and Lydia made a dash for the counter that held the tea goodies. "Kim, I called home and your cell phone and didn't get you, and I couldn't imagine where you'd gone. Cody kept talking about a meeting, and I had no idea when it was or which day or anything. You know how he is. Of course, if I'd known it was the Little Tea Committee —"

"The Tea Lovers' Club," Cody interrupted, then clapped his hand over his mouth.

"We were at the library, and we got so immersed in our research, and —" Miranda glanced over her shoulder. "Where have those kids gone now? I swear, I could wring their necks. Do you know what they did? They left Cody and me at the library and walked down the street to Lydia's friend's house. I nearly had a panic attack when I couldn't find them."

"Which friend?" Kim asked, rising. "And, Luke, when did you last check your blood?"

"They went to Tiffany's house," Miranda said. "That little tramp in all her eye makeup. I'm going to have to really work with her and Lydia both."

"No makeup, Miranda," Kim said firmly. "We told you that. Luke — what are you eating? Have you saved up enough carbs for that?"

"Lydia is almost eleven and certainly old enough to be taught correctly. You can make cosmetics look natural if you do them right. But how can I be expected to corral both twins when they won't stay where I put them? I had them settled in the children's section when Cody and I went to work on the name *Goss*. It's not a common surname, you know, but that's actually a benefit in situations like this."

Kim barely heard her mother-in-law as she hurried to the display of confections to supervise her children's snack selections.

And what was this about leaving the library without telling Miranda? Going to Tiffany's house, of all places!

A touch on Kim's arm startled her as she reached for the brownie in Luke's hand. She turned to find Brenda smiling at her.

"You'll be okay." Brenda leaned close and whispered in her ear. "I promise."

When his wife invited him to have lunch with her at the new fast-food restaurant in Tranquility, Derek jumped at the chance. First of all, he liked the meals served at the Pop-In. Other officers called it girl food. They complained that one omelet or a sandwich wrapped in parchment paper couldn't fill a man, but Derek disagreed. He didn't like to eat too much when he was working, and besides, he always carried snacks on his boat in case he got hungry.

Derek also really liked Bitty Sondheim, the owner of the little restaurant. He had grown up in St. Louis, and he felt that the Californian had a certain quality to her that he understood. She had a larger perspective on life. She had gone places and done things. And she wasn't afraid to wear whatever appealed to her, even if it didn't quite fit the local scene. Her long skirts, thick braid, dangly earrings, and sandals added a little sass to go along with her attitude.

"Well, make up your mind, Officer Finley," Bitty commanded from behind the counter that Friday afternoon when Derek and Kim met at the Pop-In. "We don't have all day, you know. Gotta keep the line moving."

At that, Bitty threw back her head and laughed heartily at her joke, because, in fact, Kim and Derek were her only customers. Unfortunately, not too many people knew what to make of eggs wrapped in paper or tortillas wrapped around alfalfa sprouts and wedges of avocado or eggplant. Derek had considered suggesting that Bitty change her menu just a little to accommodate the Missouri appetite for "home-style cookin'." That meant foods like ham, roast beef, and chicken strips. Vegetables cooked until they were good and limp. And sweet, fluffy white bread.

"I'll take the whole wheat fajita wrap, Bitty," Derek said finally. If there was one thing you could always count on for savory taste, it was fajitas.

"The same for me," Kim added.

Derek smiled at his wife. "You sure look pretty this afternoon, Mrs. Finley," he told her. It was true. Kim's brown eyes glowed as she gazed back at him.

164

"And you, too, Officer Finley." She elbowed him teasingly. "Hey, guess what good news I have. This morning I put the last load of clothes in the dryer. That means I've got the whole weekend free from laundry duty."

"Well, aren't you something else!" Derek chuckled as he leaned against the counter and studied Kim. Sometimes his wife utterly mystified him. Was getting the laundry done really cause for celebration? Laundry was a never-ending chore. But such small victories meant a lot to her, and he wanted to be supportive.

Especially after the trouble they'd had the other night. He didn't even like to think about how upset they had been.

Derek could honestly say he thought he and his wife made the perfect match. He couldn't find a fault in the woman. They rarely had sharp words with each other — in fact, he could count on one hand the times they had disagreed.

Before they married, his biggest fear had been parenting the twins. That turned out to be pretty easy too. Luke enjoyed fishing and swimming with Derek, and until recently, Lydia had been a peach.

"I'm surprised you didn't bring the kids along," he told Kim. "I'd enjoy hearing what they've been up to today."

"I would have needed to drive home and pick them up . . . or ask your mom to meet us here. And I thought it would be nice for just the two of us to have lunch. There are some things I'd like to talk about."

Uh-oh. Derek tried to keep the smile on his face. He did not want to talk about *things.* That could only mean tension. Meeting each other at a restaurant far away from everyone signaled something potentially grim.

"There you go," Bitty said as she returned to the counter with their orders in two to-go sacks. "Fajita wraps, sodas, and tortilla chips. Get your napkins over there by the door, and you two have a good afternoon."

Derek looked at the woman across the counter. Bright blue eyes set off by sun-baked skin bore testimony to many hours on Southern California beaches. He wondered how Bitty was adjusting to small-town Missouri. Had she gotten used to the country ways of folks around Tranquility? Most of all, he wondered if she might sit down with them for lunch to prevent Kim from talking about those *things* she wanted to discuss with her husband.

Too late. Kim looped her arm around Derek's and led him toward the door. "Let's eat in that little clearing down the way," she suggested. "I brought a blanket."

As they strolled past the other shops along the row, Derek wasn't sure whether to enjoy the sudden cool air that had moved in overnight, bringing the promise of rain. If it weren't for Kim's desire to talk, he would be grinning like a skunk in a cabbage patch. Time alone with his wife was rare, and often it occurred only at night, when one or both were on the brink of exhaustion. His fluctuating schedule, along with her job and the twins' needs, kept them apart too much for Derek's liking. He had hoped his mother's arrival would ease the situation, but based on the other night's conflict, he was beginning to suspect that Miranda Finley's presence in their home might be part of this discussion Kim wanted to have.

"Here we go," she said, shaking out the blanket she had brought along. "This is shady and out of the path of traffic. Someone ought to put a table and benches in here. Maybe it would help Bitty Sondheim's business."

"A lack of tables and chairs might be part of her problem," Derek said as he hunkered down on the blanket. "But I think she needs to serve something a little more hearty. Blue-collar people work hard, and they want to eat big."

"You may be right," Kim said.

Derek was lifting his fajita wrap to his mouth when he realized that Kim intended for them to pray right out in the open. He quickly bowed his head, hoping against hope that none of the other officers had decided to visit the Pop-In today.

It wasn't that Derek minded his wife's spiritual bent. In fact, he welcomed it. But religion seemed better suited to women. Neither of his parents had embraced any kind of organized church. When he was a child, his mother had read lots of self-help books and gone to weekly therapy, which she had told him was more personally meaningful than any sacred creed or ritual. His father's attitude — passed to Derek before the accident that took his life — was that religious people were weak, superstitious, and gullible.

Kim didn't fit that description at all. At the same time, she did rely a lot on God. She had been through plenty of rough water in her life, and her faith seemed to help her deal with the past.

"This is delicious," she murmured when she had finished praying and taken her first bite. "I'm going to spread the word around

Dr. Groene's office. Bitty is a fabulous cook."

"She can't hold a candle to you," Derek said, winking at his wife. "I agree, this is good, but I'd rather have a home-cooked meal any day."

Kim took a sip of her soda. She was quiet for a moment, eating and watching people enter and leave the shops along Tranquility's main road. "Is there anything you don't like about me?" she asked, just when he had gotten lulled into a soothing mood.

"Not a thing," he assured her. "You're beautiful. You take great care of the twins and me. People admire you, and you have lots of friends. You're an excellent cook — or did I already say that?"

She smiled. "Yes, you said that. But what about our house? Do you like the way it's decorated?"

Derek could sense trouble coming. It always started small, like the wake from a passing speedboat. And then before you knew what hit you, everything went wobbly and unstable, waves slammed you to the deck, and the boat that had seemed so safe suddenly felt as though it might toss you into the water.

"I don't know anything about decorating a house," Derek said carefully. "But I feel

169

completely comfortable in our home. If I hadn't, I would have said so. And, by the way, I love those living room curtains. Lace . . . nothing better for a living room than lace."

Nodding, Kim took another bite of her wrap. Derek let out a sigh. He felt confident he had passed the worst of it.

"Your mother doesn't like them," Kim said at last.

"Mom has her own ideas about nearly everything. Her own style."

"Yes, she thinks a ten-year-old girl should be taught to wear cosmetics. She thinks I should let her leave a type 1 diabetic all alone, by himself, so she can take the ten-year-old girl on shopping sprees. She doesn't approve of baked potatoes on a day when we have French toast for breakfast and sandwiches for lunch. And she's certain that lace curtains clash with leather and twill."

Derek suddenly felt like he was clinging to the side of a capsized boat. Where had that wave come from? What could he say? How could he make it all go away?

"I don't know how long your mother plans to stay with us," Kim was saying before he could think of a response. "At first it was a couple of weeks. Then she told me she

170

would stay until school started this fall. But these days she never mentions anything about going back to St. Louis. In fact, I'm pretty sure she has moved in with us permanently."

Taking a breath, Derek groped for a lifeline. He hadn't so much as discussed the time of day with his mother, let alone talked about when she might be leaving. To him, she was just part of the Finley household now, participating like one of the family.

"Is that a problem?" he managed.

"What do you think?" Kim returned immediately.

"Uh . . . I think Mom isn't really a problem, is she?" He searched his wife's face. When he didn't get an answer, he continued. "Kim, you grew up with people coming and going all the time. Folks moved in and out of your life on a regular basis. Even in adulthood, things haven't been that different. You met Joe, and then the twins came along, and then Joe left. And after that, I entered the picture. Now my mom is here. So? Is it a big deal?"

"I don't want to model my life after what I saw as a child. I hated all the moving and transition. My mother and her alcohol and all those men . . . it was awful. I'm trying to create a stable home for myself and my children. I already messed up with Joe. And, Derek . . . oh, I don't know."

He was drowning. He could feel it. Tentacles of confusion were dragging him under.

"We have a stable home, babe," he tried. "We're good parents. We love the kids. We love each other."

"Do we? Do we even know each other, Derek? I mean, what is it that you really do all day? Why won't you tell me about your work?"

"Well, what do you want to know? There's nothing that interesting about ticketing someone for carrying too many people on a pontoon boat. If there's a big event, I usually tell you."

"You say you do, but there's been this drowning, and you haven't told me a thing. Did you know your mother is trying to help Cody locate his family? The other day they were in the library most of the afternoon. They missed the TLC meeting completely, even though Cody kept telling her he wanted to leave. She wouldn't listen. She doesn't listen. She just says what she thinks. And you know what she thinks? She thinks all religions lead to God. That's what she told our children, Derek. Your mother said she had looked into every kind of faith, including paganism! And she actually had the gall to say that one religion was no more valid than any of the others. She said it right in front of Luke and Lydia! That's not what I want them to hear. Is that what you believe, Derek? What do you really believe about God, and why don't I know?"

He was utterly sunk. No doubt about it. Somehow those lace curtains, his mother, Cody, makeup, religion, and type 1 diabetes had all conspired to drag him to the bottom. He had no idea how to get out of this tangle.

"Religion," he began. He could feel himself beginning to panic, his heart beating just a little too fast. "Uh . . . I don't think about it much. It was never a part of my life before I met you, and it still isn't. That's the truth, Kim. I do my job, and I love you and the twins, and that's about it. I wish I could tell you I was deeper and more complex, but that's all there is."

"You prayed the other day at the table."

"Yeah, but . . ." He wadded up the paper in which his fajita had been wrapped. "Well, I believe in some kind of a Creator. I have trouble thinking that a blue heron or a purple coneflower could have evolved out of a blob of amoebas. I'm sure someone created the world and set it in motion. Some

173

higher being. I don't know what else to tell you about religion, babe. You heard my mother. I wasn't brought up that way."

"Neither was I, but it's important to me."

"Does it have to be important to me, too?"

At that, Kim caught her breath. "Brenda said it was all right for us to be different. You be you. I'll be me." She paused. "But not about God. I think we ought to be united. Would you come to church with the kids and me, Derek?"

Not only was he drowning, but a noose had somehow gotten wrapped around his neck, and it was growing tighter by the second. "Church?" he forced out, his voice quavering like a teenager's. "I'm usually working on Sundays."

"You could request a shift change."

"It would throw everyone else off schedule."

"Please, Derek," she said. "My faith is a huge part of my life. I need for you to understand that. And will you tell me about the drowning?"

He ran a finger around his collar. "We don't know much. I think they're bringing in the Major Case Squad on this one."

"Then it's been ruled a crime?"

"I'm not supposed to talk about it, Kim."

"I'm your wife!"

174

"I know that, but . . ." He rubbed his eyes. "Okay. We know it was a woman, but we don't know what did her in. The fishing line may be throwing us off track. It was probably an accident, but it could have been a homicide."

"Who would do such a terrible thing?"

"We have no idea. You know how peaceful it is around here most of the time. If we have a crime, it's usually because someone's been drinking. Intoxicated boaters, family feuds, trespassing. We've been seeing more drugs around the lake than usual, but alcohol is still the main issue. I'm not telling you anything you don't already know, am I, Kim?"

She shook her head. "Not really."

"I don't keep things from you. Not if I can help it." He fiddled with the edge of the blanket. "There's just not a whole lot to tell. This morning, I ticketed a kid riding without a life jacket on a personal watercraft. Over the past weekend, we chased down a couple of drunk speeders, and we cited a few females for indecent exposure. Later this month, we'll be setting up a barricade to check for licenses, boating while intoxicated, and things like that. My work is interesting to me, because one day is always a little different from the next. But, Kim, it's not like you're missing a big drama. If you went out on the water with me, you'd be flat bored a good part of the time."

"I wish you'd tell me things, though," she said. "I'd like to know more about your daily life."

"I suppose I can log in with you at the end of the day, but it won't take more than a couple of minutes." He reached for her hand. He wouldn't mind sharing more of his life with her, but there were some things she was just better off not knowing. "Kim, is this really what's got you all worked up? Me not reporting on my day? Me not going to church with you and the kids? This stuff never bothered you before. What's wrong?"

"I didn't say anything about it earlier, but that doesn't mean I didn't care." She sighed, and Derek wondered if she was done. But then she looked up at him again and continued in a softer tone. "Remember I told you about the social worker at the shelter who helped me sort out my feelings after I left Joe? She told me that for a relationship to succeed, both people need to feel safe expressing their needs. Derek, can't you see how scared I am to rock our boat? I want you to be happy, and I live in fear of upsetting you. But I do need for you to talk to me."

"What else do you want to know?"

"Why is it so hard for you to talk openly? Why do you evade me? Why do you walk into another room when someone calls you on your cell phone? Who keeps calling you, anyway?"

"Kim, you know phone calls are a part of my work. I've told you all I can. What more do you want?"

"I desperately want you to go to church."

Here she sucked down a breath that sounded almost like a sob. Derek had thought he was about to reach dry ground, but the quaver in her voice sucked him under again. Didn't Kim realize she had done a lot more than rock their boat? She was drowning him.

He crossed his arms over his chest and focused on the sign over Patsy Pringle's beauty salon in the distance. Just As I Am. That was all he needed from his wife — that she accept him, flaws and all.

Derek didn't mind telling Kim about his day. He might even venture over to her church once in a while to see what was going on inside. One of the other officers, Larry, talked about God all the time. Some of the men kidded Larry about it and tried to get his goat, but Derek respected his friend. If Larry and Kim were good examples of the way Christians lived, then it couldn't be too bad.

Derek glanced surreptitiously at his watch. He needed to be getting back on the water, but he sure didn't want Kim to wind up in tears at the end of their picnic. All the same, he had a bad feeling that she had uncovered the top of a sandbar, and no matter what, their little boat was destined to run aground on it.

"It's your mother," she blurted out suddenly. Covering her eyes with her hands, she shook her head. "Oh, Derek, it's been really hard on me these past few weeks. How long is she going to stay with us? I don't know if I can take much more of her criticism and interference."

He stiffened. His mother might be called a spendthrift or a gossip or even a meddler, but she meant well. At her own suggestion, she had left her home and her busy social life in St. Louis, and she had driven down to the lake to help out with Luke. What right did Kim have to be so hard on her?

"If she's not criticizing my curtains or my cooking," Kim was telling him, "she's dragging the twins off to who knows where. The outlet mall, the library. And then she doesn't even watch them!"

"Let's be grateful we have her help,"

Derek told his wife firmly, hoping to put an end to the discussion. "Mom's not the world's expert parent, but she's doing her best, Kim. She only had one child to practice on, and that's me. She took on the twins when they were nearly eight years old. You know she would never hurt Luke and Lydia. If anything, the incident at the library was their fault. They skipped out on my mother and ran over to Tiffany's house."

"That never would have happened if your mother hadn't taken them to the library and then left them so she could look for Cody's missing family! Your mom has no idea how to be a real grandmother!"

"Well, she might if you'd ever consider having another baby, like I've asked you a thousand times."

Derek took his sunglasses from his pocket and put them on. He couldn't imagine where that comment had come from, but it was the truth. Ever since they got married, he had been asking Kim to give him more kids. He loved the twins, but he wanted a bigger family. He longed for babies with his genes, his features, his blood. When he asked, Kim always told him she would think about it, but then she never said another word. How many times had he brought up the subject of more children, only to be dismissed with a laugh or a wave of the hand? If she wanted his mother to be a better grandma, Kim ought to be willing to produce a baby or two for her to learn on.

"I've got to get back to work," he told Kim. "I'm late already."

Kim sniffled as Derek got to his feet. More than anything, he wished he could wipe out everything he had said. He wanted to please his wife. He loved her with his whole heart. But what was all this stuff she had suddenly decided to throw at him? How much could a man take before he hurled something back?

As he stood over Kim, he tried to think of something to say to make it all better. Finally he let out a breath, shrugged, and walked to his truck.

CHAPTER EIGHT

Pete Roberts had broken just about every one of the Ten Commandments several times, plus any number of other offenses. Since drying out, taking some college classes, opening Rods-N-Ends, and starting to attend church, he had managed to rid himself of almost all these vices. But there was one he couldn't avoid.

Every time he saw Patsy Pringle, Pete could feel himself heading straight for the devil's workshop. He wanted to hold that woman in his arms. He wanted to kiss those sweet, sweet lips. And he wanted to —

"Pete? Are you coming, or are you just going to stand there looking like a big, hairy goon?" Patsy swung around, her hips aswaying as she sashayed toward the dessert table at the Fourth of July picnic.

Pete stood at the edge of the green, grassy expanse near the lake and stared. Never in his whole life had he seen anything like this

Fourth of July celebration. It was better than the Christmas parades his mother had taken him to when he was a kid. It was better than the day his father got out of prison and the whole family went to McDonald's for lunch. And it was a whole lot better than Pete's two weddings, both of which had happened more or less by accident — being as it was hard to make a clear decision when you were drunk as a skunk.

On this beautiful summer day, everyone in Deepwater Cove had turned out for the festivities. Pete counted eleven grills loaded with pork steaks, sending up an aroma that would make a horsefly dizzy with joy. All fifteen of the neighborhood's golf carts were decked out in red, white, and blue bunting. A giant flag had been strung up on one of the mud poles beside the dock. All that, not to mention the row of tables groaning with salads, chips, dips, sodas, and desserts of every flavor and color. It was enough to make a grown man break right down and cry.

"What're you hanging back for, Pete?" Patsy waited for him to catch up and bumped him with her hip. "Help me carry this watermelon before I fall off my shoes."

The moment Pete laid eyes on Patsy that afternoon, his already high blood pressure had shot up like a bottle rocket. She had bleached her hair until it was almost white, added some long blonde ringlets that must've come out of a package, and pinned sparkling red, white, and blue stars in among the curls. Her red shirt and blue shorts might have been ordinary enough, but her little feet were perched up on a pair of wedgy high-heel sandals pretty enough to make a man's heart stop.

Before Pete could drop dead on the spot, Patsy shoved a watermelon into his midsection and set off ahead of him. Stumbling after her, Pete balanced the watermelon on the cusp of his somewhat substantial paunch. He wished he didn't have that beer belly, and he denied it as much as he could. But truth to tell, once a man had got himself one, it was awful hard to get rid of.

"Where do you want the watermelon to go, Patsy?" Pete asked as he stepped up beside the fount of perfume and hair spray that drew him like a bee to honey.

"Where do you think?" She shot those big blue eyes at him and pointed with a long red fingernail. "Over there under the tree with the other watermelons. I swear, Pete Roberts, are you blind?"

No, he sure wasn't, Pete thought as he made his way to the watermelon cart. He saw those pretty calves and tiny ankles swaying on top of Patsy's high-heel shoes. He saw those red lips that matched her long fingernails. In fact, usually when Pete saw Patsy, he couldn't see much else.

He liked to give her a hard time about her hair, but the truth was plain enough. It didn't matter if she dyed it orange, black, pink, or polka dot, Patsy's hair simply fascinated him. Around Patsy, Pete felt like he had been shot straight through the heart by Cupid's arrow — a sensation he'd never had before in his life. And he wasn't at all sure what to do about it.

"Hey, Pete, how's business at Rods-N-Ends these days?" Steve Hansen was beckoning him over to where a group of men were seated in lawn chairs minding their grills. They wore ball caps and bib aprons with sayings such as *Grill Sergeant* or *Le Chef de BBQ* on the front. Each man held court with a pair of tongs, a bowl of whatever special secret sauce he had concocted, and a flyswatter.

"Didn't I tell you things would pick up during the summer?" Steve asked. "That you'd be so busy you wouldn't know whether you were coming or going?"

"You were right," Pete replied, settling into a chair with frayed webbing. He wasn't real confident it would hold his weight, but he decided if he dropped through, he'd deal with it somehow or other.

"I bet the high gas prices don't hurt," Steve added. "Keeping gas in our cars is about to kill the real estate business."

Pete nodded. "You were smart to buy that hybrid when you did. But I won't accept any blame for my gas prices. They get passed on down the line from the oil wells in Alaska, Oklahoma, or wherever in the world we're buying it from these days. Nope, boys, if you want the honest truth, I make a bigger profit selling minnows."

The other men chuckled.

"At least the minnows are homegrown." Charlie Moore was an avid fisherman. He dropped by Pete's minnow tank nearly every day. He was waving a flyswatter around his head as he spoke. "If I had my way, Esther and I would buy everything we need right here in the Ozarks. Or grow it ourselves. There's nothing like a fresh tomato right off the vine or a taste of my wife's strawberry jam."

"Who has time to take care of a garden except retired people?" Brad Hanes, a good-looking young fellow who had worked construction so long that his skin was the color of oak, had joined the older men. Pete didn't know Brad too well, though the kid always bought gas for his big new truck at Rods-N-Ends. Brad's favorite thing was to ask when Pete was going to start stocking beer and lottery tickets, and the joke was getting a little old.

"Ashley buys everything at the discount store in Camdenton," Brad was telling the others. "She tries to make our meals unless she can talk me into eating out. But at the rate she's learning how to cook, we'll owe our souls to Bitty Sondheim's place one of these days. I think Ashley has run up a mile-long tab there."

"Kim and I ate at the Pop-In the other day." Now it was Derek Finley's turn to speak. Pete liked the Water Patrol officer as much as any man he'd ever met. Derek was fair, firm, and friendly. He was tending a grill lined with hot dogs for the children.

"Bitty brought sushi appetizers," Derek informed the men as he gestured toward the colorfully clad Californian in the distance. "I'm not sure about eating raw fish on a hot summer day, but I like those omelets Bitty cooks at her restaurant. And her fajita wraps fill a guy up pretty well too."

"Not if he's been hammering shingles onto a roof all morning," Brad observed. "I don't know how many times I've told Bitty she's got to start serving platters with ham, eggs, hash browns, toast, and butter if she expects my crew to eat at the Pop-In. We don't mind her not having chairs and tables. We're used to sitting on the back of a pickup with our sandwiches and water coolers. But I can buy four or five of Pete's hot dogs for what I'd pay for one of Bitty's veggie wraps. Besides, who wants to eat eggplant and alfalfa sprouts for lunch?"

"Might as well go out to graze," Charlie agreed. "In my day, we'd step off the back porch and gather a few turnip greens or plantain leaves. Maybe some spinach if we were lucky. Mother would fry up a mess of greens for us, and we'd eat that along with ham hocks or whatever she happened to have on hand. We didn't pay a nickel for any of it, either. Those were the good old days, and I mean that for a fact."

As the men went on chatting, Pete began a surreptitious survey of the women. He hadn't seen Patsy since he left her for the watermelon wagon. She ought to stand out with her blonde ringlets and those red, white, and blue sparkly stars in her hair, but the whole lakeside was a sea of patriotic clothing. If folks didn't have on a plain red T-shirt, they wore something with the St. Louis Cardinals' red baseball logo. In the

Ozarks, rooting for the Cards was considered as patriotic as saluting the U.S. flag. Even the kids had gotten into the spirit of the celebration, waving sparklers as they chased each other back and forth alongside the swimming area just off the shore.

Pete spotted Derek Finley's twins, Luke and Lydia. Cute kids. Too bad about the boy having diabetes, though it didn't appear to be slowing him down any. He was racing after his sister with a red water balloon, and she didn't stand a chance.

On a bench under a tree, the Hansens' two knockout daughters sat watching the kids play. Brenda had brought them with her to Pete's place when she was buying gas the other day. The Hansen girls were blonde, trim, and as sweet as pecan pie. Hard to believe one of them was planning to become a missionary.

What was a missionary, anyhow? Pete wondered as he continued his search for Patsy. Some kind of religious work, Brenda Hansen had told him. Her daughter was going to study at a training center nearby and then head off to live with a remote tribe in the jungle. Pete thought missionarying sounded more like a man's job than something fit for a pretty young lady. Jennifer Hansen had explained that she wanted to tell the natives about Jesus Christ. She hoped to bring them the message of salvation so they could be born again.

Born again. That phrase.

Pete borrowed Charlie's flyswatter and slapped it down on a particularly pesky fellow that had been bothering him ever since he joined the men near the grills. As he handed the flyswatter back to Charlie, Pete had to admit to himself that he'd been doing some thinking ever since Patsy had told him he needed to be born again. And the fact was, he'd botched up his life so bad the first time around that he didn't have the heart to start all over. Oh, sure, he was doing his best not to repeat his previous mistakes. But there was simply not much hope for a man with his past.

"Whoa!" The exclamation escaped Pete's lips the moment he spotted Patsy standing near the salad table. Mercy, that woman looked good in a pair of shorts and high heels.

"Something wrong?" Steve Hansen asked, elbowing Pete. "Or did you just notice Patsy Pringle?"

The other men guffawed as if this were the funniest thing they'd ever heard.

Pete leaned back in the lawn chair and grinned. "As a matter of fact, I believe I do have my eye on the prettiest gal in Deepwater Cove."

"Now, hold on there," Steve spoke up. "Patsy's pretty all right, but I'd have to vote for my beautiful Brenda as the belle of this ball."

All the men focused on the lovely blonde whose smile shone like the summer sun. Brenda was obviously talking to the other women about her daughters as she gestured toward the two young beauties who favored their mother to a tee.

Pete agreed that Brenda Hansen was very attractive, and he was glad to hear her husband speak up for her. But Patsy Pringle —

"Aw, come on, Steve," Brad Hanes said. "My Ashley's the hottest hottie out here. Look at those long legs on my woman."

The men shifted a little uncomfortably as they all made an effort *not* to look at the young redhead's legs. Pete began to wish the topic of women had never come up. Brad shouldn't have drawn the fellows' attention to his wife's legs. Not even Pete was that ignorant, and he decided it was time to steer toward a safer topic than a comparison of one woman's attributes with another's.

"A pretty lady will get my thumbs-up any time and any place," he said. "In fact, I think this little corner of the world has got the pick of the crop. Look at those gals. Esther, Brenda, Ashley, and Patsy — fairest flowers of the land."

"Speaking of pretty women, where's that mother of yours, Derek?" Charlie Moore asked. "And come to think of it, I don't see Kim, either."

Pete glanced over at Derek, who was shifting a little uncomfortably in his lawn chair. "They, uh . . . they had a little problem in the kitchen. Kim's bringing one of those seven-layer dips."

"Got in a fight about which layer went first, huh?" Brad asked with a laugh.

The look on Derek's face told Pete that was exactly what had happened. Charlie gave an awkward harrumph and pretended to search for his wife. Steve reached across his grill with a pair of tongs to turn over his pork steaks. Who would have thought a bunch of good-for-nothings like these fellows sitting around on the Fourth of July could manage to make each other so uncomfortable?

Pete knew women talked nonstop and everyone felt just peachy when they parted company. Before he had built a soundproof wall between his tackle shop and Patsy's salon, Pete had heard the women next door jabbering away day after day. In fact, their constant chitchat had been partly what prompted him to start up a chain saw every now and then. Anything to drown out that racket.

But men? Men didn't really know how to talk to each other. They couldn't very well admire each other's hairdos or trade chicken soup recipes. What this bunch needed was a woman to sit among them and stir up some cordial conversation. But as it was, the men fanned themselves with their flyswatters or checked their grills until Pete finally brought up what everyone was thinking.

"How about them Cardinals?"

"I couldn't believe the pitcher in yesterday's game," Brad Hanes muttered.

"Did you fellas see that drive down the right-field line?" Charlie Moore asked.

And that was all it took. They discussed the ins and outs of the game, weighed the players' talents, mentioned statistics from the past, and generally talked the subject half to death.

That was okay with Pete. He focused on Patsy Pringle, who was balancing on her high-heel wedges as she picked her way across the grass toward some destination Pete couldn't see. Adjusting her gold ringlets, she began to smile as if she'd just gotten a glimpse of heaven itself. Slightly disturbed at what might have captured Patsy's attention other than himself, Pete leaned forward. The plastic webbing under his backside crackled a little as he scanned the scene, and finally he noticed goofy ol' Cody Goss half skipping and jumping toward Patsy.

"Hey, Patsy," Cody cried, clapping his hands as he greeted her. "You have stars in your hair!"

"It's the Fourth of July, honey!" she exclaimed.

"Happy America!" he said, dancing around her. "Merry Independence! Long live July!"

Patsy laughed and hugged on Cody like he was her long-lost best friend. Then she turned and pointed out the watermelon wagon, the shore where all the kids were playing, the tables lined with salads and desserts, and finally the grills. As her eyes settled on Pete, he decided he'd heard more than enough about baseball. He beckoned Patsy and Cody.

"Look, there's Pete Roberts!" Cody called out. "He makes hot dogs at Rods-N-Ends. Hi, Pete!"

"Hey there, Cody ol' fella; how're you doing today?" Pete pushed himself out of the lawn chair and ambled over to them. "I see you're wearing a flag T-shirt."

"This is the USA flag," Cody explained, laying his hand on his chest to indicate the printed banner. "Brenda and Steve gave me this shirt. The flag has stars like in Patsy's hair. I like those stars. Do you?"

"I sure do," Pete said. "Patsy always looks pretty as a picture."

"A picture? She's prettier than a picture, because this is really her."

"Aw, Cody," Patsy murmured, blushing like some shy schoolgirl. "You are so sweet. And you're handsome, too! Look at that clean-shaven chin. Gracious sakes, young man, who would ever have thought it!"

"Pete should shave, huh, Patsy?" Cody asked. "You told me he looks like a shaggy bear."

Cody glanced from Patsy to Pete, assessed their expressions, and then covered his mouth with his hand. "Oops," he said. "I think I just did bad social skills."

"It's all right," Patsy told Cody, patting his arm. "Pete knows how I feel about that awful beard."

Suddenly grouchy, Pete combed his fingers through the thick mat of dark hair that had been with him since he couldn't remember when. He snorted and hooked his hands in the pockets of his jeans. "A person ought to be able to see beyond a little facial hair, is what I say. Looks aren't everything."

"Oh, really?" Patsy retorted. "Seems you've been doing plenty of looking in my direction today, Mr. Roberts. If you want me looking back, you'd do well to shave off that musty old clump hanging from your chin."

Cody cackled and slapped his thighs. "Musty old clump! At least you don't have mice in your hair like I did when I first got to Deepwater Cove, Pete. Hey, look who's coming now! It's Mrs. Finley and the other Mrs. Finley."

Sure enough, here came Kim and her mother-in-law, Miranda, each carrying a clear glass bowl of seven-layer dip across the lawn toward the gathering. Pete didn't want to make a big deal of it, but he noticed right away that neither woman looked the least bit happy about making an appearance at the Deepwater Cove Fourth of July celebration. As Kim and Miranda set their bowls on the chip-and-dip table, Pete left Patsy's side and wandered over to fetch himself a plate of appetizers. No point just dawdling around when there was good food to be had.

"Afternoon, Miz Finley," he greeted

Derek's mother.

Both women looked up at the same time and gave pained smiles.

"Hi, Pete," Kim Finley spoke up first. "Glad you could make it to the celebration."

"Try my seven-layer dip, Pete," Miranda Finley suggested, spooning a dollop onto a paper plate and giving it to him. She dug a handful of tortilla chips from a bag, ran one through her dip, and pushed it between his lips. "I always put the sour cream on top, because that way it's the first flavor to hit your taste buds. Sets the mood, don't you think? With guacamole, cheese, and refried beans all in perfect order under the sour cream, you can almost picture yourself lounging on a Caribbean beach."

Pete tried to talk around the bite of chip and dip Miranda had put into his mouth, but he couldn't manage it. He wanted to say that it didn't matter to him which came first, because eventually the flavors all blended together. But as he started to speak, a sliver of chip flew down the wrong pipe.

As Pete began to cough, he noticed what Kim was doing. Standing beside her mother-in-law, she pursed her lips tight and ladled a large helping of her own seven-layer dip into a bowl. Swigging down some soda to clear his throat, Pete noted that Kim had put the shredded cheese on top, followed by layers of beans, guacamole, olives, and — somewhere down at the bottom — sour cream.

Grabbing a bag of chips under one arm, Kim carried her dip toward the men gathered around their grills. Pete could see the battle unfolding right before his eyes. If anyone declared Kim's appetizer to be delicious, it would undercut Miranda's before she'd even had a chance to show it off. And no doubt those sweaty gents in their barbecue aprons were going to dig into Kim's dip with gusto.

As she realized her daughter-in-law's ploy, Miranda let out a whimper of dismay. She snatched up her bowl of dip, seized a second bag of chips and marched toward the men.

Pete took one look at Derek Finley's face and realized that this unfolding conflict would put the poor man in the hot seat, no matter what. "Hey, Patsy!" he called. "Yo, Patsy!"

If only he could get the blonde in her wedgy sandals and sparkling stars to saunter over to the grills, she might just be able to distract everyone. Then maybe Patsy's kind demeanor and sweet words could defuse the oncoming clash. Determined to keep peace, Pete hurried over to where the salon owner was helping Bitty Sondheim and Opal Jones arrange carrots and sweet pickles in neat rows on a glass tray.

"Patsy," Pete said, sidling up and whispering in her ear. "You've got to come with me right now, and I mean it. No dawdling around, gal. There's trouble afoot."

Before she could respond, Pete took her arm and ushered her toward the battlefront.

"What are you up to now, Pete Roberts?" Patsy challenged him. "Bitty and I were helping Opal fix her relish dish! You know how bad Opal's arthritis gets, and she asked us to —"

"Patsy, get over there and eat some dip," Pete instructed as he propelled the woman across the grass. "Try 'em both, and then talk about something else like hairstyles or whatever comes to mind."

"Pete, let go of my arm this minute! Why, I ought to —"

Patsy caught her breath as Pete pushed her down onto the lawn chair he had recently vacated.

"Look who's here," he said. "It's Patsy."

Pete was turning to scoop dip from the two rival bowls when the unmistakable sound of ripping plastic caught his ears. He looked back in time to see the webbing give way beneath Patsy Pringle's ample backside and drop her right through the aluminum chair frame onto the ground.

Patsy let out a shriek that would curdle milk as her wedge-heeled feet flew into the air, and her sandals sailed over Pete's head.

"Incoming!" someone yelled.

Pete never would have guessed it possible, but the woman folded into that aluminum framework like a hymnbook at the end of a church service. Her legs stuck straight up, her arms waved back and forth over her head, and those sparkly stars went sailing out of her hair.

"Help!" she hollered, bare feet kicking. "Somebody help me! Pete Roberts, I'm gonna kill you!"

Horror-struck, Pete couldn't move for a full second. In fact, it seemed as though the entire Deepwater Cove gathering fell silent and turned to stare at the woman wedged into the frame of the collapsed aluminum folding chair. And then — before Pete could do his part to rectify the situation — Officer Derek Finley bent over and extricated the helpless victim from the jaws of death.

"Are you all right, Patsy?" Derek asked as he pulled Patsy to her feet.

Her blue eyes shot straight to Pete. "No, I am not all right, thank you very much! I am furious! Pete Roberts, what on earth was that all about? I ought to string you up by your thumbnails!"

"Good gravy!" Charlie Moore exclaimed. "For a minute there, I thought we'd been hit by mortar fire!"

Brad Hanes burst out laughing. "It was a blonde bombshell, all right!"

"Did you see those shoes go airborne?" someone else cried.

"I saw shooting stars right before my eyes!"

By now, all the men were grinning as they grabbed the bags of chips and dug into the identical bowls of dip. Feud obviously forgotten, Kim and Miranda Finley circled around Patsy, helping to fix her hair and find her sandals. Somehow a long curlicue had come unpinned, and Pete picked it up.

"Uh, I think you lost this," he said, holding out the blonde ringlet like a peace offering.

Patsy snatched it from his hand. "You'd better explain yourself this minute, Pete Roberts. What did you mean by jerking me away from helping Opal with her relish tray and slinging me into that broken chair?"

"Well, I was . . ." Pete gulped. "I thought maybe —"

"You made me the laughingstock of the whole place! Everyone saw me make an idiot of myself."

To Pete's horror, the feisty woman's blue eyes suddenly filled with tears. He reached out to her. "Aw, now, Patsy —"

"Don't you dare touch me, Pete Roberts!" she said, knocking his hand away. "You're pushy and mean and forward. You're just a bully is what you are! Ever since you moved to the lake, you've done everything in your power to make my life miserable. But this is the last straw. You intended to make me out to be a fool, and you succeeded — and that's the last you'll be hearing from me till the cows come home!"

"Now, listen here, Patsy," he began again.

But the sound of a child's scream drowned out his words. As Pete focused in the direction of the cry, he saw Kim and Derek Finley's young daughter sprinting toward them.

"Mommy, Mommy!" she was hollering as she ran. "Come quick! Luke fell down, and he's not moving!"

CHAPTER NINE

Kim knelt in the damp, rocky sand beside her son. Luke's brown eyes fluttered as she pressed the emergency number on her cell phone. Next to her, Derek was checking the boy's pulse and airway.

"I need a clean towel — his head is bleeding. I'm guessing he gashed it on that big rock." Derek glanced at Lydia. "What were you kids doing?"

"Just playing around, I swear!" Lydia was jumping up and down, shaking her hands, crying, and elbowing away all attempts to comfort her. "Luke told me he was dizzy and he felt like he was going to throw up. Then he started staggering down the beach, but he only got this far before he fell and his head hit that rock. Do something, Derek! Fix him! Fix my brother!"

"Nausea, dizziness, and staggering. Sounds like intoxication. Listen, Lydia, I need to know if Luke drank any alcohol,"

Derek barked at the girl as someone handed him a towel. "You'd better tell me the truth. What did you kids get into? Was it beer?"

"Luke's not drunk," Kim cut in. "It's his diabetes! His blood sugar must be off. I don't know what to do! I can't think! Where's his kit?"

She looked at Lydia, who shrieked, "I don't have it! Was I supposed to bring it? It's Luke's kit, and —"

Lydia caught her breath as her brother suddenly began to convulse. Kim let out an involuntary wail and tried to gather her son in her arms. Pressing the towel against the gash on the side of the boy's head, Derek urged everyone to calm down. And suddenly the insulin kit appeared in Miranda's hand.

"I found it in his bedroom," she huffed, out of breath. "In all the excitement of the day, he might have forgotten to take his insulin."

"Lukey's bleeding to death!" Lydia screamed. "He's going to die!"

"Someone get the girl under control," Derek shouted at the crowd as he snatched the kit and handed it to Kim. "Mom, take Lydia to the house."

"I'm not leaving my brother!" Lydia cried out. "Make him stop shaking! You have to help him!"

Kim tried to block out her daughter's hysteria as she fumbled with the insulin kit. People had crowded around, edging closer, cutting off the afternoon sunlight. She pushed at Lydia's skinny arms as the girl tried to grab her brother.

"Don't let him die!" Lydia sobbed. "He's all I have. He's my only brother. He's my best friend."

"Scoot over, Lydia," Kim ordered. Luke's convulsions had eased, but he was groggy and unfocused. "I have to test his blood."

"He didn't eat lunch, Mom!" Lydia was down on her stomach, arms around her brother. "We forgot about the snacks you sent with us. Why won't his head stop bleeding, Derek? What are you doing to him? Wake up, Lukey! Please don't die!"

"Please, God, please," Kim whispered as she tested her son's blood and read the indicator. "His glucose is low — but he shouldn't have had a seizure. Why isn't he more alert?"

"Probably the head injury," Derek said. "I'm on it."

Kim could hear a siren in the distance as she filled a syringe with insulin. "Please help my son, Lord. Please help us."

"He'll be all right," Derek was saying.

"We've got him under control, honey. He'll be fine."

While Kim injected the insulin, Derek checked Luke's pulse again. "We need to get a saline IV going. He probably needs potassium, too. Hang in there, Luke. You're doing good, kiddo. Lydia, for pete's sake, will you let your brother have some air?"

"You shut up!" Lydia shouted suddenly at Derek. "You don't know anything! You're supposed to be an officer and smart about helping people, but you're just wiping Lukey's blood and letting my mom do all the work. You can't make me —"

"Put a muzzle on that mouth, girl, or I will!"

As the emergency medical personnel clustered around Luke, Kim sensed Derek leaving her side, pressing people back, dragging Lydia away. The EMTs began asking questions, checking Luke's vital signs, starting an IV drip. Kim told them everything she knew. She watched helplessly as they lifted her son into the back of the ambulance. And then, before she could clear her head, she was inside the vehicle speeding toward Lake Regional hospital in Osage Beach.

The EMT team worked over Luke while Kim brushed back tears and tried to make sense of what they were saying. She heard words that had passed through her mind a thousand times since her son's diagnosis — *diabetic ketoacidosis, counterregulatory hormones, electrolytes, ketones.*

She struggled to answer their questions. When had Luke's blood last been tested? By the shore, she told them, ten minutes ago — or was it five?

Had he experienced a recent infection — strep throat, pneumonia, an intestinal virus, or a urinary tract infection? A cough and runny nose, she said. Oh, why hadn't she paid closer attention to her son?

Had he undergone any trauma other than the head injury in the past twenty-four hours? Nothing. Nothing she could recall, but he had been outside with Lydia since breakfast.

Kim told the team everything she knew, and it seemed not nearly enough. That morning, she and her mother-in-law had argued over the right way to make a seven-layer dip. At the sound of their bickering, Luke and Lydia fled the house and began swimming in the cove and playing with the other children. As everyone slowly gathered in the commons area and waited for the pork steaks to cook, the meal had been delayed. So what had Luke eaten that day?

When had he last given himself a dose of insulin? What had he done while she was busy in the kitchen?

"I can't believe it," Kim murmured as the ambulance stopped in front of the hospital's emergency room and the EMT team transferred Luke to the waiting medical staff. "I can't believe it. I didn't watch him. And Lydia! Where is — oh, thank God!"

Kim's breath hung in her throat as Derek and Lydia burst through the ER door and ran toward her. Miranda was right behind them, her sandals clattering on the hard floor and her blonde hair sticking out in all directions.

Still wearing her wet bathing suit, Lydia grabbed her mother and began weeping all over again. "Where's Lukey?" she sobbed. "Where did they take my brother? I hate Derek! He made me ride in the car instead of the ambulance, and he doesn't even know what ketones are!"

Kim glanced at her husband, who had leaned one shoulder against the corridor wall as he caught his breath. Obviously fighting for control, he crossed his arms over his chest and stared at Kim. And then a doctor hurried toward them. More questions. Lydia crying and raging. Miranda wringing her hands, sandals clacking along the floor as she paced. Derek, jaw clenched, staring.

The doctor vanished, and someone ushered them all to the ER waiting area. Kim had barely sat down when Lydia curled into her lap.

"It's Derek's fault," the girl whimpered. "He's supposed to know how to help people in trouble, and he didn't do anything."

"Stop that, Lydia," Miranda spoke up firmly. "You can't hold your stepfather responsible. We all played a part. This morning it crossed my mind that Luke might have forgotten to check his blood, and then I got busy with the seven-layer dip. Your mother was so insistent on doing it her way —"

"Wait — you're blaming *me* for the problem in the kitchen?" Kim stared in disbelief. "You were the one who made an issue of the dip, Miranda. In fact, you criticize everything I do. I could have put that dip together in five minutes, but I spent half the morning trying to convince you that I knew what I was doing! And you . . . you . . ." Hearing her own senseless rant, Kim burst into tears and buried her face in her daughter's shoulder.

Lydia wrapped her arms around her mother. "You should just go back to St.

Louis, Grandma Finley," she said. "And take Derek with you. We don't need either of you. It's always been Luke and Mommy and me, ever since I can remember, and we were doing just fine till you people came along."

"Lydia, no," Kim cried.

"*You*, young lady, should have been watching your brother." Miranda pointed an accusing finger at the girl. "If I didn't know about the diabetes, I wouldn't have any trouble believing you two had gotten into someone's liquor cabinet! You're both just looking for trouble, aren't you? Like the day you ran away from me at the library. How did you expect me to find you at your friend's house two streets over? The fact is, you were both raised to be wild little things. If my son hadn't married your mother and brought some order and control into your lives, you'd probably be headed for juvenile court by now!"

"That's enough, Mom," Derek growled. "Everyone be quiet for two seconds."

"How can you expect us to be detached and unemotional like you, Derek?" Kim demanded. "We don't even know what's happening to Luke! They've shut us away here in the waiting room, and the least you could do is tell them you're with the Water Patrol."

"Why would I do that?"

"So you could go in there and check on him! You're an officer. You're trained for emergencies."

"Not diabetic emergencies," Lydia tossed out. "Derek doesn't know anything about diabetes, and you know why? Because he doesn't care. I bet he never even read the printout I made. He only cares about his work. He's not our real father. Luke could die, and Derek would be glad, Mom, because that would be one less person to take you away from him. That's all he wants. Just you and his dumb job."

"Lydia." Kim tried to push her daughter off her lap, but the girl clung on tight with fingers like steel bands. "Lydia, stop being disrespectful to Derek. He loves you and Luke, and he takes good care of us —"

"No, he doesn't! He doesn't know what ketones are! All he does is ride around in his stupid speedboat looking at girls in Party Cove. Big deal! Officer Finley, Officer Finley, la-di-da! Who cares?"

"Is that the way you let your children speak to adults, Kim?" Miranda cried. "You should take that girl outside and —"

"I will deal with my daughter when this

crisis is over," Kim snapped. "At the moment, all I care about is my son's health! Derek, don't just stand there like a concrete block. Go in there and make them tell us what's going on!"

As Derek roused himself from the wall he'd been leaning against, the emergency room door burst open and in marched half of Deepwater Cove. Patsy Pringle and Cody Goss led the pack as Steve and Brenda Hansen, Charlie and Esther Moore, Brad and Ashley Hanes, Opal Jones, Bitty Sondheim, and a number of others flooded into the waiting area. Pete Roberts brought up the rear, his beefy arms wrapped around a watermelon.

The throng had nearly reached Kim when the door at the opposite end of the room opened and a nurse beckoned the family. Lydia leaped out of her mother's arms and began to run. Kim cast a backward glance at Derek, saw he was speaking to Miranda, and headed after her daughter.

"Ketones," Derek told Steve Hansen as the two men stood in the hospital room's doorway. Two days had passed since the Fourth of July fiasco, and Derek had finally succeeded in sending his wife home to bed. Luke was holding his own now. The diabetic crisis was safely behind them, and the doctor planned to release the boy the next morning. The stitches meant Luke's head would be sore, but the mild concussion should have no lasting impact. Working the late shift gave Derek the opportunity to relieve Kim, who hadn't left her son's side since his arrival at the emergency room.

"What are ketones?" Steve asked. The real estate agent had dropped by the hospital after dinner with a client at his country club. They had sealed a lucrative land deal, and Steve was in a good mood despite the late hour.

"Ketones are chemical by-products," Derek explained. Recalling Lydia's shouted accusations, he had made sure to ask the doctor everything about Luke's condition.

"Are they good or bad?" Steve asked.

Derek rubbed his temples with his thumb and forefinger. "They're bad. They affect the kidneys. Luke forgot his insulin on the morning of the Fourth. He told his mother that he'd been popping in and out of the basement bathroom all day, but he didn't think anything about it. When he got dehydrated, he felt dizzy and fell and hit his head."

"I guess I hadn't realized it could get that serious so quickly." Steve studied the sleeping boy. "Charlie Moore told us he has diabetes, but I guess his is not the same kind as Luke's."

"Charlie has type 2. That can be serious too, but it's different."

Steve clapped a hand on Derek's shoulder. "Brenda mentioned some of the things Lydia was saying to you out there on the commons. Kids can be pretty tough to handle at times, and you took on the twins sort of late in the game."

Derek shrugged. "Being a stepfather is harder than I thought. Kim says I live in my own little world."

"What man doesn't? We see our role as a job, and we do the best we can with it. For years I thought I was a good husband and dad — doing my part, playing my role. And then Brenda accused me of abandoning her."

Surprised at the frank revelation, Derek glanced at Steve. Derek liked Steve Hansen well enough, and he respected the man's dedication to his wife and children. Steve had built a good reputation as a business-man with his real estate agency. He had always seemed cheerful and his family suc-cessful.

"You abandoned Brenda?" Derek asked. "That doesn't sound like the Hansens of

Deepwater Cove."

"Well, I was gone a lot, especially when the new agency had just started to build up steam. Brenda started missing the kids and struggling over some things, and I was never around. We had a rough time, and I wouldn't ever want to go through anything like that again. But we learned a lot. Brenda and I are working hard to pull our marriage back together. I'd sure hate to see you and Kim fall into the same kind of trouble."

Derek frowned. "I don't think we have any big problems. Kim and I are crazy about each other. It's this diabetes thing . . . and my mother being around all the time. And I do have to work a lot of hours, especially in the summer. But I try."

The men fell silent, watching the lights on Luke's monitors blink on and off. Derek reflected on the arguing and shouting that had taken place at home in the past few weeks. Lydia had become a real pain in the neck, and Luke's diabetes was stressing everyone out. Kim clearly didn't like having Derek's mother in their home, but he couldn't understand why. Miranda looked after the twins so Kim could go back to work. Kim enjoyed her job, and that income was something the family couldn't surrender.

"Maybe the real problem is not you at all," Steve suggested. "Brenda had focused her whole life around our children before they left home. I'll bet Kim is frustrated over her inability to be with the twins more — especially with one of them sick. But I know Dr. Groene counts on Kim. So what do you do?"

"Turns out he's diabetic too. Type 1, like Luke. He's been great."

"Could Kim stay home with the twins permanently? That way, your mother could go back to St. Louis. Maybe then you could all get back to normal."

Derek shook his head, realizing there was so much more to the financial situation than anyone understood.

"Have you and Kim ever thought of talking to Pastor Andrew? I wish I'd listened better to his advice when Brenda and I were having trouble. He might have some ideas that could see you through this rough patch."

"The guy's been in and out of here every day visiting with Luke and Kim, but I don't feel that comfortable around him, to tell you the truth. I'm not a churchgoer, you know. I don't mind Kim and the kids attending. I just haven't felt the need."

Steve's eyebrows lifted. "Maybe not yet."

Derek glanced over at him. "I've always handled things my way, pal."

"Well, you've got our prayers whether you want them or not." Steve gave Derek a nod. "I'd better head home. Brenda and Cody baked a chocolate cake this evening, and they're waiting up for me."

At the thought of Cody's wide blue eyes, Derek smiled and his shoulders relaxed. "Eat a piece for me," he said. "Desserts are few and far between at our house these days."

"You've got a deal."

"Thanks for dropping by," Derek said. "I'll tell Kim you were here to check on Luke."

"Actually, I came to see you. I called Kim before I left the club, and she told me you were at the hospital. I wanted to visit with you awhile."

"Thanks."

Steve shook Derek's hand and headed down the hall.

Lydia settled into the soft, black vinyl chair at Patsy's station inside the Just As I Am beauty salon. Closing her eyes, she took a deep breath and said, "Cut it off."

"All of it?" Patsy lifted a hank of the girl's thick, dark brown hair. "Honeybunch, are you sure about this?"

"I'm positive. Luke and I are turning eleven in three weeks, and we're tired of being treated like little kids. We're going into the sixth grade this fall. That's middle school, in case you didn't know."

"I know how old eleven is, and I also know that you have some of the prettiest hair in Camden County. I'd put you in the running to wear Jessica Hansen's homecoming queen crown one of these days. You've got your mother's big brown eyes and your own sweet smile. You don't want to cut off your hair so close to school starting up again, do you?"

"Yes," Lydia said firmly. "Up to my ears. I want it short and sassy, like Tiffany's."

Lydia opened her purse and pulled out a school photograph of a girl who didn't have half her beauty. What had gotten into that giggly little pumpkin who used to hold her twin brother's hand as they selected goodies with their mother in the tea area?

When Lydia called the salon to make an appointment, one of the other stylists had taken the message. Now Patsy was beginning to wonder if Kim Finley even knew what her daughter was up to.

"Tiffany's got some natural wave, see?" Patsy said, pointing to the photo. "Your hair wouldn't look the same even if we did give it that style. Does your mother want me to cut it so short, honey? Or did she drop you off here just for a trim?"

As Lydia's pretty lips pinched shut, Patsy noted the film of pink lip gloss coating them. She also saw a dusting of frosted eye shadow on the girl's eyelids and some clumpy mascara stuck to her lashes. Hmmm. This was beginning to spell trouble with a capital *T*.

"I've got an idea," Patsy said. "You sit tight while I call your mom at Dr. Groene's office. She can tell me exactly what the two of you discussed."

"No, wait!" Lydia caught Patsy's arm. "I rode my bike over here by myself, and I'm spending my *own* money for this haircut. My mother has nothing to do with it."

"Really? Don't you still live at home?" Patsy swung the chair toward the mirror and snapped a plastic cape around Lydia's neck. "My parents always said I could make my own decisions when I lived in my own house and paid my own bills and ate my own cooking. Until then, I was under their thumb."

"I'm not under anyone's thumb. My real dad doesn't live with us, so Luke and I don't even have parents like yours. We live with Derek and our fake grandma, who doesn't even like us. She told us we were nothing but a gigantic pain."

"Really? Miranda said that?" Patsy began combing out Lydia's long hair. "Oh, maybe she said it that time you two ran off from her and Cody at the library and she couldn't find you. I guess she must have been pretty upset. People sometimes say and do things they don't mean when they get angry. You know what I did one time when I got mad?"

Lydia's brown eyes swiveled from gazing at herself in the mirror to focusing on Patsy. "Yes. You refused to eat a single slice of the watermelon Pete Roberts brought over to the hospital the night Luke went into the emergency room. You told Pete he could stick that watermelon in his ear."

Suddenly going warm, Patsy fanned herself with her hand. "Did I say that?"

"Uh-huh. Pete brought your watermelon from the wagon under the tree. He cut it up for everyone to eat while they waited to find out about Luke. Mom and I ate some, and even Grandma Finley said it was good — and she never likes anything she didn't do herself. But you wouldn't touch it. You said you didn't ever want to talk to Pete again."

"Oh, dear."

More than a week had passed since the

Independence Day chair incident, and Patsy had kept to her word. Once, she and Pete had passed each other in the hospital corridor while visiting Luke. Patsy had turned her head and pretended to be talking to Opal Jones, who didn't even have her hearing aids in. And Patsy had refused to speak to Pete at church last Sunday. They didn't sit together or go out to eat at Aunt Mamie's Good Food in Camdenton after the service. She hadn't thanked him for the pretty antique teacup he had left on her doorstep the previous morning. In fact, she hadn't even read the accompanying note.

"Well, it isn't every day that a man makes a spectacle of you in front of your friends," Patsy told Lydia. "I *was* mad at Pete, and I still am. But what I was going to tell you about was the time I got mad at my father for telling me I was fat. Just like you, I decided to cut my hair off so I could be a whole different person. I wasn't much older than you, and I went into my bedroom, got my scissors, and snipped off every long curl on my head."

"But you change your hair all the time, Patsy." Lydia took the comb and began parting her hair in different places. "I don't see why it's such a big deal. You style it and color it and put in extensions whenever you

220

want. That's what you do whether you're mad at someone or not."

"But you're missing my point, honey. Cutting your pretty hair off isn't going to change anything. All it'll do is give you short hair. It won't fix your brother's diabetes or bring your first daddy home or make your grandma friendlier."

"I never said it would." Lydia's voice rose. "I'm almost in sixth grade, and I want to look older. I want people to stop treating me like a little girl. I'm nearly eleven!"

"Eleven." Patsy shook her head. "I'll tell you what I tell all my clients. You should never make a big change when you're in the middle of a crisis. And you sure shouldn't cut your hair just because you're mad."

"I'm not mad."

"Yes, you are."

"Well, so are you, and look what you did. You got rid of those blonde curls you had at the Fourth of July picnic, and now it's straight and brown. So, cut my hair —" she reached for the scissors — "or I will!"

"Give me those!" Patsy snatched her shears away and crossed her arms. But when she glanced in the mirror, she saw that she and Lydia had the exact same expressions on their faces.

"Everyone keeps telling me that nothing

can fix Luke." The girl's eyes welled. "But I just want things to be different, Patsy. Starting with me."

"Real changes start inside a person. You know that, don't you, Lydia?" Patsy asked gently. "God looks at the heart, because that's what matters most to Him. And . . . well, you've helped me see that my heart is hard and cold toward my neighbor. Pete embarrassed me, and I don't know how to forgive him. But I have to change my way of thinking. And you do too. You've got to accept your brother's diabetes. You've got to realize what a good dad Derek is to you and Luke, even though he's not your birth father. You've got to accept Grandma Finley, too. She's trying to help. Everyone is doing their best."

As she spoke, Patsy had begun snipping at Lydia's hair, but it was hard to see through the tears in her own eyes. When Pete Roberts had pushed her into that lawn chair the other day, she had felt so humiliated she wanted to die right then and there. It was as if all the sensitivity and humiliation she had felt during adolescence came rushing back. In those days, her weight had gone up and down as she tried one diet after another. The time her father criticized her, she had retaliated by attacking herself — butchering her hair before she knew anything about style and color. A small voice sometimes still taunted her about it. At the barbecue, everyone had laughed at her, and she sensed that if Luke Finley hadn't collapsed on the beach, her pratfall would still be the talk of Deepwater Cove.

She had blamed Pete, but it was the Lord who had chosen to give Patsy a generous bosom and more than sufficient hips. God made her who she was, body and soul. Was she angry with Him? herself? Or Pete?

"Are you crying?" Lydia's voice was high and hollow. "I didn't mean to upset you, Patsy."

"You didn't, sweetie. You helped me take a look at my own failings, which are many. Refusing to forgive Pete is just one, but I need to deal with it."

Lydia sniffled. "What are you gonna do?"

"I guess I'll have to go next door and talk to him, won't I?" She sighed. "I have to forgive him, even though he makes me madder than a wet hen. And you? How about some wispy bangs, a couple inches off the bottom, and a few layers? You won't look like Tiffany, but why should you? You're Lydia, and I'm proud to know you."

The girl's face brightened, and she nodded. "Okay, bangs and layers. That's a good start, Patsy."

"It sure is."

Chapter Ten

Kim slipped into a pair of sandals and grabbed her Bible off the bedside table. If she didn't get the twins out the door in the next five minutes, they were going to be late for church again. It never failed — a last-minute hullabaloo as everyone searched for purses, Bibles, tithe money, matching shoes, jackets, you name it. The fuss often continued all the way to church, but by the time the service was over and the family gathered for lunch, everyone was reasonably cheerful.

After running a brush through her hair, Kim misted it with a little spray, gave one last glance through her jewelry box for her favorite pair of gold earrings, and then gave up. There was no time to keep looking. She must have laid them down somewhere else.

"Luke! Lydia!" she called into the twins' rooms as she hurried down the hall toward the living room. "Are you guys ready to go?"

As she entered the foyer, Kim was surprised to find Derek standing there in a pair of khaki slacks and a polo shirt. The last thing she had seen before heading for the shower was Derek and his mother eating blueberry muffins and drinking coffee out on the deck.

"I didn't know you were going to play golf this morning," she said. Derek rarely went out on the course unless some of the other officers needed a fourth. When he had a rare Sunday off, he usually rested most of the day.

She called down the hall again. "Lydia, Luke, you'd better get out to the car this minute." And then back to her husband. "I hope you won't play more than nine holes, honey. I've got a chicken in the oven, and I was hoping we could have a nice lunch together. I put in onions, potatoes, carrots — everything you like. And your mom promised she'd slide my bread into the oven before we get home. I hope she doesn't forget like last time. Would you please remind her?"

Luke dashed into the foyer, his shirttail hanging out and a dollop of toothpaste on his chin. "I can't find my insulin kit!"

"I've got it in my purse. I told you at breakfast." She huffed out a breath as she wiped her son's chin. "Tuck in your shirt, Luke. You're almost eleven; you should know that by now. Where's your sister?"

"She's scared to come out."

"Scared? Why?"

"She borrowed your favorite earrings without telling you, and she's afraid you'll notice and make her take them off."

"Lydia took my —" Kim shook her head as she pushed her son toward the door. "Oh, for pete's sake, Lydia, come on out. You can wear my earrings today, but in the future please ask before borrowing my things."

At the sight of Derek in his slacks and shirt, Luke let out a grumble of annoyance. "You promised to take me with you the next time you went golfing, Derek," he said. "Mom, I don't want to go to church. I want to go with —"

"We're *all* going to church," Derek announced. "All except Grandma Finley, who's in her bedroom lighting incense to her 'inner deity.' "

Kim realized she was standing there with her mouth open, but she suddenly couldn't move. Had Derek just said he was going to church? With the family?

"Can I wear your blue sweater, Mom? It matches my outfit."

Lydia came down the hall carrying the

227

delicate cashmere cardigan Derek had bought for Kim on their first Christmas. She had admired it in one of the shops in Osage Beach, but it had been way too expensive. Yet there it had lain — wrapped in gold and tied with a red bow — under the tree that perfect, snowy morning.

When Kim didn't respond to her daughter's query, Derek did. "Ask *first*," he said, holding out a hand for the sweater. "You heard your mother."

"But it matches!" Lydia stamped her foot. "You can't tell me what to —"

"Get in the car!" Derek barked. As they left the house, he called back through the door. "We're going to church, Mother. Don't stink up the place too bad." Guiding Kim with a hand on her back, he muttered, "Man, I hate that stuff she burns. Smells like a gas station bathroom."

Kim still hadn't spoken when the car rolled backward out of the drive and started toward the entrance to the Deepwater Cove subdivision. She didn't know what to think, and she certainly couldn't figure out what to say.

Derek was going to church! But why? What had happened? Was God really answering her prayers with a resounding *yes?* Or was this just a whim of Derek's? Or did he have some ulterior purpose?

"You told on me, didn't you?" Lydia accused her brother in the backseat. "I knew you'd tell her I was wearing them. You can't ever keep a secret, you blabbermouth."

"Do you think she's blind?" Luke asked. "First you sneaked off to get your hair cut. Then you went and got Mom's sweater. You think she was gonna look right past her own earrings? You're dumb."

"Don't touch me. Mom, Luke punched me in the shoulder."

"Tattletale," Luke said.

"Luke, don't you dare tell what I said about Tiffany. You promised."

"What, that she's got a boyfriend who's sixteen?"

At that, Kim's brain snapped into gear. She turned around in time to see Lydia haul off and slap her brother across the cheek. Luke snarled and drew back a fist.

Kim caught his arm just in time. "Stop it, both of you!" she cried. "Luke, don't even think about hitting your sister. And, Lydia, you're grounded. Give me those earrings."

"Told you!" Luke taunted his sister.

"You can't ground me any more than you already have," Lydia said. "I'm already up to three weeks, and that's almost the start of school."

Luke chimed in, "Besides, Grandma Finley lets her do anything she wants while you're at work, Mom. Grounding is dumb."

As she put on the gold earrings, Kim glanced at Derek. The small muscle in his jaw flickered as he drove, eyes focused on the road. She swallowed. They could *not* have an argument now — not with Derek on the way to church. This was a miracle, an obvious answer to prayer, and if the twins did anything to jeopardize it . . .

"No more arguing in the car," Kim said, "or you won't get dessert after lunch. I made sugar-free chocolate pie, so that goes for you, too, Luke."

For a few blessed moments, the two hellions in the backseat fell quiet. Kim clutched her purse, trying to think what to say to fill the silence. They were passing the row of shops in Tranquility, and she could see the church steeple in the distance.

How could she make herself sound casual when she was so excited to have Derek joining the family for church? This was no ordinary outing. This was the potential start to a whole new life. If she and Derek were united in their faith, nothing could come between them. They could pray as one, discuss problems in light of God's will, maybe even read the Bible together. They would be like Brenda and Steve or Charlie and Esther. An ideal family.

"So, was I supposed to wear a tie?" Derek asked. "I wasn't sure."

"You look fine."

He smiled. "You're gorgeous. Love those earrings, by the way."

Kim couldn't hide her grin. "I'm so glad you're going with us."

"Thought I'd better see what the fuss was about every Sunday morning. I invited Mom, too, but . . ." He shrugged.

Kim stiffened at the mention of Miranda. "Does she still have an altar in her bedroom? I specifically asked her to put that away. I know it's part of her religion, but I'm not comfortable with it."

"Just ignore my mother," Derek said. "She means well, and is she really hurting anyone with her little statues and incense?"

"All paths lead to God," Lydia intoned from the backseat. "That's what Grandma Finley says. Every religion has some truth in it. And it's smart to know about each of them and use the parts that help you find your inner holiness."

"Whatever," Derek said. "The main thing is that your mother chose Christianity, and until you move out of the house, kids, that's your religion. Then you can choose whatever

231

you want to be. Go burn incense with Grandma Finley if it toots your horn."

Luke laughed. "I'm a Christian, and I'm not changing my mind."

"You don't have any choice except to be a Christian," Lydia said. "We have to do whatever Mom and Derek say, remember?"

"Yeah, so why'd you call Dad the other day, Lydia? You know we're not supposed to talk to him except on his weekends."

"You phoned your father again?" Kim asked, turning to eye her daughter. *Great.* This was just what they needed in the middle of so much friction — Lydia bringing Joe into the mix again.

"I wanted to tell him about Luke being in the hospital. Dad should know. He's our real father."

"I told him," Derek said. "I phoned him that afternoon."

Kim glanced at Derek in time to see his hands tighten on the steering wheel.

"Dad wasn't home when Lydia called anyway," Luke said, his voice low. "She left him a message and he never called back. Both of you told Dad that I was sick, and he didn't come to the hospital."

"He might have," Lydia said. "You were asleep lots of the time. Maybe he came at night after work."

"He doesn't work at night. He goes to bars."

"Stop telling lies about our father," Lydia snapped. "We hardly even know him, because Mom and Derek won't let him near us without a big fuss."

"There are rules, Lydia — and Derek had nothing to do with them. Your father earned his reputation with the court. I've told you the situation in as nice a way as possible, but since you keep bringing it up, I'll give it to you straight. The judge took one look at your father's rap sheet, and the custody hearing went in my favor. I'm not denying him access to you. I'm protecting you from him."

Why had Lydia become so emotional about her father all of a sudden? Kim wondered as the car neared the church building. Her ex-husband made little effort to contact his children, and whenever they returned from one of their rare visits with Joe, they were always upset and off-kilter for days. But suddenly Lydia seemed taken with the man who had fathered her, and she was determined to rub his connection to the twins in Derek's face.

"What makes Derek any better than our real father?" Lydia asked. "And now — because of Derek — we have to live with

233

Grandma Finley, too. Luke and I don't have anyone but each other, Mom, because you're too busy with everyone else. I remember when it was just the three of us, and we were happy."

"Yeah," Luke chimed in. "I like Derek, but he's too strict. He never lets us do anything."

"Derek is sitting right here," Kim said. "If you want to discuss something with him, he can hear you just fine. And for your information, Derek is a wonderful man. He's always fair. If he's strict with you kids, it's for your own good."

"What did we do to deserve Grandma Finley?" Luke asked. "We think she's a witch!"

At this, both twins burst into giggles. Kim found herself searching helplessly for a reason to defend her mother-in-law. Miranda truly had made things difficult in the Finley household. She not only criticized Kim, but she insisted on changing meal plans, moving furniture around, rearranging kitchen cupboards, and worst of all, burning incense before the little statues in her bedroom. Miranda had even told the children she believed paganism was a path to God — and if that didn't put her in the witchy realm, what did?

"Derek, why don't you answer that?" Kim said finally. "Tell the children why you asked Grandma Finley to come to Deepwater Cove."

Derek pulled the car to a stop in one of the parking spaces near the side of Lake Area Ministry Bible Chapel. "My mother is here to help us," he said. "You know that. But all you three do is complain about her. She's done a lot more for us than you realize, and I don't appreciate the griping. Neither does she — and believe me, she knows how you feel about her. As for your *real* father, Luke and Lydia, last week one of the other officers ticketed him for boating while intoxicated in Party Cove. So, if that's the guy you want to admire, fine. Don't expect me to haul either of your little fannies out of jail if you decide to take after him, though, because I'm a man who believes you make your own life. You control your destiny — not your mom or me, and certainly not your dad. I've made my choices, and I'll stand by them. Now, hop out of the car, all of you. I'll be back to pick you up at noon."

Kim froze as she stared at her husband's hardened features. In the backseat, neither twin moved a muscle. Derek rarely expressed negative feelings, but when he did, it had an impact.

For so long Kim and her children had basked in this man's gentle kindness and words of support. How many times a day did Derek tell Kim she was beautiful and whisper that he loved her? How often did he go out of his way to play with the kids, to let them know he was proud of them, to compliment their schoolwork or art projects? Quietly, he had surrounded the family with protection, adoration, and encouragement. And look how they repaid him.

Her eyes filling with tears, Kim reached out to lay a hand on her husband's arm. "I'm so sorry, honey," she said. "Please come to church with us. Please don't let —"

"To tell you the truth," he interrupted, moving his arm away from her touch, "I've decided I like my mother's brand of religion better than yours. If Christianity causes people to act like this, I don't want any part of it. Maybe I'll give ol' Buddha a try."

He reached across her and pushed open the passenger door. Frantic, she brushed at her cheeks, but the tears wouldn't stop. How had things come to this?

"You kids go on inside," Kim ordered, leaning over the seat and brushing them out the door. "Meet us in the parking lot after Bible study time."

"But what about you, Derek?" Luke asked. "I thought you were coming with us."

"Not today," Derek said. As the twins raced for the church, he studied his wife. "I wish you'd go with them, Kim. I need some time to think."

"Derek, we have to talk about this," she told him, shutting the car door. "The kids, your mother, religion. You mentioned wanting a baby, and we need to discuss that. There's the whole issue of Joe and his relationship to the twins. And now we find out that Lydia's best friend is dating a teenager! Please — let's drive over to Bitty's and get some coffee."

"I've had my coffee, and I'm not interested in talking. Everything's abundantly clear to me. I'm sure it is for you, too."

"Maybe our problems are obvious, but we need to figure out how to solve them."

"You know how I solve problems, Kim? I lock them up. That's just the way I handle things."

"Sure, if you're a patrolman dealing with a —" A pounding on the car's window cut off her words. Kim turned to find Luke staring in with a pained expression. She lowered the window. "What is it, Luke? Derek and I are talking."

"My insulin kit. It's in your purse, remember?" His big brown eyes filled suddenly with tears as he glanced at the man in the driver's seat. "I'm sorry, Derek. I didn't mean what I said about you. I hope I grow up to be like you and not my other dad. I don't want to go to jail or become an alcoholic. And I like Grandma Finley. Lydia does too. It's just that we don't think she likes us. She's always reminding us that she's not our grandmother by blood, only by marriage. And when we saw those weird religious things in her bedroom, we started thinking that maybe she was a witch even though we know she's really not. But if she is a witch, it's okay, because we're not scared of her. So please don't divorce us, okay? Lydia feels the same as me; I promise."

Derek blew out a breath and leaned his head on the seat back. "Just go on to church, Luke. It's all right."

"Are you going to divorce us?"

"No, I'm not going to divorce anyone. Get going, now. You'll be late."

Luke gave his mother a final pleading glance; then he slipped his kit into his pocket and ran toward the church. Kim opened her purse and pulled out a tissue.

This was a nightmare. For a few precious moments, she had cherished such hope. A fragile hope, but a real one. Now it had vanished like flower petals in a harsh winter wind. And she wasn't even sure why.

Derek put the car into gear and backed out of the lot. Kim blew her nose and tried to blot her cheeks, but the sight of her son's face had just about killed her.

Luke was right in being fearful about the future — look what she had put her children through already. Though they had been young at the time, Kim knew the twins recalled the scenes of drunken rage and cowering fear that had occurred between their parents. When they escaped that life, Kim and the twins had lived in a women's shelter for a time. Things had been so difficult as she struggled to clothe and feed her little ones. Then she had married Derek and forced yet another adjustment on the children. Until now, she had believed their life was finally better. But Derek's angry words had sent a frightening chill clear through to her bones.

She couldn't stop shivering as she dabbed at the tears streaming down her cheeks. Derek had told Luke he wouldn't divorce Kim, but what must he think of her now? He had gone from a peaceful, independent life, in which the only thing he had to think about was maintaining order on the water. Now she had brought all kinds of turmoil and chaos into his life. His words were always kind, but did he really mean them?

"Kim, please stop crying," Derek said evenly. He had driven back to Tranquility and was parking in front of the pumps outside Rods-N-Ends. "We're running a little low on gas. I'm going to fill the tank. Try to cheer up."

Cheer up? Impossible. Nodding mutely, she held a tissue under her nose as Derek got out of the car. Pete Roberts had hired part-time help for Sunday mornings and a couple of evenings a week, but Kim noticed that today Pete was inside the store. To her dismay, he ambled outside as Derek began pumping gas.

"Howdy, Officer," Pete greeted his customer. "Playing golf this morning?"

Kim could hear Derek's deep voice. "Just out for a drive."

"I'll wash the windows for you. Nice day, ain't it? Not too hot. People are heading for the lake like bees to honey. I'm surprised you're not on the water this morning."

"Working the late shift."

"That's when the party gets going." Pete's bearded face and blue eyes appeared in the side window. "Hey there, Kim. How's the kiddos?"

"Fine," she managed. She pulled her appointment book out of her purse and studied it, hoping he wouldn't notice her swollen eyes and damp cheeks.

"I figured you'd be at church by now."

"We dropped off the twins."

"Takin' a break from religion. Sounds good to me. I thought I'd sit by a spell too. Me and Patsy used to see each other at church and go out to lunch afterward, but she won't even look me in the eye since the Fourth of July incident."

Kim frowned. "But that incident turned out fine. Luke is feeling much better now."

"Aw, it's not Luke. Patsy blames me for setting her down in that wobbly lawn chair. I mean . . . well, it *was* kind of funny when she fell through, but Patsy didn't see the humor in it. That one little thing riled her worse than all the chain saws and Weedwhackers I had revved up next door to her salon."

"She'll get over it," Derek spoke up. "Just give her time."

"I hope you're right. I couldn't take another minute of sitting on that hard pew and looking at the back of Patsy's head. You know, if you're going to claim to be holy

241

and righteous and walk around with all that sanctification oozing out, well, it seems to me you ought to be able to forgive a fellow for accidentally dropping you into a loosey-goosey lawn chair."

"I couldn't agree more," Derek said with a dry chuckle as he paid for the gas. He slid back into the driver's seat and looked across at Kim. As he put the car in gear and pulled onto the highway, he spoke gently but firmly. "I'm going to the house. I have some paperwork that I've put off too long. Why don't you drive back to church and pick up the kids? We'll eat lunch, and then I'll go to work."

"But what about Lydia's horrible attitude? . . . And all this tension between us? . . . And your mother?"

As she spoke the final words, a fog lifted momentarily and Kim suddenly saw the crux of their problems. It was Miranda. She had upset the twins. She had destroyed the balance of love and mutual support between Kim and Derek. The longer Miranda had stayed, the worse things got, until now Kim had even begun to wonder if her marriage could survive. Only one solution became clear: Miranda had to go. And Kim had to convince Derek to make that happen.

"Derek, we need to talk about your

mother."

"Kim, it's like I told Pete. Let this stuff go. Give it time. It'll pass."

"But it won't. I know we've had a lot of different things come up this summer, but one problem is affecting all of it. Your mother needs to move out of our house. We have to get back to normal, and that means she has to go. I want you to tell her that it's time to leave."

Derek groaned.

"I mean it, Derek. There's no other solution."

"You're looking at this from one angle. Don't overreact. We can handle it."

"Can we? If you really believe that, then we had better start talking. We need to figure out a way to make things better."

"You like to talk. I don't. We're different, okay?"

"No, it's not okay," she said. "We can't be different. Not with this. We have to be united. You want to lock our problems away like prisoners, but what happens when the prisoners get released or break out? And they always do."

"They get out, cause a little trouble, so we round them up and put them back in jail."

She reached for another tissue. "If you won't talk, will you at least listen to me?"

"I heard you already. You and the kids."

"Did you hear me say I want your mother to leave? Did you listen to Luke when he came back for his kit? That's how they *really* feel, honey. They love you. It's not like Lydia said."

"Kim, I'm trained to listen to people. I carry a recorder when I'm on duty so I don't miss a word. It's my job to hear things exactly as spoken."

"But you can't listen just to the words! You have to hear what's beneath them. You have to listen to people's feelings and behaviors and attitudes."

He gave her a long look. "I'm not like you, Kim. I hear what people say, and I take them at their word."

"And then you lock them up behind bars of silence."

The mute hostility continued until they finally arrived back at the house. Miranda was outside in her nightgown and slippers, snipping blooms off the tea roses that Kim had worked so hard and with such patience to grow.

Spotting the car, Miranda lifted a hand and waved. "You both came back!" she said as Derek switched off the engine and opened the door. "How nice! I'm cutting a bouquet for our luncheon table. It's so drab

244

and dreary in the dining room — all those bare windows! I thought we needed a lovely centerpiece to draw everyone's focus and brighten things up. Oh, Derek, will you fetch one of those vases from the garage? Kim has put them up so high I can't reach them."

Feeling as though her last hope had been snipped off like a rose that had just begun to bloom, Kim stepped out of the car. She clutched her Bible and fought tears once again.

"Kim, you'll be happy to hear my news!" Miranda strolled over, a large cluster of red blossoms in her basket — and the rosebush behind her completely bare. "After hearing those awful comments Derek made about my incense, I decided I should make some changes. So I've set up my altar out on the deck. That way I'll have plenty of room to perform my yoga and tai chi movements, I can meditate to the sound of the birds in the trees, and no one will be bothered by the fragrance of my patchouli incense — though I have to say, I like it better than the potpourri you've put in those little baskets around the house. See? Things just have a wonderful way of working out, don't they?"

With that she swung away and hurried

over to Kim's patch of newly opened daylilies.

CHAPTER ELEVEN

Patsy was putting the final strokes of topcoat on Ashley Hanes's fingernails when she noticed Cody sweeping up under another stylist's station. The curly-haired young man focused on his work with all the concentration of a brain surgeon. Ever since he had started helping out at Just As I Am, she noted, the salon looked fresh, clean, and tidy.

"I hear Cody's turning out to be quite an artist," Ashley said.

"It sure took me by surprise," Patsy replied. "The first thing I realized was that he had a kind of flair for organizing the styling tools. He wound their cords just so and placed gel, spray, mousse, and shampoo in neat rows."

"Didn't he work on the curtains, too?"

"Yes, Brenda Hansen taught him how to use the washing machine, and the next thing I knew, he had washed every curtain in the salon and then hung them up again. He found a long piece of ribbon, snipped it up, and used it to pull them back."

"I thought he could barely tie his shoes," Ashley said. "And now he's making beautiful bows?"

"Not only that. See those flowers on the checkout desk? I never could get them to look right. But Cody went to work on them, and now they get so many compliments that I bought more flowers for him to put into garlands and posies."

"I didn't know Cody made those! I saw they were for sale, so I bought one and hung it over our bed. Brad hasn't noticed, but I think it looks really pretty." Ashley reflected for a moment. "What got him started on painting the walls?"

"I noticed he was always looking at the hairdo magazines. He told me he would like to paint those pretty ladies, if only he could. So I bought him a watercolor pad, some brushes, and some paper — and lo and behold if Cody didn't knock the socks off everyone with his portraits. So I just decided to give him the whole wall. He works on it every day and night whenever he has a spare moment."

Both women studied the large mural. Then Ashley said, "There's something kind of weird about it. Do you know who those women remind me of?"

"Jennifer Hansen?" Patsy asked.

"Yeah. What's the deal with that? Does Cody have a crush on her or something?"

"Oh, I think he sees her when he's over at the Hansen house working with Brenda on his social skills and his reading."

"I hope he's not getting too attached to Jennifer. I heard she's going to be a missionary."

Patsy nodded. Steve and Brenda's older daughter had returned to Deepwater Cove after a mission trip to Africa. Jennifer had her heart set on living in a jungle somewhere and teaching people about God. She was beautiful, smart as a whip, and sweeter than molasses. But she hadn't even noticed the moon-eyed young man who dawdled nearby every time she came in for a trim. One of these days that girl was going to recognize herself on the wall of Just As I Am, and Patsy feared that her reaction might hurt poor Cody.

"I've made every station span," Cody announced just then, broom in hand as he walked toward Patsy. "I'll mop tonight. Would it be okay if I painted for a while?"

"It's almost time for the TLC meeting," she told him. "Don't you want to join us?"

"No thanks. But thank you anyway."

Patsy smiled. "Ashley, I'm going to go check the appointment book. You keep your nails under the dryer for a few minutes; then you're done."

Cody accompanied her across the room. "You did a great job today, as always, Cody. This place looks so good I hardly recognize it."

"Yes, you do. This is Just As I Am. It's your beauty salon."

"It sure is." She reached out and ruffled his curls. "You might be due for a trim one of these days, sugar pie. We don't want your hair getting all matted up again."

Cody gazed down at the floor for a moment as if searching for words. Then he lifted his head. "I want to tell you something, Patsy Pringle. Here it is. I want to say thank you for shaving off my hair a long time ago when I first came to Deepwater Cove. And thank you for giving me a job. And for paying me real money. And for buying me watercolors and paper. And for letting me paint your walls. And for —"

"Good gravy, that's about enough!" She laughed and gave him a warm hug. "Just seeing your smile is all the thanks I need."

"But here's the last thing I want to say. Even though you never gave me chocolate cake, I think you're a real Christian. My daddy taught me lots of Bible verses, and when I say them in my mind, I think of you because you're like the good people in the Bible. And that tells me you're a Christian."

Patsy swallowed. "Well, that's so nice."

As she had at least a hundred times a day, Patsy gave a guilty glance across the salon at the wall dividing her shop from Pete's Rods-N-Ends. She knew she ought to go over there and make peace with the man. Not only had Lydia Finley challenged her, but every Scripture she read and each whispered word in her heart told her to forgive him.

"Pete says you are an apple." Cody nodded as he spoke. "That's what he told me yesterday. He said you're mad at him, because you fell through the chair and everyone laughed, including me. We were laughing because your bare feet were sticking up in the air. It was very funny. I still laugh about it when I remember how you looked, Patsy. But Pete said you're upset, because you believe people laughed because they think you're fat. But you are *not* fat. You're an apple. That's what. An apple."

Patsy stared at the earnest blue eyes. All she could picture was a big, round, red apple, and if that's what Pete thought of her, well, she ought to just wring his neck. But Cody was standing there looking at her, watching to see what she would do.

She set her hands on her hips. "Did you come over here and talk to me about being a Christian because you know I'm upset with Pete?"

"*Are* you mad at him?"

Was Cody really as innocent as he sounded? Or was this all an elaborate ploy to prod her into doing what she'd been putting off for days?

"I wish you and Pete would be friends again."

"All right then. Enough is enough!" Patsy shook her head. "Are you sure Pete Roberts called me an *apple?*"

"Yes, and of all the fruits, that's my favorite one. Except for oranges. And watermelons. And also peaches."

Sighing, Patsy walked over to the tea area, where the women were already gathering for the meeting. She took down one of the two antique teacup sets that Pete had given her to replace those he'd broken when he first moved in next door. After filling the cup with tea, milk, and sugar, she selected two chocolate-chip cookies and put them on the saucer. Cody had followed her, nearly stepping on her heels the whole way.

Patsy swung around and poked him in the chest with a long, pink, acrylic fingernail. "You stay here." She frowned to emphasize her point. "I will do this myself."

"And it's about time you did."

Rolling her eyes, Patsy carried the teacup across the salon and out the front door. Leave it to Cody to push her into something she didn't want to do. It might be the Christian thing to do, but forgiving a person who had wounded you deeply was just plain hard.

Worse, Pete hadn't asked for forgiveness. That made things doubly difficult. If a person got down on bended knees and apologized and said how wrong he was and how bad he felt, then pardoning him would be a lot easier. But that shaggy ol' bear of a man wasn't the type to say he was sorry. No, he just told Cody and everyone how spiteful Patsy was being toward him, and then he stopped going to church just to rub it in even more. Now he was going around comparing her figure to an apple, of all things.

Well, she was woman enough to handle a man like Pete Roberts. No doubt about that.

Pushing open the door to Rods-N-Ends, Patsy noted that the store was empty. She groaned. If she could have left the teacup and cookies on the counter and made a speedy getaway, that would have been easier. Now she would have no choice but to speak to the man. Especially since he was coming straight toward her.

"Hello, Pete," she said, trying not to sound snippy. "I brought you a peace offering."

He looked her up and down and then grinned sheepishly. "This is the teacup I left for you outside your salon. I guess you read my note."

"As a matter of fact, I did not. I was too upset. But now that I've had time to calm down and consider the situation, I've made up my mind to do what the Bible teaches. I am here to speak plainly about the problem between us and get it over with. Now, as I recall the situation last Fourth of July, I was helping Opal Jones arrange her relish tray when you marched over, grabbed my arm, dragged me across the grass to where the men were grilling pork steaks, and pushed me down into a lawn chair that immediately broke. I was mortified and humiliated and even a little bit hurt, but thank goodness for Derek Finley, who helped me out like a gentleman should. I don't know why you treated me like you did, Pete Roberts, but I have decided to forgive you. So I do. I forgive you. There."

Pete stared at her for a moment. "Is that in the Bible too? The forgiving part?"

"It certainly is. It's all over the place."

"Huh." He scratched his chin for a minute, his fingers disappearing into that awful beard.

Patsy finally figured she'd done her part, and she'd had about enough of his dawdling. "Well, I'm heading back to the salon for the TLC meeting. See you later."

"Hold on, now, woman. I'm from Halfway, Missouri, and I've only got this thing halfway figured out. You need to give a fellow time."

She stood at the counter, tapping her nails on the glass and studying the window display, where Pete had neatly arranged a collection of wading boots, fishing nets, rods, reels, and water skis. He wasn't dumb, so why was this confusing? If he wanted to say something, he should just get to it and let her go to the meeting.

So far, Pete hadn't taken a sip of tea, and the chocolate chips in the cookies were melting from the heated cup. Maybe she would just pick one up and eat it while he continued the second half of his thought process.

As she lifted the cookie, Pete reached for

the cup. Their hands brushed for just a second, and Patsy jerked hers away as though she'd been shocked. And in fact, she almost felt she had been. Pete Roberts was ornery, bullheaded, somewhat hard on the eyes, and maybe even a little bit mean. So why did she feel that shiver every time she got near him? The very idea that he affected her in such a way bothered Patsy half to death.

"Good tea," Pete said, setting the cup back in the saucer after taking a sip. "Earl Grey. My favorite, of an afternoon. I prefer Irish breakfast in the morning."

Patsy felt a smile tickle the corners of her lips. "I guess a man can learn some things after all."

"Yep, and here's what I have learned today. First of all, circumstances are not always what they seem. You see, on the Fourth of July, I was trying to prevent major fireworks between the two Finley women — Kim and Miranda. I figured you, being the prettiest and kindest-hearted of all the ladies in Deepwater Cove, would be the best person to intervene. Seeing as the fuses on those two women are mighty short, I was in a hurry to get you over to where they were facing off with their bowls of dip. So I high-tailed it across to where you were arranging

Opal's relish dish, fetched you, dragged you back to the grills, where it was high noon between the Finley women, and set you down in the lawn chair I had recently vacated, which had already demonstrated its cracked and frayed webbing beneath my own personal backside. At which time, that chair up and tried to swallow you — an event that took away any need for defusing the conflict between the Finleys."

Blinking in astonishment, Patsy hadn't even managed to take a bite of the cookie as she listened to Pete. "You mean . . . you didn't push me into that chair to poke fun at me?"

"Now why would I do that?"

"Why would you start up a chain saw next to my tearoom?"

"Patsy, I might tease and pester you till kingdom come, but I will never, ever do anything to embarrass you. I would swear on my honor as a gentleman, but I don't think I qualify."

"Well —" she considered for a moment — "that's not what I thought happened."

"So here's another thing I learned today. Christians sure are different from what I first believed about them when I moved to town and started going to church."

Feeling about as low as she'd ever been,

Patsy put the uneaten cookie back on the saucer. "I don't know what you thought, but now it's my turn to apologize. I'm sorry for the way I've treated you lately, Pete. I shouldn't have quit talking to you, and I wish you would come back to church so we could go out to Aunt Mamie's Good Food for lunch on Sundays."

"Are you sure it's not so you can be a fisher of men and lure me into getting born again?"

"I won't deny that I would be very happy for you to be born again, Pete. But I really have missed talking to you and sitting with you in church. I feel awful that I ruined your good opinion of Christians."

"Well, you did. I used to think Christians were perfect — like you. You always look all gussied up, and you're so nice to everyone, and even when you used to take offense at my chain saws, you were always a lady about it."

"But I'm not perfect. I never was."

"I see that. And now I understand that Christians are just like everyone else."

Patsy started to worry that she might cry. She had marched into Rods-N-Ends as high and mighty as a queen determined to absolve a lowly peasant for his dishonorable deed. As it turned out, she was the one in

258

the wrong, and she felt just awful. Worse than awful.

"Christians are flawed like everyone else," Pete said. "Except for one difference. And here's the third thing I learned today. Christians are different because they try harder than most folks. They read their Bible and go to church and pray and do their dead-level best to be as perfect as God wants them to be. And then when they mess up, they try to make right whatever they did wrong."

"We do try, but we fail a lot. If you want a good example, you'd better look at Jesus and not at Christians. I love Him, but there's a few of us I can barely tolerate."

Pete chuckled. "I reckon you're right on that one."

"In this situation, you behaved better than I did, Pete. You gave me a china cup and saucer."

"And you filled it with tea and brought it over here."

Patsy smiled. "You'd better drink it before it gets cold."

"You gonna sit with me in church next Sunday?"

"Only if you promise to take me to Aunt Mamie's for chicken-fried steak afterward."

"All right. You've got yourself a deal," he

said, holding out his hand.

Patsy reached out and gave it a firm shake. But before she could move away, he turned her hand over and kissed it. Beard, mustache, and warm lips brushed against her soft skin. The zing went right up Patsy's arm and shot straight down to the tips of her toes. She gasped as Pete lifted his head and grinned.

"See you later, Patsy Pringle, the sweetest gal in eleventy-seven counties."

Unable to speak a word, Patsy turned and fled straight back to the salon. Barely breathing, she threw open the door, stepped inside, and sank into a chair in the waiting area. This was a very bad situation for a woman who knew her mind and always spoke it. For once in her life, Patsy felt completely bamboozled.

"Did you talk to Pete?" Cody asked. He had a smudge of black paint on his cheek and a brush in his hand as he sat down beside her. "I hope you apologized for getting mad about the chair even though Pete thinks you're as beautiful as an apple."

"I forgave Pete, and he forgave me," she said. "So it's all okay now, Cody."

"That's good. Pete would never do anything to hurt you, because he loves you, Patsy. Everyone loves you. I think you're the best person in the whole world . . . along with Brenda and Steve. And also Esther and Charlie. And Kim and Derek. And maybe some others."

Patsy glanced across to where the young man had been working on the latest version of Jennifer Hansen. "What about that pretty girl you've been painting on the wall?" she asked. "That young lady must be very special to you."

Cody studied his work. "That is a picture, Patsy," he said. "Pictures can't be special. They're made out of paint, and that's all there is to it."

Slightly more relaxed and able to breathe again, Patsy decided it was time to make her way to the TLC meeting. Wanting to make double sure her appointment book was still clear, she stood and crossed to the front desk.

"I realize what's on the wall is only a picture," she told Cody as he shuffled along behind her. "But whose picture did you paint? I think she must be someone awfully important to you, because you've painted her at least four times. In fact, I'm pretty sure I recognize her. That young lady comes in here to get her hair trimmed."

Cody leaned across the desk. "Don't tell," he whispered.

"I won't," Patsy whispered back. "But you're such a good painter that one day someone besides me is going to figure out who it is."

"Okay," Cody said. "That's when I'll tell her that I love her, and I want to get married with her."

Patsy drew closer and whispered in his ear. "She's going to be a missionary in Africa. Even if she likes you a lot, I don't think she'll want to live in Deepwater Cove."

"I don't have to worry about that," Cody said. "God will figure it out."

Patsy sighed as she shut the appointment book. Why couldn't her own faith be as simple as Cody's? Things were always so complicated, and she got herself into such tangles. Look at how much time and energy she had wasted being furious with Pete Roberts. And his opinion of Christianity had suffered as a result.

Disappointed in herself, Patsy tidied the pamphlets she kept by the cash register. All the religious tracts and Christian music and Scriptures painted on the salon's walls didn't amount to a hill of beans if a person was as hard-hearted and unkind as Patsy had been.

As she turned toward the tea area, she spotted the envelope Pete had enclosed with the teacup set he'd given her during their spat. At the time, she'd been too angry to read it. She had tossed the card onto an open shelf under the desk along with some stray curlers and a can of hair spray. But now Patsy knew she had no choice but to find out what Pete had written to her. This would certainly put the icing on the cake of her own humiliation and shame.

Patsy opened the envelope and slid out a greeting card she had seen in a turning wire rack in Pete's store. It was a photograph of a fisherman holding up a bass as long as he was — one of those silly "fixed" pictures made to look real but clearly fake. She opened the card and read the inscription: "Just wishin' we was fishin'! I MISS YOU."

Down at the bottom, Pete had scrawled a message. "Dear Patsy, I'm sorry you think I humiliated you on purpose at the July 4th BBQ. I didn't mean for that chair to break, and I hope you didn't think folks was laughing at you. Surely you know that everyone admires you, including me most of all. In fact, I think you are sweet and kind, and let me just go ahead and say that I very much admire your —"

Here Patsy had to turn the card over to continue reading.

"— ample figure. I looked it up in the

dictionary, and *ample* means 'generous, full, and abundant.' To tell you the truth, in every way I think you are ample. Love, Pete Roberts."

Patsy lifted her head and gazed into Cody Goss's blue eyes. *"Ample,"* she said.

He nodded. "I told you before. That's what Pete called you."

"You said *apple.*"

"Yes, I did. And now I've decided to change my mind about tea. Let's go have some."

Solemnly taking her hand, Cody started across the room. Patsy began to chuckle. When she caught sight of herself in a mirror at a nearby station, she paused a moment, studied her generous bosom, slightly smaller waist, and abundant hips. She decided Pete was exactly right. She was ample. Or apple. Whichever.

By the time she and Cody had filled their teacups, Patsy was giggling as she settled into the empty chair between Kim Finley and her mother-in-law.

"Well, you certainly are in a good mood," Miranda Finley observed. "Maybe it's because you missed Esther's recitation of 'old business,' which included the lawn chair incident at the Fourth of July barbecue."

Kim reached out and laid her hand on Patsy's. "Esther confessed that Charlie had hauled that chair and a couple of others out of their attic. She said those lawn chairs must have been at least twenty years old."

Patsy smiled. "Well, it gave everyone a laugh, and we all need that now and then. Pete and I talked it over. There are no hard feelings between us."

"I doubt that I could ever forgive a man who had made a fool of me," Miranda said. "You were lucky Luke's diabetic crisis came right on the heels of your calamity."

Patsy drew down a breath for fortification. She could see what Kim was up against. A tongue like Miranda's sure could spit barbs. No wonder Pete had felt compelled to come between the two women when he saw a fight about to break out.

"I wouldn't call my son's crisis *lucky*," Kim was saying, her voice stilted. "Luke's condition was very serious. That wasn't *lucky*. I don't see how you can even think such a thing, Miranda."

"Oh, I don't believe in luck," Patsy spoke up, leaning between them to take a sip of tea. "I think the good Lord permits everything that happens to us — and even the bad things can turn out all right in the end if we use them for His glory. Luke made it

265

through his problem, and we all learned a lesson about how to be more watchful. And as for Pete Roberts and me, well, I would call our friendship . . . ample."

CHAPTER TWELVE

"Here's the tomato sauce," Luke said, pushing the jar down the counter toward his grandmother. "Mr. Moore grows tarragon in his garden, and he gives us some every summer. We always put extra in our pizza sauce."

"And we don't buy the sauce with tomato chunks." Lydia was unwrapping a package of pepperoni. "I hate tomato chunks."

"We *know,*" Luke retorted.

"You won't have to worry about that tonight," Miranda told the twins. "My pizza doesn't have tomato sauce."

Kim turned from the refrigerator in surprise. She had been searching for the mozzarella cheese, but now she saw that Miranda had produced a shopping bag and was setting out ingredients she must have purchased earlier in the day.

Every Friday night, Kim and the twins baked homemade pizza. Since she'd been staying with them, Miranda had participated in the process of building the pizzas, and then she ate with the family. But this evening, Grandma Finley had asked to treat Kim and the twins to something special. She was going to teach them how to make Derek's favorite meal — her unique *gourmet* pizza.

Miranda had spent most of the afternoon outside on the deck, meditating near the collection of items that she believed fostered spiritual enrichment — crystals, a small brass Buddha, a length of sandalwood beads, and a Native American dream catcher. When her stick of incense had burned down to ash, she came inside. Still smelling vaguely of patchouli, she wore an ankle-length turquoise cotton tunic and several silver bangles, which clanged as she began measuring ingredients into a saucepan on the stove.

"To make a good white sauce," she was telling the twins, "you must have whole milk. And here we have cornstarch, salt, pepper, three cloves of garlic —"

"Wait a second," Lydia cut in. "Did you say *white* sauce? Where do you put that?"

"Right onto the pizza crust." Miranda waved her hand over the other ingredients, as if flourishing a magic wand. "Garlic salt, onion powder, oregano, and basil."

"Where's the tarragon?" Luke asked. Staring at the collection of containers on the counter, he was frowning. "I don't get it. How can you have pizza without tomato sauce and tarragon?"

"This is not just any old pizza. This is my specialty — spinach-Parmesan pizza."

"Spinach!" Lydia cried. "Huh-uh. No way. I'm not eating pizza with spinach. I hate that stuff."

"I don't like it either," Luke said, looking at his mother with imploring eyes. "Can't we have regular pizza, Mom? Grandma Finley can make her kind, but I want our usual."

"You won't even recognize the spinach," Miranda informed him before Kim could answer. "It melds right in with the cheese." She paused in stirring her sauce to unwrap a chunk of white cheese and hold it out before the twins. "Now take a whiff of this, kids. This is heaven itself."

Luke sniffed, made a gagging noise, and grabbed his nose.

Lydia took three steps backward, then began flapping her hands in distress. "It smells like vomit!" she wailed. "I'm gonna puke! What is it?"

"This is true Parmesan cheese." Miranda

glared at the twins, who were now entertaining each other by pretending to throw up. Turning her focus on Kim, she stared in silence a moment before speaking. "Do your children always have to be so histrionic?"

"Well, they —"

"The production of real Parmesan cheese comes from a restricted area in Italy," Miranda said loudly enough to cover the twins' theatrics. "It's really quite distinctive. The structure of the cheese is remarkable too. See? A true Parmesan will break into slivers. And I happen to love its delicate and fragrant aroma."

"Fragrant aroma?" Lydia was holding her nose and fanning her face. "Puke-o-roma is what you mean!"

"Puke aroma!" Luke said, doubling over in laughter. "Get it, Lyd? Puke aroma!"

Kim stood by helplessly as Lydia joined in her brother's amusement. The cheese really did smell awful, and she could hardly blame the kids for their dramatics. In fact, she was thinking of opening a window to let in some fresh air.

Clearly having decided to ignore the twins, Miranda had resumed her preparations. Between stirring the sauce, she began to coat the three circles of pizza dough with olive oil.

"Wait," Luke said suddenly. "Grandma, you're not making *all three* pizzas with that white sauce, are you?"

"I most certainly am. And if you'd like, you may begin grating this mozzarella cheese. Here's the grater. I'll need six cups. Lydia, take this knife and cut that tomato into paper-thin slices. Kim, if you would wash the spinach —"

"Mom!" Luke cried, brandishing the grater. "Not all three! We want pizza the way we have it every Friday night."

"Luke, you agreed to this," Kim reminded him. "We're going to give Grandma Finley's pizza a try."

"I don't want it! It stinks, Mom. I don't want spinach pizza that smells like vomit!"

"Luke, please."

Kim headed toward her son, but Lydia stepped between them. "Leave him alone, Mom. Lukey doesn't want to eat it. What if it makes him sick? What if his blood sugar goofs up?"

"Lydia, you know that's not going to happen."

"It might! We've never had white sauce before. It could kill him!"

"Ricotta!" Miranda sang out. "If anyone's listening to Grandma Finley, I'm ready for the ricotta."

Kim turned to find that the woman had already ladled thick, cheesy sauce onto all three pizzas. "Miranda, could you hold off for a moment? Spinach really isn't a favorite with the twins, and —"

"I'm not eating that junk!" Luke shouted. "I won't eat it, and my glucose won't be right, and I'll get sick."

"Mom, do something!" Lydia's eyes filled with tears. "Grandma Finley, stop putting on cottage cheese! We hate cottage cheese."

"This is *ricotta,* for your information. Wait until you see how the spinach and basil will blend into the white sauce. In fact, with the mozzarella and ricotta, you won't even notice them."

"But they're green!" Luke hollered. "The only green we have on pizza is tarragon. Mom, make her stop. She's ruining our supper."

"What can Lukey eat tonight, Mom?" Lydia demanded to know, tears streaming. She stamped her foot. "He has to eat the right food, or he'll get sick!"

Kim reached for her daughter. "Now, Lydia —"

"No, Mom! You have to help Luke. He's your son. You can't let Grandma Finley do this!" Sobbing, she shook her head at her mother and then turned and ran from the

272

kitchen. "I hate you! I hate everything!"

"*Now* look what happened!" Luke snarled. "Grandma Finley, don't you even care about Lydia?"

Miranda set her hand on her hip. "I'll have you know I am famous for this pizza. It's delicious. It's made of the finest ingredients. And if you and your sister would stop carrying on like a pair of maniacs, you would find out how good something new can be."

"I don't want something new! I want our same old pizza with tomato sauce and tarragon! I want everything to be normal!" With that, Luke hurled the cheese grater across the room. It slammed into a cabinet and fell to the floor, aluminum clattering on tile.

"Luke!" Kim cried as her son stormed out of the kitchen. "Luke, come back here this instant!"

"Hopeless," Miranda announced as she began washing the spinach. "Your ineffectiveness as a mother astonishes me, Kim. Those two are completely out of control."

Her temper flaring, Kim pointed a finger at her mother-in-law. "*You* are the problem here, not me. You could see right away that the Parmesan cheese was going to be an issue, but you just kept on grating. No matter what anyone says, you insist on having your way."

"We had an agreement, Kim. If you give in to children, you lose all control." She lifted her chin as she stared at her daughter-in-law. "Do you have any idea how easily a child can slip out of your hands? Do you know what it means to lose parental authority? Of course not. You've never had any power over those two. A good mother watches her young the way a hawk guards her nest. She never lets up for a moment. One wrong move and they're out of her control forever."

"For heaven's sake, Miranda, we're talking about pizza here. It's not as though my entire influence over the children rides on this one issue. I'm a good mother, and I happen to believe that it's okay to bend a little. Do you have to make all three pizzas your way? Can't you give the twins one or two crusts for themselves?"

"Give an inch, and you lose them." Miranda swung around and began to put spinach and cheese on the pizzas. "Believe me, Kim, without proper parental direction and control, a child can go off in the wrong direction. Maybe it's pizza today, but you never know what tomorrow will bring."

Kim threw up her hands in disbelief. "Oh,

this is ridiculous." She didn't know whether to start making fresh pizzas or go comfort her children. Deciding a decent supper would soothe the twins, she elected to let them console each other for now. "I'm going to make more dough," she told Miranda, "so if you'll please move your Parmesan, I'd appreciate it."

In silence, the women moved around the kitchen. As Kim began spreading tomato sauce on her newly made crusts, Miranda slid her pizzas into the oven one by one, then brushed by without a word on her way out of the kitchen.

Kim pressed the fan button on the oven hood. Maybe she could diffuse some of the Parmesan aroma and at the same time drown out the memory of her mother-in-law's insidious voice. As Kim worked, she gazed through the kitchen window at the lake. Gleaming gold and indigo, the water was as motionless as a sheet of glass. But when a fish leaped nearby, she instantly envisioned the magnificent and satisfying splash that would echo across Deepwater Cove if someone just happened to toss Miranda off the deck.

Shaking her head at the thought, Kim knew it wasn't funny. Still, imagining the expression on Miranda's face gave her such satisfaction that she was still savoring it when she took Miranda's pizzas out of the oven and put her own in to bake.

When Charlie Moore pulled his golf cart to a stop in the Finley driveway that Friday evening, Derek was chopping weeds along his ditch. Though Derek liked his retired neighbor well enough, he had no desire to make small talk.

All day he had been out on the water patrolling Party Cove and cruising the hundreds of inlets that rimmed Lake of the Ozarks. That didn't take into account the several hours spent talking to investigators about the drowning of the as-yet-unclaimed and unnamed female. Her fingerprints hadn't turned up any clues, nor had her dental information. Detectives were now discussing the possibility of hiring a forensic artist to create a facial reconstruction of the woman in order to help identify her. Derek found it hard to believe that there were no records of a missing person who fit the victim's description. He had been working with other law enforcement agencies from the start, but they had made little progress.

As if all that weren't exhausting and frustrating enough, Derek had come home that afternoon to the bleak battleground of yet another family feud — a quarrel over pizza that had left Lydia in tears, Luke furious, Kim in steely silence, and his mother out on the deck lighting incense. The combatants had told him four versions of the same event, none of which registered in his tired brain, and that's when he'd decided it might be a good time to attack the weeds in the yard.

"Things are looking mighty fine around the Finley place," Charlie drawled. He patted his dog's head as he spoke. The two went everywhere together. "Glad we had that rain the other day. Greened up all the yards."

"Brought in a little cool weather, too. I sure didn't mind that." Derek studied the cutting end of his Weedwhacker. "Well, I guess this job's done for now. I'll need more line before next time."

"Isn't that the way things are? It's always something. The trimmer runs out of line. The lawn mower needs oil. The golf cart's battery up and dies. The gutters get clogged with leaves. Spiders start to take over the eaves. A man's work is never done."

Derek nodded. "Yep, and I'd better head back inside to check my honey-do list. It's a mile long."

"How about taking a spin with Boofer and

me first, Officer Finley? Couple of things I'd like to talk over. Would you mind?"

Yes, he would, Derek thought. Listening to Charlie Moore — who had all the time in the world to do whatever he wanted and then drone on and on about it — was not Derek's idea of fun. And no matter what Charlie wanted to discuss, Derek knew he wouldn't be interested. The Moores were good people — helpful, kind, and considerate. But they put their noses in other folks' business way too often for Derek's comfort, and he wanted no part of that.

"I'll need to step inside and let Kim know," he told Charlie, "and I have a feeling she's got my evening pretty well planned out."

"Aw, we won't take long. Just a turn or two around the neighborhood. Kim won't even know you're gone."

Derek frowned. He wasn't going to get out of this. He could already see Charlie edging his dog onto the floor, dusting off the seat, and moving his flashlight to a compartment in the back. Well, maybe a trip in the golf cart would be better than heading back into the war zone his house had become.

"Settle yourself right there," Charlie said as Derek stepped into the cart. "I'll tell you what — there's nothing like a quiet ride around the lake of an evening. Boofer would tell you the same thing; wouldn't you, boy? This dog and I take a sunset ride nearly every day. It's gotten to be kind of habitual, if you know what I mean. A mail carrier establishes a routine, and it becomes a way of life. Not even retirement can put an end to that."

Derek leaned back as the cart began its excruciatingly slow journey along the narrow road that served the Deepwater Cove neighborhood. After a day in his Donzi — chasing reckless boaters and zipping from one mile marker to the next — the ride felt interminable. But Charlie wasn't in the mood to push the cart for more speed, so Derek did his best to force his muscles to relax.

"Moon's already up," Charlie intoned, pointing at the silver wedge that hung over the lake. "No sir, you just can't beat a sunset on the water. Nothing prettier, to my way of thinking. Wouldn't you agree?"

"Yep," Derek said, stifling a groan. Depending on his shift, he watched the sun settle over the lake nearly every day. Long ago the array of pink, gold, and blue had ceased to fascinate him. Late afternoon to early evening was the time that parties could turn ugly.

"The Hansen house sure looks nice," Charlie commented as the golf cart cruised by. "That Brenda sure has a way with decorations. She put on the best Independence Day display of anyone in the neighborhood. Flags, bunting, wreaths made out of shiny stars. I never saw the like. Esther pointed out that Brenda had even planted her flower beds in shades of red, white, and blue. Sure enough, she was right. Esther usually is, of course."

He elbowed his companion, who mustered a chuckle. "Sounds like a woman," Derek said. "Kim sure knows her own mind."

"Your mother does too. That must be interesting — living with two women. How're you holding up?"

This time Derek couldn't suppress his sigh. "Things are a little tense, to tell you the truth. But we're managing."

"Miranda takes good care of the twins. I see the three of them down by the lake swimming or loaded into her car heading to town. Miranda tells me they go to the library or the outlet mall, and she enjoys stopping by Bitty's place at lunchtime for some of those California-style wraps. I guess the twins have a fondness for the fajitas, but Miranda prefers the vegetarian ones, since she's watching her weight."

This was all news to Derek, and he found himself warming to the idea that his mother had embraced her new role so well. If "Grandma Finley" was doing a good job with the kids, why did she and Kim have so many problems? Both women were well liked, friendly, kind, and generous. Why couldn't they figure out how to get along?

"Those exercises she does on the deck have sure stirred up talk in the neighborhood," Charlie told Derek. "Esther thinks Miranda is doing stretching drills to get out the kinks. But Kim tells me she's performing some sort of Oriental ritual."

"I don't pay much attention," Derek said. "My mother was always a free thinker, willing to try just about anything. That goes back to her youth — the way she was brought up. Her parents were liberalminded too. Not much concerned about rules. They never understood why I went into law enforcement."

"Beatniks, huh?" Charlie said. "Miranda's a little younger than Esther and I. She must have fallen under that sixties influence — hippies, war protests, flower children. I was a mail carrier with a young family at the time, so I missed out on all that. Not to say I regret it, of course."

He was silent a moment as the cart rounded the western end of the subdivision and started back the other way. When he spoke again, it was with a tone of amusement. "I guess that would explain the incense."

"Is it bothering people?" Derek asked.

"It's no trouble. Folks were just wondering. It's not every day you see a lovely woman swaying around, listening to flute music, and burning incense. Or maybe it's the fact that most days Miranda exercises in her bathing suit."

"Her bathing suit?"

"Well, she starts out in a robe." Charlie glanced over at Derek and winked. "Mighty attractive lady, in my opinion. But some of the widows were getting a little nervous about the whole thing, especially after Lydia told Esther that her grandmother worships idols."

"Idols?" This time Derek sat bolt upright. "My mother does not worship idols."

"No need to worry. Esther has calmed the widows down, and now that you and I have cleared the air, well, it's not going to be anything to sweat about." Charlie steered the golf cart past an oncoming truck. "The real problem may be just around the bend here. I thought I ought to mention it to you

— seeing how you're an officer of the law and you might know about such situations. Of course, it doesn't pertain to water, but all the same . . ."

Derek was still picturing his mother worshipping idols in a bathing suit when Charlie braked the cart a short distance from the smallest house in Deepwater Cove. Next door to a home that was up for sale, it sat at the far end of the cove, some distance from the docks, the commons, and most of the activity. It had probably been constructed as a fisherman's retreat before the area was platted and built into a nice neighborhood. The covered deck was no longer quite level, and the shutters needed paint.

"This house belongs to Brad and Ashley Hanes." Charlie spoke in a low voice through the side of his mouth, as if confiding a deep, dark secret. "I know for a fact that they haven't been paying their subdivision dues. And I hear they're behind on their loan payments. That's their business, of course. But what has come to be of some concern is the activity going on over there to the side of the house."

In the fading light, Derek could barely make out what appeared to be a poured foundation and a couple of framed walls.

"Are they building something?" he asked.

"Young Brad works construction, you know," Charlie said. "He told some folks that he's putting up a garage for his new truck. The vehicle isn't here right now. You know, Brad spends his evenings over at that watering hole, Larry's Lake Lounge, waiting for Ashley to get home from her job at the country club. But again, that's their business. Trouble is, Ashley told Esther that they're building this addition to hold a nursery for the baby. She's not expecting yet, but she sure is hoping. That part is a secret, of course. Nobody knows but Esther."

Derek nodded. If the Hanes kids wanted to start a family, what did he care? For that matter, what was Charlie all fired up about?

"You'll notice they don't have a building permit posted anywhere on the premises," the older man continued in hushed tones. "Nobody wants to rain on their parade, but you can't add or tear down anything in Deepwater Cove without a permit. It's in the bylaws."

"Well, you're chairman of the neighborhood bylaws committee, Charlie. You'd better tell Brad before he gets too far along with the garage or baby nursery — or whatever it's supposed to be."

"Problem is, we don't know if we can really enforce our bylaws. They don't carry much weight with the county, and no one knows what the rules are way out here. Do you have any idea?"

"There are zoning laws; I'm sure of that."

"But do they apply this far out of the Camdenton city limits?"

Vaguely irritated, Derek raked a hand back through his hair. "The Water Patrol enforces state statutes, Charlie. We don't have authority where municipal or county laws are concerned. But I'm sure if anyone can find out the rules for construction in Deepwater Cove, it's you. You've got the time and the know-how."

The golf cart moved forward again. "I was hoping you'd have the answer for us. But Esther kept telling me that your jurisdiction was the lake and you might not know. A man ought to listen to his wife."

They rode along in silence with Derek slapping at the occasional mosquito. Listening to his wife was apparently his biggest failing, he thought irritably. When he got home, he would have to explain to Kim where he'd been, and she was upset already. Though he had been trying harder to communicate with her about his work and the other issues she had spelled out, he found it difficult. Derek wasn't used to talking about anything beyond whatever was happening at the time. If he was ticketing someone for a violation, he explained lake laws. If he was meeting with the Major Case Squad, he discussed homicides. If he was eating dinner, he complimented the meal. What was so wrong with that?

"Speaking of the lake," said Charlie, who didn't seem to have any problem talking about anything at any time, "Esther came up with the craziest notion this morning. Not too long after breakfast, I was trying to tell her what I was planning to do about servicing the golf cart, and all the while she was putting together one of those Jell-O salads with the marshmallows and fruit. You know the kind I mean?"

Derek nodded. He'd eaten Esther's gelled salad more times than he could count.

"Well, she wasn't paying a bit of attention to me. When I grumbled about it, she turned around and said, 'Charlie, a woman is like a fish. If you want to capture her, you've got to find the right bait, dangle it in front of her, and then reel in nice and slow.' Can you believe that? Esther — talking about fishing! The woman hasn't tossed out a line in twenty years. But this afternoon while I was working on the golf cart, I thought about it, and sure enough, Esther was right."

"You say that a lot," Derek commented.

"Because she usually is." Charlie chuckled. "I've lived nearly a lifetime with the woman, and she rarely lets me win an argument. So I've learned to pay attention when she tells me something. That fishing idea of hers, for example. Not too long after she told me about it, I had a hankering to go to Aunt Mamie's Good Food for supper. On Friday nights, Mamie's features an all-you-care-to-eat shrimp special. Sautéed, breaded, peel-and-eat — you name it. But when I suggested eating out, Esther got all upset with me — fuss, fuss, fuss. So that's when I decided to go fishing . . . for my wife."

"For Esther?"

"That's right. I wanted to catch her and get what I wanted from her — a trip to Mamie's for the shrimp special. So I sat down on the chair right across from Esther, and I looked her right in the eye — just the way you study a fishing hole before you cast your line. Then I threw out the bait. 'What's wrong, Esther, honey?' I asked, sweet as you please. Right away, she bit. She started telling me everything that was bothering her, and I shut my mouth tight. You can't talk if you want to catch a fish, you know."

Derek did know. He also knew that when Kim started talking about everything that was bothering her, the last thing he wanted to do was sit there gazing at her. He wanted to bolt in the opposite direction — as fast as he could. But Charlie was continuing his tale as he drove the golf cart along the moonlit road.

"The whole time Esther talked," he told Derek, "I kept on looking at her, studying her, not saying a word, just nodding my head. I was itching to pick up the remote and see if the ball game was on TV, but I wanted to eat at Mamie's even more. So I kept my hands still, just the way you do when you're reeling in a big ol' bass. And Esther kept talking. She said she had made that salad, and her feelings were hurt that I would prefer to eat out. She confessed that she had always been insecure about her cooking. She told me she thought Mamie's could fix shrimp better than she could, and she figured that was why I wanted to eat there."

Derek was trying to listen, but he was getting kind of drowsy. All this talk of Jell-O salad and shrimp had made him hungry, and the slow pace of the golf cart was about to put him into a trance. The more Charlie talked, the more Derek envisioned Esther

Moore as a largemouth bass. He could almost see her swimming closer and closer to Charlie's goal of eating out at Mamie's as she talked and he reeled her in.

"I didn't move a muscle," Charlie went on. "I just leaned forward and listened. She was talking about her salad, but when she pulled a tissue out of her pocket and went to dabbing her eyes, I started to realize what she was really feeling. Her fussing at me didn't have a thing to do with Mamie's. It was all about the fact that Esther's mother had never taught her how to cook, and that made her insecure about her culinary skills all her life. So you know what I said? I said, 'Esther, you are the finest woman the good Lord ever made. You learned how to be a better cook than your mother ever was — and you taught yourself. Furthermore, I prefer your Jell-O salad to all the salads in the entire universe. And I feel exactly the same about your shrimp.' You know what Esther said to that? She said, 'I love you, Charlie. Put on your shoes, and let's go eat supper at Mamie's.' And that's exactly what we did."

Derek felt as though he had just been handed that largemouth bass in a frying pan with a pat of butter and a sliced-up lemon. Charlie hadn't reeled in a trip to Mamie's.

He had landed his wife's heart — hook, line, and sinker.

When Kim heard Derek's footsteps on the porch, she decided to try to intercept him before his mother did. Somehow, Kim *had* to convince Derek to send Miranda back to St. Louis if they wanted any hope of peace in their family. Tensions were strained to the bursting point, yet the man at the center of the hurricane seemed blissfully unaware. And that infuriated Kim.

She was almost at the front door when she heard Derek's voice on the porch. Through the screened window, she could see his silhouette. He had hunkered down and was talking to Lydia, who had stretched out on the swing, one arm thrown dramatically over her eyes. Kim reached for the doorknob, but she paused as she heard Derek speaking.

"What's wrong, Lydia, honey?" he asked, laying a hand on the arm of the swing.

It had been so long since Kim had heard a gentle tone in her husband's voice that she stood unable to move in the darkened foyer. For a moment, no one spoke.

Then Lydia sniffled. "I hate this family," she said.

Derek moved over and sat down on the

wicker rocking chair near the swing. "You hate this family?" he repeated. "You mean me, Luke, your mom, and Grandma Finley? Or do you still like some of us?"

"I like Luke," Lydia said. "I like Mom, too, but it makes me sick the way she's been acting. She's such a grouch."

"Hmm." The chair squeaked a little as Derek began to rock back and forth.

Kim eased down onto a chair near the door. She watched the silhouetted shapes and listened through the open window as her husband and daughter talked. For some reason, it felt almost magical to hear their voices. His was deep and manly; hers was small and almost timid. Though Lydia spoke with belligerence, she often sounded fragile and even afraid. Kim wondered if Derek had any idea how delicate the girl was, hovering on the brink of her teens, wondering who she was, unsure of her future. She remembered feeling so much like Lydia, and yet Kim knew Derek must have no idea what to make of such a tightly wound ball of confusion, fear, and hope.

"Grandma Finley is okay," Lydia told him. "She's just weird. You know what I mean? She's got that altar on the deck. People can smell the incense — and she wears her bathing suit to do her tai chi."

"I thought she wore a robe too."

"She takes it off!" Lydia groaned. "It's so embarrassing. I could die. If Mom ever did anything like that, I would just kill her."

"*Die. Kill.* Strong words. You thinking a lot about death, kiddo?"

"Well, wouldn't you? I mean, she's your mother, Derek. Aren't you creeped out by her? You should have seen the pizza she tried to make tonight. It was all Parmesan and spinach and weird herbs. She's just strange. I don't know how you even turned out normal." Lydia fell silent for a moment. "But I don't want her to leave us. I mean, like, I wouldn't want her to really *die.* Or you either. Or Luke."

"Oh yeah. Sure, I know." Derek rocked some more.

"That's how it feels around here. Like everything's breaking apart and about to die. We already went through that, Luke and me, when Mom and Dad got divorced. It's not that I mind having you for a stepdad. But I hated it when they broke up. Even though he wasn't the best father, he was all we had. And then we had to live in that stupid shelter. And then that crummy little house with the leaky roof. Then we got you."

"Yeah, that was next."

Kim realized Derek was saying almost

nothing, yet for some reason Lydia had decided to talk to him. Calmly. She was sitting up now, her feet curled under her and her arms wrapped around the chain that held up the swing. In the rocking chair, Derek had leaned forward, elbows on his knees. He was looking at Lydia, nodding as she spoke. The intensity of his concentration almost frightened Kim. She had never seen her husband so purposefully focused.

"You're all right for a stepdad," Lydia admitted. "But why did you have to go and invite Grandma Finley here? We were doing okay without her. Every time I look at her, I remember that she's staying with us to make sure Luke doesn't die. And that just bugs me. Luke can take care of himself, and if he messes up, then I'm there to watch out for him. I mean, I do remember what happened on the Fourth of July, and I'm glad Grandma Finley was able to find Luke's insulin kit so fast. But it's always confusing around here. Who's in charge? I mean, is Grandma Finley living with us forever, or is she going back to St. Louis? It's like things never feel normal. First we lost Dad, then we got you, and now we have Grandma Finley — but we might lose Luke, or Grandma Finley might leave. Or stay. And I've heard you and Mom fighting. You guys might get divorced like she did with Dad, and then you would leave. You can't trust anyone in this family. I just hate it."

"Wow." Derek had stopped rocking. "You really do hate this family."

"No, I don't *hate* it. You're so dumb, Derek. I love this family, but how can you love something that you can't count on? It could all just shrivel up and die and blow away. It's awful. I can't stand it."

At this, Lydia began crying softly, and Kim could hardly bear to watch her daughter struggling. But as she rose to step out onto the porch, she saw Derek stretch his hands toward Lydia.

"Come here, kiddo," he beckoned. "Come sit with me a minute."

Even as he spoke, Lydia was already leaving the swing and curling into his lap as she had when she was younger.

Derek wrapped his arms around her and began rocking. "Listen up, tater tot," he said in a quiet voice. "I am not leaving this family. Not divorcing your mother. Not running out on you and Luke. No way. No how. You got that?"

"Uh-huh," Lydia sobbed, suddenly a baby again. "But what if Mom divorces you?"

"She won't. I'm not going to let her. So that's all there is to it. As for Grandma Finley . . . well, now that you mention it, she is pretty weird. But I'm used to her, because that's how she's always been. You'll get used to her too. Your grandma and your mother are going to have to figure out how to get along, because neither one of them is going away. I haven't gotten around to telling your mom that, so don't spill the beans."

What? Kim couldn't believe what she'd just heard. Hadn't they discussed it? Hadn't she made herself perfectly clear? Miranda had to leave! Now Derek was saying she was going to stay. Not only that, but he was asking Lydia to keep a secret from her mother.

Even as her anger mounted, she saw Lydia snuggle closer to Derek. "I won't tell anyone," Lydia said.

"As for Luke, you're right," Derek told her. "He's smart, and he's getting this diabetes thing figured out. Plus, he's got you to keep an eye on him. So there you go. One family — kind of stressed out, a little bit weird, sometimes sick or angry, but together. That's us."

Lydia sniffled. Kim could see her skinny arms snake around Derek's neck as her dark head nestled against his shoulder.

"You promise?" Lydia asked.

"Cross my heart."

"Hope to —" She caught her breath.

"No, I don't hope to die. I intend to live a long life, watch you and Luke grow up, be a good husband to your mother, and rock your babies just the way I'm rocking you. How's that?"

"Good," Lydia said.

Inside the foyer, Kim leaned her head against the wall and nodded. Not perfect. Not even truly acceptable. Yet in this moment, it was good enough.

Chapter Thirteen

August came in hot, just as it always did in mid-Missouri. Patsy stayed busy cutting hair short against the heat and humidity. Clients entered the salon wearing shorts and tank tops. Everyone wanted pedicures, because you couldn't go outside in anything but sandals or flip-flops. People smelled like suntan lotion or baby oil. Some of the drop-in customers were sweaty and damp, but by the time they walked out, Patsy had their hair soft, clean, and bouncy. She added three flavors of iced tea to the menu in the tea area, and they were a hit. She could hardly keep up with the demand.

In fact, things seemed pretty good all over. Next door, Bitty Sondheim's Pop-In was hopping with vacationers buying her California-style omelets and wraps to take out on the lake. Now that Pete and Patsy had patched things up, Patsy again frequented Rods-N-Ends for root beer floats and the occasional rotisserie hot dog, which she enjoyed while chatting with Pete over the counter.

His business was booming as people bought gas for their cars, RVs, boats, and Jet Skis. He kept tackle moving in and out of the shop too. His worms and minnows were said to be the healthiest and fattest around, and of course, Pete was generous in counting them out. If you asked for a dozen, you were more likely to get fifteen or twenty.

The chiropractor and tattoo places down the street both saw an upswing in their trade. People were forever flipping or flopping the wrong way in the water, and they'd come to the chiropractor for an adjustment. And the young crowd had a carefree and often reckless attitude that took them to the tattoo parlor in groups of three and four. Patsy knew they would select words or pictures they'd later regret and have them tattooed in places that would one day sag something awful. But she understood. On a dare from a group of her girlfriends, she'd had a small ladybug put on the back of her shoulder one afternoon when she was sixteen. Nowadays, she would sometimes wear a skinny-strapped top to show it off if the mood hit her.

As members of the Tea Lovers' Club

began slipping into the salon one Wednesday afternoon, Patsy realized she couldn't think of a single thing for Esther Moore to put on the agenda. Maybe for once the group would be allowed to chat in peace. Not only that, but Patsy had ushered her last customer away in plenty of time to join the TLC at the start of the gathering.

"I think we should fix some hot water," Cody suggested. He was already filling the stainless steel urn as Patsy checked on the dessert supply. "Maybe someone would want real tea," he explained. "With milk and sugar. And maybe that someone would be me."

"You don't like iced tea, Cody?" Patsy asked.

"My daddy never had a refrigerator or a cooler or anything like that. So I prefer my . . . my *beverages* . . . warm. Did I get that right?"

"Sure did. *Beverages.* That's a big word."

"I am increasing my vocabulary. Brenda thought it was a good idea, and so did I. Just so you know, I'm already up to fifth grade reading skills. Phonics and comprehension — both."

Patsy gave him a big hug. "I'm so proud of you, Cody."

It hadn't been so long ago that Cody

couldn't read at all. Brenda Hansen had told Patsy she was terribly frustrated with trying to teach him and had been about to give up. But suddenly everything clicked, and Cody began to understand letters and how they formed words. Recently Patsy had noticed him studying the magazines in the waiting area. Before, he had been looking at the pictures in order to get ideas for his wall mural. Now she realized he was probably reading the text as well.

"Fifth grade?" she said. "No joke?"

"Why would I make a joke about my reading level?" Cody asked her. "Reading skills are not funny. I'm working really hard on them, and right now, I'm reading *My Side of the Mountain,* which is a book written by Jean Craighead George. And do you know what? The boy in that book is sort of like me. He lives in the forest, and so did I. And that's why reading is good. It makes you think about yourself and figure things out. I never had a falcon named Frightful. That part is different. Also, I got beat up by some men who didn't like me. That hasn't happened to Sam. He likes living by himself in the woods, but I'm glad I live in Deepwater Cove with people around."

"We're glad you live here too." Patsy studied Cody's plugged-in water urn. "And as a matter of fact, I believe I'll have a cup of hot tea myself."

"Earl Grey or Darjeeling?" he asked.

"The latter."

Cody stared at her. "There's no ladder in here, Patsy. I'm tall enough to paint near the top of the wall without one."

She opened her mouth to explain, then decided to leave that job to Brenda. "Darjeeling, please, Cody. And I believe I'll have a lemon bar with that. It's a little more sugar than I ought to eat, but you know Pete likes me looking ample."

"I know," Cody said. "You and Pete are friends." He leaned over. "I think Jennifer Hansen is beautiful. Brenda told me she's coming to the TLC today. Do I look handsome as all get-out?"

Patsy smiled. "You sure do, honey. Ever since we cleaned you up, you get handsomer by the day. But Brenda said Jennifer is already starting her missionary studies over at Hidden Tribes Learning Center near Camdenton. I hope you're not still counting on marrying her."

"Yes, I am." Cody solemnly stirred his tea. "I'm counting on it a lot. But don't tell Jennifer when she comes to the meeting. She thinks we're just friends like you and Pete, and she doesn't know that I love her in a wife kind of way. She also doesn't know she's going to marry me. That comes later."

"I see."

As she absorbed this information, Patsy's notion of a glorious gabfest with the other ladies in the club transformed into a knot at the bottom of her stomach. This childlike puppy love Cody had developed for Jennifer Hansen could grow into a real problem. Everyone in the community understood that the young man was unusual — in an endearing sort of way. He was always helpful, kind, cheerful, and sincere.

But Cody simply didn't understand life the way most people did. He looked at the world from a different angle, almost as though his eyes and brain had been borrowed from some other creature. Often it required patience to spend time around Cody. And people didn't always have patience to spare. Patsy herself had snapped at him a few times. Though she felt bad about it, she just couldn't help herself. But Cody always forgave her immediately.

"You took the last lemon bar," he informed her now. "That's bad social skills, Patsy. But it's okay, because no one knows but me, and I won't tell on you. Hey, here comes Kim Finley and Miranda Finley. They don't look mad at each other today.

You can tell because they're both smiling. And here comes Esther Moore. She should bring Charlie. Then there would be two men in the TLC. Oh, boy, here's Brenda's car! Look, there she is! Isn't she beautiful?"

Patsy nodded as she settled into a chair. She knew Cody wasn't talking about Brenda, though the older woman was certainly lovely. Cody's focus was on Brenda's daughter. When Jennifer Hansen stepped into the salon, Patsy could see she had left her long blonde hair hanging loose around her shoulders, and she wore a simple T-shirt, a pair of khaki shorts, and plain sandals. Unlike her younger sister, Jennifer had never been the homecoming queen or the center of the social whirl at Camdenton High School. She was quiet, studious, and as sweet and wholesome as apple pie.

With a sinking feeling, Patsy watched the young woman's face light up when she spotted Cody. He gave an eager wave as he pointed to the empty chair beside him. Jennifer said something in a low voice to her mother, confiding woman-to-woman in a way that unsettled Patsy even more. Even if she genuinely liked him — which Patsy dearly hoped — he would be crestfallen when his romantic aspirations weren't returned.

"Hey there, Cody," Jennifer said brightly. She slipped into the seat he had saved as he fumbled to rise and pull it back for her. "Hey, Patsy. The salon looks great. You're really packing people in this summer."

"Just don't tell me you want to cut off that beautiful long hair," Patsy said. "I couldn't do it."

Jennifer chuckled. "Oh, don't worry. I just pin it up if I get too hot. It's easy."

Unfortunately, this comment caused her to demonstrate, which in turn drew Cody's attention like a moth to a bug zapper. He positively gaped as Jennifer flipped her hair over her shoulder, twirled it around her index finger, pulled a clip from her pocket, and secured the roll on the back of her head. It was deftly done, but Patsy knew Cody wasn't admiring the young woman's dexterity. Those bright blue eyes were glued to Jennifer's face and neck . . . and right on down.

"Wow," he said.

Jennifer shrugged. "It's easy, Cody. I've been putting it up since I was a kid. Patsy's the one who taught me how to braid. I used to do my little sister's hair all the time."

"I remember that," Patsy said. "And now you're all grown up and studying to be a missionary."

"A missionary?" Miranda Finley had somehow finagled a pair of chairs for herself and Kim at the table. "A lovely young woman like you? Oh, dear. But I suppose you're determined."

Jennifer smiled. "I certainly am. I've been praying about where to serve. I loved my mission trip to Africa so much, but I'm thinking more and more about going to New Guinea."

"Not to dash your spirits, dear, but has it occurred to you that the people in New Guinea probably have a perfectly good religion already?"

"Some of them know Christ, but there are still lots of unreached tribes."

"I have never understood why Christians are so determined to impose their religion on others," Miranda said. "I realize you're enthusiastic about your beliefs, Jennifer, but I can assure you that Hindus are very happy as they are. So are Muslims, for that matter. You'll find a great deal of zeal for Islam in the Arab world, of course. No doubt those tribes you're going to visit have a way of worshipping that's comfortable to them too. In my opinion, all paths lead to God."

Kim sighed. "Yes, Miranda, we know what you think. I'm sure everyone here has seen you and Buddha on the deck."

At that, Miranda clamped her mouth shut. But not for long. "Well, at least I'm tolerant of letting people worship however they please. I don't go around trying to convert people to my faith system. I accept *all* teachings of *all* religions."

"All except Christianity," Jennifer pointed out.

Everyone at the table turned to stare at the young woman who had spoken up. Brenda Hansen's face sobered, and she glanced across at Kim. Clearly the two women were realizing they had a couple of firecrackers at the table and there was likely to be trouble.

"What do you mean by that, Jennifer?" Miranda asked with a sweet expression. "Of course I accept Christianity. It's a perfectly valid path to God. Along with all the others. How can you say I don't accept Christ's teachings?"

"Christ insisted that there is only one way to God. He said, 'No one can come to the Father except through me.'"

"John 14:6," Cody cut in. "It's in the Bible. I've got that whole chapter by memory."

"Really?" Jennifer studied the young man for a moment, as if absorbing and filing away this information. Then she returned to

306

Miranda. "Anyway, if you agree with Jesus that He is the only way to God, you can't accept all the other religions, too."

Miranda shook her head and let out a sigh. She took a sip of iced tea, commented on the delicious flavor, and then turned back to Jennifer. "I must assure you that I do accept all the teachings of Jesus as valid. Of course He believed He was the path to God. So did Muhammad and Buddha. These three men had experienced profound spiritual revelations, and they taught valuable truths that can enlighten us on our own personal journey of self-discovery. I choose to accept them all."

"All *except* Jesus."

Brenda laid a hand on her daughter's arm. "Jennifer. Let's talk about something else. Why don't you tell everyone our news. You know . . . about your sister."

"Jessica's getting married," Jennifer muttered, and in the next breath, "Mrs. Finley, Jesus instructed His followers to go out into the world and make disciples of everyone. When you or anyone else wants to deny Christians the right to try to convert people, then you deny us the practice of our religion. And that's discrimination."

"Well, but I —"

"If you truly accepted Christianity, Mrs.

Finley, you wouldn't object to my desire to teach tribal people in New Guinea about my faith, because you would understand that evangelism is an essential part of Christianity. Christ was very clear about that."

For a moment, everyone at the table sat in silence. And then Cody began to clap. "Yay, Jennifer," he said. "That was a long speech about Jesus. I liked it. I thought it was good. You're the best Christian I ever met."

All the time Cody was speaking, Patsy was frantically trying to think of something to say that would divert the conversation away from religion. She briefly thought of asking about Jessica's upcoming wedding. But the truth was, Patsy liked what Jennifer had said, and she admired the way the girl had spoken without the least bit of hesitation. So instead of inquiring about the Hansen engagement, she heard herself echoing Cody.

"You sure are going to make a good missionary, honey," she told Jennifer. "I don't know the last time I heard such conviction from anyone but a preacher. No wonder you're going out into the world. I doubt that wild horses could keep you here in Deepwater Cove."

"But Deepwater Cove has plenty of people

who need missionaries," Cody spoke up. "People like Mrs. Finley, who dances on the deck in her bathing suit. She worships idols, and that's against the Ten Commandments, so she definitely needs a missionary." He turned to Miranda. "You should come to church with us and find out what it's like there. If you did, you would know that one day idols shall be utterly abolished. 'And they shall go into the holes of the rocks, and into the caves of the earth, for fear of the Lord, and for the glory of his majesty, when he ariseth to shake terribly the earth. In that day a man shall cast his idols of silver, and his idols of gold, which they made each one for himself to worship, to the moles and to the bats; to go into the clefts of the rocks, and into the tops of the ragged rocks, for fear of the Lord, and for the glory of his majesty.' Isaiah 2:19–21. Right, Jennifer?"

All eyes at the table turned to the young woman, who was gazing across the room with an odd expression on her face.

"Patsy, why are there five pictures of me on your wall?" she asked, pointing at Cody's mural. "Right over there. Five of them. That's me, isn't it?"

Cody grinned. "I painted them," he said. "I put beautiful ladies on the wall to show off lots of hairstyles."

Jennifer looked at him. "But the faces all look like mine. Don't they? Does anyone else see that?"

Thank goodness, at just this particular moment, Esther got up and began tapping the side of her tea glass with a spoon. "Ladies, ladies," she said loudly before Cody could whistle them into silence. Then she beamed at the young man. "Ladies *and gentleman,* welcome to today's gathering of the Tea Lovers' Club. We're thrilled to have so many in attendance on a hot afternoon. Before we return to our tea and conversation, let me just recap our old business and mention one thing new."

Esther reached into her purse for her little notebook, and Patsy took the opportunity for a quick glance around the table. It was not a comforting sight. Jennifer was staring at the paintings of herself on the salon wall. Miranda was glaring at Jennifer. Kim was frowning at Miranda. Brenda was eyeing Cody. And Cody was downing the last of Patsy's lemon bar.

"There isn't much old business to report," Esther said. "It's been a glorious summer so far. All the yards look lovely, and we ought to especially recognize Brenda Hansen, who planted red, white, and blue annuals in a tribute to our great country. As we've said before, the Fourth of July barbecue was a stellar event. The commons area and the streets were lined with nearly a hundred small flags generously donated by Ashley Hanes, courtesy of the country club. Opal provided a relish tray and several apple pies, which delighted everyone. We had more salads and side dishes than we could eat. The pork steaks were delicious, and a good time was had by all. Well . . . it looks like that's about it. Is there any other old business to report?"

When no one spoke, Esther charged on. "Then let's get down to new business. I propose we have another Deepwater Cove gathering for Labor Day weekend. How about Sunday after church? It'll still be warm enough for the kids to swim, but we could add a fishing contest at the docks. I was thinking about a hayride, but Charlie says it's too early for that. We definitely want to honor the working men and women among us, so I was thinking about a parade."

"Brad wouldn't march in a parade to save his life," Ashley said. "I'm not too crazy about it either. Would you and Steve march in a parade, Brenda?"

"I doubt that's exactly Steve's idea of

fun," Brenda said of her real estate agent husband. "Maybe the barbecue, fishing contest, and swimming would be enough, Esther."

The self-elected chairwoman of the TLC folded her hands and looked down at her notebook. "Well, if that's how you feel about it . . . ," she said, her voice trailing off. "I always loved a parade."

"A raid?" Opal spoke up. "When? I never heard any sirens."

Patsy knew everyone was thinking the same thing — Opal wouldn't hear sirens if they *did* start wailing.

"I have something to share," Brenda said. "My youngest child, Jessica, has just gotten engaged. They haven't set the wedding date, but I'm sure you'll all be welcome."

"Congratulations," several women said.

"That Jessica is so pretty," someone said. "Just like her sister."

"I'm not a bit surprised some boy snapped her up," another commented.

"I'd like to introduce some new business," Miranda said, standing so suddenly that the table jiggled and tea sloshed out of the china cups. "Esther, may I please have the floor?"

"Why, certainly, Miranda. We'd love to hear what you have to say."

For several hammering heartbeats, Patsy

was afraid Miranda intended to expound on her theory that all paths led to God. Or maybe she wanted to defend her decision to put Buddha out on the Finleys' deck. But then she smiled warmly and turned to the table where she'd been sitting.

"Cody," she said gently, "I want to announce that I have found your aunt."

A gasp went up from the entire gathering. And then everyone fell silent. Cody stared straight ahead, looking at no one, blinking rapidly.

Finally, Miranda spoke again. "Marylou Annette Goss lives in western Kansas. She's your father's sister. I have spoken with her by phone, Cody. A long time ago, before you were born, your father became estranged from his family, and they never spoke or had any contact after that. Your aunt Marylou had no idea what had become of your father."

Patsy reached under the table, found Cody's hand, and wrapped hers around it. He still wasn't moving, so she gave his hand a little squeeze. "It's a big shocker, isn't it, sweetie pie?" she murmured. "How about that? Mrs. Finley found your aunt, just like you wanted."

"I know," he said. "I heard what she said."

Miranda smiled. "I propose that the

members of the Tea Lovers' Club take up a collection to buy a bus ticket for Cody. In fact, I've already looked into it. I can put him on the bus in St. Louis, and his aunt will pick him up in Garden City, Kansas. From there, she'll drive him toward the Colorado border to the town where she lives." Miranda beamed at everyone as she seated herself again.

Patsy slipped her arm around Cody's shoulders. "Sounds like you turned up a lot of stuff when you were looking for Cody's family. I guess his aunt must be pretty excited to see him."

Miranda took a sip of tea. "Well, of course," she said. "She didn't even know he existed. I'm sure she'll enjoy him as much as we all do."

"Maybe not, if she finds out I'm kind of dumb," Cody said.

Jennifer leaned against him. "No way, Cody! You just quoted more Scripture than most of us have ever memorized."

"Your aunt Marylou didn't know your mother and father had passed away," Miranda said. "Mr. Goss didn't contact his family after Cody's mother died. He must have simply decided to take Cody and leave."

"We went a lot of places," Cody put in.

"Marylou told me she's always wondered what became of her brother."

Deciding it was time to change the subject, Patsy gave Cody a little hug. "Oh, my stars, my cup is dry as a bone. Cody, honey, would you mind getting me some more tea?"

He looked around the table, his blue eyes settling on Jennifer for a moment before he rose and headed for the hot-water urn.

As Miranda turned to Esther, Patsy noticed that the older woman's eyes had filled with tears.

Esther slipped her agenda notebook into her purse and pulled out a tissue. Dabbing her eyes, she nodded. "I think that's a wonderful idea," she said, sniffling loudly. "If Cody's aunt wants him to come . . . and if Cody wants to be with family . . . well then . . ." She gulped. "Well, let's all pitch in and make this farewell a send-off to remember."

CHAPTER FOURTEEN

"Where are the candles?" Frowning, Kim rummaged through a drawer in the kitchen. "I always keep plenty of birthday candles on hand."

"In the pantry!" Miranda sang out as she hurried through the kitchen bearing a bowl of cheesy popcorn. "I reorganized the baking supplies for you, Kim. I hope you don't mind, but that drawer you had them in was a shambles. I put everything in a lovely wicker basket on the top shelf."

Kim gritted her teeth and hurried to the pantry. No, she would not get angry. Not on this special day. A party day. A day of celebration, thankfulness, and sweet good-byes. Kim had every reason to smile. The twins were turning eleven, Cody was going to meet his long-lost aunt in Kansas, and Kim was determined to focus on her blessings instead of her woes.

True, Miranda was still staying in the Finley house and evidently would be forever. Derek had not uttered a word about the plan he had confided to Lydia that evening on the porch. So Kim told herself she still did not "officially" know that her mother-in-law wouldn't be leaving with the start of school. But she had decided to try to keep her thoughts to herself in order to keep peace in the home. She had suppressed the hurt and anger that Derek's decision — and his refusal to communicate with her — had caused.

In looking back on her own childhood, Kim could recall few good things to be thankful for — but adaptability was one. She couldn't count the times her mother had moved the family from town to town, house to apartment, man to man. People had come and gone from their lives all the time, and Kim understood the anguish Lydia had expressed to Derek on the porch. A fragmented, constantly shifting family group unsettled and frightened children. Kim knew that too well, and she was not about to put her twins through any more upheaval than they'd experienced already. But her own difficult life had taught her to adjust, to make the most of each situation, to search for blessings. And that's what she would do in order to protect her precious family.

Just when Kim heard the twins' feet pounding toward the kitchen, she found the birthday candles in a basket in the pantry. Ten minutes earlier, she had sent Luke and Lydia running to Charlie and Esther Moore's house to fetch Cody — anything to keep the rambunctious pair out of the kitchen — and they were already back.

"Eleven!" she said, poking candles into the cake as the twins breathlessly burst into the room. "Eleven years old. Yay, Luke and Lydia!"

Lydia danced around the room while her brother bounced up and down on his toes.

"I hope I get a skateboard; I hope I get a skateboard," Luke chanted.

"How soon till everyone else gets here?" Lydia asked. "I can't wait!"

"Any time now. Where's Cody?"

"On the deck with Mr. and Mrs. Moore. They followed us in their golf cart."

"Good job. Luke, I know you saved up all your carbs. Have you checked your blood sugar recently?"

"Yeah, and it's just right so I can eat cake and ice cream."

Kim smiled proudly. "I knew you'd figure it out. Okay, kids, run and open the front door for the rest of the guests."

"You made an eleven cake, Mom!" Lydia crowed before racing away after her brother. "Did you see it, Lukey? We're eleven! We're eleven!"

Kim couldn't deny how pleased she was about the large *11* she had crafted out of a pair of chocolate cake mixes. Each year since the twins' birth, she had created a cake in the shape of their age. This year, the double *1*'s iced in chocolate fudge and sprinkled with nuts were large enough to feed all the kids' friends and Cody's well-wishers, too. It would be a big group, but Kim was prepared.

"The deck table is set and ready for company," Miranda announced as she breezed back into the kitchen. "And just look at the cars pulling up along the street. Where is that son of mine? He should be home by now."

"Derek often has last-minute phone calls or paperwork. He'll be here soon."

"Paperwork? How can that be more important than his family? Especially on birthdays! I used to tell his father the same thing — family first. Eric was always off on some photographic safari, you know. But when he came home, I made it clear that his wife and son got top priority."

Kim took two cartons of ice cream out of the freezer — one sugar-free — and carried them to the counter. "I hadn't realized Eric was gone so much."

"Oh yes. The Himalayan mountains in Tibet, a volcano in Hawaii, the Rift Valley in eastern Africa. Weeks at a time. Sometimes months. It's a wonder Derek recognized his father when he came home. If I'd had any idea that marrying an internationally renowned photographer would turn me into a single mother, well . . . well, I would have married him anyway."

To her surprise, Kim laughed. The giggle was natural for once, not the forced chuckle that she so often coughed out for her mother-in-law's benefit. Miranda rarely spoke about Derek's father, and neither did her son. It was refreshing to see the woman in such high spirits and eager to chat.

"You know how you marry people for the silliest reasons?" Miranda was saying as she opened a potato chip bag and poured the contents into a large bowl. "Oh, that Eric Finley was handsome! Curly hair, blue-gray eyes, and a wonderful physique. If I'd given it two thoughts, I would have realized that his tan and all those muscles came from trekking up and down mountains or wandering through deserts. But I thought he was gorgeous. So romantic! And a photographer, too!"

"He does sound handsome," Kim said.

"To die for. In my fairy-tale vision, Eric and I were going to travel the world together, hitchhiking from one adventure to another. Then we got married, and I got pregnant — well, actually the other way around — and off he went without me. It turned out the magazines he freelanced for didn't pay for wives and babies to tag along. Worse, he didn't want company on his assignments, especially not a child. But he came from a wealthy family, and so we didn't lack for money. A handsome, absentee husband; a darling little boy; and enough to live on comfortably forever."

Kim had found spoons for the ice cream and was trying to figure out how to get the double cakes out the sliding glass door to the deck. But at the same time, she wanted to listen to Miranda. Instead of harping about Kim's choice of curtains or hinting at her failures as a mother, the woman was actually conversing.

"Derek works long hours, but he's never gone overnight," Kim said as she arranged the birthday things on a tray. "Weren't you lonely?"

"Of course I was. In those early days of

marriage, it was always Eric and Derek. Derek and Eric. And then just Derek. And finally no one at all. But money can do a lot to make up for loneliness." She shrugged. "Until I came down here, I thought that's how my existence had to be. But look — it turned out all right in the end."

"This is not the end," Kim said. "You have so much life still ahead."

Miranda paused for a moment. "Don't start me thinking about that," she said softly. "I'm focused on waiting until I can pass through this life into a new form of being."

"You're waiting to die?"

"To be reincarnated." Miranda seemed to sag as she leaned against the kitchen counter. "And please don't attack me the way that Hansen girl did at the TLC meeting the other day. If I were a Christian, all I'd have to look forward to is an eternity playing a harp and wearing a pair of angel wings. No thanks. I'll hedge my bets and keep the doors open. If I'm right about reincarnation, there's hope for a better future for me. Maybe I'll be a . . . a cat!"

At that, she winked at Kim and began to laugh. Sweeping up the cartons of ice cream Kim had just opened, Miranda headed for the door. "Oh, wouldn't I love to lie in the sun all day and bask away the hours! How lovely to be a cat!"

As Kim picked up the cake tray, she wondered how that existence would be so different from the one Miranda already enjoyed. Money. Leisure. Even a family to keep you busy — or ignore — at your whim.

But there was no time to work up any frustration toward Miranda, whose concept of heaven was so far off the biblical mark as to be laughable. Instead of resenting her mother-in-law, Kim would find compassion for her.

Despite her privileged life, Miranda obviously regretted some of her choices. She had been lonely and self-absorbed for many years. No wonder she was hard to live with. Without the Bible as a guide and the church to provide a support system in good times and bad, Miranda had learned to rely on herself and her own philosophies.

"Did I hear Miranda say something about a cat?" Esther Moore asked as she stepped into the kitchen. "I ought to warn you — your house is already very full, dear. Though Boofer is a joy, that dog takes up so much of our time. I hope you haven't gone and gotten a pet for the twins' birthday."

Kim laughed. "No pets — but we do have Miranda, who's hoping to be reincarnated as a cat."

"A cat?" Esther picked up two bowls of chips. "Goodness, not me. I'm looking forward to heaven. In fact, I can hardly wait. I won't have all these aches and pains, and I'll be able to hold my sister's hand and skip through the grass like we did when we were kids. Charlie says he's planning to sing in the heavenly choir, but I have too many people I want to visit."

At the thought of Charlie raising his voice in praise to the Lord and Esther chatting with friends and family, Kim smiled. She lifted her focus toward the sky as she stepped onto the deck with the cake. How comforting it was to know she didn't need to fear being reincarnated as a cat or a bug or even another human.

When she set the cake down on the table, Kim's eyes fell on her husband, who had just arrived. Still in uniform, Derek was speaking with his mother and obviously getting a tongue-lashing for showing up nearly an hour after the end of his shift. Kim sighed. Well, if Derek could put up with Miranda, why couldn't she?

"I'm going home."

The words were spoken so near Kim's ear that she jumped in surprise. She looked around to find Cody Goss leaning over her shoulder as she straightened the candles on the two cakes.

"Eleven," he said, reading the numerals. "Luke and Lydia are eleven years old, and that's why you made them an *eleven* cake. I never had a birthday cake. I don't know how old I am except more than twenty-one. Do you think my aunt will make me a *more than twenty-one* cake?"

"Maybe she will, Cody. Just ask her when you get there."

"I've missed a lot of cakes. If today was my birthday, I would have chocolate cake cut into squares. These cakes will be easy to cut into squares."

Kim straightened and gazed into the earnest blue eyes. "Cody, would you like to share these cakes with Luke and Lydia? They're so used to sharing everything, I know they wouldn't mind."

"Does that mean I'm eleven too?"

"No . . . but it does mean you get to eat chocolate cake in squares."

Cody's lips parted over his white teeth as he smiled. "I like that. I hope my aunt is just like you."

"No matter what she's like, she'll be so proud of you. I know that for certain. You've become such a smart, capable young man."

"Excuse me there, Cody," Derek said, tapping him on the shoulder. "Mind if I cut in? I need to talk to Kim for a minute."

"Okay," Cody mumbled, his shoulders sagging. "But I was hoping we could cut those two cakes. I want to eat some, because they're partly mine."

"No, they're not!" Miranda Finley sashayed up to the table bearing a third cake in her hands. "This is *your* cake, Cody! I ordered it especially for your going-away party. It's an ice cream cake. I've had it hidden in Esther's freezer for several days now. A secret surprise, just for you!"

She set the elaborately decorated round cake next to the fudge frosted cakes that Kim had proudly created for her twins. Miranda's cake flaunted gleaming white icing in professional scallops and swirls, a road drawn in gray icing with a yellow stripe down the center, and a miniature toy bus traveling along it. Elaborately scripted letters read *Farewell, Cody!*

The young man gaped at the cake for a moment; then he read the inscription out loud. "*Farewell, Cody!* That means me, because I'm Cody. This is my first birthday cake ever in my whole life."

Miranda touched his arm. "Honey, it's not a —"

"I wonder how old I am," Cody contin-

326

ued. He studied the table for a moment. Then pointing to the three cakes, he said, "One-one-zero. I am 110 years old. Wow!"

As the crowd laughed, Charlie Moore slung his arm around Cody's shoulders. "Come on, then, you old turkey buzzard. Step back and let the twins blow out their candles so we can dig in. That ice cream's already melting, and I'm hungry."

Kim's heart welled with emotion as Derek lit the candles. Luke and Lydia grinned happily while everyone sang "Happy Birthday." And then — with Cody joining in — they blew out the flames. Esther and Miranda moved in to cut cake and dip ice cream while Brenda Hansen poured glasses of punch.

"Kim?" Derek slipped a hand around his wife's elbow. "Can we step over here to the side for just a minute? I need to talk to you."

Concerned, she nodded and accompanied him to a bench at the far corner of the deck away from the hubbub of cake, candles, and gifts. "What's wrong, Derek?" she asked. "Did something happen at work?"

"No, it's not that." He laced his fingers together and rested his elbows on his thighs, his focus on the deck between his boots. "Well . . . it's about my mother."

"You know she's hoping to be reincarnated as a cat," Kim teased.

Derek glanced up, and for a moment his sober expression softened. "With our luck, she'll come back as a tiger — claws and all." He shook his head. "Listen, I've been meaning to talk to you about this, and Mom knows I'm putting it off. She asked me to talk to you today, before the party. I planned to come home right after work, but this morning, we finally got the facial reconstruction on our drowning victim. We've been printing flyers, talking to the media, and trying to get the word out so if anyone has seen her —"

"Derek," Kim cut in, "I know your mother isn't planning to go back to St. Louis when school starts. If that's what you wanted to tell me, I already know. I heard what Lydia —"

"She wasn't supposed to tell you," he ground out. "That ornery kid."

"It's not Lydia's fault. I was on my way out to the porch that evening when you were talking with her. I overheard you tell her about Miranda."

"You knew? All this time?"

"Yes, and I've been pretty upset that you told our daughter before you told me. Why did you do that? Are you afraid to talk to me? Do you see me as a tiger too?"

He fell silent.

"I guess that answers my question," she said, a mixture of hurt and frustration bubbling inside her. "No matter what you think about me, I deserved to hear the truth, Derek."

"I'm telling you right now."

"Here? In the middle of the twins' birthday party?"

"I've kept it from you as long as I could, but it's now or never. You know Mom is leaving for St. Louis tomorrow — taking Cody to the bus station. While she's there, she plans to hire packers, rent a storage unit, and put her house on the market. She wants to stay here permanently."

Despite her best intentions, Kim felt her anger flare. "*She* wants to stay? I thought it was your idea."

"It is. Partly." His head dropped lower. "There are things you don't know, Kim. Things I should have told you a long time ago."

"Derek, this is the twins' birthday party! What's wrong with you? You have no idea how to talk or listen or anything! How can you do this?"

She could see the muscle in his jaw flickering. "I'm sorry I'm not exactly like you, Kim. I don't talk easily. I prefer to take care of today, handle situations as they arise. It's one day at a time with me, okay?"

"No, it's not okay. Not when it affects your family. You'd better start talking — and I mean *now.*"

"I'd rather wait until after the party."

"Now," she repeated.

"All right," he groused. "Here's the deal. You know I love my mother, and I want to take care of her. But I never planned to have her live with us. *She* decided that, and I can't say no."

"Why not? Miranda has caused so much tension in the house. Of course she's been helpful with the kids, but she's also upset our whole family structure. It's all I can do to keep my spirits up when she's always on me about things. She's given both of the kids a hard time with her crazy ideas, and she's horribly permissive. She flaunts our rules — the computer, the bicycles, swimming, you name it. She criticizes almost everything about me — from my curtain fabric to the way I cook. Worst of all, she mocks our faith. You know how hard this summer has been for all of us, and I can't believe you would let her have her way in this. Especially if it's not what you really want."

"I have to, Kim. That's what I'm trying to

tell you."

"Why? You're a grown man. You're the strongest, bravest human being I've ever met. How can you let your mother walk all over you?"

"She's not walking on me. She holds me by a leash."

"What kind of a leash? What are you saying, Derek?"

"Money." He spat out the word. "It's all about money, okay?"

"What do you mean?"

He covered his eyes with a hand and rubbed his temples. "We should wait to talk about this."

"Derek, please."

He let out a hot breath. "Look, there's a part of my life I never told you about. I didn't want to believe it mattered. It happened in the past, and I decided I couldn't let it affect us. Affect *you.*"

Kim's heart sank. "Oh no," she whispered. "What happened?"

"It started when I was in college. I racked up a fair amount of debt for tuition, housing, and all that. But there's more. I used to . . . to gamble, okay? The riverboat casinos. You know they line the river in St. Louis, and I'd go there with friends — just for fun. Then I began going by myself.

Every day. Every night."

"Derek." She wanted to reach out to him, but she couldn't move.

"I don't know how to explain this, but sitting at the poker table was the only place I felt comfortable. No one demanded anything of me there. I didn't have to be the son of the late, great, world-renowned photographer, Eric Finley. I didn't have to live up to my mother's dreams and expectations for me. I knew I was destroying myself, but for some reason gambling gave me a feeling of security. False security. I figured if I won, I could have the good things in life without having to work for it or inherit it. The bottom line was that I didn't want to grow up, and I thought I could escape responsibility — to the point that it became an obsession."

"This is impossible," Kim murmured.

"It's not impossible. It's true. I barely graduated from college. I spent money hand over fist — always sure I was going to strike it rich. The next big jackpot was just waiting for me. I told myself I had a safeguard. My father's dough would bail me out, and it did. But it came with a price. I ended up owing my mother so much money I'll never be able to pay it back. She holds my debt over my head because she believes that keeps me from relapsing. She's wrong, but I can't convince her of that. My senior year of college, I started going to Gamblers Anonymous. Went to meetings more often than you've ever been to church. You want to talk about a higher power? I've got one, and her name is Miranda Finley."

As Derek spoke, Kim's entire body had stiffened. Every muscle went hard and tense; her teeth clenched; her hands knotted into fists. How could this be happening?

This wasn't true. It couldn't be. Derek would have told her if he'd had a gambling problem. He knew she was the child of one alcoholic and had married another. She had sworn she would never, ever marry anyone with an addiction.

But she had. Somehow the horrible pattern had repeated itself again. Not only was Derek an addict, but he had hidden it from her. Denied and buried his dark secret for three years!

"Sometimes I've told you I had to work late," he was saying now, "but I lied. I was at GA meetings. I have to attend, Kim. It's still hard to resist the urge. I've been away from the boats for years now, but I fight the battle every day. The guys at work will put together a football pool. Or someone's wife is having a baby, and they want me to bet on the birth date. You wonder why I never spend time on the computer? why I'm so hard on the kids about it? Now you know. There's too much opportunity to get into gambling again. Every convenience store and most restaurants have lottery machines. Scratchers. Lotto. That's why I always go to Pete's Rods-N-Ends. He doesn't sell those things, so I won't buy my gas anywhere else."

Kim couldn't speak. She could hardly breathe.

At some far distance, she could see her children tearing open birthday presents, hugging people, laughing, high-fiving each other.

And then there was this man at her side. This gambler. This addict. This nightmare.

"I survive by acting as though I don't owe the money," he continued. "You and I live off our joint income, and we make it every month. Barely. We have this nice house, food to eat, clothes for the kids, cars. But that money you think we've been saving isn't going into an account. It goes to St. Louis. To my mother. It goes to pay off my debt. When my mother dies, which isn't likely to be soon, we'll be free. In the meantime, I'm honor bound to make amends. I have to restore what I took."

Kim swallowed hard, fighting tears. "You should have told me, Derek."

"You wouldn't have married me. I knew that. I'm an addict, just like Joe."

"You're nothing like Joe." But even as she said the words, Kim realized she was kidding herself. In many ways, Derek was very much like her first husband — not only an addict but emotionally stunted, living in denial, hiding secrets. Even Derek's job with the Water Patrol revealed how important control was to him. Joe had demanded ultimate authority, and eventually he became abusive. Though Derek never lifted a finger against Kim or the twins, he had chosen a job and a life in which he could exert power and influence.

Derek had fallen silent, and Kim couldn't make herself move. So they sat on the bench, watching the children laugh and the adults eat cake and ice cream. Brenda and Steve Hansen had presented Cody with a suitcase on wheels for his trip. The Hansens looked happy together, as attractive and cheerful as a spring bouquet. Esther and Charlie were seated side by side in deck chairs, eating ice cream and laughing about something. The summer sun radiated joy from their faces. Patsy and Pete had shut down business early just for the party. He was teasing her, making her blush and swat his shoulder. The twins sat bunched in a group with their friends, examining and admiring their gifts.

Only two in the gathered group seemed less than elated. Lydia's closest friend, Tiffany, had moved a little apart, as if she sensed she was older and somehow different from these happy-go-lucky kids. And then there was Cody. He held a plate with chocolate cake cut into a perfect square by Esther, but he stood at the edge of the deck and gazed at the lake. Kim wondered if his turmoil was anything like hers.

"I'm sorry," Derek said in a low voice. "I should have told you, Kim. I should have known it would come out one way or another. But I've tried so hard to keep this in the past."

"It's not in the past, Derek," Kim heard herself snap back at him. "Not if you're going to Gamblers Anonymous meetings all the time. Not if you're still battling addiction. Not if you lie to me on a regular basis. You're telling me that Miranda controls our future. She holds you by a money leash, as though you're a puppy bound to her will. That means everything I thought about us — all that I trusted and believed in when we married — has been a sham. We're a fraud sitting here."

Derek rubbed his face and then stood quickly. "I'm going for a drive. If the kids ask, tell them I've gone to get something special for them."

"Another lie?" Kim shot out.

"It's not a lie." He looked at her, his eyes red rimmed. "I have presents for them. I'll be back."

Before she could stop him, Derek strode to the sliding door, let himself into the house, and vanished. In moments, she heard his truck starting up in the driveway.

CHAPTER FIFTEEN

"I guess they trust him completely now. Letting him ride around on that skateboard the way they do."

Esther was shucking corn on the front porch with Charlie. They had purchased several bushels at the farmers' market in town, and they planned to cut off the kernels and freeze them in plastic zipper bags. In years past, Esther had enjoyed canning the fruits and vegetables Charlie grew in their garden. She made jellies, apple butter, and even salsa once or twice. They still had rows of filled Mason jars lining their pantry shelves, but she didn't bother with the canning anymore. It was just as easy to freeze most of their produce, and it turned out nearly as tasty.

"You couldn't pay me to get on one of those things." Charlie watched young Luke fly down the sloping roadway, his arms outstretched and his knees bent. He wore a helmet, but his big smile was clearly visible. "Can't say I wouldn't have tried it a few years back, though. Looks like fun. But I reckon I've got too many twinges in my hinges now."

Esther chuckled. "I wouldn't put it past you, Charlie. If that boy came up here and offered you a ride, you'd take him up on it. There's no fool like an old fool, my daddy used to say."

Charlie laid the ear of corn in his lap and rocked awhile as he watched Luke enjoying his birthday present. If the truth be known, Charlie didn't feel nearly as old as Esther made him out to be. He still took Boofer around the neighborhood on foot and in the golf cart several times a day. He worked the vegetable garden. He fooled with his tools in the garage, and he even built something useful now and then.

More significant, he was beginning to get an itch to go somewhere. Esther never wanted to wander far from home and her favorite destinations — the beauty salon, the church, the grocery store. But Charlie had been a mail carrier, and he liked to move around a little more. He wouldn't mind visiting the grandkids in California or taking a trip to Florida to see their daughter. But he knew if he mentioned it, Esther would turn him down right away. If the family wanted to get together, she said, let them come to the lake. Why make the old folks run all over the country?

It frustrated Charlie a little. He felt like he had one foot in the grave and was already starting to molder.

"I don't know when I've seen a boy so excited as Luke was when Derek brought that skateboard to the party." Esther tossed an ear of corn into the basket and brushed strands of corn silk from her lap. "And that purse he bought for Lydia! I have no doubt Miranda picked it out. Did you see the thing? Pink leather. I never would have sent it to school with a child the way Kim did. If you ask me, that was a church purse. But I guess Miranda's influence is getting stronger by the day."

"Speaking of Miranda . . . ," Charlie said, and then his words faded as the ritual began.

The thin blonde woman stepped onto the Finleys' deck, which was just visible from the angle of Charlie's rocking chair. Within moments, a gentle tinkling music — panpipes and brass bells — drifted through the air as Miranda slipped out of her long white robe.

For the first few weeks, Charlie had resisted watching the regular evening exhibition, but he finally gave in to temptation. Miranda Finley wasn't too many years younger than Esther, but land sakes, what a few stretching exercises could do for a woman! Lithe, tanned, fit as a fiddle, his neighbor began moving around on the deck — bending this way and that, rolling her head, waving her arms — all to the intoxicating aroma of some kind of incense.

"Charlie, what are you making calf eyes at?" Esther lifted up out of her chair and leaned over in his direction. "Oh, for pete's sake! Is Miranda Finley doing her nightly belly dance? Let me see. Scoot over."

They watched the theatrics for several minutes. Charlie thought this was one of Miranda's better nights. She managed to bend over backward so far she could almost touch the deck with the tips of her fingers. But Esther kept clucking and shaking her head as if the entire performance disgusted her.

"I don't know why Kim and Derek put up with that nonsense," she said as the music tapered off. "You wouldn't want me out dancing on the porch in my bathing suit every night, would you?"

Charlie could think of several responses to that — none of which would be well received. So he picked up an ear of corn and started pulling off the husks.

"Well?" Esther demanded. "Would you?"

"I wouldn't mind you belly dancing in our bedroom now and then," he said. He waggled his eyebrows at her. "If you catch my drift."

"Oh, Charlie!" Esther giggled. "You are such a nut."

Rocking and shucking, Charlie thought he might be a nut, but he sure wasn't dead. As far as Esther was concerned, he might as well be among the dearly departed for all the attention she paid him — at least in that particular room of their house. Still, she'd been a good wife all these years, and he couldn't complain. At least not out loud.

"Here comes Ashley!" Esther said, elbowing her husband as a small car pulled into their driveway. "She's bringing me some of her handmade beads. I'm going to order necklaces for everyone I know. How about that? All the Christmas presents taken care of in one fell swoop."

"Yahoo," Charlie said.

Ashley Hanes stepped out of her car and gave her long red hair a toss. "Hey, Mr. and Mrs. Moore," she called. "What's up?"

"Not much," Charlie said, watching Miranda Finley pull her robe back on and leave the deck. "Not much at all."

"I brought my whole collection of beads for you to look at." Without being asked, Ashley settled into the third chair on the porch. She pushed a stack of corn husks off the table onto the floor. Then she set out several plastic trays with countless tiny compartments, each bearing a different type of bead.

This was Charlie's signal to head for cover, but Esther was having none of that. She caught his arm just as he tried to rise. "You sit right there, Charles Moore, and help me choose these beads."

Obedient as ever, Charlie slumped back into his rocker. Truth to tell, sometimes he felt like retirement wasn't all it was cracked up to be. Maybe if a fellow could get out and about once in a while. Or kick it up with the little woman. But here he and Esther sat, shucking corn, waiting to croak.

"I like these swirls," Esther commented. "What do you think, Charlie? Can you picture these beads on May?"

He could barely remember his wife's niece, let alone know which beads she ought to wear. He mumbled, "Sure," and turned to their visitor. "Say, Ashley," he drawled as Esther resumed hunting through the plastic containers. "How's Brad coming along with his building project?"

The young woman looked up, flushed a bright pink, and dipped her head again. "He hasn't done anything on it for a while."

"It'll make a nice garage for that new truck of his."

Esther lifted her head and frowned. "Or whatever they decide to use it for," she said, tipping her head and flashing her eyes toward Ashley, apparently to remind Charlie about the young couple's dispute over the purpose of the room.

"I guess Brad got a building permit downtown and cleared his plans with the Deepwater Cove Association," Charlie speculated. "He'd know all about that sort of thing — him working for a contractor."

"I guess so," Ashley said. "How do you like these orange ones, Mrs. Moore?"

"Not for Christmas gifts, dear. Orange is a little much; don't you think?"

Esther had laid a line of beads across the table, and Ashley was jotting who would get which necklace in a little notebook. The women discussed names, ages, hair color, and other such foolishness for females Charlie hadn't thought about in years. Clearly this was great fun for Esther, but he felt a strong urge to go inside and turn on the TV.

"Anyway, we might not finish that room,"

344

Ashley said suddenly. "At least not right away."

The idea of an unfinished construction project in the neighborhood didn't sit well with Charlie — especially when the house next door was for sale. "Brad running out of time?"

"Money," Ashley informed him. "Do you like these green stripes, Mrs. Moore? I think they go really well with the purple glass beads. Maybe with some small gold ones as separators."

Charlie studied the green, purple, and gold combo and thought it was the craziest mishmash of colors he'd ever seen. But lo and behold, Esther starting cooing like a lovebird. Said she might even want a strand for herself.

Charlie thought he'd move the conversation back a ways. "Money's always tight when you're just starting out," he commented. "Maybe you and Brad could take out a second mortgage. We did that one time when the kids were little. Wasn't easy making two house payments, but we managed."

Ashley's pretty eyes settled on him for a moment. "I'm thinking about getting another job. I could work during the day and keep my position at the country club too. I never wanted to live like my parents — with the ice cream store always on the verge of shutting down. But if these beads don't start selling better, I'll have to look around for more work."

Charlie appreciated the young woman's frankness, and he understood about financial worries. Still, it would help if Brad Hanes didn't park himself at the bar every night. And what had he been thinking when he bought that big truck? Not to mention having a mortgage and starting to add on to the house. Kids these days didn't seem to have the ability to think ahead very far.

"Pick out a nice set of beads for me, Ashley," Charlie requested. "Let's make it three strands and dip one of them down kind of long."

Esther gave a little squawk. "Oh, Charlie, are you getting me an early Christmas present, you silly goose? Don't you know better than to order a gift right in front of me?"

"Indeed I do," he intoned. "You have taught me well, woman. This necklace isn't for you. I thought I'd have Ashley create something that Cody can give his aunt for Christmas. That way, in case he forgets to buy her something, he'll be covered."

At the mention of Cody's name, all three

people on the porch fell silent. Esther messed around with the beads while Ashley wrote in her notebook. Charlie thought about the young man who had helped clean their house throughout the summer. Cody hadn't been gone long, but already the spiderwebs were starting to build up and get messy along the eaves, and the windows could use a washing.

But doing chores wasn't the main reason Charlie missed Cody. There was something special about the boy. The way he always smiled and greeted people with a wave of the hand. The way he would suddenly start spouting Bible verses or discussing his favorite subjects — chocolate cake and hot dogs. Deepwater Cove didn't seem the same without the familiar sight of a slender, carefree figure strolling along the roads from one house to another.

"I miss Cody," Ashley spoke up finally. "It's hard to believe he just up and left us."

"He wanted to go see his aunt," Esther said. "That's understandable."

"Did you get a letter, Mrs. Moore?"

"Yes, but he gave the same information to all of us. Must've just written one letter and then copied it over and over again for each person in the neighborhood."

Charlie grunted. "He ought to have told

us what he thought about his new life. The whole letter was nothing but an account of the bus ride and then a long description of his aunt's house. Moldings around the window frames and brass doorknobs. Who cares about that? I want to know if he likes the woman and if he's happy there."

"He assumes we know that," Esther said, patting her husband's knee. "Marylou Goss is his aunt. She wanted to reunite what's left of her family. Of course he likes her. You know Cody. He likes everyone."

"Well, that's true — unfortunately for us. If he could live out in the woods and eat bugs, he can survive anywhere. So I guess we might as well start getting used to it."

At the thought of never seeing Cody's curly hair and bright blue eyes again, Charlie had an awful feeling he might choke up. So he pushed himself out of his rocker and headed for the house. "Corn husks, beads, and belly dancers," he muttered. "I've had about all the fun I can stand. See you two ladies later."

Inside, he settled into his recliner and pressed the Power button on the TV remote control. Through an open window, he could hear his wife giving Ashley all the details of Miranda Finley's most recent exhibition. Thank goodness the game shows were on.

Charlie raised the volume just a tad higher than usual; then he leaned back in his chair and shut his eyes.

Working the day shift gave Derek the opportunity to share the evening meal with his family that week. He had made a valiant effort to enjoy the time with his loved ones, but Kim's long silences had erected a definite barrier between them. After his confession on the deck during the twins' birthday party, he had returned to the house bearing birthday gifts he had picked out earlier for them. Despite the kids' joy over the purse and the skateboard, Kim wouldn't even look at her husband.

The rest of the week, they barely spoke each morning, and dinners were taken up with the twins' usual banter. Miranda's quick trip to St. Louis had also impacted mealtimes. Upon her return, Derek's mother felt compelled to describe Cody's departure on the bus, her trouble with the moving and storage company, and her efforts to select a real estate agent and put her house on the market. Kim hardly said a word except to respond to questions.

That Friday's pizza night was proceeding as usual, but Derek sensed that most of the fun was missing as the family picked out ingredients and layered them onto the dough. He knew things with Kim were bad, but he had no intention of reopening that topic. Instead, he wanted to act as normal as possible. Kim and the kids had somehow worked things out with Miranda, so they had an interesting array of toppings to choose from. After the pizzas had baked, Derek tried to liven up the meal as everyone sat around the dining room table.

"Now, what is this green stuff, Mom?" he asked, pointing to a sprig on a slice of pizza. "You know how I feel about green stuff."

"That is basil, for your information." Miranda smiled at her son. "You know exactly what that *green stuff* is, young man, because I grew basil in the backyard herb garden every summer. And you used to pick it for me."

"Which kind do you like better, Derek?" Lydia asked. "Grandma Finley's pizza or ours?"

Derek could see that bullet headed his way, and he quickly dodged it. "Aren't all these pizzas ours?" He pointed to the slices on his plate. "This kind with the pepperoni and this one with the sausage and this one here with the green stuff?"

"But which one tastes best?" Lydia was swinging her legs under the table, which made her bounce up and down on the seat. "I like ours best, because it has tomato sauce. Grandma Finley's doesn't."

"Hers stinks," Luke declared.

"Hey, bud, that's no way to talk about our dinner."

"Oh, Derek, you used to the say the same thing," Miranda reminded him. "I don't know why I bothered."

"Tiffany broke up with her boyfriend," Lydia announced. "She hates him now. She burned all his letters."

"What does Tiffany have to do with pizza?" Luke asked.

"The last time I ate pizza was at Tiffany's house. Her mother's a waitress at the pizza place in Camdenton, so they have it almost every night. And that's when Tiffany told me she broke up with her boyfriend, so we burned the letters."

"You're not supposed to play with fire."

"We weren't. We burned them on the barbecue grill in the backyard. Then we burned the letters she wrote to him but hadn't given him yet. Did you know that glitter ink sparkles and crackles when you burn it? It's cool."

Derek kept an ear on the conversation and an eye on his wife. Kim was performing her usual mealtime rituals. But not once did she look at her husband.

How long was this going to continue? They had always enjoyed each other's company whenever they were together. He teased her, and she giggled. He complimented her, and she blushed. These days Derek felt like he was living with an ice cube. The chill extended from the moment he opened his eyes in the morning until the last sight of Kim's back turned toward him at night.

As the meal ended and everyone began clearing the table, the twins announced that they had decided to watch a movie together. Miranda declared that she was going to her bedroom to work. Derek wasn't certain how it had happened, but his mother had found a way to spend her free time. It seemed Esther Moore and his mother had formed a partnership that had some sort of connection to Ashley Hanes. Jewelry, he thought, but he wasn't sure.

As Kim started the dishwasher, Derek reflected on the negative changes in their marriage. Had the problems between them begun with the arrival of his mother? Or had Derek's failure to be totally honest with Kim caused this widening rift? Or could it be a combination of the things that life had tossed their way?

While he didn't know what had started them down this wintry path, Derek had no doubt what he wanted to happen. He wanted the arctic winds to cease and a summer breeze to return to his life. He longed to hold his wife in his arms again. Where had she gone? And how could he get her back?

If there was a real God and not just the invisible power Derek trusted to keep himself from gambling, why didn't He step into the lives of good people?

For that matter, Derek wondered, what kept God from feeling real? He wanted to be a part of Kim's whole world, but he couldn't figure out how. They were so different. As hard as he'd tried to convince her that those differences could be worked out, now he wasn't so sure.

As Kim walked past him toward the living room, Derek considered reaching out and taking her hand. But he didn't want to risk another confrontation.

Show me what to do. He ground out the words deep in his heart. *God, if You're there, help me. I need her. I want my wife to love me again. I need to get her love back, and I don't know how. Please make it happen.*

But of course, nothing did happen. Derek didn't know why he had even hoped it might. Whatever changes had occurred in his life were the ones forged by attending GA meetings and constantly working the steps that kept him clean. Now his participation in the organization was routine, so much a part of him that he never mentioned it to anyone and hardly gave it a second thought. In the same way, his loyalty to a higher power had been part of the process he had used to break free, and he still acknowledged it in his effort to stay that way.

With a sigh of frustration, he wandered into the living room. As usual, Kim was nowhere to be seen. Anything to avoid him.

As he settled into a recliner and flipped on the television, he heard one of the twins dashing up the stairs and into the room. It was Lydia.

"Where's our movie?" she sang out. "We can't find our movie! Where is it, Derek? Have you seen it?"

"Check the shelf under the TV," he told her.

Crazy kid. Always trailing bits and pieces of everything she touched. As she knelt in front of the bookshelf, he sat forward and flipped through a stack of movie cases on the table beside his chair.

"Here it is, tater tot," he called. He tossed

the case to her.

Lydia leaped up and caught the movie; then she headed for the basement again. As she passed his chair, she paused middash. "Thanks, Dad-o." Throwing her arms around his neck, she gave him a kiss on the cheek. "That's what Lukey and I are calling you now. Dad-o. Hope you like it!"

Before Derek could respond, Lydia had skipped off and was pounding back down the stairs to the basement. *Dad-o.* He thought about the word for a moment. Well, it wasn't bad. Through the years, he had given the twins dozens of nicknames. Nice to have one of his own. Especially one with that treasured syllable — *Dad.*

Slightly encouraged, Derek clicked through the channels. A news show. A foul-mouthed comedian. A sitcom. Maybe his talk with Lydia had actually made a differ-ence, he speculated. Come to think of it, she had been nicer to him since that night on the front porch. Neither twin had been spewing the "I hate this family" refrain lately. He pressed the channel-change but-ton again. A ball game. A crime serial. A fishing show.

Fishing.

The word hit Derek like a bolt of light-ning. His finger paused on the remote. What had Charlie told him about communicating with women? *You've got to know what you want and then fish until you catch it.* Charlie had wanted to eat shrimp at Aunt Mamie's.

Not long ago, Derek had wanted Lydia's trust. He had won it by "fishing" for it that night on the porch. He knew exactly what he wanted from Kim, too. He wanted her love.

What could he use for bait?

Charlie had used a simple query. "What's wrong, Esther, honey?"

It had worked on Lydia and Esther. But would it succeed with Kim? Something so light and obvious? And if it did — if she took the bait — what would Derek pull out of the sea of their marital discord? His wife's love . . . or an ill-tempered shark?

The very idea of trying Charlie's technique on Kim made Derek's palms sweat. Could he do it? Should he? He tried to recall the things the older man had told him. *It's just like fishing, just like fishing. . . .*

"Okay," Derek murmured out loud as he stood and squared his shoulders. It might not work, but what was the alternative? Living with a silent, angry wife for the rest of his life? Or worse — losing the marriage he had sabotaged in his determination to make it work?

After trudging back and forth through the house, even checking the garage to see if her car was there, Derek finally found Kim sitting inside the screened area of their deck. She had taken her file box out to the table and was paying bills — a chore she hated.

Bad timing, Derek thought. Better head back into the house. He swallowed, frozen for a moment; then he lifted his chin. No, he could do this. He would — but not on his own. *God, if You're there, please help me.* He said the words inside his head. But he knew the request wasn't simply a thought. It was a prayer.

CHAPTER SIXTEEN

Kim could feel Derek's eyes on her as she wrote the check for their auto insurance. He had stepped onto the deck and was standing nearby, staring at her. When she left the house earlier, she had switched on the overhead light and pulled the chain to activate the fan. That meant he could see her clearly, but she could only sense his lurking presence.

Obviously Derek wanted something from her, but Kim didn't have any intention of granting it — no matter what it was.

Who did he think he was, anyway, expecting her to acknowledge him? She knew who he was — that stranger in the shadows. He was a liar. Cheat. Gambler. Addict. Manipulator. He was selfish and egotistic. A user. A traitor. A con artist. Indifferent to religion. Unable to express emotion. Hopeless at communication. He was everything she despised and abhorred.

Trembling with anger at the thought of the man she had so foolishly married, Kim tore off the check and stuffed it into the envelope. She could hear Derek's footsteps on the deck. Moving closer, edging toward her. It didn't matter to her if he stood there all night. He might speak, but she wouldn't answer. She couldn't trust anything he would say. He was a liar.

Liar, liar, liar.

She picked up the next bill. Electricity. With the twins and Miranda home all summer, the amount was sky-high. Now she understood that all the money she and Derek earned went to pay bills and to his mother. Not a penny of it became their own. She had trusted her husband when he promised he would add what little was left each month to a savings account he had started when he lived in St. Louis. Little did she know it had instead gone into repaying Miranda for bailing him out of his gambling debts.

Now he was opening the door and stepping into the small screened area where she sat. She didn't look up.

"Hey there," he said.

Kim began to write another check. It was easier this way. Living with him in silence. Not even bothering to try to talk. She had wasted so much energy trying to plumb her husband's emotional depths — only to learn he was nothing more than a stagnant pond.

Derek pulled out one of the green metal chairs that surrounded the table. Sitting down, he let out a deep sigh. At least she didn't have to smell beer on his breath. With Joe, she'd had that constant issue to manage. Of course, Kim knew that no addiction could be managed by anyone but the addict. She had discovered that long ago in her childhood.

Clearing his throat, Derek folded his hands and set them on the table. Then he spoke. "What's wrong, Kim, honey?"

She looked up at him. *"What's wrong?* Did you just ask me *what's wrong?"*

"Yes," he confirmed in a voice that was barely audible. His eyes met hers. "That's what I said. What's wrong, Kim, honey?"

For a moment, she almost couldn't breathe as the rage rose inside her, bubbled up to the top of her throat, stung the insides of her nostrils, blistered like steam in her ears. The man was an idiot! A total idiot! This college-educated, ten-year veteran of the state Water Patrol was a complete idiot!

"Well," she said evenly. "Let's see. Hmmm. It's so hard to choose just one thing."

He leaned forward. "Okay. I understand that."

"Really? Amazing." She could hear the sarcasm dripping from her words, but she had no idea if her lamebrain husband had the ability to decipher verbal intonations.

Still staring at her, Derek nodded. She hardly knew what to make of it. He was actually looking right at her. Usually he stared at the television. At the kids or his mother. At the lake, a tree, a soaring bird. Or at the message screen on his cell phone. Now he was gazing directly at her.

"You want to know what's wrong," she stated. It wasn't a question. Just a repetition of his words to make sure she'd heard him right. "You want to know what's wrong with me."

"Yes," he repeated, nodding. His eyes were still focused on her face, and he wasn't moving even a finger.

Kim leaned back in her chair. "Why not begin with your gambling confession?" she asked airily. "Unless that was just a bad dream I had."

"It wasn't."

She straightened and pointed a finger at him. "You, Derek Finley, are a liar. The worst kind of liar — habitual and deliberate. You kept the truth from me. When you put a lie into a relationship, I don't think we call that a relationship anymore."

"You're right. I lied to you."

"You never once mentioned that you had a gambling addiction and were deeply in debt."

"You're right. I kept that from you."

"You never said you were sending all our savings to your mother."

"No, Kim, I didn't."

"You never told me that Miranda held power over you by keeping you on a leash like a little puppy. You're not the brave, strong, wonderful man I thought I'd married. You're nothing but a puppet. A mama's boy."

She could see him swallow, and she knew her angry words had hit home. At any moment, he would strike back. He would argue with her, tell her she was wrong, rationalize everything. Or maybe he would hit her, like Joe had done. She was ready for that. She could take it.

Derek knotted his fingers together, squeezing them so hard that the blood stopped and his knuckles turned white. "You . . . feel . . . betrayed by me," he said slowly. "You took a brave step in remarrying, and now you think it was a mistake."

"*You* were the mistake," she said, jabbing

her index finger at him. "You, you, you. Don't you get it? I'm repeating my own mistakes over and over again! I'm as big an idiot as you are. In fact, I'm a gambler, too. I took a foolish risk, and I never should have done that. I knew the Bible warned against marrying a nonbeliever, but I thought you were so different and amazing. I thought it wouldn't matter. But I was wrong. Your character is flawed. And so is mine. We're just a couple of stupid . . . dumb . . ."

Kim's eyes filled with tears as she continued. "We're both fools. We never should have married each other. I'm not the right kind of person to be a wife. I don't even know what it takes to make a good marriage. I have too much baggage. And now you're just one more filthy, damaged suitcase I have to lug around. Another mistake. Another terrible, awful blunder."

As the tears rolled down her cheeks, Kim pushed away her husband's reaching hands. No, she wouldn't let him comfort her. No compliments scattered like candy. No gentle hands soothing the pain. She deserved to hurt. She had given control of her life to God and then taken it back the moment she married Derek Finley.

"Kim," he was saying now, pressing his palms flat on his thighs. "You're right. I am

363

an addict and a liar. I wanted to marry you so much that I deceived you. I am flawed. And I'm powerless. I acknowledge those facts every time I step through the door at a GA meeting or fight the urge to hand over my money for a scratch-off lottery ticket. When I call you up and tell you I'm working late and then go to a meeting, I know I'm a liar. You're right to be angry with me."

Wiping her cheeks with her fingers, Kim sniffled. She couldn't believe he was admitting it. Staring at him through blurred vision, she felt she was seeing yet another side of this man she was determined to despise. Once he had been her knight in shining armor, her dream lover, her best friend. Then he had become her worst nightmare — so horribly fallen from the ivory pedestal on which she had placed him that she was sure he was broken to pieces. And now here he was . . . the broken man . . . crawling toward her . . . holding up the shards of himself. . . .

"How long?" she asked him. "How long have you been clean?"

"I got my eleven-year pin last month. Here. And here's my Combo Book." He took the pin and a yellow pamphlet from his hip pocket and dropped them onto the table. He chuckled without humor. "In

364

Gamblers Anonymous, I'm what we call a 'trusted servant.' Like a sponsor for alcoholics. People phone me, and I help them get through a bad time. There's a guy right now I'm especially worried about. I'm afraid he might be getting in too deep, and I've been talking to him a lot."

"Is that who the mysterious phone calls have been from? Why couldn't you just tell me?"

Derek sighed. "I was afraid you would leave me. GA work takes a lot of patience, and most of us are fairly unrealistic, insecure, and immature. Despite all my years, I still fit the mold pretty well." He paused and looked at the floor. "I guess you've figured that out."

Kim set her fingertips on the well-worn booklet. He must have read it every day. It must have been with him constantly. How could she not have known? Was she blind?

"You told me your mother was your higher power," she whispered.

"I shouldn't have said that. I do acknowledge an authority outside myself — and it sure isn't my mom. Having her around makes it hard to keep things in perspective. She's convinced that forcing me to repay the debt keeps me clean. I've tried to explain, but she has no idea how GA works.

She doesn't want to understand."

"Then who is your higher power?"

Derek shrugged. "Something bigger and stronger than I am. Someone. I don't know, Kim. I don't have a name for it."

She dropped her head on her arms. "Oh, why did I marry you? You're not even close to sharing my faith in God. Now here I am stuck with you and your mother. Both the same."

"My mother and I are *not* the —" As if suddenly aware of the vehemence in his voice, Derek cut himself off. He tightened his hands into fists again. "You feel like my mother and I are alike," he said. "And that makes you angry."

Kim sniffled, knowing her tears were dripping onto the utility bill. But she couldn't lift her head. "You know what's worse? The twins now love her. The other day they told me they're glad she's moved in with us permanently. I can't believe I'll have to put up with Miranda and her criticisms, her weird pizza, her tai chi, her incense. I'm faced with this wicked presence infecting me and my children for the rest of my life. Grandma Finley, spouting her phony spirituality and influencing the family in ways that terrify me. And you . . . you just sit there."

This time his exhaled breath was shaky. "Okay, I hear you," he whispered.

"What do you hear?" she fired back at him, lifting her head. "What do you even think I'm saying, Derek?"

He was quiet for a long moment. Kim was about to deride his silence when he spoke.

"You're saying you want a stronger, more influential male in the house. And you're right to expect that. I'm so used to my mother's ways that when she came here, I didn't see how she was affecting us. I didn't challenge her or stand up to her, because her presence felt normal to me, and I hoped the trouble with you would blow over. But I don't want her to dominate our family. I don't want her manipulating anyone — especially you or the kids. Or me." He stood suddenly, scraping back the chair. "And I don't want her bizarre . . ."

Before he could finish his own sentence, Derek turned and pushed through the screen door, slamming it against the side of the house. He strode onto the deck and wrenched his mother's small wooden altar from the corner under the eave where she had nailed it.

Half frightened and half in shock, Kim hurried after her husband as he snatched up Miranda's CD player, her incense burner, and her little statuettes. Cradling those objects in one arm, he reared back like a baseball pitcher and hurled the altar off the deck. The CD player and incense burner went next. Finally the statues and other items sailed one by one through the moonlight into the darkness beyond the deck.

Kim leaned against the railing as she heard a series of splashes from the lake. Gripping the wood beam, she held her breath. What had just happened? What did this mean?

"There," Derek announced, dusting off his palms. His voice was almost jaunty when he spoke again. "Now, what else? What's wrong, Kim, honey? Can you tell me that?"

She searched her mind. Suddenly all the things she had piled up against him didn't seem so huge. The gambling, the bank account, the twins, the family rules, even Miranda . . . they were crumbling, fragmenting into grains of sand as her broken husband mended and stood tall again.

"Nothing," she managed to whisper.

"Then may I have your permission to spell out the list?"

"Yes."

"Gambling," he stated. "Can I tell you about that?"

"Of course. I wish you would."

"I have to go to GA meetings. So, from now on, I'll call and tell you what I'm doing, and then I'll go. I'm eleven years clean, and I don't expect to fall off the wagon. But GA is a part of my world, and I should have shared it with you. I'll try to start doing that."

"Okay."

"*Debt.* There's no way I can erase it. I made mistakes, and now I have to pay for them — literally. But I promise I'll stop putting your money toward paying it down. Maybe one day we'll inherit my mother's estate, but until then —"

"Use my money too, Derek," she said suddenly. "If we can let this be a decision we make together, I won't mind."

He eyed her for a moment. Then he nodded. *"Church,"* he said. "Another issue. From next Sunday forward, every time I'm working the late shift or have a free day, I'll go with you. In fact, I'll request Sundays off. I can't promise to be good at doing church. I won't say I know God the way you do. But . . . but I do believe He's here . . . and He . . ." Suddenly Derek laughed. "Well, come to think of it, He came through for me tonight when I couldn't think what else to do but pray."

"You prayed?"

Spreading his arms, Derek looked into Kim's eyes. "I love you, honey. I love you so much. I'm sorry I hurt you and lied to you. I don't have any excuses. Just know that I'll do my best . . . that I already am doing my best to be the man you want. The husband you deserve. Can you try to start trusting me again? Can you love me too? Even just a little?"

Before she knew it, Kim had slipped into her husband's embrace. His arms came around her, wrapping her tightly against him. She laid her cheek on his shoulder and let the tears fall. It wasn't perfect, this marriage they had cobbled together. She saw the flimsy construction of their hastily built foundation all too clearly now. So the cracks had begun to show. Would the walls cave in next? Would the roof collapse?

"What can *I* do, Derek?" she asked him as he rocked her gently. "How can I help make us better?"

He fell quiet, and she trailed her fingers up and down his spine as he considered her question. Finally, when he spoke, his voice was low and throaty. "You could let me out of my shining armor. I'm a lot better at patrolling Party Cove than slaying dragons."

Kim nearly said something about his

mother, but she decided against it. She would forever remember those distant splashes in the night — the definite sounds of a dragon's death throes.

"You might go to a Gam-Anon meeting," he continued. "Gam-Anon is for families. Maybe if you met with other wives and husbands of gamblers, you could understand me a little better."

"Okay. I'll go. What else?"

"Try to accept our differences. Is it so bad that I'm a quiet man? that I don't have a lot to tell you about my work each day? that my inner thoughts aren't all that deep and profound? And isn't it okay that I like to show I love you by telling you how beautiful you are? My compliments aren't candy at a parade, Kim. They're the truth. Maybe I don't do loads of laundry or cook great meals to express my feelings. That's your way. My way is to say that I think you're the most wonderful, amazing, gorgeous creature on God's green earth. And I mean that."

"Oh, Derek," she said, feeling the heat rise in her cheeks. Then she spoke the words she had been pondering for months now. "How about a baby? Would that help us?"

To her surprise, he shook his head. "Let's wait, Kim. You know how much I want

371

another child. But we need some time right here. With my mother, Luke's diabetes, this new honesty . . . we need to rebuild. I need to become a better fisherman."

"What does this have to do with fishing?" she asked, puzzled.

"Talk to Charlie Moore sometime. Maybe he'll let you in on the secret."

Kim tightened her arms around her husband's chest. "I'm in the mood for rebuilding," she told him. "Or fishing. Or whatever."

At that, she felt Derek's biceps suddenly tighten. "Whatever?" he asked.

"Sure," she murmured.

With a deep chuckle, he lowered his head and kissed her. "*Whatever* sounds *great* to me."

As Patsy finished spraying Esther Moore's weekly set-and-style, she realized she did not have a good feeling about things in Deepwater Cove. Summer was winding to a close, and too many troublesome situations had been left hanging. Patsy wanted all her problems — and everyone else's — tied up with neat little bows. But that just wasn't happening.

The most recent meeting of the Tea Lovers' Club had confirmed that not a single woman had received a second letter from Cody Goss. Shortly after arriving in Kansas, he had written to nearly everyone in the neighborhood — with the exact same news in each letter. But that was it. Not another word. Patsy had considered asking Miranda Finley if she still had a phone number for Cody's aunt.

But the thought of Miranda brought up yet another issue. A big one. Derek's mother was no longer a happy camper at the Finley house. She had moved in. Permanently. To complicate matters, Derek had decided that if his mother was moving in, some other things were moving out. Permanently.

Charlie Moore had discovered one of those things washed up on the lakeshore a few mornings ago. He had taken the former altar home to Esther, who had placed the entire problem in Patsy's lap.

"Well, what do you think we should do?" Esther asked her for the fifteenth time that afternoon. "Should we return it? Or keep it? Or should we throw it away ourselves?"

Patsy covered one of Esther's ears and plastered a curlicue into place with mega-hold spray. She knew she'd hear no end of complaining if a single strand of that snowy halo wandered from its assigned position. A tornado could land on Esther Moore's head and not a hair would budge.

"The question is," Patsy said, "how did the thing end up in the lake? Are you positive Derek is the culprit? Or could it have been Kim?"

"Or maybe it was Jennifer Hansen," Esther suggested with a little gasp. "You recall how she and Miranda argued about religion a few weeks back? Maybe she crept over to the Finley house under cover of darkness and threw everything over the side of their deck. She referred to the statues as idols, you'll remember. At least, that's what Brenda told me when she related the whole argument. I wasn't a personal observer. Were you?"

"I heard the two of them discussing matters of faith," Patsy said. She used the end of a rat-tail comb to lift and define a few more of Esther's silver curls. "But I don't think that's the sort of thing Jennifer would do. She's such a sweet young woman."

"Oh, don't we know it? Every time I come in here, I see her staring down at me from those portraits Cody painted. That boy was in love, Patsy. I'm telling you, he was truly besotted. How could he just go off and leave us the way he did?"

Patsy gave the answer she had told herself over and over. "His aunt wanted him."

"I surely do miss him. In fact, I can see why Jennifer Hansen is so kind to him. He was a handsome fellow once we got him cleaned up. And he was learning so much with Brenda's help. Did you see how clear and perfect his penmanship was in those letters he wrote us? Not to mention what a fine young Christian man he turned out to be. Well, to tell you the truth, Patsy, I was halfway to loving that boy like a son."

"Cody had us all wrapped around his little finger; that's for sure." To keep from crying, Patsy turned her thoughts to the other problem weighing on her heart. Esther's use of the word *halfway* had reminded Patsy of her next-door neighbor in the strip of shops.

Pete Roberts had been back to church since their spat over the Fourth of July lawn chair incident, but he didn't seem to be one iota closer to the Lord than he'd ever been. He trudged to Bible study and worship service every Sunday morning, same as before. Then he and Patsy ate lunch at Aunt Mamie's Good Food, and that appeared to be all Pete cared to do. In fact, she had a sneaking suspicion that he had figured out a way to sleep with his eyes open during the sermon. One time he even let out a thunderous snore that startled everyone for two rows around them.

"I have to tell you that they did look like idols," Esther was saying as she preened in front of the mirror. Once Patsy finished with the do, Esther liked to take a hand mirror and check all the way around to the back to make sure each curl was cemented into position.

"During the party for Cody and the twins, I went over and took a closer look," she continued, poking a finger at a stray wisp near her neck. "You know, the big one was made out of brass. But she also had a clay one, some pink silk flowers, a few sticks of incense, and some other things. The altar floated in and got caught on a piece of driftwood near the shore. Charlie thinks the brass statue is ten feet underwater, but we both saw it at the party. Which reminds me of Cody all over again. Oh, Patsy, how are we going to get that boy out of our hearts?"

"Do we have a choice, Esther?"

The older woman stood from the chair and removed the cape from her shoulders. "I do try to count my blessings, but right now, it's all I can do to think of any. I guess we have the Labor Day barbecue to look forward to. And we can be grateful that young Luke is doing so much better managing his diabetes. I don't suppose we'll have another crisis like we did on the Fourth of

July. I guess you heard that Ashley Hanes is going to have a necklace sale at the next event. That was Miranda's idea, of course. She's behind most of the strategy for selling Ashley's beadwork. Or she was until her little religious items ended up in the lake. Charlie says he never sees her out on the deck doing her exercises, and you know how Charlie keeps an eye on things in the neighborhood."

"Yes, I certainly do," Patsy said. She led Esther toward the cash register. "I hope Miranda is happy there at home despite losing her spiritual doodads. You know how one person's mood can affect everyone else. When my mother had Alzheimer's, sometimes it was all I could do to keep my spirits up."

"Bless your heart, sweetie pie. You did have a rough time taking care of her, didn't you? Well, you're on your own now, though I don't know for how long. You and Pete look awfully cozy together on Sunday mornings."

"We're just friends," Patsy said.

"Sure you are." Esther gave a coy smile as she patted the back of her hair. "Oh, honey, nothing would make me happier than to see you get married. You have the biggest, best heart in all Missouri. And if Pete can win it,

I say good for him!"

Patsy slipped Esther's usual tip into her pocket and walked with her to the door. "I don't think Pete is trying to win my heart," she said. "And I'm not at all confident that Miranda is doing the Finley family much good. But you know what upsets me the most?"

Esther nodded. "Yes, I do."

At the same moment, the women hugged and whispered the word in each other's ear.

"Cody."

CHAPTER SEVENTEEN

Kim placed a pitcher of lemonade and two ice-filled glasses on a tray. She reached into the cookie jar and set a couple of vanilla wafers on a plate for good measure. Through the sliding glass door, she could see Miranda sunning herself on the deck.

Feeling like she was headed for the execution block, Kim lifted the tray and started toward the deck. The twins had gone boating with their stepfather that afternoon — a plot Kim and Derek had concocted together — and now it was time to do the dreaded deed. Ever since the night they had discussed their problems, Kim and Derek had felt better about their marriage. Not perfect, but better. At least they were speaking as they tried to work out the issues that had come between them.

Miranda, on the other hand, had not taken the loss of her altar lightly. In fact, she was furious. She had stopped speaking to all of them and refused to leave her bedroom except for her daily sunbathing sessions.

So it was now or never.

Tray balanced on one arm, Kim opened the sliding glass door with her free hand and stepped onto the deck. While speaking with Charlie Moore the past Sunday after church, Kim had learned the significance of Derek's "fishing" system. But in her mind, the technique could be boiled down to the simple word *listening.* She actually did it all the time.

Kim believed that most women were pretty good at paying attention. Of course, she knew there was going to be one hard part — keeping her own mouth shut. That wouldn't be easy, especially if Miranda began to criticize her. But Kim had promised Derek she would try fishing for her mother-in-law's acceptance.

"I brought us a pitcher of lemonade," Kim began, setting the tray on a small, glass-topped table between the two reclining deck chairs. "Derek just phoned to say they'll be home in about an hour. Luke has caught three crappie, and Lydia hooked into a catfish that nearly pulled her overboard."

Eyes closed, Miranda continued basking in utter silence.

Kim sat down, stretched out on the deck

chair, and tried to imagine enduring the humidity for more than a few minutes. She poured lemonade into the glasses and offered one to her mother-in-law. "Something cold to drink, Miranda?"

Not a word of response.

Kim set the glass down on the tray again and took a sip of her own drink. The lake was quiet today, glassy and bright, a green-gray color that reminded her of polished steel. Not a single bird flew in the cloudless sky. Even the trees seemed exhausted by the heat, their leaves withered at the edges and their branches saggy.

Recalling Derek's repeated insistence that Kim begin her fishing session by using the right "bait," she moistened her lips. Then she spoke the words her husband had told her to say. "What's wrong, Miranda?"

No answer.

"Miranda? What's bothering you?"

Nothing.

Forget that kind of bait, Kim thought. She already knew what was wrong. Miranda had made her feelings abundantly clear the other night. Kim decided that what might be best was a guaranteed "fishing" technique she liked to use in Dr. Groene's office to locate the exact source of a problem. When a patient came in complaining about something aching and sore — jaw, tooth, gum, lip, tongue, even throat — she listened carefully. Then she repeated exactly what she believed the person had told her.

She was often wrong.

When people were in pain, Kim had learned, they mumbled and fumbled, pointed here and there, tried to describe the indescribable. Often they babbled about things that weren't important — like where they had been when the trouble started, or how their cousin had diagnosed the problem as something he'd had years ago. It took lots of back and forth, with Kim doing her own poking, rephrasing, and echoing her patient's words, before the real problem finally came to light.

Maybe Miranda's pain and anger would emerge the same way. Kim took another sip of lemonade and cast out her own form of bait.

"Miranda, I can understand why you're upset about Derek throwing your altar into the lake," she began, reciting almost verbatim the words her mother-in-law had used a few days ago after she discovered the items missing. "You believe he did it because he was trying to please me."

Miranda finally responded, her tone icy. "Well? Am I wrong?"

Kim decided not to answer. Instead, she kept repeating her mother-in-law's own words. "I realize you think that no one in the family cares about you or is sensitive to your individuality. You believe we don't appreciate what you've done for us, and we take you for granted."

"That's exactly right," Miranda snapped. Eyes still closed, she reached for her sunglasses and slipped them on. "I might as well be a cockroach the way you treat me."

Stung, Kim thought of all the meals she had cooked, all the laundry she had done, all the times she had purposely included Miranda in family activities — not only trying to make her feel welcome and comfortable but actually providing for the ungrateful woman's basic needs. How dare Miranda say they treated her like a cockroach? That was ridiculous!

Fighting the urge to lash out or retreat into the air-conditioned house, Kim took another long drink of her cold lemonade.

"I see that you really believe we resent your presence in the house," she said. "You must think that Derek's decision to throw away your religious items is evidence of that."

"It most certainly is!" Miranda barked. "My son is an intelligent man, and he knew very well how much those things meant to me. That altar was my place to meditate and reflect on my life. It was the only way I had found to reach out and touch my inner divinity."

"Your soul?" Kim queried, hoping she had chosen the right word.

"Well, that shows just how much you understand! The soul is a Christian concept — something that lets you believe in an afterlife instead of reincarnation. The spirit of divinity, the essence of the Creator, a spark of holiness lies within every thing and every person in this world. My collection of crystals and my dream catcher were ways to receive and conserve that celestial energy. Now the box where I kept my most precious crystals is at the bottom of the lake. Buddha and my other images helped me to meditate on the things they stood for and the truths they taught. Now they're in the lake too. You think it's all about Jesus, Jesus, Jesus, but let me assure you that your narrow-mindedness keeps you from the self-actualization and self-completion available to you through other spiritual paths."

Though Kim was trying her best to hear Miranda out, she couldn't come anywhere near agreement. Countless arguments filtered through her mind. But Kim knew that if she was ever to gain her mother-in-law's trust, she had to begin with a relationship of mutual respect. Shouting their opposing beliefs back and forth at each other would get them nowhere. So Kim swallowed hard and cast out her fishing line one more time.

"I can see how hurt you are," she said as gently as she could. "Some of the things we've said have really wounded you. What Derek did the other night must have felt as though your own son had purposely injured you."

To Kim's surprise, she noticed that Miranda's lower lip was trembling. It wasn't much of a sign, but it showed that Kim's words had found their mark. And maybe, just maybe, she was close to hooking and reeling in the object of this fishing expedition: her mother-in-law's acceptance.

"Miranda, may I please tell you how sorry I am?" Kim murmured. "You came here at a time when Derek and I had run out of options, and you've done a great job with the twins. I apologize that you haven't felt our appreciation."

"No, I definitely have not."

"And you're right to be upset about what Derek did the other night. He shouldn't have thrown away your possessions. If I can explain . . ." Kim paused and took a deep breath. "You see, just a few days ago, Derek finally told me about his problems from the past. I had no idea he belonged to Gamblers Anonymous or that he owed you such a large sum of money. We've been trying to work our way through that issue, and during an intense moment, he reacted strongly. I bear as much of the blame as he does, because I didn't stop him. I should have. I wouldn't want my Bible thrown into the lake, and I ought to have considered how you would feel. Please forgive me, Miranda. And the twins, too. We've been insensitive. I know Derek would say the same thing if he were here."

When she had finished speaking, Kim leaned back in her chair and pressed the cool glass of lemonade to her cheeks and forehead. This had been an awful experience, she realized. She had hurt Miranda, and her words hadn't helped the situation a bit. She ought to just go inside and start fixing dinner. Maybe something would eventually come of the effort she had made, but clearly her mother-in-law had lapsed into angry silence again.

As Kim prepared to stand, she glanced at Miranda. And that's when she realized the trickle running down the woman's bronze cheek wasn't perspiration. It was a tear.

"I didn't want to come, you know," Miranda said in a quavering voice. "When Derek told me about Luke, I didn't even consider doing anything about it. I felt sorry for him, of course, but he wasn't my *real* grandson, and I didn't believe that I had any responsibility toward him. But then I thought about it some more — about how deeply Luke's diagnosis had distressed Derek and how hard my poor son was having to work to make ends meet and how you might have to quit your job to take care of Luke — which would put an even greater burden on Derek. So one day I called and offered to help. I expected to stay only a couple of weeks. At the most I would be here until school started. But then . . . then Luke and Lydia became . . . they somehow became important to me. I enjoyed shopping with Lydia. Since I'd never had a daughter, I didn't know what to expect of her. But we've had so much fun together. And Luke, well, he's such a sweet little guy. When he had that crisis on the Fourth of July . . ."

At this, Miranda stopped speaking and began to sob softly. Kim stared at the sleek, suntanned creature in her white bikini. For a moment, she simply couldn't reconcile her image of Miranda — that vile, heathenish dragon worthy of nothing better than to be slain with the sword of truth — with this weeping, tenderhearted woman.

Before Kim could speak, Miranda held up a hand and continued. "I realized that I truly love those two children. I enjoy being a part of a family again too. It's been so many years since Eric died. And since Derek left me. I sincerely believed I was helping my son's family. I tried to offer ideas for improving things around the house and making life easier. I brought in bouquets of roses, because I know every home needs fresh flowers, and you certainly don't have the time or the interest to decorate things properly. I tried to introduce new foods — like my spinach-Parmesan pizza and my seven-layer dip. I even thought of suggesting a different curtain fabric to bring harmony into the living area and make it more comforting for all of us. But everything I offered was rejected. Thrown back in my face, as though I'd done something terribly offensive."

By now Miranda was blotting her cheeks with her beach towel. Kim sat stone still, appalled at how her own behavior had so deeply hurt her mother-in-law. All this time, she had been looking at her children, her marriage, and her life from her own perspective. She had resented Miranda's presence and had made that obvious from the first day. Was that how a Christian was supposed to act? Would Jesus have done the same?

"You know, I gave up my friends," Miranda was saying now, gulping out the words between sobs, "and the country club and all the high-end stores I loved and the good restaurants. . . . Well, I gave up everything. I even put my house on the market. And then I found out that no one cares at all about my sacrifices. It's worse than that. . . . Not even my son . . . my beloved Derek . . . cares enough about me to respect my beliefs. I see now that I've lost everything, including my only child."

"Oh, Miranda —" Kim began to speak, but an upturned hand silenced her again.

"You think I'm cruel to keep him in my debt. I can see the resentment in your eyes. But you weren't there when he came home drunk and desperate and frightened for his life. You have no idea what I went through — trying to get him into treatment, pay off his creditors, keep him clean, get him through college. Do you know that your husband can't ever invest in the stock market? He can't buy commodities or options. He can never play the lottery. He shouldn't even flip a coin! You think I'm exaggerating, but I went to Gam-Anon meetings. For years I thought I had to keep him locked up or he'd fall right back into it. Do you see that? Do you get it at all?"

"I'm trying," Kim said. "But now?"

"Now I'm not sure. I'm just getting to know him all over again."

"I can understand that."

"I know how deeply I'm resented here," Miranda said. "But I want you to realize that I've done my best to become a part of this community. I helped Cody find his aunt, and I joined the TLC in planning the Fourth of July barbecue, and I've even started a little business to sell Ashley Hanes's beadwork. Luke helped me on the computer, and we made business cards and order forms. Lydia and I bought sample boxes for the beads. I've contacted my friends in St. Louis, and they're buying necklaces left and right. But does anyone in this family really notice me or think I matter? No, it's all been for nothing. No one cares about me. No one loves me or values me. You might as well just throw *me* into the lake."

At the very image that Kim had repeatedly — and gleefully — envisioned, she felt her own tears well. She couldn't deny that everything Miranda said or thought seemed to be about herself, but what woman hadn't indulged in a pity party now and then?

Without hesitation, she slipped out of her chair, knelt on the deck, and slid her arms around Miranda's shoulders. "No one wants you to be thrown into the lake," she said, resting her cheek against her mother-in-law's damp hair for a moment before drawing back.

"Despite what you think, Miranda, we do love you," Kim insisted. "The twins adore you, and they're excited that you want to stay permanently. Derek told me he feels so comfortable around you that he hardly even noticed when you moved in. I realize that you and I have had conflict, but I want to try to change that. I had a difficult childhood and a bad first marriage. It takes me a while to get relationships right, Miranda. But I love your son so much, and I love his mother, too. Can you ever find a way to accept me?"

Taking off her sunglasses, Miranda wiped at her eyes again and took the first sip from her lemonade. "Well," she said, sniffling a little, "when you put it that way, I suppose I can try, too. After all, Derek isn't about to part with you. He's made that clear to me again and again. And I do love the twins. I suppose . . . yes, I suppose you and I should try to do better. For Derek's sake. And the children's."

"Good," Kim said, standing. "We'll make this afternoon our new beginning. Now, if you want some more lemonade, just let me know. I'll be in the kitchen fixing dinner."

She started for the sliding glass door, but in its reflection, she saw her mother-in-law rise from the chair.

"Kim?" Miranda called. She crossed the deck, extended her arms, and drew Kim into a damp embrace. "I do accept you, dear. And I think we're all going to be just fine."

"She's at it again," Charlie observed. "Didn't I tell you?"

Esther nodded. "You were right, sweetie. I never should have doubted you."

Charlie and Esther were sitting on the front porch stringing beads onto clear monofilament. As it turned out, Ashley Hanes's necklace business had taken off like a rocket out of Cape Canaveral, and the next thing Charlie knew, he had been commissioned as an official beader.

This was not his idea of a good time. For one thing, his eyes had trouble focusing on the tiny hole through each bead. For another, his slightly arthritic fingers didn't particularly like working the line through that little bitty opening.

Oh, Charlie was plenty good with his hands — as long as the work involved running a circular saw, a router, a plane, or a drill. He could build just about anything he set his mind to, and the finely crafted shed out back of the house proved he not only knew his tools, but he was skilled at almost any kind of construction. This business of beading necklaces, though, felt too much like woman's work.

On the other hand, creating jewelry for Ashley helped fill the daylight hours, and it afforded the opportunity to sit outside and view the comings and goings in the neighborhood. This afternoon, Boofer lay sprawled at Charlie's feet while Esther sorted the beads into rows on the table at her husband's side. To her dismay, Esther had discovered that beading was not her cup of tea. She couldn't see through her trifocals well enough to thread the necklaces, and sometimes she got the colors mixed up. This meant that unless Charlie was paying close attention, he often had to start a project all over again.

"I wonder what she's using these days," Esther said. "Do you suppose she went out and bought some more?"

Sometimes they spoke this way, Charlie and Esther. It was a kind of code they had developed over the years. From his short, grunted comments, Esther knew right away that her husband had spotted Miranda Finley doing exercises on the deck. And from Esther's mishmash of a question, Charlie knew his wife was asking about the tools of Miranda's religious rituals — an altar and some rocks and statues.

"I guess she could have driven down to Springfield and bought another Buddha or two. You've gone over to orange, honeybunch, and we're still working on red. The polka-dot ones."

"Oh, for pete's sake." Esther picked up the orange beads and put them back into their compartment. "These necklaces are driving me batty. I wouldn't have joined Miranda's project, but I know it's to help keep Ashley from having to take on a second job. I'm just wondering if she will ever have that baby she wants, poor thing. I keep studying her stomach, but there's no sign of a pooch at all."

"Flat as a pancake."

"You shouldn't be looking at a woman's midriff, Charlie Moore."

"She wears those skimpy tops. What's a man supposed to do?"

Esther shook her head. "That nursery of theirs isn't coming along too well either. Last time I went over to visit Ashley, I noticed an electric saw sitting smack-dab in the middle of their living room. There's a lot of construction mess lying around in the yard too. Brad should pick up the wood he bought before the termites get it. Did you notice that the house for sale next to the Haneses' hasn't had any lookers in a while?"

"Oh, that house had a looker all right. I saw Miranda over there the other day. She was peeking in the windows, trying the doorknobs, and tromping around on the porch testing the floorboards."

"Really! Now that's interesting news. I wonder if she's thinking of buying it." Suddenly Esther let out a groan of frustration. "Are we doing orange or red, sugar bear? I can't keep it straight."

"Red. With polka dots."

"Who would wear a necklace with red polka-dot beads anyhow?"

"Some lady in St. Louis."

They worked awhile in silence.

"I think we've about got the Labor Day barbecue in order," Esther said. "Nobody liked my parade idea."

"You told me."

"Did I? Anyhow, the reaction of the TLC

395

sure surprised me; I can tell you that. I always wanted to be in a parade. But no one in the neighborhood would give my idea the time of day. Jennifer Hansen would have made a lovely Deepwater Cove queen; don't you think?"

"I don't reckon missionaries can be beauty queens, sweet pea. How about if you dress up in that old formal of yours, and I'll wheel you around the cove in my golf cart a couple of times?"

Esther laughed — the tinkling, airy sound that Charlie had fallen in love with so many years ago. She looked at him and smiled. "I couldn't fit into that formal with a shoehorn. But it's sure pretty — all that orchid organza. I know I ought to give it to some lovely younger lady, but for the life of me, I just can't part with it."

As Charlie recalled, the gown had so much prickly netting and stiff lace that he'd barely been able to get close to Esther on the night of their high school prom — a situation that had frustrated him no end. In fact, he didn't think he'd even managed to win himself a kiss. Too many petticoats. The dress was up in the attic somewhere, probably eaten up by moths, but in Esther's mind it was still a confection worthy of a queen.

"Are we doing orange beads, honey?" Esther asked. "Or pink? I can't keep it straight."

"Red," he said, watching Miranda Finley finish her exercises, slip a robe over her white bathing suit, and leave the deck for the evening. "With polka dots."

"Oh, good gravy, of course," Esther said. "How could I forget that?"

CHAPTER EIGHTEEN

Kim was so ready to go home for the Labor Day weekend that she could hardly bear to wait another minute. With her husband and mother-in-law joining her in a supreme effort to be cooperative and friendly, the Finley household was happier than it had been in months. In anticipation of the neighborhood barbecue, Derek had bought enough hot dogs to feed two armies, and Miranda was making her special macaroni-and-tofu confetti salad. The whole family had ordered Kim not to do a single thing except relax, rest, and enjoy the time off. Derek had been right that his wife expressed her love best by serving those she cared about most deeply. Still, Kim couldn't deny that the idea of putting her feet up for an entire weekend seemed positively magical.

But the last week in August wasn't over yet, and Kim pulled on her gloves in preparation for the final patient of the day.

"You're givin' me gas, Miz Kim. Ain't that right?"

A tooth extraction on a mouth like Abe Fugal's wouldn't be fun on a Friday afternoon, but there was no way around it. It would really go more easily with the patient unconscious, but Mr. Fugal had come alone to his appointment and didn't have anyone to drive him home.

"Are you sure you want gas, Mr. Fugal?" Kim asked, laying a hand on his shoulder. "Dr. Groene can numb the area without it, but if you'd prefer —"

"I don't want no needles comin' my direction! Not in my mouth nor anywhere near it. I know the doc means well, but the thought of him lungin' at me with one of them syringes gives me the heebie-jeebies."

"We can administer some gas to help you relax, but I'm afraid Dr. Groene is going to have to deaden that nerve before he pulls the tooth."

"Aw, rats. That just burns my toast. I'm sixty-two years old and never been to a doctor once in my whole life. I was born at home, and I never set foot in a hospital except for the time my wife took sick. Cancer, you know. She had to have something for the pain, right until the end. But me, I'm healthy as a horse. I never took no drugs. Not even an aspirin. And here you go wanting to let the doc put a needle in my gums."

Kim patted her patient on the shoulder.

"All right, start up the gas, honey," Abe said. "Hit me good before the doc gets in here with his needle. I don't want no part of that thing!"

Kim smiled as she prepared the small mask that would cover Abe's nostrils. "Breathe through your nose, and you'll start to calm down. When Dr. Groene comes in, I'll tell you to shut your eyes. I bet you won't even know what he's doing."

"Okay, I believe you, but only because you're so purty. Put it on me now, and crank up the knob as far as you can. Get me through this, Miz Kim, and I'll love you till the end of time."

"Please tell me if you start to feel the least bit dizzy," Kim urged him gently as he began to inhale the gas. "We don't want you getting nauseous, Mr. Fugal. If the room starts to spin, squeeze my hand." She slipped her palm over the gnarled fingers.

Abe tightened his hand around hers. Closing his eyes, he breathed in deeply. "I think you're the sweetest young thing I ever saw," he murmured.

"Thank you, Mr. Fugal." Kim was accustomed to the slightly silly, sometimes emotional expressions the dental gas unleashed. She had dealt with giggly patients, groggy patients, weeping patients, and those who professed their undying and eternal love for Ben Groene even as he drilled straight into a cavity.

"How are you feeling now, Mr. Fugal?" she asked after Abe had been lying in silence for a few moments. "Are you dizzy at all?"

"Naw, I'm just a-layin' here thinkin' about my gal. My darlin'. Her and me sure had some good times together."

"I bet you did." As Kim adjusted the dial on the gas, she pictured Abe's darling as the wife who had passed away from cancer some years before. As Dr. Groene's assistant, she had often listened to patients who wanted to share their memories.

"I can't believe she's gone," Abe told her mournfully. "Gone, just like that. Without even a word of farewell. She hollered, 'Hep! . . . Hep me, Abe,' and that was it. I tried. I done all I could to fetch her back onto the dock, but no sooner did I reach out for her, and she was gone."

"The dock?" Kim asked. A prickle ran up her spine and lifted the hair on the back of her neck. "Your wife fell off a dock? When was this?"

A tear trickled down Abe's cheek. "Not my wife. My darlin' June bug. Weren't but a couple months ago. We was havin' ourselves a little party, you know. Just a beer or two. Catchin' some fish off the dock by our trailer. And then I went back inside to fetch us another twelve-pack. It was a party, like I said. My little June bug and me used to party thataway nearly ever night."

Kim swallowed as Dr. Groene stepped into the cubicle. Against all she had been taught about keeping the patient comfortable, moving ahead with procedures, warding off unforeseen problems, she held her index finger to her lip. Pointing at Abe Fugal, she shook her head fervently at Dr. Groene.

He frowned and took a step closer.

"Abe, how did June fall off the dock?" Kim asked, making frantic, senseless gestures at Dr. Groene.

"Awww . . . she was leanin' over to pull our basket of fish out of the water, and in she went. Headfirst. She come up a-hollerin'. She yelled out that she'd got herself tangled up in fishin' line and couldn't move her arms. The line must've been driftin' around underwater — you know how it does when you hook your lure onto a snag that snaps it right off the rod?

All that flailin' around probably knotted June up, and she wasn't able to get free. I could hear her yellin', but I couldn't hardly see her no more. It was dark by that time, you know. The lake was nothin' but a big black hole. And it just swallowed up my darlin' June bug quick as a wink. She never was a strong swimmer, and with the fishin' line . . . aw, rats, I hate to think about that. I can't hardly bear it."

"Kim?" Dr. Groene asked, his brow furrowed. "What's going on here?"

Without thinking twice, Kim began to turn down the gas. "Mr. Fugal," she said, "I'm bringing you back."

"Are we done?" His rheumy eyes blinked. "Hey, you was right, Miz Kim! I didn't feel a thing. 'Cept my tooth sure does hurt. Oops, Doc, I think you missed your target. I can still feel that tooth right there where it always was."

"We haven't done the extraction yet, Mr. Fugal," Kim explained as she leaned in to where he could see her face. "I need to talk to Dr. Groene for a minute. You were telling me about June, and I don't want you to keep talking until I'm sure how to proceed."

"Aw, shucks." Abe shook his head. "You turned off that gas, didn't you?"

"Yes. You should be able to think more

clearly now."

"Clear as I ever could," he said with a wry chuckle. "Which weren't much."

"Do you remember what you told me about June?"

His expression sobered. "Yeah, I do. I didn't come in here aimin' to talk about it, but you're so purty and sweet that I decided I might as well 'fess up."

" 'Fess up to what?" Dr. Groene asked. "Abe, what have you been telling Mrs. Finley?"

"Well, I went ahead and told her about my sweet lil' June bug fallin' into the lake that night after we'd been partyin'."

"Are you talking about the woman who used to come with you to your appointments? I met her once or twice."

"Yep, you did. June done most of our drivin', bein' as I'd lost my license a while back on account of too many DWI tickets. I was in so much pain with that tooth that June convinced me to let you have a look at my chompers."

"I didn't realize she had passed away."

Kim spoke up. "Dr. Groene or I might have wanted to go to the funeral, Mr. Fugal. When was it?"

The corners of Abe's mouth turned down. "It weren't."

404

"You had a memorial service for her?" Dr. Groene asked.

"Naw. I decided not to spill the beans. Didn't tell nobody June was gone, because . . . well, if you want to know the truth, I didn't have the guts. See, we'd been drinkin' and maybe doin' a few other things we shouldn't of that night — if you catch my drift. I didn't want to get neither of us into trouble. Besides, she don't have no family other than me, and *we* wasn't even married."

"So . . . she drowned?" Dr. Groene asked.

"Didn't you hear about it on the TV? It was on the news for a while after they found her. They couldn't figure out who she was, but I knew. I knew it was poor June."

"I think it would have been better if you'd reported this to the authorities, Abe," Dr. Groene told him.

"Maybe so, but my daddy used to say, 'Dead is dead.' I figured that's the way it was with my darlin' June bug, and not a thing I could do about it. Like I told you, I was flat-out scared to own up to what had happened that night, because of the drinkin' and so forth. June used to watch them detective shows on TV, and these days they can pretty much tell whatever you've been doin' or even might have did a long time

405

ago. Not to mention that I been in the clink a time or two already, and there's somewhat of a record on my name over to the police station."

"I need to call my husband," Kim said quietly.

"Use my office," Dr. Groene said. "Abe, since you've told Mrs. Finley and me about June already, I guess you're willing to tell the police what happened now, aren't you?"

"I know I should. Yeah, I'll do it. They'll probably lock me up and throw away the key for the rest of my life. I reckon I deserve it too."

"I doubt they'll be that harsh under the circumstances."

"Well, like I said — I've done time before, so I know I can bear it. In fact, I'm glad I told you the truth. The grief was about to kill me."

Walking toward the dentist's private office, Kim could hear the two men continue to talk as she keyed in Derek's number. He would still be out on the water, but she knew it wouldn't take him long to get to Dr. Groene's office.

"Hey, beautiful," Derek said when he answered. "Is Dr. Groene letting you off early today? I was hoping —"

"Derek," Kim cut in, almost breathless

with excitement. "I'm still at work. You have to get here right away."

"What's wrong, honey? Is this is an emergency?"

"No, but it's urgent. Derek, I need your help. I don't know what to do. One of our patients is here — Abe Fugal — and he confessed something to me while he was being sedated. I turned off the gas as quickly as I could, and I think he's still willing to talk about it."

"What did he tell you, Kim?"

"He was with a woman the night she fell off a dock. He knows she died, because he saw reports about it on the news. But he never told anyone what had happened, and there was no funeral or memorial service. Derek, I don't think anyone else knows about this woman's death."

"Are you telling me the man didn't report a possible drowning?"

"That's right. They had been drinking all evening. He said she was reaching off the dock for a basket of fish when she tumbled into the water. He told me that she wasn't a good swimmer, and she yelled out that she had gotten tangled in fishing line. He tried to reach out for her, but he couldn't find her in the dark. Then he lost sight of her. He thinks she drowned."

"I'm on my way," he said. "I'll be there in fifteen minutes. Calling the police to put a stop-and-hold until I can get to you. Stay with me, Kim."

A moment later, Derek's voice became muffled as he spoke by radio first to municipal authorities and then to the Water Patrol dispatcher in Jefferson City. Kim heard him give his badge number and then say, "Jeff, I'll be off the water . . . 10-6 at the dental office of Dr. Ben Groene on Highway 5, Camdenton."

He returned to the cell phone. "Honey, are you in any danger that you know of?"

"I'm sure Mr. Fugal is harmless. He can barely see, and only one of his hands works right. But please hurry, Derek. He may change his mind and try to leave. He told us he does have a criminal record."

"Can you get me his date of birth, Kim?"

"No, his health data is confidential."

Derek spoke on the radio again. "The subject will be a possible 10-99 out of Camden County," he said, informing the office of the man's checkered past. "The name is Abe — as in Abraham — Fugal. No date of birth available. Can you run a 27, 28, and 29 on him?"

The dispatcher confirmed that Mr. Fugal's name would be checked for possible warrants as well as records on whether he might be dangerous. In moments, the dispatcher asked Derek, "Are you 10-12?"

Kim knew the code well enough to understand that Water Patrol wanted to know if he was already at the scene. That indicated they had turned up something suspicious in Mr. Fugal's documentation. Cell phone still pressed against her ear, she walked back down the hall and glanced into the cubicle to find that Dr. Groene and Abe Fugal were discussing baseball standings, particularly the St. Louis Cardinals and whether they had another shot at the World Series this year.

"Derek," Kim said as she stepped back into the hall, "I think this is it — the clue you've been looking for to identify the body you found at the start of summer. I think the woman who died lived with Abe Fugal in an old trailer around the bend not too far from Deepwater Cove. You know the one that lost part of its roof in last year's big storm? I'm pretty sure I know who she was. I used to see her here when she came in with Abe. Her name is June Bixby."

"June Bixby," he repeated. "Good. I'm on my way. Listen, I want you to know that when I get there, we may be separated. I'll need to work with the Major Case Squad, and I'm sure the police will want to question you. I doubt I'll make it home for dinner tonight."

"It's okay, Derek."

"Kim, you might not think the old guy is dangerous, but he does have a record. Be careful, honey. I don't want anything to happen to you."

"I'm fine," she murmured. "It's all right."

"I just want to make sure you know I love you. We've been through a lot lately, and I need to tell you —"

"Derek, I hear you. I understand what you're telling me." Kim paused. "And I love you, too."

CHAPTER NINETEEN

With a fair amount of trepidation, Patsy eyed the lawn chairs as she carried her plate of appetizers toward the group of men gathered near their grills. She spotted a sturdy plastic chaise lounge that would easily bear her ample figure, so she sat down on it and stretched out her legs.

"Hey, fellas," she said.

The men interrupted their discussion for a moment to greet her. "Hey, Patsy," they offered in a chorus of tenors and basses. Then they went back to talking.

It didn't bother Patsy that the men ignored her. On the Fourth of July, she'd drawn enough attention to last a lifetime. Not only had she endured that awful lawn chair collapse, but her slightly over-the-top patriotic outfit and star-spangled hairdo had only added to the spectacle.

For the Labor Day barbecue, Patsy had decided to go for a more sedate look with an autumn influence. She had returned her hair to the color closest to the one she remembered from childhood. Unfortunately, that particular hue might best be termed dishwater blonde or mousy brown or something in between. So Patsy had added a few golden highlights and then some auburn ones to brighten it up a bit.

As it was still hotter than blazes outside, she had chosen to wear a short-sleeved top with a taupe, brick red, and black leaf print. In order to give it a little more autumn flavor, she had pinned on a brooch that had belonged to her mother — a real maple leaf dipped in acrylic. Its lovely red-orange color perfectly matched the knee-length shorts Patsy wore. And the whole outfit coordinated well with the black platform sandals she had chosen from her closet.

She dipped a corn chip into the puddle of black bean salsa on her plate and chewed thoughtfully. Too bad Pete Roberts wasn't going to make it to the barbecue. He had decided to keep Rods-N-Ends open for the last of the summer gas-guzzlers passing through. She couldn't blame him. The end of the season meant a lull that nearly put the Lake of the Ozarks community to sleep. This was the time when the weakest businesses began failing left and right. Only the locals and a few off-and-on visitors kept stores and restaurants alive through the down season. Pete's first year had been rough, Patsy knew, but he thought he was going to make it.

Bitty Sondheim's Pop-In, however, appeared to be doomed. Two weeks ago, a Closed sign had appeared on the front door, and the inside of the little restaurant remained dark day and night. Patsy hadn't seen her neighbor in several days, so she was happy to spot the Californian with her long hair and swoopy, ankle-length skirts arriving at the barbecue. Bitty was in the parking area, and she seemed to be wrestling with something large in the back of her van.

"Hey, Brad," Patsy called, drawing the attention of Ashley Hanes's handsome young husband, who sat nearby. "How about you, Derek, and Steve helping Bitty out over there? Looks like she brought half her restaurant."

"Probably trying to unload her leftovers on us," Brad said. He glanced at his wife, who was selling beaded necklaces from a table set up under a tree. "Ashley keeps dragging me to the Pop-In. If I never eat another eggplant wrap it won't bother me a bit."

With that, he and several of the other men

pushed themselves out of their lawn chairs, checked the pork steaks on their grills, and then lumbered over to see if they could carry anything for Bitty. Patsy had hardly had time to sample the pimento cheese–filled celery sticks on her plate before Brad was back, more animated than she'd ever seen him.

"Charlie!" he hollered. "Patsy! All you guys, come see what Bitty's done. You won't believe this!"

Not wanting to miss out on any excitement, Patsy scrambled to her feet and hurried across the lawn to the long foldout table where Bitty was opening boxes and spreading her wares. The bad news was that she looked close to tears as she set down rows of plates and began laying one or two parchment-wrapped packages on each. The good news was that Brad Hanes had tasted one of these wraps and was about to go berserk with joy.

"Chicken-fried steak!" he exclaimed, displaying the innards of the rolled item he'd just bitten into. "It's covered in mashed potatoes and gravy — with buttered Texas toast on the outside! And she grilled it! It's good. It's delicious. You gotta try one."

"Chicken-fried steak in a wrap?" Patsy murmured, picking up a plate.

"That's not all," Bitty said in a wounded, snippy voice. She pointed to one item after another. "Right here, you've got your batter-crusted catfish. It's coated in tartar sauce and covered with a deep-fried hush puppy batter. This one is your chicken wrap. It's a large fried-chicken tender, rolled in a mixture of mashed potatoes and green beans, and then covered with baked home-made dinner roll dough. And finally, here's your ham wrap. It's got a big chunk of canned pineapple on it, along with a thick layer of applesauce, and it's been baked inside a coating of corn bread dressing."

For a moment, the men stared at the plates in stunned silence. "Where are the fajita wraps?" Derek asked. "I always en-joyed those."

"And what about that Greek salad wrap my wife liked so much?" Steve asked.

"Discontinued," Bitty said as the men began picking up the plates and biting into the strange-looking food. "Discontinued along with the eggplant wraps, the onion-and-feta-cheese wraps, the baked-lamb-and-hummus wraps, the avocado-and-shrimp wraps. In fact, all the wraps are discontinued. So are the omelets. And so is Bitty Sondheim's Pop-In."

"Now, just a minute," Patsy said. "You're

not leaving us, are you, Bitty? You've hardly given us a fair shot. One summer isn't nearly enough time to let us get used to your California cooking."

"It's long enough for me." She looked from man to man. "My out-of-town visitors liked my food pretty well, but I've heard your comments. I've seen the faces you locals make when you read my menu. I know how you feel about my California wraps. So here!" She spread out her hands to indicate the array of food she had brought. "Here's your Missouri-hearty-homemade-just-like-Grandma's-deep-fried-heart-attack *junk.* You kept telling me you wanted chicken-fried steak and mashed potatoes, so here it is. Take all you want. It's on the house."

At that, Bitty burst into tears, turned on her heel, and headed for her van.

Dismayed, Patsy set off after her. "Now, Bitty," she called, regretting her high platform black sandals with every step. "Bitty, please wait. Don't leave us like this, honeybunch!"

"I'm going back to California where I belong. Missouri is just too weird for me."

"Missouri is weird?" Patsy caught up to Bitty, who was pushing boxes and baskets into the back of her van. "We're not weird, sweetie; we're just home folks. We've been doing the same old things for years. We eat what we've always eaten, and we pretty much wear what we've always worn. Change doesn't come easy to us, but it's not impossible. Please don't run off, Bitty. Give us another chance. I was really beginning to like that humus."

"*Humus* is dirt enriched with cow manure!" Bitty wailed, turning on Patsy. Her voice rose as she spoke until she was practically screeching. "I was serving *hummus!* Hummus is a creamy puree of chickpeas and sesame seed paste seasoned with lemon juice and garlic! Everyone eats it in Greece and the Middle East! Hummus is served with bread for dipping or as a pita filling!"

"Well, all right," Patsy said, holding up both hands to try to calm Bitty. The last thing she needed was to make another big show. "Simmer down, now. I'm sorry; I didn't know the difference, Bitty. I'm sort of ignorant about these kinds of things. Most folks around here are — but that doesn't mean we can't be educated. If you'd put on your menu that you were serving chickpea paste, well . . . well —"

"You see? No one wants to eat my kind of food. You know who my best customer was? Miranda Finley — and that's because she's from St. Louis. She knows about international cuisine. She knows about healthy eating. She understands what I was trying to do. I thought I could come to the lake and set up a little restaurant and just live out the rest of my life right here where the cost of living is low and the pace is slow. But all my dreams are ruined. *I'm* ruined, Patsy! I put everything I had into the Pop-In!"

"Oh, Bitty, come here and let me give you a hug." As Patsy wrapped her arms around the woman, she suddenly realized that most of the men who'd been tending their grills were headed toward Bitty's van like soldiers on a mission. She swished her hand at them to try to ward them off, but they wouldn't be deterred.

"Bitty, we want to talk to you," Steve Hansen said. "These men have just voted me chairman of the Pop-In Revitalization Board."

Snuffling, Bitty lifted her head from Patsy's shoulder. "I already turned in my final rent check, Steve. I'm sorry to let you down, but I just couldn't make a go of it. You'll have to find a new tenant for the space."

"I'm going to have to prevent that," Derek Finley said, stepping forward and leading Bitty back toward the table, where a crowd

418

had gathered to sample her new wraps. "I'm afraid I can't allow you to shut down the Pop-In, Bitty. We don't dare risk the riot that might cause."

"What?" she asked, her voice tremulous. "What do you mean?"

Now Brad Hanes spoke as he held up what was left inside his parchment paper. "We want you to stay open and keep making these Missouri-deep-fried-heart-attack wraps. They're delicious. I mean that. I could eat one for lunch and actually get full. I'm gonna have to go swimming just to work off the one I ate, so I can be ready when the pork steaks are done."

"But they're so . . . awful," Bitty said.

"Awful *good*," Brad declared. "If you'll keep the Pop-In open, Bitty, I'll tell the other guys I work with, and we'll be there every day. I ate the chicken-fried steak wrap, but I'm a big catfish man. Charlie told me his was fantastic."

"Don't ever let on to Esther," Charlie Moore said, leaning in close, "but that catfish wrap has her batter-fried crappie beat by a mile."

"Are you serious?" Bitty asked.

"Serious as a hearty-homemade-deep-fried heart attack!" Brad said with a laugh.

Everyone was still chuckling when Charlie

suddenly elbowed Patsy. "Hey, who's that? Over yonder near the edge of the parking lot?"

Patsy's heart lurched as she searched the thick brush at the edge of the clearing. Emerging from the shadows came a tall, broad-shouldered man bearing a large box. For an instant, she thought by some miracle it might be Cody. But this was someone new. A good-looking stranger who must have noticed the gathering and decided to check it out.

"I had to park halfway to Tranquility," the man called as he sauntered toward Bitty's van. " 'Course, that's pretty much to be expected, seeing as I'm from Halfway, Missouri."

At that, Patsy gasped so loudly that everyone turned to stare at her. "Pete?" she whispered. "Is that Pete Roberts?"

It was. But it couldn't be. Where was the shaggy sheepdog? the old grizzly bear? the lumbering goof in overalls and a plaid flannel shirt?

"Hey, Patsy." He smiled, and suddenly she realized she was definitely looking at Pete Roberts's teeth. But had she ever seen those lips? that chin? the squared jawline?

"Aren't you going to speak to me?" He paused, grinning. "I brought my homemade pecan pie — a recipe of which I am most particularly proud. I hope I haven't missed the pork steaks."

"You missed Bitty's new Missouri wraps," Luke Finley said. "They're good."

"No problem, Pete," Brad assured him. "You can drop by the Pop-In anytime you want. Hey, did you lose weight or something?"

"He shaved," Patsy said, breathing out the words with a deep sigh. "Pete shaved. You shaved off your beard."

"And got myself a haircut. I should have let you do it, Patsy, but I wanted to surprise you. I closed up early to show off my new do. So, what do you think?"

When she couldn't answer, he handed the box containing his pie to Derek Finley, took Patsy by the arm and planted a kiss right on her lips. "How's them apples, sugar?" he asked.

Patsy nearly fell right off her platform sandals. All around her, the men began to cheer. The Finley twins chanted, "Pete and Patsy sitting in a tree, k-i-s-s-i-n-g! First comes love, then comes marriage —"

"Hold it right there!" Patsy said, snapping out of her trance. "If you all will excuse me, I've got to go and sit down."

As she stepped away, trying to stay balanced on her sandals, Patsy could hear the crowd laughing and murmuring behind her. Well, she'd managed to be the focus of yet another spectacle — and once again Pete Roberts had caused it. Only this time, Patsy wasn't angry. Far from it. In fact, she was so flustered, so dizzied, so downright discombobulated that she didn't know if she could make it back to the plastic chaise.

Just when she feared she might have to slump down into the grass and take off her shoes, Pete slipped his arm under hers. "Are you mad at me again?" he asked, leaning way too close for comfort.

Patsy couldn't believe it, but he smelled like heaven itself. He'd splashed on some kind of aftershave that had hints of lemon and spice, and his breath was sweet, and it was all she could do to keep from turning him around and giving him a smooch to end all smooches.

"Patsy?" he said. "Please don't get upset. I thought you'd be glad I shaved after all this time. Especially right before winter. That's when I usually let the ol' beard grow as bushy as it can. But you kept telling me I ought to shave and get a haircut, so I finally listened. In fact, I did it for you. I'd given you a few teacups, and I couldn't think of another thing that might please you. I really did want to make you happy."

Patsy paused and turned to look into his amazing blue eyes. "You did, Pete," she said. "I'm happy, but . . . but I'm kind of scared, too."

"Scared? Of what? It's just me."

"But you look so different. You're . . . well, you're handsome."

He burst out laughing. "Handsome! First time anyone ever said that about Pete Roberts. But if that's how you feel, you'll never see another whisker on my face as long as I live."

Patsy practically tumbled onto the plastic chaise, and Pete sat down beside her on the grass. She stretched out her legs, closed her eyes, and tried to make herself think straight. Pete could *not* be that handsome. It simply wasn't possible. How many beards had she shaved off men in her lifetime? At least a dozen, and what was underneath never looked as good as that. And how many men had she seen with brand-new haircuts? Thousands? But they were never as handsome as Pete Roberts.

"You'll like my pecan pie," he said, taking her hand. "I shelled the nuts myself, and I made the crust, too. It was my grandma's recipe. You wouldn't think a fellow like me could bake up a pecan pie, but if there was a fair anywhere near here, I bet I'd win first prize."

You sure would, Patsy thought. *But not for your pecan pie.* She opened her eyes a little and peeked over at him. No doubt about it. Pete was handsome. Oh, he wasn't rippling with muscles or sporting a deep golden tan. He didn't have gleaming white teeth and dimples. But that craggy face could just about stop a woman's heart.

"Before the men get back here, Patsy," he spoke up, "I want to tell you something. It's about fishing."

"Oh, Kim already told me," she said. "Charlie thought up the idea when he was trying to get Esther to go out to Aunt Mamie's. It worked so well that Charlie told Derek, and now all the Finleys are fishing left and right."

"They are?"

Patsy hesitated. "By fishing, do you mean that special way of talking to someone so you get what you want from them? Like Derek winning back Kim's admiration, and Kim winning Miranda's acceptance? And Lydia winning Luke's permission to be his diabetes buddy at school, even in front of all his friends?"

Pete scratched at what had once been his beard. Seeing as now it was just his chin, he didn't do it long. "I'm not talking about that kind of fishing," he said. "Though Derek Finley and I did discuss another kind of fishing after church last Sunday. You remember how the ladies were all bunched up talking about Jessica Hansen's wedding?"

"Yes. Jennifer is going to be the maid of honor, and they plan to wear apricot and carry calla lilies. I'm doing the whole bridal party's hair and nails. We've already scheduled it in my appointment book."

"Okay, well, while you were discussing all that stuff, some of us men lingered around our cars waiting for you to finish up. That's when I asked Steve Hansen about this 'fishing for men' business. He explained it to me pretty well, and then Derek Finley went to asking questions. And before long, Steve had up and decided to start a men's Bible study at Rods-N-Ends at six o'clock every Wednesday morning."

Patsy sat up straight. "A men's Bible study? Are you going to it?"

"Of course. It's at my store, remember? And that brings me to what I wanted to tell you. Even though I don't completely understand about being 'born again' — or exactly why anyone would want to fish for men — I'm giving it a shot. Derek said he'd come to the Bible study too. We're both kind of ignorant, but we like what we see in church. Even better, we like the people we know who call themselves Christians. So, Patsy, I may not be all I should be — or could be — but I hope you know I'm trying."

"Oh, Pete!" Unable to bear it another moment, Patsy threw her arms around the man's neck and hugged him tightly while tears flowed down her cheeks. "I'm so happy I don't know what to say! I can't believe you really listened to me. And cared about what I think. And shaved off that beard. And decided to go to Bible study. And —"

"Whoa, hang on a minute!" Pete's arms tightened around Patsy. "Slow up, girl. We've got us a potential problem here. It looks like trouble — but I think Derek's got it covered."

Patsy lifted her head and tried to see through the mist of tears that covered her eyes. "What is it, Pete?"

"There's something out in the lake. Looks too big to be a carp or a catfish. I don't think it's a paddlefish either. Why is it that every time we have a barbecue we wind up with a hitch in our giddyup?"

Still folded in Pete's arms, Patsy turned around and wiped at her eyes. She could see a dark shape a little way from the shoreline. It seemed to be drifting along at a slow pace — maybe it was a log or even a large turtle. Derek had picked up a heavy stick and was walking toward the water. Parents called their children out of the swim area, and everyone gathered in clumps with their arms around each other.

Just when Patsy had decided the object was some kind of debris, it rose straight out of the water. The whole crowd cried out and stumbled backward. The thing was standing now, wading to the shore.

"Is it a deer?" Patsy asked.

"Too hairy and tall. It might be a bear. It's too big for a raccoon. What is that thing?"

At that moment, the thing lifted a hand and began waving. "Hi, I'm Cody!"

"Cody!" Patsy scrambled out of the chaise so fast that Pete found himself holding air. Kicking off her sandals, she ran for the water. "It's Cody! Cody, you came back!"

"Hey, Patsy Pringle! Hey, Pete! Hey, Brenda Hansen! Hey, Steve! Hey, Mr. and Mrs. Moore!" Dripping, Cody Goss staggered onto the beach. His hair and beard had grown scraggly, and his T-shirt was covered with grease stains. "Hey, Mrs. Finley and Officer Finley! Hey, the other Mrs.

427

Finley! Hey, Ashley and Brad! Hey, Opal!"

Patsy rushed right up to Cody and threw her arms around his skinny, wet shoulders. A moment later, nearly every person in Deepwater Cove was making a valiant effort to hug Cody. Brenda Hansen began sobbing. Ashley Hanes started tossing necklaces over his head. Kim Finley wrapped him in beach towels as her twins danced around him. Esther and Charlie were so happy they broke into a spontaneous waltz of joy. Even Brad Hanes began to applaud Cody's arrival in the neighborhood.

"You came back to us!" Patsy said as the young man made his way onto the grass. "Oh, Cody, we've missed you so much!"

"I missed you, too." He sank onto a blanket someone had spread out, and everyone gathered around him. "I missed everyone, and let me tell you something. Deepwater Cove is not an easy place to find."

"But why did you decide to leave Kansas?" Miranda Finley asked. "We thought you would be happy with your aunt."

"I think my aunt is a very nice lady," Cody said. "She told me she liked me, and she was sorry my daddy had died. Aunt Marylou stays at her flower store pretty much all the time. She makes bouquets for weddings and funerals and birthdays and holidays and

428

church altars and hotel lobbies."

"She's a florist!" Esther said.

"Yes, and she has a big television in her house, and she told me to watch it all the time while she was gone. When she came home, we would eat together. My aunt is a vegetablearian. We ate beans and peas and lettuce and carrots. But we never ate meat. Or eggs. Or nothing interesting but nuts. We ate lots of nuts — peanuts, walnuts, macadamias, you name it."

"Yuck!" Luke Finley announced. "That's worse than my diabetic food."

"You're right," Cody said. "Yuck. Besides that, my aunt and I didn't have too much to talk about, because she was always at her shop working on flower bouquets. She said she didn't have time to teach me reading or social skills, and she didn't want me to clean anything in her house or mow her yard. Aunt Marylou always said, 'I'm glad you came for a visit. How long do you plan to stay?' I told her I was glad to have a family and a home. Anyway, one day I decided I had watched enough television to last me for a long while, because in case you didn't know, the things they do on television are not good. So I wrote my aunt a letter to say good-bye and thank you for the vegetables and come see me in Deepwater Cove sometime, because that is my real home and my real family. And then I bought a bus ticket back to St. Louis."

"St. Louis!" Patsy exclaimed, imagining the innocent young man stranded in the middle of such a large city. "But that's miles from here."

"I know. I could not find any of your houses or even Just As I Am or Rods-N-Ends. I lived in the woods for a while, just like my daddy and I used to do. But living in the woods makes you stink. And that's why . . . well, after I found Deepwater Cove a few minutes ago, I tried to get into the lake and wash off. . . . But Brenda will tell you *I am not a fish.* So, that's how come I stink."

"I don't think you stink." The voice belonged to Jennifer Hansen, who stepped between Patsy and Pete. She was carrying a plate, and she offered it to Cody as she settled down cross-legged beside him.

"Three hot dogs!" he practically shouted. "And chocolate cake!"

"Cut into squares, not triangles," Jennifer said. "Because squares are better."

Cody stared at her for a moment as if he truly could not believe his eyes. Then he picked up a hot dog. "This is the happiest day of my life," he announced. "And here's another thing I want to say. I love you, Jennifer Hansen."

The young woman smiled. "Everyone here loves you, too, Cody," she said. "Welcome back to Deepwater Cove. Welcome home."

DISCUSSION QUESTIONS

The principles and strategies illustrated in this novel are taken from *The Four Seasons of Marriage* by Gary Chapman. In this book, Dr. Chapman discusses marriage as a journey back and forth through different "seasons."

- **Springtime** in marriage is a time of new beginnings, new patterns of life, new ways of listening, and new ways of loving.
- **Summer** couples share deep commitment, satisfaction, and security in each other's love.
- **Fall** brings a sense of unwanted change, and nagging emptiness appears.
- **Winter** means difficulty. Marriage is harder in this season of cold silence and bitter winds.

1. In *Summer Breeze,* which season of the year is it in Deepwater Cove, Missouri? Which season of marriage do you think Derek and Kim Finley are experiencing? What are the signs that let you know?

2. At the start of the book, someone has drowned near Deepwater Cove. What changes does this event bring about in Derek's life? How does the drowning affect Kim? What does the news mean to Cody? Can you think of an example in your own experience in which God has used one event to bring about change in many peoples' lives?

3. What are Luke and Lydia like at the beginning of the book? How do their personalities change through the story? How does a family's structure affect children? How does the parents' relationship affect children's behavior?

4. On the way to church, the Finley family erupts into a furious argument (pages 228–235). What is the end result for each member of the family? Do you ever find your own family engaged in disagreements on the way to church? Catherine Palmer's family refers to these quarrels as "holy

wars." Why do you suppose tensions are so high at such times? Can you think of some good ways to prevent "holy wars" in your family?

5. Patsy Pringle gets angry with Pete Roberts over the lawn chair incident at the Fourth of July barbecue (page 201). How does her version of the event differ from his? What is the root cause of her anger? Twice, Patsy is challenged to forgive Pete. Why do you suppose it takes her so long to admit her wrongdoing? What does Cody say that finally propels Patsy to forgive Pete? How can we forgive others?

6. What does Miranda think of Christians? What are her own religious beliefs? How does Jennifer Hansen respond to Miranda's declarations about religion (page 307)? What do you think of Jennifer's method of stating her beliefs? Have you ever tried to share your faith with someone else? Has anyone tried to tell you about a religion different from yours? What happened?

7. In this book, Kim and Derek are dealing with Luke's diabetes. What impact can a chronic illness have on a family — finan-

cially, physically, emotionally, and in other ways? How is Kim handling the situation at the start of the book? What is Derek's attitude about Luke's problem? How has Dr. Groene chosen to deal with his diabetes?

8. In the first book in this series, *It Happens Every Spring,* Steve and Brenda Hansen's marital problems grew from within their relationship. In this book, Kim and Derek face trouble that comes from outside their marriage. They are struggling not only with Luke's illness but also with a blended family and with in-law relationships. But Kim and Derek also have trouble within their marriage. What are some of the mistakes they have made in building their relationship?

9. Strategy 3 in *The Four Seasons of Marriage* encourages couples to discover and speak each other's primary love language. The five love languages are (1) words of affirmation, (2) acts of service, (3) receiving gifts, (4) physical touch, and (5) quality time. What love language does Derek speak? How can you tell? What is Kim's response to his way of communicating love? What is Kim's love language? How

does Derek feel about it?

10. In this book, Charlie Moore teaches Derek how to "fish" (pages 287–289). "Fishing" is Strategy 4 — empathetic listening — in *The Four Seasons of Marriage.* What is the goal of this kind of "fishing"? Practical ways to do this include (1) listening with an attitude of understanding (not judgment); (2) withholding judgment on the other person's ideas; (3) affirming the other person, even when you disagree with his or her ideas; and (4) sharing your own ideas only after the other person feels understood. How did Derek begin to listen empathetically to Lydia? to Kim? How was Kim's "bait" different from Derek's? Can you describe how you might listen empathetically to your spouse or loved one regarding an area of disagreement in your relationship?

11. Think about the other couples in *Summer Breeze.* Along with Kim and Derek Finley, you have met Ashley and Brad Hanes, Esther and Charlie Moore, and Brenda and Steve Hansen. Patsy Pringle, viewing her salon as a garden, describes the season she believes each woman is experiencing in marriage (pages 150–

153). From what you have learned about these marriages, would you agree with Patsy? Why or why not?

12. During a meeting of the TLC, Cody quotes a Bible passage his father taught him, Isaiah 2:18–21: "Idols will completely disappear. When the Lord rises to shake the earth, his enemies will crawl into holes in the ground. They will hide in caves in the rocks from the terror of the Lord and the glory of his majesty. On that day of judgment they will abandon the gold and silver idols they made for themselves to worship. They will leave their gods to the rodents and bats, while they crawl away into caverns and hide among the jagged rocks in the cliffs. They will try to escape the terror of the Lord and the glory of his majesty as he rises to shake the earth" (NLT). What characteristics of God does this passage reveal? Do these traits fit with your concept of Him? What are idols, and why is God so angry about them? Idols made of gold, silver, brass, clay, and wood are still worshipped in many countries of the world, mostly in the East. Are there other things that people in the Western world idolize?

13. In this book, the character of Cody is childlike in his faith and understanding. Recall some of the truths he speaks and how they affect the other characters. What was your favorite "Cody moment"?

ABOUT THE AUTHORS

Catherine Palmer lives in Missouri with her husband, Tim, and sons, Geoffrey and Andrei. She is a graduate of Southwest Baptist University and holds a master's degree in English from Baylor University. Her first book was published in 1988. Since then, Catherine has published more than 40 novels and won numerous awards for her writing, including the Christy Award — the highest honor in Christian fiction — in 2001 for *A Touch of Betrayal.* In 2004 she was given the Career Achievement Award for Inspirational Romance by *Romantic Times BOOKreviews* magazine. More than 2 million copies of Catherine's novels are currently in print.

Dr. Gary Chapman is the author of *The Four Seasons of Marriage,* the perennial best seller *The Five Love Languages* (over 3.5 million copies sold), and numerous other marriage and family books. He is the director of Marriage & Family Life Consultants, Inc., an internationally known speaker, and host of *A Growing Marriage,* a syndicated radio program heard on more than 100 stations across North America. He and his wife, Karolyn, live in North Carolina.

Praise for
Michael Koryta's *The Prophet*

One of *Kirkus Reviews'* Best Fiction Books of 2012

"*The Prophet* is a relentless, heart-in-your-throat thriller about ordinary people caught in the middle of an extraordinary nightmare. It's about the sins of the past haunting the hopes of the present and the need to find redemption from the jury of your own conscience. It's also a quantum leap for Michael Koryta and irrefutable proof that he has enough game to one day be considered a master of the genre." —Dennis Lehane

"Koryta comes back to the crime novel but with the depth of a seasoned pro. His best book yet." —Michael Connelly

"Michael Koryta is an amazingly talented writer, and I rank *The Prophet* as one of the sharpest and most superbly plotted crime novels I've read in my life."

—Donald Ray Pollock, author of *Knockemstiff* and *The Devil All the Time*

"Elegantly written.... Koryta shows great sensitivity in examining how each brother deals with these parallel tragedies." —Marilyn Stasio, *New York Times Book Review*

"I'm just glad it's me, not Michael Koryta, who is telling my son bedtime stories. The kid needs to sleep, and the Koryta Effect is cold sweats, nightmares, and me in the next room up past two because I can't put down *The Prophet*."

—Nicholas Dawidoff, author of *The Catcher Was a Spy* and *The Crowd Sounds Happy*

"*Friday Night Lights* meets *In Cold Blood* in this powerful tale of distant brothers in a small Ohio town whose torment over the murder of their sister when they were teens is compounded by the murder of another targeted teenage girl—a killing one of the brothers is determined to avenge even if that means committing murder himself.... Koryta, who drew acclaim with his supernatural thrillers *The Ridge* and *The Cypress House,* returns to crime fiction with a gripping work. This book succeeds on any number of levels. It's a brilliantly paced thriller that keeps its villains at a tantalizing distance, a compelling family portrait, a study in morality that goes beyond the usual black-and-white judgments, and an entertaining spin on classic football fiction. A flawless performance. A compulsively readable novel about brothers on opposite sides of life."

—*Kirkus Reviews* (starred review)

"I've been an admirer of the hardworking Michael Koryta for many years. I loved *So Cold the River*'s creepy gothic tone; I was enthralled by the eerie world of *The Cypress House.* Koryta is a fantastic writer, and a remarkable storyteller. But his latest book, *The Prophet,* finds him at an entirely new level; I suspect it may be the novel that brings him the sort of widespread acclaim he's deserved all along. A gridiron metaphor would seem appropriate, given the crucial role football plays in *The Prophet.* It's as if Koryta has been wowing us with a brilliant running game for eight novels. We'd be more than happy to see him keep driving the ball up the middle, but here, suddenly, he's gone to the air: *The Prophet* is like a long, heart-stopping pass down the sidelines in the final seconds of a decisive game. It's made me want to leap to my feet and cheer him on."

—Scott Smith, author of *The Ruins* and *A Simple Plan*

"After three supernatural thrillers, Thriller Award–finalist Koryta (*The Ridge*) triumphantly returns to crime fiction with this multilayered exploration of guilt and redemption.... Like Laura Lippman, Koryta has a gift for melding a suspenseful, twisty plot with a probing, unflinching look at his protagonists' weaknesses."   —*Publishers Weekly*

"A delicious read, intricately woven, with characters who are impossible to forget. Michael Koryta excites and satisfies on every level."   —Elin Hilderbrand

"Edgar-nominated mystery wunderkind Koryta (he turns thirty this year) has earned kudos from veteran thriller writers Stephen King and Dean Koontz. He proves plenty worthy of praise in this vivid portrayal of a small Midwestern town and the evils that befall it. Koryta's recent novels (e.g., *The Ridge*, 2011) have combined suspense with horror and the supernatural, but this time he returns to his mainstream thriller roots. With its crisp writing and steady suspense, this is a must-read for his fans both old and new."   —*Booklist*

"Koryta's latest thriller powerfully portrays the angst of the dysfunctional family stretched to the breaking point by blame and guilt. The tension and suspense are relieved only by scenes depicting Kent's football team in fierce combat at the state finals. Gut-wrenching at every level."   —*Library Journal*

"Koryta's latest book shows him gaining strength as a writer of thrillers.... This up-and-coming author has produced a compelling page-turner, notable for its nuanced sense of humanity and loss."
—Laura DeMarco,
Cleveland Plain Dealer

"Koryta's eerie prologue has the reader settling in for a dark tale, an encounter with a villain as nasty as Hannibal Lecter.... A twisting, surprising, and satisfying finish that ends the story as strongly as it begins."

—Gerald Bartell, *San Francisco Chronicle*

"A compelling story...a powerful psychological portrait.... Koryta skillfully contrasts the two brothers, telling the story from their alternating points of view and ratcheting up the suspense. The book's detailed accounts of football games don't slow the action but complement it and deepen the portraits of Adam and Kent."

—Colette Bancroft, *Tampa Bay Times*

"Deliciously complicated.... With each turned page, Koryta builds the impression that something unearthly is gaining strength.... It is, in a word, chilling.... That he manages to make a football championship equally compelling is especially impressive. It's certainly an odd pairing. (Will they find the killer before he strikes again? Will the wide receiver whose girlfriend was murdered be able to concentrate in the big game?) But Koryta, who has yet to turn thirty, merges the two story lines masterfully in what is surely one of the summer's best thrillers."

—Doug Childers, *Richmond Times-Dispatch*

"Michael Koryta is a superb storyteller who counts Stephen King and Dennis Lehane among his fans."   —*Parade*

THE PROPHET

THE PROPHET

MICHAEL KORYTA

BACK BAY BOOKS
LITTLE, BROWN AND COMPANY
NEW YORK BOSTON LONDON

Copyright © 2012 by Michael Koryta
Reading group guide copyright © 2013 by Michael Koryta and Little, Brown and Company

Back Bay Books / Little, Brown and Company
Hachette Book Group
1290 Avenue of the Americas, New York, NY 10104
littlebrown.com

Originally published in hardcover by Little, Brown and Company, August 2012

First Back Bay paperback edition, August 2013

Back Bay Books is an imprint of Little, Brown and Company, a division of Hachette Book Group, Inc. The Back Bay Books name and logo are trademarks of Hachette Book Group, Inc.

The publisher is not responsible for websites (or their content) that are not owned by the publisher.

The Hachette Speakers Bureau provides a wide range of authors for speaking events. To find out more, go to hachettespeakersbureau.com or call (866) 376-6591.

The author is grateful for permission to use lyrics from "Return to Me," by Matthew Ryan, from the album *Regret Over the Wires* © Irving Music Inc./BMI.

Library of Congress Cataloging-in-Publication Data
Koryta, Michael.
   The prophet / Michael Koryta — 1st ed.
      p. cm.
   ISBN 978-0-316-12261-0 (hc) / 978-0-316-22420-8 (large print) /
978-0-316-12259-7 (pb)
   1. Brothers—Fiction.   I. Title.
   PS3611.O749P76 2012
   813'.6—dc23   2012014690

10 9 8 7 6

LSC-H

Printed in the United States of America

*To the spring baseball commissioner — deepest thanks
to a great friend*

I keep hoping for a cure,

for some medicine,

just one conversation.

I can't return to you,

you must return to me,

that's the deal.

I'm sorry.

Did I say I'm sorry?

"Return to Me"
Matthew Ryan

Part One

PLEDGES

PROLOGUE

*T*HE TOWN FEELS LIKE *home immediately, and he credits the leaves. It must be a pickup day. Plastic bags bursting with withered remains of life are stacked on the curbs, a few spilling over onto the sidewalks, flecks of crimson and copper that dot the white concrete like blood splatters on pale flesh. The air is that contrary blend: alive with a smell, but the smell is death.*

Those who pass him have their heads down and shoulders hunched, turtles seeking their shells. He stands tall as he walks, embracing the cold wind, which is wonderfully unblocked by concrete walls, unmarred by razor wire fencing. He is grateful for that. There are other people in this town who have similar feelings, memories of days when one could not embrace the wind and longed to, no matter how bitter and chill. He knows some of them, and he knows that those very memories — realities — are in some cases exactly what chased them to this town, a chance to hide from the past.

At first glance, this town feels like a fine place for hiding from reality, too: impossibly quaint, with an actual town square and a brick courthouse. It could be the stage set from some Hollywood version of small-town middle America if not for all the empty buildings.

Half the storefronts facing the courthouse have FOR RENT *or* FOR SALE *signs in dusty windows. As he moves away from the square, walking north, toward the lake, stepping carefully around those swollen bags of leaves, he encounters vacant properties, once-tidy yards filled with brown weeds, vinyl siding begging for a hose and some bleach.*

Hard times have come to Chambers, Ohio.

Five blocks farther north, the lake visible now, the smell of water pushed toward him by a steady wind, and he departs to follow the signs for the high school. Turns west, walks a few more blocks, and now he can see it. A two-story main structure with single-story wings sprawling in odd directions, indications that several additions have been made over the years.

Chambers High School, Home of the Cardinals.

A cardinal was the third creature he ever killed. Caught it beneath his grandmother's birdfeeder. He'd watched the cat's approach to this task and marveled. The cat didn't hide; it just waited with incredible, dazzling patience. There was no cover under the birdfeeder, nothing to shield a killer, and still the killer succeeded. As the cat approached, the birds would scatter. The cat was unbothered by that, content in his role and devoted to it, possessed of unusual clarity of purpose. The cat would simply settle down into the grass beside a dusting of fallen sunflower seeds and wait. And without fail, the birds would return. Even though they could see the cat, its lack of motion reassured them, convinced them that they were safe. The cat never reacted to those first birds. The cat would wait, and watch, and eventually they'd become so confident in their safety that one would come just near enough, and then there would be a blinding strike, and those around the victim would scatter.

Give them enough time, though? Then they would return. Always. Because the feeder was there, the feeder was home, and though they might be capable of remembering what had befallen one of their own in the same spot, they did not believe it could happen to them as well.

Unshakable confidence. Unshakable stupidity.

He is fascinated by the confident specimens of the helpless. He finds no fascination in the fearful.

The first bird took him longer than it took the cat, but not as long as he'd expected. The secret was in his stillness. The secret was in their stupidity. It took him only five days to get the cardinal. He killed the cat when that was done. There was nothing more to be learned from it.

He has patience for study, and hunger for it, in the way that only those truly devoted to a craft can ever possess. His craft is killing. His understanding of it is great, but he knows there will always be more to learn, and in that knowledge is his happiness. He has studied the behavior of killers, has spoken with them, has lived behind steel bars with them, and he has learned from them all.

Now, as the wind freshens and the smell of dead leaves fills air that is rapidly chilling with the promise of rain, he stares at the front of the high school long enough to observe the security guard in the parking lot, and then he walks down the block and turns the corner and the football field comes into view. Here the Cardinals make their claim to glory. It's a terrible name for sporting teams. Why not the Warriors or Titans or Tigers? How does one summon any level of confidence wearing the logo of a bird that can be killed by the squeeze of a child's palm?

There are half a dozen men sitting in the aluminum bleachers that border the field. He is not the only watcher today. They are undefeated, these Cardinals, they are the most intense pride of a town that once had many more reasons to be proud.

He slips in, leans beside the bleachers with hands in pockets, and waits for the coach to arrive. The coach, of course, is more than a coach. He has won 153 games for this school, this community. He has lost only twenty-two. On this field where his players are now stretching, limbering up against the wind and beneath the gray sky, he has a record of eighty-one wins against four losses. Just four home losses. He's more than a coach, he is a folk hero. A mythic figure. And not just because of the wins. Oh, no. Coach Kent Austin is about much more than football.

He proves it now, drawing silence as he walks across the field, still a young man and a fit one but always with the trace of a limp, the left knee refusing to match strides with the right, always yielding just a little more, a little too much. It only adds to the coach's compelling quality. Everyone else recognizes his wounds; the coach pretends not to.

It is not only the young players in uniform who fall silent as the coach makes his way across the field, it is the men in the stands, the watchers. There is a reverence about them now, because what happens on this field matters deeply to people who have not so much as walked across its surface. You take your pride where you can find it, and right now, this is where it can be found. Because hard times have come to Chambers. This much he understands well, reads it as a weather forecaster would read the dark clouds scudding in off Lake Erie. He is a forecaster in his own right.

A prophet of hard times.

The coach is far too focused to look up and see him, because the coach is at work, lost to the game that he insists does not matter, but of course it matters because it is all he really has, in the end. Empty games and empty faith. Hollow words and false promises. A child's preoccupations and distractions, carefully constructed walls to separate him from the reality of the world that owns him, that carries him in an open palm that could so swiftly turn into a closed fist. He needs to feel the first squeeze of that fist.

The prophet spent three years with a killer named Zane who murdered his wife and both of her parents with a ten-gauge shotgun. Quite a messy weapon, the ten-gauge. Before he pulled the trigger, he gave all three of them the chance to renounce God. To say that Zane was their God. A promising idea, though poorly understood. Zane was not of proper depth for such a task, but he was to be admired for the effort nevertheless. The way Zane told it, two of the victims accepted him as their God and one did not. It made no difference in their fate, of course, but Zane was interested in their answers, and so was the prophet. At one time, he was even impressed. The idea of posing that question to someone facing the final seconds before entering eternity seemed powerful.

He no longer believes this, though. Consideration has shown him its weaknesses and ultimate insignificance. The question and its answer mean little. What matters, what Zane was unable to see—he was an impulsive man was Zane—is in the removing of the question from the mind entirely, and replacing it with certainty.

There is no God.

You walk alone in the darkness.

To prove this, to imprint it in the mind so deeply that no alternative can so much as flicker, is the goal. This is power, pure as it comes.

Bring him the hopeful and he will leave them hopeless. Bring him the strong and he will leave them broken. Bring him the full and he will leave them empty.

The prophet's goal is simple. When the final scream in the night comes, whoever issues it will be certain of one thing:

No one hears.

What he has been promised in Chambers, Ohio, is strength and resiliency. He has looked into a confident man's eyes and heard his assurance that there is no fear that will not bow to his faith.

The prophet of hard times, who has looked into many a confident gaze in his day, has his doubts about that.

I

ADAM HAD HIS SHIRT LIFTED, studying the lead-colored bruise along his ribcage, when the girl opened the door. She turned her head in swift horror, as if she'd caught him crouched on his desk in the nude. He gave the bruise one more look, frowning, and then lowered his shirt.

"Want a lesson for the day?"

The girl, a brunette with very tan skin—too tan for this time of the year in this part of the world—turned back hesitantly and didn't speak.

"If you're going to tell a drunk man that it's time to go back to jail, you ought to see that the pool cue is out of his hand first," Adam told her.

She parted her lips, then closed them again.

"Not your concern," Adam said. "Sorry. Come on in."

She stepped forward and let the door swing shut. When the latch clicked, she glanced backward, as if worried about being trapped in here with him.

Husband is a good decade older than her, Adam thought. *He hasn't hit her, at least not yet or at least not recently, but he's the kind who might. The charges probably aren't domestic. Let's say, oh, drunk and disorderly. It won't be costly to get him out. Not in dollars, at least.*

He walked behind the desk, then extended a hand and said, "Adam Austin."

Another hesitation, and then she reached forward and took his hand. Her eyes dropped to his knuckles, which were swollen and scabbed. When she removed her hand, he saw that she was wearing bright red nail polish with some sort of silver glitter worked into it.

"My name's April."

"All right." He dropped into the leather swivel chair behind the desk, trying not to wince at the pain in his side. "Somebody you care about in a little trouble, April?"

She tilted her head. "What?"

"I assume you're looking to post a bond."

She shook her head. "No. That's not it." She was holding a folder in her free hand, and now she lifted it and held it against her chest while she sat in one of the two chairs in front of the desk. It was a bright blue folder, plastic and shiny.

"No?" The sign said AA BAIL BONDS. People who came to see him came for a reason.

"Look, um, you're the detective, right?"

The detective. He did indeed hold a PI license. He did not recall ever being referred to as "the detective" before.

"I'm ... yeah. I do that kind of work."

He didn't think he was even listed in the phone book as a private investigator. He was just AA Bail Bonds, which covered both his initials and gave him pole position in the Yellow Pages as people with shaking hands turned pages seeking help.

The girl didn't say anything, but looked down at that shiny folder as if it held the secrets of her life. Adam, touching his left side gingerly with his fingertips, still trying to assess whether the ribs were bruised or cracked, said, "What exactly brought you here, April?"

"I'd heard...I was given a referral."

"A referral," he echoed. "Can I ask the source?"

She pushed her hair back over her left ear and sat forward in the chair, meeting his eyes for the first time, as if she'd summoned some confidence. "My boyfriend. Your brother was his football coach. We heard from him that you were a detective."

Adam said, "My brother?" in an empty voice.

"Yes. Coach Austin."

"Kent," he said. "We're not on his squad, April. We can call him Kent."

She didn't seem to like that idea, but she nodded.

"My brother gave you a referral," he said, and found himself amused somehow, despite the aching ribs and bruised hand and the sandpaper eyelids that a full week of uneven hours and too much drinking provided. Until she walked in, he'd been two minutes from locking the office and going in pursuit of black coffee. The tallest cup and strongest blend they had. A savage headache had been building, and he needed something beyond Advil to take its knees out.

"That's right." She seemed unsatisfied with his response, as if she'd expected the mention of his brother would establish a personal connection. "I'm in school at Baldwin-Wallace College. A senior."

"Terrific," Adam said.

"It's a good school."

"I've always understood that to be true." He was trying to keep his attention on her, but right now all she represented was a delay between him and coffee. "What's in the folder?"

She looked down protectively, as if he'd violated the folder's privacy. "Some letters."

He waited. Could this take any longer? He was used to fighting his way through personal stories he didn't care to hear about, used to deflecting tales of woe, but he did not have the patience to tug one out just so he could *begin* deflecting it.

"What precisely do you need, April?"

"I'd like to get in touch with my father."

"You don't know him?" Adam said, thinking that this wasn't the sort of problem he could handle even if it interested him. How in the hell did you go about finding someone who'd abandoned his child decades ago? It wasn't like chasing down a guy who'd skipped out on bail, leaving behind a fresh trail of friends, relatives, and property.

"I've met him," she said. "But he was…well, by the time I was old enough to really get to know him, he was already in prison."

Adam understood now why she'd gone to the trouble of telling him that she was in a good school. She didn't want him to form his understanding of her from this one element, the knowledge that her father was in prison.

"I see. Well, we can figure out where he's doing his time easily enough."

"He's done. He's out."

Damn. That would slow things down.

"What I've got," the too-tan-for-October girl said, "is some letters. We started writing while he was still in prison. That was, actually, your brother's idea."

"No kidding," Adam said, doing his damnedest to hide his disgust. Just what this girl needed, a relationship with some asshole in a cell. But Kent, he'd have found that a fine plan. Adam's brother had gotten a lot of ink for his prison visits over the years. DRIVEN BY THE PAST, one headline had read. Adam found that a patently obvious observation. Everyone was driven by the past, all the time. Did Kent's past play a role in his prison visits? Of course. Did that shared past play a role in Adam's own prison visits? Better believe it. They were just different sorts of visits.

"Yes. And it was a *wonderful* idea. I mean, I learned to forgive him, you know? And then to understand that he wasn't this monster, that he was someone who made a mistake and—"

"He stopped writing when he got out?"

She stuttered to a stop. "No. Well, he did for a while. But it's an adjustment."

"It certainly is," Adam said, thinking *That's why most of them go right back.* She was so damn young. This was what college seniors looked like? Shit, he was getting old. These girls seemed to be moving backward, sliding away from him just as fast as he aged away from them, until their youth was an impossible thing to comprehend.

"Right," April said, pleased that he'd agreed. "So some time passed. Five months. It was frustrating, but then I got another letter, and he told me he'd gotten out and explained how difficult it was, and apologized."

Of course he did. Has he asked for money yet?

"So now he writes, but he hasn't given me his address. He said he's nervous about meeting me, and I understand that. I don't want to force things. But I'd at least like to be able to write back, you know? And I don't want him to be...*scared* of me."

Adam thought that maybe he didn't need coffee anymore. Maybe he needed a beer. It was four in the afternoon. That was close enough to happy hour to count, wasn't it?

"You might give him some time on that," he said. "You might—"

"I will give him time. But I can't give him anything more than that if I can't write back."

That's the point, honey. Give him nothing but time and distance.

"He explained where he was living," she said. "I feel like I should have been able to find it myself, honestly. I tried on the

Internet, but I guess I don't know what I'm doing. Anyhow, I'd love it if you'd find the address. All I want to do is respond, right? To let him know that he doesn't need to be afraid of me. I'm not going to ask him to start being a *dad*."

Adam rubbed his eyes. "I'm more of a, uh, local-focused type. I don't do a lot of—"

"He's in town."

"Chambers?"

She nodded.

"He's from here?"

She seemed to consider this a difficult question. "We all are, originally. My family. I mean, everyone left, like me to go to college, and..."

And your father to go to prison. Yes, everyone left.

She opened the folder and withdrew a photocopy of a letter.

"In this, he gives the name of his landlord. It should be easy to come up with a list, right? He's living in a rental house, and this is the name of the woman who owns it. It should be easy."

It *would* be easy. One stop at the auditor's office and he'd have every piece of property in this woman's name.

"Maybe you should let things take a natural course," he said.

Her eyes sparked. "I have plenty of people who actually know something about this situation who can give me *advice*. I'm asking you to give me an *address*."

It should have pissed him off, but instead it almost made him smile. He hadn't thought she had that in her, not after the way she'd crept so uneasily into his office, scared by the sound of the door shutting behind her. He wished she'd come in when Chelsea was working. Not that Chelsea had a gentle touch, but maybe that was why it would have been better. Someone needed to chase her out of here, and Adam wasn't doing a good job of that.

"Fair enough," he said. "May I see the letter?"

She passed it over. A typed letter, the message filling barely a quarter of the page.

Dear April,

I understand you're probably not very happy with me. It just takes some time to adjust, that's all. I don't want you to expect more of me than I can be. Right now I will just say that it feels good to be back home. And a little frightening. You might be surprised at that. But remember it has been a while since I was here. Since I was anywhere. It's great to be out, of course, just strange and new. I am living in a rental house with a roof that leaks and a furnace that stinks when it runs, but it still feels like a castle. Mrs. Ruzich — that's my landlord — keeps apologizing and saying she will fix those things and I tell her there is no rush, they don't bother me. I'm not lying about that.

It is my favorite season here. Autumn — so beautiful. Love the way those leaves smell, don't you? I hope you are doing good. I hope you aren't too upset about the way I've handled things. Take care of yourself.

Jason (Dad)

Adam read through it and handed it back to her. He didn't say what he wanted to — *Let it breathe, don't force contact because it will likely bring you nothing but pain* — because that argument had already been shot down with gusto. The landlord's name made it cake, anyhow. Ruzich? There wouldn't be many.

"I just want to write him a short note," April repeated. "Tell him that I'm wishing him well and that he doesn't need to be worried about my expectations."

Definitely beer, Adam thought. *Definitely skip the coffee and go right to beer.*

"Can you get me an address?" she asked.

"Probably. I bill for my time, nothing more, nothing less. The results of the situation aren't my responsibility. All I guarantee is my time."

She nodded, reached into her purse. "I'm prepared to pay two hundred dollars."

"Give me a hundred. I charge fifty an hour. If it takes me more than two hours, I'll let you know."

He charged one hundred an hour, but this would likely take him all of twenty minutes and it was good to seem generous.

"All right." She counted out five twenty-dollar bills and pushed them across the desk. "One other thing—you have a policy of being confidential, don't you? Like a lawyer?"

"I'm not a lawyer."

She looked dismayed.

"But I also am not a talker," Adam said. "My business is my own, and yours is your own. I won't talk about it unless a police officer walks in this door and tells me to."

"That won't happen."

She had no idea how often that *did* happen with Adam's clients.

"I just wanted to be sure...it's private, you know," she said. "It's a private thing."

"I'm not putting out any press releases."

"Right. But you won't even say anything to, um, to your brother? I mean, don't get me wrong, I really respect Coach Austin, but...it's private."

"Kent and I don't do a whole lot of talking," Adam said. "What I will do is find some potential addresses and pass them along to you. The rest is between you and your dad."

She nodded, grateful.

"How do I get in touch with you?" he said.

She gave him a cell phone number, which he wrote down on a legal pad. Beside it he wrote *April* and then looked up.

"Last name?"

She frowned, and he knew why she didn't want to give it. If she still carried her father's name, and he was betting that she did, then she was afraid Adam would look into what the man had done to land in prison.

"Harper," she said. "But remember, this is—"

"Private. Yes, Miss Harper. I understand that. I deal with it every day."

She thanked him, shook his hand. She smelled of cocoa, and he thought about that and her dark skin and figured she'd just left a tanning bed. October in northern Ohio. All the pretty girls were fighting the gathering cold and darkness. Trying to carry summer into the winter.

"I'll be in touch," he said, and he waited long enough to hear the engine of her car start in the parking lot before he locked the office and went to get his beer.

2

KENT KNEW WHAT THEY were hearing and what they were reading: this was their season, the stuff of destiny, and they were too good to lose.

It was his job to make them forget that.

This week, that would be a little more difficult. They'd played a good team on Friday, a ranked team, and handled them easily, 34–14, to complete the first perfect regular season in school history. They'd won every statistical battle, and while Kent didn't believe in paying much attention to statistics, he knew that his boys watched them carefully, and he was happy to use that tendency against them. In four short days they'd play again, the first playoff game, and there would be pep rallies and television cameras and T-shirts announcing their unbeaten season.

All of those things scared him more than anything the opponent might do. Overconfidence was a killer.

So, knowing that their confidence would be a difficult thing to shake, knowing that they'd be looking ahead to the school's first state championship in twenty-two years—an undefeated championship, no less—he sought out drills that would show their weaknesses.

Colin Mears would be all-state at receiver for the second year in a row. The fastest kid Kent had ever coached at the position, and the most sure-handed, Colin would run routes all practice long with a smile on his face. Colin would not block long with a smile on his face. His lanky, lean frame made it difficult for him to get low enough quick enough to set the kind of block that contributed, and the Cardinal linebackers were happy to demonstrate that to him. Damon Ritter in particular, who ranked among Kent's all-time favorite players, a quiet black kid with an unmatched ability to transfer game video to on-field execution, as bright a player as Kent had ever had at middle linebacker. Lorell McCoy, likewise, would be all-state at quarterback for the second year in a row. He had the touch that you didn't see often in a high school quarterback, could zip it in like a dart when needed or float one up so soft in the corner of the end zone that his receiver always had time to gather his feet. What Lorell didn't have was Colin's speed. He had unusual pocket presence and read gaps well enough that he could gain yards up the middle consistently, but he had no burst. On a naked bootleg, then, taking the snap and sprinting around the end, he would nearly always be lacking the gear needed to make the play a success, and on the bootleg, Colin Mears had to block, his least favorite thing.

They ran the naked bootleg for the last twenty minutes of practice.

Kent didn't have any intention of beating Spencer Heights on Friday night with this play, but he did intend to beat Spencer Heights, and this reminder of the things that his boys *couldn't* do well was important. This unbeaten team needed to leave the practice field with a sense of fallibility. The attitude you needed to win football games was a difficult balance. Confidence was crucial; overconfidence killed. Success lived on the blade's edge between.

Up in the bleachers, thirty people were watching. It was cold and windy, but there they sat anyhow. Talents like Mears and Ritter and McCoy were on their way out of the program, and their like might not pass through Chambers again. This much Kent understood better than anyone. He'd been the head coach for thirteen seasons now and had reached the state championship game twice. He had never had a team like this.

Watching them now, he wanted the lights on and the ball in the air. Wanted game day. That was unusual. Like most coaches, he was always wishing for one more practice day. You were never prepared enough. This week, though, this season, this team? He found himself wanting to be under the game lights. Wanted it over, so he could begin wishing that it had never ended. Because if he couldn't close out that elusive state championship with *this* kind of talent?

It's a game played among boys, he reminded himself while Matt Byers, his defensive coordinator, walked into the middle of the field to make a point about leverage, *and the reason you're here is to use this game to help these boys. You're not here to put a trophy in that case. Never were, never will be. That trophy's absence doesn't say a thing about your measure as a man, and its presence wouldn't, either.*

This season, though? This season that was difficult to remember.

He let Byers say his piece and then he called them over, everyone circling around him, forty-seven players and six coaches, and told them they were done.

"Keep your heads down," he said, the same thing he said to end every practice and locker room talk until the season was finished. Then he'd tell them to lift their heads up and make sure they held them high. Only then.

The practice officially over, Kent walked to midfield and most of the team followed. He offered no instruction for them to do so, and this was critical — the school board had required this of him after a complaint from a parent four years earlier. Praying with a public school team, he'd been told, was a violation of the separation of church and state. He couldn't require it of his players. And so he did not. He prayed to end every practice, but participation was voluntary.

The players took a knee and Kent offered a short prayer. Football was not mentioned. Never was, never would be, never should be. The closest he came was when he prayed for their health, though he caught himself drifting too close to the game sometimes this season even as the words were leaving his lips. A swift, sharp desire to make it specific: *Not Damon's knee, Lord, not his knee. God, please watch over Lorell's throwing shoulder…* Silly things, desires for which he would chastise himself privately, but still they arose.

Because this season…

"Amen," he said, and they echoed, and then they were on their feet and headed for the locker room at a run — no player walked onto or off of the field, ever. Kent watched while Colin Mears made a beeline to where his girlfriend, Rachel Bond, waited at the fence. One kiss, quick and amusingly chaste for hormonal teenagers, and then he rejoined the others. It was a deviation from the team-first routine that Kent ordinarily wouldn't have allowed, but you needed to understand your players as something beyond cogs in the gridiron machine. That girl had been through a great deal, and Colin was a light in the darkness for her. He was what Kent wanted them to be so badly: not only about more than football but also about more than the self.

Kent let the assistants follow the team to the locker room while he headed directly to the parking lot. This wasn't standard, but today he had places to be. A prison waited.

Standing behind the end zone, hands tucked in his pockets, was Dan Grissom, a local minister. Together, they would make the drive down to Mansfield, to one of the state's larger prisons, and there Kent would speak to a group of inmates. There would be some talk of football; there would be more talk of family. Truth be told, Kent had winced a little when he saw Grissom arrive, the reminder of his required task. He wanted to put it off until after the season, after playoffs. But responsibilities were responsibilities. You weren't allowed days off.

"They're looking good!" Dan said, gushing with his usual enthusiasm, and Kent smiled a little, because Dan didn't know the first thing about football. He knew plenty about encouragement, though.

"They should be," Kent told him. "It's that time of year."

"I can't believe you have a crowd in the stands just for a practice."

Kent turned and glanced into the bleachers, saw the faces, some familiar, some not. The watchers grew as the season went on, as the wins stacked up and the losses stayed at bay. Definitely more strangers on hand. Curious about what the Cardinals had. What they could do.

"It's a big deal in this town," he admitted.

"Alice and I would like to have you and Beth and the kids over for dinner," Dan said. "To celebrate the season."

"Let's wait until the season's done."

"I mean to celebrate how well it's gone so far," Dan said, and Kent wasn't sure if he imagined the uneasiness, the sense that Dan didn't expect it to close out as well as it had begun.

"I appreciate it. But dinner right now, it's tough. With practices, you know."

"We can eat late. Be fun to get the kids together. Sarah's the same age as Lisa, you know. I think they'd get along well."

"After practices, there's film," Kent said. And then, after

catching a glance between disappointment and reproach from the minister, he said, "I'm sorry, Dan. But this time of year I get a little...edgy. I'm not much of a dinner companion. So as soon as we're done, okay?"

"Sure thing," Dan said. "Win, lose, or draw, we're doing that dinner at season's end."

But there are no draws, Dan, Kent thought. *Not in the playoffs. It's win or lose.*

They were in the parking lot when they passed Rachel Bond, who caught Kent's eye and smiled, lifting a hand. He nodded and tipped two fingers off the bill of his cap. She was a prize. A convict for a father and an alcoholic for a mother and she'd risen above it all. It was unbelievable how much some of these children had to bear, so young.

But life? It didn't card you before it sold you some pain. Kent had been given the most personal of examples in that lesson. It was why he devoted so much of himself to a game. Sometimes a game was what you needed — mind, body, and soul. That much he'd known for years.

3

THERE WAS A TIME when Chambers County had produced more steel by itself than forty-six states. It had been home to mills for five major companies that exported worldwide, and the steel industry had employed more than half of the county's workforce.

That time was a whispered recollection now.

The steel industry was gone, and a decade since the last plant closed and two decades since the writing on the wall had been clear, nothing had been found to replace it. Chambers had boasted one of the highest unemployment rates in the state for years, and most of those who could leave did. The population had dropped by twenty-five percent since 1950, one of the few places in an always-growing country that had experienced such a thing. A manufacturing town that found itself without anything to manufacture.

While the census reported a declining population, the county jail reported a rising one. It had been remodeled and expanded twice. The core of the town's troubles — economic woes and absence of jobs — also provided the core of Adam's business.

Only two things were flourishing in Chambers of late: high school football and bail bonds.

Because he was busy, he had to determine focus areas. Nature of the beast, simple as that. A skip with a $10,000 bond was a priority. A girl with a hundred bucks and a missing father was not. April Harper got one call, and one call only, from Adam on the morning after her visit. She didn't answer her cell phone, so he left a message informing her that there was only one Ruzich in town who might own a rental property. Her first name was Eleanor, and she owned two homes: one that was assessed at three hundred thousand, pricey for Chambers, and another well outside of town, a place on a small private lake that looked like a seasonal property. If she was renting out a place with a leaking roof and a failing furnace, he told her, it was probably 7330 Shadow Wood Lane, the lake cottage.

He told her to call with questions and then hesitated for just a moment, tempted to remind her again that if her ex-con father wanted communication to be a one-way street, she might be well advised to agree. Then he remembered that the hundred dollars in his pocket had been paid for an address, not advice, and he disconnected the call. He hadn't allowed himself to look up Jason Harper's criminal record, because he knew what he'd think if he did, knew what he'd be tempted to tell his client: *Your father is toxic, and you need to stay the hell away from him.* Unlike his brother, he wasn't in the pro bono therapy business.

The average person — hell, the average client — viewed Adam as part of the criminal defense system. You needed an attorney to beat your charges, but you needed a bondsman to pop the locks on that cell while the attorneys played their games. In that part of the role, and only in that part, did Adam live up to the standard perception: he helped secure temporary release.

Emphasis on temporary. Adam did not view himself as any part of the criminal defense side of the spectrum. He viewed himself as a free-world jailer. Convictions might not yet have been made in the cases, but charges had been. After the good felons of Chambers County scraped together enough money to secure a surety bond, they walked back into the free world, entering a process of trial delays and plea bargains designed to keep them out. Maybe it would work, maybe it wouldn't. But during that process? During that process, they belonged to Adam. They weren't free, they were his. In nineteen years, more than three hundred of his clients had jumped bail. He'd found all but four. It wasn't a bad winning percentage. Those four, though? There were days he'd catch himself grinding his teeth over them.

The entire bail process was uniquely American. There were only two countries in the world that allowed a private business-man to pay to secure a prisoner's release—America and the Philippines. Criticism of the idea lay in the fact that defendants paid a nonrefundable sum to get out of jail, presenting an unfair burden on the innocent. Adam wasn't interested, and never had been, in the moral merits of his profession. What he was inter-ested in was the promise made with every bond he posted: he'd see that his wards faced their day in court. It was a small role, maybe, and hardly glamorous, but it counted. He knew just how much it counted.

Any curiosity he had over April Harper faded as the week progressed. On Thursday, which was a busy day on the Cham-bers County criminal court dockets, two of his own failed to show up for their hearings. One was facing his third round of charges for drunk driving. The second had a more serious charge, prison time likely, for selling OxyContin and Vicodin. Many people couldn't fathom the idea of simply failing to appear for a court date in a criminal case. They expected that the police would come after you then, expected SWAT teams kicking in doors and detectives sitting in surveillance vans, everyone vigorous and vigilant until the missing offender was caught. Much of the time, though, that would never happen. There were too many warrants, too many inmates, too many active cases. Police were overworked, prisons were overpopulated, and if you didn't show up for your court date, law enforcement wasn't necessarily going to come looking for you unless you were a high-profile offender. Enter Adam Austin, owner and operator of AA Bail Bonds.

He'd come for you.

The class of people Adam posted bond for didn't work nine-to-fives and didn't own alarm clocks. They didn't go to sleep; they passed out. They didn't fear missing a court date, because they were in no hurry to listen to their public defender explain why a plea bargain was the best option. Most of them simply paid their surety and walked out the door, and then they either showed up for court or they didn't. When they didn't, Adam got the call, and went hunting. Like with most forms of hunting, you had your best luck if you understood your prey and knew their territory. Adam was an excellent hunter. He'd float between bars and trailer parks and he'd intimidate when he could and open his wallet for bribes when he could not and he would work every angle until he got a lead that counted. It was a game of diligence, and Adam had diligence to spare. That had been put in him long ago, and it hadn't faded over time.

Never would.

On Friday after April Harper's visit, Adam learned that he had one skip missing, a painkiller-dealing gent named Jerry Norris. It was the third time Adam had held a bond for Jerry and the third time he'd gone missing. Adam wasn't overly worried about tracking him down, but he did know it would make for a late night, because he wouldn't be able to start until after the football game. The last place he wanted to be was at Chambers High School, but tonight was a playoff game, the first, and he would not miss a playoff game for his brother. He had never missed one before and he would not start now. Marie wouldn't let him. Marie might not have approved of what Adam was, but he attended to the things he knew she'd have demanded, and watching her little brother's team take a run at the state championship was one of them. Marie wouldn't allow Adam to miss the playoffs, no matter the circumstances. He'd tried it once, but he'd felt her ghost heavy around him, and the most frightening of ghosts is a disappointed one.

When the lights came on, he'd be in the stands.

One of Kent's preferences for a football game was that the kickoff be handled routinely. Big plays to open the game excited the fans, but not him, not even when they went his way. He'd just as soon see the ballgame get its start with a first and ten from the twenty every time out. High school kids were emotional atom bombs, and it was good to settle them down early.

His team didn't give him that chance tonight. Instead, Colin Mears decided that it was a good opportunity for the first fumbled kickoff of his career. It slipped through his gloved hands and between his legs and skittered backward, rolling all the way down to the five-yard line, and there Spencer Heights recovered. No first and ten from the twenty for Kent tonight; it was first and goal from the five, and his defense was taking the field in front of a suddenly hushed crowd.

Wonderful.

The defense held, stuffing three straight running attempts to the strong side, swarming to the ball carrier, and then the crowd was back into it, because holding Spencer Heights to a field goal from that starting position was no small feat.

Only they didn't go for the field goal. They lined up again,

THE PROPHET · 29

going for it on fourth down, and Kent had to admit that while he never would have made that call — he took points whenever he could — he liked the guts of it. What he didn't like was the way his safeties bit on the subsequent play-action fake, the way they came roaring in expecting another running play as a Spencer Heights receiver glided into the end zone on a seam route and caught the ball untouched.

The crowd was silent again, the Cardinals were down a touchdown, and Colin Mears was going to have his second attempt at catching a kickoff in just a matter of minutes. Kent thought about going to him, then dismissed it. Sometimes you showed your faith through silence.

Colin secured this one, though he didn't do much with the return, and then they had their first down and Lorell McCoy was under center and things were surely about to improve.

They didn't, though. His 10–0 squad was rattled, and spent the rest of the half proving it. Lorell and Colin misfired on several plays, the Spencer Heights pass rush was better than anybody — including Kent — had expected, and late in the second quarter the Cardinals' junior tailback, Justin Payne, fumbled the ball on what should have been a big gain, holding it low and away from his body as he tried to spin away from a tackler. Instead, the ball spun away from him — *high and tight, high and tight!* Kent shouted, sick of watching fundamental mistakes at a point in the season when fundamental mistakes should not be made — and then Spencer Heights went to work making them pay for the turnover again. It was 14–0 at the half, and the home crowd was silent.

Not this year, Kent thought as he walked to the locker room. They had made mistakes, yes, far too many of them, but they were correctable mistakes. They *would* be corrected, and his team would not lose this football game. As he left the field,

Kent's focus was on his own demeanor. Steady stride, steady stare. No pleasure in his face, of course, but no anger, either, no disgust, and above all else, no fear. While some coaches liked to feed players a testosterone-fueled fury, Kent wanted to teach them how to drain it away. The approach he wanted wasn't wild aggression, it was clinical discipline. If you prepared well enough, if you studied and anticipated and understood the opponent, there was no need for fear. When your opponent saw calm, when your opponent saw understanding and preparation, your opponent could not find fear. And so they felt it themselves. In the strength of your will, in your composure, they felt it.

Outside the locker room, the coaches paused for a few minutes, broken up into offensive and defensive sides of the ball. Here they had a brief opportunity for technical adjustments, a chance to look at the charted plays from the first half and consider what wasn't working, and why it wasn't. Once inside, Matt Byers took the first speaking role and started it off by punting an empty Gatorade jug across the room. This was standard fare. Byers was a holdover from the days when Kent himself had played on this field, a thirty-three-year assistant, and to say that his style differed from Kent's was a laughable understatement. Kent was cool precision, Byers was hot emotion. Matt could — and did — intimidate the hell out of the kids with furious and profane reactions to mistakes, theatrical demonstrations, and imposing size. They butted heads, sometimes so much so that the rest of his staff took bets on the likelihood of a firing, but in the end, Kent needed Matt. He'd let someone else throw clipboards and scream himself hoarse — it delivered a message to the boys, certainly, but what it also did was emphasize the occasions when Kent was the one shouting. Those caught more attention because it was not a constant. Players learned to tune out the consistently raving coaches. When Kent's voice rose, the field went silent fast. That was how he liked it.

Matt was in the midst of an explanation of how the team's performance apparently demonstrated that the players were not only pussy sons of bitches but also lacking in so much as a shred of respect for their fans, parents, state, and country when Kent rose from his chair. This was the signal, and this was where they'd had their greatest clashes. When Kent stood, Byers was to shut up and sit down. Immediately. He stopped in mid-tirade, which always distressed him, and said, "Listen to the head coach, now. Damn it, *listen*."

Kent stood and faced his team, let them all sit in silence, hoping they'd absorb two things from him: calmness and disappointment.

"Who thinks I'm upset with the numbers on that scoreboard?" he said eventually. His voice was low enough that those in the back leaned forward to hear.

Nobody raised a hand. They knew better; it was not a game of points to him, it was a game of execution. The points were a product of proper execution, and proper execution was a product of proper focus. He turned to Damon Ritter and said, "What am I upset with, Damon?"

"We're giving them their points."

"Correct. I want you boys to be generous, but not with the football." He swiveled to look at Colin Mears. "Colin, are you afraid of losing tonight?"

"No, sir."

"You ought to be," Kent said. "Tell me why that's true, Colin. Tell me why."

His star receiver said, "Because we aren't getting beat, we're losing the game."

This difference was critical; this difference was the focus of their season.

"Do me a favor, Colin. Read that poster on the wall behind me. Read it out loud."

The poster said, THERE IS A DIFFERENCE BETWEEN ACCEPTING A LOSS AND EARNING ONE. The boys were sick of hearing that little slogan. Kent watched while they heard it one more time.

"You've earned ten wins this year," he said. "Haven't earned a loss yet. If we have to accept one, we will. But, boys? Let's not earn it. Let's not do that."

He was looking at Colin, who nodded emphatically. There was something off with him, though. Something wrong with his focus. Of all the players to have playoff jitters, Colin was the most surprising. Kent decided they'd feed him the ball early in the second half, see if they could settle him down through repetition and ritual.

"We're going to run a lot of thirty-one flood at them," he began, and from then on their focus was on the technical details. He hoped.

If you focused on your individual responsibilities, good things happened as a team. Early in the third quarter, the Chambers safeties no longer biting on that play-action fake, Spencer Heights threw an interception. Then the offense finally got going, with Lorell and Colin connecting up the seam for a quick touchdown. They also scored at the start of the fourth, and when they got the ball back, it was a tie game with six minutes left. Lorell marched them down the field patiently, taking what was offered, letting the defense chase frantically after Colin on the vertical routes and then throwing into the windows underneath. They had first and goal from the three, and Kent looked at the field and thought, *What the heck, we practiced it,* and called for the bootleg. Lorell jogged in without a hand on him.

That was how it finished: 21–14. Kids and parents alike came streaming down out of the stands and onto the field and the band boomed away and Kent spoke to the opposing players, telling them all the reasons they might find victory in defeat. Through it all, he could already feel the squeeze in his chest. He knew the teams that awaited would be better, each week they would be better, and four teams and four weeks stood between Chambers and a trophy.

He was going to get it this year. He was going to get it.

4

W HAT KENT TOLD THE BOYS in the locker room — *Enjoy this one, all right? Don't look ahead yet. Tonight, relish the opportunity you've had to play ball this season with your best friends. But keep your heads down. We aren't done* — was something he believed. They were entitled to a night of celebration. The intensity of focus he demanded on the field needed to be released when they stepped off it. This was a game, and these were kids, and they needed to enjoy it.

For him, though, there would be no celebration. There had been an alarming number of mental errors made, fundamental mistakes, and those sickened Kent. He could tolerate many things, but not those that should have been handled by preparation and practice.

The digital age was a beautiful thing for a football coach. Less than an hour after the game concluded, he and his assistants already had the chance to watch a high-definition replay. Coffee had been made and cans of soda opened. No alcohol was allowed on school grounds, but after this session, most of his assistants would go out to drink together. Kent rarely joined, for two reasons: one, he didn't drink, and two, far more important, he understood that his staff often needed the opportunity to vent without him around. Or, more aptly, the need to vent about him. His was not a relaxed coaches' room, nothing about it was low-key, not even after victory, and he understood that this wore on them. He did not intend to address that by relaxing the tone, but he did know that it needed to be addressed. So they'd invite him out to join the festivities and he would decline, and it was better for everyone that way.

Before he released them, though, they'd assess the night's performance and agree to responsibilities for the next day's video breakdown. Tonight he knew that they wanted to get out early. Byers was hosting a celebration, and because of that, Kent would hold them a little longer. There were four games left, and they could refresh themselves on that notion before they refreshed themselves with a Budweiser.

While they all looked at their watches and then at the door, he hooked up the laptop to the projector and suggested they have a quick look at some key plays.

The first key play was that fumbled kickoff, and even though they knew it was coming, everyone shook their heads. Colin Mears didn't make mistakes like that. He just didn't.

"Won't happen again," promised Steve Haskins, who coached the receivers and special teams units. "First playoff game, lot of crowd energy, he was trying to show off a little, that's all. Break a big one for his parents, for his girl."

Kent nodded, but something felt off about the explanation.

"Something was up with him tonight," Kent said.

"He came back fine," Haskins said. "Big second half. Big."

"Yeah," Kent said, but still he was bothered. Maybe that's why it didn't come as a total surprise when he got the call from the police.

* * *

It was almost midnight and they were still watching the game video. The ringing phone got an immediate reaction, because one of the swiftly understood rules of Kent's locker rooms was that cell phones did not exist. He didn't hold his staff long, but when he had them there, he demanded focus. Each year there would be some new assistant who'd decide it was acceptable to send a text message or check an e-mail during a meeting. That would happen once. It would not happen twice.

This call came on the locker room landline, which almost never rang. All of the coaches were given the number at the start of the season with specific instructions to share it with family. You never knew when someone was going to need you for something bigger than football. Kent answered the phone, heard a man identifying himself as a lieutenant, and closed his eyes. It was not the first call from the police to this locker room, nor would it be the last. Boys got in trouble, even good boys.

So it wasn't the caller's identity that rattled Kent but the player's name. Colin Mears. *Something was wrong with him,* he thought. *Something was wrong and I could see it but I didn't ask, why didn't I ask?*

"What's he gotten into?" Kent said, and his voice drew attention from the other coaches. The next thing he said—whispered, really—was *"Oh, Lord,"* and then Byers grabbed the remote and shut off the video.

"Of course," Kent said into the phone while his assistants stared at him, trying to read the situation from the one-sided conversation. "Of course I can provide witnesses. Fifty of them."

That got a visible reaction, everyone turning to look at one another.

"I'll come down," he said. "You tell his parents I'm going to come down. Please."

He hung up, the room silent, everyone waiting.

"Rachel Bond is dead," he said. They all knew who she was. It was a small school and a smaller football program. When you had an all-state receiver on the roster, your coaches knew his girlfriend. "They've got Colin down at the jail."

"No way," Haskins said. "Absolutely no way on earth could that boy have —"

"Of course not."

"But they think?"

"I don't know," Kent said. "Probably not. He'd be one of the first to look at, that's all. I guess they need me to confirm where he was this afternoon and tonight. They want to see me."

Byers said, "First to look at. You're not talking a car wreck. Someone killed that girl?"

Kent nodded.

There was a hushed pause. Kent picked his keys up off the desk, stood, and said, "Get on home, gentlemen. Go see your families."

He drove with the windows down and the radio off and he prayed aloud, as was his habit when he drove in the darkness. He prayed for Rachel Bond and her family and for Colin Mears and for the police tasked with the investigation. Prayed for everyone he could think of except himself, because of all the people deserving, he was well down on the list.

Prepared for this, he told himself, flicking a glance at the mirror. *You are unusually, terribly prepared for this. Every horror has its purpose, and this...*

He prayed for his sister then, and her name rose through him and passed his lips like a strand of cold barbwire tugged from a coil within. *Marie Lynn.* How it hurt to let that go, as if by saying it aloud he was releasing her into a world that would not return her, and he knew that but did it anyhow. Memories of the dead. You wanted them close; you needed them far.

The police station was bright, clean limestone, the sidewalk marred by scattered leaves. Kent crunched through them and went up the steps to where the Mears family waited.

Looking for a leader, he reminded himself. It was important to know that people were watching. You carried yourself differently when you remembered that, carried yourself better. There under the bright lights when the crowd was watching, you could become a different man, the one you knew you should be. How much better would the world be if everyone operated under the lights and before the crowd, if they were not granted moments alone in the dark?

The police led him through a hall and into a room where Colin Mears and his parents sat at a small round table. Colin's face was a winter pallor with anguished and unbelieving eyes. Kent said, "Let's do what we have to do to help her, son. Let's do that first."

He meant doing *this:* the police station, the questions. He meant holding his head above the waters of grief for just a little longer. The boy understood.

"Yes, sir," Colin Mears said. "I'm trying."

Kent reached across the table and laid a hand on his shoulder, gave it a squeeze, and Colin's mother, Robin, said a soft "Thank you for coming." Kent nodded and stepped back and looked at the police officer who'd brought him in, a Lieutenant Salter.

"Anything you need from me, or my staff, I can get you immediately. Beyond my statement, and verification that he was with our team, what can we offer that will—"

"Hang on, Coach," Salter said. "We don't need any of that from you. We know where Colin was, and we understand that can be verified several hundred times over. What we need is a little more personal to you."

"Personal?" Kent said, and he thought, *Here it begins, the shared experience. They will want you to tell the boy how to carry this weight, because you had to once before.*

"Yes," Salter said. "Do you have any idea how we might get in touch with your brother?"

Kent swiveled his head a quarter turn, as if he'd had his ear in the wrong place and missed the question.

"My brother."

It wasn't Lieutenant Salter who answered but Colin.

"He helped her, Coach. But she wasn't... I don't think she was honest with him."

"Helped her," Kent said. "My brother helped Rachel."

He was squinting at the boy now.

"You have a number for him?" Salter asked. "We haven't been able to reach him. Sent someone out to his house, but he's not there."

"Probably a little early for that."

"It's past midnight."

"Yes," Kent said, and then he looked at Colin, catching up now. "You went to him for help with her father?"

"He wrote to her that he was out of prison. She wanted to find him. She believed him. We both believed him. And so I suggested..."

His words were swept away from him then like flimsy things in a gust of wind, and Kent said, "What do you mean, you believed him?"

Salter answered for the boy.

"Rachel's father never left prison, Coach. We don't know much yet, but that part is clear. So whoever your brother found for her... well, it was not her father."

"She didn't tell me she was going alone," Colin said, the tears spilling now. "I wouldn't have let her do that. She promised me I could go with her. I got a message just before the game, she said she was going to see him and would meet me at the game, but she wasn't there. She was missing at the start and she..."

Was missing at the end. Kent didn't need the boy to finish that sentence. He thought of the fumbled kickoff, the kid standing there alone waiting on a football to float through the air to him and trying to tell himself that it mattered. Why hadn't he told anyone? What might have been avoided if he'd spoken?

But of course he wouldn't have said anything. Kent's demands on the field were consistent: total focus. Total.

"The place where...where she was located," Salter said, choosing his words with gentle care, "is not where she was sent. This is why we need your brother. To find that place."

Kent lifted a hand, squeezed the bridge of his nose, and told himself to focus. He could not think of the full weight of it yet, could not allow himself to consider the scope of this night, the way it was spreading away, seeping into corners he'd never imagined it would touch.

"I can give you his cell phone number," he said. "I just can't guarantee that he'll answer."

Salter took the number and left to make his call and then, for a few minutes, it was just Kent and his star receiver and the boy's parents. Kent said, "Tell me how we got here, son."

It started in the summer, Colin explained, and this much Kent already knew. Rachel was around their house often because she was their regular babysitter and because Kent's wife, Beth, had taken a special interest in her. Mostly, Kent left her to Beth. The exception was in the situation with her father, who'd never been a figure in her life and was currently in prison. She was interested in Kent's prison visits, asked about them often, from details of the cells to what he thought of the men inside. She told him that she wanted to see her father again. It had been nearly ten years since their last encounter, when he stopped by to drop off a birthday card days after her seventh birthday, a crumpled ten-dollar bill inside, and Rachel's mother, a woman named Penny Gootee, chased him off. Kent's advice was to start with a letter. He warned her not to expect an answer.

She'd received one.

Short, curt, and to the point. Jason Bond was sorry they did not have a relationship. He appreciated her taking the time to write. He hoped her mother was well. Things for him were as good as could be expected. She was to stay in school, take care of herself, and make better decisions than he had.

Kent remembered this letter. He also remembered that the four Rachel sent back went unanswered. He'd tried to counsel her through that, tried to remind her that she represented guilt to the man, and that you could not rush a relationship along, could not force one into existence.

He was unaware of other letters. He hadn't pressed after learning that those beyond the initial attempt had been ignored. Then the season began, and while he was focusing on football, she was focusing on her father. Letters had been exchanged regularly, according to Colin, who had seen most of what Rachel's father had to say: apologies, always couched in the warning that he did not want to fail her again and perhaps they should not be in contact. There was talk of guilt, talk of almost everything Kent had explained to her earlier in the summer.

There was also talk of a pending release.

By September the letters were more frequent, and more detailed. Jason Bond said he was back in Chambers, close enough to tantalize the daughter who wanted to meet with him. But he would not be rushed. He urged her to understand that one-way communication was best, urged her not to discuss the situation with her mother because that was another relationship that he was not ready to handle just yet, if ever.

Not a bad ploy, because Rachel Bond's relationship with her mother was hardly a strong one. Penny Gootee was an alcoholic, given to struggles with depression and greater struggles with maintaining employment. Her only words for Rachel's father were soaked in bitterness. If there was one person to whom Rachel was unlikely to rush for guidance, it was her mother.

So she rushed to her boyfriend, to Colin. He had an idea. If she wanted to find a way to return her father's letters, she would have to locate him. And Coach Austin? He had a brother who was a detective.

5

HASLEM'S HAD A single TV mounted in the corner above the bar, an ancient, heavy thing in an age of sleek flat screens. Nobody ever complained, because what people came there to watch wasn't on television but cavorting across the stage and swinging around a stainless steel pole.

Adam Austin watched it for ten minutes, though. At 11:20 he asked the bartender, Davey, to tune it over to Cleveland's ABC affiliate.

"Volume?" Davey asked.

"No."

It was the sports segment of the local news, and all Adam wanted to see were the scores ticking by at the bottom of the screen. He wanted to know who was coming at his brother's team from the other side of the bracket. The only team in the state that posed a real risk was probably Saint Anthony's, a program that had dominated Kent's squad consistently. They'd won, of course. By forty points. A confident thrashing. Chambers, on the other hand, had advanced with a win that felt more like a sigh of relief.

"Too close, Franchise," Adam muttered as he thought about it, using a nickname that only one other person in the world had ever called his younger brother. "Way too close."

Kent had probably spent the past week preaching them up instead of teaching them to hit. That was his way. But they'd gotten the job done, they were 11–0, and the state title was no longer a dream for this town, it was an expectation. How his brother would handle that remained to be seen. Perhaps some of the Psalms would be forfeited in favor of the lessons of Lombardi, and the teachings of Paul would come to mean one man and one man only: Paul Brown.

Behind Adam there were three girls working the stage and maybe two dozen rednecks shoving bills at them. Every now and then somebody who'd just sold a used jet ski or some such bullshit would get giddy over his fortune and flash a twenty, but mostly these girls were dancing for dollars quite literally. Adam kept his back to them. He was waiting for the appearance of one Jerry Norris, who hadn't deemed Thursday's court appearance worth his time. Jerry hadn't shown yet, which suggested one of two things: he was too wasted to make it to the titty bar, or he had been tipped off to Adam's presence by a friend.

Adam meant to leave at midnight, but Davey poured him a shot of Jim Beam on the house, and it was sacrilege to pass on free whiskey. By the time it was gone, he felt a little less tired and a Drive-By Truckers song was playing on the computerized bastard imposter of a jukebox and he thought he might as well have one more last beer.

He'd had three last beers before the phone call came. He felt no surprise; the calls that came for him often came at this time of night. It was late and he was tired, but this would be money calling, and when money called, it didn't matter if it was late and you were tired. Hell, in his business, money rarely called at other hours. When it turned out to be Stan Salter, he was surprised but not stunned. He dealt with police too often for that.

"Which one of my favorites has done what?" he asked.

"It's not that kind of situation," Salter said. "We're going to need to talk to you in person, Adam. You good to drive in, or should I send someone out to get you?"

"The hell you talking about?"

"Homicide," Salter said. "When I say I need to talk to you, I mean *now*."

This wouldn't be the first time one of Adam's charges had killed somebody — it would, in fact, be the third — but it was never a pleasant experience.

"Who did it?" he asked.

"Adam, it's not that kind of case. We need to talk to you about the victim. I've been told you spoke with her recently."

"Name?"

"I said we're going to need to speak in person."

"And we will. I can still hear the damn name."

There was a hesitation, and then Salter said, "Rachel Bond."

"Don't know her," Adam said. He wouldn't have forgotten posting bond for someone named Bond. That shit would stick with you.

"We're hearing otherwise."

Rachel, he thought. *Rachel. Was that the woman who came in all bruised up, asking to get her husband out?*

"Blond chick, 'bout thirty?" he said. "Husband's name is Roger?"

"No," Salter said. "Brunette, and she wasn't about thirty. She was exactly seventeen. Came to you to ask for help finding her father."

"That's not right. No. That girl...her name was April. She was a college student."

But he was remembering the way he'd looked at her and thought that he was getting old fast, because college girls were beginning to look impossibly young.

"That may be what she said," Salter told him, "but that's not what she was. And she's dead now, Adam, and we need to talk about it. We need to talk *tonight*. I'll ask you again—can you make the drive or do I need to send someone?"

"I can make the drive," Adam said, thinking that she'd brought the letters in one of those plastic-covered folders that students carried. Not college students. And the nail polish. Red with silver sparkles. She'd painted her nails for the Cardinals.

"Then get down here. I'll be waiting on you."

Salter hung up, and Adam set the phone onto the bar and stared into the mirror in front of him. With all those rows of bottles, all he could make out of the reflection were his eyes and receding hairline.

"Fuck me," he whispered.

He didn't remember the address, to the great frustration of the men in the room with too-bright lighting and the smell of new plastic, a digital recorder running on the table.

"It was out in the country," he said. "On a lake. It was... Shadow Lane. No, Shadow Wood Lane. I don't remember the number."

"You're sure of the road?"

"Shadow Wood. Yes."

One of the detectives left then, and it was just Stan Salter and Adam.

"Do you think she was killed there?" Adam said.

"We're going to find out. Did you see the place?"

"No."

"Just gave her the address?"

Adam wasn't sure if Salter's tone was really loaded with contempt or if he was imagining it. He couldn't have blamed the man either way. He was remembering that while the girl had teeth that were straight and white, she'd smiled in an odd, careful way, lips-only most of the time, as if she'd worn braces until recently and was still trained by muscle memory and teenage insecurity to hide those now-perfect teeth...

No, she didn't. She didn't have that smile at all. That was a different girl. You cannot think of them together, Adam, you cannot do that.

"Yes. I gave her the address in a phone message. Said she could let me know if it didn't pan out, and then we'd try again. I never heard back. She told me her name was April Harper. She told me she was a college student."

"You make no habit of checking identification?" Salter asked, and Adam had to make an effort to focus on the question. He kept losing himself to that nail polish, that plastic folder, that smell of coconut that told him she'd been to a tanning bed.

"On my clients?" he said. "No. Who does? I wasn't letting her board a plane or even drink a beer, I was agreeing to do a job. Checking her age, that's not my responsibility."

But he was thinking—*seventeen, seventeen, seven-fucking-teen*—and the liquor was stirring in his belly like acid.

She'd looked it, too. He couldn't pretend otherwise, couldn't even grasp at the pathetic shield of claiming she'd been one of those girls who looked older than her age. If anything, she maybe looked a little younger. Would've been carded for cigarettes by any gas station clerk. Went out of her way to tell him she was a senior at Baldwin-Wallace, and while his eyes had said *No*, his brain had said *Who gives a shit* and her money had said *Just do the job, Adam.*

"You didn't think," Salter asked, "that she might be lying to you?"

"Everyone lies to me, Salter. All the time. Did I think she might be lying? Sure. But caring about *why* she was lying, that's just...look, she said what she wanted me to do and she had a reason for it and she had the letters."

"And the cash," Salter said.

Adam felt like breaking the smug prick's nose, Salter sitting there with his bristling military crew cut and hooded eyes and his badge, looking at Adam as if he were one of the dancers back at Haslem's, empty of dignity and hungry for a dollar.

"You don't need a paycheck?" Adam said. "You don't need to keep the mortgage paid?"

Salter's gaze didn't waver. "I'm not interested in the idea that you wanted work. I'm interested in the idea that she paid cash."

Right. Because cash suggested her age, at least to Salter, who expected an adult would have written a check or asked if Adam accepted credit cards.

"In my business," Adam said, "cash transactions aren't unusual."

This was true. A lot of people came to him with higher IQs than credit scores, and that wasn't to say they were bright.

"I see." Salter made a notation on his pad, and then said, "Let's talk about the letters she had. You read them?"

"Yeah." *Seventeen. A child. A corpse.*

"Did you make copies?"

"No. She'd already done that. What she had, they were copies. I never saw the originals. And I saw only one of the letters. But there were others."

"What did that letter say?"

"It was from her dad. He was—he'd been—in prison. Got out and then I guess he didn't write anymore for a while. She was upset about that. Then he started back up, but he wouldn't say where he was, wouldn't give a return address or anything. So it was just, you know, a one-way street. She wanted to be able to respond. Asked me to find him. An address, I mean."

"You're qualified for this sort of work?"

"I'm a licensed PI, you know that."

Salter didn't respond.

"It's what I do," Adam said. "Same thing I do every day. People skip out on bond, and I go find them. I bring them back. You know this."

"Nobody had skipped out on a bond here."

"Skill set," Adam said. "Same skill set."

"I see. So you used that skill set, and you found an address?"

"That's right."

"Do you remember it?"

"No."

"But you have records?"

"Yeah. Yes."

"She didn't give you a physical address? Just the phone number?"

"Just the phone number. She said she was a student at—"

"Baldwin-Wallace," Salter said. "Yes. She say how she picked you for the job?"

"She said she had a referral." Adam wished he'd stopped for a mint or some gum. He was breathing beer out with every word, and it made them seem flimsy, pathetic.

"We understand this part," Salter said. "Her boyfriend told us. The referral, if we can call it that, came from him. He plays football for your brother."

"Plays?" Adam said. "Like, right now? On this team?"

"Like right now," Salter said, nodding. "Colin Mears? I gather he and his family are pretty close to your brother. There was some conversation about you, and I guess Colin understood you to be a detective."

Adam let that glide by. *Understood you to be*, not *understands that you are.* Who cared? Who cared what Salter thought? What mattered here was a girl with glitter nail polish. What mattered was finding the sick son of a bitch who'd killed her, finding him and ending him. Because if you didn't...if he just stayed out there...

"It's a shame she lied to you," Salter said, "and a shame you didn't ask for any sort of identification. Because if you'd been operating with her real name, you'd have found her father easily. At Mansfield Correctional."

Adam stared at him. "He never left?"

"Never left. He's been there seven years. We've got people interviewing him right now. He says he wrote his last letter in August. So whoever kept writing? Whoever it is you found for her? We need to find *him*. Fast."

"Makes no sense," Adam said.

"What?"

"It doesn't make sense, Salter. I saw the letter, okay? The guy who wrote it was trying *not* to see her."

"Really?"

"Yes, really. I read the damn—"

"You've told me that. But it seems like he was tossing a lot of breadcrumbs out for someone who didn't want anyone following the trail. Telling her he was in town, then giving her his land-lord's name? This to a girl who was actively seeking contact with him? That doesn't strike you as contradictory?"

These were fair points, but still Adam shook his head.

"He knew where to find her, clearly. So what's the point in that kind of a game?"

"I'm not sure," Salter said. "But games aren't uncommon with stalking. Not at all."

"It's so patient, though," Adam said. "Waiting to see if she'd respond? If she'd look for him? It's too damn patient."

"Maybe he wasn't so patient. Maybe when she showed up at his door, it rushed him."

Adam remembered the numbers then. They floated toward him on a black breeze: 7330. On Shadow Wood Lane, yes. That was the address, that was the door at which she'd arrived.

That was where he'd sent her.

6

WHEN BETH CAME DOWNSTAIRS to greet Kent, it was past two in the morning but she didn't show any surprise. During the season, hours like this were no cause for alarm for a coach's wife, and in the years before they'd had children, hours like this had been Beth's norm. She'd been an ER nurse and intended to return to it once Lisa and Andrew were old enough. The night shift had never ebbed away from her; Kent sometimes found her making coffee at four in the morning simply because she knew better than to fight for a return to sleep.

Tonight, though, she'd been asleep. He could tell that from her foggy smile and the way her long blond hair was fuzzed out from the pillow. "Still perfect," she said. "Nice work, babe."

He'd opened the refrigerator to get a bottle of water and in the shaft of white light she saw something that made her say, "Hon?" in a concerned voice.

He took the water out and let the door swing shut and they were standing in darkness when he told her that Rachel Bond was dead.

"Someone killed that poor girl? Murdered her?" she said, her reflex response to bad news, stating the facts and considering them, the practiced reaction of someone who had been required to show poise in the face of crisis. Tonight it chafed. *Scream,* he wanted to say, *cry, shout, break down,* because no quality was so annoying in someone else as the very one you didn't like in yourself. He'd spent the whole night trying to offer calm and strength and to repress emotion. He was tired of that.

Beth crossed the kitchen and took him in her arms then and the irritable edge that sorrow and fatigue had given him melted into her warmth. He held her while he told her about the police station, all that had been said, Stan Salter and Colin Mears and the news about Adam.

"Adam sent her to him?" Beth leaned back, searching his eyes. *"Adam?"*

He nodded. "You remember the night that Colin asked me about him? Saw him in the team photo from the championship year and asked where he'd gone? Well, I told him he was still here, and I said...I said he was a private detective. He remembered that, apparently. And when Rachel decided to try and find her father..."

"She went to Adam."

"Yes."

They were silent. Kent finished his water. Neither of them turned on the lights.

"She was such a beautiful girl," Beth whispered. "In every way. Too mature. You know I used to tell you that. Like she'd never been a *girl,* always had to be an adult."

"I know."

Beth wiped tears from her eyes with her fingertips. "She was going to do so much, Kent. She was one of those...you could just tell that she was going to do so much."

Her voice trailed off and he reached out and stroked her hair as she took a shaking breath, folded her arms tightly around herself, and said, "By tomorrow morning, people will have heard what happened. Maybe before practice."

"We won't practice. I'll say a few words, send them home." He leaned against the counter and removed his baseball cap and ran a hand through his hair. "They'll try to connect it to football. Make her a symbol, start dedicating games to her. I wish they wouldn't."

"They're just boys."

"It's not going to be only the boys. It'll be the parents, the fans, the guys on the radio. It'll be the cheerleaders and the teachers and the janitors and even the police. All of a sudden a bunch of kids playing a game are going to represent something they should not."

"Maybe that won't happen."

"Trust me," he said. "It will."

The police had finished with him before three, but Adam didn't make it home until the sun was up. He went to his office—a convenient trip from the police station—and then he drove north to the lake. There, on the tumbled slabs of rocks that formed the breakwater, in the shadow of an empty mill that had once produced steel and now stood as a tired symbol of an age that had been gone for generations but that people still mourned as if it had just ended, he sat in the cold and drank from the bottle of whiskey he'd removed from his office. It was very good whiskey. Auchentoshan Three Wood, a fine Scotch. He kept only good stuff around his home and office. You didn't drink the good stuff as fast, couldn't afford to.

He drank it fast now.

Didn't get much of it down.

As the moon went pale and then faded beneath the dawn's

lead light, Adam Austin vomited fine Scotch into Lake Erie and then he let himself weep, slipping down until one arm and one foot were in the frigid water, the wind heedless and unforgiving. This would make him sick, being both unprepared for the cold and unwilling to step out of it. It would infect him in time.

Why again? he thought. *Why wasn't bearing it once enough? How can it not be?* He crawled back up the rocks and stared out at this lake that touched three other states and one other country in places he couldn't see, this lake that was always cold, when you needed it to be and when you didn't. Watched the horizon take shape and then, when it was bright enough or as close to bright as this day seemed inclined to get, he returned to his car and drove home. It was the only home he'd ever known, the home his parents had brought him to from the hospital, their firstborn son, firstborn child, eldest of three. He'd remodeled when he could afford to, replaced what he cared to. Other than the basics of the structure, there wasn't much left to the house that recalled what it had once been. He'd changed almost everything.

Except for one room.

He walked to it now, stood in the dim upstairs hallway, and reached for the knob. Laid his hand on the chill metal and read the handwritten sign: MARIE LYNN AUSTIN LIVES HERE — KNOCKS REQUIRED, TRESPASSING FORBIDDEN! THANKS, BOYS! He shook his head. Not yet. He couldn't enter like this, nothing more to show her than a drunk man with wet shoes and bile on his shirtsleeve and blood on his hands. More blood.

Instead, he went down the hall and peeled off his clothes and turned on the shower, looking into the mirror as the old water heater took its time limbering up and preparing for action. His eyes were dry now. They'd stay that way. He knew that.

"I'm coming for you," he whispered, and then he thought that was a strange thing to tell your own reflection, and turned away.

7

WORD SPREADS FAST IN Chambers, Ohio. There was nothing in the morning newspaper, but his kids already knew, anyhow, and Kent was not surprised. It is a small town, close-knit. Or invasive. You picked the word depending on your role in it, the way it impacted you. The familiarity, the way everyone knew everyone else, either wrapped warm arms around you or pried with cold, cruel fingers. One of the boys on his team had a father with the police. Another had an uncle with the coroner's office, a third had a mother who worked as an emergency dispatcher. It would have started with one of the three. Or maybe one with a connection he didn't even know about, and it ultimately didn't matter; somewhere, somehow, one of them would have heard, would have issued a late-night call or text message or e-mail, and that would have spawned a dozen like it, and most of the town probably woke to the news.

The weight of it was visible on them as they took to the field, parents walking down with their sons, parents who would ordinarily have sent their sons out into the cold day alone. This was one of the things that he liked about Chambers. It was small enough that people considered everything a shared experience. There was a positive to that. There was also a darkness. Those who never knew Rachel, who wouldn't have recognized her in a grocery store checkout line, would today claim to remember her quick laugh and generous smile and kind spirit.

Except for the truly dark ones. For those exist in Chambers, too, make no mistake. Kent remembered them well. By noon today, someone would have voiced the first rumor—*She was a little slut, you know.* Or maybe it would be even worse, tinged with more of the things they attach to disaster in their private moments—*I heard she was running around with some Mexican boy.*

Only some of them would have memories of Rachel, but *all* of them would have a theory.

He stood in the center of the field as they gathered. There were a few nods exchanged, a few whispers, but no one actually said words of substance. They were waiting on him.

Remember Walter Ward, he thought, and he wished his old coach were here so bad it stung him, a child's need, desperate and weakening. *Take this one for me, Coach Ward, take this one and handle it the way you did once before, please.*

But Walter Ward had been in Rose Hill Cemetery for six years now. By then he was more than an ex-coach, he was family, Kent's father-in-law, and Kent had stood beside the open earth and delivered the eulogy. That earth would not offer his old coach back today. Kent had accepted the job from Ward, and all that came with it. This was one of those things. He'd never imagined it would be, and yet somehow he felt as if he couldn't be surprised. Everything circled. Everything with teeth, at least, everything that snapped and bit and drew blood.

When the full team was gathered, he spoke. The crowd was well over a hundred deep. Lots of adults. Parents, mostly, but there were faces in the group he didn't recognize.

"I expect most of you have heard," he said, "but just in case you have not, let me explain that there will be no practice, and why not."

And so he told them the news they had already heard. One of their own had been taken from them. The word choice was key. He would never forget the way the word *lost* had seared him when used with Marie, as if she had been misplaced, a set of car keys, a remote control, a pair of shoes. No, she was not lost.

She was taken.

"We know," he said, "that this game is of the barest importance. This morning we are all reminded of that in a way I hoped we never would be. Let's remind ourselves of something else now: we draw strength from one another. Sometimes, we need to take more than we can offer. You boys have to be aware of that now. There will be those—Rachel's family, her friends, your teammate Colin—who will need more than they have within them. They will need it from you, from me. We have to remember that, and offer it.

"We've spent months—years—discussing what this game represents, and what it does not. Today, it represents nothing. Understand that. Be clear on it. And remember... There is no fear or loss so mighty that it can break faith."

A chorus of agreement, one of the loudest coming from a man in the back of the crowd, and when Kent's eyes flicked his way the man dipped his head immediately. He was wearing a baseball cap and now his face was down but he was familiar. For a moment Kent stuttered, then looked away and refocused.

"No practice today, no football. Be with your families, be with your friends, be with your thoughts. Make sure those thoughts are directed toward the people who need them." He paused, then said, "I'll say a prayer now for those who would like to stay for it."

They all stayed.

* * *

Kent hoped to make it home without comment to the press, but Bob Hackett, the community's venerable sports editor, three decades on the job and still going, caught him at his car. He'd been there when they won their state title in Kent's freshman year, he'd been there when they lost the title game with Kent at quarterback his senior year, he'd been there through everything that had happened in between.

Today he was waiting beside Kent's Ford Explorer, and they leaned together against the car and stared at the ball field that had mattered so much only a few hours ago.

"I'm sorry," Hackett said.

"Lots of people are deserving of sympathy right now, but I'm not among them."

"Kent? Someone is going to want to talk with you about it soon enough," Hackett said. "And I'll tell you this: it's easier if you talk to me. If I write it first, the AP will grab it. Then when somebody else calls, you can say you gave your one interview on the topic and want to leave it at that. If you don't give any, though, everyone will get to bend it their own way."

So let them, Kent wanted to snap. *It's got nothing to do with anything, it's so long ago, so far away.*

But that wasn't true. It wasn't far away, never would be.

"You know me well enough to understand I'm not hunting for the scoop," Hackett said. "If you don't want to say a word about her then I'll —"

"No," Kent said. "Let's get it done. Let's talk about my sister."

Hackett looked away, and Kent appreciated the man's genuine discomfort. He didn't always agree with the sportswriter's columns, but he always appreciated the way he went about his job. He didn't treat it as writing about coaches and athletes and games. He treated it as writing about people.

"Go inside?" Hackett said.

Kent shook his head. "Why don't we sit on the bleachers."

It was maybe thirty-five degrees, the morning sun not yet doing much to warm the gray day, and Hackett didn't have a hat covering his bald head, but he nodded and led the way.

8

CHELSEA CALLED AROUND noon.

"I just heard," she said, no preamble, no questions about why Adam hadn't returned to her in the night, why he was not at the office now, Saturday mornings traditionally being busy.

"From who?"

"Police. Came to get the file on her. There wasn't much to it. They had a little trouble believing that."

"They're hopeful. I don't blame them. I wish there was more in it, too. I wish..." He couldn't continue, and he hoped she thought he was drunk. Somehow, that seemed better. Safer, less vulnerable. *Adam? He's not broken, he's just drunk. Worthy of your scorn, sure, but don't waste pity or sympathy on him, please.*

"Where are you?" she said. Her voice very soft.

"Home."

"Your home."

"Only one I've got."

"Yeah?"

He was silent. He'd spent maybe thirty nights in a row at her place. Maybe forty.

"We're holding paper on three after this morning," she said. "That's probably all we will see today. The Friday night drunks are out. I'm closing up. Somebody needs us, they can call."

"Sure, whatever."

"Let me see you, Adam. Please?"

"All right."

They hadn't talked much in the years after high school. Ten of them passed without contact at all. She'd been in Cleveland for a time, and then she'd been back, and she'd been married. Travis Leonard. Ex-Army, dishonorable discharge. The first bust he took in Chambers was for selling stolen goods. She came to Adam for the bond, checkbook in hand, and he'd been angry with her, furious, because she was so much better than that guy, that life.

"This is where you ended up?" he said. "Really?"

She closed the checkbook, tilted her head, and looked around the dingy office.

"This is where *you* ended up, Adam? Really?"

They finished the paperwork in silence. Travis Leonard hit the streets, then promptly missed his court date. Adam came around. Travis was gone, Chelsea was home.

"You're better off waiting inside," she said, and that was the first time. Well, second time. First time in a decade. She kissed Adam full on the mouth as she slid off him in the predawn, then kissed her husband on the cheek as Adam slid him into the back of the Jeep two hours later when he finally came home.

There were no phone calls for a few days. He didn't want to see her, didn't want to see any more of what she'd become, or for her to see what he'd become. Nobody needed that.

Then one night he was on her porch. She opened the door again. And so it went.

* * *

Her house was his favorite hated place. Hated because the title was in her husband's name but she paid the mortgage and the taxes while his dumb ass sat in county lockup; hated because it was filled with the dickhead's snakes—he bred pythons, had sixty or seventy of them in the house at any given time, and Adam had always loathed snakes; hated because he wanted so badly to be there, always. Hated because she deserved so much better, and Adam was part of that collapse from the start.

And favorite because she was there. That part was simple, clean. The only thing that was.

It was not her fault that she carried memories. That didn't wipe them clean, though, didn't stop him from feeling sick with himself every time he pulled into the driveway, didn't stop him from sometimes squeezing his eyes shut when she touched him.

She'd been seventeen when they met, a transfer from Cleveland's West Technical High School. Her father had taken a bust and she'd left the Clark Avenue house they'd rented to move in with an aunt in Chambers. Chelsea and her mother and three sisters. Word about her had spread through the halls and the boy's bathrooms in under an hour on the first day of school, hormonal kids tearing neck muscles to get a second glance. Winner of a genetic lottery on both sides, with an Italian mother and a Puerto Rican father, Chelsea had a different look from most of the girls in Chambers. Had a different look from most of the girls anywhere. And she had *command,* too, bored by childish attentions but able to lock you down and melt you with one long, amused exchange of eye contact.

She was the only distraction from football that year. Girls always were some level of distraction, but in such a small school most of the top-flight talent was paired off with somebody by senior year—all those photographs to worry about, homecoming and prom and graduation, being a single senior was a real bitch for the yearbook — but this was different, this was the *new* girl, and she neither carried baggage nor knew who else did, so everyone could imagine they had a shot.

Adam won.

Took a few weeks, too. Longer than he'd have liked. Longer than he was used to. The only surefire Division 1 prospect on the team, standing six-four and 215 pounds of ripcord muscle, dark hair and dark blue eyes and an easy smile, Adam was not used to the chase. He'd had to chase her, though, and at first that was part of the fun, it was a competition and Adam loved to compete. Then he got to know her, and saw all there was beyond honey skin and radiant hair and a body that promised all of the things he'd imagined since puberty. And be damned if he didn't actually love this girl, awfully fast. Fast in the way it can go only when you're eighteen years old.

That was the fall of 1989.

He'd been after her since mid-August, but it was September before he got the first date, a week later the first kiss — he was no stranger to girls then, but his legs trembled when he kissed her, the way they did after running the bleachers, muscle gone liquid, and he reached up and cupped the back of her head with his right palm to steady himself. She remembered that; later she told him that she thought it was a sign of his gentleman's expertise, but he'd never told her the real reason for it, which was that he didn't want her to feel him shaking when they kissed.

What followed was hardly so elegant. Heated make-out sessions and groping, backseats and picnic tables. They talked about having sex. He was no virgin, she'd had a bad attempt at it two years earlier and that was that.

No pressure, he joked, but when a girl kept you awake at night, when she made concentration an impossible thing, you'd better believe there was pressure. He was not Adam Austin the Ohio

State recruit with Chelsea Salinas; he was a kid whose legs shook when he kissed.

Then came October 2, 1989. The Cardinals practiced late, and the daylight faded and the lights came on and everything smelled of leaves and wood smoke and autumn, everything smelled of *football,* the bullshit summer drills a faded memory, the real season under way, Adam's last, and before Chelsea appeared, it was a perfect night. They were playing clean and fast and hitting hard and Coach Ward was pleased.

Then she was there. Ward called for a water break, looked at Adam, and said, "Get your girl away from my field before you start tripping over your hormones, Austin."

Adam jogged over and said *what's up,* excited because she never came to watch him practice, and he was feeling *fast* that day, the savage kind of fast, a wolf in snow, a shark in dark waters.

She laid her hand over his on the fence and said, "I need to see you," and that was the first time in his adrenaline-fueled excitement that he saw the tears glittering against her eyes.

"What?"

"I'm going back to Cleveland."

"What?"

"You have practice. Finish it. I'll explain. I'll wait at your car?"

All he could do was nod.

She walked away and he put his helmet on and jogged back to the field, the same autumn breeze that had seemed so perfect ten minutes ago now feeling chill and hostile.

They'd gotten through the practice, though he didn't recall much of it, just that it had gone on too long and he was cursing Coach Ward under his breath for every extra rep. Then finally it was done, they broke for the showers, and he was rushing, toweling off his chest with one hand and pulling his pants on with the other when Kent showed up. Only a freshman but already the backup quarterback, everyone seeing the promise there, half the town ready to ditch their starter for the kid, even though their starter had lost only one game. If it were up to Adam, any of the standard big brother attitude, the wait-your-turn, don't-steal-my-thunder posturing would be damned, too, and Kent *would* be under center. He was that good. Put Kent out there leading the offense and let Adam slaughter on defense, and state was guaranteed. But Coach Ward did not bench seniors for freshmen. Ever.

"Marie's waiting," Kent told him.

Adam was actually puzzled — no, Chelsea was waiting, and how in the hell did his little brother know? — but then he got it. Yes, Marie was also waiting. Marie had cross-country practice and Adam had the car and thus the responsibility of getting her home.

"Can't do it," he said.

"Huh? They got done an hour ago, man. She's been waiting."

"I just said I can't do it," Kent said, anger showing itself, except it wasn't really anger, it was fear, it was *no, no, Chelsea's wrong, she's not leaving, she can't be leaving.*

"Well, I've got to stay with the coaches. They want me watching tape. You knew this. I can't walk her home."

And then came the words that still woke Adam in the night two decades later, the words that on three occasions had led him to go so far as tasting the barrel of a gun, cold steel and oil on his tongue:

"It's five fucking blocks, Franchise. She'll make it."

He left then. Jogged out of the locker room and into the night to meet the most important thing in his eighteen-year-old life.

Marie was walking away from the school when Adam drove out of the parking lot with Chelsea. He passed her in the dark, her head down, backpack on, walking through the chill night toward a car that no longer waited, and he thought that he would deal with that problem in the morning. She'd be angry, but he could always joke his little sister out of anger fast enough, could always raise a smile even when she desperately wanted to refuse him one. His dad was tougher, but that, too, could be dealt with, and what *really* mattered right now was the fact that Chelsea was being taken from him.

You had to prioritize.

He drove Chelsea to the pier. Put his letter jacket around her slim shoulders and held her when she told him that her father was going to be released in November and that meant she was gone. They'd go back to Cleveland, and they'd stay there. The city was an hour's drive away, but that night, the idea of it was a world apart. They were standing in silence at the edge of the pier, water slapping on the pylons below, when she pulled her face away from his neck, looked into his eyes, and said, "Can we go somewhere?"

He had two blankets in the trunk of his Ford Taurus. There was a county park not far from the pier, up on the bluffs where you could see out to the lake, popular for summertime barbecues and sunsets but empty on this night, the first cold evening of autumn, with that menacing wind pushing down from Canada. They had no trouble with the cold, though. Two eighteen-year-olds, first time together? No, cold was not an issue. Snow could have been flying and they wouldn't have cared. There was a moment, as they lay on their sides, her back to him, his hand tracing her breast, side, hip, that he knew it was going to be a night that lingered, something they would talk about when they were old, because the first time with the right one, the one that lasted? There was nothing else like it on this earth. Tonight would linger with him, always. He was sure of it.

He made it home by eleven.

The first of the police cars was in the driveway.

Twenty-two years later, as he drove to her husband's house

through a light rain, he remembered the police questions, the look in his father's eyes, his mother leaving the room.

The last five hours, you've been where?

The pier and the park.

Doing what?

Talking, man, hanging out.

You just forgot to give your sister a ride, is that it?

Well, no, my brother reminded me. But it was kind of an emergency.

Marie was still gone at three, and then at six, and then any half-hearted hope that she might have gone to a friend's house and fallen asleep or broken an ankle or, hell, even run off with a boy to do the same damn thing Adam had done was gone. The questions grew more pointed, the truth more painful.

Yes, I was supposed to take her home.

No, I did not.

I got in the car with Chelsea Salinas and drove away. We were at the pier, then the park. We had sex on a blanket.

No, I did not call to tell my parents I'd left Marie to walk home alone.

Yes, I passed her heading out of the parking lot.

No, I did not stop to speak to her.

No, I did not see her on the street when I came home.

But he felt that he had. In fact, he felt that she was still there, that on the right night, with the right half-moon rising behind charcoal clouds above the lake, walking into the right cold breeze, he might find her heading into the parking lot in search of the car he'd driven away from her. Felt that if he hit all of those elements just perfectly, he'd see her marching through the dark and toward the lights of the football field, backpack on, and she'd turn and look at his slowing car and flash the cautious smile before remembering that the braces were gone and then finally letting the smile go wide and radiant. She would slide into the passenger seat, call him a jerk, and he'd get her home. Back to her bedroom, where the sign warned away trespassers. It was still possible, somehow, it had to be, because if it wasn't? Well, fuck this world, then.

He was sitting with his head on the steering wheel, his eyes dry but closed, when Chelsea opened the driver's door and laid a cool hand on the back of his neck. He eased out a slow breath, kept it from shuddering with an effort, but left his forehead on the wheel and his eyes closed.

"It was five blocks," he said.

She rubbed his neck, silent.

"Half a mile," he said.

Her fingers found a knot, kneaded it.

"Rachel Bond was seventeen," he said. "Did I know that? No. Should I have seen it? Yes. You would have. If you'd been there, if anyone but me had been there..."

She stopped kneading, let her fingertip rest on the knot, gentle but steady pressure, like a doctor trying to draw infected blood. Something faded from him and into the touch, but not the right thing, or not enough of it.

"Seventeen," he said again.

"Come inside," she told him, and moved her hand away from his neck.

He shut off the Jeep's engine, climbed out, and followed her up the steps and through the door to see the snakes.

9

THE DESIRE TO KEEP calling the police caught Kent off guard, and it was impossible to shake. Every ten minutes his mind returned to it: *Maybe they know something more now. Maybe Salter will tell you. Maybe there's some question you can answer that they haven't thought of yet. Maybe you can ask them to confirm that Gideon Pearce had nothing to do with this.*

It was the last part, the ludicrous one, that stalked him with the most diligence, utterly absurd yet utterly relentless. The man who had murdered his sister in the autumn of 1989 died in prison years later, convicted of the crime, and rightfully so. The rational mind reminded Kent of this over and over, but the heart frequently shows nothing but disdain for rationality, and his heart called forth the question time and again.

Two murdered girls, separated by twenty-two years. How many people had been murdered in this country since 1989? This state, this county, this town? They weren't all linked. But in Kent's heart these two were.

He did not call the police. If they needed him for anything, they would call. Until then, he would serve only as a distraction and a hindrance. So he turned to football, to the best of his ability. They had lost a practice during a playoff week, and while it had been the right thing to do, it was also a costly thing. The team didn't meet on Sundays, just the coaches, and that meant player preparation would not begin until Monday. Kent's team was already forty-eight hours behind the opponent. Forty-eight of 144 prep hours gone before they even started. That was the sort of thing that lost you football games.

The burden of making up that lost time belonged to him.

At the start of his coaching career, he'd spent hours charting plays and breaking those plays down into percentages, until he could show Walter Ward that he understood an opponent's tendencies better than the opponent did.

"They blitzed thirty-six times when the ball was between the twenties," he'd inform Ward. "But if it was in the red zone, they never brought pressure on first down. Not once."

Ward believed in precision, he believed in preparation, but he often dismissed Kent's detailed scouting reports with a flat smile, altering his own game plan little. If they *just played Chambers football,* he'd always say, things would work out fine.

These days, under Kent's leadership, Chambers football meant being the most prepared team in the state. And thanks to computers, the ability to understand your opponent was available in a way it had never been before. The team subscribed to a database called Hudl that was used for sharing game video. It wasn't a cheap program, but one of the boosters, a dentist named Duncan Werner, covered the cost. Kent loved Hudl. Not only could he easily watch video for every situation he desired, but also the stat breakdown was remarkable.

Blitzes by field position was one click away. *Blitzes by down and distance* was another. Want to know the percentage of running plays an opponent used on first down? Or maybe how often they passed out of a specific formation? Just click. By Friday morning,

Kent would be able to quote these tendencies without pause. He would understand the mind of the opposing coach, what he wanted and what he feared. From that he would be prepared to avoid their strengths and hammer their weaknesses. You would not surprise him on the football field, you would not surprise his team. They would see teams that were bigger, stronger, and faster, but never would they see a team that was better prepared.

Never.

On Saturday afternoon he sat on the living room floor with his back against the couch, a laptop computer to his left, a notepad to his right, and, every few seconds, a Nerf basketball in his lap. He was tossing it around with Andrew, who approached the task more like a rabid German shepherd than a budding athlete, and Lisa was doing homework, though she had none to do. That was her thing these days, always announced formally — she was going to do her homework now. Just so you knew. Then she'd arrange books at the table and spend her time drawing. Kent's favorite touch, the one that he and Beth laughed themselves silly over when their daughter wasn't around, was the slide rule. She'd come across the antiquated math device at a neighbor's garage sale, purchased it with her own money, and insisted on keeping it at hand, finding the look much more sophisticated than a calculator.

The idea of being a student had suddenly appealed to her. A recent perfect score on a multiplication test prompted her to announce with gravity that she was hoping she could get a scholarship because she understood the Ivy League schools were very expensive. Kent asked where she'd heard of an Ivy League school and was met with a sigh.

"They're the good ones, Dad. The *really* good ones."

All right. He'd told her if they were that good, then yes, a scholarship was probably a great idea, because his bank account was not nearly so good.

"Dad? You're not watching."

This from Andrew. Kent flicked his eyes up from the screen, said, "Playoffs, champ. Playoffs. We multitask now, okay?"

The word *multitask* left his son blank-faced, but then Kent tossed the ball and Andrew charged after it, banging down the hallway. Kent looked back at the script again. Hickory Hills was an option-heavy team, and fast enough to pull it off against most of their opponents. He wasn't worried about his team's speed, though. They'd just have to widen their gaps on the line, and shade to the strong side because that's where the quarterback wanted to go most of the time.

"Hackett's article is up on the website." Beth had emerged from the kitchen, her gentle blue eyes grim.

"It's bad?"

"No. But they mention Adam."

"What do you mean?"

"The police explained that she was trying to find her father. And that Adam...that he got it wrong."

Kent let out a breath and tossed the Nerf basketball one last time, Andrew chasing after it wildly, nearly wiping out an end table in his pursuit, and then he rose and went into the kitchen where she had the laptop open on the granite-topped island.

The home page of the newspaper's website was devoted entirely to Rachel Bond. Pictures of her were now joined by pictures of a desolate cottage surrounded by investigators. Five stories were linked around the photographs, one headline reading: TRAGEDY FAMILIAR TO KENT AUSTIN.

He closed his eyes for a moment, bracing. Reading your own press was always an uncomfortable thing. Kent never felt anything but uneasy dread over it. You weren't in control of the way you were about to be presented, weren't in control of the context of your remarks or, with many reports, even the accuracy of your remarks. You were someone else's version of yourself, fed to the public to create their version of you, a disturbing disconnect. *We will build a new you, thanks. The one we want.*

He'd spent his life in the public eye of the town, and so far the town hadn't snapped on him. He always felt as if it might. You drifted around in front of enough people for enough time, eventually someone would take a swipe, and then the rest would join in. Eagerly.

He worried more for his family than himself when it came to the media. He'd seen good coaches, good men, turned into objects of scorn with swiftness and alarming hunger, and he always thought it went harder on them if they had children old enough to be aware of it. Lisa was nine and Andrew was six. They were excited to see their father in the paper, particularly this season, when his team was unbeaten. He wasn't sure what he'd do with this story. They understood a little about it, but now they would want to know more. They would want to know the very sorts of things he didn't wish them to hear, ever.

Your sister was murdered, Daddy?

Yes.

Did he do anything else to her?

Yes.

He could hear Beth talking to the kids now, everyone's tone light, theirs in a natural way, hers in a forced way, and he blocked it out and clicked on the link and read the story.

CHAMBERS—He's won six regional titles and has his team in position to claim another, but on Saturday morning Kent Austin sent the Cardinals home with a prayer and no practice.

It was not a day for football.

The horrific Friday night slaying of a classmate has the students of Chambers High School reeling, and a school that was once basking in gridiron glory is now awash with tragedy.

It's an experience all too familiar for Austin.

When the Cardinals coach was 15, his older sister, Marie, was abducted and killed.

Marie Austin, 16 at the time of her death, was last seen walking home from school on the evening of October 2, 1989. Confusion within the family left her without a ride, and she attempted to walk home. She never made it.

Three days later, her body was found in the Lake Erie shallows. Her killer, Gideon Pearce, was not apprehended until January of 1990. A Chambers native who'd moved to Cleveland, Pearce was already facing charges for the assault and battery of a minor at the time. His trial in that case had been scheduled for September 22, but Pearce, out on bail, disappeared in early summer and did not surface again until the Rocky River Police Department stopped him for driving a truck with an expired license plate. They soon discovered that the truck was stolen, that Pearce had an active warrant, and took him to the Cuyahoga County Jail. There, when his belongings were confiscated, they found a football card, part of a set made for the previous year's high school all-state team. The player was Adam Austin, Kent and Marie's older brother, an 18-year-old star defensive back. The card had been in Marie Austin's possession on the day of her disappearance.

It was the first lead in what ultimately became a quick trial and conviction. More of Marie Austin's belongings were found, and Pearce confessed within 48 hours of his arrest. He avoided the death penalty but was sentenced to life in prison, and he was still in custody at the time of his death from cancer in 2005.

Now, 22 years later, tragedy has revisited the Austin family. Kent Austin was familiar with Rachel Bond, and, according to police, Bond contacted Adam Austin for help in locating her father after a series of letters led her to believe that he'd returned to the Chambers area.

Kent swore under his breath. It wasn't Hackett's fault—reporting the facts, salting his retrospective with all relevant connections—but all the same, Kent wished his brother's name had not come up. Hackett treated it gently, but this would be only the start. There would be more calls, and more articles, and they would not be so gentle.

Adam Austin could not be reached for comment and, understandably, Coach Kent Austin does not discuss his sister's death often. When he does, though, he acknowledges that it shaped his life.

"Everything that I've done," he says, "I've done because of what happened to Marie."

Austin's primary passion is in ministry. Specifically, prison ministry. He makes one visit each month to lead a Bible study in the same prison that housed his sister's murderer.

"Comfort was a hard thing to find, after losing Marie," he says. "I found what I could in two things: football and faith."

Nine years after his sister's murder, Austin sat down with her killer.

"It was not easy," he admits. Asked what the conversation consisted of, Austin pauses and wipes the back of his hand over his mouth. "I prayed for him."

And Pearce?

"He laughed at me."

Asked if he regrets the visit, Austin shakes his head emphatically. He's made many other trips. Working now with Dan Grissom, a minister from Cleveland, Austin has made dozens of visits to the state's prisons, meeting with inmates who have been convicted of the same crime—murder—that took so much from Austin and his family.

"It's the right test," he says. "The critical one. I could harbor hate or spread love. I don't think there's anything in between, coming out of something like that. I really don't."

Just Friday night, Austin was asked if he considered the unbeaten regular season his team had just completed to be a defining moment in his career. With his unique blend of patience and bristle, a hallmark familiar to those who have covered the coach, he answered that he didn't care much for the term "defining moment," and that if he did have one, he hoped that it wouldn't come on the football field.

For a man who doesn't believe in defining moments, though, he speaks of his visit with Gideon Pearce as a critical decision, if nothing else.

"It changed some things in me that needed to change," he says. "Hardest thing I've ever had to do. From the decision itself, to the execution of the decision…hardest thing I've ever had to do. I knew who he was and what he had done. I knew what my heart called me to do, and I knew what my faith called me to do, and I didn't like that those things were at odds."

When he returns to his team after a prison visit, he'll bring some stories with him. Reminders of good men who made bad decisions.

"To spread my faith among the people who had challenged it seemed imperative," he says of his mission. "We've done good work over the years. We've seen men change. I'm proud of that, more proud of that than anything we've done on the football field."

Austin has always made it clear that victories are not the priority of his coaching career. Preparing young men to make the right decisions, to consider the effects of each action and choice, is what the game offers to him.

"This is not a game won by individuals, and it is surely not a game won by selfish choices," he says. "We're concerned with the weight of responsibility. We're concerned with the idea that your individual mistake, your poor decision or poor effort, impacts many more people than yourself. We understand that this is a game of little consequence. We also understand that the lessons of the game are not empty."

Something else Kent Austin understands is playing through grief. The investigation into his sister's murder took time. During that time, the Cardinals—Kent was not playing with the varsity squad yet, but Adam Austin was a senior and a star and Kent was on the sidelines as a backup quarterback—reeled off six straight victories and claimed the state championship, the last in school history. Tributes to Marie Austin were made before every game. Players wore her initials on their jerseys. Fans lifted signs bearing her name in the stands. Moments of silence were held.

"Of course it meant a great deal," Austin says. "The team, the community, they meant a great deal to us as a family."

Now, as this current undefeated team pursues its first title since that year, its head coach says that he hopes the community is prepared to respect the wishes of Bond's mother.

"That's a family choice," he says. "We are all thinking of Rachel, and the family, we are praying for them. We will not confuse the game of football with the realities of life, however. Our scoreboard does not alter anything, our scoreboard is of no consequence. I don't think anyone's mind is on football right now. What we as a coaching staff are not concerned with is what happens on Friday night. We are concerned with helping these young men cope with a tragedy."

There is no one more prepared to offer that help than Kent Austin.

10

ADAM HAD TURNED OFF his cell phone after the first dozen calls from reporters. His own house was probably crawling with media by now, but they hadn't found Chelsea's — not yet at least. He lay on his back with her curled against his chest, her long dark hair cascading over his neck and the side of his face, and through the open bedroom door he watched the snakes shift in their boxes. Cheap plastic tubs, slid into homemade wooden shelves that were just tight enough to provide air while still keeping them in.

Most of the time. There had been an escape or two.

In the room that should have been the pantry was a large cage of rats. The python food of choice. Chelsea handled their care while her husband was in jail. She liked the rats more than the snakes, she said, but her responsibility was to the snakes.

Adam thought that was a hell of an unpleasant loyalty to have to pick.

His own house, the home he'd grown up in, was meticulously tidy. Adam was regimented; in that way he was not so far from his famous little brother across town. He got his hair cut every ten days, he ironed every shirt, he refused to leave the office with any loose paperwork on the desk. All of that bled over and into the house, where no dishes were ever left in the sink, where weeds did not encroach on flowerbeds and grass clippings were always blown back toward the lawn and not out to the sidewalk. Maybe it would have been this way anywhere he lived, but he had lived in only one place, and that was Marie's home. Something Adam had come to understand was that nobody ever left a true home, so it was still Marie's home. Still Kent's, too, and sometimes he thought it was a shame that Kent would no longer visit the house, but Kent had another home now. Marie, like Adam, did not and would not. So he tended it carefully, because he did not want to dishonor her.

Chelsea's house was a different matter. Travis Leonard's house. Dirty dishes gathered and waited until Adam washed them whether he'd used them or not, the carpet carried ancient stains, cobwebs hung like décor in the corners of the ceilings. In the bathroom, where lime and mold were thick enough to be approached with a chisel, a long strip of flypaper dangled in the summer months, covered with dead bugs.

She took care of the snakes and the rats, kept their cages clean, but the rest of the house seemed to escape her attention. Her own condition was always flawless—marred, perhaps, some might think, by the many tattoos and piercings, but that was a personal preference, and what no one could argue with was the sheen she had, from hair to teeth to body, every ounce of her polished.

In this, Adam saw only what he already understood about his own home. You didn't leave it behind. You just carried it with you into new places. Chelsea at thirty-nine was more similar to Chelsea at seventeen than she would like to admit. A creature of organized beauty in a home of chaos, owned by an inmate.

She had not asked him about the police. Had not asked him about Rachel, hadn't asked him a thing. She would let him speak of it when he chose, or she would force him to when needed, but she would never press ahead of time.

He waited until the evening shadows had lengthened enough to keep him from making out the coiled bodies and flickering tongues inside those milky-white plastic tubs, and then he slid out from under her and dressed. She opened her eyes, watched him.

"You'll be back?"

He nodded.

"Should I know where you're going?"

He shook his head.

She turned away from him then. Had her eyes on the headboard as he slipped out of the bedroom, walked to the front door, and exited, car keys in hand. The only thing that had kept Adam from the house at Shadow Wood until sunset was the knowledge that police would be there, processing the scene. By now he hoped it was done. They'd have had all day, the news crews would have taken their footage, the photographers would have snapped their pictures. It was dark now, the way it had been when she arrived, and they would have left.

He hoped. If not, it would make for an uncomfortable scene, but he needed to see the place for himself. See where he had sent her.

The drive wasn't long. Northeast out of town and winding along Lake Erie, then dipping south, into the woods. Another six miles and he caught a road sign just in time to bring his Jeep to a fishtailing stop and make the turn onto a gravel road. Shadow Wood Lane. PRIVATE RESORT PROPERTY, boasted an ancient sign, pocked with rounds from a .22.

Maybe it had once been a resort, but those days were well past. Adam had trouble imagining that even in the summer this place was much more than a haven for drunks who wanted to have a rollicking white trash party somewhere secluded enough that police were unlikely to disturb them. The lake was coated with leaves, dead cattails clogging the south shore, the northern shore lined with decrepit cottages. They were probably fifty years old and perhaps repainted once since their original construction. The docks tilted, and anyone who ventured down them barefoot would quickly have enough splinters to impress a porcupine. Adam parked and walked down an overgrown path to the cabins on the opposite shore, carrying a flashlight but leaving it off, the gloaming enough for him to see all that he cared to see. He was feeling a chill that had nothing to do with the wind, imagining Rachel Bond making these same steps, walking toward the same place. Had she been fearful? Of course. But she had been determined, too. And brave. And armed with an address.

Damn you, Adam. Damn you, damn you, damn you.

It was not hard to determine the proper cottage. Police tape and padlocks announced that. He walked to the edge of the porch but not onto it, just leaned against the railing with his hands on the weathered wood and stared at the door as the wind rippled by, pushing the low-lying branches of an untrimmed hemlock across the shingles of the roof, the sound like a broom on floorboards.

This was where she had died.

This was where he had sent her.

He looked at the door for a long time, wondering if she'd been greeted at it or if she'd had to knock. Did she hesitate? Did she even try to leave? How long had it taken her to realize how terrible a mistake she had made?

How terrible a mistake you made. You made it, Adam. Own that. Own it.

He turned from the door and blew out a long breath and studied the lake. Took out a cigarette and lit it and let the wind blow the smoke back into his face and sting his eyes. When it was half done he dropped it to the ground, stamped it out, and made his first circle of the cottage. The building was secured,

but the police had not boarded the windows. That seemed foolish, seemed like something they would have wanted to do—or
hang blackout curtains at least—but it helped him. Using
the flashlight he could see into both of the bedrooms, most of
the small living room and adjoining bathroom, and all of the
kitchen.

The place was empty. Bare-bones empty, not so much as a
blanket on the beds. Unless the police had carried everything
out, it would have been empty when she arrived, too. So she had
not been given time to run. It would have been over quickly for
her. Part of it at least. The chance of escape. That had been gone
fast.

He returned to the front porch and stared at the other cottages. They were close; two were within fifty feet, all five were
within two hundred. A scream would have echoed through their
paper-thin walls. But that would not have mattered, because
they would have been empty. It appeared the entire place would
have been empty when she arrived. A baited trap.

*He didn't give her the address, though. She had to find it. I had to
find it.*

The letters were just a game.

Maybe, Salter had said, *he wasn't that patient. Maybe, when she
showed up at his door, it rushed him.*

Adam smoked another cigarette there in the quiet and the
cold and then he left to start things the right way.

11

I**N THE FIRST TWO YEARS** after his daughter's death, Hank Austin had put on forty-five pounds. After-dinner beers became after-dinner twelve-packs. Morning coffees became morning Bloody Marys. A half-pack of cigarettes a day became two packs, a slice of pizza became six, and on and on. Excess defined him. When the heart attack took him, it was an August afternoon with a heat index of 105 and he'd decided to sand the deck by hand.

When Adam found him, he felt relief amidst the sorrow and the shame. His father hadn't been able to bear the loss, but he'd been a touch too strong to run from it, too. Just a touch.

Adam was twenty-two then, working as a bail agent in Cleveland. The one semester at Ohio State was a distant memory. Kent was a sophomore in college, a starting quarterback for a small but quality program. Adam was still living at home, if living was the right word. It was where he slept, from time to time. Usually during the day, when his parents were gone. He did most of his hunting at night. His boss loved that, and it suited Adam. He was a nocturnal sort.

After his father died, his mother moved into an apartment. It had been Adam's suggestion.

You're not happy here, he told her. *There's too much pain all around you. You know that.*

She agreed. Moved into an apartment near the bank where she worked, and Adam stayed in the house. She remained in the apartment for nine years, and then the first stroke came, and a month later the second, and her final four years were in an assisted living facility. The house was left to Adam and Kent jointly, and Adam had three separate appraisals conducted and then offered his brother half of the average, a fair share.

Kent refused it. Told him they needed to sell the place not for money, but for purposes of moving on. Adam declined. Each month he sent his brother a check for what he deemed half of fair rent on the home. Each month the check went uncashed.

Once his father was dead and his mother had moved, Adam finally got the room back the way he wanted it. Hank Austin had been firm—the day Marie's body was found, turning the inevitable into the official, he'd begun to pack her things away, working alone, no sounds but the shrieks and tears of the packing tape and the occasional soft sob.

Adam understood both the idea and its futility. It was tempting to try, maybe, but it was hopeless. You couldn't put her into boxes and seal them shut.

The boxes had gone into the attic above the garage. Sometimes Adam would slip up there and go through the artifacts, handling them carefully, taking in the smell of her, amazed by how it lingered. He was alone with her then, felt close to her in a way he could not anywhere else, and he was certain that she was there with him, somehow aware of the communion and appreciative of it. They talked a little. He couldn't get through much at first, the tears came too fast. Over time it got better. He apologized often—too often for her, he knew that, but how did you stop? — and he told her what news there was to share. He told her about every skip he tracked down, everyone who jumped bond and tried to hide. He got them all, he was remarkably diligent, his boss in Cleveland was already talking about turning the business over to him, but Adam wanted to come home. He wanted to be in Chambers County.

They talked about that, too. Whether maybe what he needed was exactly the opposite, what he needed was to get *out*. In the end, though, that just didn't feel right. The debt Adam owed had been left here on Beech Street in Chambers, Ohio. There were advantages to leaving town — the stares wouldn't follow him in other places, the whispers would never be heard, no one would remember because no one would know. Sometimes that seemed so beautiful, so desirable, that it could nearly bring him to his knees. But he would not run, and that was all it amounted to. Those stares, those whispers, those memories? Adam had earned them. They were necessary reminders, needles of agony that refreshed the heart and kept him focused. He was here to offer atonement. That was not a painless task, and it was not one from which you could run.

He made some promises, up there in the attic surrounded by the boxes that testified to a vanished life. He intended to keep them.

When the house was his, no one left to object to a little rearranging, Adam moved Marie back in. It was a painstaking process. The large objects were no problem, he remembered where they belonged, but on smaller issues, the order of the books on the bookshelves, the arrangement of posters on the walls, he had to stop and think and, sometimes, simply ask for her approval, apologize, and put the things where they seemed to fit. He had not paid enough attention to the details when he'd had the chance, but he was certain that Marie understood and forgave him.

When he was done, when he'd hung her sign on the door, the last step, he felt cleaner than he had in years. She would not be boxed away, would not be forgotten.

Kent had problems with it. That had been one of their true blowups, second-to-last of the effective end of their relationship. He came in and saw the room and said it was a sick thing to do, that Adam needed help, needed to learn how to move on, and that there was no honor for Marie in what he'd done. They'd disagreed strongly on that point. Then came Kent's visit to Gideon Pearce. Adam found out about that in the papers. He'd gone to Kent's house, and would always regret that. He shouldn't have allowed it to happen with Beth present. That argument ended with blood. Since then, they'd circled each other with carefully preserved distance.

Adam knew that Marie hated that, but he did not know how to make it right. Maybe in time. Maybe it wasn't meant to be made right.

Adam returned from Shadow Wood Lane clear-eyed and sober. He drank a glass of water at the sink, rinsed and spat, trying to rid his mouth of the cigarette smoke, and then he took a deep breath and climbed the stairs to his sister's room. Knocked twice. Paused. Turned the knob, opened the door, and entered, then shut the door behind him.

The twin bed was in the corner, with a white comforter that had been a recent change from the pink she'd had for most of her childhood, a step toward maturity, tired of anything that suggested a little girl. Stuffed animals vanishing from the room, replaced with stained-glass pieces and candles. The stained glass was a mixed collection, some professional items, some her own handiwork. She'd fallen in love with it at a camp that summer, started taking lessons. Her favorite was a giant turtle with a multi-colored shell; she'd done all the cutting and soldering herself, and while it was a beautiful piece, it was too big to hang in the window, so she had settled on resting it on the top of the book-shelf just below, where it still caught sunlight and sparkled. She called the turtle Tito. Nobody knew why, and she was content with that.

The candles were the other obsession of her final year, and a constant source of friction with their father, unusual in their relationship. She'd been her daddy's girl, didn't make many moves that raised his ire, but he was certain she'd burn the house down with the candles. For her last Christmas, Kent and Adam had gone in together on a set of wall-mounted candles with mir-rors behind them. They threw the light around the room and caught the stained glass and painted everything with surreal, tinted glows. Marie loved them.

He lit all the candles now, one at a time. There were thirty-three in the room, from small tea candles to a massive stump-shaped thing that crackled like a wood fire. Initially, he'd debated whether he should light them, knowing they'd burn down eventually and have to be replaced, and he did not want to replace anything that had been sacred to her. But she'd loved to have them lit, loved the flickering glows and the incense mix of smells, and so he decided that was best.

When they were all lit, Adam sat on the floor with his back against the wall, facing the bed, the way he used to on the nights she called him in to talk, or when he simply barged in to pester her. She hated that—hence the sign she'd put on the door—and that made it all the more entertaining for him. If he heard her talking on the phone, he'd beeline for the room, crash through the door, and loudly say the most embarrassing thing he could think of.

Marie, the doctor called to say your toe fungus is contagious.
Marie, you left your training bra in the bathroom.
Marie, Dad's pissed that you stole his porn again.

Then there'd come the shout of indignant outrage, the thrown shoe or book or whatever was handy, and the cry for their father. Hank Austin would come up the steps and, depending on his mood, kick Adam out with a smile or with true irritation. Then Marie would slam the door but not lock it—locked doors weren't allowed in the Austin house—and when she finally emerged, Adam would look at her and smile. She'd try to keep the anger, she'd try so damn hard, but it always melted. She was not someone who could hold anger.

He sat on the floor and looked at the bed, remembering tossing a football back and forth with her and giving her hell about boys, watching the flush rise in her cheeks as she hotly denied every suggested crush. He'd made a lot of jokes about chaperoning her to dances and sitting behind her at the movies. Protective older brother, that was his role, and he played it so well.

Until the night it mattered.

"Hi," he told the empty room. Silence answered. Colored lights danced as the candles burned amidst the stained glass. "I've got something to tell you. You won't be happy. It's bad, Marie, but I'm going to make it right. I promise you that. I'm going to make it right."

His voice had thickened, and he didn't like that, so he paused. He wanted a drink, but he would never drink in this room. Never. When he felt steadier he said, "Good news first, okay? Kent won. They're undefeated. They should have a shot at it, Marie, they really should."

He always gave updates about Kent, told her the results of every game, and this return to normalcy helped a little. He could breathe easier and his voice was his own.

"All right, then," he continued. "Let me tell you the rest. Let me tell you what I did, and what I will do to fix it."

He bowed his head and spoke to the candlelit floor. He told

her all there was to tell, and then he told her that he was sorry, again and always, and he got to his feet and blew out the candles, one at a time. Once the last of the light was extinguished and the room was lost to darkness he slipped out, closed the door behind him, and went to see Rachel Bond's mother.

12

ADAM HAD IMAGINED THAT the girl with the glitter nail polish had grown up somewhere pretty and safe and secure. When he saw the shitty apartment building, one in which he had two current clients and countless former, he was at first surprised. Then he remembered why she'd come to see him — her father had been in prison for years, her background was not anything that suggested upscale living — and realized that he was doing it again, the thing he could not do: he was turning Rachel Bond into Marie Lynn Austin.

There was a van from one of the Cleveland news stations parked in front of the apartment, but the crew appeared to be loading up equipment. Adam cracked the window and smoked a cigarette and waited until they were gone. Then he got out of the Jeep and went to the door to make his promise.

She would have heard a lot of them by now. None quite like his.

The first response to his knock, shouted, was, "I told you I got nothing more to say!"

"Not a reporter, Mrs. Bond."

There was a pause, then the sound of footsteps and the ratcheting of the deadbolt. The door opened and a small dog, some sort of mutt with a shiny black coat, rushed forward and shoved his nose against Adam's jeans. Above the dog stood Penny Gootee, a thin, weary-looking blonde with red-rimmed eyes. She was wearing jeans and a white sweater that was covered in dog hair. Beyond, Adam could see an open beer on the coffee table, a cigarette smoldering in an ashtray beside it, and, on the couch, a worn comforter and a giant stuffed penguin.

Those last two would be Rachel's things, he knew. Penny had been on the couch with her daughter's blanket and stuffed animal, having a beer and a cigarette. Adam felt a red pulse behind his eyes, had to reach out and put one hand on the doorframe.

"Mrs. Bond," he said, "my name is Adam Austin. I came to—"

"Ah, the great coach."

"I'm not the coach."

She tilted her head, and when she did, her neck cracked. "Who are you, then?"

He willed his eyes to stay on hers as he said, "I'm the guy who gave her the address. I'm the guy who told her where she could find the man who was pretending to be her father."

"Fuck you," Rachel Bond's mother said.

Adam nodded.

Tears tried to start in her eyes but didn't find the mass or the energy needed to spill over. The dog jumped up and put his front paws on Adam's legs and licked his hand, tail wagging.

"She lied to me about her name and her age," he said. "I wish she hadn't. But I should have been paying better attention."

Penny reached out and pulled the dog down from Adam and back to her, held his collar.

"I want to be alone," she said.

"I understand that." He was struggling for his voice now,

wanted to turn from the sight of her grief as if it were a bitter winter wind. "I just had to come by to say a few things."

"You're sorry, right? Well, great. I'm real glad to hear that. I'm real damn glad, that just means the world, you have no idea how much that helps."

"Yes, I'm sorry. And, no, that's not worth a damn. I came here to make you a promise."

She knelt to wrap both arms around the dog. When she spoke, her voice was muffled against his fur.

"She's in heaven now? Is that your promise? Or is it that you're going to help them catch the son of a bitch who killed my daughter? I've heard both of those a lot today. They mean as much as your apology. Not shit, Mr. Austin. Not shit."

"I'm going to kill him," Adam said.

For a moment she just held the dog. When she lifted her face, her eyes focused on his for the first time. She looked as if she intended to speak, but whatever she saw in his eyes closed her parted lips. She just sat there on her knees on the dirty carpet holding the dog.

"I will find him," Adam said, "and I will kill him. That task is all that I am now. It is all that I will be until it's finished. He will die for what he has done. That's the only thing anyone can give you, and I will give it to you. I promise."

The dog whined, pulled toward Adam, and Penny Gootee tightened her arms around him and held. She hadn't spoken. Adam reached in his pocket and removed a business card.

"I'll find him on my own," he said. "But it may be faster with your help."

He extended the card, but she just looked at it, then back at his face.

"I'll call the police," she said. "They need to know what you're talking about. Coming here, bothering me, saying things like that...they need to know."

"Tell them," Adam said. "When they come to see me, I'll make the same pledge to them. I'll make it to anyone who asks. It's not idle talk. I'm going to find him, and I'm going to kill him, and before the end he'll know why I came."

She reached out and took the card. Held it in one hand and the dog's collar in the other as behind her the room filled with smoke from the still-burning cigarette, a trail of it rising above her daughter's blanket, draped there on the edge of the couch.

"He's still out there," Adam said. "And as long as he is, I will be, too."

He turned and left then, and she did not call after him or shut the door. When he started the Jeep she was still there on the threshold, on her knees.

13

IN THE YEAR THEY'D WON the state title, Adam's position coach was a man named Eric Scott, who wanted one word to be tattooed onto the brains of his linebackers: motion.

Coach Scott valued strength, yes, but he worshiped speed. Players who pursued the ball relentlessly were prized. You couldn't wait for contact; you had to initiate it. Victory belonged to those in pursuit of it. Life was motion, he would tell them; you had to keep moving or you'd die. Some players rolled their eyes at that, until they realized that their flat-footedness had landed them on the bench. Then, playing careers dead, they'd consider it with a different eye.

On Sunday morning, Adam rose with motion on his mind.

Something he knew he'd have to admit from the start—he wasn't a detective. Had never been police, had never worked as a PI despite holding the license, had never built an investigation into any sort of crime, let alone something as complex as a homicide. But what he *was,* what he'd devoted his adult life to becoming, was a hunter. And this was a hunt. His challenge now was not only to do a job for which police were far better prepared and equipped, but also to do it faster.

Speed and pressure. He had to find ways to apply them.

He was as good as anyone at finding people who were trying to hide. The problem was that he always knew his targets. Not just their names but personal information, a sense of their lives, of who they were. That helped the hunt. In this situation, he had absolutely none of that, and it threatened to freeze him, a bloodhound being told to start the search without being offered an initial scent. How in the hell did you begin?

Because he was used to pursuing someone with an identity, and because the lack of one was troubling to him, he decided to offer his target a name. Gideon worked nicely, felt just right. Gideon Pearce was dead, but Adam had not been afforded the opportunity to bring about that end. So his new target should be named Gideon. He could not afford to confuse Rachel Bond with Marie Austin, but blurring her killer and his sister's into one being? That felt right.

He read the public details available, and after review, he decided to start with the isolated camp on Shadow Wood Lane, the one that had been dangled in front of the girl's face so gently, a lure with every hook hidden. It was the furthest thing from an arbitrary location.

Eleanor Ruzich lived in a two-story brick house with a detached garage on the northwest side of town, apple trees lining one edge of the property, filling the air with a sweet scent. Her husband had been a doctor, dead now, and she lived alone in the sprawling place. A woman in her mid-sixties, gray hair cut short and stylish, trim figure, sharp eyes, intelligent face. She accepted his private investigator's license without the reluctance he'd feared, and he soon understood why: she was horrified, and eager to help.

"I can't begin to imagine going back there," she said, the two of them sitting at the kitchen table, Adam with his notepad and pen out, Eleanor Ruzich with a cup of coffee. "It's been empty for a long time now, but it could still bring back nice memories. Sometimes when my kids come back in the summer, we'll run up there for a day or a weekend. It's changed so much, it's a very different sort of place than what it was when we bought it and they were still children. Different people. A lot of drinking, a lot of…carrying on. The kids want me to sell it, but what could I get out of that place? This economy, this market, and that lake in the shape that it's in? I just don't see the point. So I say that I'll hold onto it, the taxes aren't so much, and maybe someday the right people will come in and clean the lake up and it will be like it once was again. I've kept ours up, just had the roof replaced this summer, had it painted summer before that. It's still in excellent shape, but it's about alone in that regard. Sad, really."

"You'd never heard of Rachel before?"

"Not until the police came to see me, no."

"And did you ever rent the place out? Or was it strictly for family use?"

"Family and friends. As I said, it's been empty for a long while now."

"The friends who knew about it…"

"Wonderful people, all of them. And elderly, now. My husband's colleagues, mostly, and he was eight years older than me. So if you think a senior citizen committed this heinous—"

"What about kids?"

She frowned. "Pardon?"

"The friends who used to visit. Did they bring children?"

"Sometimes. They were wonderful families, though."

"I'm sure they were. All the same, the names would help. Maybe one of those kids mentioned the place to the wrong person. I'm not saying it's likely, Mrs. Ruzich, I'm saying it has to be checked. You chase every possibility."

She took a deep breath and nodded. "You want a list?"

"If you can provide one, yes. Anyone who spent time at the property, over the years."

She motioned for his notepad, and he slid it over.

"I understand the idea," she said, "but I can't believe it will help. And it's not as if whoever did this was staying there, anyhow. They picked the spot because it was empty, right? Empty and isolated. So it's far more likely that it was someone who happened by it recently, thought about breaking in, maybe *did* break in. But of course they didn't take anything. Nothing had been disturbed, they just used it for ... for *that*. Just used it as a place to kill that poor girl."

Adam sat quietly, letting her talk and write. This was good. She was telling him things that he did not know, telling him things that she would have learned from the police.

"The mailboxes out there," he said when she fell silent, scribbling names, "are all bunched together at the end of the road. Correct? No mail goes to the actual cottages?"

"Correct. All of the boxes are together. We never used them except to send postcards or letters out, occasionally. It was a place to go with the children and get some sun and swim and fish. A place to relax. It was never any sort of home. And now ..."

Yes. And now.

"So no one checks the mail?"

"No. Not even when I *do* go out there. There's a box and an address, that's all."

There would also be a local carrier, and on a rural route like that, it would be a consistent carrier, most likely. The rare breed to whom a handful of letters might stand out, particularly when placed in an ancient box that had not seen mail before.

Eleanor Ruzich slid the notepad over to Adam, fifteen names written neatly in a column.

"I think that's everyone," she said. "I also think that it's a waste of your time. I understand the need to, what did you say? To chase every possibility. I understand that, of course. I just think there have to be more fruitful possibilities."

"I think so, too. But it's good to have this one if I need it. I appreciate your cooperation."

She nodded. "I will give that place away rather than set foot inside it again."

"I understand that feeling. I'm sorry it happened there."

"A pale concern in the grand scheme of the tragedy, but I'm sorry, too, Mr. Austin. I am, too." She tilted her head, focusing on him again, and finally asked the question she should have asked before she let him through the door. "Who was it who hired you? The girl's mother?"

He shook his head.

"So who sent you here?"

His stock answer, the one he'd been ready to offer at the start, was that his client's identity was confidential. It didn't come, though.

"I'm here on behalf of my sister," he said, and then he got to his feet, thanked her again for her help, and left the house.

None of the names offered much potential. He ran them all through criminal records checks and got nothing more exciting than a speeding ticket. That wasn't to say they were innocent — Rachel's killer didn't have to have a criminal history — but there were no scents that seemed promising enough to start a chase, either. For the most part, the names she'd provided belonged to people in their sixties or older. They lived nice lives in nice homes and did not intersect with the Jason Bonds or Penny Gootees of the world. Knowledge of the family seemed imperative. Only one was familiar to Adam: Duncan Werner, a local dentist and one of the football team's prominent boosters.

That sent him back to the start then, but he willed down the frustration. You had to keep your motor running, had to pursue, pursue, pursue even if you weren't having the opportunity to make plays. Those opportunities did not come to those who waited.

On Monday afternoon, he waited at Shadow Wood Lane for two hours until the mail carrier arrived.

"Minute I saw all those cars down here on Saturday, I was curious," the man said. He was an older man with a gray mustache and hound dog jowls. "Trying to figure out which cottage it was, you know, because there are some problems down here in the summer, but the place is pretty much dead the rest of the year. I don't deliver much of anything."

"I'd imagine. You been delivering much of late?"

"Letters to 7330."

Adam nodded. He was wearing sunglasses and jeans and a plain brown baseball cap and a matching jacket. No logo on any of them, but he knew that he looked like a cop, and he knew how to carry himself like one, too, and how to talk like one. From the postal worker's cooperation, he was fairly certain that the man believed he was police, but that was safe, because he had not been misinformed. Adam had a recorder running in his jacket pocket, and if this became an issue, they would not be able to say he had identified himself as law enforcement.

"The last one, you remember when that was delivered?"

"Wednesday," he said confidently. "Only thing that went in any of the boxes. Like I said, it stands out. This place is pretty well shut down after Labor Day."

This is what Adam had counted on. He nodded, thinking that Wednesday would have given enough time for an immediate response by mail, but also that Rachel Bond had probably offered a cell phone number. Cell phone, e-mail, one of the fashions of communication preferred by a teenage girl, particularly one in a hurry. From Wednesday's letter to Friday's meeting, details could have been arranged quickly.

"When did they start?" he asked. "Or was that the only one?"

"Only one coming in." The mail carrier had no hesitation. This was the great thing about rural routes: everything stood out. Adam couldn't help feel some petty tug of pride that the man clearly hadn't been interviewed by police yet.

"But there were some going out."

"Yes, sir. Round about Labor Day, I think. I hadn't put a damn thing in that box for a good while, and then the letters started coming, so it sticks in my mind, you know?"

"Sure. How many, would you say? How often?"

"Once a week, maybe twice. I'd say I picked up, oh, a half-dozen."

"Any chance you remember the handwriting?"

"Typed."

"Never saw anyone put them in the box?"

"Never saw a soul. I'd come out, flag was up, and that was that. Always surprised me. I'm in the habit of blowing right by here, you know." He sighed and spread his hands. "I wish I had more to tell you, Officer."

Adam let him go then, because he didn't want to push the police impersonation any further, and he didn't feel the man had anything left to offer. When the mail truck was gone, Adam walked back down to the cottages, watching the quiet pond ripple under the wind, sun-speckled and beautiful, and he wondered what it had been like when she arrived, tried to recall the weather on Friday afternoon. It had been colder then, and overcast. The pond would have been bathed in shadows and the decrepit cottages would have looked forlorn and ominous, and still she'd pulled in and gone to finish her task.

A brave girl, and a determined one.

"I'm working on it, Marie," Adam whispered. "I'm working on it."

It wasn't until the words were out of his mouth that he realized he'd meant to say Rachel.

What next? Where else to look? There was the prison, possibly, but he doubted that Jason Bond would be willing to see him, and knew without question that approaching the man would trigger police attention to Adam's quest that would only slow him down. Likewise with any effort to interview Rachel's friends. But maybe it was time. There were not many other options.

He turned and gazed around the cottages with frustration. He'd been sure this was the right way to start. The kill site had not been random. Everything about it worked too well, from the isolation to the opportunity to send the letters from an active address but a vacant home. It had been carefully selected, and that required knowledge of the place, but none of the names Eleanor Ruzich had given him seemed promising. Who else might have known about the cottage? There were the neighbors, of course. He hadn't pursued them yet. It would be hard to determine which cottages had actually been used recently, they were all so run-down. Except for Eleanor Ruzich's. She had not exaggerated when she said she was alone in her efforts to keep the place in good shape.

He'd turned full circle, his back to the pond again, and was staring at the cottage.

I've kept ours up, Eleanor had said. Yes, she certainly had. He called her from the dock and found her at home again. He told her he was still working on the Shadow Wood leads and was now searching for potential witnesses.

"You had some maintenance done recently," he said. "The roof was replaced, isn't that what you said?"

"Yes. Roof replaced this summer, the exterior painted last summer."

"Do you recall what company did that work? It seems that the activity with your address began in the summer, so I was—"

"It wasn't a company," she said. "It's a man who's been our caretaker for years out there. He works for the hospital in some sort of maintenance job. My husband met him there."

"What's his name?"

"Rodney Bova," she said. "That's spelled B-O—"

"I know Rodney," he said.

"You do? How?"

He hesitated, then said, "I played football with him once. A long time ago. Thanks, Mrs. Ruzich. Maybe Rodney will be able to help."

14

Rodney bova was a ghost's name, an attachment to
vague and receding memories. He'd been one of those kids
who flitted around the periphery of Adam's life but never
stepped into focus.

His place among the memories had been etched by rumors
and gossip. Adam couldn't recall his face, his voice, his family, or
even what position he'd played. He remembered only two things
about Rodney Bova — he'd been on the team briefly, and he'd
left it when he was sentenced to a juvie lockup. He had, for a
short time the summer before Adam's senior year, taken a star-
ring role in the team's conversation by getting himself arrested.
There was a live-in camp every August, the first week of practice, the kids practicing twice a day and spending the nights in
sleeping bags on the gym floor, a bonding-by-boot-camp exercise
that Walter Ward designed. As Adam recalled, Bova was missing during live-in camp, and nobody was sure why, but some of
the kids had heard rumors. Adam's interest in the situation was
minimal, Bova being a couple of years younger than him and
not a starter. Had a contributor been arrested, had they lost a

playmaker, that would have been different. Bova was a nobody, though, and so his flare of fame had faded fast.

Rodney Bova, the caretaker at 7330 Shadow Wood Lane.

Maybe it shouldn't have felt like so much. Maybe the mind was teasing him into believing this connection had value simply because it was the *only* connection he'd found, an unanticipated link to the past and to crime. Maybe the right thing to do was simply to give old Rodney Bova a call and ask the questions — when had he logged his hours at Shadow Wood this summer, who had he seen, which of the neighbors were talkative, which were suspicious.

Somehow, though, that didn't feel like the move to make.

The voice that whispered in Adam's head when he was chasing skips, the one that was usually right, was telling him to circle Rodney Bova, and do it quietly.

At least to start.

The team began approaching practice with distraction where passion belonged, and while Kent understood it, he also had to fix it.

Rachel Bond's murder was in all of their heads, he knew that. Grief and gossip, faith and fear. The conversation inside the school would be swirling amidst those four cardinal directions right now, and it would be ceaseless. There were a few on the team — Colin Mears foremost among them — to whom the loss was truly and deeply personal. There were more to whom it was distant and would now be made personal. That strange magnetic pull of tragedy. Kent had known it too well, for too long. Classmates who'd never spoken to his sister began reminiscing over time spent with her. Strangers in town would approach him in the grocery store or at McDonald's or on the street, tears in their eyes. Often, they wanted to touch him while they offered their condolences. He was struck by the frequency of that—hands on the arm, pats on the back, awkward embraces. Seeking some contact with the tragedy, but minimal, of course. Minimal. As if somehow that offered a vaccination. If they got just the right amount of contact, incubated just the right amount of terror and horror in their own hearts, they'd be protected.

You had to find your refuge. The place of consistency in a world gone mad. For Kent it had been the football field. Walter Ward had understood so well what nobody else seemed to: Kent and Adam needed some level of normalcy. Had to have it. Kent did, at least. Adam started missing practices. Never missed a game, and never played better than he did down the stretch after Marie was killed, but until kickoff he was uninterested. Kent had gone the other way. Taken more reps, watched more film. Immersed himself. Ward had helped him to do that.

Now, twenty-two years removed, Kent watched Colin Mears in the receivers line, saw him glancing over his shoulder, and followed the boy's look. Three of his teammates engaged in earnest, whispered conversation. Kent could guess the topic, if not the specifics.

He turned away, his cap pulled low, and chewed furiously on his whistle. It was a lifeguard's whistle, soft, waterproof rubber, and he liked it because he could bite on the thing so hard that it was almost like having a mouthpiece back in, almost like having the helmet on and lining up under center with the crowd in your ears and the lights on your face.

We are going to lose, he thought. *We are going to lose.*

Byers was barking and pacing and cussing, but Byers always barked and paced and cussed, and so the kids paid him little mind. Kent watched his linebackers run through a drill, banging off the tackling sled with cursory attention, nobody coming close to earning a bruise, which made him furious—this point in the season, the point that mattered most, and they didn't want to hit? Then he swiveled his head and watched his offensive line-men execute what was supposed to be a zone-blocking scheme but looked like blindfolded kids being chased by bees, and he knew they were going to get beat.

Again.

Just like every other year.

Hickory Hills might not beat them, even if Chambers extended this passionless effort from the practice field to the game. But on the opposite side of the bracket waited Saint Anthony's, a school Kent had never beaten, led by a coach, Scott Bless, Kent had never beaten. There was no team in the state he wanted to beat more desperately. In his two state championship appearances, Saint Anthony's had marched off the field with the trophy two times.

Kent's jaw was beginning to ache from chewing the whistle. He turned downfield, watched his receivers, who were working on snap counts, Steve Haskins trying to confuse them with a mix of cadences, making sure they'd jump only when they were supposed to, and Colin Mears bristled with energy, crisp on every play, then back in line, slapping helmets and demanding focus and providing reminders.

Kent blew the whistle, and most of the field went silent, but not enough of it. Not enough. His defensive secondary was laugh-ing through their drill, and it was the worst kind of laughter to have on the football field. Cocky laughter. The kind that sug-gested they thought they'd already won, when they'd never walked off the field at the end of a season without a loss.

"*This is funny to you?*" he screamed, and now he was walking toward them and everyone was backing up. "Practicing for the playoffs is entertainment? Is that what I'm to understand?"

A chorus of "no, sirs" came, but he was already turning away from them in disgust.

"Colin, Lorell, Damon! Get down here."

In came his three senior all-state studs. When Kent stared them down, they all met the gaze, but Colin did it with hunger, almost as if he'd been hoping it would go this way. Kent understood. There was an excruciating fatigue that came when every pair of eyes that looked your way seemed to read a FRAGILE: HANDLE WITH CARE label on your forehead.

"What do you think of your team's effort today?" Kent said.

There was a murmured "Not great" from Damon, a "Poor" from Lorell, and a nearly shouted "Awful, sir!" from Colin.

"So no one is impressed?"

Three heads shook.

"Anyone feel like we're ready to win with this effort?"

"No, sir."

"All right then. We're going to keep at it down here, and while we do, you can hit the bleachers to demonstrate the sort of effort that you want, as captains. Move."

They moved—off the field and through the fence and into the bleachers and began to run, six feet hammering on the aluminum in unison.

"When they see enough from you," Kent said, turning back to his team but shouting loud enough for the benefit of the three running the bleachers, "they'll come back down to join us."

He saw heads turning from him, eyes drifting away, and for an instant he was enraged—they were *still* not going to give him focus?—but then he saw the police uniform by the fence, and he, too, was distracted. It was Stan Salter.

"Coach Byers, get these boys fired up," Kent said, and then he walked over to Salter.

"How's your team doing, Coach?"

"Could be better. How's your investigation going?"

"Could be better."

Kent nodded and waited. Salter had sunglasses on, and he looked from Byers up to the rattling bleachers. Damon Ritter stumbled, slipping in the burgundy leaves that were raining silently down. That would be perfect, wouldn't it? Kent's best defensive player blowing out a knee running sprints to make a point to the team.

"That the Mears boy you got running?" Salter asked.

"It is."

"How's he holding up?"

"This will help him."

"Yeah?"

"Yeah."

Salter nodded, took a deep breath, and said, "You spoken to your brother?"

"I have not." Kent was still staring into the bleachers.

"I could use your help with him."

"He's not going to be any more cooperative with you if I'm the middleman. If anything, it will make things more difficult for you."

"You don't know that he's investigating Rachel Bond's murder, I take it."

Kent turned to Salter, seeing his own reflection in the cop's sunglasses.

"Investigating?"

Salter nodded. "I got a call today from a woman of . . . potential value to the investigation. Seems your brother went out to interview her yesterday morning, then called again today. Told her he was a private investigator. She didn't think much of it at the time, because his name didn't resonate with her. Then she talked it over with a friend this afternoon and realized how disturbing an answer he'd given her when she asked who he was working for."

"Who *is* he working for?"

"His sister," Salter said. "That's what he told her, at least. He said he was working on behalf of his sister."

Kent leaned on the fence, tightened his right hand around the chain link. "He said that?"

"Yes."

Neither of them spoke then. Behind them the coaches shouted instructions and the kids grunted with effort and the tackling sleds slapped and rattled on their frames. Beside them the bleachers shook and Colin Mears screamed out encouragement as he took the steps — *Come on, show them something, show them how we do this!* The wind was pushing across the field in strong gusts, fat orange and crimson leaves tumbling.

"I would like," Stan Salter said, "for your brother not to jeopardize my investigation. I understand that the two of you are not close. But I need you to understand that I can't have him doing what he's doing."

"On behalf of his sister," Kent repeated. "That's what he told her?"

"Yes."

"And what did his sister want, Lieutenant?" Kent's voice was choked, the whistle back in the corner of his mouth now, teeth grinding against it. "Do you know?"

"Suspects."

"Suspects." Kent nodded. Spit the whistle out. Looked away. "Tell you what, Lieutenant. You let me talk to my brother."

"Thought you didn't do much of that."

"I don't. But it's time."

15

IN THE YEARS SINCE HE'D faded into the mists of memory, Rodney Bova had drifted out of Chambers County and then returned, with stops at three jails and one prison in between.

The first bust—at least the first available to the public, his juvenile record was protected—had been in 1994, for selling weed. He did thirty days in jail in Sandusky and then got out and migrated back east, pausing in Cleveland to be arrested for trafficking with an inmate at the Cuyahoga County Jail and sentenced to three months. Back out again, long enough to sniff the fresh air and decide he didn't like the smell, and then through the revolving door and into the Lorain County Jail for a three-count conviction involving assault, drug possession, and an unlicensed firearm after he was arrested during a bar fight. The judge in that case had less patience with young Rodney and sent him to prison for an eighteen-month stay. Mansfield Correctional had been his home from the autumn of 1998 to the spring of 2000.

The facility had also been home, those years, to Gideon Pearce.

And, later, to Jason Bond.

Something began to tick inside Adam as he read through the arrest records and constructed his timeline. It wasn't a bad feeling. Not at all. More like the application of a match to a part of him that longed for heat, ached for it.

He was lost in the web of overlapping names and dates and prisons when his phone began to ring, and he silenced it without a glance, didn't look at the display until the second call, an immediate, impatient follow-up effort, and then it froze him.

Kent was calling.

Kent did not call.

Five rings before voicemail, and he let it get to four before he picked it up.

"Yeah."

"It's me."

"I noticed that."

Silence. Kent said, "We need to talk, Adam."

"Do we?"

"Yes. I'd rather it be in person." There was a hard edge to his younger brother's voice. The coach's tone, that's what it was, the ruler of young men, captain of the ship, and it raised a bristle in Adam. Always did. *Coach your boys, Kent, don't coach me,* he'd said more than a few times, back in the days when they spoke.

"I'm not at home."

"That's fine. Tell me where you are."

"Busy."

"That's not a place, Adam."

"It's a condition, Kent. So you're right. But it's still true."

"True for me, too. I've got a game tomorrow, I've got two kids and a wife at home, and I've got police calling me, looking for you. But I'm making time, and you will, too."

Adam let a few seconds and a few responses float by, and while he did that, Kent said, "Tell me where I can find you, all right? Just do that much."

"Let's go to Haslem's." This was designed to get a rise out of him, just the sort of needle Adam couldn't bring himself to put down with Kent, even when he tried.

"I'm not meeting you at a strip club."

"The house, then."

The only place that would appeal to Kent less than the titty bar was their childhood home. You could practically see his skin crawl when he crossed over the threshold. How long had it been since he was inside? Adam couldn't remember.

"Okay," Kent said after a pause, and then Adam pulled back on the offer, a poker player immediately regretting his bluff.

"Like I said, I'm not there. Tell you what, Coach, I'll come out to the school. Meet you in your office. That way you can get some work done while you wait."

"I don't want to wait."

"Then I'll hustle right along," Adam said, and hung up. He bounced the phone in his palm and stared at the wall and eventually he became aware of a pain in his jaw and realized how tightly he was clenching his teeth. He set the phone down and opened the refrigerator. There were five beers left in the twelve-pack he'd bought last night.

"See you in five, Franchise," he said aloud, and then he opened one of the Coronas and took another in his free hand and walked outside to drink in the cold.

Kent was glad Adam had picked the school. He didn't want to chase his brother through the town's grunge bars and he certainly didn't want to see him at either of the two places he called home: one that belonged to a married woman with an inmate husband, or one that belonged to bad memories. Carefully preserved bad memories.

He knew when he hung up that Adam would take his sweet

time appearing. He had to do that, had to try to establish the alpha status in whatever sad way possible. Kent had said he did not want to wait, and that meant he would be made to wait.

The coach's office and locker rooms at Chambers were in a single-story concrete-block building behind the end zone. When he pulled in and parked in the empty lot he could see posters and silver and red streamers covering the walls, handiwork of the boosters and parents and cheerleaders. PLAYOFFS: WIN OR GO HOME! one of the signs shrieked.

He was so sick of going home with a loss he could hardly bear it, so sick of uttering the same damned reassurances of how he was proud of his kids and proud of their character and proud of the season, the season that had ended with his kids watching their opponents celebrate.

It wasn't supposed to happen again this year. Not with this team. They were too good, they were too well prepared, they were too experienced. Every part was there, every element a championship squad needed was in place. They were the best this town had ever seen. Better than the '89 team by a mile. But the '89 team had put a trophy in the case, they had rings on their fingers. Their work was done. His was not.

He had one of those rings himself, but it didn't count. He'd been a freshman that season, never took a snap in the playoffs, just stood on the sidelines with a clipboard and charted plays while Pete Underwood, the senior starter, ran the careful, plodding offense, the world's most boring offense, a two-running-back set that asked very little of the quarterback beyond the ability to complete a handoff. It was tedious to watch, but Walter Ward was not interested in entertaining, he was interested in wins. They had a big bruising line and a committee of big bruising backs, and they just wore teams down. In the state championship they'd used fifteen straight running plays on their final drive. Fifteen. The opposing defense had everyone down in the box, essentially ignoring the threat of a vertical passing route, committed to stopping Chambers up front, confident that if they did that, they'd win the game, because Underwood was not going to beat them with his arm. And Coach Ward had looked at that, at the way his team was being dared to pass, and he'd kept running the ball. All the way into the end zone.

Prophet right.
Prophet left.
Prophet right.
Prophet right.
Prophet right.

Never showing a trace of emotion, no hint of fear, not even when they got to fourth and two, just kept calling those plays in a flat, steady voice, everyone in the stadium knowing exactly what was coming, including the defense, all of it on Adam, who was the prophet, who was the telltale blocker out front, promising contact. Coach Ward just stood there with his arms folded across his chest and gave it to them again and again, relentless and confident — *You must stop this, and you will not be able to.*

How the fans had loved that! You wanted to talk about smashmouth? Watch a fifteen-play drive against the state's best defense in which the ball was never passed. Adam had been out in front of the ball carrier the whole way. He'd played every down of the state championship game, both sides of the ball, and somewhere in Ohio there were ex-linebackers with loose teeth who remembered him well. They used four different running backs on those fifteen handoffs, but just one lead blocker for all of them. It was the point of the play — promise package, they called it. When Adam came in on the offensive side of the ball, you were going to get a run, and you were going to have him out front. Every time. Usually he rotated, usually Ward saved most of his strength for defense and short-yardage situations, but not that drive. Fifteen straight.

The way the crowd had roared after that drive...Kent hadn't heard anything else like it in high school football. Doubted he ever would again. It had been ugly football, mean and nasty, but somehow it connected with hearts in the stands because of that. It took Kent a while to understand the reason exactly, and with it came a better understanding of the game, why it inspired such a fierce pride in towns like Cleveland and Green Bay and Pittsburgh. Like Massillon. Like Chambers.

The way they'd roared that night—people cried in the stands, he remembered that, would never forget it, people *cried*—wasn't just because Chambers had won the game. At that point, in fact, victory had hardly been assured; there were three minutes left to play, and the top-ranked team in the state had the ball and a last chance to regain the lead. No, it was because they'd started with their backs against the wall, jammed against their own goal line with a deficit and a ticking clock and then lined up in a way that said, *We will have to take a beating with this approach, there is no other way,* and then they'd taken it, and taken it, and taken it, until suddenly they were administering it.

That was why people cried in the stands.

It had taken Kent a long time to understand it.

Tonight he was in the locker room alone, and when he flicked on the overhead fluorescent lights, the place picked up a white glow, and at the end of the locker room he could see the photograph of the 1989 team, the only team picture that he'd ever allowed to hang in the locker room. It was not all about wins and losses, he reminded his boys every day, but then there was just the one team picture hanging in the room.

Because they won. Right, Coach? Why else? And you're in that picture but you don't belong in it, and all of the pictures you do belong in, well, they don't belong on the wall.

He went through the locker room and into his office, fired up the computer and projector and began to watch video. A little more than an hour passed before Adam arrived.

In through the locker room door without a knock, and then Kent could see him standing out there, gazing around. The door to the coach's office was open and the lights from the video painted it and its lone occupant with that white glow, but Adam didn't even glance that way, just stood with his back to the office and took in the rest of the room, and Kent knew he was both remembering old ghosts and assessing the ways in which it had changed since the days when they were not ghosts at all.

Kent rose from the chair and walked out to join him. Adam looked at him for a minute. "Not even a handshake, Franchise?"

They shook hands. Adam's grip was stronger. One of the reasons he liked to shake hands. He enjoyed intimidation in all of its forms, brutal to subtle. Kent was not a small man — six-two and 190 pounds that still saw several hours a week in the weight room — but around Adam he was not just the little brother in terms of years. When he'd signed with Ohio State, Adam had stood six-four barefoot, with a forty-five-inch chest and thirty-one-inch waist. Ridiculous proportions. He ran the forty in 4.7 seconds, which wasn't blazing speed, not Colin Mears speed, but was awfully damn fast. Twenty-two years had taken the speed from him, but it had hardly made a dent in the muscle, and somehow that annoyed Kent. Maybe his brother was always in a gym, and he just didn't know it. He doubted it, though. So how did he do it? How could a man drink like that and live like that and still look like *that*?

"How you doing?" Kent said, already awkward, the handshake somehow removing the sense of focused control he'd had when he walked over to meet his brother.

"I'm all right. You?"

"Tired."

"Going to get more tired, if you're any good. Should have a few weeks left. Undefeated season's never been done in this school. Going to get it for them?"

"We'll try," Kent said. "Listen, I didn't bring you in here to talk football."

"Should have. I could help your Pollyannas. Teach them how to play with blood in their eyes."

"Adam, listen, we need to —"

"You remember the last time you called me?" Adam said. His dark blue eyes held a faraway sheen, and Kent could smell beer on his breath.

"You've been drinking tonight, haven't you?"

"I drink every night. Now, do you remember the last time you called me?"

Kent thought about it, said, "Your birthday."

"That doesn't count. Remove the obligatory holiday calls and then tell me."

They were obligatory only to Kent; he did not receive holiday calls from Adam. But his brother's eyes had gone serious and for some reason he was compelled to go along with it, to try and remember. He couldn't do it. Adam saw that in his face and smiled humorlessly.

"Don't worry," he said. "I couldn't recall it myself."

Kent said, "A girl was murdered, Adam, and the police are calling me about it."

"I've heard from them, too."

"Apparently they don't hear back." Kent stepped forward, forced himself into Adam's wandering gaze, and said, "Did you really tell some woman you were working for our *sister?*"

It went very quiet then. In his office the video played, and flickers of light and shadow bled out of the room and danced over Adam's lean face as he looked down into Kent's eyes.

"I said I was there on her behalf," Adam said, and his voice was slow and cold. "That's what I said, and that's what I meant. Would you like to take issue with it?"

"Yes," Kent said, not backing down, not on this point, not when Marie's name had been invoked. "I take issue with it. I don't know what sort of scheme you had in mind at the time, but it boils down to a lie, and you can't tell me it doesn't. You're not a detective, and nobody's hired you to do anything. So you're out masquerading as one and telling people that *Marie* sent you? The first half is pathetic, the second I take personally."

"You take it personally." Adam's voice had gone absolutely empty.

"That's what I just said."

Adam gave a small nod. "And you're entitled to do that. Because she was your sister."

"She was *our* sister. I don't understand how you could use her name like that, how you can even suggest that, twist her into whatever lie—"

"Not a lie."

"I'm sorry?"

"Keep calling it one, Kent. That's fine, but it won't become one. You say I'm not a detective? I've got a state license that says otherwise. You say I wasn't there on Marie's behalf? You better *believe* you're wrong on that count. You better know that."

Kent stepped back, put one hand on a locker, and leaned against it. Let a few seconds pass, trying to let the building anger ebb away. Then he said, "What are you doing, man? What in the world do you think you're doing?"

Adam sat down on one of the long benches in front of the lockers, braced his forearms on his knees and looked at the floor and took a deep breath. Kent could see his back muscles spread out under his T-shirt, could see his big shoulders rise. *Loading dock muscle,* Coach Ward had called it. *That's the kind that moves freight, boys. That's what we want. I don't give a damn if you look pretty in the mirror, I want you to move freight.*

"What did they tell you about the situation?" Adam said.

"Which situation? The woman you interviewed? Or Rachel Bond?"

"Rachel."

"I know that she went to you looking for help finding an address. I know that she lied to you about her age, and the police probably didn't cut you much slack on that, but you'll cut yourself less slack on it." He was almost surprised he'd said that; it wasn't a thought he had expressed to anyone else. "I know that you gave her an address."

"And you know what happened when she went there."

"Yeah. Yes."

Adam nodded again.

"So that's what I know," Kent said when it was clear his brother was not going to speak. "Today, I was told about your contact with some woman who the police don't want you dealing with. I was told what you said to her. I didn't like what I heard."

"I can imagine not."

"Tell me, then. Tell me what you're doing, Adam."

Adam lifted his head. "I'm going to find him."

Kent stared at him. Adam's eyes were clear and cool.

"Rachel's murderer," Kent said.

"Gideon."

For a moment Kent thought: *There he went. Finally. All the way over, it was bound to happen, he was bound to tip and now he has*—but then Adam added, "That's what I like to call him. I needed a name. That one works."

Kent was scared for him now. Anger had faded to fear, and he said, "Don't talk like that."

"The name helps me."

"No, it doesn't. Adam, they are not the same person."

"The hell they aren't. One abducted and murdered a teenage girl. So did the other. They're close enough to share a name, at least. Shit, you and I do, and how much do we have in common? They can share a name."

Kent said, "He's dead, Adam. The man is dead."

"Marie's Gideon is dead. Rachel's is not."

Kent wanted to tell him to shut up, stop using names, but that wasn't going to accomplish much. He couldn't look into that unsettling, empty stare anymore, and turned to face the white light in the office as he said, "Don't get in their way, Adam. Please."

"The police. You don't want me to get in their way."

"That's right."

"Because you don't think I can find him."

"I don't know if you can or not, but I know it's not your place to try. I know you'll cause problems if you do, I know —"

"The police," Adam said, "looked for Marie's killer for four months."

"And they found him."

"Police in another town made a random stop and caught a break. The police assigned to find Marie's killer, though? They were not close, Kent. They were not close. And he was supposed to be in prison the whole time. He'd been missing for months, and how good a job did the police do then? How quickly did they find him?"

Kent reached up and rubbed his eyes. He hated to think of it, hated to remember it, but Adam lived in a temple of memories, he could not move forward, his past was his present.

"Don't do this. Even if you could help, they won't let you. It'll only make things worse."

"Because it's not my place."

"Because they're cops, Adam, and, yes, they will be upset because it is not your role."

"That's where you're wrong. It is my role, it's the only one for me. So this, this is my place. Because this Gideon? This one belongs to me."

"Stop calling him that."

"It's the right thing to call him."

Kent dropped his hand, looked at him, and said, "Please, Adam."

"What did they want from you? What were you supposed to accomplish? Just get me to step away? Get me to call Salter back? What?"

"All of the above. But I called you because...because I didn't like what I'd heard."

Adam said, "You should see the place."

"What?"

"Where she died, Kent. Where I sent her. You should see it. Desolate, empty, dangerous. If I'd bothered to give it a look first, she never shows up there. If I'd known where I was sending her, everything changes. I sent her to a place I did not know. That's why it happened."

"No, Adam. Whoever did this...he wouldn't have just gone away."

"Maybe not. But, Kent? Read your own damn slogan." Adam pointed at the banner above the locker room door, the one the players passed under ahead of every game, every half, every practice. THERE IS A DIFFERENCE BETWEEN ACCEPTING A LOSS AND EARNING ONE.

Kent shook his head, frustrated but running out of words, because words never seemed to work on his brother. At least not Kent's.

"Funny, you being in this locker room still," Adam said.

"Keeps it all fresh to you, I bet. For me, it's been a while. A lot of shit that went down in here I can hardly remember. Being in here brings it all back, you know?"

Kent was happy that he wasn't talking about Gideon Pearce anymore, so he rolled with it, said, "Yeah, I'm sure it does."

"There was a kid, had a locker right over there..." Adam pointed into the corner. "Rodney Bova. Got thrown off the team for trouble with the police. You remember him?"

"Sure."

"What was that he did?" Adam was squinting, thoughtful. "Stole a car, maybe?"

"Set it on fire."

"No shit?"

Kent nodded. "They sent him to a juvenile detention center."

"He was your age?"

"Yeah."

"Any good?"

"No. Wanted to play receiver but couldn't catch a cold. Ward moved him to defense but he never played." Why in the world were they talking about Rodney Bova? All the things he needed to say to his brother, all the people they needed to discuss, and somehow they were locked in conversation about a random kid they'd played with more than twenty years ago? He tried to steer them back to what counted. "Adam, you've got to understand that Stan Salter is going to return to talk with me, and when he does —"

"When he does," Adam said, "you can tell him the truth. Tell him you've washed your hands of me. Tell him good luck and God bless, and that it doesn't involve you. Then let it sit."

"I wish you would —"

"Then let it sit," Adam told him again, and he rose from the bench and walked out of the locker room. The field showed itself, dark and windswept, for a moment when he opened the door, and then it clanged shut and Kent was alone in the pale white light, surrounded by his quotes and posters and bits of inspiration. Outside, Adam headed away from him and into the night. Kent wondered where he was going. It was impossible to know.

He wondered if he should have asked.

16

CHELSEA WAS IN THE YARD when Adam returned, pouring sunflower seeds into a birdfeeder, fumbling in the dark, spilling half of the seeds into the leaves as she struggled to balance the weight of the bag in one arm and the position of the feeder with the other. He braced the feeder for her and said, "Why in the hell couldn't this wait until morning?"

"One died."

"What?"

"It was on the porch. Flew into the window. You know how they do that sometimes."

"So it flew into the window. It didn't starve to death."

She shrugged, indifferent to that logic. "All the same, I thought I should fill the feeders."

She was wearing loose sweatpants and a tank top, nothing else, hadn't bothered to put on a jacket before she stepped into the cold night. This wasn't atypical. She liked the cold, embraced it. He'd found her on the porch one winter morning in the predawn wearing just jeans and a bra, exhaling long breaths and watching them fog. When he asked her what the hell she was doing, she just smiled and said there was nothing like lung-care advice from a smoker.

Once the feeder had been filled she turned to face him and said, "Where have you been?"

"Talking to my brother."

"Really?"

He nodded, still looking at her standing there barefoot in the dead leaves, her nipples taut against the thin fabric of the tank top, and, as was often the case, he found himself overwhelmed with desire for her. It was one of those things that was supposed to wane over time, wasn't it, that teenage hormonal rush? Somehow it never had, with her. And if he'd been able to control that back when he was a teenager, if he'd just taken care of his responsibilities...

"What did Kent have to say?" Chelsea asked.

"Not much." Adam took her in his arms as she gave him a skeptical glance.

"Kent just wanted to have a casual talk?"

"Yeah." He kissed her, and she returned it for a few seconds before breaking away.

"What did he *really* want, Adam?"

"To tell me not to get into trouble," Adam said, and then he wrapped his fingers in her hair, a touch like satin, and pulled gently, forcing her head back in the way she liked, and put his lips to her throat.

"Don't do that," she said.

"Do what?" he whispered, tracing her collarbone with his tongue, his hands sliding down her back and over her hips, her body pressed against his.

"Try to distract me. It doesn't work." But her voice had gone softer and deeper and now she had her arms around him, too, her fingernails biting into his back, pulling him tighter.

"Thought you wanted my mind in other places. That's what you said last night."

"What I want right now," she said, "is not your mind. We'll get to that."

He picked her up then, and she wrapped her legs around him and locked her ankles behind his back as he carried her into the house. She was light and he could have gotten her all the way to the bedroom easily, but they didn't make it there. The living room floor was closer.

They made it to the bed eventually, though, and they were there, still sweat-covered and breathing hard, when she placed her palm flat on his chest, put her face just above his, her lips hovering so close he could feel her breath as she spoke, and said, "What changed?"

"What do you mean?"

"Your mood. I'm not complaining, trust me. But what changed?"

Purpose, he thought. *I know where I'm running now.* But he said, "I just need you. Okay? Don't interrogate me about it."

She didn't respond, still searching his eyes.

"You're usually tense after talking to your brother. Why not tonight?"

"Maybe because I had the good sense to drink first," he said, and then, because a drink sounded like a hell of a nice idea, he got up and poured a Scotch and returned to bed.

"Let's try this again," she said. "And this time, why don't you tell me the truth?"

It was silent for a moment. She took the whiskey glass out of his hand and took a swallow. He traced the tattoo she had just over her hip, low on a stomach that shouldn't be so flat and taut on a woman in her late thirties. It was a cat's eye, shaded golden and outlined in bold black. She hated cats. Loved dogs, hated cats, had a cat's-eye tattoo. It made sense to her, if nobody else.

She just liked the look of it, she said. It had a hold on him, but not an altogether good one. He knew the tattoo artist who'd done it—her husband—and there that eye was, watching him in the night. Reminding him at all times that he was in bed with a married woman, and that Travis Leonard was coming back eventually. Then what? Would Adam sit back and hold his breath, waiting for the good news that they'd caught Travis with a stolen car, that he was going back to jail, a good long bust? What a beautiful life he had. What a beautiful damned life.

Chelsea said, "You didn't kill the girl, Adam."

"Rachel."

"What?"

"Use her name. She's not *the girl,* she's not a body in the morgue, she's—"

"You didn't kill Rachel," she said, and that stopped him before the boil. He closed his eyes. The tattoo would never close its eyes, but he could close his.

"I know. But I didn't help."

"There's a lot of difference. And you're going to deal with it by, what, disappearing?"

"I'm not going to disappear. I'm going to make sure that he doesn't."

"He?"

"Whoever did it."

"Let the police do their job."

"I don't want to do their job. I want to do one that's a little different."

"Adam..."

"Gideon Pearce should have been in jail the day he murdered Marie."

"So you're a vigilante now, that's it? That's the right thing?"

"If I'm going to pull a trigger, I'd rather the barrel be in his mouth than mine."

She looked at him for a long time and said, "It'll be in both at once."

"Better than just the one of us."

She lifted his chin with her index finger to make him look her in the eyes. It was dark in the room, though, and all they could exchange were shifting shadows.

"Get some help, Adam. Talk to someone."

"I'm going to find him."

"That's not what I mean by *help*. I mean you need to find a —"

"A shrink, a priest, a doctor with an open prescription pad. Yeah, I know what you meant."

She dropped her hand from his face, and for a moment it was quiet. Then she said, "It won't take long for the police to learn what you're trying to do. And then you'll have problems."

"I know it."

"You can't stop, though? Not even for a few days, not even for long enough to step back and realize that all of this —"

"No, Chelsea. I can't stop."

He took the whiskey back from her and finished it and they lay together in the silent dark.

Warm breath on his ear, a cool palm on his chest. Something whispered. Adam wanted to respond, but his brain clung to drunken sleep and reminded him that he was going to be hurting tomorrow, that he'd hit the Scotch a bit too hard before the end, and Scotch, as was its generous way, might have let him slip off into sleep tonight but would certainly make him pay the bill come morning, with interest.

Sleep on, then. Burrow deeper, darker.

The palm was on his shoulder now, and it grew fingers, and the fingers had nails, and they squeezed. The whisper again, rising, nearly a full voice.

"Baby. Adam."

He tried to turn away, but Chelsea shook his shoulder and now she'd won, sleep was on the retreat.

"Let me be," he said, or tried to say. His voice was hoarse and choked.

"It's Rachel's mother."

He opened his eyes, turned to see that Chelsea was pressing his phone to her chest, the bluish light of the display spilling over her breast.

"What?"

"She called five times. I finally answered. She wants to talk to you."

He sat up, the hangover already throwing a few experimental punches even though the alcohol was still too thick in his bloodstream to be called into the ring yet.

"Here," he said, holding out his hand. His voice croaked again, and he cleared his throat, tasting the smoke from his last cigarette. She passed him the phone and he climbed out of the bed. The alarm clock said it was twenty past three. He walked out of the bedroom and into the living room, where the darkness faded to light from the heat lamps that sustained the snakes.

"Hello," he said, and he was pleased with his voice—it sounded clear and sober enough to get by, at least.

"Didn't want to wake you," Penny Gootee said, "but figure if you were any bit as good as your word, you wouldn't care. So it's the right time to call, maybe. Just right."

Hers was a voice that was not clear or sober enough to get by.

"It's a fine time. Are you all right?"

"No, I'm not all right. You really just ask me that?"

"I'm sorry."

He paused, waited.

"They bury my daughter this week," she said. Her voice

reminded him of her eyes the last time he'd seen her, shot through with misplaced blood.

"I know it."

She let it go for a few seconds before she spoke again. This time she seemed to be trying harder, a drunk's careful tightrope walk over the treachery of words, wielding a thick and clumsy tongue as the balancing rod.

"You meant what you said, didn't you?"

"That's right."

"You think you can do it?"

"I'm going to."

"You really going to find him? And kill him?"

"Yes. I'm going to kill him."

He saw a shadow move, knew that Chelsea was in the bedroom doorway watching him, but he didn't turn to face her. He watched the snakes in their slumbering coils and he waited to hear what Rachel Bond's mother had left to say.

"Promise me something else," she said. "Promise me that if you get him, you'll tell me. Will you do that? Will you tell me?"

"I will get him," Adam said. "And you will know when I do."

She hung up before he could say another word. When Adam turned back to the bedroom, Chelsea was already gone, and the door was shut.

17

R ODNEY BOVA LIVED IN A rental house three blocks from the hospital where he worked as a maintenance supervisor. He was not home on Tuesday morning, and Adam walked the block twice, staring at every car. The possibility of police surveillance could not be ignored. No one appeared to be watching, though. It was for damn sure that no one had a view of the back of the house. He approached from that side, cleared the privacy fence, and used a thin metal carpenter's ruler to shim the lock on the sliding glass door.

Wearing a pair of latex gloves and working methodically, Adam soon came to know a good deal more about who Rodney Bova had become in the years after he set his stepfather's Cadillac on fire and disappeared from the halls of Chambers High. He followed horse racing, enjoyed pornography, and was an impulse shopper—there was a wide array of fitness equipment in the apartment, all of it the gimmicky shit they sold on late-night commercials for $19.99, and if you *acted right now!* you, too, could look like a Navy SEAL. According to photographs scattered around the house, Rodney Bova's belly suggested he was well into his second trimester, so it seemed he was more inspired to buy the devices than to use them. That was the problem in shifting from viewing porn to viewing home fitness commercials. *With twenty minutes a day on this discount device, I, too, could have a woman like those I was just watching...*

Bova's computer was password protected, and Adam didn't have the faintest idea how to subvert even simple computer security. That was a shame, because the computer might be of use. For a while he entertained the idea of stealing it and finding someone who could get around that password, but in the end he ruled that out, at least temporarily. For the time being, it was better that Bova's life not be rattled in any way. Adam needed him operating with a sense of comfort and security.

Instead he took a step backward in technology, digging through stacks of old mail and paperwork, scrutinizing the innocuous and irrelevant in hopes of finding something that spoke to a connection with Rachel Bond. He was just beginning to feel hopeless about his prospects when he opened a Visa bill from July and saw a $100 debit to Mansfield Correctional.

He stood there in Bova's kitchen and stared at the bill in confusion, trying to figure out the charge. Too low for bail even if it had been a county jail, but it was a prison. You didn't bond out of a prison, not for a million dollars, let alone a hundred. Then he got it: the commissary. You could mail funds to an inmate's commissary account, so surely you could transfer money to one electronically as well. Long after he himself had been released, Rodney Bova had been making contributions to the prison's commissary, supporting someone.

Who?

The rest of the bills told the same tale — a hundred dollars a month, every month, for as far back as Bova had bills, which was more than two years. He'd never missed a contribution. That was dedication. That was loyalty.

The loyalty payments ended in August. Only two logical options there: either Rodney Bova had decided to stop making his diligent payments, or the recipient had left Mansfield.

End of summer, start of the letters to Rachel. Maybe the inmate stayed with Rodney for a while. Maybe he worked with him, made a trip out to Shadow Wood Lane to nail shingles to a roof.

"Who do you know, Rodney?" Adam whispered.

He replaced the bills carefully, took a final pass through the house, making sure nothing looked disturbed, and then he exited and returned to his car and called Penny Gootee and asked if he could see her.

"Fine," she said. Her voice sounded sober today but hollowed out. "You can watch the police on TV like everybody else will be."

"What are you talking about?"

"Press conference," she said. "They're going to tell everyone how my baby died. How she was killed."

She wore an oversized hooded sweatshirt and seemed to disappear inside it. She had to have slept at some point, but there was no indication. When he stepped inside, the television was on, an empty podium in the center of the screen. Penny said, "You can watch it. I don't want to," and then she went into the bathroom and closed the door behind her. Adam knew better than to pursue. He sat on the couch beside the comforter from Rachel Bond's bed and watched Stan Salter step forward and occupy the podium, eyes grim as he adjusted the microphones, glanced at his notes, and then faced the cameras and provided the details that the public was so desperate to know, the ones they somehow felt they deserved. There had been a time, maybe, when Adam could have been able to get his head around that idea, the way a community could decide that the victim of a tragedy belonged to them, that because they were interested, they were a part of it, but that time was far gone.

Today, though, with Rachel Bond's case, he listened with the same interest shared by all the rest who considered the murder a spectator sport. Only he was no spectator.

The autopsy results had been completed, Salter said. Rachel Bond had been asphyxiated, with marks on her neck indicating the use of a plastic bag wrapped in place with duct tape. The bag had not been found at the kill site, but they believed it to be of clear plastic.

Adam thought about that, and what it meant. The sick bastard had wanted to watch her go. That had been important to him, to see it happen. No guns, no knives, no bludgeoning, not even any blood.

Just a slow, horrific expiration, a final gasp that found no oxygen, the sudden removal of one of those universally promised things: you will have air to breathe.

In the end, she had not. That had been taken from her.

Salter explained that the property owner was not a suspect, that the house was vacant. He explained that Rachel had gone there in hopes of reuniting with her estranged father, and that someone had been impersonating her father in a series of letters. He said the investigating team was gathering leads and analyzing forensic evidence and would reveal more information when it was prudent to do so. Adam found the remote and turned off the television. When the volume was gone, the bathroom door reopened and Penny Gootee appeared.

"Heard enough?" she said.

"Yeah."

She came back down the hallway and sat on the couch at his side and wrapped Rachel's blanket around her.

"I want you to do it," she said.

"I know. I'm going to need your help."

"Just tell me how."

"Do you know more than they just shared? Have they asked you about suspects?"

"They've asked me if I have ideas. I don't. They haven't shared any names with me."

"No questions about people who were in Mansfield with your husband?"

"Jason was never my husband. Don't call him that. I don't have his name."

"Did they ask you any questions about people who were in prison with Jason?"

She shook her head.

"Does the name Rodney Bova mean anything to you?"

A frown, then another shake of the head. "No. Why? Who is he?"

"Just a guy who might have crossed paths with Jason," Adam said. "Probably nothing more." He didn't want her to focus on the name, not yet, so he did not tell her that Bova also was connected to the house where her daughter had been killed. Instead, he asked her if she'd seen any of the letters.

"Yeah. That's all they've shown me. I've got photocopies."

They would have wanted her to spend time with the letters, to read them and consider them and see if, through prolonged study, any suspects suggested themselves.

"Can I see them?" he asked.

"Yes." She rose again and returned with a small stack of papers. "That's Jason," she told him, isolating two of the photocopies, moving an ashtray aside to spread the documents out. "I can recognize him, no problem. Can smell the shithead rising right off the page."

The first letter had been innocuous enough:

Thanks for writing, your mom probably doesn't know you did, does she? I bet you've never heard a good word about me, not from her at least, so I'm sure she doesn't know. Glad to know you are turning into such a great girl. Hope life keeps going your way. Don't waste your time worrying about me. This isn't a place I'd like you to visit, and I don't know what I could tell you that you haven't already heard from other people. Not proud of myself, and sorry if you've grown up ashamed of your father. Can't go back, though, Rachel, I can't go back and make anything right, so I'll just say I'm sorry and you take care of yourself. Sounds as if you make lots of good choices. Keep on doing that.

Jason

"Shithead," Penny proclaimed again.

The second letter was even shorter. A curt thanks, a reminder that Rachel's mother wouldn't like any contact between the two of them, a repeated request not to visit, and then an instruction to get good grades in school and be careful with boys.

It was the third letter that Penny deemed someone else's work.

"See how he starts acting sincere?" she said. "Jason can't fake sincere. Jason doesn't give a damn about anyone, and he doesn't care enough to fake it."

The tone was different, yes, but only slightly. There had been no rush to suggest contact, just a careful building of the relationship. Patient, that was the word that kept rising to mind; whoever had taken up writing as Jason Bond had been very patient.

The next letter raised the cautious suggestion that he would soon be released.

Bet your mother didn't tell you, and maybe you shouldn't tell her. She and I shouldn't see each other again. I need you to understand that. For her if not for me.

That had been the first test. If Rachel had been paying close attention herself, or if she'd had anyone else looking out for her, she'd have known that he wasn't eligible for parole yet. Whatever she wrote back, though, had clearly established that she was in this alone, and was accepting his news without verifying it.

None of her letters existed. Jason Bond had discarded the two that reached him, which said everything Adam needed to know about him. The others might still exist — in fact, they probably did; whoever killed her was the sort who kept souvenirs — but there was no way to know what Rachel had written. You could guess at some of it from the responses, but it was impossible to know for sure. The only person she'd discussed the matter with, apparently, was her boyfriend. And Kent.

His brother was even referred to in the later letters.

I'm so glad you decided to begin writing, Rachel. It was a very good idea. You should tell the football coach that I appreciate his understanding, his encouragement. There aren't many men who would do that. He's something special.

"He could have told me," Penny said. "Your damned brother could have thought to talk to her *mother* before he encouraged her to do something like that."

Adam didn't argue. "Did she tell anyone else about these? Beyond Colin Mears and my brother? Who else would she have trusted?"

"Should have trusted me. But she didn't, and it's my fault. She knew how I felt about Jason. Maybe I shouldn't have been so harsh, you know? Maybe I should have...you got to understand, he's a hurtful man. Hurt me worse than anyone ever had, until this. And I just wanted to...shield her. I didn't want him to have the chance to hurt her the way that I knew he would. But maybe I should have said, Rachel, let's go see your dad. Let's talk about all the reasons you need to stay away from that man. Maybe——"

Her voice was rising, tears chasing behind, and she lowered her face, fingered the zipper on the sweatshirt. "I could have told her, you know? But she hid the letters. Because she knew I wouldn't like it. That was Rachel, she never wanted to upset me."

Adam watched a tear fall onto the back of her hand. He made no move to reach for her.

"Tell you the truth?" she said, looking up again, her eyes bright with tears. "I'm pretty shitty at a lot of things. Drink too much, smoke too much, can't hold on to a decent job, don't keep the house up the way I should. But something I was always good at? Loving that girl. Might be a lot of people who don't see it that way, who don't see me as a good mother, but——"

"She loved you," Adam said. "You know that. You just said it. She was trying to protect you, and you were trying to protect her. There's no blame inside these walls, and the only things that happened between you happened because you were trying to take care of each other. Remember that, Penny. You need to remember that."

She used the blanket to wipe away tears and said, "I keep thinking it's done. Keep thinking I'm dried out, there's none left."

He was silent. She wouldn't dry out. She'd think she had, and then she'd find herself down in the frigid waters of Lake Erie weeping into a cold dawn. He let her sit and cry while he lit a cigarette and smoked in silence.

18

I T WAS MATT BYERS WHO first expressed concern with Colin's approach to practice. They were halfway through drills when the defensive coach sidled over to Kent and spoke in a low tone.

"He's going to burn himself out in ten more minutes like this, Coach. Look at him."

Kent had been looking at him. They were running no-contact drills—as the playoffs lengthened, as he hoped they would, contact would be less and less common in practice as he tried to protect fatigued bodies—but still the kid was burning jet fuel, smoking through every pattern and then returning to his spot at the rear of the line to run in place or do jumping jacks or push-ups. It was a cool afternoon but the sweat dripped out of his helmet.

"He may need to burn himself out, Matt." Kent was fairly certain that he did, in fact. Today, Colin was coming off a sleepless night after hearing the details of his girlfriend's murder. Today, every one of his teammates and classmates was whispering about what they'd learned. They all knew how she had died, and if

Colin had not shown up at practice, Kent would almost have been relieved.

Colin was trying to sweat it all out. To empty himself of all that he carried, and while it was not possible, it might help. If he broke himself down enough to sleep through the night, that might help.

"He's freaking these guys out," Matt said.

Kent looked at him, the bills of their caps close together, voices still low. "*He's* not what's freaking any of them out. They understand it, Matt. They know. Let him give what he can today. When he's done, I'll stop him. Okay?"

Byers nodded.

Over in the receivers line, Colin, never a vocal leader, had begun to shout. Demanding faster feet, better hands, more effort. Slapping helmets as his teammates went by, and, yes, all of them looked a little shaken. No one more so than Lorell McCoy, who threw a few awkward passes, his always-polished release hurried, responding to Colin's frenetic energy.

Kent left them there and walked down to the other side of the field, where the offensive and defensive lines were working on their splits. Hickory Hills ran an option offense, and did very little with it except pitch the ball to the fastest kid on the team and try like heck to open a hole for him, rarely with much success. This meant their offense would play with wide gaps, trying to spread out the Chambers front line, and hope they could get around the end faster than the Cardinal defenders.

They could not. He was sure of that, but he was also sure that his defense would see the same option plays, the same veer approach, soon enough, and there would be much greater speed to it then. Hickory Hills was in many ways a perfect opponent, because they would give Chambers a chance to polish fundamentals before running into a higher level of talent.

Kent was pacing, nudging at the feet of his offensive linemen, when he heard Steve Haskins, the receivers coach, shout for a trainer.

Kent turned then and saw that Colin Mears was on his hands and knees on the fifty, throwing up.

He did not rush to him. Every one of the kids was watching anxiously, and Kent tried to communicate calm to them through patient motion. By the time he reached midfield there was already a trainer with Colin, wiping his face down with a towel and offering a bottle of Gatorade. Colin took a sip, swished it in his mouth, and spit it back onto the turf. His chest was heaving.

Kent knelt and laid a hand on his back.

"You all right?"

Colin nodded. Retched again, brought nothing up, and then spoke between gasps.

"Good to go, Coach. Good to go."

"Go sit down. I'll tell you when you're good to go."

"No, sir. I'm fine. I'm—"

"Son, you want to tell me what you just said?"

Colin spit again, then turned back to him. "I said that I'm fine, I'm ready to—"

"Let's take another look at this situation, a little slower. I told you what I wanted from you. And you did what?"

Colin's breathing was beginning to steady, but his eyes were confused.

"You did what?" Kent said again, making sure his voice was clear enough to be heard by others, trying his best to stare the boy down the way he would have at any other practice, any other day.

"Argued," Colin said.

"That's right. You're a senior, am I correct?"

"Yes, sir."

"How many times have you seen someone have luck arguing with me on my football field?" Voice rising now. Let them all feel this day was normal, from Colin to his teammates, let them find some familiarity in this practice so that they would not lose their heads.

"None, sir."

"That's right. It won't start today. Go sit your ass down. I'll tell you when you're ready to go."

Colin rose on wobbly legs and went to the sidelines. Kent stood and looked up and down the field, saw all the uneasy faces watching, and shouted, "That's what we call effort, gentlemen. You might want to remember it. I suspect you'll need it to win a few more football games."

They got back to work, Colin sitting on the grass just off the field, his helmet still strapped tight. Kent walked to him and knelt, spoke out of the side of his mouth, his eyes still on the field.

"You tell me the truth, son. What helps you more — being here or being home?"

"Here, sir."

"You know this doesn't matter," Kent said. He waved a hand at the field. "You understand that, don't you?"

"It matters. I need it."

Kent nodded. "I'll be here, Colin. I can't promise you anything that will help, but I can promise you I'll be here. You have something you need to tell me, or want to tell me, do not hesitate."

"Thank you, Coach." He was crying now, and though Kent knew it he pretended otherwise.

"Whenever you feel like going," he said, "you go."

He stood up and began to walk away then. Colin Mears beat him back to midfield.

* * *

There were few things Kent imagined more unenviable than being a coach's wife with two young children during the season. He tried hard to help, tried hard to ease the burden when he could, but the reality was that his evenings and nights were gone to the game for months at a time, and at this time, playoffs looming? The few hours became fewer.

It was past ten when he got home Tuesday, and that wasn't anywhere near as late as many coaches would push it. Not as late as Kent was tempted to, either, but he'd built his program on regimented behavior, and that carried off the field and into the coach's room. You did not waste minutes in Kent's program, you did not waste even seconds. *Focused attention, focused attention, focused attention.* The kids heard it constantly, but what they did not realize was that the coaching staff heard it, too. Maybe more often. Other coaches could keep their staffs up into the wee hours watching game video with one eye, drinking beer and swapping jokes, but that would not happen at Chambers. Despite the even-keeled demeanor for which he was known, Kent had lost plenty of assistant coaches over the years because he wasn't much fun. That was fine by him.

He came home, slipped into a dark house, kissed his sleeping son and daughter on the forehead, and went into the bedroom to have his wife tell him that Lisa had been hearing stories in school about her aunt.

"She asked me about Marie today," Beth said. She was in bed with a Pat Conroy novel held against her chest and the TV on across the room. Something they bickered about with consistency and good nature. *You can't watch TV and read at the same time,* Kent would say. *It's simply impossible. Pick one.* Then she'd say, *Funny, every now and then I'll start doing* other *things with the*

TV still on and you never complain about that. And of course she had him there.

He sat on the bed beside her. "What did she say?"

"Some kids told her Marie was murdered. She wanted to know if it was true. Then she said that she'd heard it was in the newspaper. She wanted to read about it."

Her voice was tired, and Kent laid a hand on her leg, sympathy and apology in the touch. It was an inevitable conversation that she'd had with their daughter, but it was also his to have, and she'd been forced to do it because he was gone. While he was demanding focused attention on videos of teenage boys playing a game, Beth had made dinner for two children and explained a homicide to one. There were times when his occupation felt almost foolish, when all of the *We're building character, we're about more than the game, these kids are learning life lessons on the field* felt absurd, and this was one of them.

"How'd she take it?" he asked, because he did not need to ask what Beth had told her. He knew there would have been neither coy games nor excessive detail, just gentle honesty.

"She wanted to know why you don't talk about Marie. Why you never told her about it before. She seemed a little hurt by that."

"Probably a fair response."

"I told her that it hurts you to talk about it, and that a sister is a lot like a daughter and talking to her about it would probably hurt even worse because of that."

He felt a thickening in his throat, looked away from her eyes and out to the dark window, bare limbs showing beyond the reflected light of the room. He let out a breath and swung himself onto the bed beside her, leaned his head against the pillow, and looked in her eyes. He could find peace in them, always had been able to, so many years of seeking things from within her now, so many years of having those things granted.

"I'm sorry," he said.

"It might be best that I talked to her."

"Did Andrew hear?"

"No."

"Will she want to talk to me about it? Should I volunteer something?"

"You'll need to talk to her. I don't know if she'll press it, but she's curious. She was surprised she didn't know. Thinks she's far too old and mature to have it kept from her. I just said that it hurts you and that you're very good at hiding the things that hurt you."

When she said this, she reached out and squeezed his left knee, the bad one. He looked at her slender fingers working on the soft, damaged tissue below the kneecap.

"I'll talk to her," he said. "She thinks it's unfair, and she's probably right, and she deserves to understand her own family better than the kids at school do. I never wanted that."

Beth said, "She's also got another question I'll let you field."

"Yeah?"

"She wants to know if it has something to do with the reason we don't like Uncle Adam."

His gaze left her hand and returned to her eyes. "What?"

Beth nodded. "That's exactly how she phrased it. *We* don't like him. As if it's something just understood. A family rule. We don't like the Pittsburgh Steelers. We don't like Uncle Adam. Casual."

He passed a hand over his face, rubbed his forehead.

"All right," he said. "I'll talk with her."

"Good," Beth said. "What about Adam?"

"Huh?"

"Will you talk more with him?"

"No."

"Really."

"I said all I could say. You're surprised? He and I don't talk much, Beth."

"I know that, Kent. I know that. All this, though?" She shook her head. "I just can't believe one of you hasn't picked up the phone."

"To say what?"

"I have no idea. A girl's murdered, you're both talking to the police, you both knew her, and the whole town's relating it to your sister. You're right, Kent. Nothing to talk about."

She released his knee, rolled over, and picked her book back up. He looked at her, frustrated, and said, "I'm trying to refocus and move forward, Beth. Trying to help my team do the same thing. Those are not Adam's strengths. He circles, circles, circles. I can't get caught up in that. I can't."

19

ADAM'S HOPE WAS THAT Rodney Bova did not live alone. That by evening someone else would join him in the house, someone who'd earned parole from Mansfield during the summer.

It wasn't going to be that easy, though.

Bova was alone Tuesday night, and all day Wednesday and Thursday. He drove to work, parked in the hospital garage, logged his eight hours, then drove home and turned on the TV. At peace and oblivious.

And wasting Adam's hours.

Adam was violating his own protocol. His motion had stopped, he was stagnant now, waiting for Bova to take action instead of taking it himself. He couldn't afford to do that, but he also didn't want to initiate direct contact. Not yet. Finding out who the man had been sending money to for all those months was critical, but Adam couldn't risk flushing his quarry. He had to find other ways to pursue the information — go to the prison, interview Jason Bond, try to find and bribe a source within the commissary, something. To do all of those things, though, he would have to leave the man untended.

There were ways around that, though.

In the state of Ohio, like most states, a bail bondsman holds unique authority. Adam could outfit skips with tracking devices, in the right circumstances he could perform warrantless searches, he could generally invade their lives and privacy in ways prohibited not just to the general public but to the police. You owned a piece of them once you held that bond, more than they realized in their frantic rush to sign whatever papers necessary to get the locks popped on the jailhouse doors.

He often considered the monetary value of the bond, but he'd rarely considered the power that came with the signature. *I'm yours to watch,* the offender was acknowledging. *I'm yours.*

On Thursday morning, exactly one week after he'd set out to look for him originally, Adam returned to searching for Jerry Norris, his outstanding skip.

The first two times Jerry Norris had skipped, he'd crashed at his cousin's house, a pattern he'd given up since, but Adam knew damn well that Rick Tieken, the cousin, would know where he could be found. He'd tried bribes with Tieken in the past and had some success. Family mattered to Tieken, sure, but not as much as cash. Priorities.

Tieken worked for an auto parts store and was behind the register when Adam walked in. He looked up when the bell over the door rang, recognized Adam, and smirked. Probably had been waiting on him for days.

"How's it going, Teek?"

"Just fine, man, just fine. The Jeep letting you down again?"

"Serpentine belt," Adam said. "Got a feeling it's about done. Got a match for me?"

"I'm sure we do. What's the year on that?"

"Oh-four."

Tieken clicked away on the computer, wrote down a number, and vanished into the back. Came back with a belt in a plastic bag.

"This should do the trick, chief."

"Great. You mind coming out to take a look with me?" Adam said, taking a pointed glance at the other employee in the store. "Want to be sure I'm not wasting dollars. A professional opinion might help."

Tieken's smirk widened. He knew the drill.

"You seen your cousin recently?" Adam said as they walked around the corner of the store to the Jeep. It was parked behind the store's van, out of sight from the road.

"Hillary? Yeah, we played cards just the other night."

"Funny. But you know I mean Jerry. Where is he?"

"Oh, Jerry?" Tieken ran a hand through his red hair, pursed his lips, mock-thoughtful. "Man, I thought that old boy was in jail. You mean he's not?"

"He needs to be," Adam said. He opened the driver's door, then popped the hood. "And I've got ten grand invested in seeing him back there. Think you can help?"

"Ten grand? Boy, that's a lot."

"It is." Adam lifted the hood, set the brace. "And the thing is, Teek? I need this one settled fast. Like, *today*."

What he needed settled had nothing to do with Jerry Norris, but Jerry was an important means to the end, and Adam could not afford to waste time getting there. He took the bag from Tieken's hands, tore open the plastic, and slipped out the belt. A long loop of very strong rubber, V-ribbed. He pulled on the ends, felt the satisfying tension.

"You want to entertain yourself with this bullshit, or do you want to make a little money?" he said. "Pick fast, Teek. It's two hundred dollars you won't have in about thirty seconds. So pick fast."

"Two hundred? I thought he was worth ten grand to you. I mean, if you spent five to get him back, just breaking even, that would help, wouldn't it?"

Adam dropped the serpentine belt over Rick Tieken's head, jerked it backward, and twisted. Tieken's grunt of surprise was the last sound he got out before his air was gone. He fumbled at the belt and Adam twisted it again, cinching it tighter, and then slammed him forward, pressed his face down against the engine block, which was not hot enough to sear, but still hot enough to be awfully uncomfortable. Adam leaned down and spoke with his mouth close to Tieken's ear.

"I do not have time to waste on you. Just don't have it."

He hit him again, and Tieken tried to let out a sob but couldn't get enough air, just strangled a little more. Adam stepped back and loosened the belt. Tieken fought to clear it from his neck, and Adam obliged, slipping it back over his head, then coiling the belt in his hand. When Tieken fell, gasping, into the parking lot, Adam whipped the belt back and lashed it off his ribs, watched him double over and drop onto his face in the gravel.

"Son of a bitch." Tieken wheezed. "I'm calling the cops, you piece of—"

"Do that and I'll come back here and when I leave again you'll be toothless. Now tell me where to find your brain-dead cousin. I promise you, if you see me again, it will not go well."

Tieken looked up at him, and Adam smiled and looped one end of the belt tight in his fist, let the rest dangle in front of the man's eyes.

"You want to have me arrested, you better believe I'm going to earn it."

Tieken gave him an address through shaking breaths.

"That better be accurate," Adam said.

"It is."

"I'll go find out." Adam dropped the belt onto his chest in a loose tangle. "I don't think I need that. Restock it, would you?"

The address checked out. Jerry Norris was lounging in a trailer on the south side of Chambers, watching *SportsCenter* and throwing Doritos at a fat pug who sat on the couch with him. He looked out the window when Adam knocked on it, made eye contact, and then abandoned the couch and sprinted down the hallway. The dog moved on the Doritos immediately, was face-first into the bag in under three seconds. On another day, Adam might have laughed. There were skips you actually worried about, guys you wanted off the street and in jail, and then there were skips like Jerry. Eating Doritos with a pug at nine in the morning.

"Jerry?" he called. "We just looked at each other. It's safe to say I spotted you in there. I can wait outside and call the police, or you can open the damned door."

Silence. The pug had fallen off the couch with the chip bag on his head. Adam squeezed the bridge of his nose and closed his eyes.

"Jerry. Come on."

Now he heard the click of a door opening, and Jerry Norris came down the hall and back into the living room. He looked at Adam through the window, spread his hands, and gave an awkward smile.

"Instinct," he said.

Adam nodded. Instinct.

"Let me in."

Jerry unlocked the door and swung it open. Adam stepped inside, looked around the trailer, watching the pug push the chip bag out of the living room and into the kitchen, and said, "Whose place?"

"Girl's name is Christine. Works on the turnpike. I met her at the tollbooth."

Adam had to give Jerry a little credit here; picking someone up at a tollbooth was kind of impressive. He assumed it had been a light traffic day.

"She know you're violating?"

Jerry shook his head.

"Good thing you've got going with her? Think you can stick it out if you're not in jail?"

"Maybe."

"Think you can stick it out if you *are* in jail?"

"Doubt it."

"Well, then," Adam said, "let's talk."

Jerry gave him a puzzled look. They had never discussed options before; Adam just cuffed him and hauled his ass in.

"You'll do a minimum of ninety days if I bring you in," Adam said. "Minimum. They might go for a year. No more Christine. Doesn't sound like much fun, does it?"

Jerry waited, curious or confused or both.

"I will drive away and leave you here," Adam said, "if you can do me a favor. I would like some drugs."

"You're shitting me."

"I am not."

Jerry laughed. "Oh, man. You got to be kidding me. What do you need?"

"Something in the heroin, meth, or coke families would be terrific," Adam said. "But if that's hard for you to come up with, I'd settle for OxyContin, provided the quantity is substantial."

The smile left Jerry's face and his eyes narrowed. "Screw this, man. Entrapment, that's what this bullshit is."

"Only police can entrap you, Jerry. And I'm quite serious. I would like whatever you can give me. Right now. Or we go to jail. Right now."

There was a long pause while Jerry studied his face and *SportsCenter* ran and the pug wrestled with the chip bag somewhere out of sight in the kitchen.

"I can give you some OxyContin."

"I'd like more than a hundred."

"What? Why?"

"Jerry—again, we could be on our way to jail now. I'm frustrated by the need to continue to reiterate that idea. What I am telling you is this: I will officially lose interest in your bond if you make sure you give me at least 101 pills. Understand?"

Jerry understood perfectly. That extra pill was the difference between illegal possession charges and trafficking charges. Between jail time and prison time.

"No way," he said, shaking his head. "I'm not letting you trap me, man."

"Trap you? Jerry, I've *got* you. What I'm offering is to release the trap. Your call."

Jerry Norris sighed, looking unhappily at Adam, not liking the situation but not liking the certainty of several months in jail if he didn't roll with it, and then he said, "Hang on," and went down the hall and into a bedroom and closed the door. When he came back, he had four orange prescription bottles.

"One twenty," he said. "There's a lot of money there. Maybe we could talk about that?"

Adam almost laughed. The dumb son of a bitch had a pair of brass balls on him, you had to admit that.

"Jerry," he said, "you probably have one hell of a battle of wits going with that dog who is currently stuck in the chip bag. I'm going to let you get back to it now."

He pocketed the pill bottles, left the trailer, and drove to the hospital garage where Rodney Bova parked his truck every day.

* * *

The hospital parking garage was a risk-versus-reward scenario. On the one hand, it was a far more potent opportunity than Rodney Bova's house; on the other hand, there would surely be security cameras in place. Adam addressed this problem as best he could by borrowing a jacket, hat, and set of car keys from Bova's home. He was even more pleased to find that Bova had an extra security tag, complete with his photograph. It was outdated, but Adam doubted they'd changed the design much. He was a good deal taller than the man, but if he kept his head down and the cap pulled low and moved fast and with confidence, he'd make it hard on anyone studying the tapes, at least.

He left his own car nine blocks away, where no camera would track it, and then walked in, staring at his feet as he entered the hospital, careful not to lift his face to the cameras. Once inside, he found a restroom, where there would be no cameras, and waited for a full hour, giving those security videos a long lapse to deal with after his entrance. All of this would not fool a diligent detective, but it was unlikely that a police detective would buy the "someone planted this stuff" story enough from a guy with priors to pursue it to such lengths.

When he entered the parking garage through the attached walkway, he moved fast, and then he was in the poorly lit space and headed down to the second floor, where he'd seen Bova park the previous day. The F150 was right where it belonged. He used Bova's spare set to unlock it, then reached out with a gloved hand, opened the door, and placed the bottles of OxyContin in the glove compartment, then removed a Colt .38 revolver from the jacket pocket. An acquisition from one of his previous skips — Adam had taken it after the guy threatened him but then backed down. The gun's serial number was filed off, and it had probably floated through dozens of hands over the years. Today it was loaded, and wiped clean of prints. He added the weapon to the glove compartment, then locked the car again.

He was out of the garage in under two minutes, back at Bova's house in ten, the jacket, hat, and car keys replaced exactly as they had been.

It was another two hours before Rodney Bova left for lunch. Adam, now parked with a clear view of the hospital, slipped in behind him, followed him to a Burger King, and called the police from a disposable cell phone — *burners,* his skips liked to call them, guys who didn't want to have a number attached to their name — and gave the location and license number, then said that the driver seemed impaired and was armed.

"I honked, you know, because he was so erratic, and he held a gun up," Adam said, speaking high and with a shop towel held between the phone and his mouth, enough distortion to get by. "Pointed that thing right at me, I thought he was going to shoot."

They asked for his name, of course.

"Hell, no," he said. "No way, no way. That guy just pointed a *gun* at me, do you understand? I'm not going to be part of this. I don't want him coming to my house, threaten my wife, my kids, how do I know what he'll do? You just pull him over and see if I'm lying. He's going to leave the Burger King on Lincoln Avenue in about five seconds if you don't hurry. The guy's drunk or stoned and he's waving a gun around. Do something about it."

He hung up. A defense attorney would have a field day with this anonymous call, but Adam didn't care what happened in court, he cared about providing probable cause for the vehicle search.

When the F150 pulled out of the Burger King, Adam passed it driving the opposite direction on Lincoln, then banged a left so he was running on a different street but parallel. It was maybe a mile before he saw police lights come on through the houses beside him.

He made another call then, this one from his own phone. Called the Chambers County Jail and asked for one of the booking agents he knew best, a guy who regularly sent business to AA Bail Bonds in exchange for a small commission. There were only three bond agencies in the county, but Adam wasn't about to take a risk on missing this one.

"I'm listening to scanner traffic right now," he said. "You're going to see a boy in there soon on possession charges, maybe weapons, too. Sounds lucrative. I need it. Understand?"

"Yeah."

"A grand in cash tonight if you can send him my way. I need this one. And if anybody else comes in today on high-dollar shit, consider the offer matched. When you recommend me, though, don't use my name. Just say Double-A Bonds."

"A *grand*? Shit, you got it, Austin."

"Thanks," Adam said, and then he hung up and drove to the office. Chelsea was behind the desk.

"Jerry Norris back in jail yet?"

"He is not," Adam said. "But I'm done chasing for the day. We got any calls?"

She frowned. "None. Slow day."

"Maybe it'll pick up," he said.

20

I T WAS JUST PAST THREE when Rodney Bova called from the Chambers County Jail, seeking bond and release. Adam listened while Chelsea ran over the basics and promised him she'd be at the jail in fifteen minutes to secure his release.

"Good news," she said when she hung up. "Fifty-grand bond on a guy named Bova who's in on drug and weapons charges. That's a nice five-grand day for us."

"Very nice," Adam said. "I'll go down and handle it."

"I can do it."

He shook his head, getting to his feet. "I probably ought to put in an appearance."

"You sure?"

"Positive," he said, and then he gathered the required paperwork and walked out of the office to the jail.

There was a conference room at the jail designated for bail meetings, and when Adam arrived, they brought Rodney Bova in to meet him. To say the man looked shaken was an understatement. His face was pale and his hands actually trembled when he accepted the papers from Adam. He looked as if he might throw up, in fact, or faint. If he recognized Adam, he did not show it.

"This is crazy," he told Adam. "Someone put these things in my truck. I don't know what to do. I called a lawyer, but I don't know if he even believed me. I don't—"

"You remember me?" Adam said.

Bova looked genuinely puzzled. "Huh?"

"Adam Austin. We went to—"

"Oh, shit. Yeah, yeah. High school. You were the football star."

"And you transferred out, right?"

Bova's expression flickered. "Right, I got transferred. But, listen, I need to figure out what to do here. Someone set me up, man."

"Did they?" Adam said, going for bored and dismissive, which was easy enough to fake, because half of the guys in this office claimed to have been set up. "Why?"

"I don't know, man. I don't know. But this thing, it's not an accident, right? Someone is taking a shot at me."

When Adam did not respond, Bova ran a palm over his face. It came back sweaty. "Let's just get the paperwork done, okay? Let's just get me loose, and I'll deal with it."

"Fair enough," Adam said, and he had to use effort to stay casual. He wanted all the secrets that this man held, wanted to bang his face off the wall until he provided them, as if the truth would leak out with the blood, but that was not the way to do this. "Your bond is set at fifty thousand dollars. The way this works is I guarantee the bond, and in so doing, I guarantee that you'll appear in court or I eat that debt. Understand?"

"Yeah."

"Now, the way I make money, which is what I need to do in order to take the risk of insuring your bond, is that I am paid a premium. This is a nonrefundable amount. It's what keeps my light bill paid. Whether you're convicted or not, whether the charges are even prosecuted or not, you do not receive a refund on the premium."

"Ten percent?" This was the voice of a regular offender, someone who knew the drill.

"Yeah. So, five thousand dollars."

Bova winced. "This is bullshit. I got set up, man, and—"

"That's not my concern, Mr. Bova. My concern is making sure you appear in court. To get out of jail, you'll have to pay someone a bond premium, and the standard is ten percent. Now...I can bring it down a lot if you're willing to agree to help me on my end."

"What do you mean?"

"I can't afford to have you skip out on me, right?"

"I'd never—"

"I don't think you will," Adam said. "Your credit is decent, you're employed, all that good stuff. Because of that I will offer a premium reduction of ten percent to one percent if you're willing to wear an ankle bracelet. We'll have to file the paperwork as if it's the standard ten, but I'll charge you a different amount."

Bova seemed uncertain. "I don't know if that's something I'd want."

Interesting, Adam thought. *You'd prefer throwing thousands away to wearing a tracking device? Why's that, Rodney, old buddy?*

He said, "Well, you think you're going to get out of these charges, right?"

"Absolutely. Yes, absolutely."

"Okay. When I hear that, it makes me happy, because I don't have to worry about chasing you. Now, I worry even less about chasing you if you're wearing the tracking bracelet. That's why I can charge so much less."

The only unprecedented move here was the price drop. Adam

would sometimes require ankle bracelets from offenders with a history of skipping, or on particularly high-dollar bonds. He'd never offered to drop his fee in exchange for one. It wasn't even legal.

Bova was still hesitating.

"The other element to consider," Adam said, "is that your willingness to wear the tracking bracelet might help in court. It proves that you're not a flight risk."

The court didn't give a damn what someone agreed to with a bail bondsman, but it sounded good, and he was immediately glad he'd played the card, because that's what seemed to convince Bova.

"All right," he said. "Sure. Yes, I'll wear one so long as you promise me that people won't notice it. It doesn't go off like an alarm or anything, right? And nobody can see it?"

"Unless you wear shorts, nobody will have any idea, Mr. Bova. I think it's a good option. Saves you a lot of cash."

They completed the paperwork, Adam accepted credit card payment for the five hundred, and then, once they'd gotten the jailers to open the doors and send Rodney Bova back into the free world, he walked him down to his Jeep and got out the ankle bracelet he'd brought along.

"Nice and thin," he said. "Won't be a problem for you at all, and once you've gotten this mess cleaned up, you'll be glad you saved all that money, won't you?"

Bova rolled up his jeans and let Adam clasp the bracelet high on his ankle, just above the sock.

"So it...follows me?" he said.

"No. It just lets me know if you've left the county." This was a lie — the bracelet sent out a GPS signal that would follow every step Bova took and return it to both Adam's computer and his phone, tracking him on digital maps. He'd tested it at the office before Bova even called, putting in fresh batteries and making certain that it showed up on the map software. It did. He'd know every step Bova took.

"It's got tamper detection," he said. "So don't get cute and try to cut it off. I'll know immediately, and then you'll be right back in jail for violating the terms of your release."

That, too, was total bullshit—the monitoring was Adam's private arrangement, not court-mandated—but he wanted to keep the already-scared Rodney Bova as scared as possible about trying to remove the thing. It was a bitch to cut off, but it could be done. What he wanted Bova to believe was that he had no interest in where he went. That was imperative.

"I won't mess with it."

"Good." Adam straightened up, looked at him, and said, "My role in this is simple: just make sure you show up in court. Don't make that a problem for me. Deal?"

"Yeah. Deal. Thank you."

Adam nodded. "Okay, Rodney. You're free to go now. Can I offer you a ride somewhere? I assume your truck was impounded."

"That's right," Bova said. He'd clearly forgotten. "I've got to figure that out. But I'll...I'll take a cab. Or walk. Thanks, though."

"Fair enough. Good luck."

Adam got into the Jeep, slid his iPhone out of his pocket, and logged into his monitoring system's application. A few seconds later he was looking at a map of Chambers and one slow-moving red dot.

"All right, Rodney," he said. "Go find him for me."

21

FRIDAY AFTERNOON, DURING the pep rally, Lorell McCoy took the microphone and told the student body what Kent had been anticipating for days: the season was officially dedicated to the memory of Rachel Bond, and when the Chambers Cardinals took to the field tonight, they would wear her initials on their cleats and on their helmets.

The crowd cheered, faculty joining the students, and Kent wanted to look away but he was standing out there in front of the whole school, and there were many eyes on him, so he just gave a small nod and kept his hands folded in front of him, head down.

Colin Mears did not address the fans, and Kent was glad of that, but Lorell had said his piece for him, and now Lorell led the school in a moment of silence in Rachel's memory, reminding them all that while the Cardinals intended to go out and win a state championship, none of that really mattered. What mattered was Rachel.

All the right things to say. He sounded good, poised and mature and well reasoned. Kent should have been proud of him, probably. Instead he just felt uneasy.

They had their moment of silence, and then the pep band started to play. Just like that. One murdered child recognized, one game to play. On to the next one. There was nothing wrong with it. How else were they supposed to do it? You put one foot in front of the other, you honored the past while you went to meet the future, that was the only way. Otherwise you turned into...into Adam.

That was the end of the day, there were only fifteen minutes left before the final bell rang, and Kent let them walk out of the gym with its smells of trapped sweat and polished hardwood and go on to do whatever it was they each did before kickoff. He made no claims on them before five thirty, when they were required to arrive in the locker room. He didn't even make claims on his coaching staff before five thirty. As he told them every year, if we aren't ready to go by Friday morning, we're already beaten.

His own game day rituals were simple. A run, a shower, and then a retreat into his office until game time. He went to the locker room and changed clothes, put on shorts and running shoes and a hooded sweatshirt and a soft, flexible brace for his left knee, and then he went out into the fall day.

Perfect football weather. Perfect. The sky was cobalt blue, a fringe of dark gray encroaching from the northwest, but not here yet, and the clouds were high and clean and white. There was a breeze that carried the scents of autumn out of the wooded neighborhoods past the school and down to the field, and the temperature was mid-fifties, brisk enough to energize. Kent stretched in the end zone, then paced off to the sideline, where he would not cross the playing surface, and began to run.

There was a track that ran between the bleachers and the field, but he never ran the track. He loved the feel of the turf beneath his shoes, loved the memories each step brought. The track featured gentle curves, too, and by running around the field in rectangles, he was forced to make hard, ninety-degree cuts, each one putting a stab of pain through his left knee. He needed that.

The knee had ended his playing career. He'd played D-1 ball but for a small school. The knee began to give him problems his freshman year, when he was a backup. Over the summer he visited a joint specialist in Cleveland and was told that it wasn't so serious, he had a partially torn MCL and some damaged cartilage that needed to be scraped, but once that happened, he'd have only a couple of months of rehab and be back on the field, good as new.

A couple of months took him out of the starting competition, though. A couple of months set him back maybe a full season.

He didn't let them scrape the knee. Thanked them and said he'd make an appointment but never did. Showed up in the fall and won the starting job, and the team won four of their first five games before he began to hobble. Trainers recommended an MRI. This time the test showed that the cartilage damage was getting worse, should already have been removed, and that the ACL had begun to fray because it was absorbing extra stress from the already weakened ligament on the inside of his knee. They braced him up and shot him full of cortisone and he tore both ligaments all the way through in the third quarter of the final game of the season. Missed a year rehabbing it, and there was a big, strong-armed kid behind him who claimed the job and never relinquished it. Kent finished his career pacing the sidelines with a clipboard in hand, validating what he'd always known, the reason he wouldn't take the time off for proper treatment—there was always somebody better than you waiting just behind you.

After college he'd come right home. Walter Ward had a position waiting for him, and it was supposed to be a temporary gig, a filler, because Kent was done with football, and willing to let the game own him for only a few more months, while he determined the best course of action for the future.

Then he met Beth. Well, got reacquainted with Beth. He'd known her during his high school years, but Walter Ward's daughter was three years younger than him, and *nobody* was dumb enough to look too long at the coach's freshman daughter. By the time he was part of the staff, Beth was in college, and Walter Ward approved, on one condition — Kent needed to get his ass into church. Case closed.

Between the church and Beth, Kent found things to fill holes that the game could not. As his family disintegrated around him, first with his father's death, then his mother's slow, sad, booze-soaked decline, and Adam's inability — no, *refusal* — to move beyond Marie's death, these were critical new pillars raised to support Kent. The flares of emotional pain faded to a dull, manageable ache, the surges of anger became soft waves of sorrow, and he was able to turn, for the first time, back toward the loss of his sister instead of away from it. And then, finally, to move on, marked by loss but not defined by it.

It was Walter Ward's idea to bring Kent into a prison. It was him walking out with Kent when he couldn't take the place, on that first trip. But they went back. And back again, and then, several years later, Kent sat down with Gideon Pearce and prayed for him while the man laughed.

But still he had his games. The mission he'd given himself at twenty — find a way to live that didn't require football as oxygen — had never truly been accomplished. He insisted, and believed that he succeeded much of the time, on diminishing the importance of the game, that he had turned it from a pathological need to win into something truly healthy, and the boys who came back each year with degrees or good jobs or fine families or simply good attitudes, they were the result that mattered, the only reward he needed.

He lengthened his stride, a good sweat coming now, and tried to tell himself that he didn't want to win as badly as he felt he did, tried to tell himself that it wouldn't prove anything about him. A win or a loss made no difference. Chambers had enjoyed a good year and he was sending good boys out into the world better prepared to be good men.

More wins did not matter.

But, oh, how he wanted them.

I will not be defined by a trophy, he often said, but it was easy to say you would not be defined by something you didn't have.

It was a packed house, and by arriving late, Adam and Chelsea lost any chance at finding a comfortable seat in the bleachers with a decent view. He didn't like crowds, anyhow, so they just stood at the fence, positioned behind the end zone. If Chelsea minded having to stand, she didn't say anything about it. Casual fans loved to be centered up on the field — ticket prices for pro games rise every ten yards between the goal line and the fifty, the fifty being considered the best seats in the house. But in Adam's opinion, the difference between someone who just enjoyed football and someone who truly knew the game was that someone who knew the game wanted to watch from a position that put him in synch with the action. The game moved vertically, so why sit in a position where you were always at right angles to the action? There was such disconnect. Adam had played middle linebacker, and the way he wanted to see the game was the way he'd always watched it unfold from the field — facing down the quarterback and the offensive line, reading his keys, trying to determine the play calls.

Walter Ward Field had bleachers for twelve thousand. Not bad for a small town, but it wasn't Massillon, either, where the population was the same but the stadium seated almost twenty thousand, the band was essentially a Rose Bowl Parade every week, and there was a live tiger on the sidelines. Massillon had won fifteen state championships in twenty years at one point. Their rivalry with Canton McKinley was, in Adam's mind and much of America's, the greatest high school rivalry in history. Both schools were in Stark County, and during one thirty-two-year stretch, the two combined for twenty-eight state championships. It was the gold standard of high school football, and his brother was obsessed with the program's history, always had been, but their field hadn't been good to him. His division played the championship game at Massillon. He'd lost both of those tries on the hallowed ground he so adored.

Now, the pep band banging away and cheerleaders screaming and twelve thousand people clapping and shouting, Adam stood with his arms folded behind the north end zone and watched his brother's squad. They'd gotten the kickoff but somehow did not have the ball any longer; it appeared they'd punted. Kent's script, of course. Another Walter Ward technique, and one Adam hated. Football was played best when it was played fast and loose, and scripts were the enemy of fast and loose.

The Chambers defense was solid, though Adam thought they should be playing a 4–3 base and not the 3–4 that Byers always used. The 4–3 allowed for better flexibility and adjustments and, the way Adam would approach it, more aggression. Chambers had enough athletes and hitters to put better pressure on the quarterback than they did. All that said, the kids didn't make mistakes. They knew their responsibilities and upheld them. Nobody prepared a team quite like Kent. If he ever let the kids know that it was okay to *want* it, to really play with a desperate need to win, he'd start putting trophies in the case. But to do that he'd have to admit it to himself first.

Hickory Hills punted; Chambers got the ball back in great position and went to Colin Mears on a stick route — sprint ten yards out, spin back, know that the ball would be there. The ball was there, but he didn't catch it. Adam watched him slap his helmet and didn't like what he saw. Too much tension.

In the rest of the half, they threw to Mears five more times. He caught one of them — barely. Bobbled it and probably would have dropped it again if he hadn't taken a shot from the cornerback that actually drove him back toward the floating ball, and he got his right hand on it and pulled it in when he went down. The crowd gave that a standing ovation, and Adam could tell the kid hated it. Sympathy applause. The kid understood just what it was, and it hurt him.

The running game was strong, though, and the defense was better, picking off two passes and forcing a fumble. It was 20–10 at the half. All was well with the Chambers Cardinals.

Most of them, at least.

"Rachel's boyfriend doesn't look too good," Chelsea said.

"No," Adam answered. He didn't speak much during the games, and she never intruded. Now that the action was paused, though, she turned to him and said, "Do you miss it? Being out there?"

"Hell, yeah."

"Did you ever want to coach?"

"I would have liked to coach with my brother. Defensive coordinator, that's what I would have liked."

"You could have let Kent be your boss?" She said it like she didn't believe it.

"Absolutely. Nothing about being head coach appeals. All the bullshit that goes with it, the school boards and the parents and the boosters, the media, that's not for me. Kent's good at that stuff, he's got the right temperament. He needs a good defensive coach, though. Byers isn't bad, but I'd be a hell of a lot better. He doesn't see enough. You watch the second half, you won't see many defensive adjustments. It's why they need to score so damn much. Kent likes that, of course, he's good at it. The passing game, he's in love with that. Most men dream of women and riches. My brother dreams of the play-action post."

She was watching him with a curious gaze, and he said, "What?"

"I'm surprised you would have been willing to work for him."

He shrugged. "Would have been fun, I think. He's the right head coach. I could have helped, though. I'm pretty sure I could have helped."

In the locker room, Kent praised his secondary and chewed out his defensive linemen for not getting better pressure on the quarterback, reminding them that Hickory Hills was going to have to try to pass their way back into the game, and the less time they had to do that, the better. He made a few changes offensively, instructing Lorell to be aware of the way they kept shading a safety over the top to help on Colin—it was leaving opportunities in the slot that he was missing. Lorell nodded, but he wouldn't look at Colin, and Colin wouldn't look at anyone. They were all thinking the same thing: it was unlikely that safety was going to be helping out on Colin in the second half, not when he couldn't catch anything.

"You've got to close it out," Kent said. "This is a team that can put points on the board in a hurry if you give them chances. Let's not give them chances."

There were claps and shouts and then they were on their feet and headed out, and Kent got a hand on Colin's shoulder as he went by.

"Look at me, son. Look at me."

Colin lifted his head. "I'm sorry, Coach. I'll get it fixed."

"I know you will. Drop it down a gear, okay? You're running routes like there are scouts with stopwatches on you. Run them like it's a football game instead. Your fourth gear is more than those guys can handle, anyhow. Slow it down, start with the football and *then* think about the end zone. All right?"

"Yes, sir. I'll get it fixed."

They left the locker room then, and Kent held back, turned to Steve Haskins, and asked if he'd heard a halftime score in the Saint Anthony's game. Haskins always checked the scores, and Kent had chewed him out for it before, so he wasn't surprised to see a flicker of a smile in his assistant's eyes.

"They're up ten."

Kent nodded.

"Here they come, right?" Haskins said.

"No." Kent shook his head. "Here we come."

Chambers scored twice in the third and ate the clock in the fourth.

Four times, McCoy found Colin Mears. Four times, Colin Mears couldn't handle the pass. Adam wasn't surprised. Had expected this after the first drop, seeing the boy's reaction to a ball he'd always caught and somehow had missed. After the last drop, Mears got into a shoving match with the Hickory Hills cornerback and got flagged for unsportsmanlike conduct. Kent took him out then. Mears stood at the end of the sideline, alone, and refused to take off his helmet.

When it was 34–13 and Lorell McCoy took a knee, Adam left the field as the rest of the crowd rose in raucous applause. He passed behind the home bench on his way out, but Kent had his back turned.

22

AND SO THEY WERE UNDER WAY. A dominant win over a quality opponent, the perfect season continuing without so much as a hiccup.

Unless you'd watched the game.

There'd been a hiccup, and his name was Colin Mears, and Kent wasn't certain what he wanted to do about this. The kid ran the same routes he always ran, Lorell McCoy delivered the ball to him in stride just as he always had. The only thing that had changed was Colin's ability to catch the ball. Kent wasn't surprised. Some kids were able to use the game as therapy, to cleanse their minds on the field, but others brought emotional burdens between the lines with them. Colin, the product of a secure, untroubled childhood, likely fit into the latter category. The issue was finding a way to get him to understand that it was fine, which was no easy task, because the boy had already determined that his performance on the field meant something, was some form of atonement.

"He's caught too many balls for too long," Kent said when he met with the coaches that night. "He's not going to keep dropping them. He'll be back."

"Maybe you try a gimmick," Matt Byers said.

"Such as?"

"Take his gloves off, maybe."

"He's going to have an easier time holding onto the ball without gloves?"

"Technically speaking, no. Mentally? Maybe."

Kent thought about it and nodded. "We'll try it. Change is good for him. Distraction is good. We'll give it a try." He looked at Haskins. "You got a final in the Saint Anthony's game?"

"They won by twenty-four."

"No surprise there," Byers said. "But this year we've got them. This year we're going to run their asses into the ground. Provided Mears can start catching the damn ball."

"He'll be ready to go," Kent said. "And *we* need to be. This one won't be easy."

It wouldn't be. This year, Chambers had the better team. But still Kent felt dry-mouthed thinking about Saint Anthony's. He knew that Scott Bless was already looking at video, already considering moves he could make that he hadn't made all season, ways to leave Chambers flat-footed and unprepared. The coaches were watching Kent, everyone well aware of what he was thinking. Bless was his nemesis. Kent had one of the best career records of any active coach in the state, but he had a goose egg against Scott Bless.

"Meet at nine," he said. "Have your film watched, have your reports ready. This one won't be easy."

It wouldn't be, but he was excited, excited because he believed he had the better team, excited that they'd gotten through this week and put another win on the board and things were, finally, starting to feel right again.

Matt Byers returned to his office with a note just as Kent was preparing to turn off the lights. A sealed envelope addressed *For Coach Austin.*

"This was on the floor," Matt said. "Someone slipped it under the door."

Kent tossed it into his bag among the play scripts and the notes. It might be fan mail or it might be a complaint from disgruntled parents who wanted more reps for their son, but it would not be imperative.

He should have gotten to the letter earlier, but he was distracted the next morning by a phone call from Colin's mother, Robin Mears, asking him what his thoughts on Colin were.

"Robin, you can't expect him to play like normal. He's not normal right now. He can't just drop all of those burdens off on the sideline and check in to the game. I'd love it if he could, and I know that he's trying to, but the reality is the game used to feel natural to him, and right now, nothing in the world feels natural to him. Everything's out of balance."

"He was so upset, Coach Austin. I don't think he slept at all last night. I found him in the yard at three in the morning, just sitting on the picnic table, crying. I tried to talk to him, but he wouldn't talk. Couldn't."

"That's how it'll go, for a time," Kent said gently. "He'll need space for some of it. Other times, he's going to need you. You're doing all the right things. Be ready when he needs you, and step back a little when he needs the space. There's no quick fix for loss, for grief. You're doing all the right things."

And so it went, for forty-five minutes of conversation, and he hung up feeling wrung out, because he could explain it to her, but he couldn't make her *know* it, *feel* it, couldn't do anything for her except offer words, and the words felt hollow. So he offered a prayer next, because prayers were never hollow, and then he tried to get to work.

We'll try getting him to play without gloves, he thought as he drove to the school. *Maybe Matt is right, maybe that will help.*

Then, as he pulled into the parking lot, he found himself feeling self-loathing over that, because his thoughts had ebbed, quickly but totally, from concern over the boy's mental and emotional health to concern about what the Saint Anthony's defense might do if they realized he was no longer the threat he had been. Their coaches would be watching the game video; they'd be watching those stunning drops. And remembering them. Come next Friday night, if he dropped a few more? If they saw early in the game that Colin Mears was not worthy of double coverage and began to jam the box? Then the Cardinals would be in real trouble.

Can't think about that, Kent told himself. *It's pathetic, Austin, it's shameful.*

But still it was happening. Because he wanted to win this game, and all those on the other side of it. Wanted it more than he could dare show, wanted it so bad it was hard to sleep and hard to breathe and hard to remember the things he should remember, because while the only thing that really mattered about Colin Mears right now was in his mind and soul and not in his hands, the first things Kent wanted fixed, in the darkest corner of his heart, were the hands. *Catch the ball, son, and then we'll put the rest of you back together. But first start catching the damned ball.*

He'd stop that. He'd find a way to get it in check.

Saturday practices weren't practices so much as prep sessions. They'd watch some video, then put the boys through a light workout, running and stretching, designed to speed recovery, loosen the aching and bruised muscles after the previous night's combat, and then return to the locker room to watch more video.

He was running late, delayed by Robin's phone call, but still half an hour ahead of the team, enough time to gather his thoughts. Went into his office, turned on the lights, and shut the door. Ninety-five percent of the time, the door to Kent's office stayed open. When it was shut, though, everyone understood, players and coaches alike—he wanted privacy for a reason, and if you interrupted, there'd better be good cause and you'd better knock.

He was organizing his notes when he discovered the letter, tucked in with the preliminary scouting reports. His mind was still on Saint Anthony's when he slit it open.

Later, he would be surprised by how immediately he thought about fingerprints. How carefully he set the envelope down, handling it now by the edges, even though it was probably too late to help. There was no moment of stunned pause, just sick understanding.

There were three items inside. The first was a standard sheet of printer paper, cut in half, a short message typed across it.

Wonderful win, Coach. Wonderful. A beautiful autumn night, too. Though I have to be honest and tell you that I preferred last week's autumn. That was special. I'll tell you more about it soon, I promise.

You told me once that I was welcome to contact you at any point. I have taken you at your word on that. Is your word good, Coach? Do you welcome this contact? I have not forgotten your visits or your message. There's no fear that can break true faith, isn't that right? I always admired your conviction. Your foolishness. Will you forgive me, too, Coach? Will you pray for me? Will you remain unbroken?

I wonder if you regret telling me about the girl who had forgiven her father. I wonder if you're still so convicted as you were this summer. I wonder if you possibly believed it when you looked into my eyes and told me that you had already

*passed your greatest test, that forgiving the man who raped and
murdered your sister was that test. I disagreed with you then. I
still do, Coach. There are greater tests coming.*

Kent read it three times, a chill spreading through his chest
and out to the rest of him, until his temples and fingertips felt
tight and tingling. The other two items were cards: a business
card for AA Bail Bonds and a weathered sports card with perfo-
rated edges, Adam Austin kneeling in full pads, helmet resting
beside him, staring into the camera with a loose, easy grin.

Gideon Pearce's wallet. The random traffic stop, the first clue.
This was the football card that started him on his way to prison,
the football card that brought Kent to him all those years later, saying he forgave him, telling him he'd like to say a prayer together,
Pearce laughing—a wild, mocking laugh—as Kent got through
it, head bowed and eyes shut, his voice shaking and his hands
folded together so tightly the nails left half-moons of blood.

He shifted his eyes back to the business card. It was
nondescript—cheap stock, gray, the name and address and two
phone numbers. He used the letter opener to turn the business
card over. Blank. He turned the football card over next and then,
for a long time, a very long time, sat in frozen silence at his desk.
When the door banged open, he rose to his feet and rushed into
the locker room. Steve Haskins, playbook in one hand and cup
of coffee in the other, nodded at him.

"If you're ready, I was hoping we could go over—"

"I'm going to need you out of here for a while," Kent said. "Kids,
too. Everyone. Make sure nobody comes in here. Practice is yours."

"Coach?"

"Practice is yours," Kent repeated. "And keep people away
from that door until the police are here."

He went back to his office then and called Stan Salter to tell
him that he knew who had killed Rachel Bond.

Part Two

LAST WEEK'S AUTUMN

23

ADAM WAS ON HIS WAY to Mansfield Correctional to interview Jason Bond when the phone began to ring. Chelsea, calling from the office, so he expected she would be calling about business. He did not care about business, and let her calls roll to voicemail three times. It wasn't until the fourth that he finally gave in with a sigh.

"Yeah?"

"Where in the hell have you been?"

"Working. What's up?"

"Police are searching your property, Adam."

"Not surprised. Salter's unhappy. Let them do their thing."

"They aren't here. They're at your house."

A tenth of a mile rolled by, two tenths, three, and Chelsea said, "Adam? You hear me?"

"They're searching my house?"

"That's what I've been told. Based on new evidence."

"What new evidence?"

"They don't volunteer that, Adam. They just show the warrants. We got one here, too."

"They broke down my door?"

"No. Your brother gave them a key."

"Gave them a key."

"Yes. The deed's in both of your names. He's allowed to grant them access, legally."

Chelsea was still talking, but his mind was empty, the world empty, consisting of nothing but gray pavement and the far-off sound of Chelsea's voice.

"Adam? Do you want me to go there? Or call a lawyer?"

"No," he said. "No, I'll handle that myself."

He hung up. He was thinking of the closed door with the handwritten sign, thinking of police entering the room, and ahead of him the highway seemed to narrow like a tunnel and pull him underwater, swift and silent.

In his entire coaching career, Kent Austin had missed one practice. That was the day his son was born, and he was back the next morning.

Today he missed his second, spent it with a sergeant from the Chambers Police Department and an FBI agent named Robert Dean. Kent wondered why the FBI was here already, recalling how long it had taken for them to get involved in Marie's disappearance. His father had shouted for them, screamed for them, as if they were mythical problem solvers, would walk in and listen to the situation and produce his missing daughter immediately, tip their caps, and go on their way. By the time the FBI actually got involved, though, most of the heart had gone out of Hank Austin, the shouts turning to numb musings, as if he'd already checked out of his life and was studying it sadly from afar.

He kept up those musings for the rest of his life, but only Adam was allowed in. Not Kent. That was his brother's rule, though, not his father's. The two of them would sit in the kitchen, sharing a bottle of Scotch and an ashtray, and his father would tell tales of revenge. Never mentioning Marie's name. They were always historical, or anecdotal, or flat-out apocryphal. He'd talk about how the Apaches would bury enemies up to their necks in the sand, coat their eyes with sweet sap from cactus, and wait for the ants to come. Talk about spies who'd had their tongues cut out, soldiers who had been left impaled on stakes in Vietnam.

There was a time when Kent felt that he should sit with them. Adam wouldn't allow it.

"Get your ass down to the weight room," he'd say when their father began to get warm, began to tip the bottle a little more frequently, glass clinking off glass. "Go see Coach Ward."

Kent would go. Always with a shard of guilt, a sense that he belonged there, three men sharing their alcohol and their pain, and that he was slinking away from it like a coward. Once, and only once, his father tried to get him to stay. Poured a third glass and slid it across the table and told him to have a seat. Adam caught the glass, and told Kent to go see Coach Ward.

"Ah, he can stay," Hank Austin had said. "It doesn't always need to be football."

"For him it does," Adam said, and he looked their father in the eye and his voice was hard. There was a long pause, a frown but no argument, and then Adam spoke again, not looking at Kent. "He's not worth a shit right now, anyhow. Dances in the pocket, throws high on the first pass after anybody gives him a good hit, and if he's checked down to a third read in his whole damned career I've never seen it."

That had been the end, the cue to leave, and Kent popped open the door and slipped out into the night and walked to the Wards' house, where he was eating dinner more nights than not, where he listened to the family say grace before each meal, where he watched game tapes and talked to the coach and tried to pretend he was oblivious to Beth, that he didn't live for a moment of eye contact with her.

Right up until the end, his father remained entranced by revenge stories. They weren't always so dark, but he had an unerring ability to return to the concept. Talk about a baseball game, he'd segue over into the memory of a pitcher who'd thrown a beanball at someone who slid into a base with spikes up. Mention football, and it was a savage late hit delivered in retaliation for the way a teammate had been treated. His daily scans of the newspaper became a quest, a search for reminders of balance in a world that had ceased to offer it to him.

It always comes back around, he'd say, whether the topic be sports or war or an embezzling business partner. *You always pay your dues.* There was a tragic hopefulness to the assertion. He needed to believe that pain circled. If you caused it, you caught it.

Today, Kent believed that pain circled. The only problem was that all he did was catch it. He found himself thinking, as he answered questions, that he was relieved his father was dead.

"Clayton Sipes?" Robert Dean said.

"Yes. I believe that letter is from him."

"And you know this man how?"

"I met him in prison. This summer. I was there on a speaking visit."

"Tell us about that interaction, please."

Something in the question caught Kent's attention; it reeked of preparation. He appreciated a prepared man. But Dean shouldn't be prepared for this.

"You're already aware of this name, aren't you?" Kent said.

"Why do you say that?"

"It doesn't seem to have caught you by surprise."

"We have a list of everyone who was paroled from Mansfield around the time those letters started. Everyone who might have had access to Jason Bond or awareness of the contact with his daughter. Sipes is on that list. He is not alone on it, but he's on it."

"Have you interviewed him?"

Dean tapped his pencil, eyes down, and shook his head.

"Why not?"

"Because he's missing."

"Missing?"

"He's made none of the required contact. There's an active warrant for parole violation."

Kent closed his eyes. "When was he paroled?"

"In August."

"When the letters resumed with Rachel. The false letters."

"Yes."

Kent rubbed a hand over his face and said, "He was in for assault, wasn't he?"

"How do you know that?"

"I asked the director of our outreach program to find out for me. His name is Dan Grissom. He said it was assault. Is that correct?"

"It is. Sexual assault, stalking, violating a restraining order. Why are you so sure he wrote this letter?"

"Because it's a repeat conversation."

"Pardon?"

"I've done a lot of prison visits," Kent said. "There are men who listen, and men who don't. Men who mock, men who get on their knees and pray with you. I've seen them all by now. Or I thought I had. I'd never seen anything quite like him, though. He was...combative, I guess that would be the word. But not in an angry way. The best way I can describe it is...intensely interested."

Focused attention was the phrase that first came to mind, but that was his coaching mantra, and he could not transfer it to Clayton Sipes, refused to do so.

"Interested in your message?" Dean said.

"Interested in challenging my message. Interested in challenging the very idea that I believed in a God, but he wasn't content to keep that debate theological."

"Explain that."

"It was personal," Kent said. "Immediately. When I go to a prison, I tell a personal story, of course. I talk about my sister, the way I had to learn to bear that grief. I talk about my own journey. But his reaction…" Kent paused and shook his head, remembering the man so vividly, shaved head, wiry muscle, neck and left arm covered in brightly colored tattoos. "His reaction was disturbing. It was as if…as if I woke something up in him. He was all dull eyes and boredom and then he just kept… intensifying. I don't know the best way to describe it. The way his interest grew as I talked was unsettling. Like it was this dim light when I walked in the room and with every detail I shared it got brighter and brighter, right? Not in a healthy way."

"You simply observed this? Or was there direct interaction?"

"Oh, there was direct interaction. He asked to speak with me alone when my talk was done. What he wanted from that conversation was specific. It was very important for him to hear me say that my faith couldn't be broken."

"But you didn't think he was taking reassurance from that?"

"No. I thought he was taking a challenge from it. I know that he was."

"Did you mention Rachel Bond?"

"No. I'd never have done that. She was a child."

Dean frowned. "The letter seems to indicate otherwise."

"Well, I mean, I didn't use her name. I didn't identify her."

"But you discussed the situation?"

"To an extent."

"What extent?"

"Minimal." Kent realized how defensive he was becoming,

realized that he was acting as if he were being accused of a crime, and for the first time understood exactly why. He felt guilty. What Dean was asking about wasn't speculation, it was the truth. Clayton Sipes had found his way to Rachel Bond through Kent.

"I'm going to need a little more than —"

"I was talking about forgiveness," Kent said. "And family. Those are regular points for me. Usually I keep it focused on my own experience. But this summer, the situation with Rachel and her father was fresh. She'd been so relieved to make contact. She'd replaced something that was missing, you know? So I used her" — he stuttered then, hating the word choice, *used* — "as a, uh, an anecdote. A lot of those men have lost ties with family. Maybe through their choice, maybe not. Many of them have isolated themselves from family because of guilt and shame. I wanted to talk about that, and . . . her situation was fresh. It was relevant."

Dean scribbled on his pad and said, "The two cards, the football card and the business card. Why would he have sent those?"

"To make me suffer. He was fascinated by the idea that I said I'd found peace with my sister's murder. He took issue with that."

"You don't believe it was designed to make you feel doubt?"

Kent paused. "Doubt in what?"

"Gideon Pearce's guilt."

The silence built and hung. Kent swallowed, leaned forward, and said, "I feel no doubt about the guilt of Gideon Pearce."

"I didn't ask what you felt. I asked if it was possible that's what he was going for."

"Perhaps." The twenty-two-year-old football card was already haunting him, because it had come from one of two places: the evidence collection from Gideon Pearce's case, or the inside of Kent's childhood home. They'd printed a few thousand of those cards in 1989, but there were only two in the world with the number 18 inked on the back in his dead sister's handwriting. It was Kent's number. There had been no football card for him in 1989 because he was not all-state, was not even a starter, but she hadn't wanted him to feel left out, so she kept two of Adam's cards and wrote Kent's number on both. One had been in her room when she went missing. The second had been found with Gideon Pearce after she was murdered.

"So the recollections in the letter," Dean said, "they're accurate? This doesn't strike you as a possible imitation?"

"Absolutely not. They're accurate. I talk about forgiveness, faith, all of the things that were mentioned in the letter. About Gideon Pearce. I invite them to contact me if I can help."

"What about your brother?"

"Pardon?"

"Do you talk about him during these visits? The cards are directly connected to him."

"I don't know if I used his name. I talked about what my family went through. And the card, I talked about that. The way it felt when we learned about Pearce."

"Are you aware of any people you might consider enemies of your brother? Deep-seated problems, threats, things of that nature?"

"I don't know what that has to do with Clayton Sipes."

"Probably nothing. But we can't just shut off all other possibilities. Clayton Sipes can be considered a suspect, but right now all we've got is your recollection of an odd conversation. So let's look wider, please. Are you aware of anyone who has problems with your brother?"

"No. I'm sure in his business there have been some."

"Why do you say that?"

"He brings people back to jail. I would imagine many of them resent that."

"True. But that's not a personal thing, is it?"

"No. I'm just saying... listen, I am not qualified to talk about my brother's life."

"You're not close, I take it."

"No."

"Why not?"

Kent felt his jaw clench. "Personal differences."

"Any particular incident? Something to do with Gideon Pearce?"

The sound of the name put a chill through Kent. Always had, always would.

"Gideon Pearce is dead."

"I understand that."

"Then why would you ask —"

"Someone gave you a football card identical to the one found in his possession after your sister was murdered. He seems relevant."

"Okay. All right. Yeah, it had to do with Pearce. I went to see him, in prison, long after he had been convicted. My brother didn't approve. He came by my house to express that, and... we got into it pretty good."

A scar along the left side of Kent's lip, which stood out more when he smiled, a stark white line, testified to just how well they'd gotten into it. Nine stitches had been required. Beth still recalled it uneasily. *He could have killed you, Kent. I really thought he could have killed you.*

"So Sipes would have been aware of the football card, your brother's feelings about your visit with Pearce, all of that? You speak about this in your visits?"

"Yes. I describe how Pearce laughed it off."

Kent could see the son of a bitch so clearly, the gap-toothed smile. *I forgive you,* Kent had told him. *I want you to understand what you have taken from me, and so many others, but before we begin with that, I need you to understand that I forgive you, and I would also like to say a prayer.*

The laughter had started then, and Kent remembered a drifting sensation, his anchors loosening and sliding free into a current of wild rage, and he'd bowed his head and prayed and waited for the anchors to catch again as Pearce laughed and laughed, a truly delighted sound.

"Coach?" Robert Dean said. "Mr. Austin?"

He lifted his head now, having bowed it again unaware, and nodded. "Yeah. I'm good."

24

THERE WERE FOUR CARS—three cruisers and one unmarked detective's car—parked on the street when Adam arrived. A photographer knelt on the sidewalk. He wasn't in uniform, and he was keeping his distance from the cops. Media. As Adam exited the Jeep and went through the yard to the front door, one of the officers shouted at him, and a flash popped from the photographer and Adam ignored them both and went into the house. Stan Salter was waiting for him, warrant in hand.

"We tried to call you first. Let's talk it through."

"Talk it through? You're in my house."

"With legal authority and sound reasoning. Let's talk about the reasoning."

"You consider me a suspect?" Adam said. "You out of your mind?"

"Didn't say suspect. Said we have sound reasoning for a search. Could have talked with you about it before now, if you'd answer the phone or return a call. We need to—"

There were two officers moving through the kitchen and into the living room, and Adam had been watching them, but when he heard the sounds from upstairs he lost all track of Salter's words, and the pulse was pounding behind his eyes again.

"What are they doing up there?"

"Their job. Let's you and I step outside and talk. Or if you want to watch them now and then talk, fine. I won't stop you from watching. But either way, we're going to need a level of cooperation from you that we haven't received to this point."

Adam started for the stairs. Salter moved to block him but Adam shrugged that off easily and kept on going. He could see that the door was open. Marie's door. Salter's voice was chasing him but it had no meaning, the words were part of a surrounding fog, the only clear shape in the gathering mist was Marie's open door. KNOCKS REQUIRED, TRESPASSING FORBIDDEN!

He reached the top of the stairs and turned and then he saw them in there, two of them, one taking pictures and the other kneeling beside Marie's closet. He had blond hair and wore gloves and he was moving things out of the closet and stacking them on the floor. A tower filled with cassette tapes was in his hand. Her favorite on top, the one that had been released that summer, her last summer, the one that they'd all listened to, Adam and Marie and Kent, Tom Petty's *Full Moon Fever*. She'd loved that tape. "Free Fallin'," "Love Is a Long Road," "I Won't Back Down." The last was the song they blasted in the locker room from start to finish that championship season. *You could stand me up at the gates of hell, but I won't back down...*

"Free Fallin'," though, that was Marie's favorite. She had a decent voice but was too shy to sing in front of people, so Adam and Kent would constantly try to catch her at it, always embarrassing her to a flushed silence and a defensive *What? It's a great song!*

Now, twenty-two years later, Adam watched as the blond detective slipped the tape out, checking the ancient cassettes as if they were of value to his current investigation.

"Put that down," Adam said. Salter had caught up to him and was standing in the doorway, one hand on Adam's arm, and the grip was supposed to be firm but the contact meant nothing to Adam. The blond detective on the floor looked up at them.

"We're just executing the warrant, sir. Lieutenant Salter can explain. Nothing's —"

"Put that the fuck down," Adam said, and then he stepped through the door and into the room, dragging Salter with him, and though his words were soft and his steps were slow, the detective rose abruptly, saying, "Lieutenant?" in an uneasy voice.

He still had *Full Moon Fever* in his hand. It did not belong in his hand. Adam reached for it, and when he did, Salter made the first truly aggressive attempt to keep him back, grabbing his bicep and pulling his arm down. Trying to, at least. Adam twisted free, and the motion frightened the cop who held the tape. He said, "Hey, hey, relax," and then he took a fast step backward and banged into the bookshelf.

On top of the bookshelf was Tito, Marie's prize, the stained-glass turtle she'd spent weeks on her last summer, coming home with cut fingertips and pride as she worked those multicolored speckles into his oversized shell. The turtle tottered, fell forward, hit the hardwood floor.

Shattered.

It broke in one quick snap, but the sound did not end the same way in Adam's brain. It came on and on in echoing waves, windows blowing out in a skyscraper, too many to count, too many to comprehend.

All he heard was shattering glass when he broke the blond cop's nose.

As the cop went down the blood sprayed from his nose and found Marie's bed. The new comforter, the one she'd had changed from pink to white, because she was becoming a woman and she wanted the room to look elegant, not childish. The one

Adam hand-washed once a month even though nothing had so much as creased it in nearly two decades. Crimson bloomed across its surface as Stan Salter shouted for help and slammed into Adam's back, trying to get some sort of combat hold on his arm and neck. He didn't succeed. Adam shook free and took a handful of the blond cop's shirt and jerked him back to his feet, then pivoted and threw him toward the door, wanting him out, needing him out, trespassers were forbidden in this room, couldn't he fucking read? Another cop was already coming through the door, though, and they banged together and both of them went into the wall and then the blond one was down on his knees dripping blood on Marie's floor.

Just before he felt the first staggering jolt from the Taser, Adam became aware of his own voice, slow and soft, saying, "I'm sorry, I'm sorry, I'm sorry."

He hoped that she could hear over the chaos. Then the volts found his spine again and climbed giddily up into his brain and he was falling and the world was falling with him, spinning down onto the floor, and despite the indescribable electric pain he felt a sliver of glass enter his palm, one of the shards from the stained-glass turtle, cutting deep, sinking fast.

I'm sorry.

25

K ENT SHOULD HAVE ANTICIPATED it. Should have prepared the police for his brother's reaction. Or prepared his brother for the police visit. One or the other. Instead he'd just given them the key and sent them out there to look for the card. When his interview was interrupted by the news that Adam had been arrested for assaulting a police officer, he did not need details in order to understand.

"They were in her room, weren't they?" he said.

"Whose room?"

"My sister's," Kent said.

TRESPASSING FORBIDDEN! THANKS, BOYS!

"I'm not certain. Do you intend to bail him out?"

Kent blinked at him in surprise. "That's what he does."

"For other people, yes. He might need help when the situation is reversed."

It was so obvious that it was embarrassing, but somehow Kent had just expected that Adam could handle the process on his own.

"I guess he'll need me to, yeah," he said. But who was he

supposed to call? Adam bailed people out; Adam was the one you called.

Salter unlocked the handcuffs and tossed them on the table, then went and sat on the other side and ran a hand over his face and through his close-cropped hair.

"The hell were you thinking, Austin? It was a damned search warrant, and we had permission from your brother, who is one of the homeowners. What were you thinking?"

"That's the wrong way to back me off," Adam said. "You don't like me doing what I'm doing, but trying to intimidate me by forcing bullshit warrants and—"

"It was not a bullshit warrant."

"I suspect I'll disagree on that point."

"Whoever killed Rachel Bond may have been in your home," Salter said, voice quiet.

Adam had always played football fast, had required a high motor, a sense of savagery. But there were times, few and far between, when the gears stuck. When everything went slow and syrupy. Those were the times when the offense fooled him completely, when he roared into a play expecting one thing only to be given another. Now, staring at Salter, he felt it again.

"Explain that," he said.

"Someone wrote your brother a letter. Included in it were two items: your business card and a football card with your picture and what appears to be your sister's handwriting."

Adam said, "Top left drawer of the desk."

"What?"

"Top left drawer of the desk. That's where it should be. Is it not?"

Salter shook his head.

Under the table, Adam folded his hands like a man in prayer, squeezed the left tightly against the right, trying to find the old ache, to use the pain to ground the electrical current of his rage. The bones had knitted so long ago, though, and he could not call up the pain now.

"It was sent to Kent?" he said.

"It was left for your brother, yes. We're not prepared to say that it was from the killer, but we have to acknowledge —"

"Yes, it was. You know damned well that it was."

Salter looked at him, tapping a pencil on the edge of the table, and said, "Who could have gotten into the house?"

"I don't know."

"Who is in it regularly, other than you?"

"No one."

"Come on. Give me a starting point, no matter how vague. Friends, visitors. Who comes over to watch a ballgame or have a beer, who —"

"No one," Adam said again. "That house is not where I socialize."

"Your brother has a key."

"Yeah. The one he gave to you."

"No one else? You couldn't call someone to, say, let you in if you were locked out?"

Adam started to answer, then stopped. Salter's eyes glimmered at the hesitation, having seen Adam observe first the bait and then the trap.

"The letter went to Kent. Not to me."

"Correct. But the football card came from your house. That's your own statement, not mine. You believe it was in the desk."

"Yes, it was."

"Okay. So let's stick with that. Who else has a key?"

"Chelsea."

"Chelsea Salinas. Let's talk about her a little, yes. She has access to the home?"

"It's not worth discussing, Salter. This has nothing to do with Chelsea."

"But she does have access to the home?"

"She's got a key."

"Now, we're being honest here, so let's avoid the bullshit and get this out in the open—Chelsea Salinas is a married woman, and you're sleeping with her. And her husband is in jail. I believe you held bonds on him in the past?"

Adam felt a bristle of anger. "Travis Leonard is in jail," he said. "You're right about that. So he's not a suspect, and this isn't worth discussing."

"Does he know that you're sleeping with his wife?"

Adam stared at him. It was the first time anyone had directly challenged him on his relationship with Chelsea. Of course Salter would know, of course he'd have done that much checking, and it was not a hard thing to determine, but still it made Adam uncomfortable.

"Not to the best of my knowledge. She hasn't told him. I haven't told him."

"We'll have to look at it."

"He's in *jail*," Adam repeated.

"He has friends who are not."

"Friends who would kill a seventeen-year-old girl to, what, screw with my head? Punish me? No, Salter. No, that's not the scent you want to chase. It's the wrong direction."

Salter didn't respond.

"The letter," Adam said, "went to Kent."

"I understand that."

"Rachel's contact with her father started from Kent's suggestion. Am I correct?"

Salter gave a small nod.

"Then why aren't you interviewing Kent?"

"Other people are."

"Who?"

"We have multiple investigators working on —"

"You're the lead, Salter. And you've been at my house, and now you're here with me. That's a waste of time that you can't afford. You should be talking to my brother."

"The FBI is talking to your brother."

Adam opened his mouth to say more, then shut it. He was finally understanding what Salter was looking for. He was not a dumb man, was Salter, he was probably a pretty damned good detective, in fact, far too smart not to understand that if Rachel Bond's killer had wanted to antagonize Jason Bond or Adam Austin, he would have gone directly to them. Instead, he'd gone to Kent. It was about Kent. It had been from the start.

But why?

"They're talking to him," Salter said, watching Adam, "and you and I can talk about him. You have any thoughts on people who would want to take this sort of head shot at your brother?"

Adam nodded. "Sure. Pick a murderer. He's made friends with plenty of them."

"Sounds like that bothers you."

"Yes. He started with Gideon Pearce. It bothered me then, and it continues to bother me."

"My understanding is that you threatened to kill Mr. Pearce."

"No," Adam said. "I *promised* to do it. Unfortunately, I wasn't given the chance."

"Your feelings on that situation…who have you discussed them with? Who understood the depth of your feelings about him?"

"Who understood the depth of my feelings about the man who murdered my sister?" Adam stared at him. "You think I needed to *discuss* those feelings to have them understood?"

"I'm asking. Who did you talk about the idea with?"

"My father. Who is dead. And my mother. Who is dead."

And my brother, he thought, *who is not dead. And who is currently with the FBI. I'm not, but he is. So when the FBI floated in here and pulled rank, they went to Kent. Why? Because they think he's of more importance than me.*

"Do you know if anyone you've held bond on ended up meeting your brother in prison? On his, um, speaking tours?"

Adam studied him. "No. Was that indicated in the letter?"

"It was not."

"But the prison visits are important to you?"

"It's just a question, Austin." But Salter's eyes danced away when he said that.

26

IF CHELSEA SALINAS WAS ANY happier to see Kent than he was to see her, she hid it well. There was a moment of frigid silence when she opened the door for him, and when he put out his hand, she hesitated. Held his eyes the whole time—she'd always been steady like that, so contained and cool, he remembered her at Marie's funeral, remembered thinking, *I wish that bitch would at least cry*—but seemed not to trust his hand. Finally she took it, though, her grip stronger than half of his defensive backs', and said, "He doesn't want you to be involved, but you have to be."

"It's a felony, right? What he was charged with?"

"Right now."

"It changes?"

"He can plead it down. He doesn't want you to have to deal with it, but they set the bond high, and he's got to put the house up. He can't do that without you. Because you're both—"

"I understand the situation with our house," Kent said. He willed down the anger. He'd put so much behind him, he'd looked Gideon Pearce in the eye and told the man he was forgiven, and somehow the idea of doing the same with Chelsea Salinas seemed an impossible challenge. Terribly unfair, he understood that and always had, but the heart was not a fair thing, that was why you had to fight it. The heart was not pure; it required resistance. Demanded it. Follow your heart, people said, but people were wrong. Control your heart. That was the rule.

Adam wouldn't have left her before you were there, Kent thought, studying the woman. *He had his head on straight until you came along, he made the right decisions, he was devoted to the right things. There was never a more protective older brother in the world than Adam. Then you arrived, and he drove past her with you in the car, he drove right past her in the dark and the cold and you sat and watched and let it happen. Caused it to happen.*

But Chelsea had been seventeen, too. Why couldn't he remember that?

"So what do I need to do?" he said.

She walked past him and around the desk. She still looked good, tall and lean and firm, and if she covered up the tattoos and took the damned rings out of her eyebrow she'd be a beautiful woman instead of having that sad look of the middle-aged trying to preserve a fading and forgotten youth. *You're almost forty,* he wanted to say. *Why do you insist on looking like a roadie? It's not even fifty degrees out and still you're wearing a tank top?*

She sat behind the desk, pushed her dark hair back over her ears, and said, "You really don't like me, do you Kent?"

For some reason his first instinct was to tell her to call him Coach. Or Mr. Austin. Or sir. He simply didn't like the sound of his first name on her lips.

Instead he said, "I don't even know you."

"You did once."

"Not really. Now would you please tell me what I need to do?"

She looked at him for a moment, her gaze hardening, and

said, "I wish you didn't have to do a thing. I should be able to cover it. I'd put up my own house, but..."

"But it's not your house. It belongs to your husband."

For the first time, her granite façade showed fissures, and she glanced away, began shuffling through paperwork on the desk.

"You'll have to sign over your share of the house. It's not as if anything will happen to it. You won't lose anything unless Adam skips, and that won't happen, obviously. They set the bond very high. Higher than I've seen for similar cases. It's because of the publicity that will be around this, probably."

"How high?"

"A hundred thousand. There's a cash surety, too. Ten thousand. We've got enough liquid cash for that. We can't cover the whole thing without the property, though. I'm sorry."

"It's not your fault. You didn't punch a police officer in the face."

She looked back up. "He's struggling with this. Do you understand how much?"

"I haven't seen him since it happened. I imagine he's not real proud, or pleased."

"I don't mean what happened today. I mean with that girl, with Rachel Bond. He's breaking under it. Do you realize that? Do you talk to him enough to see it?"

"I'm seeing it happen," Kent said. "More clearly today than before. I've already told him what I can tell him. I guess I can repeat it, but he ignored it then and he will ignore it now."

There was a moment, right then, when the look she gave him could have come from Beth. A soft scrutiny that seemed too knowing, too intimate.

"Right," she said. "So, you want to sign papers and get on your way, is that it?"

"Unless there is something else for me to do."

She began to slide papers across to him. "No. I guess there isn't."

"Anything I need to understand about what I'm signing here that I don't already?"

"It's straightforward. Financial guarantee that he makes his scheduled appearances. As far as the court is concerned, you're now responsible for him. Your brother's keeper."

He signed the last three pages faster, an illegible scrawl.

By the time Chelsea got Adam released, darkness had settled and the streetlights were on and a chill wind whistled through town. He was wearing only the T-shirt he'd had on that afternoon, when the sun was high and the fall air was warm. Chelsea had brought his jacket, handed it to him without a word. He pulled it on and started to zip it up but she slipped her arms inside the jacket and wrapped them around him and held him, put her head on his chest. For a moment he stood there awkwardly, wanting to step away from her touch, wanting to show that he did not need it, that he could bear this alone just fine, but the warmth of her and the smell of her hair got to him and he returned the embrace and lowered his face until his cheek rested against hers.

"I'm sorry," she said. "I should have gone there with you. I shouldn't have let you go alone, not when I knew they were at the house."

He tried to tell her not to worry about it, but words weren't coming easily, and so he just stood there and breathed in the smell of her and did not speak. They swayed a little, and for a moment they could have been dancing together, cheek to cheek and happy and in love, somewhere far from here. It would have to be somewhere far from here. Then a door banged open behind them and he knew it was one of the cops and so he released her and began to walk.

"They set it awfully high," he said. "I figured they would go fifty, not one hundred."

"I know."

"How'd you cover it?"

"Your house. I can't sign over mine. I pay for it, but it's still—"

"Yeah," he said. "I know."

"Your brother came down. He called me; I didn't have to call him."

Somehow this surprised Adam. They reached her battered car, an old Corvette that had so much rear-wheel-drive torque that it was absolutely impossible to drive in northeastern Ohio winters, a decision that said—*Chelsea!*—in flashing neon lights. It had been July when she bought it, and in July it worked great, so why worry about winter?

"I'm going to need to talk to him," Adam said as she gunned the big motor to life.

"He didn't put up any of the cash. Just signed what he needed to for the house."

"I'm not worried about that. It's about the reason all of this shit came down today. Whoever killed Rachel Bond doesn't have interest in her father. He has interest in Kent."

She turned to him. "In *Kent?*"

"The guy is contacting Kent for a reason." In the side view mirror Adam could see a cop standing outside the jail, watching, and he said, "Let's get out of here."

"You want to go home?"

"Eventually. First I want to see my brother."

There were countless reasons that Kent loved his wife and that he'd been attracted to her from the start, but central among them was strength. The calm kind of strength, the most rare and most difficult to obtain. She'd fostered it in her career, of course, but it had been there for as long as Kent had known her. She was unflappable.

That night he came up the stairs and found her standing on the threshold of Lisa's room, her hand tight on the doorframe and her head bowed. He knew the nature of the prayer, saw it in every tense muscle. She was praying against fear.

"They'll find him, Beth," he said.

She kept her head down for a moment, then lifted it and stepped away, leaving the door cracked open even though their daughter was adamant about sleeping with the door closed.

"I know they will," she said. She had moved to Andrew's door, and Kent joined her there, watched his sleeping son. A nightlight kept a dim glow, shadows around it. Earlier that fall, Kent had been talking on the phone while Andrew played in the driveway with a basketball that was far too big for him. It was getting on toward evening, and when Kent turned to the window he saw his son on the pavement with pools of blood spreading away from his head.

He dropped the phone in mid-sentence, and the plastic case cracked when it hit the tile floor. Was out the door with a scream in his throat when Andrew sat up and smiled at him.

It had been shadows, nothing more. The way he was lying there in the fading light, they'd looked like blood all around him. Kent carried Andrew in, picked up the phone, and apologized, tried to joke it off. "You've seen the kid's balance — it was a reasonable concern." Then he excused himself, went into the garage, and sat on the workbench stool until his hands stopped shaking.

Not my children, he'd thought that night, a desperate plea, *not mine, not mine, not mine. Tragedy will make its daily appearance, I know that, but please, God, not at my door. Not again.*

"What are you thinking?" Beth said.

That Sipes could have started with us, he thought. *That instead of Rachel, it might have been Lisa.*

"Maybe we should leave," he said.

"What?"

"For a while. Until they sort it out. Give the police time to find him."

"You want us to hide somewhere? Take the kids out of school? You quit coaching?" She shook her head. "If the police thought that was necessary, you'd know it."

It was what he needed to hear her say, it was the return to the calm strength he needed, the kind she'd provided to him so many times over so many years. And yet, somehow, it didn't steady him the way it usually did. She hadn't met Clayton Sipes. She hadn't seen his eyes.

Beth was saying, "We don't even know for sure that it's him," when there was a hammering on the front door. Three rapid reports—*thud, thud, thud.*

For a moment they both looked at each other uneasily, and then a voice called, "It's just me, Franchise," as if Adam could see through the walls of the house and knew exactly how they were reacting, knew that they were scared.

"Adam," Kent whispered, and when he turned to go to the door, Beth reached out and caught his arm. He looked back at her and said, "It will be fine," though he wasn't sure how he knew that. The last time Adam had come to their home it had not been fine.

He went downstairs and opened the door. Adam stood with his hands in his jacket pockets, and beyond him there was an old Corvette. Kent could make out Chelsea sitting behind the wheel. The engine was still running. Evidently they did not intend it to be a long stop.

"Hey," Kent said. "I'm sorry. It unfolded fast, but I should have called you."

Adam lifted his hands, palms out, a placating gesture. "Not a problem. Not a problem. It was a rough situation all the way around."

There was something false in it. He was too conciliatory. Allowing access to Marie's room was a cardinal sin, Kent knew that.

"You doing okay?" Adam asked.

"Yeah." Kent hesitated, then said, "You? How serious are those charges?"

"Ah, we'll figure it out, right? I mean, I'm clean, so they'll plea bargain."

"If there's anything I can do to help…"

It sounded pathetically formal, stilted. Adam gave a wan smile, glanced back at Chelsea in the car, and then returned his focus to Kent, and the smile was gone.

"Who left the letter?"

Kent was silent. His only operating instructions from the FBI were not to disclose his suspicions about the identity of Rachel Bond's killer.

Adam leaned his head to the side. "Kent?"

"I don't know."

"Bullshit," Adam said, and there was bite to his tone that made Beth come down the steps. He looked over Kent's shoulder and saw her and there was a pause as they studied each other, Kent trapped in the middle of the gaze.

"Relax," Kent said, and he wasn't sure which one of them he meant to direct it to.

"Salter told me the guy who left you the letter was one of your buddies from the prison," Adam said. "Someone who was in *my home*. Tell me who he is, Kent."

Kent said, "I haven't even talked to Salter."

"No. You talked to the FBI."

He knew that much, then. What detail they had provided to him Kent couldn't guess beyond the obvious fact that they had not inquired about Clayton Sipes directly. Kent took a deep breath and said, "Adam, I'm sorry. For all of it. But you need to go home, keep your head down, and stay out of trouble. There's nothing in this for you but—"

"He killed her, you son of a bitch," Adam said, the words rising in volume but not in speed, no rush to temper, just a steady climb toward the summit of rage. "At least I'll admit that I sent her to him, but you *brought him here.* How are you going to handle that? Are you going to pray with him again, Kent? *He put a bag over that girl's head and watched her drown inside it, do you understand that? Do you have…*"

He had just taken his hands from his pockets and coiled them into fists when he came to a stammering stop. Whatever words — or punches — had been about to come were lost as fast as embers beneath rain. Kent saw the change and turned his head to follow his stare.

Lisa was awake. Standing at the top of the stairs in her pajamas, eyes bleary but concerned, staring down at them. Watching her uncle.

Kent said, "Beth," but Beth was already moving, taking their daughter and shuffling her toward the bedroom, whispering that everything was fine. By the time Kent looked back to Adam, his brother was stepping away.

"You need to think about them," Adam said, gesturing at Kent's wife and daughter. "I know what you believe, Kent, I know how you are, I know who you'll trust. Salter, the FBI. And I know that you look at me and you see… shit, I don't even know what you see. But I can tell you that it's wrong. What I'm thinking about is exactly what you *should* be thinking about. I'm going to have to answer for what I've done. You will, too."

There was no heat to his words. His eyes were still on the spot where Lisa had just been standing, and he looked as troubled as Kent ever remembered seeing him, as unsteady.

"We're both going to have to answer for it," he said, and then he turned and walked off the porch and back to the Corvette.

27

ONE OF KENT'S STRUGGLES, and they were many, was with his language. Locker room talk was a product of testosterone, nerves, and macho competition. Always had been, always would be. Kent, who had been raised in locker rooms, and whose father had been one of the most impressively profane individuals he'd ever known — *The secret, boys, is in the verbs. Everyone uses the adjectives, but you've got to pick unique verbs* — wanted to run a clean locker room. That started by keeping his own tongue in check, which was a far more difficult ordeal than anyone probably would have guessed. He'd been nurtured on profanity; it came as a reflex.

That morning he got as far as "worthless cock —" and was about to employ the unique verb when he saw his son's head snap up. Kent bit down the rest of the sentence, and that was too bad in a way because it was one that would have impressed the heck out of his coaches, who didn't think he had it in him. Neither, though, did his son, and he wanted to preserve that for as long as possible.

"Daddy?"

"Sorry, buddy. I'm good. We're all good."

But his hands were fists at his sides down below the kitchen island, where Andrew couldn't see them, and when he brought in a breath it was through his teeth.

The arrest had made the front page of the paper. Kent shouldn't have been surprised—there weren't many big stories in Chambers right now. There was his undefeated high school football team, and there was Rachel Bond. Of course her case would stay on the front page.

He hadn't counted on the photograph, though.

In the photograph, Adam was in handcuffs, head down, a cop on either side, and just in front of him another officer stood beside a cruiser with a bloody towel held to his face.

LOCAL BAIL BONDSMAN ARRESTED AFTER SEARCH IN BOND HOMICIDE CASE

Adam Austin, 40, of Chambers, was arrested on preliminary charges of assaulting a police officer, resisting law enforcement, and battery after police attempted to serve a search warrant at the local bail bondsman's house as part of the investigation into the murder of 17-year-old Rachel Bond. Police said that Adam Austin, brother of Chambers High School football coach Kent Austin, has not been named as a suspect in the homicide, but that his professional interaction with the girl provoked "avenues of interest," according to Lt. Stan Salter of the Chambers Police Department.

Salter deemed the incident an "unfortunate situation" and declined further comment, saying the pending criminal charges against Austin are a separate matter from the Bond homicide case. Salter also said he could not provide details as to what led police to seek a search warrant for Austin's home and office, and was unable to confirm whether any articles of evidentiary value were confiscated during the search.

"This is part of a process," Salter said. "It is one of many searches conducted in that process. We will release more information when it is suitable to do so."

The rest of the article included a short biography of Adam, and that of course carried a mention of Marie. No accusations were made, careful journalistic distance was upheld, and yet in the gaps between what police confirmed and what they did not, dark suspicions would flourish. Why would the police have sought a warrant? Why would anyone possibly try to prevent the search if there was nothing to hide? Why would any man of pure heart do anything but assist? That photograph — Adam in cuffs, a bleeding officer at his side — would tell people more than the text. Or so they would think.

It's not about Rachel Bond, Kent wanted to tell them all. *You've got to understand that it is about my sister, and when it comes to my sister, Adam is not quite right. You cannot expect the same reactions from Adam if it involves my sister. You'd understand a little better if you realized that all they needed to do was stay out of her room.*

While his children shouted at each other upstairs — Andrew had apparently walked into the bathroom while Lisa was *"working on my hair!"* — Beth emerged around the corner, stepping into the kitchen, and headed for the coffee. She stopped when she saw his face.

"What's wrong?"

He slid the paper across the countertop, and she did what everyone in Chambers would do: looked at the photograph first.

"Kent…this is going to be really bad for him, isn't it? This is going to be really bad."

"Yeah."

"Do you think he'll be ready to see it? Handle it?"

"I don't know what Adam's ready for," Kent said. "I really do not know."

* * *

There was always a newspaper on the counter in the morning; Chelsea brought it in before she fed the snakes, and Chelsea was always up ahead of Adam. It was usually turned to the police beat column, jail bookings being of paramount importance to them. Today there was no paper in sight. Adam poured his coffee and walked to the sink, where she stood washing dishes, wearing one of his sweatshirts and a pair of loose cotton pants. Soft music played from the little iPod dock on the counter. A dark, brooding rock tune by Brian Fallon. *I kept my secrets far from your condition. And in the explosions, they both were just powders...*

He leaned down, kissed the back of her neck, and said, "You can let me see it."

She rinsed a glass, dried it, and her shoulders rose and fell with a deep breath.

"It's not good."

"You can let me see it."

She went into the garage to get the paper then, which had already been tossed into the recycling bin, leaving him alone with the soft sad song. *Did you say your lovers were liars? All my lovers were liars too.*

When she brought the paper back inside, she dropped it on the table without a word. Adam studied the picture and, in a perverse twist of the mind, found himself thinking, *I look big, and I look mean,* with a touch of pride. Old habits, maybe. Memories of the days when his picture was in the paper often, and the bigger and meaner he looked, the better. That was an acceptable version of the traits; this was not. He pushed the paper aside.

"Thought you wanted to read it," Chelsea said.

"I said I wanted to see it is all," Adam said, and felt like a child. He had thought he wanted to read it. The headline and photo were enough, though. Seeing the spread scared him, but not for any of the reasons people might expect—public perception or jail time. The thing that scared him was that Rodney Bova was unlikely to miss this, and if Rodney Bova understood, then Adam's best hope for success was dead.

He said, "I should talk to Rachel's mother. I'll need to clear some things up."

"Or let it go." Chelsea had her back to him, standing in the living room, and when he looked at her, he saw that she'd taken one of the snakes out of its tub. The python coiled around her arm, then slid up her shoulder, its wedge-shaped head bobbing, gliding past the row of silver loops that lined her right ear. She knew that he hated the snakes, never wanted to touch them, and he couldn't help but feel that she'd removed it to keep him at a distance.

"No," he said. "No, I cannot do that."

She didn't answer. The snake's tongue flickered, its eyes on him, its thick body slinking past her neck now as it slithered from one shoulder to the other. *Why does she have to come with the snakes?* he wondered, and then he looked down at the photograph of himself and thought she was probably asking herself something similar.

"I can't, Chelsea."

"You could," she said. "But you don't." She put the snake back into its plastic tub and slid it into place against the shelves. "I've got to see Travis today."

"Why?"

"He's my husband."

"Why?"

"Is that a new question or a repeat?"

"Both."

She turned and faced him then, folding her arms under her breasts. "He knows by now, Adam. I need to address that in person."

He hated the idea, but what could he say about it? It was her husband.

"You want me to go with you?"

"No, I do not."

He was glad of that, and didn't know why he'd even offered. "Why haven't you left him?" Adam said.

"He's in jail."

"Wonderful reason to stay with the guy, yeah."

She didn't waver. "I didn't think it was the best time to hand him papers, at least."

"Otherwise you would have? If he was out, you'd be divorced?"

"I don't know."

"How in the hell can you not *know?*"

She shook her head as if it were a foolish question. He felt anger rising, and though most of it was directed at him, he wanted to push it outward, and there she was. He turned from her and found the wet dishtowel and squeezed it, bleeding water out.

"Fair enough," he said. "I've never understood why you were with him, so I guess it's reasonable that I don't understand why you won't leave him."

"I was with him," she said, "because when he told me he loved me, he meant it. And you know what, Adam? Back then, it felt like something. It felt like enough."

"And now?"

"Now, I'm..." she stopped, shook her head again, and waved her arm around at the house, and him. "Now I'm this. I don't know what else to tell you."

"What do you want from me?" he asked.

"For you not to have to ask that damn question, Adam."

"Huh?"

She shook her head. "Forget it."

"No. What?"

"You just do what you want. I'm curious to know what it will be. Have been for a while."

"Meaning?"

"You want me to be with him, Adam? With Travis?"

"Of course not. It is what it is. I deal."

"You deal."

He nodded.

"If you don't want me to be with him," she said, "why not ask me to leave?"

I believe my trouble and your trouble shook hands, Brian Fallon sang, and Adam snapped off the music.

"That's not my decision, Chelsea. You married him. You want to leave him? Then do it. You haven't so far."

"And you haven't asked."

"I'm supposed to, what, propose divorce? You want me down on one knee? Do I take the ring *off* your finger, is that the tradition?"

"Forget it, Adam."

He started to argue. Started to say that, no, he wouldn't forget it, they needed to finish this conversation, needed to understand each other, needed to finally put into words all the things that should have been said long ago but never were.

Instead, though, he let her go.

28

GHOSTS AND GOSSIP FLOATED like vapors around Kent on Monday. He heard the names — Rachel, Adam, Marie — in flickering whispers and then they were gone as he turned to face the source, everyone looking away or offering awkward encouragement: *Hang in there, Coach.*

He was used to attracting attention from the students as he passed through the halls, those who were impressed by him or those who wanted to impress peers by showing their contempt for the football coach. Today was different, though. The teachers almost as bad as the kids. Several who had expressed no interest in the team before stopped him to talk about the upcoming game. Others who usually would have settled instead for quick nods and averted eyes.

That afternoon he left a message for Dan Grissom, the minister who had joined him on the speaking visit that included Clayton Sipes, asking for a call back. It came quickly.

"I'm trying to verify my own memory, Dan," Kent said.

"What does that mean?"

"Do you remember my encounter with Clayton Sipes this summer?"

"I do," Dan said, low-voiced, steady, the way he always was.

Kent closed his eyes and said, "Did I taunt that man, Dan?"

"*Taunt* him?"

"Yes. He was...challenging me. And I'm just trying to remember what I said. I can remember it all fine from my perspective, but I need yours. I need some objectivity."

"You didn't taunt him," Dan said. "I would not use that word, no."

"Well, what word would you use? I know that you told me to be careful with him. I remember you saying that, it's vivid, because you'd never said that about anyone else before."

"Yes. That's true."

"Why did you with Sipes, then?"

"I didn't like the way your exchange went."

"On which end?"

"Both. He was disturbing. I won't deny that; I'd been around him before and he'd exhibited the same behavior then. But with you...he, well, I'd say he got a little more intense."

"I used the same word today with the police. When you told me to be careful, though, I had the sense that you thought I'd already made a mistake. I'm looking for honesty, Dan. This guy may have killed a girl, and he may have sent me a letter about it. Don't worry about my feelings. Tell me the truth."

"I thought you'd made a mistake, yes."

Kent nodded as if Dan could see him.

"But I thought you made a mistake as a minister, as a witness, not in any sort of dangerous way. When I told you to be careful with him, I meant that your response was too combative. It's a fine line, what he asked you to tread, and I just thought...I thought it was indicative of a problem you might have in the future. You want to show firm faith, but quiet strength, I think.

That's a personal opinion. And with Clayton Sipes, you treated it more like..."

"Like what?" Kent prompted.

"I was looking for a better word, but what I was going to say was a trophy. You asked if you taunted him, and the answer is no. But you carried your faith like a chip on your shoulder. I don't fault you for that. Responding to aggressive questioning about your faith is hard. I just saw no gain to the way you approached it with Clayton. You just held firm ground."

"I should have yielded?"

"No. You should have engaged. Tried to find a better dialogue. These were the thoughts I had at the time, and they were relating to your ability to make an impact, Kent. That's all. What you're wanting to know now, I'm afraid, is whether you could have brought this down upon yourself in some way. Whether your response to Clayton Sipes that afternoon makes you *responsible* for something he might have done afterward. No, Kent. No. Don't let your mind go down that road. It's treacherous ground."

"All right."

"You've done good work," Dan said. "Don't lose sight of that. You've done good work."

It was the same message Kent had for his team after every season-ending loss.

Rodney Bova was home when Adam dropped by, answered the door with a nervous expression and kept it cracked just enough for conversation.

"What's the problem?" Bova said.

"I'm hoping there isn't one."

"Then why are you here?"

"Because it's my job. You've got a preliminary hearing this week. Going to make it?"

"Yes. Of course."

"Good," Adam said. "I can't afford to have anything go wrong. I'm crossways with the police myself right now, actually."

"I saw that," Bova said, and Adam watched him very carefully, looking for any sign that he'd been informed that his Mansfield connection was of interest in the Rachel Bond homicide investigation. There didn't seem to be one. This was good. This was critical.

"Feeling your pain, in other words," Adam said. "First time I've been in this situation. You doing all right otherwise? You need anything?"

"What I need is for my attorney to prove that somebody set me up."

"Any luck with that?"

"Finding out who did it? No. Not yet."

Adam gave that a thoughtful look, as if he were really brooding over the problem, and leaned against the wall, gazing up the street.

"Issue is, why would someone have the desire to bring this kind of trouble to you? I mean, this thing, it's not fooling around. A pretty serious takedown attempt. And for what?"

"I have no idea."

"Regardless of whether you've got an idea, you're going to have to *create* one, right? You can't just sit back and plead for mercy, Rodney. The judge doesn't listen to that sort of shit. What you need to do is put pressure on the prosecution. Create a sense of doubt. Then maybe they drop the charges. I've seen that happen a hundred times."

Now Bova was interested. "How?" he said. He'd opened the door a little wider.

"Suspects, Rodney. Suspects. Who do you know who's been in trouble? Who can you use to distract the police from yourself?"

"I'm not rolling on anyone."

"Rodney?" Adam held his eyes for a long beat. "Better be damn certain of that choice. Because sometimes, even the people we trust let us down. Even the people we love. So I'd have some long conversations if I were you, and I would try to see who might be bullshitting you. Otherwise, brother, you're looking at a long stretch. I know your judge. She's not forgiving with weapons charges. Not a bit."

Bova looked sick. Adam grabbed his arm. "Listen," he said, "you do what you want on your defense. Got nothing to do with me. But you miss that court date, and I'm coming for you."

"I won't miss it."

"I'm glad to hear it," Adam said. "Good luck, brother."

He turned and left.

The tracking device had logged four locations for Bova's movements during the weekend, and Adam visited them all after he left Bova's house. A Home Depot, a grocery store, a Walmart, and a Wendy's. Bova had spent the day running errands, nothing more.

Unless, of course, his Mansfield Correctional friend was at one of those places. Maybe they'd met in a parking lot. Maybe the unknown friend from Mansfield worked at the Wendy's. That would be easy enough to determine, if Adam had the name. All he needed was the name. And his brother had it and would not share it.

Adam sat in his Jeep after the addresses had been exhausted and thought of Kent's refusal and felt the fury building again and tried to will it aside. There were other ways to learn the man's identity. He had to pretend Kent wasn't even an option. Pretend he had no brother at all.

Being alone was not the same as being helpless.

He drove to Mansfield to get the answers he needed.

* * *

Adam had been to the prison before, but he didn't know any of the corrections officers there. Nobody said a word to him about his recent media appearances as they checked his ID and listened to his explanation that he was working for the family. He felt something strange in that silence, thought they should have shown more interest. He was hopeful for Jason Bond's cooperation but not guaranteed of it. If the man called off the interview, there was nothing Adam could do. Bond had agreed to see him, though, and that was something.

They were left alone in a visitation room, glass between them, and Bond looked a great deal different from the photographs Adam had seen. His hair was short and gray now, he was clean shaven, and he weighed a good forty pounds less than he had at the time of his booking. He took his seat, studied Adam through the glass, and said, "Penny hired you?"

"That's right."

"She don't have money to waste, would be my guess."

"She's not spending any."

"Yeah? Who pays you then?"

"Nobody."

Jason Bond thought that over and nodded. "I'm glad to hear it," he said. "Because you can't be very good. I've already said all I can say. Got nothing new for you."

"It's all new for me, Jason. There's a difference between police and a PI. What you've told them, they don't necessarily tell me."

"What I've told them, I won't necessarily tell you."

Adam nodded, then leaned forward. "She came to me," he said. "With your letters. The real ones, and then the fakes. She wanted an address, wanted to be able to keep contact up with you. I found it."

Bond didn't say anything.

"She went to the place I told her to go," Adam said, holding the man's stare. "Do you understand that? I cannot let that go unsettled."

"Should have stayed the hell out of it. You and your brother both."

"I've got nothing to do with my brother."

"No? He was the one who told her to write. You were the one who helped her keep it up. That's a coincidence?"

"It actually is," Adam said. "Small town, Jason. Small town."

"Your brother's been here."

"You meet him?"

"Nah. Came in to preach, basically. Had the Bible and all. Wasn't really for me."

Adam nodded. "Who do you know who *did* go to hear him?"

"I'm not sure."

"You need to be. I need you to be. Think about it. Remember it."

Bond said, "Whoever killed her, you think they knew your brother? Met him in here?"

"Yeah."

"Why don't you ask him, then?"

"I'm asking you."

"Man, I do not know the answer. Like I said, I wasn't there. He came in the summer. Reason it stood out to me then was because he's from Chambers. The coach, you know. I follow the team, see the scores, at least. But I didn't meet the man."

"Does the name Rodney Bova mean something to you?"

"No." He said it firmly. Adam was waiting for a sign of a lie, but he didn't find one.

"You're sure."

"I've never heard the name. Yes, I'm sure."

Adam considered, trying to think of what else he could ask, how he could ensure that this visit had not been wasted, fruitless.

"When my brother came here," he said, "was there word about it beforehand? Some sort of opportunity to sign up? You said you chose not to go."

"It's optional, yeah. Like any of those groups. Outreach shit. They bring in all kinds, man. Preachers, sure. Football coaches. People who want us to grow plants, pet dogs, whatever. Everyone has an idea, right? Everyone's got a cure. And most of us, hell, the only get-right meetings we care about are called parole board."

"But there's an official posting, something like that?"

"We know when they're coming, at least."

"The prison would have records, then. They'd know who went to what program?"

"Yeah, I'd expect so."

Adam nodded. They would not turn the records over to him. They could be subpoenaed, though. Maybe. It would take Penny and an attorney, but maybe he could make that happen.

"Do me a favor," Adam said. "You ask around. See who was there when my brother came. See what they remember. If anybody stands out. More importantly, you see if they remember anyone who was released this summer. Can you do that?"

"I don't know. I'm not a big talker."

"Someone murdered your daughter," Adam said, "by impersonating you."

He let that sit between them for a moment, and then he said, "Ask around, Jason."

Jason Bond nodded. "I've been trying to figure it out, you know. A reason some asshole would have targeted my daughter? Would have even given a damn where I came from, what I've left on the other side? Nah. I can't figure that."

"You wish you could," Adam said.

"Hell, yes, I wish I could."

"You can rest easy on one part of that. Whoever did it wasn't targeting you."

"You say that like you're sure."

"I'm sure."

Bond nodded again, and Adam could see that this disclosure mattered to him. It was a comfort of some kind. One he needed.

"All I know is, I hope when they get him, whichever one it was, they send him back here. And then he's dead. Because, buddy? I might not have known her. But that was my daughter. That was my daughter."

Adam said, "You won't have the chance to kill him."

"Yeah, I know, they'll send him somewhere else."

"Not what I mean. I'm not going to leave that chance on the table. For you, or anyone else."

Jason Bond looked at him for a long time. Then he said, "I hope you're just as nasty as you look."

"Haven't let anyone down yet," Adam said. "Not on that front."

29

I**T WAS OBVIOUS FROM THE MOMENT** Chelsea returned that
she'd been drinking. Adam watched as she tried—with
slower hands than normal—to catch the rats and feed the
snakes.

"How'd it go?" he asked finally.

"He wasn't happy."

"How are you?"

She caught one of the rats on the fifth try, then held it in a
cupped palm as she moved toward the snakes. Slid out one of the
tubs, dropped the mouse inside, then slid the tub back into place.
The rat scampered, searching for an exit that did not exist, and
the python lifted its head and studied it, tongue flicking, but
made no move. Yet. He knew that he didn't have to hunt in this
place. The rat would be there. When he was hungry, he would eat.

"How are you?" Adam repeated.

"Ashamed. Angry. Relieved."

"Where did you leave it?"

"He told me not to come back."

"I'm sorry."

"They were my vows, not yours."

"I'm sorry," he repeated.

"Where were you today?"

"Mansfield."

She turned to face him. "The prison?"

"Yeah."

"You saw her father?"

"Yeah."

"Had to be tough." She crossed the room to join him. Lay down on the couch, curled up like a child, and rested her head on his lap. Closed her eyes. He was surprised at how vulnerable she looked, how fragile. She always put out strength like body heat, and he'd grown content in that, relaxed by it, comforted by the knowledge that she didn't *need* him. Because of that, he could not fail her. Love without burdens. Or could that really be love?

"I've got something to show you," she said. Eyes still closed.

"What's that?"

She opened her eyes and looked into his for a long time. Then she rose and walked to the bedroom. When she returned, there were a few sheets of paper in her hands. She dropped them onto his lap and went into the kitchen to get a beer, removing a second one for him. He took his eyes off her and looked at the papers in his lap. He didn't need to read much. The heading identified it as a petition for divorce.

"You filed?"

"I haven't yet. I'm going to." She returned and handed him the beer. Her dark hair was pulled back into a ponytail, and she looked so young, a decade younger than she was.

He didn't know how to answer, so he looked back at the papers, read the legalese as if somehow it had significance beyond that single word. Divorce. Finally she said, "Adam, it's not a riddle. There's no paragraph in there that will tell you how to respond. So... just respond."

He said, "It's too fast. He just found out yesterday. You just got hit in the mouth with this. Don't rush the decision because of that."

"Don't rush."

He nodded.

"Take a look at the date on those, please."

The date at the top, which he'd read right over, was May 1.

"You had these drawn up in May?"

"Yes."

"And didn't move on it."

"No. But I'm going to now. Don't worry, I'm not asking for your encouragement. I'm not going to ask anything from you. It's the right thing to do, and I should have done it before. I shouldn't have kept this sad state of limbo going. I'm embarrassed that I have for so long. When you say I just got hit in the mouth yesterday, you're right. That doesn't mean it made my decision for me, though. The decision had already been made, but…apparently I needed to be pressured to follow through on it. Sometimes that's not a bad thing. A little pressure can help."

He said, "Coach Ward loved it when teams blitzed Kent. He thought he played better if he had less time to think."

For a moment she just stared at him, and then she started to laugh.

"What?" he said.

"I tell you I'm leaving my husband and you reinforce it by equating it to a linebacker?"

He felt a smile creeping onto his face, which seemed impossible for this moment that had been so heavy. "Sometimes it's a safety on the blitz," he said. "Even a cornerback."

"I stand corrected," she said, and then she put her hands on his face. Kissed him once and said, "No pressure's coming at you, though. Understand that? I'm doing what I needed to do. I'm not asking anything of you."

"You're not asking me to stay."

She shook her head. "Not asking you to go, either. Definitely not that. We'll see, right?"

"Yeah," he said. "We'll see." It was hard to keep the smile off now. He looked down at the papers in his hand and realized for the first time how long he'd hoped to see them. He wanted to be something real with her. It was startling to feel just how badly he wanted it.

"It won't be easy on you," he said.

"I'm aware of that."

"All right."

"I also just lied to you," she said.

He raised his eyebrows.

"Not about this. When I said I wasn't going to ask anything of you. I won't when it comes to us. I'm going to with something else."

He waited.

"Let the Rachel Bond thing go," she said.

He didn't answer. She wouldn't look away from his eyes and finally he lifted the beer to his lips, drained the rest of the bottle.

"It's dangerous for you, Adam," she said. "You're facing felony charges. You'll get those reduced without much of a problem. Clean record, and *that* situation, people searching Marie's room? You'll get it pled down. As it stands now. If you keep pushing, though? If you keep pushing, it'll get bad. Fast. And for what?"

"For *what*?" he echoed.

"Yes," she said, calm. "For what?"

"Someone killed that girl, Chelsea. Someone pretended to be her father, baited her with her own damn heart, trapped her and taped a plastic bag over her head and watched her try to find air that wasn't—"

"Stop," she said, looking away, one hand raised. "Please. I

don't need that. I understand all of that. It's terrible. It must be dealt with. By the police."

He exhaled and looked away from her and she reached down and forced his face back toward her, forced his eyes back on hers.

"Please," she said. "Give them some time. Step back. Breathe. Understand that it wasn't your fault, that she's not Marie, and that you can't atone for anything here. They don't take any points off this scoreboard, Adam. I won't tell you all of the things you refuse to hear and have refused to hear for more than twenty years. I'll just ask you this: please, step back."

"In the right way," he said.

"What?"

"I can step back if it's done in the right way."

This wasn't the answer she'd been looking for, so he tried again.

"I want to move on," he said. "Understand that? I do."

Her eyes doubted him. He kissed her forehead to break the stare, then went for a second beer.

"Here's to moving on," he said, and she seemed to find more comfort in him this time, because she smiled as they clinked bottles. He hoped she believed him. He was serious about this, more serious than she knew. He wanted to move on. There were just a few things to be done first. He could try to explain that to her, or he could simply do what she had done back in May — have things in place when the time came to act. When it did, then he, too, would be clean and able to move on. She was correct that you could never set the past right, but you had to part ways formally with your mistakes, just as she had done. He did not want to live with her amidst secrecy and lies, but he could make his own plans, and when the time came to act, he would tell her. He promised himself that, then realized that he was still holding her divorce papers as they toasted and drank, reluctant to let them go.

30

222 MICHAEL KORYTA

THE COACHES HAD A GROUP film session after practice that night, and it went late. Kent had told Beth not to expect him for dinner, but he hadn't intended to be as late as he was. Part of that was inability to focus. He'd broken his no-phones policy five times, calling to check in with her. Was everything all right, were the doors locked, was the alarm on?

His staff asked no questions, but he could tell from their exchanged glances that they had their suspicions about the situation, and he felt like Colin Mears, the target of everyone's silent sympathies and worries, striving for a normalcy of routine that was impossible to achieve.

He didn't know how much progress they had made. The defensive strategy was sound, but on the other side of the ball, so much depended on Colin Mears. Would he make catches?

He was pulling into his driveway when the headlights of the Explorer passed over the front door and he saw the man waiting for him on the front porch.

For an instant, he wasn't sure how to react. It was so startling that he didn't have the good sense to be afraid. In this neighborhood, where he'd lived for nine years without so much as hearing of a burglary or a domestic dispute, where he'd raised his family in peaceful suburban security, he lacked even the instinct of fear. All he felt was confusion until the man rose from the stoop and walked into the lights, toward Kent, who registered his face before he registered the gun in his hand.

Clayton Sipes.

Clayton Sipes was at his home. Beth and Lisa and Andrew were here.

"They're fine, Coach. Everybody's fine so long as you want them to be."

Sipes spoke loudly, no fear of attention from the neighbors, as if he, too, had assessed the environment and determined it without threat. He was the alpha predator here, and he knew it, and was comforted by it.

Police, Kent thought, *call them, call for help.*

But even as he reached for the phone, Sipes rounded the front end of the car and pointed the barrel of the gun at Kent's head.

"It's up to you, Coach. What happens to them tonight is up to you. Choose wisely."

Should have driven into him. Should have floored it while he walked in front of the car, what's the matter with you, the chance was there and you missed it and now it's too late.

"My suggestion," Clayton Sipes said, "would be to turn off the car, get out, and talk with me. Now, that's only a suggestion. The decision is yours. I'll wait while you make it."

Kent didn't move. He had his foot on the brake and his cell phone in his hand, and he was still trying to think of ways to use them, was considering the car alarm—Could you set it off while you were inside? Did the panic button even work if the key was already in the ignition?—when Clayton Sipes waved his free hand toward the dark house where Kent's wife and children slept and said, "They're waiting, too, Coach."

Kent shut off the car. The lights stayed on while he opened the door and stepped out but went dark a few seconds after he swung the door shut. Then they were alone in the night. The autumn wind blew steady and cold. Sipes stood five feet back, far enough away to avoid grappling, close enough for an easy kill shot on Kent.

"If you've hurt my family, I will—"

"No," Sipes cut him off. "No, that's not one of your options, Coach. You don't get to offer threats. You want to use the word *if*, then I can use it for you. *If* I pull this trigger, your children may grow up with the memory of finding their dead father in the driveway. *If* I pull this trigger, they may not grow up at all. *If* you insist on acting like you have any control over this moment, I may introduce myself to your wife tonight. There you go. There are some *if*s for you."

His voice was as it had been in the prison. Amused menace.

"You remember me, Coach?" Sipes said when Kent had been silent for a while.

"Yes."

"You remember my name?"

"Yes."

"Have you said it recently?"

Kent hesitated, a mental double-clutch, looking at two options and not liking either but knowing he had to let the ball go in one direction or the other, and then he shook his head. "No."

"Coach." Sipes sounded thoroughly disappointed, a scolding parent. "Imagine if I had decided before this moment that I'd kill your children if you told a single lie. I could have done that. I still could. Now, would you like that answer back so you can try it again?"

Kent nodded. His hands were trembling.

"Have you said my name recently?"

"Yes."

"To whom?"

"The police."

"And why did you say it?"

Kent's eyes were adjusting to the dark now, and he could make out the man's features, the slick shaved head and the ring of blue ink tattoos around his neck, his skin pale, body lean and strong. He was wearing jeans and a black T-shirt that fluttered in the wind. He should have been cold, but he showed no trace of it, looked comfortable and at ease.

"I said it because you left that letter."

"You called the police over a letter? That's strange. Do you often contact the police with concerns about your mail?"

In the house, just above Clayton Sipes's head, a light flickered on. A television. Beth was awake. Awake but oblivious.

Look out the window, Kent thought. *Please look, please see.* But did he really want her to? Or was that the worst possible thing, was that—

"Coach?"

Kent's eyes returned to Sipes. It was harder to speak now, knowing that Beth was awake. He said, "I called them because I thought you killed Rachel Bond."

"There you go, Coach. An honest man is better received on earth and in heaven."

Turn the TV off, Kent thought, afraid to look at it now, the pale light seeming impossibly bright. *Please, Beth, turn it off.* He didn't want Sipes to be reminded that there was other prey here; he wanted nothing from his family but darkness and silence.

"Why do you believe I'm here?" Sipes said. "Why do you think I came for you?"

"I don't know."

"You've forgotten me?"

"No."

"Well, that was the implication. Words can wound, Coach.

You should be careful with them." Sipes had lowered the gun. It was pointed at the driveway now, and Kent could reach him before he lifted it, but he would not try, not with Beth and the children inside.

"I came," Sipes said, "to test the strength of your promises."

"I don't understand."

"When you met me, what did you offer me?"

"Help," Kent said.

"Help?" Sipes gave him mock astonishment. "I recall it differently. I recall a promise. That was what you called it, at least. You told me that there was no fear so strong that it could break your faith. Is that correct?"

"That's what I said."

"Is it what you believe?"

"Yes."

Sipes smiled, and Kent was terrified by how genuinely pleased the man looked.

"Good for you, Coach. Good for you." He spread his arms wide, the gun rising with him. "I'm here to see if that's true. You should appreciate that. Every man learns so much about himself in a crucible. You told us that. I believe you felt you'd learned all you needed."

"No. That's not —"

"I was in your sister's room," Sipes said, and Kent fell silent. "Interesting, how your brother preserved that. Do you visit often?"

Kent shook his head.

"Somehow, I didn't think that you would," Sipes said. "I'm curious, Coach, do you know who Gideon was in the Bible? Do you recall his significance?"

Kent loathed the name Gideon. But, yes, he knew.

"I've read the story," he said.

"So have I. Gideon was God's own chosen warrior. What was

the phrase? 'For the sword of the Lord and of Gideon,' I believe. Does that sound right?"

Kent didn't answer.

"Do you think Gideon Pearce was the sword of the Lord, Coach? Was he God's chosen warrior?"

"He was a different man than the one in the Bible."

"Astute. I think there's more than a little irony in the names, though. If Gideon was the sword, Coach, then I'm the prophet. I think you'll remember my words often in days to come. I suspect you already have been remembering them. What was it that I told you the day we met?"

"You promised me that you could replace my faith with fear."

"And what did you say?"

The wind was stinging Kent's eyes, but he didn't look away. "I disagreed."

"You certainly did. And now we'll see, won't we?" Clayton Sipes said. "We'll see. I probably should be on my way. Unless you'd like me to go upstairs and watch TV with Beth?"

The twin terrors of realization that he knew she was awake and that he'd said her name froze Kent. He offered no response at all, and Sipes smiled again, then put out his left hand.

"Keys, please."

"What?"

"To the car, Coach. It doesn't seem prudent for me to walk."

Kent hesitated again; he wanted the man gone, but his house keys were on the same ring as his car keys.

If he wanted in tonight, he'd already be in, he told himself, the worst kind of reassurance, and then he passed him the keys. When Sipes accepted them, their hands brushed, and Sipes smiled at the touch.

"You think you're learning already, don't you?" he said. "I can see it in your face. Already trusting your decisions. Wonderful stuff, Coach. Wonderful."

He walked around Kent, with the gun lifted, and stood with his back to the driver's door.

"Go on up to the porch," he said.

Kent headed for it, stepping sideways, and Sipes shook his head.

"Prove you trust me," he said. "Turn your back, Coach."

For an instant Kent thought about charging him, though this was the worst opportunity he'd had since he arrived, Sipes was too far away now.

"Trust me," Sipes whispered.

Kent turned and walked for the house and waited for the shot. When the car door opened, he tensed, bracing his body for pain that never came. He kept moving, was up the steps and onto the porch when the engine roared to life and the headlights spread his silhouette over the front door. He stopped there, stood with his back to the street until he could no longer hear the tires on the pavement. He turned back then and saw the taillights of his car vanishing up the street, and the strength went out of his legs and he had to put his hand on the wall to steady himself. He watched the dark empty street and waited for balance to return and then, when it did not, he knocked on the door of his own home and cried out hoarsely for his wife.

31

IT TOOK STAN SALTER ONLY ten minutes to arrive, but when he got there, he informed Kent that none of his cars had located the Explorer yet. Kent had called 911 maybe ninety seconds after Sipes drove out of his neighborhood, but already he was gone.

"We'll locate it," Salter said.

"He won't be in it by then."

"Maybe he will."

Kent just shook his head. They were standing in the living room and Beth was upstairs with the kids, who'd woken to the sound of their mother's panicked voice as their father called the police for help. She'd composed herself quickly, or pretended to, at least, and she was with them now, calming, soothing, assuring them that everything was fine downstairs, the police just needed to talk to Dad for a few minutes, that was all, no problem, nothing to be scared of.

In the living room, Kent dropped onto the couch and braced his forehead with his hands as he told Salter what had happened.

"Did he explicitly say that he murdered Rachel Bond?" Salter asked.

"It was clear, yes."

"Did he admit to it, though? Or was he content to let you think that?"

"He didn't lift his right hand and swear to it on the Bible, Salter, but he had no problem acknowledging it."

Salter let him snap, watching him without judgment, and somehow in the man's patience Kent found only more fury.

"If you find him now, he'll be happy to discuss it with you, I'm sure. But you need to *find* him, damn it." His voice rose too loud at that, went into coaching tone, and he regretted that immediately because he knew it would carry upstairs, undermining every soothing word Beth was offering to Andrew and Lisa.

"Was there anything in the conversation," Salter said, carrying on as if Kent hadn't spoken, "that felt foreign to you?"

"Foreign?" Kent stared at him. "The man was pointing a gun at me and talking about murder. It all felt a little foreign, yes."

"I mean anything that didn't ring true to your past conversations. To the letter he left."

"No. It was the same guy, using the same words, with the same sick mind. Only this time he was holding a gun and he was at my home. Those were the elements that changed. Just two of them, but a significant two."

"The exchange about Gideon Pearce—was that in keeping with what you'd discussed on your visit to the prison?"

"Absolutely. He didn't mention the biblical version then, but I'm sure he's had plenty of time to read since I last saw him. And he admitted to breaking into Adam's house. He said that he'd been in my sister's room, described the way Adam has...has re-created it."

"Offer any sense of *when* he was in there?"

"No." Kent stood, walked to the window and looked at the dark street, then said, "I should tell Adam about that."

"I'd prefer you didn't."

"What?"

"This is a complex investigation, Coach. We've got to be extremely cautious in how we proceed. You understand that. You've told me repeatedly how intelligent Clayton Sipes is."

"If the man was in my brother's home, Adam has a right to —"

"Not from you," Salter said. "We will handle discussions with your brother. I would think you'd understand, after his latest response, the need for discretion in approach."

"I'm not asking you to put up a billboard announcing the guy is a suspect. I'm asking you to disclose to my brother the identity of the person who broke into his house. I don't think that's unreasonable."

"Nor do I. But let us do it. I'll consult with Agent Dean and we'll discuss it with your brother. Until then, we need your cooperation."

"My cooperation," Kent echoed. "Well, you've got it, Salter. When a murderer shows up at my door, the first person I call is you. There's cooperation. What I need from you is *protection*. Can we discuss that?"

"You'll change the locks? Keep the alarm in use at all times?"

"Obviously. But I don't consider that proper security at this point. We're talking about a murderer, someone with a history of stalking. I'd like to hear some better ideas for protecting my family than 'use the alarm.'"

"We'll have patrols in your neighborhood regularly. Multiple passes per hour."

"Can't we have someone here around the clock?"

"We don't have that sort of manpower. I'll make sure we have a *very* visible presence, but I can't promise twenty-four-hour surveillance."

"Are you getting closer to finding him?"

"We're moving as fast as we can in every facet of the investigation."

"That's evasion. Not an answer."

"We're working with the FBI and the Ohio Bureau of Criminal Investigation and we're making progress. Your continued cooperation can only help."

Kent nodded, but he couldn't look at Salter anymore, was feeling more detached from the man with every word. *It took them four months to find Marie's killer,* Adam had reminded him, *and then it was police in another town who caught a lucky break.*

He couldn't argue with that. He'd tried to once, and now he wondered why.

Part Three

TROPHY HUNTERS

32

Adam and Chelsea were just out of the shower, coffee brewing but not yet poured, when they heard the sound of a car pulling into the driveway. Chelsea looked out the window, and Adam said, "Who is it?"

A pause. "Your brother."

"What?"

She nodded.

He'd had all the conversation he cared to have with Kent in the locker room the other night, and he didn't like him showing up at Chelsea's house. It felt invasive. Why couldn't he have just called?

"I'll deal with it," Adam said, and then he went outside, closing the door behind him.

"What are you doing here?"

Kent said, "For what it's worth, I wish I'd called you before I gave the police the key."

Adam stared at him. "All right."

"I wish I'd called," Kent repeated, and he was jingling his car keys in his hand. Restless, nervous. Adam figured this visit had to be Beth's idea. Kent didn't want to be here. Kent was even driving Beth's car instead of his own. The obviousness of it was infuriating.

"Came all this way because you need to apologize? Shit, Kent, just because I've been charged with a crime doesn't mean you need to start making your standard visits. Wait until I'm in jail, with the rest of your favorite people."

It was unnecessarily harsh, he was trying to pick a fight, but he just wanted Kent gone. He didn't need to be preached at, didn't need apologies, didn't need whatever attempt this was to make real a relationship that no longer existed.

"Focus on your football team," he said, losing some of the edge. "My problems are not your fault or your concern, and I won't keep you off the front page for long, don't worry. I intend to be a little more silent running at this point. I won't give them anything else to—"

"I would like to borrow a gun," Kent said.

Adam stopped talking, tilted his head, and stared. "Say that again?"

"The man who killed Rachel Bond was at my house last night. While I was gone, while Beth and Lisa and Andrew were alone inside."

Adam said "Holy shit" in a soft voice, and now he came down the steps to join his brother. "Did he try to get in, or—"

"He waited for me. He was on the front porch. Stole my car. Just drove away, and they haven't found him, and I don't think they will. I've called the police, and they're doing patrols. I've done everything I can think to do, but I...I..." Kent stammered, swallowed, and gathered himself. "He was at my house, Adam. With my wife and children inside."

Adam felt the sensation he'd had when the stained-glass turtle broke in Marie's room, a pool of rage with no drain, seeking any fissure, any release.

"We can't have that," he said. "No. We will not have that."

Kent wiped a hand over his mouth. "I'm trying not to scare Beth. But I ... I'd just like to know there was a means of protection if we needed it. Do you have a gun? May I borrow one?"

"I have plenty. But do you know how to shoot a gun, Kent?"

"I was hoping you'd teach me. I'm not asking to become a marksman overnight. I just need to be able to ... if I needed to use it, I'd want to know that I could."

Adam nodded. "All right," he said. "You got some time now, we can go to the range."

"I've got time."

"Hang on."

Adam went back inside, and Chelsea gave him a questioning look.

"Finding the son of a bitch who killed Rachel Bond might be easier now," Adam said. "He's apparently stalking my brother."

"You're serious?"

"Yeah." He took a deep breath, feeling the aches left from the Taser, and then he said, "I'm going to be late getting to the office, Chelsea."

She did not argue.

He took Kent to a private range south of town. It wasn't really a range at all, just property belonging to a gun nut who'd devoted several acres of field to shooting, put in a berm, and let friends come by. Adam was a friend. The guy wasn't home, but Adam knew he wouldn't care.

"You're not going to be a marksman overnight, just like you said," he told his brother. They'd driven separately; Kent said he wanted to follow. "So the right choice is going to be something that can do a lot of damage without requiring a lot of accuracy. I like this one."

He handed Kent a revolver with rubber grips and a short stainless steel barrel. "Kind of a unique piece," he said. "It's a pistol that will shoot both shotgun shells and .45-caliber bullets. Holds five rounds. We'll load it with two shells, and then three of the .45s. If the guy is anywhere near you, you'll put him down with the shotgun shells."

Adam had dragged out a sheet of plywood, something they used for holding targets in place. He stood fifteen feet in front of it, pointed the revolver, and fired twice. Clouds of woodchips flew into the air.

"Trust me," he said. "That'll put him down. And then..." He walked over to the plywood, placed the barrel just an inch away from its surface, and fired again. This time a .45-caliber bullet blasted through. "You make sure he stays down."

He looked back at Kent. "Can you do that? Because you're going to need to. The shotgun rounds will drop him, but they won't keep him down. Not a four-ten shell, which is what this takes. So you'll need to be able to finish it. Can you do that?"

"I hope not to have the opportunity to find out."

"Can you do it?" Adam said. "Because otherwise, there's no point, Kent. Go buy some pepper spray and hope the neighbors hear when Beth screams."

Kent winced. Then he extended his hand for the gun.

"If he is in my home, and I need to defend my family, yes, I can put him down. I will."

Adam nodded, then spun the cylinder open to reload.

"Let's see how you like it," he said.

Kent shot thirty of the shotgun shells and fifty of the .45 bullets. His hand was steady and his aim wasn't bad at all. An old quarterback. The hand-eye coordination hadn't left him yet.

"If you can do that," Adam said, watching him, "you'll be fine. Just remember to *finish* it. Don't leave him on the floor and go for the phone. Finish it."

Kent turned the gun over in his hand, studying it.

"Pretty nasty weapon."

"It is. Not a very accurate pistol, but for close-range self-defense, I think it's the best thing out there."

"What kind is it?"

"A Taurus. The model is called the Judge."

Kent seemed uncomfortable with the name, which was funny, because it had never struck Adam as having any significance. "The idea was that a judge would wear it in court, I think," he said. "Close-quarters protection, you know, if some lunatic rushed the bench or whatever."

"All right. Listen, I appreciate it. The gun and your time."

"Stop, Kent. It's my niece and nephew you're talking about. I know you don't want to worry Beth, but I could work nights outside the house. She'd never know I was there."

"I don't know if it's a good idea, with the police going by all the time. They'd notice you, and with the situation you've got right now..."

"I'll deal with it," Adam said. The wind was blowing hard, flattening the dead grass around them, a few raindrops beginning to spit out of a gray sky. "Keep this in mind, though: you don't want to come across a day when you wish you'd asked me. Remember that."

"You're willing to?"

"I'd like to."

"I can pay you. It's a job, and I wouldn't—"

"Are you really saying that to me?"

Kent stopped talking and nodded. "Sorry. And, yeah, if you don't mind...maybe just tonight at least. Until I hear from the police. I'm sure it will be soon."

"Right," Adam said. "It will be soon. Now, do you want to tell me about this asshole? You say you *saw* him. Spoke with him."

"Yes."

"Do you know him? Can you identify him?"

"I know him."

"Yeah?" Adam's heart rate had been up all morning. Now it seemed to slow, as if his blood had thickened, and he had to wet his lips before he spoke again. "If you're so confident, and the police already are looking at this guy, why hasn't there been an arrest?"

"He's missing."

"Missing."

"Was released from prison this summer. Hasn't made his parole meetings. There was already an arrest warrant. They're looking for him."

Of course there was already a warrant. Of course they had already been looking for him. Of course they had fucking lost him and not bothered to find him before this.

"Who is it?" Adam said.

Kent was silent, eyes back on the gun, still turning it over in his hands, adjusting his fingers around the grips as if they were laces on a football. Adam remembered the way he'd looked when he knew the defense was going to bring a blitz. So restless, so amped. He'd execute against it just fine, but Adam had always hated the body language he displayed in the pocket when pressure was coming. Even though he could handle it, he looked like he couldn't. He looked scared. Today Adam watched him handle the gun and thought, *He knows, damn it, he knows this prick's name, and he will not tell me.* The anger began to surge and he fought it back, reached out and grabbed Kent's shoulder and squeezed.

"Tell you what, Franchise. You asked me for a favor, and I granted it today. I'm going to do the same now."

"Adam, the police told me that I had to—"

"Let me get the favor out before you say no," Adam said.

Kent glanced at the hand that was still on his shoulder. The flesh over the knuckles was swollen and dark. "What is it?"

"There's a place I'd like you to see."

"What's that?"

"The spot where Rachel Bond died," Adam said.

"I don't need to see that, Adam. And you shouldn't be there."

"I'd like you to have a look."

After a long time, still staring at Adam's bruised hand, Kent nodded.

33

They sat on the dried, cracked wood of the dock across from the cottage, where they could face it but not have to be on the property. The fall winds had torn most of the leaves from the surrounding trees, and already the place was dull and colorless. None of the cottages were in use. The lake was as gray and still as concrete. Kent didn't like to look at the house, the kill house, the spot where Rachel Bond had sought a final, impossible breath, so he kept his eyes on the water while he told Adam about the visit to Mansfield in the summer.

He didn't need to worry about confiding in his brother, his brother with whom he had no real relationship, his brother who had been on the front page of the paper in handcuffs, a bloodied police officer beside him. The police might have asked Kent not to share theories about Clayton Sipes, but Kent was, after all, his brother's keeper now. Chelsea Salinas had said so herself as he signed the paperwork. Kent had failed to inform Adam of the police search, and he had seen the result. Adam was in trouble because Kent had not prepared him. It could not happen again. For Adam's own good, Kent needed to keep him informed.

Prepared.

"Gideon Pearce was never at Mansfield," he said.

"What's that got to do with anything?" Adam asked.

"I've been wondering if they knew each other. If the card...
that connection to Marie, if that came from research, or from
Pearce. It wouldn't have been hard to find out about. A little while
with old newspapers. But I wonder if they knew each other."

"It's possible."

"I found out that you met Pearce."

"Yeah?"

"Police told me. You went in to promise him you'd kill him."

Adam cleared his throat and spat into the water. "That's right.
If I could have gotten to him that day, I would have done it then.
That son of a bitch's eyes, Kent...shit, I'd have killed him for
the eyes alone, just for the way he looked at me."

"Amused," Kent said.

"Yes. That's the word."

"Did you mean it?"

"Mean what? That I would kill him?"

Kent nodded.

"Hell, yes, I meant it. One of the saddest days of my life was
when he died, Kent. Really. Because I'd been waiting. I wanted
the chance. I didn't care how long it took. If Gideon Pearce had
come out of that prison a white-haired old man pushing a walker
and hooked up to a frigging oxygen tank, I would have cut his
throat."

His voice was steady. No shouting, no rage, no choked-down
tears. Just steady and firm.

Kent stared at the house where traces of crime scene tape lay
limp along the weathered porch railings, where a man he'd met
months earlier had set a trap for a child and ended her life. The
wind pushed in a short, chill gust, flapping the tape and putting
a momentary gray glitter over the pond. Then it was still again.

"Why'd you ask me that?" Adam said.

"I'm worried about you, man."

"Worried?"

"Yeah. You do a lot of talking about killing. First Pearce, now…now the man who killed Rachel. The other day when you came to the locker room, it was the same talk. I understand the anger, I just…you know, I want you to find a way to be at peace."

Adam was watching him with an odd smile. "You want me to *be at peace?*"

"Of course."

"All right. I'll work on it. You know what would help put me at peace today, Kent?"

"The name."

Adam nodded. "Yes. I would like the name."

"I was told not to share it. That the police would."

"You're worried about your family," Adam said. "Already told me that. Beth's scared, you're scared."

"We'll be fine."

"I hope so. But let's remember something — this son of a bitch also came into *my* home. He got that football card from inside the place where I live. And you don't think I'm entitled to a name? Suppose this guy is hanging around. Following me, following Chelsea. Wouldn't it be useful if I could recognize him? Now, if something happens, and you know that had you just shared a name and let me find a few photographs, it might have prevented things…how will that sit with you, Kent?"

It was a shrewd argument. Adam had always been shrewd, and he'd always understood how to motivate Kent.

"I'll spend every night outside your house watching for this bastard if you want me to. Every night. You have a chance to do the same. To help protect me."

For a long time, Kent was quiet. The image from the front

page of the newspaper returned, that glimpse of his brother's flat eyes and bloodied hands. *If Gideon Pearce had come out of that prison a white-haired old man pushing a walker and hooked up to a frigging oxygen tank, I would have cut his throat.*

"Clayton Sipes," Kent said. He'd expected it to come out in a whisper, but his voice was clear and strong.

"Clayton Sipes." Adam echoed the name in a measured way, like someone tasting wine before accepting the bottle.

"I brought him here," Kent said, and then he told him all that had happened, from the first prison encounter to the previous night. "He's here because of me."

"Seems that way." Adam's voice was tight. He removed a cigarette and lit it, and it took him five tries to get the flame steady, his thumb trembling on the lighter's flywheel.

"You want to say something about the circumstances, get it out now," Kent said. "Go on and tell me that if I didn't go parading into prisons with a Bible, none of this would have happened. Go ahead and tell me that and whatever else—"

"Shut up, Kent."

Kent looked at him, watched Adam exhale a wreath of smoke.

"You're thinking it," he said. "And in this case, at least, you're not wrong."

"All I am thinking," Adam said, "is that a man who killed a seventeen-year-old girl is out there, free. And he walked into my home—into *our* home—and removed our sister's property. That's what I'm thinking."

Kent didn't answer. The sun hadn't so much as creased the clouds but still he had his Chambers High cap pulled very low over his eyes.

"Do what you say," Kent told him, "take precautions, stay vigilant. But the other ideas…Stay away from those thoughts, Adam."

"It's hard to stay away from thoughts, Kent. They have a way of chasing you down, you know? It's awfully hard to relocate from your own mind."

It was quiet for a moment. Adam blew smoke into the wind, and then he said the name again, soft. "Clayton Sipes." He nodded, and he looked calm when he rose to his feet and offered Kent his hand. "You did the right thing, telling me."

"I hope so."

"Trust me," Adam said. "You did the right thing."

34

CLAYTON SIPES HAD EARNED his sentence at Mansfield for sexual assault and stalking. He'd been twenty-nine when he went in, was thirty-four when he walked out.

And vanished.

August. The same month Rachel Bond's supposed father had contacted her to inform her of his release.

While he read about Sipes, Adam smoked four cigarettes in the time he usually allotted for one, not realizing it until he picked up the pack and was startled to find it empty. There was a tightness along the back of his skull. Too much nicotine, too fast.

The tightness didn't go away when he stopped smoking, though. It spread into his neck as he sat at the computer and studied the newspaper accounts. Sipes was from Cleveland, and had been arrested there, a janitor at Case Western Reserve who'd taken an unhealthy interest in a twenty-one-year-old engineering student at the school. The first complaint from the victim had been made three years prior to the final arrest, proving that it was not a passing fancy. Clayton Sipes, the Gideon who'd

258 · MICHAEL KORYTA

tracked Rachel Bond, was a patient man. Devoted, diligent. Kent was not likely wrong in his assessment of the man's guilt. Sipes fit the profile.

After multiple unsettling encounters with Sipes, the victim had finally contacted the campus police, saying she felt intimidated. Sipes was warned to keep his distance, but he was not charged. Five months later, having failed to keep his distance, he was fired from the school and charged with harassment. The charges were dropped, but Clayton's interest in his victim was not. Over the following two years, he appeared again and again. Calls were made to the police, investigations were conducted, but Sipes had alibis, and no further charges were filed. It wasn't until three years after he first showed interest in the woman that he was finally arrested on her porch, carrying a .357 and wanting to talk to her about the way she was ignoring her destiny, while fondling her breasts and smelling her hair. She managed to hit redial on her cell phone while it was in her pocket; a friend picked up and, thankfully, amazingly, listened instead of dismissing it as an accidental call. Heard enough to hang up and dial 911 and the police found them there on the porch. Sipes was charged with violating a restraining order, sexual assault, stalking, and attempted kidnapping. The last charge was dropped, and he was sentenced to eight years, which meant with good behavior he'd walked in five.

Adam's first step was this background gathering. He had to understand Sipes before he began to hunt; that was imperative. He had to know as much as possible about the man. There was a hot anger in his blood as he looked at the booking photographs, saw the smirking, taunting eyes projecting indifference to the camera.

Lost him, he thought. *They lost him.*

How? How could you take your eyes off a sick son of a bitch

like that? How could you just let him wander away, show no real concern over it until a girl was dead in a ditch?

He could not set things right. He understood that was beyond his grasp; there was no way to make such a thing right. But there was penance, and there was punishment, and those things he could administer.

He wanted to begin the search now, but by the time he'd finished his information gathering, it was edging toward dusk and he knew he needed to be at his brother's house. Days he would hunt, nights he would stand guard. And if Sipes would cooperate and make another appearance, then the hunt wouldn't even be necessary.

Come to me, Adam thought as he slipped on a shoulder holster and put a Glock semiautomatic into it. Chelsea watched with unsettled eyes.

"You think this is a good idea?" she asked.

"The son of a bitch showed up at their house already, Chelsea. He may come back. I will not leave them alone to face that. I can't."

She accepted that with a nod, then kissed him and held him. A little too tight, a little hard. Not happy that he was leaving, and he understood that, but there was nothing else to be done.

"I've got to go," he said, pulling free from her. "I'm sorry."

That night Beth kept calling Kent back to bed.

"Please," she said. "You're just making me more nervous when you pace like that."

He wasn't pacing, he was trying to make sure they were prepared. He checked the alarm, he checked the windows, he watched the yard. Stood on the porch with his fingers wrapped tightly around the rubber grips of the Judge — he had not shown it to Beth; she was opposed to firearms and he doubted even in this situation would be accepting of one in their home—and stared into the shadows, listening to the dry leaves whisper over the boards of the privacy fence, every one of them sounding like a potential footstep at first, and then, when he realized it had not been, more like a soft, taunting laugh.

"I won't sleep ten minutes if you keep wandering the house," she said. "The police are making their patrols. Trust them."

Right. The only problem with that was he'd observed only two passes from a police car in the last three hours. They were present, sure—Salter had been good to his word on that—but the gaps in between patrols went thirty or forty minutes. That was so much time. Kent, who spent his life watching games decided in a matter of seconds, who had once lived with his sister only a ten-minute walk from their own high school, understood just how little time it took for things to go terribly wrong.

"Get some rest," Beth told him.

He promised her that he would, and then he lay beside her and watched the bare limbs cast dancing shadows over the windows and kept his eye on the jacket pocket in which he'd left the Judge. When he could tell from Beth's breathing that she was asleep, he slipped out of the bedroom once more, went downstairs, and called Adam.

"You out there?"

"I'm here."

"Nothing's happening?"

"Police cruise by pretty often. If they're aware of me, they aren't bothering to stop and talk. If they're not aware of me... well, that's hardly encouraging."

"I appreciate it," Kent said. "Really. The extra presence is a good idea."

"I'd have been here regardless of whether you agreed to it. You make sure you're carrying that gun from here on out, though."

"I just want it at night."

"You don't need to worry about nights. Nights I'm here. Days, you should carry it."

"I'll keep it in mind. Listen, if the police stop to talk to you, please tell them —" He was interrupted when a shadow moved on the steps, nearly shouted before he realized it was Beth, watching him. "I've got to get back to my family," he told Adam. "Thanks again."

"Sure thing, Franchise."

When he hung up, Beth said, "Who are you talking to?"

"My brother."

"At one in the morning?"

"He's outside."

"What?"

"He's watching for Sipes."

"Just…sitting in his car?"

"I guess so, yeah. It was his idea, Beth. And I thought it was a good one."

"Why outside?"

"Huh?" He honestly couldn't follow the question.

"Why did you make him watch from outside? If you think it's a good idea to have him here, let him be *here*. Inside the house."

"I didn't want to frighten the kids. Or you."

"You were just asking him if the police had stopped him, Kent. And he was just arrested for fighting with the police. You think the best idea is to have him outside in the car? Open the door and let him in."

Adam could not remember the last time he'd been in his brother's home. He hadn't crossed the threshold since the day he punched Kent in the driveway.

Now he stood in the living room in the dark, wearing a Glock pistol in a shoulder holster, unconcealed by a jacket, and shook hands with Beth, who was making an obvious effort not to stare at the weapon. Obvious and unsuccessful.

"You don't have to do this," she told him.

"I think it's a good idea. And I was fine in the car, that didn't bother me at all."

"That doesn't make any sense," she said.

He didn't argue.

"Well ... I'm going to bed," she said. "Thank you, Adam."

"Of course. Get some rest, Beth."

She went to the bedroom then, leaving him alone with Kent in the living room.

"How you doing, Franchise?" Adam asked. "Holding up?"

"I'm all right."

"How's the team look?"

"I hardly saw them today, honestly. Mind was elsewhere."

"Relax on that," Adam said. "Focus on them, let me deal with this."

"You and the police."

"Right." Adam nodded and said, "Tough one coming up. Saint Anthony's."

"Big game."

"Probably the biggest. You get past them this week, you ought to be in pretty good shape if your boys stay healthy. Think you can do it?"

"I need Mears to make some catches."

"You ought to play him at corner. Or let him play defensive special teams at least."

"What?"

"I watched that kid. Tell you what he needs: to do some hitting. Tough for a receiver, right? But if he gets the chance to knock somebody down, put blood in somebody's mouth, he'll come back around. Right now he's got to leave some emotion out on that field. He wants to play fast and mean. It's hard for him to do that split out wide right. The kid needs to hit."

"He's never lined up at corner in his life, Adam."

"He's played against them his entire life. Let me ask you this: if that kid had arrived on your team with stone hands, where would you have played him? He's, what, six-two and runs the forty in four-point-four?"

"Four-three."

"Okay. Now imagine that he couldn't catch a cold if you spotted him a sneeze in the face. Where do you use him?"

"Corner, sure. But I can't move him over there now."

"In press coverage, you could. He knows all the routes, he's got all the right skills. If it's just him covering another kid running the same routes, with less impressive skills, he'd be fine."

Kent shook his head, then said, "Why are we talking football?"

Adam smiled. "Following your own advice, Franchise. Let's distract ourselves, right?"

"Right."

"Wait on the police to do their jobs."

"Yes."

"It's a damn good plan," Adam said. "Now, go back to your wife, and get some sleep."

"Feel bad, making you stay up."

"I won't have any trouble with it."

That was the truth. It was as he'd explained to Chelsea: the four people in that house were all that he had left of a family.

When Kent went upstairs, Adam sat alone with his hand on the butt of his gun and watched the street, and he had no trouble staying awake.

35

HIS TEAM LOOKED CRISP on the field, polished, and Kent almost wished that they weren't. He felt swollen with emotion and wanted to find an outlet, release his fear and frustration into a shouting session about poor effort or technical shortcomings. The kids didn't grant him that, though; they were precise and intense, and it was a short practice because most of the time would be devoted to watching video, the only chance all week that the coaches would have to review video of the opponent.

They went into the school, breaking up into offensive and defensive units to study football, sitting at desks in the same classrooms they'd so eagerly left an hour earlier.

The assistant coaches ran the video sessions so Kent could drift between the two groups and offer input to both sides of the ball. Today he started with the offensive group, where Steve Haskins ran through the various defensive fronts Saint Anthony's had played during the season. Unfortunately, there were a lot of them. Scott Bless liked to mix it up.

"Any additional thoughts, Coach?" Haskins asked Kent.

"Their cornerbacks are not fast enough to keep up with

Colin," Kent said. "They'll play a safety over the top, like we've seen all year, but these kids are a half-step behind, all the time. We're still going to have the vertical game there if Lorell can put the ball in the right spot. Think you can do that, Lorell?"

This was by design, of course. He wanted everyone to think his only question was with his quarterback's ability, that Colin's hands offered him not even a flicker of doubt.

"I can do that, yes, sir," Lorell said, but he was looking at Kent with a knowing stare. Colin wasn't looking at anybody.

"Glad to hear it," Kent said, "because those kids cannot keep up with him."

He nodded at Haskins, who moved on to blocking schemes for inside runs, and then slipped out of the offensive classroom, paused in the hall, and called Beth.

"Hey."

"Hey."

"Everything good?"

"Yes."

"Just checking," he said. It was the fifth call of this sort he'd made today. He was trying not to make so many, not to feed her paranoia with his own, but it was hard. He'd be focused on something and then he'd see Clayton Sipes, remember the intensity of his eyes and the way the prison's fluorescent lights had cast a shine on his shaved head, remember the way he'd smiled when Kent told him that there was no fear that could break his faith.

"Everything's good," Beth said. "Kids home, doors locked, alarm on."

"I'm not trying to scare you."

"I know."

"Home soon."

"Love you."

"Love you, too." He hung up and started for the defensive group, thinking about Agent Dean, who knew damn well that

Clayton Sipes had killed that girl. How in the hell could they not find him? It was the FBI, it was what they did, why couldn't they go out there and get it done? And why in the hell had Kent gotten into it with Sipes in the first place? Dan Grissom was right; he'd responded to the man's attack in the wrong way. He'd worn his faith like a chip on his shoulder and promised Sipes that nobody could knock it off, and now Rachel Bond was dead and Kent was calling his family every thirty minutes and if he'd just...

He paused halfway down the hall between the offensive and defensive classrooms, thinking of how many calls he'd made out of fear today and trying to remember how many times he'd prayed. Had he prayed? Surely he had.

But he couldn't remember.

He was preparing to kneel there in the hallway, a quick prayer but a needed one, when he heard the squeak of wheels on tile just before the janitor's cart appeared.

"Hey, Coach."

"Hey," Kent said, straightening. He didn't want to be seen on his knees, not even in prayer. It felt like weakness to him today. He listened to the wheels of the cart approaching down the hallway, found himself thinking, *Clayton Sipes was a janitor at a school, just like him, he was just like him,* and then he held the man's stare for a long moment, gave him a curt nod, and walked on toward the defensive classroom, head high, no longer bowed.

Adam slept for two hours in the morning, then went in to the office, where Chelsea was already at work, and began the hunt in the only way he knew how, treating Sipes not as a murder suspect but as a skip. He printed out an address history report, developed a list of neighbors from that, found phone numbers...

and stopped. Stared at it, shook his head, and swore softly. Chelsea looked up.

"What's the problem?"

"He's been in prison for years. Such a cold trail."

She leaned back in her chair, let out a long breath, and pushed her hair back over her ears.

"This would be Clayton Sipes you're talking about. Not one of our own skips."

He didn't answer.

"Adam, the police will —"

"No," he said. "No, Chelsea. I'm sorry. I understand what you're going to say, and why you're going to say it, and why I should listen to it. I do. But you need to know…" His voice faltered then, the way it did sometimes in Marie's room, and he turned his eyes from her and said, "A seventeen-year-old girl walked through that door and asked me for help. And, circumstances be damned, excuses be damned, I sent her to a man who murdered her. He's still out there. Not only is he still out there, he came to my brother's house with a weapon. My niece and nephew asleep upstairs. So, no, Chelsea, I'm sorry but I cannot listen even if I should."

She was silent for a moment, and then she said, "What do you need? To find him, what do you need, how can I help?"

He turned back to her then, and, God, how he loved her.

"It can't be neighbors," he said. "I've got to find someone close to him, someone with the sorts of ties that don't break no matter what happens. No matter what he did. I've got to find that person, and I've got to do it in a way that doesn't attract police attention. They'll jam me up, they'll make it so damn hard, make it hopeless. So I'm trying to think of a way to find that person. Nobody will turn over prison visitation. I've got one guy who I think might be it, but nothing's panned out there, so maybe I was wrong."

"How'd you come up with that person?"

"Looking for people who knew the property at Shadow Wood," he said, and he was thinking of what it would mean if indeed he had been wrong. Bova's court date was this week, his charges were serious. How in the hell did Adam go about putting that genie back in the bottle? He rubbed his eyes. He needed more sleep. Needed coffee. Needed a drink, needed—

"Find someone like you," Chelsea said.

"What?"

"You already said how to do it. You need to find the sort of person who would stand by him no matter what he did, right? Well, somebody had to post bond for him at some point. It wouldn't have been a stranger."

He lowered his hand, looked at her, and said, "You're brilliant, you know that?"

She didn't smile. Instead she said, "Be careful, Adam. Please."

Sipes had been arrested in Cuyahoga County, and his bail agent was someone Adam had known for years, Ty Hampton, a black guy who went about six-six and three hundred pounds. Adam had always figured Ty had fewer skips than the average agent because he wasn't the sort of man you'd want to come looking for you.

"He ran on you, eh?" Ty said when Adam explained what he wanted.

"A little worse than that," Adam said. "He's threatening my brother."

"Really?"

"Yeah."

"Man, I'm not all that surprised to hear it. Never did like that creepy asshole. I didn't have any trouble with him, I just didn't like him."

"I'll pay you whatever you think is fair," Adam said.

"Stop it. If I called you with the same problem, would you want my dollars? Just give me a few minutes. I'll find it, call you back."

It took him less than ten minutes.

"Got your name," he said, "and I hope it helps. Bond was posted by his half brother. Now, this is old information, but I've got an address and a phone number. His name is Rodney Bova, and his number was —"

"I've got his number," Adam said.

"What? Damn, not a new name for you, huh? I'm sorry, man. Hoped I could help."

"You did," Adam said. "Ty, you absolutely helped. Half brother, you say?"

"Yeah. Same mother, different fathers, that's what I've got in my notes. You sure you don't need anything else?"

"No," Adam said. "I've already got that gentleman's number. I keep hoping it will pay off."

"Good luck, Austin."

"Appreciate it."

Adam hung up, and Chelsea raised an eyebrow. "Nothing new?"

"Nothing new," Adam said, and then he pulled open his tracking software and stared at the red dot that represented Rodney Bova's existence. He'd been right.

Move, damn it, he implored the dot silently. *Move. Go to him.*

36

AFTER PRACTICE KENT AND his staff met for an hour to discuss the offensive game plan, considering tight end seam routes and quick slants and bubble screens and all of the things that might work if their number-one receiver was done catching the ball. Then they emerged from the locker room and found Colin Mears sitting on the hood of his car, pointing toward them like an accusatory finger.

"What's he still doing here?" Byers asked, and then Haskins said he'd go talk to him, but Kent shook him off.

"I've got it. Go on home, guys."

He crossed the grass to Colin's car alone. It was cold out, and the boy's breath fogged the air. He'd been waiting a long time.

"You all right, son?"

Colin nodded. He had a tennis ball in his right hand. Squeezing rhythmically. Working on his grip strength.

Kent propped one foot on the tire of the boy's Honda. "Why are you sitting here in the cold, Colin? Last thing we can afford is for you to get sick."

Colin shifted the tennis ball from his right hand to his left, kept squeezing.

"I want you to know I'll make plays this week."

"Don't doubt it, son. You always have."

"Not Friday night."

"You worry more about your stat line or the scoreboard?" Kent said. He was studying the worn tire treads, not looking at the boy.

"Scoreboard."

"Then you ought to be happy."

"Yes, sir." He stopped squeezing the tennis ball, passed it from hand to hand, and said, "What's the deal with your brother, Coach?"

"Pardon?" Kent looked up now.

"Why were they searching his house?"

Kent was quiet, looking into the kid's intense eyes, and then he said, "Because they thought it might help. That's all you need to know."

"What more do *you* know?"

"Excuse me?"

"You have to know what they were looking for. It's your brother."

"The police don't always tell you what they're looking for, Colin. Sometimes they don't even know. It's about gathering—"

"What sort of person punches a cop?"

Kent stopped talking. He stared at Colin for a few seconds and then turned his face back to the field, where the blank scoreboard stood in ghostly silhouette, bare-limbed trees weaving in the wind beyond, and, out farther, the gray-on-gray line of the horizon, Lake Erie.

"Adam has some issues with his temper. Always has."

"The police went there looking for something, and he didn't want them to find it. He *punched a cop,* Coach. Who does that?

Instead of helping them, he tried to stop them. Why didn't he want them there? Why didn't he —"

"They were going through my sister's things," Kent said, and his own voice was angrier than the boy's, it was his lace-up-those-shoes-and-head-for-the-bleachers voice. "That's one of the things you don't understand, son, and you should begin to consider them before you start theorizing. Tell me this — how would you feel if someone started going through Rachel's room without explaining it to you? That's how Adam felt. I'm not defending his reaction, and I won't. It was a poor choice. He'd admit that. But he's got some problems with his temper, and the police found a sore spot. That's what happened. That's all. He's as committed to helping find this guy as anyone, Colin. I can promise you that."

Colin nodded. "Okay. It just... it surprised me."

"It shouldn't have. You understand the situation better than most. Rachel went to see him asking for help and she... she was less than truthful. You already know this."

"Yes, sir. I just wondered if he knew something. If you knew something. Because if there's anything you can tell me, it would help so much to have an idea of what's —"

"Police don't make a practice of sharing information with civilians. I know that it's hard. Remember that. I've been there. I wish to God you weren't there right now, but there's no stepping backward. We put our heads down and move forward. That's the only choice."

"I'm trying."

"I know you are. It's not a matter of effort, son. It's not something you can control."

The tennis ball slipped from Colin's hand. He tried to catch it on the bounce, missed, and then it rolled under his car. Kent blocked it with his foot, picked it up.

"How many of those have you done?"

"Had three thousand when you came out. Lost track then."

Kent had been ready to head home, but he looked at the kid now and then tilted his head in the direction of the locker room.

"Let's watch some video, shall we? A lot to work on."

Colin slipped off the hood of the car and they walked together into the locker room.

"You want to see Adam?" Kent asked, the words out of his mouth without a thought.

Colin looked both surprised and afraid. "Talk to him?"

"No. I mean on tape. See the kind of player he was."

The kid looked anything but enthused, but he said, "Sure."

"I'll just show you the last drive," Kent said. "Then we'll look at Saint Anthony's."

He wasn't sure why he wanted Colin to see it so badly. Maybe it was just a chance to leave a different image in the boy's mind from the one on the front page of the paper. That image wasn't fair to Adam, it was a preserved lie, nothing more.

The man's name is Clayton Sipes, Kent wanted to say. *He killed her, and I brought him here. It's got nothing to do with Adam.*

He couldn't say that, of course. He could play the video, though, could show Colin what Adam had been once, before he'd been the man in handcuffs and bloodstains on the front page. Kent hadn't watched it in years. He didn't like watching it. Hadn't even at the time, really; the only person in that stadium from Chambers who had not enjoyed every moment of the championship-winning drive was now their head coach. He'd had the tape converted to DVD years earlier, and now he slipped the disc into the player and turned on the projector and then it was 1989 and the Cardinals were playing Angola Central, the unbeaten and top-ranked Tigers.

"He played both sides of the ball. Fullback on offense. Best blocking fullback I've ever seen in high school. If you stayed behind him, you'd gain a lot of yards without breaking a sweat." He fast-forwarded through the first three quarters—Chambers had scored first, Angola answered with two in the second quarter, then fumbled to start the third and Chambers converted and it was all tied up. The Tigers made a beautiful drive, meticulous and precise, put it in the end zone early in the fourth and then went for two and got stuffed: 27–21 with 10:41 left in the game.

"Here we go," he said, and pressed PLAY.

The Chambers return man botched the kick, then got lit up and driven into the turf at his own four-yard line. The Angola fans were going crazy, and on the sidelines Walter Ward stood with his arms folded and his eyes flat. Kent was there, too, clipboard in hand, and he remembered that he'd felt sick, that he was suddenly just fine being the backup.

"What you're about to see," he said, "is not the brand of football we play. But it worked."

Adam was the last one out, his teammates already lined up as he entered with trademark slow swagger, a gentle bounce to his step, shoulders swaying side to side, head bobbing.

"Promise package," Kent said. "That's what this was called."

One wide receiver, split out right, one tight end, and a three-man backfield: two tailbacks, one left and one right, and a fullback ahead of them, a fullback who would never touch the ball, who was there just to lay the wood. That was Adam.

"Why 'promise package'?" Colin asked.

"Because we never lied out of it. Never tried to fool the defense. It was Coach Ward's baby that year. He loved it. From the first practice, he told us that we would never give them anything but what they expected when we went to that formation. It was a psychological thing, it was pure intimidation. We were saying, *Here we come, and you can't stop us.* The fullback is Adam. We called him the prophet. Those were the plays — prophet left and prophet right."

"Prophet?"

"When he took the field offensively, he told the defense exactly what was coming, that we intended to run it right down their throats." The name caught on Kent's ear now, though, it called up a memory of Clayton Sipes: *If Gideon was the sword, then I'm the prophet.*

Colin said, "Coach? What are you thinking?"

"Nothing," Kent said, but what he was thinking was that he'd talked about this play in his visit at Mansfield, he'd talked about this season and this play and the way being steadfast and diligent led to victory, the way you had to absorb the hits and shake them off. Prophet right, prophet left, he'd explained it all, explained the reward of the grind, the reward of endurance.

Colin's stare brought him back, and he tried to shift his mind from Sipes to football.

"It was a strange approach, because usually you treat play calling like a chess match. Out of this set, though, Coach Ward wanted it to be clear to every team that we were essentially saying, *Stop this if you can.* They usually couldn't, and that's the height of frustration for a defense. It breaks you down. Physically, sure, but more so mentally. Once you break their spirit, you own the ballgame."

First snap, and on the first run, Adam caught a linebacker who was standing too high, planted him in the turf, and Chambers was out to the twelve already, eight yards on the play.

"Wow, he could hit," Colin said.

Kent nodded. "Big kid, but just *hard.* Not gym muscle. There's a difference. You know that. Some guys are naturally hard. Coach Ward always called it loading dock muscle."

Second snap. A brutal collision. Three yards. First down. Now out to the fifteen.

"I was waiting for a change here," Kent said. "I figured we'd gotten our backs away from the goal line, would open it up a little bit more. But…"

Prophet left.

This time Angola brought a safety on a blitz, and he got through the line almost simultaneously with the handoff and dropped the runner. Chambers went back into promise package, back to prophet left. Gained four yards. Walter Ward refusing to blink.

Sixth carry, prophet right, fifteen yards, first down. Adam hit an Angola linebacker so hard going around the end that, two decades removed, Colin Mears winced. Seventh snap, prophet left, a bigger hole this time, fourteen yards gained, getting across midfield. Even on the poor audio of the old tape, you could hear the buzz in the stands, because everyone got it by now — Ward was going to make Angola prove they could stop this.

Eighth snap, nine yards, and the Chambers fans were beginning to roar.

"He has a broken hand from this point on," Kent said.

"Your brother?"

Kent nodded. "I was the only person who knew something was wrong."

"How did you know?"

Kent picked up the remote and rewound. "Adam used Jim Brown's technique."

Colin understood, because they'd talked about it before. A lot of kids — a lot of pros, even — liked to pop up after suffering a massive hit, to show how tough they were, show that they weren't hurting. The problem with that approach was that sometime you *were* going to be hurting. Then the defense knew, and they fed on it, grew strength from your pain. Jim Brown, the Cleveland legend, who took more abuse from defenses than maybe any other running back in history, had developed a system for that: he stayed down, rose slowly, and limped back. Every play. The defense never knew when he was hurting because he looked the same after every hit. He gave them nothing emotionally, nothing they could feed on. It was very different from the way Kent coached football—speed, speed, speed—but if you had the hitters, it was effective. Demoralizing. The defense played to hurt you, and they wanted to know when they had.

"Adam had a lot of adrenaline," Kent said. "Getting up slow was hard on him. So he developed this technique where, once he was down, he'd make himself squeeze the turf, first with his left hand, then with his right. It slowed him down. On Saturday mornings, he had to spend twenty minutes digging dirt out from under his nails. Because of course he refused to wear gloves. Or long sleeves under his jersey. He was one of those. Now watch what he does here."

On the replay, Adam cleared the hole, then got blown up by a linebacker and tumbled to the turf. One of the Angola players looked down—pointedly, obviously, and stepped on his right hand, then twisted the cleats.

Colin hissed in a breath. "Nobody saw that?"

"No. I missed it, even. But I saw this."

Adam was down, supporting his weight with his right forearm. He reached out and dug the fingers of his left hand into the field, then reached out and did it again.

"Left, left," Kent said. "He'd never done that before. That was when I knew."

Back on his feet and back to the line, and now it was prophet right, six yards, Adam dropping a 250-pound defensive tackle, just splintering him as the tailback scampered through behind, clear and untouched until he stepped out of bounds.

Angola thirty-two-yard line now, clock under six minutes, and the Angola coach was screaming at his guys. *They can't run over us! They can't run over us! Show some heart!*

Prophet left, twelve yards, and Colin said, "They're not even watching your vertical routes anymore. Those guys are open by ten yards."

He was right. The safeties were in the box and now even the cornerbacks were cheating down, trying to help stop the bleeding. All Pete Underwood had to do was throw it out there. But promise package was promise package. It told no lies.

Adam was the right player for it, no question. Last one into the formation every time, always with that bouncing swagger, and if anyone spoke to him he didn't respond, his focus was total, and he warned you of it with every step. *I am the hammer. You'll feel me shortly.*

"Coach Ward told me once that Adam should have been a boxer," Kent said. "That he would have been a nightmare, because he fed on the taste of the canvas."

"Meaning, what, he liked being knocked down?"

"It fired him up, at least. We scared teams with him out there. You'll see it by the end."

On the screen the action had paused, because Angola took a timeout. The defensive coaches were screaming at their guys, telling them this was it, stiffen up and shut them down, *show us some heart!*

The first play after the timeout was from the twenty-six, and it was prophet left, the eleventh straight running play, and on this one the instruction from the Angola coaches during the break showed itself. The linebackers weren't trying to separate the ball carrier from the ball anymore, they were trying to separate Adam Austin's head from his body. Two hits from two different directions, one a blatant helmet-to-helmet shot, and Adam rocked up and over and was on his back under the lights as the ball carrier ducked and spun and carried it to the fourteen.

Down on the field, Adam rolled over until his face mask was resting on the ground, and reached out with his left hand. Squeezed the turf twice. Rose.

Second and two, clock under five minutes. Prophet right and they lost a yard — the Angola defenders driving Adam straight backward and into the ball carrier to make the tackle.

Facedown again, two squeezes with the left hand, then back up. Third and three. Prophet right. The offensive line blew it again, they were getting tired. Gained a yard.

Fourth and two.

The Chambers crowd was quiet. Down on the sidelines Ward stood impassively, arms folded, and next to him a fifteen-year-old Kent Austin stared at the ground.

"Watch this," Kent said softly. "Watch what Adam does."

Back into promise package, only Adam didn't get down into his stance. He stood up tall and began bouncing on the balls of his feet, and against his sides he shook his hands.

"He was *screaming*," Kent said. "You could probably hear it at the top of the stands. Everyone thought he was just getting them fired up, and he was, but it was from the pain, too. See what he's doing with his hands? He's got broken bones sliding around at this point, and he started to shake his hands like that to call up the pain. He wanted to feel it, needed to feed on it. This was it, this was the ballgame, we *had* to get two yards."

The crowd saw Adam and heard him and found confidence in him, and now the roars were back, and feet were hammering on the aluminum bleachers and the play clock was counting down, and finally he dropped back into his stance, and then they went prophet right.

Helmet to helmet, the impact staggering, and then one

linebacker was down and another rose to replace him but fell as Adam drove forward and Evan Emory, the tailback, came in tucked behind him, chasing the tornado's wake. They blew out of bounds with a gain of four — first and goal from the nine.

For just a moment they'd been together then. Adam and Kent. The force of the play had carried Adam down out of bounds and right to where Kent trailed Coach Ward. When Adam got up, they were face-to-face, and Kent had said, "Nice hit," and he remembered that his voice had seemed impossibly small and weak. Adam spit out his mouth guard and a streamer of blood came with it, and he said, "We're almost there, Franchise. Almost there."

Back to the field, and Angola was broken. After that fourth and two, Angola's defense was done and they knew it.

"I wish Ward hadn't run it every play," Kent said. "Or he could have let him have a carry. Adam was on the field for every snap, we ran him fifteen straight times, seven of them with his hand broken, and on the stat line he never gained a yard. On the stat line, he's standing still." His voice had thickened, so he coughed to clear his throat and said, "Watch what the safety does here."

They took the snap, fifteenth of the drive, first and goal from the nine, and the line opened a nice gap and Adam came through it and the Angola safety, who'd dropped down in the box to stuff the run, winced ahead of the contact, stiffened up and turned his head a bit just before Adam hit him, just before Chambers cruised into the end zone for the score.

"He tried to get out of his way," Colin said. "He didn't want any piece of him."

"No, they did not. Not by then."

"They make it close on the next possession? Have a chance?"

"Nope. Turned it over on downs." Kent was suddenly regretting his choice to screen the game, and he didn't know why. He'd wanted to show Colin the way his brother played football, and Colin seemed impressed, so why did Kent wish he hadn't watched that tape?

"Let's look at Saint Anthony's," he said, getting to his feet. "That Angola game's more than twenty years old. We've got our own to work on."

37

THAT NIGHT ADAM WAITED until Kent called to tell him that the kids were in bed, and then he returned to the house to occupy his post.

"You haven't heard anything from the police?" Kent said. "Still?"

"Not a word. You get any updates?"

"Not today. They don't seem to be making much progress."

Adam didn't say anything to that. He was looking at the pictures in the living room and was amazed by how old Lisa was getting, how tall Andrew was. He never saw them. Lisa would remember him, but he wasn't sure that his nephew would recognize him. Adam had visited the hospital when he was born, and come by on his first birthday with a gift, but never again. He looked at the photographs and thought that the kid was getting old enough to be some fun.

"They're great kids," Kent said.

"I'm sure they are." He almost said *I'd like to get to know them,* but he stopped himself, turned away from the photos, glanced out at the street, and touched the butt of his gun as if to physically remind himself why he was there.

"You don't need to stay awake all night," Kent said. "Stay in the guest room if you'd like, or at least stretch out on the couch and get some—"

"I'm good."

"Okay." Kent hesitated, then said, "I watched the Angola game today."

"What? Why?"

"Wanted to show Colin Mears. You know, last time the school won state, all that."

"You'll get it this year."

"We'll try." Kent shook his head and said, "That was a hell of a game you played. That last drive…I mean, I remembered it, but watching it again was impressive."

"All I did was open some gaps. Evan Emory did the running."

"You opened craters. He could have done the walking, still would have scored."

Adam shrugged. "How's Mears?"

"Struggling."

"I'm telling you, let him hit."

"I know, I know."

Kent seemed to regret having brought it up now, which wasn't Adam's goal, but he didn't know what he was supposed to say about a twenty-two-year-old football game. He searched for something, some lighter memory from the pitch-black year that was 1989, the only year they had played together, and said, "You remember Tater?"

Kent smiled. "Tater Phillips? Yeah."

Tater was a backup offensive lineman who had earned his nickname for an unfortunate resemblance, in shape and speed, to a potato.

"I'll never forget the day Ward about killed him with the sled," Adam said.

That brought a laugh from Kent, and Adam was smiling, too, couldn't help it. Walter Ward had purchased a used tackling sled at an auction, which he then proudly set up in an open grassy area just outside the field—and at the top of a gentle hill. Featuring six angled tackling dummies connected through a steel frame, the sled was a massive piece of equipment, weighing hundreds of pounds. And mounted on wheels. Ward hadn't experimented with his acquisition yet, confident that he understood all there was to understand about a tackling sled, but he did not understand the locking brakes. They'd run through a few rounds of hitting before the sled began its trembling slide. Ward's first reaction when he realized it was going to roll down the hill was to tell everyone to get out of the way. It was about two seconds later, enough time to allow it to build a good head of steam, when he spotted Tater Phillips lumbering up the hill, late to practice after a trip to the trainer, his helmet on and head down.

"I thought I had heard Ward scream as loud as anyone could scream a hundred times before that," Kent said. "But that was when he was angry. When he was *scared?* Wow, he hit a different level that time."

Adam nodded. "It looked like some piece of farm machinery going at Tater. A combine or a thresher. Tater somehow oblivious to the whole thing."

"Tater usually couldn't get out of his stance in under three seconds, but I swear he covered fifty yards in three seconds when he finally saw it coming. He dodged it by an inch and then it wiped out the side of Byers's truck. Always so lazy he insisted on parking it at the curb instead of the parking lot. He's been in the lot ever since. I haven't given him grief about that in years. I'll need to do that tomorrow."

"Give him my regards," Adam said. They held the shared laugh for a few seconds longer, but then it was gone, and Adam was conscious of the holstered gun again, conscious of his job in this house. "All right, Franchise. Go to bed. I should be paying attention to the street."

The street stayed empty. Clayton Sipes made no appearance. Rodney Bova did not leave his home. They were patient. That was fine. Adam could be patient, too. There was another word for his kind of patience — relentlessness.

They would break at some point. One of them. And he'd be there when they did.

The next day, while Adam sat in the office and watched a red dot, Chelsea went to prison to tell her husband that she was going to file for divorce. Before she left, she told Adam that she was going to let Travis Leonard keep the house.

"You're the one who's been paying the bills on it for years," he said. "Why in the hell would you give up the house? It's the only thing he's got."

"That's why," she said. She was dressed unusually formally, black pants and a long-sleeved white shirt, crisp and ironed, as if she felt a responsibility to look professional delivering the news. "He had two things. Me, and the house. I'm not taking them both from him."

Adam gave that a slow nod, then said, "Where will you live?"

"It'll take some time to get everything done, to move out. It will take some time. But when it's done...we can talk about that, Adam. We've essentially lived together for a long time now. I'd miss that, wouldn't you?"

"Of course. I was expecting you'd stay with me."

She looked him in the eye. "Not at your house."

"What?"

"I can't live there," she said, "and I think it's time for you to consider moving on."

He didn't speak.

"You remember your sister, you think of her daily, you carry her with you," she said. "That's all good. Honorable, healthy. What you've created in that house is not healthy. Your brother is right about that. You've got felony charges to prove it."

"Cops break into my home and I'm supposed to —"

"They did not break in, and you knew they would be there. Let me ask you this: Why did you *really* swing on that guy? Because he was in *your* home? Was that really the reason, Adam?"

It was not. It was because the son of a bitch had been in Marie's room. Chelsea watched and waited and Adam looked away without answering.

"Okay," she said softly. "These are things to think about. It's time to move forward for me. I want to do it with you. But that's going to require both of us being willing to move."

She came around the desk, dropped to her knees, and sat with her hands on his waist and waited until he turned back to face her. Her dark eyes searched his, dancing as if she knew she needed to evade some of the things his eyes would show her to find the things that were true.

"Talk to Marie about it," she said.

His throat tightened. He had never told her, had never told *anyone* about his conversations with his sister. Chelsea would never have overheard so much as a whisper of Marie's name, and yet there was no doubt to her voice. She knew that he spoke to Marie, and she was not alarmed by this, or even surprised. The realization, and the way she'd just suggested he talk to her about this, crippled him. Before he'd chosen not to answer her; now he could not.

"Consider it," she said. "Talk it out. But be fair to me on it,

Adam. If you decide it isn't the right thing for you, okay. I'll
stand by you. But give it fair consideration. I want us to be
together, and that is not the right place. We need to find a new
one, and make it ours."

He nodded. She studied him, then rose, leaned over to kiss
him, and left. He stared at the door for a time, shook his head,
returned his attention to the computer screen, and pulled up his
tracking program. The red dot that was Rodney Bova held
steady.

He had not returned to the house since his arrest. Had planned
to every day but found an excuse every day, and there was work
to be done, searching for Sipes and guarding Kent's house and
trying to snag a few hours of sleep in the time between. This
afternoon he found no police in sight, no media, no curious
neighbors. He parked on the street and let himself in the side
door, which opened into the kitchen. He'd had new appliances
and countertops put in, replaced the floor tiles, but still it was the
kitchen of his childhood; you couldn't remodel that away. He
could almost see his father at the table, the bottle of whiskey sitting between the two of them, could almost smell his mother's
Pall Mall smoke wafting out of the living room.

It was a warmer afternoon, maybe sixty degrees, and he
cracked some windows and let the fall breeze fill the house.
Paused at the bottom of the stairs and took a deep breath and
then went up, knocked, and entered Marie's room.

Nothing looked disturbed. Unless you knew where the stained-
glass turtle belonged, you'd never have known it was gone. The
police had been unusually respectful in their search, actually,
although the cleanup probably improved substantially after Adam's
arrest, when they knew they were going to have to defend their
conduct against his response in court. They'd swept up the

broken glass. He wondered where it had gone. Probably into the trash somewhere. A shame, because he might have been able to put it back together. It would have taken time and care, but he might have been able to do it.

He lit the candles one at a time, then cracked this window, too—autumn was Marie's favorite season, no surprise in a football-crazed family—and let the fresh air come in and stir the flames. Took his customary seat on the floor, back to the wall, and began to talk.

"I'm sorry I've been gone," he said. "I'm so sorry they were here, and I'm sorry I've been gone. I wish it hadn't happened in your room. I really do."

His head was bowed and his eyes closed now.

"Let's start off with good news, all right? Your little brother's winning football games. They're an awfully good team, Marie. They should get it done. There are some distractions that might be a problem, but I'm trying to help with that, and if anyone can focus through these sorts of distractions, it is your little brother. This week's a big one. Saint Anthony's. I'm scared for him against that team, but I'm also glad he drew them. I think he has to go through them if he's going to get it. That's part of it. He's got to beat them. I think he will."

He paused, covered his closed eyes with his bruised hand, and said, "Now for the bad news. There's been some trouble with Kent. It's nothing you need to worry about. I promise you that, Marie. I'm watching out for him. I will not let anything happen to him, or to Beth and Lisa and Andrew. I won't. It's a bad situation, but I'll get it fixed. I can still get this one fixed."

Her favorite candles had smelled of cinnamon, and the scent was heavy now, drifting toward him on the gentle breeze, and he felt as if she'd pushed it his way, trying to relax him. He stopped talking and breathed it in for a while.

"Chelsea wants me to move," he said, and his voice was

choked, so he cleared his throat and gave himself another minute. "She's not pushing me on it, that's not her way. She's so patient, Marie. I wish you'd gotten to know her better. I think you'd have liked her. I really do. I think everyone would have liked her."

Another pause, wiping a hand over his mouth, and then he said, "I think she might be right. I think it might be time to go. If you're unhappy with that...I hope you find a way to let me know. But I think she's right. It could be...could be a good thing for me. For us."

He'd expected a greater sense of guilt and betrayal, but felt little of either. Felt clean, actually, far better than he had when he'd entered.

"We'll see what happens," he said. "This is what I'll promise you, though: I'm not going anywhere until I've taken care of the things that I need to take care of. When I know I can leave Kent alone at night again, when I know I can make a call to Rachel's mother, we will see what happens. But I will set that right first."

He sat in silence for a moment, and then he blew out the candles, told her that he loved her and that he was sorry, and left the house. He needed some sleep before he returned to Kent's, and, these days, he slept much better at Chelsea's place.

38

IT WAS BETH'S IDEA TO invite Adam to dinner.

"We're sleeping while he sits down here awake," she said. "And you know what, Kent? I've been *able* to sleep. He's the only reason. I'd like to try and show him that. Not just slip him in and out under the cover of darkness."

"I don't know if he'll like the idea," Kent said.

"One way to find out."

So Kent called him. His brother seemed uncertain but said he'd make it. There was a woman's soft voice in the background, and only after he'd hung up did Kent think that perhaps he should have extended the invitation to Chelsea Salinas as well. She probably wouldn't have accepted, but he should have asked.

One step at a time, though. That was fair.

Adam arrived at seven, and when the doorbell sounded, Kent realized that he hadn't reminded his brother not to bring the gun into the house when the kids were awake. It wasn't there, though; he wore just a blue button-down shirt, and had a shopping bag in his arms. Lisa and Andrew approached hesitantly, and Adam's smile seemed equally uncertain.

"Hey, guys."

They both said hello, and he set the bag down and said, "Well, I've missed a couple of birthdays, haven't I? Figured I'd do something about that."

"Adam, you didn't need to—," Kent began, but his brother cut him off.

"Don't worry, no money spent. I'm going cheap on them today." He looked up at the kids and winked, and Lisa's smile was genuine. She'd always liked him. She didn't remember the day in the driveway. "Just some old stuff."

He reached into the bag, removed a weathered football, and extended it to Andrew.

"Come on, big guy. Let's see your grip."

Andrew beelined over. Adam was holding the ball easily in one of his massive hands, and Andrew had to cradle it in both arms.

"Your father," Adam said, "set a school record for touchdown passes with that ball. Hit a kid named Leo Fitzgerald on the slant, a fifteen-yard pass. Put it right in his hands, soft as I just gave it to you."

Kent was astounded that he remembered the play, let alone that he'd kept the ball. Kent remembered the pass, remembered the record—Lorell McCoy had broken it in week five of this season—but he'd never seen the ball, had no idea that Adam had claimed it.

"Say thank you," he told Andrew.

Andrew thanked his uncle, dropped onto his butt on the floor, and began to study the football. Adam returned to his shopping bag, and this time he used both hands.

"Lisa, this is for you. Your aunt made it a long time ago. I'm sure she'd like you to have it."

It was one of Marie's stained-glass pieces. Fall leaves in brilliant reds and oranges, tumbling down from the wiry black outline of a tree. Kent watched his brother hand it to his daughter and he couldn't meet anyone's eyes, not even Beth's.

"It's so pretty," Lisa said. Almost whispered. "She *made* this?"

"Yeah," Adam said. "She was pretty good, right?"

Lisa nodded. For a moment they were frozen there together, each of them with their hands on the stained glass, and then Adam released it and rose from the floor.

"Dinner smells good," he said. "What is that, spaghetti?"

"Lasagna," Beth said.

"Ah, good stuff. I wanted to contribute something..." He'd removed a bottle of red wine from the bag, and now he looked down at it and gave an awkward smile. "Um...you guys don't drink, though, do you? I'm sorry."

"I'd love a glass of wine," Beth said. Kent didn't recall her having any alcohol in years, not since the kids were born, and not often before that. She met his surprised stare and smiled. "I think it sounds great."

"Yeah," he said. "Thanks, Adam. Let's eat, gang. I'm hungry."

He asked Beth to say grace before dinner. He wasn't sure why, because he was always the one who said grace. She took the request in stride and offered a prayer and Adam sat with a bowed head and said a soft *amen* when she concluded with a request that Rachel Bond's family be granted peace.

It was a good meal. The kids, shy at first, grew more vocal as things went on. Adam joked with them easily. Beth and Kent each drank a small glass of wine. Then Beth took the kids upstairs to get ready for bed, and Adam began to load the dishes into the dishwasher.

"She's a great cook. Going to be harder for me to stay up tonight, after a meal like that."

"I'm sorry we haven't done it before," Kent said. "I hate that it took circumstances like this to get us here, but sometimes you can get to a really good place out of..."

His voice trailed off because Adam had looked up with a hard stare. The gaze softened a touch, and Adam returned to the dishes and said, "Sometimes, yeah. I guess that's the truth."

Silence followed, and Kent tried to break it by saying, "I'm going to watch some video on Saint Anthony's. You want to have a look with me?"

"Know what Saint Anthony represents?" Adam said, head still down.

Kent was embarrassed to admit that he didn't. It felt like the sort of thing he should know, but he was a Protestant, not a Catholic, and the notion of saints was a foreign thing.

"I don't."

"Patron saint of lost things," Adam said, closing the dishwasher and turning to face Kent.

"Yeah?"

"Yeah." Adam nodded, drying his hands on a towel. "I gave him a few tries once."

Kent didn't know what to say to that.

"I was going to watch film," he began again. "You might see some things there that I—"

"Watching film is your job," Adam said. "Watching the street is mine."

They went into the living room then, and Beth came down to join them. Adam thanked her again for the meal while he stood and surveyed the darkness beyond. He said, "I'll bring the gun in when the kids are asleep."

"Thanks for thinking about that," Beth said.

"Of course. I don't want them to be scared." Adam's head was moving in a slow swivel, taking in the silent street. "I wish he would come."

"That's the *last* thing we want," Kent said.

"I don't mean that I'd like him to be here. But if he just came by and I could follow him to wherever the hell he's hiding..."

"You would call the police," Beth said. "Right?"

Adam didn't answer. Kent was watching his wife's face and knew that she was going to push the issue and for some reason he didn't want her to, did not want her to derail his brother's focus, despite knowing that it was a dangerous focus. He interrupted then, trying to change the direction the conversation had taken.

"Funny you remember that pass was to Fitzgerald. He didn't catch many, but he got open on that one. I wonder whatever happened to him. I think he joined the Army, but I could be—"

"You remember if Rodney Bova had family down here?" Adam asked.

Kent was confused. This was the second time Adam had brought the name up now, and it was hard to imagine a more irrelevant name from their playing days.

"No," he said, "I don't. Why do you keep asking about him?"

"He's still around," Adam said. "Got into some trouble, I came across him. I don't remember him well, you know? I wish that I did. I just remember that he got sent to juvie, but I couldn't come up with the details to save my life. You reminded me that he set fire to the car. I wouldn't have been able to—"

"He didn't set fire to the car," Beth said, and they both looked at her with surprise. She was standing between them with her arms crossed under her breasts, watching Adam with curiosity. "It was his brother. He tried to take the blame for it."

"How do you know that?" Kent asked.

"Dad talked about it. He was disturbed by the whole thing. Police interviewed him, or a counselor maybe? Somebody interviewed him, and—"

"His brother?" Adam said. His stare was heat-lamp intense, and Kent looked at him and said, "What's this about? Why do you care so much?"

Adam considered the question for a long time before he said, "I'm responsible for him now. So he matters to me."

"You posted bond for him?"

"Yeah."

"What did he do this time?"

"Drug charges. Weapons possession." Adam was looking at Beth again. "I didn't remember that he had a brother."

"He was younger. Dad thought he was going to be real trouble. Said he seemed to influence Rodney, not the other way around. Which is strange, because the older brother usually" — she hesitated — "sets the tone."

"Usually," Adam agreed. "But I thought Rodney went to a juvenile detention center."

"I don't think so. Maybe he did. He went into the state's care, somehow, some way. But when it came to that fire, it wasn't him. His little brother did it, and Rodney took the blame. His story didn't hold together very well, though. Dad went to see him, and I think he might have suspected it pretty early, just like the police did. He was just trying to protect his brother."

"I see," Adam said, and then they were all quiet, and Adam waved a hand at the window. "Is it okay if I bring my gun in now?"

"That's fine," Kent said. "You should probably have it."

At one thirty that morning, as he sat on his brother's couch in the dark, Adam's phone alarm went off, notifying him that his GPS tracker was in motion.

He logged in to the program and watched the dot move away from Rodney Bova's house and could not decide what to do. He wanted to go after him, because this sort of movement, so late at night, was interesting. To pursue him, though, would require leaving Kent's house unguarded.

"Damn it," he said aloud, and set the phone down, torn. This could be it. This could be the meeting with Sipes, his first chance and perhaps his only chance.

But upstairs, his only brother slept with his family. Adam's niece and nephew were in their rooms. If Bova was not meeting Sipes, if Sipes was on his way to their home right now . . .

No, he could not leave. He could investigate the location tomorrow, but he could not leave his post tonight.

The dot was sliding across town and toward the steelyards. A rundown area, one Adam knew well, home to more than a few of his clients. It stopped at 57 Erie Avenue.

"That you, Clayton?" he whispered. "Is that where you're hiding?"

Ten minutes passed. Fifteen. Twenty. Adam continued to refresh the screen, keeping the display lit. It was hard not to move, he wanted so badly to drive out there and see what was happening. A glance up his brother's staircase, to where his family slept, calmed him, though. He could not leave, and he would not.

At ten past two, after a half-hour stay, Rodney Bova left 57 Erie Avenue and went into motion again, this time heading southeast. Back home.

Adam set the phone down, kept his hand on his gun, and waited for dawn.

39

By the time adam was born, there were only two steel mills still going in Chambers, and now there were none. Many of the structures remained, though, including the old Robard Company plant, which had once employed Hank Austin. Its blast furnace carved the skyline with ancient smokestacks, and at its base, rows of abandoned rails, rusted and overgrown and untouched by a train's wheels in years, ran like the lingering scars of an old addiction. To the east and west of the plant, the streets made a slow shift from industrial to residential, brick and iron giving way to narrow wood-framed houses. The sidewalk had been jackhammered out in a three-block stretch but not yet replaced, lined by orange plastic fencing, footpaths worn into the weeds beside it. A low-rent district in a low-rent town.

Number 57 Erie Avenue had boards over the ground-floor windows, but the glass upstairs was exposed and unmarred by blinds or curtains. At first glance most people would say that the house had not been occupied in many years. There was plywood over the broken windows and weeds protruded through torn porch boards, no car parked outside, no lights on inside. But Adam had found plenty of people staying in less hospitable-looking places, and Rodney Bova had visited this address in the middle of the night and stayed for thirty minutes.

He parked across the street, took a series of photographs of the property, and then sat with the engine off as the chill seeped into the car, staring at the house and trying to determine his next move. Did he go in, or did he wait to see if someone came out?

Sometimes you could enter a place easily enough and leave without a trace, as he had at Bova's house, but Sipes was on guard. This was a hiding spot for him, a safe house, and he would likely be attuned to any signs of danger checking for intruders. The last thing Adam wanted was to put him on the run again if in fact he was staying here.

He decided to give it time. If Sipes was in there, he'd have to move at some point, and if he was already gone, with luck he might return.

This decision meant a grudging pact to settle in for a lengthy wait, but it didn't take long. Just twenty minutes after Adam arrived, the side door of the house opened and a man stepped out and walked down the driveway to the sidewalk, then up the road to a white Buick Rendezvous. Adam's adrenaline spiked at the sight of him, then fell. It was not Clayton Sipes. Not even close. Too heavy a build, a head of thick dark hair instead of a shaved scalp, no tattoos. Adam took five photographs of him as he got into his car, then decided to follow. It would be good to know who Rodney Bova had visited in the night. It had not been Sipes, but maybe it was someone connected to him. You had to chase the leads you found.

Still, he couldn't help feeling defeated. It had seemed like a promising chance, and now that it hadn't panned out, he had to consider the possibility that it might never pan out, that Rodney Bova could be a dead end. He started the engine and pulled down the street, wondering how long he should pursue this. The glance he gave the house at 57 Erie was a distracted, indifferent flick of the eyes.

But it was enough to see the man in the window.

Somehow he avoided hitting the brakes. It was his first instinct, and it was strong, but he overrode it and managed to keep on driving.

The man had been watching the street from the upstairs window, the one that had neither boards nor curtains, and the view of him was clear. He had a shaved head and he stood shirtless in front of the glass and colored tattoos ran the length of his left arm.

Adam drove to the end of the block, reached the stop sign, and stared in the rearview mirror. He could still see the house but not the figure in the window, not from this distance. He turned right, heart hammering, and lapped the block, sliding into a new parking spot on the other side of the street. Unholstered his gun and set it in his lap.

He'd found him. Clayton Sipes was inside that house.

Watching and waiting no longer felt like the best option. Not at all. Not with the son of a bitch so close, not now that Adam had actually laid eyes on him. The patience he could force himself to have on the hunt was evaporating, because he'd seen the prey, he'd seen the target. The hunt was over. All that remained was finishing it.

I will find him and I will kill him.

That was the promise. He had not wavered when he spoke the words. He could not waver when the chance to deliver on the promise came. Should not, at least. But it was on him fast now, the hunt had reached a sudden end, and after all the days of hungry anticipation, he found himself unprepared for it, uncertain.

Kill him? He was really going to kill him?

Yes, damn it. Do what you promised you would do.

He removed the holster with his Glock and put on a pair of thin black cotton gloves. Then he retrieved a new weapon, this one from under the seat, another gun he'd stolen from a skip, similar to the piece he'd left in Rodney Bova's truck. It was easy to acquire guns from skips if he caught them armed; most of them knew damn well the possession charge might add years to their jail stay. Often the guns were cheap, poorly maintained crap, but this was a Ruger .45-caliber in mint condition. He preferred the Glock, but the Glock was registered to him. The Ruger was not.

He ran his gloved thumb over the stock of the gun. He was so familiar with them and yet not truly familiar at all. He'd shot them, cleaned them, oiled them, experimented with ammunition and shooting stances and grips and speeds. He'd done everything one could possibly do with a gun except the one thing for which it was designed.

He ejected the magazine and checked its load even though he knew it was full. Slipped it back in, racked the slide, and heard the click of a round chambering. One trigger pull away.

His eyes drifted from the gun to the cell phone.

Just call it in.

So simple. He could stay right here, right where he was, and he could call Stan Salter. They'd send out a SWAT team, they would not let Clayton Sipes escape from that house. He would be arrested, back behind bars before the day's end.

Would he be convicted, though? Would they find evidence of a homicide inside that decrepit home, or would they find only a very smart and very evil man? He would serve some time, no question. How much time was harder to say. When would he walk back out? When would he return to the world?

That's why you don't call it in, Austin. That's why you made the promise in the first place, and that's why you have to come through on it now. Because if the system was worth a shit, your sister would have made it home, and so would Rachel Bond.

He started the engine and moved the Jeep, then went five blocks east until he was parked on the other side of the old steel mill. Out of the car and across the abandoned plant's grounds, stepping through weeds and over old cinders as he followed the railroad tracks up to Erie Avenue. There he crossed the street quickly, keeping his head down, and entered a narrow alley four blocks down from the house where Clayton Sipes waited. There he turned left, the wind off the lake blowing gravel dust into his face, and slid behind a low concrete wall that separated the old homes. He followed that until he reached the back of 57 Erie Avenue, and then he broke across the small backyard without pause, went into the driveway and up to the side door.

The gun was positioned in the pocket of his sweatshirt so that the muzzle was pointed straight out from his waist, his right index finger curled around the trigger, as he knocked on the door with his left hand. The aluminum frame of a storm door still remained, but all of the glass had been broken out, so he had to reach through the frame to find anything solid. He rapped his knuckles off the wood in three calm strikes. Not aggressive, just clear and loud.

Come on down, Clayton, he thought. *Or I can come in. It's totally up to you.*

Footsteps. Just like his knock — measured, steady, and clear. Sipes was not trying to hide his presence inside the house, and he was not trying to run. He was coming to the door. Adam's breathing and heart rate had slowed at the sound of the approaching steps, and his finger tightened on the trigger, adding a few pounds of pull, bringing it to the brink.

You can hold him here. Hold him here and call the police, you'll be a damned hero, everyone will see your picture in the paper again and this time they will think different things.

Then the door opened, and the slender man with the shaved head and the ring of tattoos around his neck looked at Adam and smiled, and any thought of holding him here and calling the police evaporated. Sipes was still shirtless—he had a sheen of sweat across his torso and his chest and arms were swollen, as if he'd been working out—and his smile was amused, taunting, and he held a gun in his left hand. Unlike Adam, though, he held his pointed down.

"He sent you instead of coming himself?" Sipes asked.

"You know who I am. Good for you."

"Yes, Adam, I know who you are. Your brother sent you instead of coming himself. An interesting choice. Not a surprising one, but a little disappointing, don't you think?"

If being discovered rattled him in the slightest, Sipes didn't show it.

Adam said, "I would like to talk with you."

"Weapons aren't conducive to good conversation, Adam."

"That didn't stop you from using the same approach with my brother."

"Come on in then. Enter, please."

Adam shook his head. "We'll walk together. The guns go away, and we walk."

Sipes considered this, the two of them staring at each other through the empty storm door frame. Beyond him the chipped, mildewed linoleum stairs led up to darkness.

"Fine, Adam," he said. "We will walk. If you'll allow me to put on a jacket, then—"

"You're good," Adam said. "I think you can stand the chill, Sipes."

The smile returned, and Sipes pushed open the storm door

frame and stepped out to join him, Adam moving backward and keeping the gun up. He shut the door behind him, and then he tucked his pistol into the waistband of his pants, looked at Adam with mock reproachfulness, and said, "What was that promise about the guns?"

Adam slipped the Ruger back into the pocket of his sweat-shirt but did not remove his finger from the trigger.

"There we go," he said. "Let's walk, Sipes. We'll walk, and talk, and then you'll leave."

"I'll leave," Sipes echoed, leading the way out of the yard and to the sidewalk. When he was in front of Adam, the gun tucked into the back of his pants was visible for the first time. He made no move to reach for it, and offered no comment about it. A car passed but no one looked at them. "That sounds like an ultimatum."

"It is."

"How very Wild West. I like the touch. Your idea or the coach's?"

"Mutual."

They were moving north on Erie Avenue, the steel plant to their right, the dead end ahead, and the great gray lake beyond.

"My understanding was that you were not close with your brother."

"We're brothers," Adam said. "It does not get much closer."

"Are you proud of him?"

Sipes was three feet ahead of him and just to the left, walking exactly as Adam wanted him to without requiring any instruction. The butt of the gun protruded above the waistband of his jeans. Sweat ran down the small of his back toward it.

"I think you're confused on a few things," Adam said.

"How so?"

"I'm not here to answer your questions, Sipes."

"I'm sure that you're not. I assume your intent today is to threaten, perhaps to assault? Because you didn't come here without the police to do anything within the bounds of the law, did you? That wouldn't make much sense."

They'd covered several blocks and the dead end was approaching. Sipes said, "I'll need to know where we're going, Adam."

"All the way to the end of the street. Through the fence. I'd like to look at the lake."

"Then let's have a look." They reached the end of the road, and Sipes stepped through the weeds and pulled loose one of the torn sections of chain link and ducked through. Adam kept the gun pointed at him while he did this, but Sipes made no move to reach for his own weapon. Adam was tensed as he slid through the fence himself—this was the best opportunity for Sipes to strike—but the man made no attempt, just stepped over a broken vodka bottle and continued on, out to the slabs of rock where the lake slapped and sloshed, some of the waves breaking high now and then and trapping themselves in puddles behind the stones.

"What interests me," Sipes said, "is that he sent you and not the police. That seems so unlike him. Unless the fear is beginning to extract its pound of faith, of course. Unless the—"

"Kent did not send me," Adam said.

"Forgive me if I call you a liar on that point."

"Kent did not send me," Adam repeated. "My sister did. And so did Rachel Bond."

Sipes nodded in approval. "That's wonderful stuff. Wonderful. I told your brother you might be more fascinating than him, and I think I was right. It's a shame we haven't met before."

They were alone on the lakefront. A few miles out, a low shadow on the horizon, a freighter moved northeast for the Saint Lawrence Seaway and the ocean at its end. Sipes spread his arms wide.

"Here we are," he said. "You have your view of the water. You have your captive audience. Let's hear what you came to tell me, Adam. What you were *sent* to tell me."

Adam ran the tip of his tongue over his lips. "Why Kent?" he said.

"Because he said he could not be broken," Sipes told him. Voice calm, patient. "Because he believes it."

"That's enough reason for you to murder a girl who had nothing to do with him?"

"*Nothing* would be a stretch, I think. He promised me that his faith could weather any challenges, Adam. I've come to see that for myself. Tell me, do you agree with your brother? I've heard otherwise. I've heard that you were anything but pleased with his decisions."

Adam was listening to the waves break on the rocks. It was so quiet out here today. Usually it was, this time of year. The day they'd found Marie, the quiet broke, though. There'd been helicopters, Adam remembered that, television cameras watching from above. It had been maybe two miles from this spot. Not far. Not all that far.

"There's something I would like to know," Sipes said. "Is your brother aware of this?"

Adam shook his head.

"That's a shame," Sipes said. He seemed to mean it.

Shoot him, Adam thought, and he wanted to, but he couldn't. So close, so close, all he needed was to add that last bit of pressure. Find a way to call it up. Somehow.

"Go ahead and take your gun out, Sipes."

Sipes smiled and shook his head. "I'm fine, thanks."

Adam's hand was starting to tremble. He tightened his grip, felt old aches. He'd broken that hand once, a long time ago. The bones knit back together fine, but sometimes, in cold weather like this, you still had the aches.

"You're here to protect your brother," Sipes said. "That's the idea?"

"I'm here to make you accountable," Adam said.

"For what?"

"All that you've done."

"You know nothing about what I've done, Adam. You know nothing. I understand all that you are, and you understand not the first thing about me. You're not here for your brother, or even for Rachel Bond. You're here for your sister, you said that much yourself, and you know what? I didn't kill her. I never laid eyes on the girl. Now, I do feel some level of . . . closeness, I think that's the word. You've preserved her so well in that bedroom that when I entered it I honestly *felt* her presence. It was remarkable. I'm sure you understand that, though. You and I are certain to agree on that point. She has a remarkable presence after all these years, doesn't she? And yet I never saw her. Pictures, that's all. You look a bit alike. The eyes, certainly. The cheekbones. There are traces of her. And in your niece, well, that's quite different. More than traces there. They look *so* similar, it's almost as if—"

Adam brought the trigger home, and the Ruger blew a .45-caliber bullet through the center of Clayton Sipes's chest.

Sipes did not show any panic, not even surprise. The smile was gone, at least, the smile was gone as if it had never existed, but he wasn't panicking. He took a stumbling step away, and reached behind his back for the gun he'd believed he did not yet need, and Adam shot him a second time. This time the bullet caught him higher, just below his throat, and he went down, and life went with him.

The thing that had once been Clayton Sipes existed no more in this world.

Adam used his shoe to roll the body over, and then he wiped the gun on his sweatshirt, pulled his arm back, and whipped it toward the water, flinging the Ruger into the lake like a discus.

The wind was with him and it carried well out, splashed, sank. He considered dragging Sipes out into the water but saw no point. The waves would carry him back fast enough. Adam's gunshots had echoed loud over the water, and it was time to move, and move fast.

He turned on his heel and left the way he had come, walking fast but not running, crossing the rocks and sliding through the fence and returning to Erie Avenue. There were no sirens yet. He thought someone might have been able to hear the shots up here, but maybe not. Or maybe it didn't even matter if they had. It was a bad neighborhood, and most of the people who would be occupying it in the middle of the day were not the type who would rush to call the police.

He walked to the old Robard Company plant where his father had once worked, and then, finally out of sight from the street, he began to run.

40

OCUS HAD NOT COME EASILY all week, and Kent was struggling to attain it Thursday afternoon as he considered the use of a six-man defensive front, wondering if it might allow Chambers to put enough pressure on Rob Sonnefeld, the Saint Anthony's quarterback, to force him into mistakes, when Stan Salter arrived.

His first thought at the sight of the cop was fear, but he hadn't even finished the question before Salter answered it.

"Your family is fine, Coach. Nothing's wrong."

Fear quelled, what replaced it was a vague irritation. *If nothing is wrong then leave me alone in here, I'd finally gotten away from it all, can't you let me stay in here with the door shut?*

"How can I help you, then?" Kent said.

"You probably can't." Salter was leaning against the doorframe. "I just wanted to let you know that Clayton Sipes will trouble you no more."

The statement washed over Kent like a breaking fever.

"You got him?"

Salter shook his head. "We have him. We didn't get him. Someone else beat us to that."

"What do you mean?"

"Clayton Sipes was found shot to death by the lake this morning."

Kent stared at him. *Adam,* he thought. *How did he get him? How did he find him?* Video of Saint Anthony's was still running on the screen, and he clicked the projector off.

"You don't know who killed him?"

"Not yet."

"There were no witnesses, nobody who saw—"

"Too early to say. We're working on all of that, obviously. We just got the positive ID back. I figured you ought to know."

Kent opened his mouth, then closed it. Salter raised his eyebrows and said, "Yes?"

"I was about to say that I was sorry to hear it happened like that," Kent told him. "But you know what? That's hard for me. Right now I'm just...I'm just glad to hear he's gone."

"Understandable. But there are some difficulties presented because of it."

"Such as?"

"Resolution for Penny Gootee for one," Salter said. "I've got a homicide investigation to close. That doesn't go away with Clayton Sipes."

"Not the way you want it to, at least."

"Not in any way," Salter said. "That case is not closed. Now there's another one. I need to find out who killed Sipes, too, regardless of what he was. I still need to know."

Kent nodded.

"Your brother staying with you as some sort of protective measure?" Salter asked.

It was said casually, but Kent felt invaded. "How do you know my brother's been staying with us?"

"You wanted us to pay extra attention to your home, Coach. I told you we would. When somebody pulls into your driveway these days, we're running plates. That's to help you. I thought it was what you wanted."

"Sure," Kent said. "I just…I hadn't heard from you."

"Well, we've been watching."

"Great." He didn't know why the word sounded so hollow. "Yeah, Adam has been a sort of security blanket for us. I know you're not a fan of his right now, but he's more experienced with this sort of thing than I am. I just felt better having him around in case Sipes came back."

Salter nodded. "Fair enough. Well, Sipes won't be back."

"I'm not going to pretend I'm sorry to hear that."

"I'm not going to ask you to," Salter said. "I didn't come here with the idea that I was going to be breaking bad news to you, Coach. I know tomorrow's a big day for you, but I hope you can make yourself available to Agent Dean."

"Dean?"

"The FBI."

"Yes, I remember him. Why would he need me?"

"I don't know that he will," Salter said. "But I wouldn't be surprised. You'll cooperate with him, I'm sure."

"Of course. I don't know what I can say that would matter at this point."

"He may have some ideas about that," Salter said.

"I'm here if he needs me. I'm just glad that it's resolved."

"There's a lot left to resolve," Salter said. "For me, at least. There's a lot left." He said it absently, then shook his head, as if to remind himself that Kent was still in the room, and swung his body away from the doorframe. "I've got to get back to work, Coach. You do the same. Everybody's rooting for you. Everybody wants a win tomorrow night."

"Yeah," Kent said. "We'll try to get it."

* * *

He left the school and drove to Adam's bail bond office. His brother was inside with Chelsea Salinas, their desks angled to face each other.

"Hey, Chelsea."

"Hello, Kent. You doing all right?"

"Hanging in there, yeah."

Adam was shepherding him toward the door. "I need a cigarette. Let's talk outside."

It felt like an obvious move to force the conversation into a private exchange, and Chelsea seemed to read it the same way but let it pass with a quizzical stare and a shrug of her lean shoulders, returning her attention to the computer. They went outside into the fall day, and true to his word, Adam shook a cigarette out and lit it.

"You've heard?"

"Yeah. I didn't know if you had."

"I work a block from the police station, Kent. I've heard."

"Salter come to see you?"

Adam shook his head and said, "I've got a source. People always talking, you know."

"Sure." Kent looked at him and tried to find the words. How did you ask something like this? "Are you worried about the investigation?" he said finally.

Adam exhaled a stream of smoke and said, "What?"

"Somebody killed Sipes. They'll be trying to determine who."

Adam looked at him with flat eyes and said, "Yes, I'd expect so. I'm sure as hell not going to worry about it, though. What I was worried about was *him*."

Twin engines of relief and guilt began to turn over within Kent, and he said, "Right, I just meant…you made a lot of threats, you know, you did a lot of talking."

"Talk's an empty thing," Adam said.

"Okay. Good."

Adam leaned forward and put his hand on Kent's shoulder. "Relax, Franchise. The problem is gone. Don't you get that? Your problem is gone."

Yes, it was. Kent took a deep breath, let his lungs empty, and said, "I wish I didn't feel so happy to know that the man is dead, but after the things he —"

"You should be damned happy," Adam said, his voice harsh. "Anyone who knows anything about it should. That son of a bitch is gone, and we're better off for it. Everyone. Not just you, or me, or your kids. Everyone."

Kent nodded. "I'd like to think otherwise, but maybe you're right. With Clayton Sipes? Yeah, you're probably right, Adam."

Adam put the cigarette back to his lips, looking not at Kent but up at the police station, and said, "I hope they find enough to tell Rachel's mother that it was the right guy."

"They're working on it. I don't know anything about the place where they found him. Whether he was staying there, or what the situation was. I don't even know if Salter had any idea yet. But hopefully there's something there. She needs the closure."

"Yes," Adam said. "She certainly does."

"Listen, Adam, I want you to know how much we've appreciated —"

"No worries, Franchise. I don't require a thank-you card, either. I'm just glad it's done."

Kent paused, unsettled by the curtness, and then said, "Okay. Just know that it was appreciated. And don't stay away."

"You'll see me around. I'll be at the game tomorrow night, for one thing. Put up a win for me, would you?"

"I'll try." Kent hesitated again. "Listen, I've got your gun in the car. Beth's car, that is. Mine is still missing. I figure…not much need for the gun now. I appreciated having it, but now, I guess I'd rather clear it out of the house. Too easy for something to go wrong, especially with kids."

"Sure. It was there when you needed it, and if you ever do again, say the word."

"I hope I never do."

"Likewise."

They walked out to the car, and Kent opened the door, unlocked the glove compartment, and removed the Taurus Judge pistol. Passed it over to Adam carefully, still not liking the feel of the thing. It fit Adam's hands so much better.

"I didn't mean to interrupt your day," he said. "I just wanted to tell you, and to thank you. Your willingness to be around when we needed you . . . it meant a lot. To all of us."

"I'm a phone call away, Franchise. Remember that."

"I will."

"You let me know if you hear anything else from Salter, or the FBI, or anyone. I'd like to know what the situation is."

Kent promised him that he would, and said that he hoped it would go fast. The quicker all of this went public, the quicker other people could begin to find the same sort of peace Kent was feeling right now.

He called Beth as he drove, and he told her that it was done.

"It's terrible," he said. "Hearing that someone was murdered and finding some pleasure in it. But I can't help that."

"It's a human reaction, Kent. He was a threat, and the threat has been removed. We can't blame ourselves for finding some comfort in that. It's not as if we just wished death upon someone. We just wished for protection, for safety."

"Yes. No sin in that."

"Does Adam know?"

"Yes. I've just come from seeing him. He's been at the office all day, but I guess someone with the police told him."

"Good," she said, and he knew from her voice that she'd held the same questions he had. "I was afraid of what we were doing to him, you know."

"What we were doing to him? I don't follow."

"Asking him to sit down there with his gun, asking him to be ready to do things we weren't ready to do ourselves, it just felt—"

"He's better at it," Kent said. "That's what he does, he deals with criminals, he handles weapons, he's prepared for what we were facing."

His voice had risen too loud, too fast, and Beth's silence condemned him for it.

"I'm sorry," he said. "You hit a nerve. I was worried about it, too. I just didn't want to..."

"Say it out loud?" she finished when he did not.

"Yeah."

"It's done now," she said. "That's what matters. It's done, and Adam is okay."

"He's fine."

She was silent for a moment, then said, "Tell him not to stay away, please."

"I already did."

"He helped me. More than I probably wanted to admit. Knowing he was there helped."

"Yes," Kent said. "It did."

Only half of the promise had been fulfilled. It felt like more than that, certainly, but you couldn't consider promises things of balance, things that you could tilt enough to count. You either did what you said you were going to do, or you did not.

He had promised to find Rachel Bond's killer and destroy him, and that was done. He had also promised to tell Rachel's mother when it happened.

Today, this part seemed almost more difficult. It was an admission of guilt, a confession, impossibly foolish.

It was also what he had promised. And when she'd called him

in the night, it was all she had asked of him. He thought about his mother and father, searching for some resolution in the unending smoke of sorrow, afraid to venture away from phones that did not ring, remembered his mother opening a letter from amidst the stacks of useless tips and finding an anonymous complaint from someone who found all of the posters of Marie around town to be depressing, to be *just a little too much,* and he knew he had to follow through on his word. He could not keep Penny Gootee waiting.

He called her from one of the disposable cell phones he kept, a different model than he'd used on the Bova setup. She answered on the first ring, and again he thought of his parents, of the long, terrible wait.

"Hello?"

"Hello, Penny. I'm the man who made you a promise not long ago. Do you understand?"

A pause. "Yes."

"It's done," Adam said.

When she finally spoke again, her voice didn't have its sea legs.

"You really mean it? You're telling me that the man who—"

"I'm telling you that it's done," Adam said, and then he hung up. His hand was shaking when he tossed the phone into a nearby Dumpster.

41

A DAM WAITED FOR THE POLICE to come, but they never did. The day dwindled away without contact. He ran the police scanner in the office and heard nothing but the standard traffic. Whatever was taking place was not running through dispatch and radio calls. They'd be processing the scene now. Interviewing the neighbors, looking for security cameras that might have seen something.

AA Bail Bonds had no skips, nobody who required hunting. No one came in during the day to process a bond, either. All quiet. Chelsea occupied herself with financial spreadsheets; Adam spent some time on the computer, browsing real estate websites. At four thirty, while the sun was still up, he grabbed his keys and asked her if she wanted to go for a ride.

"A ride?" she said, looking at him with one arched eyebrow and sweeping her hair back from her face, tucking it behind her ear.

"Please."

She took his hand and got to her feet. "What is going on with you today?"

He didn't answer. On the drive to Amherst Road he felt tense, forcing himself through silly small talk that she indulged, all the while refusing to ask him where they were going. It was a gorgeous afternoon—blue skies had slid in behind the last front, and fat white clouds rolled through on a warm southern breeze. An Indian summer day, full of sunshine and bright colors and the last gasps of warmth. An illusion. He'd seen the forecast and knew it was going to break overnight, that by tomorrow morning the wind would be blowing hard out of the north and driving rain with it. Still, today was so perfect it was almost hard to believe that. Easy to ignore it, at least. Easy to put the forecast aside.

The house was a stone ranch with a detached garage and a full basement. It looked too suburban to Adam, lacked character, but the property appealed. Eighteen acres, all of it wooded except for the lawn, old-growth oak and walnut trees. A few white pines near the back deck.

"Foreclosure sale," he told her as they got out of the car and stood in the fading sunlight, the trees beyond the house alive with color. "There are a lot of them around here right now."

She was watching him in silence, the warm wind fanning her hair out behind her.

"You've decided," she said.

He nodded.

"Is it what *you* want, Adam? Don't do it just for me. If you're not ready to leave that house, or if you don't want to, then please do not—"

"I'm ready," he said. "And I want to. It's time." He looked away from her and added, "It's probably well past time."

She reached out and put her hand on his arm, and he felt a tingle along his spine and wondered how that was possible, how such a familiar touch could continue to provoke sensations like that. Why didn't it wear off, like so many other things did?

"It's a good spot," she said.

"It's just an option. Like I said, there are lots of them. This economy, it'll be a hell of a lot easier to buy one than it will be to sell the ones we've got. We'll have to figure that out." She was making clean breaks, she was moving forward. He would do the same. "Who will take care of the snakes?" he asked.

She looked at him in surprise. "You care? I thought you hated them."

"I'm not a fan. But, still, they're out there. Someone has to take care of them. We can't just pretend they don't exist."

"Someone will take care of them," she said. "Don't worry about that."

He nodded. They were walking through the side yard now. He waved a hand at the house. "Whether this is right for us, I don't know. I just wanted to see it, because I like the idea of the space. It's almost twenty acres. Good privacy. No neighbors looking over your shoulder."

"Pioneer mentality," she said. "All you midwestern boys are ranchers at heart. You want *land*. The more the better."

"Privacy," he repeated.

She smiled. "I like privacy. Good deck for a hot tub. I'd *really* like privacy if we put one of those in." She leaned over and kissed his neck, her tongue gliding over his skin.

"I'd actually want neighbors for that," he said.

"Yeah?"

"Athletic past. I perform better in front of a large crowd."

"You do all right in the bedroom when it's just the two of us."

"Just the two of us? I've got cameras all over the place in there."

She smiled, then tugged on his belt, bringing him to a stop, and her eyes went serious. "I love you," she said.

He told her that he loved her, too, and he meant it. Had never stopped meaning it. As he kissed her there in the yard, he thought that this might actually be the place. They could make it work here, where they had some space, where they were far enough from home but not gone from it completely. He knew better than to try to run from his sins—and it was in his sins that Adam's past and present joined hands, their embrace as intimate as the one he now shared with Chelsea—but he also believed, maybe for the first time, that you could build something clean in their shadows.

Part Four

AUTUMN'S END

42

GAME DAY.
Kent had slept deeply the night before; he knew this because Beth told him so in the morning.

"You're usually so restless on Thursday nights," she said. "Last night, you slept like Lisa. Only with additional snoring."

"I gather you did not sleep as well?"

"As I said, there was the snoring."

They could afford to be light again, afford to joke. The front page carried news of the murder of Clayton Sipes, a recently paroled felon from Cleveland. There was no mention of Rachel Bond yet, but he hoped there soon would be. Stan Salter and Robert Dean would do their jobs. Until then, he would be grateful for the comfort of his private knowledge.

"Bad football weather," Beth said. The sun that had set the previous day seemed to have chosen not to rise; the sky was a deep gray and rain splattered in nickel-colored drops on the driveway.

"There is no such thing," Kent said, "as bad football weather."

*   *   *

Rodney Bova came by that afternoon, and Adam knew instantly that it wasn't good. The man's eyes were red-rimmed and he was humming with tension. The first words out of his mouth were "Did you help them?"

Adam said, "Help who?"

"The police. Did you help them?"

Behind him, Chelsea stirred, and while Bova didn't turn, Adam saw her hand going under her desk, down to where she kept a snub-nose .38 Special. He'd insisted that she keep the weapon there, but she never paid attention to it. Something about Bova was already putting her in a state of high alert.

"If there is one thing I am not right now," Adam said, "it is a friend of the police, Rodney."

"Why did you put the tracking bracelet on me?"

Now Chelsea's eyes rose from the pistol and found Adam's. He looked away fast, and got to his feet.

"Let's go outside," he said. "I'll hear you out, Rodney, but I will not allow you to shout in my office. I've got a business to run."

He moved for the door without waiting for Bova's agreement. And without meeting Chelsea's eyes. They went out into the rain that had replaced the beautiful Indian summer weather in less than twenty-four hours. Adam stopped walking under the overhang of his building, where the rain didn't reach, and took a cigarette out and lit it. They were standing in front of the dust-filmed plate glass window of what had once been an insurance office and bond business rival. It had been empty for three years. Adam lifted the cigarette, drew in smoke, and held it for a few seconds before letting the cold wind peel it away from his lips.

"Why did you put the tracking bracelet on me?" Bova repeated.

"I told you the reasons. It was better for you. I could not have been clearer about that."

Bova looked torn, and Adam took the opportunity to keep talking, to keep the pressure on him, force him not to dictate the situation but to react.

"You told me the police set you up," Adam said. "You never told me why. You don't have to. But if there's one thing I can assure you, Rodney, hell, that I can assure *anyone,* it's that I didn't share your information with the police."

Bova was silent. Adam was thinking about the tracking bracelet and knowing its risk, and he said, "You want it off, we'll take it off. I've got a reputation to worry about here. I can't have you talking like this."

"Take it off, then."

"I will. But first tell me why?"

"My brother was killed. They were looking for him and now he's dead. And I . . . I saw him. I went to see him before he was killed, I mean. I didn't know what they thought he'd done, but now that I do, then —"

"What did your brother do? Why did the police want him so bad?"

Bova looked away. "That's personal."

"You're the one who came to me."

"I knew they were looking for him," Rodney Bova repeated softly. "But I didn't know why. It's bad. But they don't understand him. He was a lot of things, he was a lot of trouble, but he wouldn't have done this. Not what they're going to say he did."

"Were you close with him?"

"We didn't talk often. But he was my brother. We went through a lot together, a long time ago. I got my feet under myself a little faster. He took a different road. But I know what he was, and who he was, and —"

"I get all that," Adam said. "Just tell me this: Did you lie to the police about him at any point? They ask where he was and you said you didn't know, that sort of thing?"

"Yes. He was on parole violation. That's all I knew. But I wasn't going to turn him in."

"Did you tell them where he was staying after they came to you with the news?"

"No. I haven't said anything yet."

"Why not?"

"Because I want to understand what happened. Not from them. I want to know what happened myself."

"And then?"

Bova wet his lips, looked away, didn't speak.

"I haven't told them anything," Adam said. "And I won't. But they can get a warrant for those tracking logs. Do they know about the bracelet?"

"No."

"Then we'll take it off now, and you should be careful how much you tell them. Don't get yourself into trouble."

"I'm not worried about that. Not now."

"You should be," Adam said. "Because if they're ready to accuse him of something as heavy as this sounds, dead or alive, and you were involved with him, they'll try to drag you into it. You've got to realize that. The heavier it was, the more they'll want somebody living to take the fall. So whatever it is you're talking about, are you prepared to become involved in it?"

Bova didn't answer.

"Whatever your brother did," Adam said, "be careful not to let it pull you down, too."

Chelsea watched in silence as Adam removed the tracking bracelet from Bova's ankle, but as soon as the man was gone, she wanted to know what it was about.

"We posted bond for a guy who's being looked at in a murder case," Adam said. It was not a lie. It was disturbing how much that was starting to matter to him lately, how often he was struggling not to lie while still not saying anything close to the truth, as if there was some honor in that.

"Why'd you have a tracking device on him?"

"High bond."

"You didn't mention that to me."

"My mind's not really been on business, Chelsea. You know that."

She was watching him skeptically.

"Are you in more trouble, Adam?"

"I intend to leave all my troubles behind me. You know this."

She didn't pursue the question any further. He looked at the clock.

"You about ready to head out?" he asked.

"To the *game*? It's four hours away. We're going to stand in the rain for three hours waiting on a football game?"

"We'll grab an early dinner. I'd like to get over to Murray Hill, hit one of those little Italian places. Haven't been there in a while."

"It's four hours away," she repeated.

"When I played, the buses left at three thirty. That's my tradition. Humor me?"

"My mission in life," she said, and slipped on her jacket.

The game was a sellout, more than ten thousand tickets claimed by Friday morning, and the weather would not scare them away. Not in northeastern Ohio. Plenty of people would travel from Chambers, but the crowd would be largely hostile, and loud. Saint Anthony's fans were used to seeing wins, particularly against Chambers. They would feel blood lust watching the Cardinals take their field with an undefeated record and a number-one ranking.

Kent intended to give the team the standard fare in the locker room. To keep things balanced and steady. *Head down, head down, head down.* It felt wrong tonight, though. So in the final moments before they took the field, after he gave them his usual reminder — *Know how lucky you are right now, about to play the best game ever invented with the best friends you'll ever have* — he challenged his seniors.

"You're going to take your uniforms off at some point this season for the last time," he said. "You'll never wear them again. Realize that. Every autumn has its end. Now let's make sure you leave a trophy in the case before this one does."

The team roared.

Chambers won the coin toss and Kent elected to defer the kick-off. Ordinarily he preferred to take it. He liked to put points on the board early, forcing the opponent to play from behind, but he expected this to be a close game and that extra second-half possession might be valuable.

Also, truth be told, he was worried about Colin botching the return.

Kent paced the sidelines, nodding at his players and slapping helmets and telling them they had to play fast and smart. Opposite him, on the Saint Anthony's sideline, Scott Bless conferred with Rob Sonnefeld, his quarterback, and Kent couldn't help but glance at them, thinking, *Let's get this started, let's see what you've got.*

It was raining steadily, the wind coming in gusts, the temperature in the forties. Weather that was better suited for the power game of Saint Anthony's, but that was fine, Kent wasn't in the business of making excuses. His team was prepared to win in any conditions, and should.

Five snaps later, the confidence was already ebbing. Sonnefeld had passed four times, completed three of them, and the ball was at the Chambers twenty-five. So much for the power game. Kent had expected Bless to use two tight ends and test the Chambers front line, so instead Bless had spent the whole week spreading the field and preparing to test their secondary.

On the sixth snap Sonnefeld went with a play-action fake and Ritter, Damon-the-best-linebacker-Kent-had-ever-coached Ritter, bit on it, jumped away from the number-two receiver, his coverage responsibility, who promptly caught the ball behind him and then six points were on the board, Chambers losing already.

"What are you doing?" Kent shouted as Damon came off the field, head down. "Where were your eyes? You're looking in the backfield! Don't you *ever* look at Sonnefeld! You know better than that. *We don't make that mistake!"*

Ritter said *"Yes, sir,"* retreated, and Kent shook his head in disgust and paced away as the extra point sailed in: 7–0. He'd never held a lead against Saint Anthony's. Not even a *lead*.

"We've still got this ballgame," he said into the headset, and his assistants nodded, but nobody was looking at him. It was a bad start and they all knew it.

The offense gained one first down on three straight carries by Justin Payne, all part of the script, designed to settle things down, force Saint Anthony's to respect the running game. When Lorell took his first snap out of the shotgun, he pump-faked, and there was Colin on a hitch route, the ball coming in high and soft and right in stride.

He caught it.

Then bobbled it. Kent had a fist raised already, wild with excitement both for the kid and for the knowledge that this was about to be a tie ballgame, because they would not catch Colin from behind.

But they did. He was juggling the ball, fighting for possession, and his feet went unsteady on the wet turf, and then the corner-back caught him with a sweeping right hand and the ball was out and bouncing free and as Saint Anthony's scooped it up Kent thought, *Please tell me he dropped that one, too, please rule it incomplete.*

They ruled it complete. Fumble recovered by the defense on the forty.

Kent went out onto the field to meet Colin, grabbed his helmet, and forced his face up. "You'll have that play all night long," he said. "You're going to make it every other time. You believe that?"

"Yes, sir."

"Do you believe that?"

"Yes, sir!"

Kent slapped the side of his helmet and returned to the sidelines and watched Sonnefeld direct a precise, balanced drive that chewed seven minutes off the clock and featured another effective fake, this time on a reverse, and again Chambers chased the ball and forgot their gaps. They held them to a field goal, but it was already 10–0.

"We're going to get fucking beat," Kent said through clenched teeth. It was too soft for the players to hear, but his headset microphone was on, and every assistant heard it. He saw their heads snap up, the Kent Austin profanity-free-football-field myth having officially crumbled, and he thought about apologizing but decided against it. Wiped the rain off his face with the back of his hand and walked to the farthest end of the sideline, shaking his head.

43

As HIS BROTHER PACED AND muttered, Adam circled the field, bumping through throngs of kids with painted faces and ducking an errant trombone slide from a pep band member, trying to reach the opposite end zone and a clearer view. Chelsea came with him, and they stood in the south end zone, where the wind blew cold rain into their faces.

"Some date you are," she said. "Walked right past the concession stand and you don't even offer me popcorn?"

"Who wants to eat wet popcorn?"

"Fair point." She was watching the Chambers sideline. "Your brother doesn't look happy."

"He shouldn't." Adam folded his arms over his chest, then saw the way Chelsea was ducking against the rain and moved to stand behind her and wrap his arms around her. She leaned back, pressing her weight against him.

On Chambers's second and third possessions, Scott Bless started rolling his safety down into the box instead of helping over the top on Mears, as if the one fumble had been enough to confirm what he'd hoped was true, that Mears was now an empty threat. Lorell McCoy tested the belief, found Mears three times, put the ball in his hands with each pass, and the kid never came close to holding on to one. Chelsea covered her eyes on the third drop. The Chambers defense had stiffened up, maintaining their gaps, no longer biting on the play action, and they forced yet another punt. When the teams took the field again, the Saint Anthony's safety was shading four yards farther in and five yards closer to the line of scrimmage, hovering nakedly in the flat. Outright ignoring Mears, trusting their slow-ass cornerback to handle him. It shouldn't even have been an option. Tonight, though, it was simply the right decision.

Chambers worked the ball downfield patiently, McCoy looking poised, picking up blitzes and moving well in the pocket, gaining first downs on sweeps and veers. Twice he saw Mears wide open, hesitated, and then checked down and threw underneath. Mears stood downfield with his arms up, wanting to know where the ball was. Adam could hardly stand to watch the kid.

The drive stalled on the fifteen and they took a field goal: 10–3. Saint Anthony's answered with a field goal of their own, making it 13–3 as the rain began to pour. They had control of the game but hadn't put it out of reach, and with only two minutes left in the half, Adam thought that it wasn't as bad it could have been.

Then they went for an onside kick, and he said, "Holy shit."

What a call. What a bold play call. Saint Anthony's recovered, and while the move had certainly caught Chambers off guard, it also seemed as if two of Saint Anthony's special teams players had gotten one hell of a jump on the kick, and Adam looked for a penalty flag but didn't find one. Then Chelsea said, "Uh-oh. Your brother…" and then he saw Kent storming onto the field, screaming, tearing his headset off and hurling it behind him.

"Come on, Franchise," Adam whispered. "Don't go down like this. Not like this."

"That is offsides! He was offsides by five steps! Are you out of your mind? How did you not see that!"

Kent was near midfield now, and he was aware that his headset had shattered when it hit the aluminum bench but didn't care, he was too focused on fury.

"Coach, go back to the sideline."

"How did you not see that!" Kent screamed. His face was inches from the official's, rain stinging his eyes and dripping into his mouth. He spun and kicked the ground and the turf was so wet he tore a furrow through it, sent a divot flying into the air, and drew a roar from the crowd.

"Back . . . to . . . the . . . sideline," the official repeated.

"You're standing on the line and you can't see him jump? Are you kidding me? You're *right on top of it! That is all you need to watch! That is your only responsibility!"* The official was trying to walk away but Kent was keeping pace with him, still screaming, still face-to-face, and when the flag finally came out he should not have been surprised, but it further incensed him.

"This is bullshit! This is absolute bullshit!"

He felt a hand on his arm then, started to tear free from it, but it was Matt Byers and his grip was firm. "Coach, get back now. Don't get thrown out of this game."

He let Byers pull him back to the sidelines as the Saint Anthony's crowd booed and Scott Bless regarded him with what appeared to be genuine surprise. Kent picked up his headset, saw that it was in pieces, none of the indicator lights glowing, and dropped it again. One of his assistants was offering him a new one but he brushed it off and paced away as the chain crew moved their markers another fifteen yards downfield in honor of his penalty. He stood alone with his arms folded, his hat lying somewhere in the mud, and watched as Sonnefeld completed four straight passes and then scored from the one on a quarterback dive as the clock wound down.

20–3 at the half.

"You have got to be kidding me," Kent shouted, his voice breaking, as he looked at the rain-swept scoreboard. Not again. Not again.

Adam stepped away from Chelsea as the team jogged toward their locker room, heads down all around, and his brother remained on the sideline, his chin resting on his right hand as he studied the scoreboard as if it were a code he could not decipher. Adam wanted to go to him, say something. He didn't know what. He just wanted to speak to him.

But he couldn't get to him. Kent had walked out to the middle of the field, into the jeers and boos from the Saint Anthony's fans. In the Chambers bleachers, the crowd was silent. Stunned by the score and by the meltdown from their always-impassive head coach. Adam could see Beth sitting with the kids, one on either side of her, the three of them nestled in the center of the friendly crowd. He stopped trying to reach his brother and stood at the fence, watched as Kent crossed the field and found the officials. A hand was extended to the one who'd missed the call and received the tirade, a few words whispered in his ear, a quick pat on the back. The official nodded, apology accepted. The Chambers fans applauded; Saint Anthony's fans continued to boo. Kent walked off the field with his head down, alone in the pouring rain, and Adam's throat tightened as he watched him go.

"Good for you, Franchise," he said. "Good for you."

Damn it, he was proud of him.

* * *

The rest of the coaches were waiting for him outside the locker room. They usually spoke there while the kids caught their breath alone inside, talked about potential adjustments. Tonight Kent walked straight for the door.

"We are not done," he said. Those were the only words he had for his staff.

Usually the locker room hushed when he opened the door; tonight it was already silent. He went to the whiteboard, took one of the markers, and wrote the number 3 as large as he could. Turned and faced the team and said, "What's that mean to you?"

"How many points we've got," Lorell McCoy said.

Kent shook his head. "How many touchdowns we need. Now let me show you one more number." He turned and wrote another 3 on the board. "Anybody know what that one is?"

Silence.

"That's the fewest amount of touchdowns we've scored all year," he said. "The most is eight. The average is five. The *average* is *five*. Does anyone doubt we can get three?"

Nobody did. He put the cap on the marker and set it down and said, "We will win this football game, gentlemen. They played a good half. We will play a better one now. And we will not lose composure. I've done that for you. I apologize. You need to be better than me now, understand that? You need to be better than me."

Intense eyes watched him from every corner. He took a deep breath, cleared his throat, and said, "They'll keep throwing the ball. Bless will not take his foot off our throats until it's out of reach. With our offense, he cannot feel that it's ever out of reach. And he is correct. Agreed?"

They agreed.

"We are going to get downfield and put that ball in the end

zone on the first possession," he said. "Two-score game then. And when they get it back, we are bringing the house. Linebackers, are you ready to hit?"

Shouts of "yes, sir!" echoed around him. He nodded. "Blow those kids up, understand me? Blow them up. Does a blocker get credit for a tackle or a gained yard?"

"No."

"Does a blocker make the play happen?"

"Yes, sir."

"If we don't leave people on the ground, we don't deserve to be on this football field."

There was some fire coming back, he could see it, could feel it.

"We are not taking a loss from this team tonight," he told them. "It's not happening."

They were shouting now, clapping, and Matt Byers was grinning in the back of the room, and Kent was almost frightened by just how good he felt, how alive.

"I want to see hitters out there," he told them. "I want to see hitters."

Adam had feared a blowout was in the offing, but what he saw was aggression and execution. They didn't look hurried, didn't look bothered by the deficit, Lorell McCoy so calm in the pocket you would have thought he'd just emerged from meditation. He got hit twice for losses, and twice Mears dropped balls that could have been big gains, but each time McCoy came back without a trace of frustration and converted. They scored to cut it to 20–10, and then the defense stunned Adam and everyone else in the stadium—including Sonnefeld—by blitzing on three straight downs. Saint Anthony's punted, McCoy drove Chambers right back, and as the fourth quarter started, it was 20–17.

"Ball game here," Adam whispered in Chelsea's ear. "We've got a ball game here."

Saint Anthony's regained momentum with a pair of first downs but then Damon Ritter blew through the middle, sacked Sonnefeld, and forced a fumble. Chambers came out in the shotgun immediately and scored on one play. The extra point was good: 24–20, Chambers.

The crowd was going insane, and Adam heard Chelsea laughing and looked down.

"What?" he said.

She held her arm out, pulled up her shirtsleeve. Goosebumps. He smiled, squeezed her shoulders, and said, "Let's see if he can finish."

Kent knew they'd score again. His defense was playing superbly, swarming to the ball, but Scott Bless had not coached his way to two state titles without a few tricks up his sleeve.

He used one now, a double reverse that gained forty yards, and then on the next play Sonnefeld rolled right, looked downfield, and found nothing. He was a half-step away from a sack when he cut back inside, seeing a hole that only great players see, and then he was free and into the end zone.

"We're all right," Kent said. "We're all right."

He believed it, too. They were dominating this half in the way Saint Anthony's had the first, and the extra point was going to make it 27–24, meaning they only needed to get into field goal range to force overtime. Then Saint Anthony's came out and lined up to go for two, and Kent looked at Matt Byers and said, "Is he serious?"

If they didn't make the two-point conversion, Chambers could win on a field goal. Bless had no interest in overtime, it seemed. He was ready to finish it, one way or the other.

Saint Anthony's scored on a jet sweep, blocking perfectly, the running back never touched: 28–24. Touchdown mandatory now. Across the field, Scott Bless leaned forward, hands on his knees, impassive, and Kent felt a wild desire to tip his cap to the man.

"They asked for it," he told his offense in the huddle, "now let's give it to them. That was a risky play call, and do you know why they made it? Because they're scared of you, gentlemen. They're scared. Show them why."

When Saint Anthony's got into the end zone for two, Adam said, "Son of a bitch," lowered his face, and buried it in Chelsea's hair.

"I thought they'd kick it," she said.

"Yeah." Her and everyone else. Chambers had to put it in the end zone now, and with that clock running, they'd have to pass to do it.

"I hope he makes a play," Adam said, looking up again. "Damn, I hope he makes a play."

"Rachel's boyfriend?"

"Yeah." His mouth was dry. He'd forgotten just how much it could mean, this game, had forgotten the way your heart raced and your fingertips tingled and your lungs couldn't fill. He wanted to be out there, he wanted to make a hit, and he was forty damn years old. Was that wonderful, or was that sad?

"Let's go, Franchise," he said. "Don't panic. You got time."

Chambers took the field with Colin Mears split out wide right, tensed and ready. It was clear that he still thought he would make the catches. He really did. It could break your heart, watching him.

* * *

"First down," Kent shouted to Lorell. "That's all we need right now. Play patient."

Lorell played patient. Handed the ball off to Justin Payne for six, then picked up five with a pass to the slot receiver. Payne again, four more, and then Lorell got loose on the outside but was tackled short of the first down and couldn't get out of bounds to stop the clock. Now time was an issue; the clock was under a minute and still rolling.

"Get a yard," Kent said. "Just get one."

Lorell got two before being knocked out of bounds. First down, clock stopped. Twenty-one seconds left. Ball on the Saint Anthony's forty-two.

Lorell came to the sidelines, looking for a play call, and Kent told him the formation and then said, "Take what they give you, son."

What they gave him was Mears. Colin exploded on the same hitch route he'd run to start the game, when he'd caught the ball but fumbled. Lorell looked right, saw him, and drew his arm back. Then tucked the ball and ran. Darted upfield, gained twelve yards, and called the team's last timeout. On the five-yard line, where he'd ended up uncovered, Colin turned and stared at his quarterback with hands on hips.

"Bring it in here!" Kent shouted. There were only eleven seconds left, they were out of timeouts, and they needed a touchdown. Had to put the football in the air, because an incomplete pass would stop the clock and give them another chance, but a run would not. The offense came over, huddled, and before Kent could get a word out, Colin Mears said, "I'll catch the ball."

For a moment, nobody answered. Colin had been looking at Lorell, but now he turned to Kent. "I'll make the catch. I'm telling you, I will make the catch."

Kent squinted into the rain. Nodded once. "I know you will. What play do you want?"

340 • MICHAEL KORYTA

"Slant. He takes my outside hip every time. I can kill him on a slant."

"All right," Kent told his team. "You heard the man."

They broke the huddle, and Colin led the way out onto the field, clapping his gloved hands. Kent hesitated for a split second, then ran two steps out and snagged Lorell's arm.

"Check down to Justin," he said.

"Coach?" Lorell's dark eyes were confused but focused, ready to listen, ready to execute as instructed. Kent grabbed the back of his helmet and pulled their faces together.

"Play action to Justin, stay out of trouble, and then hit him going up the seam. They'll lose him after the fake. They'll pursue the ball, and he'll be open. Got it?"

"Yes, sir."

Kent slapped him on the back and returned to the sideline. His team lined up, Lorell barked the count, took the snap, turned, and faked the handoff. Nobody was fooled, they knew Chambers wouldn't run in this situation. They chased after Lorell, pursuing the ball, and Payne slipped up the middle. Colin had executed a perfect route, digging hard, right to left, wide open on the slant just as he'd predicted. Wide open. Lorell glanced at him as he slid backwards, away from the defenders, and then he brought the ball back and fired it away.

Payne up the seam. Justin caught it, secured it, barreled forward. Took a hard shot on the one-yard line but it wasn't enough, he was across and through.

Touchdown.

Ball game.

Kent raised his arms, signaling the score, and then Byers was screaming in his ear—*We finally got the bastards!*—and the band was playing and the crowd was roaring.

Final score, 30–28. Saint Anthony's vanquished, Scott Bless

finally beaten. Two games left to play, and then the trophy was in the case.

In the end zone, where he'd found himself free and clear, running the route he'd guaranteed would work, Colin Mears walked first to Justin Payne, then to Lorell McCoy, and hugged them both.

Chelsea was screaming like one of the kids. When she spun to face Adam, her eyes were bright, her smile wide.

"They won!" She put her hands on his shoulders and shook him. "They won! You aren't even going to *smile?*"

"Two games left to play," Adam said. "Don't rush the smile."

"You can let yourself be a *little* happy, can't you?"

"A little." He knew that he should be happy. This was a huge win for his brother, this was the win he needed most. Or wanted most, at least. He'd called it perfectly, too. That route to Justin Payne was brilliant. It had surprised everyone, even Adam. Maybe Adam more than most, in fact, because Adam had watched Colin Mears blow clear on the slant, had seen him crossing the end zone with nobody in reach, and had been certain that Kent would put the ball in his hands, to win or to lose. Foolish football, with the way Mears had been playing, but even so Adam had been sure Kent would give him the chance.

He couldn't figure out why he felt so strangely sad that Kent had gone the other way.

44

K ENT DID NOT LIKE parties after games. He let his staff have them, he could not and would not attempt to control that, but he almost never attended. Tonight, though, when Matt Byers told him there was barbecue and beer waiting at his house, he said he'd be there.

"What if we'd lost?" he asked on the noisy, elated bus.

Byers grinned. "You can always freeze barbecue," he said. "But, Coach? We didn't lose."

Kent couldn't keep the smile off his face. "No, we sure didn't."

He called Beth from the bus and asked her to join him.

"It'll be a late night for the kids," she said.

"They can survive one late night."

And so it was, because of the party and the late night, that it was just past one in the morning when they returned to their home and found the photographs of Rachel Bond's corpse taped to their front door. Beth was driving—Kent almost never drank, but he'd indulged in three beers tonight, and three beers to a non-drinker felt like a lot—and she saw them first. Kent had his head down, looking at his iPad, where video of the next opponent was already available, when she said, "There's something on our door."

He looked up with only idle interest, expecting some sort of banner or congratulatory note. That happened, sometimes. Once, after a rare string of three losses, a FOR SALE sign had also appeared in the yard, a favorite trick of fans who wanted a coach removed, but nobody was going to want to relocate Kent Austin after tonight's come-from-behind win.

When he saw the odd collection of papers scattered over the door and realized that they were printed-out photographs, though, a sense of alarm that had been absent since Clayton Sipes was found dead by Lake Erie returned.

"Stop the car," he said. He kept his voice low; both kids were asleep in the backseat. He wanted them to stay that way until he had a look.

"What are those?" Beth said.

"I'm not sure. Stay here, I'll check." When he got out of the car, he punched the lock button before he swung the door shut. The rain had stopped but the temperature was still falling, down into the low thirties now, and his breath fogged as he made his way to the porch. He was suddenly wishing he had not returned the gun to Adam.

The porch light was off, so the door was illuminated only by the glow of the headlights, but it was enough. He stopped on the steps, didn't need to get any closer and didn't want to.

He was looking at photographs of Rachel Bond, taken after life had left her.

There were longer shots and close-ups, pictures of her body and one of only her eyes shown through the haze of a plastic bag, and they registered in rapid fire because his eyes were already drawn to others in the mix. Lisa. Andrew. Beth. Pictures of them in the yard, in the bleachers, and one of Beth dropping Lisa off at school. He recognized the outfit—it was what she had on today. It had been taken that morning.

He moved off the stairs, looking back at his family. They had to leave, fast. Sipes could be here, he could be waiting, he could—

But he could not be. Clayton Sipes was dead.

"Kent? What is it?" Beth had gotten out of the car, and Kent lifted a hand and shook his head.

"Don't."

"What?"

He crossed the yard to her, saw that Lisa had woken up and was leaning forward in her seat, curious about why they were waiting in the driveway. Kent put his hand on Beth's arm and said, "Get back inside the car, and drive them somewhere safe."

"What are you talking about?"

"Please take them away from here," he said. "I'll call you after I call the police."

She stared at him, her blue eyes beginning to show understanding that he hadn't even fully achieved himself.

"It's not done," she said.

"No."

"How can that—"

"I don't know. Please get away from here now, though. We can't have Andrew and Lisa here. We can't let them see this."

She didn't go far. Took the kids across the street, woke the neighbors, and explained the situation. By the time the police arrived she was back, standing with him in the cold. He told her not to look at the pictures, and she didn't.

"They're of Rachel, aren't they?"

"Yes," he said. He did not tell her about the others. Could not.

The police took pictures of the pictures. Kent watched with numb detachment as lights went on around the neighborhood and doors opened, everyone curious, everyone watching. The yard was bright with lights and a crowd was gathering and Kent stood before them. It felt almost familiar, except for the helplessness. He had no control here. He could make no adjustments, he could affect no outcome.

Salter arrived just as officers with gloved hands were removing the photographs from the front door. It had been more than thirty minutes; other officers had conducted the first round of interviews and then told him to wait on Salter. Why Salter was taking so long was not clear. When he finally appeared, Kent looked at him and said, "I thought it was done."

"It's not," Salter said. His voice was tired. Sad, even. He watched his officers at work and then said, "I guess I'll need to see if they're the same."

"The same?"

"You were not the only recipient, Coach. Photographs were also left for Rachel Bond's mother. That's where I've been."

Kent just stared at him. Beth whispered, "Dear God."

"Her mother," Kent said, and he thought that he would be sick, those three unfamiliar beers roiling his stomach.

"Yeah," Salter said, and there was no mistaking the man's fatigue and sorrow now. "Let me review the pictures, and then we need to go somewhere away from here to talk."

"All right."

Salter crossed the yard and went to speak to his team, and across the street a neighbor called out to Kent, asking if everyone was safe. He didn't answer. Beth lifted a hand and nodded but did not speak either. She wrapped an arm around Kent and lowered her face to his chest and said, "Who is it? Who is doing this?"

He had no answer. He thought he had known, he'd been sure

of it, but the only certainty now was that the terror had not ended.

Salter studied the photographs, said a few more words to the officers on the porch, and then returned to them.

"We're going to take you to a hotel, Mrs. Austin. You and your children, if that's all right with you. I'd like to be certain of where you are, and I'd like to have one of my officers with you."

"Okay. Yes, that's okay."

"What about Penny Gootee?" Kent said.

"She refused, unfortunately. She asked us to leave. Demanded it."

"She's alone."

"Yes. We have a car nearby, though." Salter ran a hand over his face and said, "If you could come back to the station with me, Coach, it would be a help."

Kent said good-bye to Beth, gave her an empty kiss, and watched as a uniformed officer escorted her across the street to get their children. Salter put a hand on his arm and guided him toward his car. Up and down the street, the neighbors watched.

"He's dead," Kent told Salter, as if the lieutenant were unaware.

"Clayton Sipes is dead," Salter agreed. "That doesn't mean Rachel Bond's killer is dead."

"He did it," Kent said.

"No, Coach, he did not." Salter opened the passenger door of his unmarked car for Kent. "In fact, he was at your football game the night she was murdered."

Kent was in the seat and the door was closed before he could respond. When Salter got in on the other side and started the engine, Kent said, "He was at the game? That night?"

"Yes."

"How can you be sure?"

"We went through the newspaper's photographs. They ran two pictures of the game, but they took about a thousand. He's in three of the crowd shots."

The rain started again as they drove away. Kent sat in stunned silence. He did not speak until they were out of the neighborhood. Then he said, "He could have been at the game and still killed her."

"Not based on the scenarios the coroner gave us. Certainly not very likely."

"You found him in pictures? Why wasn't I told?"

"That was the FBI's decision, not mine. I suggested it, and I was overruled. I understood their position, though. We're trying to resolve a complex situation, and updating civilians is not a priority, nor is it a help, necessarily."

"But he came to my house, with a gun. He admitted that he had killed her."

"You said that he did not. I asked you specifically, and you said that it was implied, not stated outright."

"I know that, but, still...it had to be him, Salter. He could have left the game and—"

"No." Salter shook his head. "The timeline does not make that likely, and other evidence suggests it is even more improbable. He wasn't working alone, Coach. And what happened tonight should remove your doubts. Clayton Sipes did not put those pictures on your door."

He certainly had not. Kent stared at the dark road ahead and listened to the windshield wipers thump.

"He didn't just show up out of nowhere," he said. "He had to be involved."

"He was clearly involved. But he didn't kill the girl."

"Then who did?"

"Agent Dean would like to talk to you about that. I'll let him handle it. It's become part of his investigation."

"Part?"

Salter nodded. "You're a piece of a complex situation, Coach. You and Sipes both. And while it might have seemed like a very good thing to you to have Sipes removed, it ultimately might be a problem."

"How?"

"He was a link we needed," Salter said. "He was someone who understood, and who maybe could have helped. Maybe. Now that's gone."

45

ADAM WAS IN BED BUT AWAKE, Chelsea curled on his chest, when Penny Gootee called. The sound of the ring woke Chelsea, and she murmured unhappily and tried to burrow deeper in his chest, then grudgingly moved and opened her eyes when he reached for the phone, recognizing the number.

Shit, he thought, *don't call me to talk about it. We do not need to talk about it, ever. Just know that it is done, and take what comfort you can from that. But we cannot discuss it.*

He thought about ignoring it, but he couldn't do that, not to this woman, so he answered, sitting up in bed as Chelsea slid off him and rolled onto her side. He was trying to get away from her, this not being a conversation he needed anyone to overhear, but he thought he'd have time to get out of the room before they began to speak in earnest. He was not prepared for the scream.

"You told me he was dead! You told me he was dead!"

Even if he'd made it out of the room, Chelsea might have heard. It was that loud. As it was, she was at his side, and the words were clear. She grabbed his arm and spoke his name in a harsh, questioning tone. He pulled free and stumbled out of the bed and into the living room, banged into one of the snake shelves, heard an immediate strike against the plastic.

"Penny, you can't do this. You can't call me and say —"

"You told me you'd done it." She was sobbing. Adam pulled up short in the dark living room, frightened now, wondering what in the hell had gone wrong.

"I did," he said. He'd feared saying something so damning over the phone, but now, listening to the woman's hysterical sobs, he no longer cared. He just needed to understand.

"No, you didn't! That sick piece of shit is still alive, because he brought me *pictures*. He brought me *pictures of my baby!*"

No, Adam thought. *No, he could not have done that. He's in the morgue now. I left him in the rocks and the water and he was dead, Penny, I am sure of it, he was dead. I put a bullet through the man's heart. He is dead.*

"He must have sent them before," he said. "That's the only possibility."

"He didn't *send* anything. He left them in an envelope at my front door!"

This was not possible.

"Someone else did," Adam said. "I'm sorry, Penny. I'm so sorry. But it was not him. Someone else —"

"I don't believe you." Her voice was choked with tears. "I don't believe you did a damn thing. You lied to me, and what sort of evil are you that you would lie about *that?*"

"I did not lie."

"Go to hell," she said. "Just go to hell, you and him both, you belong together."

She hung up and then he was alone in darkness and disbelief.

For a moment there was no sound but the soft rustling of the shifting snakes. Then Chelsea said, "Why did that woman think the man who killed her daughter was dead, Adam?"

He turned to her as the display light faded out on his phone and left him in blackness.

"Because he is," Adam said. "He is. He was supposed to be, at least. I don't understand, someone else had to do this for him because —"

"You know who it was?"

"I thought I did." He could not lie to her, not now, he had no energy left for lies. Hardly had the energy to breathe. He had finished it, he had made good on every promise, but now Rachel Bond's mother said that nothing was fixed, nothing was finished.

"How? Who told you?"

"Kent gave me the name. He gave it to the police, and to me."

Kent saw him, he thought. *Kent knew that it was true, he was certain.*

Chelsea had slipped into a sweatshirt, and she approached him now and put her hands on the side of his face, holding him as if to prevent him from turning from her, though he had no desire to do so.

"What did you do, Adam?"

"I killed him."

She took her hands away from his face. Whispered his name. That was it, just his name.

"He came to my brother's house with a gun," Adam said. "He threatened his family, and he talked about Rachel Bond's death. He did it, Chelsea, he did it, so I don't know who gave these photographs to Penny, but the man I killed was the right man."

"You shot him? Murdered? Just went out and —"

"He had a gun, too," Adam said.

"You murdered him," she repeated.

"I did what I promised I was going to do. What needed to be done."

She stepped away from him, then slid down the wall until she was sitting on the floor, her bare legs stretched out in front of her. She wasn't looking at him anymore. Didn't seem to be looking at anything.

"How did you even find him?"

"I was getting close by myself," he said. "Then Kent took it home for me. He gave me the man's name, and I'd already found his half brother. Rodney Bova."

"You used his brother?" she said. "That's how you found him? By putting a tracking device on his brother?"

"Yes."

"Rodney Bova didn't just happen to get arrested in time for this." Her voice was soft and distant and impossibly sad.

"No."

"So you...what did you do? Just call in a tip after you found out he had drugs on him?"

"I did a little more than that."

"*Adam.*" She put her face in her hands.

"I intended to fix that at some point."

"How?"

"I don't know, Chelsea. But I will make that right. I always was going to. I just needed him. And it worked, damn it. He led me right to him. It worked."

"You could have called the police. When you found him, you could have—"

"When Gideon Pearce killed my sister, the police had been looking—"

"*This isn't about your sister!*" she screamed.

He didn't answer. It was silent for a while, and then he sat down on the floor, too. Not close to her, though. Across the room, widening the distance, staring at her from the shadows.

"They'll find out, Adam," she said. "Someone will talk. Bova, Penny, someone."

"They'll be suspicious. They won't be certain. There's a difference."

"To a guilty man, I guess there is."

What could he say to that?

"Can they prove it?" she asked finally.

"That won't be as easy for them as connecting it back to me was."

"What will the tracking logs show them?"

"That Rodney Bova went to a house on Erie Avenue where Sipes was staying, and that I knew about it. It will be hard to prove anything beyond that. Possible, of course. But harder."

Chelsea didn't speak. Adam said, "He killed that girl, Chelsea. Murdered a child."

"It sounds like maybe he didn't."

Adam couldn't begin to wrap his head around that. He'd known it was true. He'd walked all the way down to the lake with Sipes and Sipes knew what he believed and he'd never said a word, never issued a denial. Why?

"He was a predator," Adam said. "Even if somehow we were wrong, and I don't know how we could be, he was still a threat. He'd stalked a woman for years and ended up in prison because of it, and as soon as he was back out, he began to stalk my brother and his family. He came to their home with a gun in his hands, Chelsea. He was a predator."

"And so you decided to become one, too."

"What do you want from me?" he said. "I'm asking honestly. Tell me what you think I should do, and I will do it. Do you want me to confess? I can call them now."

"I want you to be with me," she said. "And I want you to be right, Adam. To be the person you really are, not the person you've let yourself become."

"I may need an alibi," he said slowly. "If it comes down to that, if they push hard enough, I'm going to need to be able to say where I was."

"I'll do it."

"I don't want you to."

"Who else will, Adam? Who else?"

"My brother, maybe," he said.

46

As he followed Salter down the sidewalk, up the steps, and into the police station, Kent recalled the trip after the first playoff game, the night it all started. How terrible that night had seemed. How impossible for it to get any worse.

Robert Dean was waiting for them. The agent showed not a trace of Salter's fatigue. He hummed with the same quiet energy he'd had in their first meeting. *Good motor,* Kent would have said of him if he were a football player. He just struck you as the sort of guy who could run a long time without rest.

"I understand your family is secure," Dean said.

"They are," Salter answered for Kent.

"Good." Dean nodded. He had the notepad and pencil out again. He looked at the pencil and not at Kent when he said, "I'm sure you will not share my opinion after the encounters you had with the man, but I consider the loss of Clayton Sipes rather disappointing."

"I don't wish death on anybody," Kent said. "I want to know what I haven't been told, though, and why things were hidden from me."

"You're entitled to your frustration, but I don't agree with the categorization. I did not *hide* anything from you, Mr. Austin."

He was the only one who didn't call Kent "Coach." Salter couldn't help himself, it seemed; in this town, Kent was the coach. Robert Dean was not from this town.

"Clayton Sipes was a very dangerous man in some ways," Dean said. "He was certainly a troubled man. He had an ill mind and it is becoming more than apparent that he did not receive the proper sort of help. That's a shame. But he was not a violent man, Mr. Austin."

"He *pointed a gun at me!*"

"He did not use it."

Kent almost laughed. It was that insane a comment. Instead he shook his head and said, "He was in prison for a reason. He'd been convicted of assaulting a woman. What is that if not violent?"

"He fondled her breasts while he held an unloaded weapon. Criminal, yes. Disturbing, yes. It is sexual assault, but I'd hesitate to call it *violent*. He did not attack her, did not leave so much as a bruise. In the many months — years — he spent stalking that poor woman, he did not take truly violent action. He seemed to prefer the game of it. In his history we find stalking, voyeurism, even arson, but we do not find an inclination toward violence. His psychological evaluations support this. A love of it, yes, a fascination with it, but more as a spectator sport."

"You could have said that before. You knew I believed that he killed Rachel Bond."

"You and I were each operating with limited understanding at that time. We have new information today. It started when Sipes was killed. When we found the apartment where he was staying in Cleveland, we found evidence suggesting that while he was a participant in the Rachel Bond homicide, certainly some level of collaborator, he was not alone. In fact, it appears he was very much under the control of another man. I would venture to guess, at this point, that you were actually of greater interest to this suspect than you were to Sipes."

"Who are you talking about?"

Dean glanced at Salter, then extracted a piece of paper from the back of his notebook and slid it across the table to Kent. It was a photograph of Dan Grissom. Kent's first reaction was to shake his head, dismiss it as a mistake. Clearly, Dean had given him the wrong photograph. Then he saw the agent's face and understood it was anything but a mistake.

"I don't believe that," Kent said. "Dan's a minister, he's a counselor, he's —"

"No," Dean said. "He is not. Daniel Grissom holds a degree in theology, but he is not a minister with any church. In fact, he was expelled from a seminary six years ago. He also holds a degree in psychology, but he has never practiced in a clinical environment. Aside from the degrees, the résumé he offered when he began his prison ministry was largely falsified. It was, unfortunately, also unquestioned. He was not a corrections officer; he was not being given weapons or keys or anything that might have required that thorough a background investigation. He was not even employed by the state. His organization was a voluntary effort. He said he was there to help, he had a convincing story, and he was believed."

Kent was staring at the photograph. He'd been visiting the prisons for years with other people when Grissom reached out to him. So compelling. So earnest. He told Kent that he found his efforts fascinating and hoped Kent would consider working with him.

"How long have you known this?"

"Me, personally? A matter of hours. I've already interviewed three other targets of Mr. Grissom."

"People like me?"

"No," Dean said. "People like Sipes. I haven't found anyone else like you yet, though I'm sure there are some. His primary interest in the false ministry seems to have been in recruitment. Control. Daniel Grissom likes to compel men to follow him. That seems to be a high priority. In your situation, for example, what he saw was an opportunity to test two men, to explore their boundaries. You, and Clayton Sipes."

"You know all this, yet you haven't arrested him?"

"I've learned all of this in the past day, after the discovery of evidence linking Sipes to Grissom. I'm working as fast as I can, Mr. Austin. We all are. And much as with Clayton Sipes, arresting Grissom first requires finding him."

"What are you talking about? Grissom isn't hiding."

"He is now. He has been since September, in fact."

"But I just talked to him."

"When?"

"Maybe a day after I talked to you. I called him to ask what he remembered about Sipes. He was—" *Very encouraging,* Kent wanted to say. "He seemed normal. Seemed the same as he always had. And he answered his phone. So what do you mean he disappeared?"

Dean leaned forward. "Did he answer the phone? Or did you leave him a message?"

Kent had to think about that for a second. "A message. He called right back, though."

That seemed to deflate Dean.

"He was still close to the phone," Kent said. "And the only number I have for him is a landline. So—"

"We've already pursued this route," Dean said. "It appears to be how he maintained contact with Sipes as well. It looks as if he checks his messages from a safe line, and then he apparently returns the calls from yet another number. He paid the bill a year ahead. He was anticipating that he might be pursued, clearly, and preparing for it. We're going to keep the line active and hope he makes a mistake, but I'm not counting on it."

"Why would he go through the motions of returning my call if he thought he could already be a suspect?"

"I'm not at all surprised to hear that he returned your call. I suspect he was intensely interested in what you had to say. You may hear from him again. Previously, Sipes was able to offer updates about you. That's no longer the case. Grissom made a decision to take control."

"How?"

"Sipes is dead, Mr. Austin, and contact is still being made with you. Once the contact came from Sipes, now it does not. Do the simple math. If there was a falling-out between them, and it would appear that there was, then Grissom killed his partner and assumed total control. And immediately he felt the need to reach out to you."

"Reach out to me. That's what we're calling those photographs?"

"The question," Dean said as if Kent hadn't spoken, "is whether he understands his cover is already blown. It's hard to say. My fervent hope is that he believes killing Sipes might have added a layer of protection. Two men walked out of a house with a secret, one man remains."

"Why not run, then, hide, whatever? Why not let it rest?"

"I'd say he enjoys the idea of what he's putting you through. He knows you suspected Sipes. Beyond that, he knows that you *believed* it was Sipes. Then Sipes was killed. It doesn't seem to be in keeping with his goals to let you live with the peace of that, the sense of resolution. Whether he runs now or stays with it, I'm certain he wanted to provide you with the knowledge that you were wrong. He wanted to take the evil you thought was gone and resurrect it."

"That's all Sipes," Kent said. "I know he couldn't have put up the photographs, but the ideas you're talking about, the goals, that is all Clayton Sipes."

"Dan Grissom had visited with Clayton Sipes on five occasions before he arrived at Mansfield with you. Sipes wasn't taken aback by you, he wasn't reacting. He was prepared."

"Five times?"

Dean nodded. "Six more after your visit and before his release. They'd formed quite a bond. Shared a similar worldview, it seems. So whatever Sipes said to you, he probably believed, Mr. Austin. But that doesn't mean the ideas were of his own mind. They could have been put there. After the interviews I conducted today, I suspect they probably were. There was a partnership at play here. Originally, Dan Grissom had his job — Rachel Bond — and Clayton Sipes had his: dealing with you. Dealing with you, and deceiving you. He did it well. But once Rachel was gone, Grissom didn't have his own game to play anymore. I've wondered if there could have been a territory battle."

"Over me."

"Over the goal of breaking you, yes. Grissom protected himself by letting Sipes take the lead at first, but it's quite possible he wanted it back. He seems to value control."

Kent was remembering the photographs again, Rachel Bond's eyes seen through the milky plastic, his own daughter's seen bright and smiling and oblivious.

"You need to find him," he said. His voice was hoarse.

"Agreed. We're hoping you can help. If you can bring him to the surface...that's what we need, Mr. Austin. We need him to appear. For you he might, even if he is concerned that his cover is blown. You seem to be of great value to him, great excitement. Will you help us?"

"You want me to bait him?" Kent didn't like the idea, wanted no part of it.

"Yes. We'd like you to call him again, at least. Just as you did before, when you were unaware of the situation. Leave a message, wait and see if he responds. We'll talk about what you say, and we'll work on how you say it. Are you willing to do that?"

"You'll keep my family protected?"

"Absolutely. Of course."

Kent took a deep breath and nodded. "We can try."

"Thank you. It may help."

"If it does," Kent said, "if I can bring him to the surface, as you termed it, are you prepared to convict him?"

"We're building a very strong case."

"You *are building*? That implies that it is not yet built. That you do not have the evidence you need to convict. Can you prove he killed Rachel Bond?"

"I believe we will, yes. We have DNA samples from the house and from her body that do not match with Sipes. If they match with Grissom, and I think that they will..." He spread his hands, his point made. Then lowered them to the table and said, "I will see that man convicted, Mr. Austin. Have some faith in me, please. I'll see that it's done."

Kent was quiet, and when Dean spoke again, his voice was gentle, soothing.

"What's on your mind, Mr. Austin? I'm trying to give you answers this time. I'll offer what I can."

"I believed in him," Kent said.

"He had a convincing story."

Kent shook his head. "Not just the story, Dean. I believed in him."

"What he is," Dean said, "is a false prophet, Mr. Austin. And a convincing one."

47

HE CALLED GRISSOM AT SIX in the morning, after some coaching from Robert Dean, who liked the feel of an early call, the sense of need it would create.

"If you seem emotionally desperate," he said, "it could be very appealing to him."

Seeming emotionally desperate was not a difficult task for Kent. Keeping his voice steady and not shouting at the son of a bitch who'd taken photographs of his family less than twenty-four hours earlier, this monster who'd left a beautiful girl dead in a ditch and then sent Kent tokens of the horror, that was the difficult task.

He got through it. Called from his cell phone while Dean listened. Kent had told Dean that admission of fear would matter. If Sipes had been acting at Grissom's request, then fear was paramount. They'd wanted to break him. Dean suggested that Kent ask Grissom to pray for him. That was the only thing Kent refused to say. His voice did not waver as he left the short but carefully choreographed message.

Dan, it's Kent Austin. You're probably asleep, and I'm sorry if I woke you, but... I could use you right now. If you have a chance, I'd appreciate a call back. Clayton Sipes is dead, Dan, but this thing is not. I don't know what to say or what to do. The police seem to be blaming me, almost, but I saw Sipes, so I don't know how they can fault me for what I told them. Whoever's doing this is targeting my family. I'm afraid for them, Dan. I'm truly afraid.

If you've got time to get together, or at least time for a phone call, it would mean a lot to me, he told the murderer, and then he disconnected.

"We'll see if he bites," Dean said.

Yes. They would see.

Dean wanted him to go about his routine that day. To coach his team, play his games. Police would be watching, he said.

And so he did. He stopped by the hotel where they had his family, he held Beth in an exhausted embrace, and he kissed his children and told them that it was all going to be fine soon, it was just a bad day and they'd have to get through it. Part of growing up, he said. They were going to have some bad days now and then, and it was important to learn how to get through them. You had to keep your head down. You had to endure.

He coached in a fog. His staff had heard about the chaos at his home in the night, and half the kids had, too. He was a well-known man in a small town. It was not a situation for privacy, let alone for secrets, and still he had tried, and hoped. He told his coaches that he couldn't talk about the matter, as required by the police, and asked for their help in keeping the kids focused. They tried. Everyone tried.

It should have been a euphoric few hours on the field. They were coming off the biggest win in their careers, they'd defeated the second-ranked team in the state, they were two wins away from a championship. Instead, the mood was hushed, everyone sharing whispers about what was going on with Coach, everyone confused and uncertain. Kent's involvement was minimal. Byers ran most of the practice, while Kent stood on weary legs and chewed on his whistle and watched his undefeated boys. When practice was through, he began to walk directly to his car. The team gathering at midfield confused him somehow, even though it was the daily routine, and it wasn't until he saw players taking a knee that he realized he still had the prayer to lead.

The words didn't come easily. He prayed for their health and thanked God for the opportunity to be surrounded by this group for another week. Kept it short, then tried to disappear from the field, but didn't make it. Colin Mears caught him before he could, and told him that he wanted to be benched.

It would have mattered, once. It would have been extremely important, a star player suggesting that he no longer deserved to be on the field during a playoff game. This morning Kent looked at him and could hardly register why anyone might think that this football field and what happened on it was significant.

But it is, he reminded himself, thinking of the days after Marie disappeared, of the long walks to watch film with Walter Ward, of the hours spent wearing his shoulder down to rubber, flinging a football at nothing. It had mattered to him then, and it mattered to Colin now.

"We're not benching you, son," Kent said.

"I'd like you to. Please. I'm not helping the team out there anymore. You know it, Coach, everyone does. I promised we'd win state for her. I promised that. I'm not going to help us. I wish I could, but I'm not going to."

Kent hadn't slept in thirty hours, had gone from the biggest victory of his career to the most stunning of personal horrors, and he had nothing left in the emotional tank. He was emptied, or as close to it as he had been in many years.

"We've got all week, Colin. We'll talk things through. Okay?"

He squeezed the boy's shoulder, moved past the locker room without entering, and went into the parking lot to find Chelsea Salinas waiting at his car. He was a few steps away from her still, far enough that he wasn't ready to speak himself, when she said, "How could you give him the name?"

"What?"

Her eyes were red and her usually mocha skin looked like a winter sky. She said, "You knew what he wanted to do, Kent. He'd *told* you. And you just gave him the name and stepped aside, you didn't even think to warn me? I might have been able to help. You might have been able to help. Instead you just let him go out there and—"

Her voice was rising to a scream, and Kent put his hand on her arm and whispered, "Stop shouting, Chelsea. What are you talking about? What happened to Adam?"

She shrugged off his touch. "So far? Nothing. Soon, though? Soon you'll get to visit him in prison. And you could have stopped it."

He'd been lost from the start—this morning, the act of thinking was like wading against a strong current—but suddenly it took shape and he saw it clearly and was horrified.

"Sipes," he said. That was it, just the last name, and she did not respond, but her eyes told him all that he needed to know.

"Where is he?" he asked. "Where is my brother?"

"He's gone to talk to your sister," she said. A tear had seeped free and was gliding over her cheek. "And, Kent? You damn well better help him."

"How can I help?"

"By giving him an alibi. Whatever he says he was doing when Sipes was murdered, you better be prepared to back him up." She saw something in his face that seemed to infuriate her and said, "Yes, you'd better be prepared to lie. You better lie your ass off, Kent, because it's the only thing that might save him, and you owe him that much at least. You let him go on when you could have stopped him. I know you'll never forgive either of us for driving away from Marie that night, but you let him drive away this time."

"Chelsea, I didn't have any idea —"

"Bullshit, Kent. He told you exactly what he intended to do."

"And I told him *not to do it*."

"At first," she said. "When Sipes showed up for you, though? What did you do then?"

"He offered to help. He offered —"

"You came to him for a gun," she said. "And you were looking for one, all right, but you also were looking for someone to pull its trigger for you. Tell me I'm wrong."

"I didn't think he would actually do this."

She shook her head in disgusted disbelief. "It's worse than what we did to you, Kent. It's worse. Back then, we didn't know what might happen. This time? You knew."

48

S HE WAS NOT WRONG.

Kent accepted that as he drove. His instinct was to defend himself, to rationalize. The only thing he'd ever said to Adam about killing Clayton Sipes was to tell him not to do it, not even think about it. Those had been his instructions, and he could hide behind them if he wished.

Just as he'd hidden behind Adam since the moment Sipes arrived.

He would not do that now. There are different layers of honesty — the truth of what you said and the truth of what was in your heart when you spoke the words. They did not always share a path.

There were things that stood out to him from the day he'd revealed Sipes's identity to Adam. The photograph of his brother with another man's blood on him. The bruised and swollen hand. The way he'd not so much as blinked when he declared his disappointment that he'd not had the chance to kill Gideon Pearce.

I knew what he would do if he could, Kent thought. *I knew that.*

He remembered the unease he'd felt watching the old game film with Colin Mears. He hadn't been able to explain it at the time, or hadn't wanted to search deeply enough and honestly enough to do so. The reason was clear to him now, though. He'd watched the way they'd played that game — put Adam out there in front and let him do the hitting, let him do the savage work, with the understanding that if you stayed behind him you'd be untouched and unharmed — and he'd seen the truth of what he was doing with his brother and turned away from it.

I didn't know he could find him.

That much was true. But he'd known damn well what Adam would do if he *did* find him.

Chelsea had requested an alibi. Kent could offer that, but he thought that he could offer one better. He understood things that Adam did not, and in those things was a chance at making this right, at removing his brother from a hell that belonged to Kent. He'd brought Grissom here, Grissom and Sipes both, and it was time to own that. There would be no more running, there would be no more turning away from the conflict. Any hitting that was left to do, Kent would do himself, the way he always should have.

Adam didn't have words for Marie today. He'd done all of the right things, had knocked twice, had lit the right candles in the right order, but he couldn't call up any words.

So he just sat on the floor, thinking about all that he had done. Rodney Bova, framed for a felony. Clayton Sipes, shot and left dead by Lake Erie. These things had always been horrible, but they'd had purpose. They were required acts, the only means of atonement that carried any weight in this world. What he had done was brutal, but it was righteous.

Now he had been told it was the wrong man. What did that leave behind?

"I'm sorry," he told Marie finally. They were usually the last words he had for her, but today they were the only ones.

Someone knocked downstairs. At first he thought *police,* but then the knock came again and he realized it was not the front door but the side door. His family had always come and gone from the side door; visitors came and went through the front door.

Kent was here.

He got to his feet and left Marie's room without extinguishing the candles. Went downstairs and through the kitchen and pulled open the door and saw his little brother standing there and wished he couldn't see him, because Kent looked that bad. Looked wounded.

"Chelsea talked to you," Adam said.

"Yeah."

Somehow Adam wasn't surprised.

"What did she tell you?"

"All there was to tell, I think," Kent said, stepping inside. Adam closed the door behind him and moved to sit at the kitchen table. Kent joined him, sitting where their father belonged. Adam had always tried to keep Kent away from those long night sessions at the kitchen table, Scotch disappearing like water, bloodshot eyes taking aim at impossible targets. Adam would tell his brother to get his ass down to the field or the weight room or Walter Ward's house. The position opposite their father at the table on those nights was Adam's place, Adam's burden. He'd tried to keep Kent away from it, and for a long time, he thought he had succeeded. But here they sat. Their father was gone, and Kent was where he'd been once, and the realization made Adam sad.

"I wish you hadn't done it," Kent said. He didn't ask whether

Adam had done it. Clearly, Chelsea had left him no room for doubt. "Adam, you should have —"

"I know what I should have done," Adam said. "And what I shouldn't have done. I put a bullet in an innocent man's head, Kent. That's where it stands now, am I correct?"

Kent nodded.

"Great." Adam took a deep breath. "He was a piece of shit. A predator. But I deal with the same kind of people all the time. I'm not putting a gun to all of their heads. I wanted him because of what he'd done. Only he never did it. So what I'm left with..." He ran a hand over his face, falling silent.

"We will keep you clean," Kent said.

"*Clean?*" Adam looked up. "A bit late for that, Franchise."

"I mean with the police. We can't change what you did, no. We can change who knows about it, and what happens because of it. We can still control that much."

"I don't even know if I want to," Adam said. "But regardless, I'll take care of myself. Chelsea probably said you needed to help me. I've decided I don't want that, though. Stay away from the wreckage, Kent. I'll take care of —"

"If we can find him, we can keep you out of prison," Kent said.

Adam stared at him. "Find who?"

"I know who it is, Adam. This time I *really* know. I spent the whole night with the FBI."

"Tell me," Adam said, and then he listened as his brother explained the whole thing, the sociopath who'd impersonated a minister, who'd walked in and out of the prisons in which he belonged and sought recruits. Found one. Clayton Sipes.

Adam lit a cigarette but couldn't smoke it. The inhalations were too hard, so he set it back in the ashtray and let it burn itself out.

"They believe Grissom killed Sipes," Kent said. "Right now, there's not even a doubt in their minds. You're not a suspect."

"It'll change fast. Bova was already suspicious, and if he starts talking, and at some point he will, they'll get to me. When they realize I knew about the house where Sipes was staying, they'll begin to press. Then it's a matter of whether I can hold up against the pressure."

"How long did you follow him before...before you killed him?"

"Bova?"

"Sipes."

"I never followed him. I found him and I killed him."

Kent frowned. "Sipes was staying in Cleveland."

Adam shook his head.

"No," Kent said. "I'm not wrong on this. They told me they got to Grissom through evidence found in an apartment in Cleveland. That's where Sipes was living."

Adam looked at him for a long time. Said, "He was in Cleveland?"

"Yes."

"He had to have a place to operate here. Did they not mention that yet?"

"No. It's not a long drive, Adam. He probably just—"

"How did they find the place in Cleveland?"

"I have no idea."

"Find out."

"Adam, why does it matter?"

"Find out."

Kent called his contact with the FBI, got an immediate answer, and Adam listened to one side of the conversation. Kent played it well. Surprisingly well. Led with questions about Grissom, about the security plans for his family, said that no, he had not heard from Grissom, but, yes, he did have one question. How did they know where Sipes was staying? From his end, Adam couldn't hear the answers, but he could get a sense that it had something to do with a phone. He hadn't searched Sipes, not for a phone or a wallet, not for anything. Why would he have? There had been nothing left to hunt once Sipes was facedown in the rocks.

"Who did he call?" Adam asked when Kent hung up.

"Dan Grissom, for one. The same number I have for him, the one he only uses for messages. And his landlord. Promising money for rent. I guess they'd been threatening eviction. Maybe that's why he came to Rodney Bova. Looking for cash?"

"That would be consistent," Adam said, and his voice sounded distant even to his own ears. "So he was staying in Cleveland?"

"Yes."

Adam got to his feet. Kent said, "Where are you going?" but he didn't answer. He went outside, unlocked the Jeep, and found his camera. Came back inside, turned on the display and clicked backward through his recent photographs, then passed the camera to Kent.

"Is that him?"

It was a picture of the man who'd left the house at 57 Erie Avenue just before Adam began to drive away and spotted Sipes in the window. Sipes had been looking out at the street, and Adam had thought at the time he might be keeping an eye on things, checking his safety. Maybe not, though. Maybe he'd been watching his messiah depart.

Kent was staring at the display window of the camera.

"Is it him?" Adam repeated.

"Yes." Kent's voice was barely audible. He moved back through a few pictures, then went forward again, to the close-up of the man who'd left the house. "That's Dan Grissom. When did you take a picture of him?"

"Thursday morning."

Kent looked up. "Just before…"

"Yeah."

"Where was he?"

"With Sipes. It's the place where Sipes was staying."

"Not in Cleveland."

"No. So if he had a place in Cleveland, and Grissom is missing, then…"

Neither of them said anything for a minute. Kent was staring at the camera, and Adam thought that he was trying to place the house. Kent would not know that house, though. Kent would not know the street. They'd been on it a few times, when they were kids, when the steel mill was still alive and their father worked there. But in the years since, Adam doubted that Kent had ever had occasion to drive back through. He'd coached some fine players from the neighborhood — Erie Avenue was home to hitters, the kind Kent liked — but he would not recognize the houses. It was not his world.

"Do you know whether Sipes was staying there alone?"

"I don't. Bova went there in the middle of the night. I was at your house, so I didn't want to leave. I waited until morning and then I went to check the address out. This guy came out and drove away, and Sipes stayed behind. I got him then."

The phrase made Kent grimace, but he said, "This has to be where he is. Sipes would have come to him, not the other way around."

"You think?"

Kent nodded. "Control is big to Grissom, according to the FBI. It's critical."

"I wonder if he's gone now. If I scared him off by killing Sipes."

"Yeah," Kent said. "I wonder." He finally set the camera down, and now his attention was on Adam and his face was thoughtful. "Can I have that gun back?"

"Why?"

"Same reason I wanted it before. In case I need protection."

"Bullshit, Franchise. Tell me what you're thinking."

Kent was silent. Adam spread his hands. "Come on, Kent."

"I'm thinking," his brother said, his brother who was on the front page of today's paper with his arms upraised, signaling victory, "that if Grissom is dead, he takes the Sipes case with him. They're already assuming he's responsible for that. If he's around, they'll have to investigate it hard, because he won't admit to doing it. He may know damn well that *you* did it."

Adam shook his head. "Stop."

"I can do it," Kent said. "I'm the right one to do it. In so many ways."

"Stop talking like me," Adam said. He'd never meant anything more.

"He's taking pictures of my family, Adam. Last night I got home and found photographs of a murdered girl beside photographs of my daughter."

Thirty minutes earlier, Adam had thought his ability to feel righteous fury had been extinguished, probably for good. He'd been sure of it. But it rose now like a rogue wave.

"Fuck it," he said. "I'll take him down. I went this far to do it, I might as well finish."

Kent was shaking his head. "Let me."

"Hell, no. Kent, look at what you've got to lose. Look at what I've got—it's already lost."

"I could get away with this. You can't. After the night I've spent with the FBI, if I say he approached me and I killed him in self-defense, everybody buys it. Everybody."

"Stop," Adam said again.

Kent fell silent. They looked at each other for a long time, and then he said, "At least let me give the address to the police, Adam. Don't let them get it from you. If it comes from you, everyone is looking at it different. If it comes from me, they'll believe it."

"How will you claim you got it?"

"I'll say he called my cell. They're hoping that he will. They don't have it tapped, though, so they can't record what's said."

"They'll know whether a call came in."

"Then I'll call myself from somewhere. A pay phone, some-place in that neighborhood, whatever. What happens after that, they will believe."

Adam felt sick, listening to him. He'd always hated their dif-ferences. He'd hated Kent for the way he approached Marie's murderer, going into the prison and praying for the son of a bitch. It had seemed, back then, that no response could be worse. There was one, though.

This was worse.

"We'll give the address to the police," Adam said, "and let them take it from there."

"That'll end with you in prison. Maybe with Grissom there, too, but definitely you."

"Maybe it does, maybe it doesn't. But we'll let them finish it."

Kent leaned forward and rested his forehead on the edge of the table. He looked exhausted. Worse than that, actually. He looked beaten.

"It's on me, Adam. The whole damn thing. I brought it all here, and you were right all along. I should have been like you from the start."

"It's here despite you. Look at what you've done with your life, Kent. Look at what you've built for yourself, for other people. You actually wish you'd gone my way? Then you're a stupid son of a bitch."

Kent looked up but didn't say anything. Adam said, "I don't begrudge you, Kent. What you did with Pearce. It turned out well for you. It was the right thing."

"Turned out well? Look at where we are now!"

"That's got nothing to do with it, and the only person who

wants you to think that it does is the sociopath who's responsible for all of this. Don't start agreeing with him."

Kent leaned back in his chair with a weary sigh. Rubbed his eyes, got to his feet, and said, "Can I please have the gun?"

"I thought we were going to the police."

"We are. Well, *I* am. Let me come up with a way to tell them where you saw Grissom. Maybe they find him there, maybe not, but let it come from me."

"Fair enough. What do you need the gun for, then?"

"Protection. Just in case. The guy's a killer, Adam, and he's here for me."

"Just in case," Adam echoed. "Okay. Sure."

"You'll give it to me?"

Adam nodded. "It's still in my car."

"All right," Kent said. "You give me the gun and the address where you took this picture. I'll make a phone call to myself, just to log one so the story holds up. Then I'll go to the FBI and I'll give them the address. Say he asked to meet me there. Hopefully, he's still there. If he's not, then it'll still be a clue. It will be a lead. Evidence. Somewhere for them to start."

Kent had never been much of a liar. Just didn't have the capacity for it, even when he wanted to. Gave himself away so easily, because he simply could not look you in your eyes and tell you a lie. He wasn't looking at Adam now.

"That's what you're going to do?" Adam said. "Give the address to the police? You're not going to do anything stupid? Not going out there by yourself?"

"I'll give it to the police. Meanwhile, though, you need to go find Chelsea. Or someone. Just find someone to be with today, all right?"

"Why?"

"So they can't blame the phone call on you."

"The phone call."

Kent nodded.

"All right," Adam said. "Sure."

He went to the door, and Kent followed. They walked across the yard, mud and leaves clinging to their shoes, everything saturated from the previous day's rains, and out to the Jeep. Adam got the Taurus Judge out of the glove compartment, checked the cylinder, and then passed it to his brother. Kent took it almost eagerly. It seemed as if he'd grown comfortable with the feel of the weapon. Adam had never expected to see that.

Kent said, "I'm sorry, Adam. For all that's happened, for getting you into this, I'm—"

"That's not allowed in our family," Adam said. "If anybody knows that, it's me."

"What?"

Adam waved a hand back at their childhood home. "No apologies accepted in the Austin house, Kent. Nobody ever let me say it. Not you, not Dad, not Mom. Nobody. I drove off and left Marie and then nobody would even let me say I was sorry."

"That's because it wasn't your fault."

"I was supposed to bring her home, and I did not. Of course I didn't know what was going to happen, but that doesn't change anything. Instead we all sat around pretending I wasn't to blame."

"You weren't."

"I was supposed to bring her home," Adam repeated. He slammed the Jeep door shut. "She's the only one I've ever been able to say it to. The rest of you wouldn't let me, but I can say it to her."

Kent was staring at him, the gun in his hand, not saying a word.

"So don't you apologize for a damn thing," Adam said. "None of this is your fault, Kent. You didn't ask this sick bastard to come to town. Stop acting like you did."

"Okay." Kent nodded, then looked down at the gun and said, "I'm going to need the address."

Adam thought of Rachel Bond, the firm set of her jaw when she'd told him she didn't need advice, she needed an address. He'd given her the address instead of advice, and away she'd gone.

"Adam?" Kent prompted.

"Take it to the police," Adam said.

"I will."

"Okay," Adam said, and then he gave him the address. Kent repeated it, murmuring the numbers like a prayer, and then he said that it was time for him to go, and repeated his request that Adam go find Chelsea and stay close to her.

"We'll talk soon," Kent said.

"I hope so."

"Be safe," Kent said.

"You, too. Keep your head down, Franchise."

His brother nodded, and then walked to his car, got behind the wheel with the gun in his hand, and drove off down the street. Adam watched the taillights disappear.

"I love you," he said aloud, but the car was gone then and the street was empty.

He went inside to say good-bye to Marie and put out the candles.

49

KENT WANTED TO TELL NO LIES. Never did, but certainly he did not want to now, and certainly not to Adam after all he'd endured. So he'd chosen the forked tongue of honesty again, had told true words and true facts and concealed the reality of his heart.

He would tell the police. He would give them the address.

But first he would go there himself.

He believed in his theory, he believed it would work. If Dan Grissom died at his hand today, Robert Dean and Stan Salter and every other investigator on the case would not be surprised. Kent was, after all, the target of the man's assaults, and they also knew Kent. The whole town did. They knew him and believed in him, their understanding of his character was firm, and it would help him. Because he had made so many proper decisions for so long, the world would struggle to believe that he was capable of making so terrible a choice now.

The choice had been made, though. He was going to end it, for his family if not for himself. For Beth's safety, and Lisa's, and

Andrew's, he would remove Grissom from this world if he could. For Adam, who had already tried to do the same for Kent.

He kept the gun in his lap as he drove, and he prayed. It was the strangest prayer he'd ever offered. He asked for strength to do the wrong thing, and then forgiveness for doing it.

He knew that he would need both.

He prayed while he drove, and kept only his left hand on the wheel, the right occupied by the pistol. He felt as if letting it go, even for an instant, might derail his determination. He followed the car's navigation system as he wound through areas of town he hadn't seen in years, and then the soft instructional voice that guided him to the street announced that he was approaching and that his destination waited on the left.

He stopped praying then, tightened his hand around the pistol, and slowed. The street sign above him promised that his navigation system was correct: he'd arrived at the address Adam had given him.

The only problem was that 2299 Amherst Road was not the home in the photograph. It was a brick ranch alone on acres of property, a FOR SALE sign in the yard, not the least bit like the house Adam had captured in his photograph of Dan Grissom. Kent hadn't questioned him because Adam hadn't hesitated. He gave both the street and the numbers as if they were sacred to him.

He'd also given Kent the wrong address.

There had been a tradition, years ago, that steel workers named the blast furnaces that produced their product. Adam wasn't sure if such a thing remained in those few towns that still manufactured steel, but he remembered that the blast furnace of the Robard Company plant had been named Becky.

He parked beside the abandoned structure, his Jeep alone on

the property, overgrown train tracks snaking away from him and the massive tubing of the blast furnace casting shadows where the sun fought heavy dark clouds scudding in on a western wind. For years he'd taken a strange pride in the smoke that rose from the weathered stacks, because his father had taken pride in working there. For a moment, when he opened the driver's door, he swore he could still smell the smoke. Funny how the memory could taunt the senses.

He wore his standard jeans and boots and a black jacket that he left unzipped so he could reach the Glock holster easily. There was no drop piece today, no unregistered street weapon, just his own.

Maybe he's gone, Adam thought as he walked away from the steel mill and out to Erie Avenue. *Maybe he flushed after I killed Sipes, and we won't see him again.*

He paused when he reached the sidewalk and looked up the road. A white Buick Rendezvous was parked at the curb. The same car Grissom had left in the day Adam took the pictures.

For a time he stood where he was. Then he turned to his right, gazing out to where the lake stretched off toward Canada in an endless expanse of harsh water. He could see the fence that he and Sipes had passed through forty-eight hours earlier. A few gulls circled just above the spot where Sipes had died, scouring for food, dipping down to inspect, then finding nothing to their liking and returning to the sky.

Something buzzed, a warm hum on the silent street. His phone, vibrating in his jacket pocket. He slipped it out. Kent was calling.

He did not need to answer to understand that his little brother was calling from Amherst Road. Adam had known that he would go, and while it disappointed him, it also vindicated his decision. He'd sent Kent to the right place. There was no harm in 2299 Amherst Road. Adam was certain of that. He had stood in the yard and he had seen the things that were already there and others that could be there in time, and harm was not among them.

He held the phone until the last vibration was gone and the display went dark again, and then he put it back into his pocket and turned left, the lake to his back and 57 Erie Avenue ahead.

"Is my brother with you?" Kent said, phone in one hand and gun in the other, his car still running, the peaceful brick ranch house on Amherst Road still in front of him.

"No," Chelsea Salinas told him. "Kent, what's wrong?"

"I think we need to find him," Kent said. "Fast."

"What's wrong?" she repeated.

"If he's not with you then I think I know where he is, but you're going to have to help me find the place. It's a spot where Rodney Bova went in the middle of the night. That would have been Thursday morning. Adam had a tracking device on him."

"Why is he going there?"

"To keep me from doing the same thing," Kent said. "Chelsea, I need to know that address. Can you find it?"

"If the tracking device recorded it, then I can find it. Hang on."

"Hurry," Kent said. "Please."

She didn't question him. Set the phone down and he could hear things shifting in the office and could hear her fingers clicking over keys, and soon she was back, her voice fearful but firm.

"Fifty-seven Erie Avenue," she said. "What's happening, Kent?"

"I need to get there," he said. "Fast."

But Erie Avenue was all the way back across town, by the old steel mill. He could not make that drive fast. His brother had led him too far afield; he would never make it back in time.

"Call the police, Chelsea," he said.

"The police." She was hesitant, and he knew why. She was thinking of Adam and Sipes, of murder charges and prison cells, and as he slammed the car into reverse and began what he knew would be a too-late drive, she said, "I'm close. I'll go find him."

"Don't do that," he said. "Chelsea, just call the police."

She'd hung up.

He dropped the phone and pressed the accelerator to the floor and blew through a stop sign without a care, looking at the map on the navigation screen and knowing well that he would not make it in time. Whatever was happening, Kent would arrive too late, just as Adam had designed. He called his brother again while he sped along the rural roads. There was no answer.

He returned to the side door, where Grissom had exited the house back when Adam had no idea who he was, where Sipes had come down to meet Adam, shirtless and smiling, in the minutes before his execution. The empty aluminum frame of the storm door hadn't been pulled all the way shut, and it shifted in the gusting wind, a soft, steady knock.

Whap, whap, whap.

Adam's phone buzzed again as he approached the door, and this time he silenced it instantly, without bothering to check the display. He removed the Glock from its holster, studied the closed door, and wondered how to approach it. Sipes had opened it peacefully, had agreed to walk and to talk. There was no guarantee that Dan Grissom would do the same.

It seemed to Adam that the time for knocking on doors was past.

He drew his foot back and drove his right heel into the door just beside the knob. It was a perfect shot, fast and hard, and the frame splintered and tore and the door swung open, revealing the dimly lit linoleum stairs that led up from the driveway and into the kitchen. As Adam shoved the remnants of the storm door out of his way and took the first of the steps, gun in hand, he heard someone rushing into motion inside, the sound to the left of the kitchen. He cleared the steps and spun to the left, in a shooter's stance now, saw a blur of movement as Dan Grissom rushed out of the living room and down a hallway. Adam took one shot and only one; he knew even as he fired that he'd been a half-second too slow reaching the top of the stairs. The bullet caught air where Grissom had just been and then buried itself in the wall in a cloud of plaster dust.

It was just three strides from the top of the stairs to the threshold where the kitchen opened up into the living room, and Adam dropped to one knee as he reached it, then turned left again, saw that Grissom was at the end of the hall and, turning toward him, saw the shotgun in his hands and thought *I wish it was a different weapon* just before they both fired.

Adam's nine-millimeter bullet hit Grissom in the right side of his jaw, drilled him against the wall, and then dropped him to the floor, blood and bone and flesh streaking the dusty yellow paint. It was a perfect head shot, clean and pure and deadly.

Grissom, both more panicked and less skilled, had not possessed similar aim.

The shotgun compensated for him, though, fired at fifteen feet, with a double-ought load. The thin layer of plaster between Adam and the muzzle did not impede the nine solid lead pellets that scattered from the shell. They tore through the wall and found his left side and opened it and spilled his blood. There was a reason why Adam had advocated for his brother to use the shot shells first if he needed them. They did not require precision.

He fell onto his right side but did not release the gun, keeping his eyes on Grissom, down at the end of the hall. Dead at the end of the hall.

Make sure, Adam reminded himself, and then he took careful aim, focusing through the pain that was catching him like a rising fog, and squeezed the trigger again. The Glock bucked once more in his hands, and another bullet found Dan Grissom, this one centered in the chest. The only reaction from the body came when the bullet passed through it. Dan Grissom was dead.

Got him, Kent, he thought. *I got him for you.*

Dizziness overwhelmed him then, and he put the Glock down and braced his right hand on the floor and sucked in a breath against the agony.

Be strong for just a while longer, he told himself. *Call it up, Austin. Find it. Damn it, you've still got some in there, now call it up.*

He gave a strangled cry as he pushed himself upright, got high enough so that his feet were under him and then he could use his right hand on the wall to steady himself. There was an instant when he thought he would faint, but he willed it down, and then he was moving back through the kitchen, taking care not to slip in his own blood.

He made it down the stairs and through the door and into the cold wind before he allowed himself to look at the wound.

All he could process was that he could see too much. Parts of him that should not be visible were, and the side of his jacket and his jeans were bright with blood. He used his right arm to pull the jacket tighter around him, and then, awkwardly, he zipped it up, as if that might help. He stood there for a moment, uncertain where to go. He would not make it far, but he did not want to stop here, either. He did not want to go down in this place, this evil house.

He spotted the brick smokestacks then, and he walked toward them, vaguely aware that they represented the place from which he had come, though he was no longer certain exactly how they did, or even where that place was. When he got to the sidewalk, he saw someone staring at him from the porch of a neighboring house. Words were shouted at him but they did not register. He hesitated again, looking at the smokestacks and realizing that while it had once seemed a good idea to return to them, they were too far away. He'd never reach them now.

He turned left and began to weave down the sidewalk. Ahead he could see Lake Erie, could see the gulls, still circling, creatures of diligence, able not just to survive the chill winds but to benefit from them. He remembered the rocks and the waves and the shallow pools that formed there where cold waters were trapped behind stones and thought that was the right place, and close enough to be reachable.

It took him a while to make the first block. His feet were not obedient and balance alone was a struggle, let alone forward progress. There were still shouts behind him, but he had no interest in trying to decipher them until one of the shouts was his own name. He stopped then, looked back, and saw Chelsea.

She was out of her car and running toward him.

Of course, he thought, hot pain easing toward warm relief, *of course.* She had come for him, and he should have known that she would, he should have remembered this, felt bad that he had not. He turned to meet her, but turning was a bad idea, it was too difficult a task for the uncooperative bastards that his always-strong legs had become, and they tangled and gave out beneath him and then he was down on the sidewalk.

When she reached him and took him in her arms, he saw that he was getting blood all over her, staining her with it, and he did not like that. There were tears on her face, and those were bad, too. She was telling him something about an ambulance, and he wanted to listen because it clearly mattered to her, but all that drew his attention were the tears and the blood. He wanted to clean them from her, but he was out of strength for that now, she'd have to do it on her own.

"I'm sorry," he told her. He was sure the words made it to her, he was sure they were clear, but she did not respond to them, she was still talking about the ambulance. He didn't answer, couldn't think of anything to say, but then she told him that she loved him and he knew what to say to that, that one was easy, because he loved her, too, always had. He was glad that she was there with him but wished it didn't have to be like this, with the blood and the tears.

"I'm sorry," he said again, and this time she seemed to understand how hard the words came, how much they took. She laid her hand on the side of his face, her palm a soothing cool in a world that had grown far too hot.

"I know, baby," she said. "I know. It's all right. It's okay."

50

$\mathbf{A}$ DAM WAS IN THE AMBULANCE by the time Kent arrived, but the police did not delay him long. They took him to the hospital without much pause, and so it was there that he learned his brother was dead.

A surgeon told him. Dead on arrival, he said, one hand applying what was supposed to be a reassuring touch to Kent's arm. Shotgun wound. He was very sorry. The police could explain more than he could. All he could say was that it was over.

Agent Dean was there by then, and Stan Salter. They did not ask questions yet, and for that Kent was grateful.

"He got Grissom," Dean told him. "We don't know much more yet. Grissom was dead inside the house, though. Your brother made it out, but did not make it far."

Kent nodded and asked if he could have a moment before they spoke any further. Dean said of course, he could take whatever time he needed, and asked if he wanted them to call Beth or if Kent wanted to do that himself. Kent said he would do it himself, and then he walked down the long, brightly lit corridor, his shoes slapping off shining disinfected tile, and out into the parking lot. His legs held up long enough to get him beyond the rows of cars and then he knew they would not last much longer, and he sought the closest place that looked dark and alone. There was a loading dock nearby, the doors down, no trucks in wait, and he made it that far, lowered himself onto the pavement, put his head between his knees, and wept for his brother.

He wasn't sure how long he remained there. He was aware of Dean and Salter coming to the hospital doors, and though they saw him they did not approach. Eventually his eyes ran dry, because that was the way it went; they had no other choice. He looked at Robert Dean and thought of what he'd said just hours earlier, when he filled Kent in on the relationship between Grissom and Sipes, of his theory that one had murdered the other.

Two men walked out of a house with a secret, and one remains.

He stood up, brushed the dirt from his pants, and walked back to where the police waited, back to explain how it was that his brother had come to die.

Inside the house at 57 Erie Avenue police found items belonging to Rachel Bond, and identified the deceased Dan Grissom and Clayton Sipes as the primary suspects in her homicide. Privately, Dean told Kent that the story had produced three calls from current inmates and one from a former inmate wishing to discuss Grissom. He believed that these accounts and forensic evidence from the house would be enough to close the Bond case, certainly, and, he hoped, several others. Kent asked if they would have been able to convict Grissom had he lived. Dean said they'd have had a strong shot.

Penny Gootee, Rachel's mother, told any news outlet that asked that she was pleased with the results and that Adam Austin had promised her the very killings he had delivered. That story went national fast. International, even. Kent received calls from reporters in France and England. That Sunday he met with his coaching staff and told them he'd step back for the remainder of the season, because his team didn't need that kind of media scrutiny, and he wanted to be with his family. He named Byers the acting head coach. He left them to the work that needed to be done then, closed the door of the conference room behind him, and left the locker room, pausing for one look at the picture of the 1989 championship team, the two Austin brothers standing together.

They buried his brother on Tuesday morning, just after dawn, in a private ceremony that was to be attended only by Kent's family and Chelsea Salinas. Stan Salter asked Kent if he could be there as well. Kent agreed. It was a swift, simple ceremony. The goal was to avoid media attention, and they managed that. When they left, Kent sent Beth on with the kids and asked Chelsea if he could have a minute with her.

She was wearing an elegant black dress and heels, but when they reached her battered old Corvette, she slipped the shoes off and then slid herself onto the dirty hood of the car. Kent stood before her in his suit and asked her what it had been like for his brother at the end.

She told him all that she could. Her voice wavered sometimes but never broke. Adam had known he was dying, she said, but she thought that he was glad to see her. He did not seem afraid, he seemed sorry. She wanted to remove that from him, to give him some peace as he went, and she was not sure if she'd succeeded.

"I'm glad you made it to him," Kent said, and he meant that. "But I wish I had, too."

"He would not have wanted to see you," she said, and on that point her voice was firm. "He did not want you to have to go near it."

"It was mine to deal with."

She pushed her hair back over her ears, stared at the cemetery grounds, and said, "He never could stop trying to make up for Marie. It's sad as hell, but it's also one of the reasons I loved him."

"I could have helped," Kent said, "and I did not. If I'd made some different decisions, or involved him more in those, then—"

"You know what he told me the other day, Kent? He told me that he wished he'd been able to coach with you. He wouldn't have wanted to be the head coach. I believe he wanted the defense only. And you know what that tells me? He was proud of your decisions. Maybe not all of them, that's impossible. But as a rule, he trusted them."

Kent worked on an answer and couldn't get to one.

"Should he have done what he did?" Chelsea said. "No. But he didn't do it for himself."

She looked away from the cemetery grounds and back to him and said, "Can I ask you something?"

"Of course."

"The place he sent you. The address he gave you. Was it outside of town? Amherst Road?"

He nodded. "How did you know that? What's the significance?"

For the first time, tears pooled in her eyes. She wiped them away and shook her head. "I just had a feeling," she said, and though he wanted to know more, he sensed that he should not ask. This one stood between his brother and Chelsea, and should remain there.

"I've been told he has no will," Kent said. "But I want you to be involved, because he would have wanted that."

She shook her head. "Trust fund for his niece and his nephew.

All of it. That's what he would have wanted. And a few other things. A few priorities. I can handle one. That's clearing Rodney Bova. I'll take care of that. The other one I think should come from you."

"Which is?"

"You can tell your sister what happened."

"Talk to my sister."

"It's what Adam did," she told him. "He'd like her to know, I think. I believe that would matter a lot to him."

Once this would have struck Kent as madness, but no longer.

"You know I could have gotten her home," he said.

Chelsea regarded him silently.

"Adam was supposed to drive her," he said. "But he'd told me he wasn't going to. He'd decided to let her walk. And all I was doing was watching game film. I could have walked her home myself, run back, it would have taken ten minutes. It all fell on Adam, but I knew the situation, and I made the same call he did. I said it was five blocks, what could go wrong. He wasn't the only one who failed to look out for her."

Chelsea said, "You ever tell him that?"

"No," he said, and his voice was unsteady. "No, I never did. But I wanted to tell you."

Chelsea's palm was cool when she touched his arm. "Tell your sister," she said. "Tell her that, and all the rest. It would have mattered to Adam."

"I'll do it," he said. "Will you be around, Chelsea? If we could talk at some point... I think we should. Please."

She looked away. "We can talk, Kent. But I don't think I'll be around for long."

"Where are you going?"

"I have no idea," she said. "But it's time for me to leave. I know that much. He was ready to, and so was I, and now... well, now

I'm what's left, right? But we weren't wrong about its being time to leave."

She slid off the hood of her car, and they said good-bye then, all that could be said, but she paused with her hand on the driver's door.

"I read in the paper that you're done coaching for the year."

"That's right. I don't belong on a football field right now, Chelsea."

"Your brother," she said, "would have kicked your ass over your shoulders for that."

Those were the last words she said to him before she got into the old Corvette and drove away. Kent took his wife and children home, and then he went to Adam's house, alone, to tell his sister that her brother was dead, and explain how he had gone, and why.

Matt Byers coached the team through the week. Kent did not make any appearances at practice. He wanted the news crews to go away, to leave his boys alone, and his presence there would not help. He stayed in a hotel with Beth and the kids until Thursday, when they finally ventured home. The cameras were gone. Some neighbors came by, but most people kept their distance, gave the family some space.

"You've got to be at the game," Beth told him. "You know that."

He knew it. They went together and sat in the stands, the first time he'd been in the stands for a Chambers game since he was a child, and watched as Byers used a run-heavy offense and a blitz-heavy defense to guide the Cardinals to a 14–10 halftime lead over the Center Point Saxons, a program known more for its marching band than its football team until this season. Lorell tried to connect with Colin Mears on two plays, both unsuccessful. He did not go back to him in the second half, and though the offense couldn't generate anything, the defense played brilliantly, giving up only a field goal to preserve a 14–13 win and earn a berth in the state championship game in Massillon.

The next week was supposed to be the same. He met with his coaching staff on Sunday and said that they'd done great work, and that he offered nothing but a distraction and that he needed to be with his family and not his football team. They told him they understood, and he told them that he knew they would get a win, and that was supposed to be the end of it. He'd sit in the stands in Massillon, that hallowed ground he'd dreamed of all year, and he'd watch from a distance.

On Monday evening, though, the doorbell rang and Kent went to answer it expecting a reporter and found Colin Mears instead.

"Can I have a minute, Coach?"

Kent didn't want to give him a minute. He didn't want anyone in his home except for his family, but of course he could not say that, so he let the boy in and listened as Colin told him that Kent needed to return to the team.

"I appreciate it," Kent said. "I do. But right now is not a time for me to be involved with football. You need to understand that."

He realized as he said it that if anyone understood, it was of course this seventeen-year-old boy.

"I'll be there to support you," Kent said. "You know that. But, son, I just don't have much to contribute right now."

"You've seen me play," Colin said. "You've seen exactly what I've contributed to these games. Nothing. But, Coach? I didn't quit on anybody."

"I'm not quitting on you," Kent said, but it was a hard position to defend. He'd chosen the stands over the field. It was the right choice, he thought, but how to make that clear to Colin, he was not sure.

"I promised Rachel we'd win it," Colin said. "You told me that didn't matter."

"It doesn't."

"When you promised me you'd be there regardless, did that matter?"

The boy was bristling with anger. It went beyond anger, actually. Betrayal, that was the word. Kent looked at him, told him he'd consider the request, and took him to the door. When he closed it, Beth was waiting.

"You heard?" he said.

"Yes."

"And?"

"You told him you need to be with your family now," Beth said. "But that team is part of your family, Kent."

And so he returned. He was at the field when the team arrived for Tuesday's practice, and nobody said a word to him, not coaches or players, they just waited to hear what he'd come to say.

"I'm not in a very good place right now," he told his team. "I don't know how much help I'll be to you. But I'd appreciate it if you all would let me be around to watch you finish what you started."

He let Byers run practice, and he helped with the position drills, commenting on technical details, not saying much, just observing. That night he watched video for the first time. Their opponent, Center Grove, was very good. They had a fine quarterback and skilled receivers and they spread teams out and scored lots of points. Their number-one receiver was a great route runner with sure hands, and their number two, a kid named Shepherd, was not so reliable, but he was fast. He could fly, and that threat opened the field. Kent spent an extra hour watching him.

On Wednesday he called Colin aside and asked if he'd watched video from both sides of the ball. Of course Colin had. He watched everything.

"If we needed you to," Kent said, "could you play press coverage on Shepherd? Could you stick with him?"

Colin stared at him. "You mean at cornerback?"

Kent nodded. "He's going to give us trouble with his speed. I know you can run with him, and we don't have anyone else who can. But are you able to play the position if we asked you to go man-to-man on a few plays? Be honest."

"I know all the routes," Colin said. He was giving the idea careful consideration, and he nodded. "I can play it."

"We might never use you," Kent said. "But it's an idea."

They were three minutes into the second quarter when Colin Mears caught his first pass—from the opposing quarterback. The game was tied at seven, and it was the third time they'd rotated him in to play press coverage as a cornerback. Kent was limiting him to down-and-distance situations where he knew they would pass. The first time he chanced it, they ran a draw instead of passing, but Colin flew to the ball without hesitation, coming in wild but fast, laying himself out to assist on the tackle. It took self-sacrifice to hit like that; you couldn't offer contact without taking some yourself. The next time he lined up at corner, they tried a pass to the tight end, and then, on the third attempt, Center Grove finally tested him. They sent Shepherd on a go route, pure speed down the sideline, and the quarterback put it out in front where only he could get it.

That was the idea, at least. But Colin was with him, it was speed on speed, and while the ball was in the air, he pulled a full stride ahead of Shepherd, eyes up, a receiver's instincts taking over now, forgetting his man to play the ball.

Just knock it down, Kent thought. That was all he needed to do, just knock it down.

Instead, he caught it. Pivoted and looked surprised, then saw open field ahead of him, and took off. Brought it back to midfield before he was tackled. On the sidelines the kids mobbed him, and Colin was smiling and Kent realized it had been five weeks since he'd seen a smile on the boy's face. It would not last, but it was there, and he was glad.

"Reward one, risk zero," Byers said in Kent's headset.

"My brother's idea," Kent answered, pacing down the sideline. The headset went quiet then, none of the other coaches sure what to say, but that was fine. Kent said, "Let's make them pay, gentlemen," and then it was football once more.

They led 14–7 at the half, and early in the third quarter, Lorell tried a pass to Colin on a slant route. The Center Grove fans seemed confused by the roar that went up from the Chambers crowd when he caught it for a simple gain of seven yards. He caught another just two plays later, and then Lorell scored on a run, and it was 21–7 and Byers asked Kent if he wanted to try Mears at cornerback again.

"I think we're good," Kent said.

It was never a ballgame in the second half. The final score was 35–10.

Beth met him at midfield, the kids at either side, and Kent said, "Why are you crying?" but then her arms were around him and he was crying, too. She reached up and pulled the brim of his hat down to shield them, her face pressed against his, her tears on his. She held him for a long time, and then she leaned back and wiped his face clean with her hand and said, "Go talk to your team."

He went to them. They circled at midfield, the way his teams had in so many season-ending games before, but this one was different. He did not need to tell them where the victory was tonight, where they might find it. The trophy was making its way through the ranks, everyone wanting a hand on it, and Kent watched and tried to prepare the right words.

"Gentlemen," he said, "I know this feels like a moment of pure celebration, and celebrate we will, but first I need to…"

He stopped then. *Remind you,* that's what he'd been about to say, *remind, remind, prepare, prepare.* But they had been reminded and they had been prepared and tonight they had won. Tomorrow might bring different things their way, but tonight they had won.

"I need to thank you," he said. That was all he had for them, tonight.

The prison occupies just over eleven hundred acres, most of that covered with pavement or buildings, tall fences and razor wire protecting the perimeter. It's a bleak place on the most beautiful of days, but in February, beneath gray sky and above week-old snow, it's particularly foreboding. Hundreds of people make their way to and from the brick buildings each day for work; more than two thousand remain inside. For them it is home.

The man and the boy are just visitors. The man is familiar with the place, the boy is not. They check in, pass a security screening, and follow a corrections officer down a winding corridor and through a series of doors that lock behind them as they pass. The boy, tall and lean and agile, looks at each door as it closes. The man asks him if he's certain he wants to do this, to be here.

The boy says he is.

All you have to do is listen, the man says. You don't have to say a word unless you want to.

Let's see how it goes, the boy tells him.

They're through a final door then, and in this room a group of

men in orange uniforms are seated on plastic chairs in all directions.
The corrections officer addresses them, says that the coach is here.
The man asks that they call him Kent, not Coach. He says that he's
not here to talk about football, that there are other things to discuss
today. He's here to tell them about his family, about his sister and
about his brother and about himself, here to tell them that they are
not so far apart, these men behind the bars and the razor wire and
the man who has earned his fame on a football field. They are not so
far apart at all, and it is important to know that.

I would like to tell you, he says, about the time I went to kill
a man.

I would like to tell you what I have learned.

ACKNOWLEDGMENTS

This book would never have been written without the generous support of the Bloomington High School North football program. To Coach Scott Bless and the rest of his staff, my deepest thanks for allowing me to be part of the program for the 2011 season, and for enduring all of my questions.

Tyler Abel deserves the lion's share of thanks, as he both facilitated my contact with the Bloomington North program and was forced to hear by far the most questions. He helped carry the book from an idea to a reality, and for his insight and friendship I am deeply indebted.

Thanks also to all of the players from that team, who provided a wonderful and dramatic season for me as I conducted my research. Nice conversion in overtime down in Columbus, guys.

Don Johnson of Trace Investigations was, as always, an invaluable resource, as was George Lichman of the Rocky River Police Department, and Gideon Pine was a tremendous help on the research front. Anything I got right is a credit to people like them.

On the book front, it's the usual suspects, but their critical roles cannot be overstated. To Michael Pietsch, David Young, Sabrina Callahan, Heather Fain, Vanessa Kehren, Victoria Matsui, Miriam Parker, Tracy Williams, Eve Rabinovits, and countless others at Little, Brown, thanks for the tremendous support you have provided these books. The Inkwell agenting team, David Hale Smith and Richard Pine and Kimberly Witherspoon in particular, also deserve grateful recognition, as do Angela Cheng Caplan and Lawrence Rose.

Deepest gratitude is reserved for all of the early readers who made it into something better than I could have on my own.

And for Christine. Always.

ABOUT THE AUTHOR

Michael Koryta is the author of eight previous novels, including *Envy the Night,* which won the Los Angeles Times Book Prize for best mystery/thriller, and the Lincoln Perry series, which has earned nominations for the Edgar, Shamus, and Quill awards and won the Great Lakes Book Award. His work has been translated into twenty languages. A former private investigator and newspaper reporter, Koryta lives in Bloomington, Indiana, and St. Petersburg, Florida.

BACK BAY · READERS' PICK

Reading Group Guide

THE PROPHET

MICHAEL KORYTA

DEAN KOONTZ INTERVIEWS
MICHAEL KORYTA

DEAN: Your new novel, *The Prophet,* is a crime novel, a suspense novel, but also a good novel about brothers and family relationships. I know you a little, and I'm 99 percent sure that you weren't cloned, that you have a family, but I don't know about siblings. You write so well about brotherly relationships that I wonder — do you have any? And football — playing it, coaching it — serves both as a background and as a solid metaphor for the value of traditions. Did you play football in school? Have you coached any?

MICHAEL: I was a natural athlete. Played every sport, and the responses from my coaches were unanimous and emphatic. Whether it was a basketball or football or baseball bat or golf club in my hands, they'd say, "Son, I think you should be a writer." It's good to have consensus. So, no, never played football beyond pickup games — I bruise too easily and lack fundamental coordination — but I was hopefully able to bring some authenticity to the book due to the tremendous level of help and access I received from Scott Bless, Tyler Abel, and the rest of the Bloomington High School North coaching staff. I spent a full year with them in coaching meetings, practice fields, and on the sidelines, and it was tremendous and fascinating. The bad news for them is I'm hooked now and currently drawing up plays. If they'll just give me a chance…As for brothers, I have none. Just friends who feel like brothers to me, in the good ways and the infuriating. And I have a sister who brings only the positive side.

DEAN: You quickly built a reputation for crime/suspense, and then went for a touch of the supernatural in *So Cold the River, The Cypress House,* and *The Ridge.* Did your agent freak out? Many years ago, when I first began ricocheting from genre to genre, I received more than a few heartfelt lectures about how I was destroying my career. Now, *The Prophet* has no supernatural edge. What is it with you, pal? Easily bored? Creatively restless? Enjoy walking a cliff's edge? Multiple personalities?

MICHAEL: Dean, please stop answering the questions before I can. Yes, yes, yes, and, certainly, yes to those last four. As for the genre ricocheting, I had a supportive agent. I lost a publisher, but that'll happen, and somehow I fell into the hands of Michael Pietsch at Little, Brown, who I think is one of the all-time great editors. Can't say enough about the team over there. They've indulged my flights of fancy, and I know it isn't easy, and I've heard plenty of lectures from other parties about the career suicide I'm cheerfully carrying out, but I'll always say the same thing here: You've got to tell the story that wants to be told. That's the joy of it, the privilege of it, and, I'd argue, the responsibility of it. To write the best story you can. That won't always fit in the same tidy box. And to try to do so seems far too close to actual work. I'm not cut out for actual work.

DEAN: When researching *The Ridge,* you became interested in big-cat rescue — lions, tigers, nothing as safe as your common tabby. Now you participate in rescues. In a way, your fiction entered your life and became part of it. The same has happened to me with Canine Companions for Independence and other things that I wrote about and subsequently became involved with. Tell us why big-cat rescue so appeals to you. And are there other examples of research/writing changing your life?

MICHAEL: The experience of working with the Exotic Feline Rescue Center is one of the truly special things in my life. I couldn't imagine *not* having those cats and those people in my life at this point. It's an amazing mission and deserving of support and, as you did with Canine Companions, I simply fell in love. I'd drop anything to go on a big-cat rescue, and will continue to do so as long as they'll have me. Research is forever changing my life and bringing new interests and new people into it, and that's one of the great privileges of this craft, the chance to visit so many different worlds.

DEAN: You're young. From my perspective, you're a puppy! Yet you've already published nine substantial novels and are at work on number ten. In your book-jacket photos, you often look intense, driven. In person, you're not like that; you're relaxed and easygoing. Which is the real Michael Koryta? Or are they both real — professionally driven but personally at ease? Given the commitment that's required to write well, do you find it difficult to strike the right balance between writing and downtime?

MICHAEL: I simply cannot take a good picture. If I smile for a photograph, I look evil. Possessed. Since I don't want to reveal this truth, I try to look brooding, haunted by remarkable stories and gorgeous prose. Now, they're not my stories and prose, of course, but no one need know that truth, either. Professionally driven? Absolutely. It's a privilege to have the chance and I want to do it well. Better than well. I'm not anywhere as close as I'd like to be. Personally at ease? Depends on the day. Striking the right balance isn't terribly hard, or hasn't been so far. The only real cost to all this is sleep. I've been a chronic insomniac since I began writing seriously, and I've given up on that ever changing.

DEAN: You're writing a novel about wilderness-survival training, so you went to a survival school. Presumably you survived. I went to Las Vegas so I could write about it, and I have drunk numerous California Cabernet Sauvignons so I could write about them. But I have my limits. Do you? Is there anything you wouldn't do yourself—aside from commit a crime—so you could better write about it? At survival school, did you have to eat grubs or rodents?

MICHAEL: I shouldn't have committed the crimes? Oops! I do love field research, though. That traces back to my PI days and reporter days, but I'd much rather step into the world I'm writing about than Google it. You simply can't achieve the same level of understanding if you go from the outside in. You'll find no gold if you don't pan for it, right? That sounds like a fortune cookie at a bad steakhouse. Such is my gift with words.

I did not eat grubs at survival school, though I did learn which ones were edible, and I also learned that if I came to the point where I needed to eat them, then I'd screwed up in every other lesson I'd been taught. As far as further research goes, I'm always on the hunt for something bizarre and fascinating. I see those chances as a tremendous gift that comes along with being able to do this for a living. I'd like to learn at least a little about as many things as possible. It's the journeyman approach, I suppose, but there are so many fascinating things in the world to me, from people who rescue big cats to people who fly airplanes to people who understand how to replace the leaf spring on a farm truck. These are all things I can't do, they're all fascinating, and I'd like to learn a little about as many worlds and skills and trades as I can.

DEAN: Most of us grab the chance to adapt our books to film. But film writing is highly collaborative, with every executive a potential master. I found I really liked the screenplay format, its fluid nature and ease of revision, but disliked everything else about the film process. Have you done some film writing? If so, how close to madness did you come? How close to homicide? Or are you one of the lucky ones who feel comfortable in both worlds?

MICHAEL: Past madness, short of homicide. I love the form. I've been fortunate to work with great writers and producers, genuinely good people. But if your novel becomes an irrelevant piece of source material, with an entirely new cast of characters and story, then it's awfully tough, not just letting go — you would probably not be surprised to discover how easily I can do that! — but because you've got to love a story to write it well, and supposing you don't love the one that's handed to you? It's tough. It's a grind, everything in it is foreign, and the emotional investment between writer and characters and story that is imperative for good work is one that can't be forced. Delivering quality work from that place is difficult for me. Every circumstance is different, though. I love movies, always have, always will, and one of these days it sure would be fun to see one of my stories break through to the big screen. We'll see.

DEAN: You were once a private investigator. I have a good friend who's a rather celebrated PI — there have been TV shows about a couple of his cases — and he seems to thrive on the challenge of bringing a case to a good resolution and on the occasional adrenaline rush. Did you enjoy the work? At what point — and why — did you give it up?

MICHAEL: I loved the PI work, particularly when the investigation was such that a resolution made a tangible difference in someone's life — child custody cases come to mind. I gave it up when I was able to make a living as a writer, because I think to do anything well you've got to commit at as deep a level as you can. I think the PI work would have suffered as the publishing schedule became more demanding, and that's not fair to clients who come to you with too much on the line. I do miss it, though.

DEAN: Do you ever suffer writer's block? For a day, a week, longer? If so, how do you trick yourself into getting on with the book? If not, why do you think you haven't been thus plagued? I know from time to time you suffer heavy self-doubt, as I do. I think I know you well enough to say that you use your self-doubt in some constructive way. Am I right?

MICHAEL: I suspect you smiled as you typed "Am I right?" because you've talked me off a ledge or two in the past. Yes, every book comes from a place of self-doubt, from the thought "When will I be exposed as a talentless fraud, when will they take my writer's permit away?" And in this is the thing that has thus far kept the writer's block away. I'm always anticipating the need for heavy, heavy revisions because I'm always convinced that what I'm creating is dreck. So I write every day, because I don't understand any way to improve other than to continue to work. And I also write every day because I love it. There's a quote from the songwriter Josh Ritter on my desk: "I sang in exultation, pulled the stops, you always looked a little bored / But I'm singing for the love of it, have mercy on the man who sings to be adored." I love that. It's a guiding light.

DEAN: I would never put a writer on the spot by asking him which living authors he most admires — which always leads to at least one friend having been unintentionally forgotten. But what deceased writers do you most admire, and why?

MICHAEL: There was once this guy named Dean R. Koontz. Had a middle initial, a mustache, and a bald head. I don't know what happened to him, because dust jackets tell me he is long gone, but I loved his stuff. Let's see, in all seriousness, keeping the list to a respectable length: Raymond Chandler, John D. MacDonald, Ross Macdonald, Dashiell Hammett, F. Scott Fitzgerald, Charles Dickens, G. K. Chesterton, Mark Twain, Ray Bradbury, Ira Levin, Robert Louis Stevenson, Sir Arthur Conan Doyle. Why? Because I think they were all storytellers first, and writers second. The story was the thing.

DEAN: We share some tastes in writers. As for Dean R. — now let's be fair, he wasn't bald but balding. You might find this funny, so indulge me. Being a tad vain, I long considered a state-of-the art surgical procedure along with transplants, by a specialist. I did not go forward when I was told the several procedures would take months and would be painful. Then when I changed dentists, I learned that I had for years been brushing my teeth too hard and, in the process, had worn away my gums. I needed to undergo eighteen months of gum transplants, and the tissue for the gums would be carved out of the roof of my mouth! My instant reaction was that the gum surgeries would be so painful that I wouldn't notice the scalp surgeries, which proved to be true. By the time my mouth was set right, I had a full head of hair. But the periodontist wasn't able to save one of my molars, which kept abscessing. I went to his office at 5:00, and he said I'd be out by 5:30. Instead, when he pulled the tooth, the roots proved to be fused to the bone, and they broke off. He wanted to sedate me, because Novocain wouldn't be effective when he was drilling in the jawbone, but I didn't like being put to sleep, so I remained awake for the three hours it required to remove the roots. When it was done, he told me that I had the highest pain threshold he'd ever seen — and I told him I needed to use the restroom really bad. Standing in front of the bathroom mirror, I saw one side of my face swollen as round as a basketball — and because the periodontist worked on that tooth from every imaginable angle, all of my glorious hair was disarranged and standing straight out from my head like Christopher Lloyd's in *Back to the Future,* like any cartoon character struck by lightning. I thought it was so funny that I didn't even try to comb it but paid the bill and went home that way. I'm not sure which was the better painkiller that night: the medication the doctor gave me, or the sight of myself in any mirror, which reliably cracked me up.

Now, a final question for you, Michael. When your doorbell rings long after midnight, who do you think will be standing at your threshold: (a) some thug I have hired, (b) my periodontist with a drill in hand, (c) my dog Anna wearing her stainless steel attack teeth, (d) me wearing my stainless steel attack teeth, (e) an IRS accounting squad to whom you will have to explain all those foreign bank accounts that have shown up in Credite Suisse files, (f) Wile E. Coyote with an Acme killing machine that will finally work? Also, what are your two favorite Ira Levin novels? My first is *A Kiss Before Dying,* and second is *Rosemary's Baby.*

MICHAEL: You realize I had to make that remark in 2012 when I had the chance, because my hairline is retreating faster — and with less hope of success — than Custer at the Little Big Horn. But my answer would certainly be, (c) Anna, because she is kind, forgiving, and blessed with a fine sense of humor.

And hopefully remembers that I once brought her a treat. As for Levin, the two titles you mention would be my favorites, but I have always thought that *The Boys from Brazil* is a sadly overlooked gem of a thriller. Many thanks for allowing me the chance to do this interview, and, if you will excuse me, I'm off to lock the door and hire a security sniper.

QUESTIONS AND TOPICS FOR DISCUSSION

1. Discuss the title, *The Prophet*. What is its meaning, and why do you think this is the killer's moniker? How does the title influence your conception of the book?

2. "Everyone was driven by the past, all the time," Adam thinks when he first meets Rachel (p. 12). To what extent do you think this is true for the characters in the book? Is it possible to break free from the past, or only to change your relationship to it? Cite specific examples from the book.

3. The book alternates between Kent's perspective and Adam's. Which brother did you feel closer to as a reader? In what ways is this Adam's story? In what ways is it Kent's?

4. At the opening of the book, Kent and Adam Austin are estranged brothers who lead very different lives. Kent is a football coach, and Adam is a bail bondsman. How does their shared tragedy affect their individual career choices?

5. How does Adam's guilt over the murder of his sister shape his life and his decisions? How does guilt play a role in the

book as a whole? Have you ever experienced long-lasting guilt?

6. Adam warns Bova, "Whatever your brother did, be careful not to let it pull you down, too" (p. 326). In what ways does Adam's advice apply to his own life and his relationship with Kent? Do you believe that family members should stick by each other no matter what? Or are there circumstances under which one needs to separate from one's family?

7. Compare the bonds between team members with the bonds between family members. In what ways is a team similar or dissimilar to a family? Do you think Kent gains something from his team that he can't get from his family?

8. What moment in the book scared you the most? What moments made you feel the most emotional? Why?

9. When Adam confesses to Chelsea that he killed Clayton Sipes, he justifies his actions by explaining that Sipes was a predator. Chelsea responds, "And so you decided to become one, too" (p. 353). Do you see Adam in this moment as a savior or a predator? Is it possible to be both at the same time?

10. Discuss the final scene of the book, which is written in italics, like the opening scene. From whose perspective do you think the final section is written? Did you find the ending hopeful or unsettling? Why?

A PLAYLIST FOR *THE PROPHET*

I write to music, and below are some of the songs that made the regular playlist while I wrote *The Prophet*. Although my books are always influenced by music, I felt this novel was perhaps unusually connected to certain songs, and I'm grateful to the artists who provided them.

> **"Return to Me," by Matthew Ryan.** I've never felt such a strong connection between a song and a novel as I did with this haunting number by one of our most talented songwriters. It seemed to me like Adam Austin's personal anthem.
>
> **"Juarez," by We Are Augustines.** A close runner-up in that sense of the personal connection. With lines like "Tell my sister I've gone and to find someone, 'cause I won't come back no more" it felt surreally close to my fictional world.
>
> **"Free Fallin'," by Tom Petty.** One for Marie Lynn Austin. Provided the inspiration for what became one of the turning-point scenes in the book.

"No Harm," by the Boxer Rebellion. Look close enough and you'll find the phrase "no harm" in a critical moment of the novel.

"After the Storm," by Mumford & Sons. Plenty of tracks from this standout album lived in my headphones during the writing, but none made more frequent appearances than this number.

"Bloodbuzz Ohio," by the National. A favorite song from a favorite album. I saw the National play live at a point when I was struggling with the book, and this song connected that night and many times after.

"I Believe Jesus Brought Us Together," by the Horrible Crowes. If Matthew Ryan provided the theme song for *The Prophet,* then the Horrible Crowes provided the bulk of the soundtrack. The album *Elsie* arrived when I was nearing the homestretch, and I felt as if it had been written by the characters in my book. In this song's case, by Chelsea and Adam.

"Blood Loss" and "Ladykiller," both by the Horrible Crowes. And the beat goes on . . . with lines like "I can leave the wound wide open, and maybe see if I can tough it out" you'll understand why I was feeling this album. It's a haunting but propulsive rock 'n' roll masterpiece, and these are songs that Brian Fallon seems to sing from his bones.

"Carolina," by M. Ward. This would be the Kent Austin anthem of the mix, I believe. The story of a man divided, walking backward to the place where he's come from, "but that ain't enough, no, you want me to run."

"Lines on Palms," by Josh Pyke. Another one of the "Kent" tunes, and one of the few upbeat, pop numbers in the dark mix! Josh Pyke is a wonderful Australian talent, and this is a lyrical gem. The opening lines defined Kent Austin to me.

Also by Michael Koryta
So Cold the River

"An icy, terrifying winner." — Dennis Lehane

"Creepy....Michael Koryta swigs from the fount of Stephen King with *So Cold the River*."
— Thom Geier, *Entertainment Weekly*

"A supernatural mystery that intensifies the suspense by thickening the atmosphere. *So Cold the River* is a superior specimen, with its eerie tale of a lovely valley in Indiana where at one time an elixir known as Pluto Water bubbled up from the underground springs."
— Marilyn Stasio, *New York Times Book Review*

"This book builds like a summer storm. *So Cold the River* is guaranteed to put the cold finger down your spine."
— Michael Connelly

"A chilling supernatural tale....Michael Koryta's novel is being compared to the writings of Stephen King and Peter Straub. He lives up to the comparison in this dark novel."
— Carol Memmott, *USA Today*

Back Bay Books
Available wherever paperbacks are sold

Also by Michael Koryta
The Ridge

"Powerful....Koryta has created a vivid world that's hard to shake for days after the book is finished."
— Paula L. Woods, *Los Angeles Times*

"Michael Koryta is an immensely gifted storyteller, and this new novel confirms that he gets better and better with each new book. Once I started *The Ridge,* I couldn't put it down."
— Ron Rash, author of *Serena* and *The Cove*

"An eerie tale....A dark and compulsively readable story.... Koryta's prose is observant and streamlined, and his characters are believable and complex....Reading *The Ridge* is a fine way to chill down a hot summer night. But you'll want to leave the lights on." — Colette Bancroft, *St. Petersburg Times*

"A chilling supernatural thriller by a rising literary star."
— Alexandra Alter, *Wall Street Journal*

Back Bay Books
Available wherever paperbacks are sold